The Best Ghost Stories

The Best Ghost Stories

Authors Include

E.F. BENSON

J. SHERIDAN LE FANU

E.M. FORSTER

M.R. JAMES

H.P. LOVECRAFT

EDGAR ALLAN POE

IVY LEAF

This volume first published in Great Britain in 1990 by
The Octopus Group Limited

This edition published in 1990 by
Ivy Leaf
Michelin House
81 Fulham Road
London SW3 6RB

Reprinted 1990

This edition produced exclusively in Great Britain for Bookmart Limited

ISBN 0 86363 008 1

Copyright © 1990 Arrangement by The Octopus Group Limited

Printed in Great Britain at The Bath Press, Avon

CONTENTS

EDWARD BULWER-LYTTON	The House and the Brain	7
EDGAR ALLAN POE	The Masque of the Red Death	39
EDGAR ALLAN POE	The Facts in the Case of M. Valdemar	45
EDGAR ALLAN POE	Ligeia	53
JOSEPH SHERIDAN LE FANU	Carmilla	66
GUY DE MAUPASSANT	Was it a Dream?	126
GUY DE MAUPASSANT	The Horla	131
M.R. JAMES	Count Magnus	151
M.R. JAMES	An Episode of Cathedral History	162
M.R. JAMES	Casting the Runes	176
O. HENRY	The Furnished Room	194
W.W. JACOBS	The Monkey's Paw	200
ARTHUR MACHEN	The Great God Pan	209
EDWARD LUCAS WHITE	Lukundoo	253
E.F. BENSON	The Man Who Went Too Far	265
E.F. BENSON	Negotium Perambulans	283
SAKI	Gabriel-Ernest	295
SAKI	The Music on the Hill	301
E.M. FORSTER	The Story of a Panic	306
KAREN BLIXEN	The Sailor-Boy's Tale	324
H.P. LOVECRAFT	Pickman's Model	333
H.P. LOVECRAFT	The Dunwich Horror	344
H.P. LOVECRAFT	The Rats in the Walls	381
	Acknowledgements	399

Edward Bulwer-Lytton

The House and the Brain

A friend of mine, who is a man of letters and a philosopher, said to me one day, as if between jest and earnest, 'Fancy! since we last met I have discovered a haunted house in the midst of London.'

'Really haunted? and by what – ghosts?'

'Well, I can't answer these questions; all I know is this: six weeks ago I and my wife were in search of a furnished apartment. Passing a quiet street, we saw on the window of one of the houses a bill, "Apartments Furnished." The situation suited us; we entered the house, liked the rooms, engaged them by the week, and left them the third day. No power on earth could have reconciled my wife to stay longer; and I don't wonder at it.'

'What did you see?'

'Excuse me; I have no desire to be ridiculed as a superstitious dreamer, nor, on the other hand, could I ask you to accept on my affirmation what you would hold to be incredible, without the evidence of your own senses. Let me only say this: it was not so much what we saw or heard (in which you might fairly suppose that we were the dupes of our own excited fancy, or the victims of imposture in others) that drove us away, as it was an undefinable terror which seized both of us whenever we passed by the door of a certain unfurnished room, in which we neither saw nor heard anything; and the strangest marvel of all was that for once in my life I agreed with my wife, silly woman though she be, and allowed after the third night that it was impossible to stay a fourth in that house.

'Accordingly, on the fourth morning I summoned the woman who kept the house and attended on us, and told her that the rooms did not quite suit us, and we would not stay out our week. She said dryly:

' "I know why; you have stayed longer than any other lodger. Few ever stayed a second night; none before you a third. But I take it that they have been very kind to you."

' "They – who?" I asked, affecting a smile.

' "Why, they who haunt the house, whoever they are; I don't mind them; I remember them many years ago, when I lived in this house not as a servant; but I know they will be the death of me some day. I don't care – I'm old and must die soon anyhow; and then I shall be with them, and in this house still."

'The woman spoke with so dreary a calmness that really it was a sort of awe that prevented my conversing with her further. I paid for my week, and too happy were I and my wife to get off so cheaply.'

'You excite my curiosity,' said I; 'nothing I should like better than to sleep in a haunted house. Pray give me the address of the one which you left so ignominiously.'

My friend gave me the address; and when we parted I walked straight towards the house thus indicated.

It is situated on the north side of Oxford Street, in a dull but respectable thoroughfare. I found the house shut up; no bill on the window, and no response to my knock. As I was turning away, a beer-boy, collecting pewter pots at the neighbouring areas, said to me, 'Do you want anyone at that house, sir?'

'Yes; I heard it was to be let.'

'Let! Why, the woman who kept it is dead; has been dead these three weeks; and no one can be found to stay there, though Mr J— offered ever so much. He offered mother, who chars for him, one pound a week just to open and shut the windows, and she would not.'

'Would not! and why?'

'The house is haunted; and the old woman who kept it was found dead in her bed with her eyes wide open. They say the devil strangled her.'

'Pooh! You speak of Mr J—. Is he the owner of the house?'

'Yes.'

'Where does he live?'

'In G— Street, No—.'

'What is he – in any business?'

'No, sir, nothing particular; a single gentleman.'

I gave the pot-boy the gratuity earned by his liberal information, and proceeded to Mr J— in G— Street, which was close by the street that boasted the haunted house. I was lucky enough to find Mr J— at home; an elderly man with intelligent countenance and prepossessing manners.

I communicated my name and my business frankly. I said I heard the house was considered to be haunted; that I had a strong desire to examine a house with so equivocal a reputation; that I should be greatly obliged if he would allow me to hire it, though only for a night. I was willing to pay for that privilege whatever he might be inclined to ask.

'Sir,' said Mr J—, with great courtesy, 'the house is at your service for as short or as long a time as you please. Rent is out of the question; the obligation will be on my side, should you be able to discover the cause of the strange phenomena which at present deprive it of all value. I cannot let it, for I cannot even get a servant to keep it in order or answer the door.

'Unluckily, the house is haunted, if I may use that expression, not only by night but by day; though at night the disturbances are of a more unpleasant and sometimes of a more alarming character. The poor old woman who died in it three weeks ago was a pauper whom I took out of a workhouse; for in her childhood she had been known to some of my family, and had once been in such good circumstances that she had rented that house of my uncle. She was a woman of superior education and strong mind, and was the only person I could ever induce to remain in the house. Indeed, since her death, which was sudden, and the coroner's inquest, which gave it a notoriety in the neighbourhood, I have so despaired of finding any person to take charge of it, much more a tenant, that I would most willingly let it rent free for a year to anyone who would pay its rates and taxes.'

'How long ago did the house acquire this character?'

'That I can scarcely tell you, but many years since; the old woman I spoke of said it was haunted when she rented it, between thirty and forty years ago. The fact is that my life has been spent in the East Indies, and in the civil service of the East India Company.

'I returned to England last year, on inheriting the fortune of an uncle, among whose possessions was the house in question. I found it shut up and uninhabited. I was told that it was haunted, and no one would inhabit it. I smiled at what seemed to me so idle a story.

'I spent some money in repainting and roofing it, added to its old-fashioned furniture a few modern articles, advertised it, and obtained a lodger for a year. He was a colonel retired on half pay. He came in with his family, a son and a daughter, and four or five servants; they all left the house the next day; and although they deponed that they had all seen something different, that something was equally terrible to all. I really could not in conscience sue, or even blame, the colonel for breach of agreement.

'Then I put in the old woman I have spoken of, and she was empowered to let the house in apartments. I never had one lodger who stayed more than three days. I do not tell you their stories; to no two lodgers have exactly the same phenomena been repeated. It is better that you should judge for yourself than enter the house with an imagination

THE BEST GHOST STORIES

influenced by previous narratives; only be prepared to see and to hear something or other, and take whatever precautions you yourself please.'

'Have you never had a curiosity yourself to pass a night in that house?'

'Yes; I passed, not a night, but three hours in broad daylight alone in that house. My curiosity is not satisfied, but it is quenched. I have no desire to renew the experiment. You cannot complain you see, sir, that I am not sufficiently candid; and unless your interest be exceedingly eager and your nerves unusually strong, I honestly add that I advise you *not* to pass a night in that house.'

'My interest *is* exceedingly keen,' said I, 'and though only a coward will boast of his nerves in situations wholly unfamiliar to him, yet my nerves have been seasoned in such variety of danger that I have the right to rely on them, even in a haunted house.'

Mr J— said very little more; he took the keys of the house out of his bureau, and gave them to me; and, thanking him cordially for his frankness and his urbane concession to my wish, I carried off my prize.

Impatient for the experiment, as soon as I reached home I summoned my confidential servant – a young man of gay spirits, fearless temper, and as free from superstitious prejudice as anyone I could think of.

'F—,' said I, 'you remember in Germany how disappointed we were at not finding a ghost in that old castle which was said to be haunted by a headless apparition? Well, I have heard of a house in London which, I have reason to hope, is decidedly haunted. I mean to sleep there to-night. From what I hear, there is no doubt that something will allow itself to be seen or to be heard – something perhaps excessively horrible. Do you think, if I take you with me, I may rely on your presence of mind, whatever may happen?'

'Oh, sir; pray trust me!' said he, grinning with delight.

'Very well, then, here are the keys of the house; this is the address. Go now, select for me any bedroom you please; and since the house has not been inhabited for weeks, make up a good fire, air the bed well; see, of course, that there are candles as well as fuel. Take with you my revolver and my dagger – so much for my weapons – arm yourself equally well; and if we are not a match for a dozen ghosts, we shall be but a sorry couple of Englishmen.'

I was engaged for the rest of the day on business so urgent that I had not leisure to think much on the nocturnal adventure to which I had plighted my honour. I dined alone and very late, and while dining read, as is my habit. The volume I selected was one of Macaulay's essays. I thought to myself that I would take the book with me; there was so much of healthfulness in the style, and practical life in the subjects, that it would serve as an antidote against the influences of superstitious fancy.

Accordingly, about half-past nine I put the book into my pocket and

11

THE HOUSE AND THE BRAIN

strolled leisurely towards the haunted house. I took with me a favourite
dog – an exceedingly sharp, bold, and vigilant bull-terrier, a dog fond of
prowling about strange ghostly corners and passages at night in search of
rats, a dog of dogs for a ghost.

It was a summer night, but chilly, the sky somewhat gloomy and
overcast; still there was a moon – faint and sickly, but still a moon – and
if the clouds permitted, after midnight it would be brighter.

I reached the house, knocked, and my servant opened with a cheerful
smile.

'All right, sir, and very comfortable.'

'Oh!' said I, rather disappointed; 'have you not seen nor heard anything remarkable?'

'Well, sir, I must own that I have heard something queer.'

'What? – what?'

'The sound of feet pattering behind me; and once or twice small noises
like whispers close at my ear; nothing more.'

'You are not at all frightened?'

'I! Not a bit of it, sir!'

And the man's bold look reassured me on one point, namely, that,
happen what might, he would not desert me.

We were in the hall, the street door closed, and my attention was now
drawn to my dog. He had at first run in eagerly enough, but had sneaked
back to the door, and was scratching and whining to get out. After I had
patted him on the head and encouraged him gently, the dog seemed to
reconcile himself to the situation, and followed me and F— through the
house, but keeping close at my heels, instead of hurrying inquisitively in
advance, which was his usual and normal habit in all strange places.

We first visited the subterranean apartments, the kitchen and other
offices, and especially the cellars, in which last were two or three bottles
of wine still left in a bin, covered with cobwebs, and evidently, by their
appearance, undisturbed for many years. It was clear that the ghosts
were not wine-bibbers.

For the rest, we discovered nothing of interest. There was a gloomy
little back yard, with very high walls. The stones of this yard were very
damp; and what with the damp and what with the dust and smoke-
grime on the pavement, our feet left a slight impression where we passed.

And now appeared the first strange phenomenon witnessed by myself
in this strange abode.

I saw, just before me, the print of a foot suddenly form itself, as it
were. I stopped, caught hold of my servant, and pointed to it. In advance
of that footprint as suddenly dropped another. We both saw it. I
advanced quickly to the place; the footprints kept advancing before me;
a small footprint – the foot of a child; the impression was too faint

thoroughly to distinguish the shape, but it seemed to us both that it was the print of a naked foot.

This phenomenon ceased when we arrived at the opposite wall, nor did it repeat itself when we returned. We remounted the stairs and entered the rooms on the ground floor – a dining-parlour, a small back-parlour, and a still smaller third room that had probably been appropriated to a footman – all still as death.

We then visited the drawing-rooms, which seemed fresh and new. In the front room I seated myself in an arm-chair. F— placed on the table the candlestick with which he had lighted us. I told him to shut the door. As he turned to do so, a chair opposite to me moved from the wall quickly and noiselessly, and dropped itself about a yard from my own chair, immediately fronting it.

'Why, this is better than the turning-tables,' said I, laughing; and as I laughed, my dog put back his head and howled.

F—, coming back, had not observed the movement of the chair. He employed himself now in stilling the dog. I continued to gaze on the chair, and fancied I saw on it a pale, blue, misty outline of a human figure; but an outline so indistinct that I could only distrust my own vision. The dog was now quiet.

'Put back the chair opposite to me,' said I to F—; 'put it back to the wall.'

F— obeyed.

'Was that you, sir?' said he, turning abruptly.

'I – what?'

'Why, something struck me. I felt it sharply on the shoulder, just here.'

'No,' said I; 'but we have jugglers present, and though we may not discover their tricks, we shall catch *them* before they frighten *us*.'

We did not stay long in the drawing-rooms; in fact, they felt so damp and so chilly that I was glad to get to the fire upstairs. We locked the doors of the drawing-rooms – a precaution which, I should observe, we had taken with all the rooms we had searched below.

The bedroom my servant had selected for me was the best on the floor; a large one, with two windows fronting the street. The four-posted bedstead, which took up no inconsiderable space, was opposite to the fire, which burned clear and bright: a door in the wall to the left, between the bed and the window, communicated with the room which my servant appropriated to himself. This last was a small room with a sofabed, and had no communication with the landing-place; no other door but that which conducted to the bedroom I was to occupy.

On either side of my fireplace was a cupboard, without locks, flush with the wall, and covered with the same dull-brown paper. We examined these cupboards; only hooks to suspend female dresses – nothing else. We sounded the walls; evidently solid – the outer walls of the building.

Having finished the survey of these apartments, warmed myself a few moments, and lighted my cigar, I then, still accompanied by F——, went forth to complete my reconnoitre. In the landing-place there was another door; it was closed firmly.

'Sir,' said my servant in surprise, 'I unlocked this door with all the others when I first came in; it cannot have got locked from the inside, for it is a—'

Before he had finished his sentence, the door, which neither of us was then touching, opened quietly of itself. We looked at each other a single instant. The same thought seized both: some human agency might be detected here. I rushed in first, my servant followed. A small, blank, dreary room without furniture, a few empty boxes and hampers in a corner, a small window, the shutters closed – not even a fireplace – no other door but that by which we had entered, no carpet on the floor, and the floor seemed very old, uneven, worm-eaten, mended here and there, as was shown by the whiter patches on the wood; but no living being, and no visible place in which a living being could have hidden.

As we stood gazing round, the door by which we had entered closed as quietly as it had before opened; we were imprisoned.

For the first time I felt a creep of undefinable horror. Not so my servant.

'Why, they don't think to trap us, sir; I could break that trumpery door with a kick of my foot.'

'Try first if it will open to your hand,' said I, shaking off the vague apprehension that had seized me, 'while I open the shutters and see what is without.'

I unbarred the shutters; the window looked on the little back yard I have before described; there was no ledge without, nothing but sheer descent. No man getting out of that window would have found any footing till he had fallen on the stones below.

F— meanwhile was vainly attempting to open the door. He now turned round to me and asked my permission to use force. And I should here state, in justice to the servant, that, far from evincing any super-stitious terror, his nerve, composure, and even gaiety amid circum-stances so extraordinary, compelled my admiration and made me congratulate myself on having secured a companion in every way fitted to the occasion. I willingly gave him the permission he required. But, though he was a remarkably strong man, his force was as idle as his milder efforts; the door did not even shake to his stoutest kick.

Breathless and panting, he desisted. I then tried the door myself, equally in vain. As I ceased from the effort, again that creep of horror came over me; but this time it was more cold and stubborn, I felt as if some strange and ghastly exhalation were rising from the chinks of that rugged floor and filling the atmosphere with a venomous influence hostile to human life.

The door now very slowly and quietly opened as of its own accord. We precipitated ourselves on to the landing-place. We both saw a large, pale light – as large as the human figure, but shapeless and unsubstantial – move before us and ascend the stairs that led from the landing into the attics.

I followed the light, and my servant followed me. It entered, to the right of the landing, a small garret, of which the door stood open. I entered in the same instant. The light then collapsed into a small globule, exceedingly brilliant and vivid; rested a moment on a bed in the corner, quivered, and vanished.

We approached the bed and examined it – a half-tester, such as is commonly found in attics devoted to servants. On the drawers that stood near it we perceived an old faded silk kerchief, with the needle still left in the rent half repaired. The kerchief was covered with dust; probably it had belonged to the old woman who had last died there, and this might have been her sleeping-room.

I had sufficient curiosity to open the drawers; there were a few odds and ends of female dress, and two letters tied round with a narrow ribbon of faded yellow. I took the liberty to possess myself of the letters. We found nothing else in the room worth noticing, nor did the light reappear; but we distinctly heard, as we turned to go, a pattering footfall on the floor just before us.

We went through the other attics (in all four), the footfall still preceding us. Nothing to be seen, nothing but the footfall heard. I had the letters in my hand; just as I was descending the stairs I distinctly felt my wrist seized, and a faint, soft effort made to draw the letters from my clasp. I only held them the more tightly, and the effort ceased.

We regained the bedchamber appropriated to myself, and I then remarked that my dog had not followed us when we had left it. He was thrusting himself close to the fire and trembling. I was impatient to examine the letters; and while I read them my servant opened a little box in which he had deposited the weapons I had ordered him to bring, took them out, placed them on a table close at my bed-head, and then occupied himself in soothing the dog, who, however, seemed to heed him very little.

The letters were short; they were dated – the dates exactly thirty-five years ago. They were evidently from a lover to his mistress, or a husband to some young wife. Not only the terms of expression, but a distinct reference to a former voyage indicated the writer to have been a seafarer.

THE HOUSE AND THE BRAIN

The spelling and handwriting were those of a man imperfectly educated; but still the language itself was forcible. In the expressions of endearment there was a kind of rough, wild love; but here and there were dark, unintelligible hints at some secret not of love – some secret that seemed of crime.

'We ought to love each other,' was one of the sentences I remember, 'for how everyone else would execrate us if all was known.'

Again: 'Don't let anyone be in the same room with you at night – you talk in your sleep.'

And again: 'What's done can't be undone; and I tell you there's nothing against us, unless the dead should come to life.'

Here was interlined, in a better handwriting (a female's), 'They do!'

At the end of the letter latest in date the same female hand had written these words:

'Lost at sea the 4th of June, the same day as—'

I put down the letters, and began to muse over their contents.

Fearing, however, that the train of thought into which I fell might unsteady my nerves, I fully determined to keep my mind in a fit state to cope with whatever of the marvellous the advancing night might bring forth. I roused myself, laid the letters on the table, stirred up the fire, which was still bright and cheering, and opened my volume of Macaulay.

I read quietly enough till about half-past eleven. I then threw myself dressed upon the bed, and told my servant he might retire to his own room, but must keep himself awake. I bade him leave open the doors between the two rooms. Thus alone I kept two candles burning on the table by my bed-head. I placed my watch beside the weapons, and calmly resumed my Macaulay. Opposite to me the fire burned clear, and on the hearth-rug, seemingly asleep, lay the dog. In about twenty minutes I felt an exceedingly cold air pass by my cheek, like a sudden draught. I fancied the door to my right, communicating with the landing-place, must have got open; but no, it was closed.

I then turned my glance to the left, and saw the flames of the candles violently swayed as by a wind. At the same moment the watch beside the revolver softly slid from the table – softly, softly – no visible hand – it was gone. I sprang up, seizing the revolver with the one hand, the dagger with the other: I was not willing that my weapons should share the fate of the watch.

Thus armed, I looked round the floor: no sign of the watch. Three slow, loud, distinct knocks were now heard at the bed-head; my servant called out:

'Is that you, sir?'

'No; be on your guard.'

The dog now roused himself and sat on his haunches, his ears moving quickly backward and forward. He kept his eyes fixed on me with a look so strange that he concentred all my attention on himself. Slowly he rose, all his hair bristling, and stood perfectly rigid, and with the same wild stare.

I had no time, however, to examine the dog. Presently my servant emerged from his room; and if I ever saw horror in the human face, it was then. I should not have recognized him had we met in the streets, so altered was every lineament. He passed by me quickly, saying, in a whisper that seemed scarcely to come from his lips:

'Run! run! It is after me!'

He gained the door to the landing, pulled it open, and rushed forth. I followed him on to the landing involuntarily, calling him to stop; but, without heeding me, he bounded down the stairs, clinging to the balusters and taking several steps at a time. I heard, where I stood, the street door open, heard it again clap to.

I was left alone in the haunted house.

It was but for a moment that I remained undecided whether or not to follow my servant; pride and curiosity alike forbade so dastardly a flight. I re-entered my room, closing the door after me, and proceeded cautiously into the interior chamber. I encountered nothing to justify my servant's terror.

I again carefully examined the walls to see if there were any concealed door. I could find no trace of one – not even a seam in the dul-brown paper with which the room was hung. How then had the THING, whatever it was, which had so scared him, obtained ingress, except through my own chamber?

I returned to my room, shut and locked the door that opened upon the interior one, and stood on the hearth, expectant and prepared.

I now perceived that the dog had slunk into an angle of the wall, and was pressing close against it, as if literally striving to force his way into it. I approached the animal and spoke to it; the poor brute was evidently beside itself with terror. It showed all its teeth, the slaver dropping from its jaws, and would certainly have bitten me if I had touched it. It did not seem to recognize me. Whoever has seen at the Zoological Gardens a rabbit fascinated by a serpent, cowering in a corner, may form some idea of the anguish which the dog exhibited.

Finding all efforts to soothe the animal in vain, and fearing that his bite might be as venomous in that state as if in the madness of hydrophobia, I left him alone, placed my weapons on the table beside the fire, seated myself, and recommenced my Macaulay.

Perhaps, in order not to appear seeking credit for a courage or rather a coolness, which the reader may conceive I exaggerate, I may be pardoned if I pause to indulge in one or two egotistical remarks.

THE HOUSE AND THE BRAIN

As I hold presence of mind, or what is called courage, to be precisely proportioned to familiarity with the circumstances that lead to it, so I should say that I had been long sufficiently familiar with all experiments that appertain to the marvellous. I had witnessed many very extraordinary phenomena in various parts of the world – phenomena that would be either totally disbelieved if I stated them, or ascribed to supernatural agencies.

Now, my theory is that the supernatural is the impossible, and that what is called supernatural is only a something in the laws of nature of which we have been hitherto ignorant. Therefore, if a ghost rise before me, I have not the right to say, 'So, then, the supernatural is possible,' but rather, 'So, then, the apparition of a ghost is, contrary to received opinion, within the laws of nature, namely, not supernatural.'

Now, in all that I had hitherto witnessed, and indeed in all the wonders which the amateurs of mystery in our age record as facts, a material living agency is always required. On the Continent you will still find magicians who assert that they can raise spirits. Assume for a moment that they assert truly, still the living material form of the magician is present; he is the material agency by which, from some constitutional peculiarities, certain strange phenomena are represented to your natural senses.

Accept, again, as truthful the tales of spirit manifestation in America – musical or other sounds, writings on paper, produced by no discernible hand, articles of furniture moved without apparent human agency, or the actual sight and touch of hands, to which no bodies seem to belong – still there must be found the medium, or living being, with constitutional peculiarities capable of obtaining these signs.

In fine, in all such marvels, supposing even that there is no imposture, there must be a human being like ourselves, by whom or through whom the effects presented to human beings are produced. It is so with the now familiar phenomena of mesmerism or electrobiology; the mind of the person operated on is affected through a material living agent.

Nor, supposing it true that a mesmerized patient can respond to the will or passes of a mesmerizer a hundred miles distant, is the response less occasioned by a material being. It may be through a material fluid, call it Electric, call it Odic, call it what you will, which has the power of traversing space and passing obstacles, that the material effect is communicated from one to the other.

Hence, all that I had hitherto witnessed, or expected to witness, in this strange house, I believed to be occasioned through some agency or medium as mortal as myself; and this idea necessarily prevented the awe with which those who regard as supernatural things that are not within the ordinary operations of nature might have been impressed by the adventures of that memorable night.

As, then, it was my conjecture that all that was presented, or would be presented, to my senses, must originate in some human being gifted by constitution with the power so to present them, and having some motive so to do, I felt an interest in my theory which, in its way, was rather philosophical than superstitious. And I can sincerely say that I was in as tranquil a temper for observation as any practical experimentalist could be in awaiting the effects of some rare though perhaps perilous chemical combination. Of course, the more I kept my mind detached from fancy the more the temper fitted for observation would be obtained; and I therefore riveted eye and thought on the strong daylight sense in the page of my Macaulay.

I now became aware that something interposed between the page and the light: the page was overshadowed. I looked up and saw what I shall find very difficult, perhaps impossible, to describe.

It was a darkness shaping itself out of the air in very undefined outline. I cannot say it was of a human form, and yet it had more of a resemblance to a human form, or rather shadow, than anything else. As it stood, wholly apart and distinct from the air and the light around it, its dimensions seemed gigantic; the summit nearly touched the ceiling.

While I gazed, a feeling of intense cold seized me. An iceberg before me could not more have chilled me; nor could the cold of an iceberg have been more purely physical. I feel convinced that it was not the cold caused by fear. As I continued to gaze, I thought – but this I cannot say with precision – that I distinguished two eyes looking down on me from the height. One moment I seemed to distinguish them clearly, the next they seemed gone; but two rays of a pale, blue light frequently shot through the darkness, as from the height on which I half believed, half doubted, that I had encountered the eyes.

I strove to speak; my voice utterly failed me. I could only think to myself, 'Is this fear? it is *not* fear!' I strove to rise, in vain; I felt as weighed down by an irresistible force. Indeed, my impression was that of an immense and overwhelming power opposed to my volition; that sense of utter inadequacy to cope with a force beyond man's, which one may feel *physically* in a storm at sea, in a conflagration, or when confronting some terrible wild beast, or rather, perhaps, the shark of the ocean, I felt *morally*. Opposed to my will was another will, as far superior to its strength as storm, fire, and shark are superior in material force to the force of man.

And now, as this impression grew on me, now came, at last, horror – horror to a degree that no words can convey. Still I retained pride, if not courage; and in my own mind I said, 'This is horror, but it is not fear; unless I fear, I cannot be harmed; my reason rejects this thing; it is an illusion, I do not fear.'

With a violent effort I succeeded at last in stretching out my hand towards the weapon on the table; as I did so, on the arm and shoulder I received a strange shock, and my arm fell to my side powerless. And now, to add to my horror, the light began slowly to wane from the candles; they were not, as it were, extinguished, but their flame seemed very gradually withdrawn; it was the same with the fire, the light was extracted from the fuel; in a few minutes the room was in utter darkness.

The dread that came over me to be thus in the dark with that dark thing, whose power was so intensely felt, brought a reaction of nerve. In fact, terror had reached that climax that either my senses must have deserted me, or I must have burst through the spell.

I did burst through it.

I found voice, though the voice was a shriek. I remember that I broke forth with words like these, 'I do not fear, my soul does not fear'; and at the same time I found strength to rise.

Still in that profound gloom, I rushed to one of the windows, tore aside the curtain, flung open the shutters; my first thought was, LIGHT.

And when I saw the moon, high, clear, and calm, I felt a joy that almost compensated for the previous terror. There was the moon, there was also the light from the gas-lamps in the deserted, slumberous street. I turned to look back into the room; the moon penetrated its shadow very palely and partially, but still there was light. The dark thing, whatever it might be, was gone; except that I could yet see a dim shadow, which seemed the shadow of that shade, against the opposite wall.

My eye now rested on the table, and from under the table (which was without cloth or cover, an old mahogany round table) rose a hand, visible as far as the wrist. It was a hand, seemingly, as much of flesh and blood as my own, but the hand of an aged person, lean, wrinkled, small too, a woman's hand. The hand very softly closed on the two letters that lay on the table; hand and letters both vanished. Then came the same three loud measured knocks I had heard at the bed-head before this extraordinary drama had commenced.

As these sounds slowly ceased, I felt the whole room vibrate sensibly; and at the far end rose, as from the floor, sparks or globules like bubbles of light, many-coloured – green, yellow, fire-red, azure – up and down, to and fro, hither, thither, as tiny will-o'-the-wisps and sparks moved, slow or swift, each at its own caprice. A chair (as in the drawing-room below) was now advanced from the wall without apparent agency, and placed at the opposite side of the table.

Suddenly, as forth from the chair, grew a shape, a woman's shape. It was distinct as a shape of life, ghastly as a shape of death. The face was that of youth, with a strange, mournful beauty; the throat and shoulders were bare, the rest of the form in a loose robe of cloudy white.

It began sleeking its long yellow hair, which fell over its shoulders; its eyes were not turned towards me, but to the door; it seemed listening, watching, waiting. The shadow of the shade in the background grew darker, and again I thought I beheld the eyes gleaming out from the summit of the shadow, eyes fixed upon that shape.

As if from the door, though it did not open, grew out another shape, equally distinct, equally ghastly – a man's shape, a young man's. It was in the dress of the last century, or rather in a likeness of such dress; for both the male shape and the female, though defined, were evidently unsubstantial, impalpable – simulacre, phantasms; and there was something incongruous, grotesque, yet fearful, in the contrast between the elaborate finery, the courtly precision of that old-fashioned garb, with its ruffles and lace and buckles, and the corpse-like aspect and ghost-like stillness of the flitting wearer. Just as the male shape approached the female, the dark shadow darted from the wall, all three for a moment wrapped in darkness.

When the pale light returned, the two phantoms were as if in the grasp of the shadow that towered between them, and there was a blood-stain on the breast of the female; and the phantom male was leaning on its phantom sword, and blood seemed trickling fast from the ruffles, from the lace; and the darkness of the intermediate shadow swallowed them up – they were gone. And again the bubbles of light shot, and sailed, and undulated, growing thicker and thicker and more wildly confused in their movements.

The closet door to the right of the fireplace now opened, and from the aperture came the form of a woman, aged. In her hand she held letters – the very letters over which I had seen *the* hand close; and behind her I heard a footstep. She turned round as if to listen, and then she opened the letters and seemed to read: and over her shoulder I saw a livid face, the face as of a man long drowned – bloated, bleached, sea-weed tangled in its dripping hair; and at her feet lay a form as of a corpse, and beside the corpse cowered a child, a miserable squalid child, with famine in its cheeks and fear in its eyes. As I looked in the old woman's face, the wrinkles and lines vanished, and it became a face of youth – hard-eyed, stony, but still youth; and the shadow darted forth and darkened over these phantoms, as it had darkened over the last.

Nothing now was left but the shadow, and on that my eyes were intently fixed, till again eyes grew out of the shadow – malignant, serpent eyes. And the bubbles of light again rose and fell, and in their disordered, irregular, turbulent maze mingled with the wan moonlight. And now from these globules themselves, as from the shell of an egg, monstrous things burst out; the air grew filled with them; larvae so bloodless and so hideous that I can in no way describe them except to remind the reader of the swarming life which the solar microscope brings before his eyes in a drop of water – things transparent, supple, agile, chasing each other, devouring each other – forms like naught ever beheld by the naked eye.

As the shapes were without symmetry, so their movements were without order. In their very vagrancies there was no sport; they came round me and round, thicker and faster and swifter, swarming over my head, crawling over my right arm, which was outstretched in involuntary command against all evil beings.

Sometimes I felt myself touched, but not by them; invisible hands touched me. Once I felt the clutch as of cold, soft fingers at my throat. I was still equally conscious that if I gave way to fear I should be in bodily peril, and I concentred all my faculties in the single focus of resisting, stubborn will. And I turned my sight from the shadow, above all from those strange serpent eyes – eyes that had now become distinctly visible. For there, though in naught else around me, I was aware that there was a will, and a will of intense, creative, working evil, which might crush down my own.

The pale atmosphere in the room began now to redden as if in the air of some near conflagration. The larvae grew lurid as things that live in fire. Again the room vibrated; again were heard the three measured knocks; and again all things were swallowed up in the darkness of the dark shadow, as if out of that darkness all had come, into that darkness all returned.

As the gloom receded, the shadow was wholly gone. Slowly as it had been withdrawn, the flame grew again into the candles on the table, again into the fuel in the grate. The whole room came once more calmly, healthfully into sight.

The two doors were still closed, the door communicating with the servant's room still locked. In the corner of the wall, into which he had convulsively niched himself, lay the dog. I called to him – no movement; I approached – the animal was dead; his eyes protruded, his tongue out of his mouth, the froth gathered round his jaws. I took him in my arms; I brought him to the fire; I felt acute grief for the loss of my poor favourite, acute self-reproach; I accused myself of his death; I imagined he had died of fright. But what was my surprise on finding that his neck was actually broken – actually twisted out of the vertebrae. Had this been done in the dark? Must it not have been done by a hand human as mine? Must there not have been a human agency all the while in that room? Good cause to suspect it. I cannot tell. I cannot do more than state the fact fairly; the reader may draw his own inference.

Another surprising circumstance – my watch was restored to the table from which it had been so mysteriously withdrawn; but it had stopped at the very moment it was so withdrawn; nor, despite all the skill of the watchmaker, has it ever gone since – that is, it will go in a strange, erratic way for a few hours, and then come to a dead stop; it is worthless.

Nothing more chanced for the rest of the night; nor, indeed, had I long to wait before the dawn broke. Not till it was broad daylight did I quit the haunted house. Before I did so I revisited the little blind room in which my servant and I had been for a time imprisoned.

I had a strong impression, for which I could not account, that from that room had originated the mechanism of the phenomena, if I may use the term, which had been experienced in my chamber; and though I entered it now in the clear day, with the sun peering through the filmy window, I still felt, as I stood on its floor, the creep of the horror which I had first experienced there the night before, and which had been so aggravated by what had passed in my own chamber.

I could not, indeed, bear to stay more than half a minute within those walls. I descended the stairs, and again I heard the footfall before me; and when I opened the street door I thought I could distinguish a very low laugh. I gained my own home, expecting to find my runaway servant there. But he had not presented himself; nor did I hear more of him for three days, when I received a letter from him, dated from Liverpool, to this effect:

HONOURED SIR,—I humbly entreat your pardon, though I can scarcely hope that you will think I deserve it, unless – which heaven forbid! – you saw what I did. I feel that it will be years before I can recover myself; and as to being fit for service, it is out of the question. I am therefore going to my brother-in-law at Melbourne. The ship sails to-morrow. Perhaps the long voyage may set me up. I do nothing now but start and tremble, and fancy it is behind me. I humbly beg you, honoured sir, to order my clothes, and whatever wages are due to me, to be sent to my mother's at Walworth: John knows her address.

The letter ended with additional apologies, somewhat incoherent, and explanatory details as to effects that had been under the writer's charge.

This flight may perhaps warrant a suspicion that the man wished to go to Australia, and had been somehow or other fraudulently mixed up with the events of the night. I say nothing in refutation of that conjecture; rather, I suggest it as one that would seem to many persons the most probable solution of improbable occurrences.

My own theory remained unshaken. I returned in the evening to the house, to bring away in a hack cab the things I had left there, with my poor dog's body. In this task I was not disturbed, nor did any incident worth note befall me, except that still, on ascending and descending the stairs, I heard the same footfall in advance. On leaving the house, I went to Mr J—'s. He was at home. I returned him the keys, told him that my curiosity was sufficiently gratified, and was about to relate quickly what had passed, when he stopped me and said, though with much politeness, that he had no longer any interest in a mystery which none had ever solved.

I determined at least to tell him of the two letters I had read, as well as of the extraordinary manner in which they had disappeared; and I then inquired if he thought they had been addressed to the woman who had died in the house, and if there were anything in her early history which could possibly confirm the dark suspicions to which the letters gave rise.

Mr J— seemed startled, and after musing a few moments, answered:

'I know but little of the woman's earlier history, except, as I before told you, that her family were known to mine. But you revive some vague reminiscences to her prejudice. I will make inquiries, and inform you of their result. Still, even if we could admit the popular superstition that a person who had been either the perpetrator or the victim of dark crimes in life could revisit, as a restless spirit, the scene in which those crimes had been committed, I should observe that the house was infested by strange sights and sounds before the old woman died. You smile; what would you say?'

'I would say this: that I am convinced, if we could get to the bottom of these mysteries, we should find a living, human agency.'

'What! you believe it is all an imposture? For what object?'

'Not an imposture, in the ordinary sense of the word. If suddenly I were to sink into a deep sleep, from which you could not awake me, but in that deep sleep could answer questions with an accuracy which I could not pretend to when awake – tell you what money you had in your pocket, nay, describe your very thoughts – it is not necessarily an imposture, any more than it is necessarily supernatural. I should be, unconsciously to myself, under a mesmeric influence, conveyed to me from a distance by a human being who had acquired power over me by previous *rapport*.'

'Granting mesmerism, so far carried, to be a fact, you are right. And you would infer from this that a mesmerizer might produce the extraordinary effects you and others have witnessed over inanimate objects – fill the air with sights and sounds?'

'Or impress our senses with the belief in them, we never having been *en rapport* with the person acting on us? No. What is commonly called

mesmerism could not do this; but there may be a power akin to mesmerism and superior to it – the power that in the old days was called magic.
That such a power may extend to all inanimate objects of matter, I do
not say; but if so, it would not be against nature, only a rare power in
nature, which might be given to constitutions with certain peculiarities,
and cultivated by practice to an extraordinary degree.

'That such a power might extend over the dead – that is, over certain
thoughts and memories that the dead may still retain – and compel, not
that which ought properly to be called the SOUL, and which is far beyond
human reach, but rather a phantom of what has been most earth-stained
on earth, to make itself apparent to our senses – is a very ancient though
obsolete theory, upon which I will hazard no opinion. But I do not conceive the power would be supernatural.

'Let me illustrate what I mean, from an experiment which Paracelsus
describes as not difficult, and which the author of the *Curiosities of
Literature* cites as credible: A flower perishes; you burn it. Whatever
were the elements of that flower while it lived are gone, dispersed, you
know not whither; you can never discover nor re-collect them. But you
can, by chemistry, out of the burnt dust of that flower, raise a spectrum
of the flower, just as it seemed in life.

'It may be the same with a human being. The soul has as much escaped you as the essence or elements of the flower. Still you may make a
spectrum of it. And this phantom, though in the popular superstition it
is held to be the soul of the departed, must not be confounded with the
true soul; it is but the eidolon of the dead form.

'Hence, like the best-attested stories of ghosts or spirits, the thing that
most strikes us is the absence of what we hold to be soul – that is, of
superior, emancipated intelligence. They come for little or no object; they
seldom speak, if they do come; they utter no ideas above those of an
ordinary person on earth. These American spiritseers have published
volumes of communications in prose and verse, which they assert to be
given in the names of the most illustrious dead – Shakespeare, Bacon,
heaven knows whom.

'Those communications, taking the best, are certainly not of a whit
higher order than would be communications from living persons of fair
talent and education; they are wondrously inferior to what Bacon,
Shakespeare, and Plato said and wrote when on earth. Nor, what is more
notable, do they ever contain an idea that was not on the earth before.

'Wonderful, therefore, as such phenomena may be (granting them to
be truthful), I see much that philosophy may question, nothing that it is
incumbent on philosophy to deny, namely, nothing supernatural. They
are but ideas conveyed somehow or other (we have not yet discovered
the means) from one mortal brain to another. Whether in so doing tables

walk of their own accord, or fiend-like shapes appear in a magic circle, or bodiless hands rise and remove material objects, or a thing of darkness, such as presented itself to me, freeze our blood – still am I persuaded that these are but agencies conveyed, as by electric wires, to my own brain from the brain of another.

'In some constitutions there is a natural chemistry, and these may produce chemic wonders; in others a natural fluid, call it electricity, and these produce electric wonders. But they differ in this from normal science: they are alike objectless, purposeless, puerile, frivolous. They lead on to no grand results, and therefore the world does not heed, and true sages have not cultivated them. But sure I am, that of all I saw or heard, a man, human as myself, was the remote originator; and, I believe, unconsciously to himself as to the exact effects produced, for this reason: no two persons, you say, have ever told you that they experienced exactly the same thing; well, observe, no two persons ever experience exactly the same dream.

'If this were an ordinary imposture, the machinery would be arranged for results that would but little vary; if it were a supernatural agency permitted by the Almighty, it would surely be for some definite end. These phenomena belong to neither class. My persuasion is that they originate in some brain now far distant; that that brain had no distinct volition in anything that occurred; that what does occur reflects but its devious, motley, ever shifting, half-formed thoughts; in short, that it has been but the dreams of such a brain put into action and invested with a semi-substance.

'That this brain is of immense power, that it can set matter into movement, that it is malignant and destructive, I believe. Some material force must have killed my dog; it might, for aught I know, have sufficed to kill myself, had I been as subjugated by terror as the dog – had my intellect or my spirit given me no countervailing resistance in my will.'

'It killed your dog! That is fearful! Indeed, it is strange that no animal can be induced to stay in that house; not even a cat. Rats and mice are never found in it.'

'The instincts of the brute creation detect influences deadly to their existence. Man's reason has a sense less subtle, because it has a resisting power more supreme. But enough; do you comprehend my theory?'

'Yes, though imperfectly; and I accept any crotchet (pardon the word), however odd, rather than embrace at once the notion of ghosts and hobgoblins we imbibed in our nurseries. Still, to my unfortunate house the evil is the same. What on earth can I do with the house?'

'I will tell you what I would do. I am convinced from my own internal feelings that the small unfurnished room, at right angles to the door of the bedroom which I occupied, forms a starting-point or receptacle for the influences which haunt the house; and I strongly advise you to have the walls opened, the floor removed, nay, the whole room pulled down. I observe that it is detached from the body of the house, built over the small back yard, and could be removed without injury to the rest of the building.'

'And you think that if I did that—'

'You would cut off the telegraph wires. Try it. I am so persuaded that I am right that I will pay half the expense if you will allow me to direct the operations.'

'Nay, I am well able to afford the cost; for the rest, allow me to write to you.'

About ten days afterwards I received a letter from Mr J—, telling me that he had visited the house since I had seen him; that he had found the two letters I had described replaced in the drawer from which I had taken them; that he had read them with misgivings like my own; that he had instituted a cautious inquiry about the woman to whom I rightly conjectured they had been written.

It seemed that thirty-six years ago (a year before the date of the letters) she had married, against the wish of her relatives, an American of very suspicious character; in fact, he was generally believed to have been a pirate. She herself was the daughter of very respectable trades-people, and had served in the capacity of nursery governess before her marriage. She had a brother, a widower, who was considered wealthy, and who had one child about six years old. A month after the marriage the body of this brother was found in the Thames, near London Bridge; there seemed some marks of violence about his throat, but they were not deemed sufficient to warrant the inquest in any other verdict than that of 'found drowned.'

The American and his wife took charge of the little boy, the deceased brother having by his will left his sister the guardian of his only child, and in the event of the child's death the sister inherited. The child died about six months afterwards; it was supposed to have been neglected and ill-treated. The neighbours deposed to have heard it shriek at night.

The surgeon who had examined it after death said that it was emaciated as if from want of nourishment, and the body was covered with livid bruises. It seemed that one winter night the child had sought to escape; had crept out into the back yard, tried to scale the wall, fallen back exhausted, and had been found at morning on the stones in a dying state.

But though there was some evidence of cruelty, there was none of murder; and the aunt and her husband had sought to palliate cruelty by alleging the exceeding stubbornness and perversity of the child, who was declared to be half-witted. Be that as it may, at the orphan's death the aunt inherited her brother's fortune.

Before the first wedded year was out, the American quitted England abruptly, and never returned to it. He obtained a cruising vessel, which was lost in the Atlantic two years afterwards. The widow was left in affluence; but reverses of various kinds had befallen her; a bank broke, an investment failed, she went into a small business and became insolvent, then she entered into service, sinking lower and lower, from housekeeper down to maid-of-all-work, never long retaining a place, though nothing peculiar against her character was ever alleged.

She was considered sober, honest, and peculiarly quiet in her ways; still nothing prospered with her. And so she had dropped into the workhouse, from which Mr J— had taken her, to be placed in charge of the very house which she had rented as mistress in the first year of her wedded life.

Mr J— added that he had passed an hour alone in the unfurnished room which I had urged him to destroy, and that his impressions of dread while there were so great, though he had neither heard nor seen anything, that he was eager to have the walls bared and the floors removed, as I had suggested. He had engaged persons for the work, and would commence any day I would name.

The day was accordingly fixed. I repaired to the haunted house; we went into the blind, dreary room, took up the skirting and then the floors. Under the rafters, covered with rubbish, was found a trap-door, quite large enough to admit a man. It was closely nailed down with clamps and rivets of iron. On removing these we descended into a room below, the existence of which had never been suspected.

In this room there had been a window and a flue, but they had been bricked over, evidently for many years. By the help of candles we examined this place; it still retained some mouldering furniture – three chairs, an oak settee, a table – all of the fashion of about eighty years ago.

There was a chest of drawers against the wall, in which we found, half rotted away, old-fashioned articles of a man's dress, such as might have been worn eighty or a hundred years ago, by a gentleman of some rank; costly steel buckles and buttons, like those yet worn in court-dresses, a handsome court-sword; in a waistcoat which had once been rich with gold lace, but which was now blackened and foul with damp, we found five guineas, a few silver coins, and an ivory ticket, probably for some place of entertainment long since passed away.

But our main discovery was in a kind of iron safe fixed to the wall, the lock of which it cost us much trouble to get picked.

In this safe were three shelves and two small drawers. Ranged on the shelves were several small bottles of crystal, hermetically stopped. They

contained colourless volatile essences, of what nature I shall say no more
than that they were not poisons; phosphor and ammonia entered into
some of them. There were also some very curious glass tubes, and a small
pointed rod of iron, with a large lump of rock crystal, and another of
amber, also a lodestone of great power.

In one of the drawers we found a miniature portrait set in gold, and
retaining the freshness of its colours most remarkably, considering the
length of time it had probably been there. The portrait was that of a
man who might be somewhat advanced in middle life, perhaps forty-
seven or forty-eight.

It was a most peculiar face, a most impressive face. If you could fancy
some mighty serpent transformed into man, preserving in the human
lineaments the old serpent type, you would have a better idea of that
countenance than long descriptions can convey; the width and flatness of
frontal, the tapering elegance of contour, disguising the strength of the
deadly jaw; the long, large, terrible eye, glittering and green as the
emerald, and withal a certain ruthless calm, as if from the consciousness
of an immense power.

The strange thing was this: the instant I saw the miniature I recognized a startling likeness to one of the rarest portraits in the world; the
portrait of a man of rank only below that of royalty, who in his own day
had made a considerable noise. History says little or nothing of him; but
search the correspondence of his contemporaries, and you find reference
to his wild daring, his bold profligacy, his restless spirit, his taste for the
occult sciences.

While still in the meridian of life he died and was buried, so say the
chronicles, in a foreign land. He died in time to escape the grasp of the
law; for he was accused of crimes which would have given him to the
headsman. After his death the portraits of him, which had been
numerous, for he had been a munificent encourager of art, were bought
up and destroyed, it was supposed by his heirs, who might have been
glad could they have razed his very name from their splendid line.

He had enjoyed vast wealth; a large portion of this was believed to
have been embezzled by a favourite astrologer or soothsayer; at all
events, it had unaccountably vanished at the time of his death. One
portrait alone of him was supposed to have escaped the general destruction; I had seen it in the house of a collector some months before. It had
made on me a wonderful impression, as it does on all who behold it – a
face never to be forgotten; and there was that face in the miniature that
lay within my hand. True that in the miniature the man was a few
years older than in the portrait I had seen, or than the original was even
at the time of his death. But a few years! – why, between the date in
which flourished that direful noble and the date in which the miniature

THE HOUSE AND THE BRAIN

was evidently painted there was an interval of more than two centuries. While I was thus gazing, silent and wondering, Mr J— said:

'But is it possible? I have known this man.'

'How? where?' cried I.

'In India. He was high in the confidence of the Rajah of —, and well-nigh drew him into a revolt which would have lost the Rajah his dominions. The man was a Frenchman; his name De V—; clever, bold, lawless; we insisted on his dismissal and banishment. It must be the same man, no two faces like his, yet this miniature seems nearly a hundred years old.'

Mechanically I turned round the miniature to examine the back of it, and on the back was engraved a pentacle; in the middle of the pentacle a ladder, and the third step of the ladder was formed by the date 1765. Examining still more minutely, I detected a spring; this, on being pressed, opened the back of the miniature as a lid.

Within-side the lid were engraved: 'Mariana, to thee. Be faithful in life and in death to —.'

Here follows a name that I will not mention, but it was not unfamiliar to me. I had heard it spoken of by old men in my childhood as the name borne by a dazzling charlatan, who had made a great sensation in London for a year or so, and had fled the country on the charge of a double murder within his own house – that of his mistress and his rival. I said nothing of this to Mr J—, to whom reluctantly I resigned the miniature.

We had found no difficulty in opening the first drawer within the iron safe; we found great difficulty in opening the second: it was not locked, but it resisted all efforts, till we inserted in the chinks the edge of a chisel. When we had thus drawn it forth we found a very singular apparatus, in the nicest order.

Upon a small, thin book, or rather tablet, was placed a saucer of crystal; this saucer was filled with a clear liquid; on that liquid floated a kind of compass, with a needle shifting rapidly round; but instead of the usual points of a compass, were seven strange characters, not very unlike those used by astrologers to denote the planets.

A very peculiar, but not strong nor displeasing, odour came from this drawer, which was lined with a wood that we afterwards discovered to be hazel. Whatever the cause of this odour, it produced a material effect on the nerves. We all felt it, even the two workmen who were in the room; a creeping, tingling sensation, from the tips of the fingers to the roots of the hair.

Impatient to examine the tablet, I removed the saucer. As I did so, the needle of the compass went round and round with exceeding swiftness, and I felt a shock that ran through my whole frame, so that I dropped the saucer on the floor. The liquid was spilt, the saucer was broken, the compass rolled to the end of the room, and at that instant the walls shook to and fro as if a giant had swayed and rocked them.

The two workmen were so frightened that they ran up the ladder by which we had descended from the trap-door; but, seeing that nothing more happened, they were easily induced to return.

Meanwhile I had opened the tablet; it was bound in plain red leather, with a silver clasp; it contained but one sheet of thick vellum, and on that sheet were inscribed, within a double pentacle, words in old monkish Latin, which are literally to be translated thus:

On all that it can reach within these walls, sentient or inanimate, living or dead, as moves the needle, so works my will! Accursed be the house, and restless the dwellers therein.

We found no more. Mr J— burned the tablet and its anathema. He razed to the foundation the part of the building containing the secret room, with the chamber over it. He had then the courage to inhabit the house himself for a month, and a quieter, better conditioned house could not be found in all London. Subsequently he let it to advantage, and his tenant has made no complaints.

But my story is not yet done. A few days after Mr J— had removed into the house, I paid him a visit. We were standing by the open window and conversing. A van containing some articles of furniture which he was moving from his former house was at the door.

I had just urged on him my theory that all those phenomena regarded as supermundane had emanated from a human brain; adducing the charm, or rather curse we had found and destroyed, in support of my theory.

Mr J— was observing in reply, 'that even if mesmerism, or whatever analogous power it might be called, could really thus work in the absence of the operator, and produce effects so extraordinary, still could those effects continue when the operator himself was dead? and if the spell had been wrought, and, indeed, the room walled up, more than seventy years ago, the probability was that the operator had long since departed this life' – Mr J—, I say, was thus answering, when I caught hold of his arm and pointed to the street below.

A well-dressed man had crossed from the opposite side, and was accosting the carrier in charge of the van. His face, as he stood, was exactly fronting our window. It was the face of the miniature we had discovered; it was the face of the portrait of the noble three centuries ago.

'Good heavens!' cried Mr J—, 'that is the face of De V—, and scarcely a day older than when I saw it in the Rajah's court in my youth!'

Seized by the same thought, we both hastened downstairs; I was first in the street, but the man had already gone. I caught sight of him, however, not many yards in advance, and in another moment I was by his side.

I had resolved to speak to him, but when I looked into his face I felt as if it were impossible to do so. That eye – the eye of the serpent – fixed and held me spellbound. And withal, about the man's whole person there was a dignity, an air of pride and station and superiority that would have made anyone, habituated to the usages of the world, hesitate long before venturing upon a liberty or impertinence.

And what could I say? What was it I could ask?

Thus ashamed of my first impulse, I fell a few paces back, still, however, following the stranger, undecided what else to do. Meanwhile he turned the corner of the street; a plain carriage was in waiting with a servant out of livery, dressed like a *valet de place*, at the carriage door. In another moment he had stepped into the carriage, and it drove off. I returned to the house.

Mr J— was still at the street door. He had asked the carrier what the stranger had said to him.

'Merely asked whom that house now belonged to.'

The same evening I happened to go with a friend to a place in town called the Cosmopolitan Club, a place open to men of all countries, all opinions, all degrees. One orders one's coffee, smokes one's cigar. One is always sure to meet agreeable, sometimes remarkable persons.

I had not been two minutes in the room before I beheld at table, conversing with an acquaintance of mine, whom I will designate by the initial G—, the man, the original of the miniature. He was now without his hat, and the likeness was yet more startling, only I observed that while he was conversing there was less severity in the countenance; there was even a smile, though a very quiet and very cold one. The dignity of mien I had acknowledged in the street was also more striking; a dignity akin to that which invests some prince of the East, conveying the idea of supreme indifference and habitual, indisputable, indolent but resistless power.

G— soon after left the stranger, who then took up a scientific journal, which seemed to absorb his attention.

I drew G— aside.

'Who and what is that gentleman?'

'That? Oh, a very remarkable man indeed! I met him last year amid the caves of Petra, the Scriptural Edom. He is the best Oriental scholar

I know. We joined company, had an adventure with robbers, in which he showed a coolness that saved our lives; afterwards he invited me to spend a day with him in a house he had bought at Damascus, buried among almond blossoms and roses – the most beautiful thing! He had lived there for some time, quite as an Oriental, in grand style.

'I half suspect he is a renegade, immensely rich, very odd; by the by, a great mesmerizer. I have seen him with my own eyes produce an effect on inanimate things. If you take a letter from your pocket and throw it to the other end of the room, he will order it to come to his feet, and you will see the letter wriggle itself along the floor till it has obeyed his command. 'Pon my honour 'tis true; I have seen him affect even the weather, disperse or collect clouds by means of a glass tube or wand. But he does not like talking of these matters to strangers. He has only just arrived in England; says he has not been here for a great many years; let me introduce him to you.'

'Certainly! He is English, then? What is his name?'

'Oh! a very homely one – Richards.'

'And what is his birth – his family?'

'How do I know? What does it signify? No doubt some *parvenu*; but rich, so infernally rich!'

G— drew me up to the stranger, and the introduction was effected. The manners of Mr Richards were not those of an adventurous traveller. Travellers are in general gifted with high animal spirits; they are talkative, eager, imperious. Mr Richards was calm and subdued in tone, with manners which were made distant by the loftiness of punctilious courtesy, the manners of a former age.

I observed that the English he spoke was not exactly of our day. I should even have said that the accent was slightly foreign. But then Mr Richards remarked that he had been little in the habit for years of speaking in his native tongue.

The conversation fell upon the changes in the aspect of London since he had last visited our metropolis. G— then glanced off to the moral changes – literary, social, political – the great men who were removed from the stage within the last twenty years; the new great men who were coming on.

In all this Mr Richards evinced no interest. He had evidently read none of our living authors, and seemed scarcely acquainted by name with our younger statesmen. Once, and only once, he laughed; it was when G— asked him whether he had any thoughts of getting into Parliament; and the laugh was inward, sarcastic, sinister – a sneer raised into a laugh.

After a few minutes, G— left us to talk to some other acquaintances who had just lounged into the room, and I then said, quietly:

'I have seen a miniature of you, Mr Richards, in the house you once inhabited, and perhaps built – if not wholly, at least in part – in Oxford Street. You passed by that house this morning.'

Not till I had finished did I raise my eyes to his, and then he fixed my gaze so steadfastly that I could not withdraw it – those fascinating serpent-eyes. But involuntarily, and as if the words that translated my thoughts were dragged from me, I added, in a low whisper, 'I have been a student in the mysteries of life and nature; of those mysteries I have known the occult professors. I have the right to speak to you thus.' And I uttered a certain password.

'Well, I concede the right. What would you ask?'

'To what extent human will in certain temperaments can extend?'

'To what extent can thought extend? Think, and before you draw breath you are in China!'

'True; but my thought has no power in China.'

'Give it expression, and it may have. You may write down a thought which, sooner or later, may alter the whole condition of China. What is a law but a thought? Therefore thought is infinite. Therefore thought has power; not in proportion to its value – a bad thought may make a bad law as potent as a good thought can make a good one.'

'Yes; what you say confirms my own theory. Through invisible currents one human brain may transmit its ideas to other human brains, with the same rapidity as a thought promulgated by visible means. And as thought is imperishable, as it leaves its stamp behind it in the natural world, even when the thinker has passed out of this world, so the thought of the living may have power to rouse up and revive the thoughts of the dead, such as those thoughts *were in life*, though the thought of the living cannot reach the thoughts which the dead *now* may entertain. Is it not so?'

'I decline to answer, if in my judgment thought has the limit you would fix to it. But proceed; you have a special question you wish to put.'

'Intense malignity in an intense will, engendered in a peculiar temperament, and aided by natural means within the reach of science, may produce effects like those ascribed of old to evil magic. It might thus haunt the walls of a human habitation with spectral revivals of all guilty thoughts and guilty deeds once conceived and done within those walls; all, in short, with which the evil will claims *rapport* and affinity – imperfect, incoherent, fragmentary snatches at the old dramas acted therein years ago.

'Thoughts thus crossing each other haphazard, as in the nightmare of a vision, growing up into phantom sights and sounds, and all serving to create horror; not because those sights and sounds are really visitations from a world without, but that they are ghastly, monstrous renewals of what have been in this world itself, set into malignant play by a malignant mortal. And it is through the material agency of that human brain that these things would acquire even a human power; would strike as with the shock of electricity, and might kill, if the thought of the person assailed did not rise superior to the dignity of the original assailer; might kill the most powerful animal, if unnerved by fear, but not injure the feeblest man, if, while his flesh crept, his mind stood out fearless.

'Thus when in old stories we read of a magician rent to pieces by the fiends he had invoked, or still more, in Eastern legends, that one magician succeeds by arts in destroying another, there may be so far truth, that a material being has clothed, from his own evil propensities, certain elements and fluids, usually quiescent or harmless, with awful shapes and terrific force; just as the lightning, that has lain hidden and innocent in the cloud, becomes by natural law suddenly visible, takes a distinct shape to the eye, and can strike destruction on the object to which it is attracted.'

'You are not without glimpses of a mighty secret,' said Mr Richards composedly. 'According to your view, could a mortal obtain the power you speak of, he would necessarily be a malignant and evil being.'

'If the power were exercised as I have said, most malignant and most evil; though I believe in the ancient traditions that he could not injure the good. His will could only injure those with whom it has established an affinity, or over whom it forces unresisted sway. I will now imagine an example that may be within the laws of nature, yet seem wild as the fables of a bewildered monk.

'You will remember that Albertus Magnus, after describing minutely the process by which the spirits may be invoked and commanded, adds emphatically that the process will instruct and avail only to the few; that *a man must be born a magician!* – that is, born with a peculiar physical temperament, as a man is born a poet.

'Rarely are men in whose constitutions lurks this occult power of the highest order of intellect; usually in the intellect there is some twist, perversity, or disease. But on the other hand, they must possess, to an astonishing degree, the faculty to concentrate thought on a single object – the energic faculty that we call WILL. Therefore, though their intellect be not sound, it is exceedingly forcible for the attainment of what it desires. I will imagine such a person, pre-eminently gifted with this constitution and its concomitant forces. I will place him in the loftier grades of society.

'I will suppose his desires emphatically those of the sensualist; he has, therefore, a strong love of life. He is an absolute egotist; his will is concentred in himself; he has fierce passions; he knows no enduring, no holy affections, but he can covet eagerly what for the moment he desires; he can hate implacably what opposes itself to his objects; he can commit fearful crimes, yet feel small remorse; he resorts rather to curses upon others than to penitence for his misdeeds. Circumstances to which his constitution guides him, lead him to a rare knowledge of the natural secrets which may serve his egotism. He is a close observer where his passions encourage observation; he is a minute calculator, not from love of truth, but where love of self sharpens his faculties; therefore he can be a man of science.

'I suppose such a being, having by experience learned the power of his arts over others, trying what may be the power of will over his own frame, and studying all that in natural philosophy may increase that power. He loves life, he dreads death; *he wills to live on.* He cannot restore himself to youth; he cannot entirely stay the progress of death; he cannot make himself immortal in the flesh and blood. But he may arrest, for a time so long as to appear incredible if I said it, that hardening of the parts which constitutes old age.

'A year may age him no more than an hour ages another. His intense will, scientifically trained into system, operates, in short, over the wear and tear of his own frame. He lives on. That he may not seem a portent and a miracle, he *dies,* from time to time, seemingly, to certain persons. Having schemed the transfer of a wealth that suffices to his wants, he disappears from one corner of the world, and contrives that his obsequies shall be celebrated.

'He reappears at another corner of the world, where he resides undetected, and does not visit the scenes of his former career till all who could remember his features are no more. He would be profoundly miserable if he had affections; he has none but for himself. No good man would accept his longevity; and to no man, good or bad, would he or could he communicate its true secret.

'Such a man might exist; such a man as I have described I see now before me – Duke of —, in the court of —, dividing time between lust and brawl, alchemists and wizards; again, in the last century, charlatan and criminal, with name less noble, domiciled in the house at which you gazed to-day, and flying from the law you had outraged, none knew whither; traveller once more revisiting London with the same earthly passion which filled your heart when races now no more walked through yonder streets; outlaw from the school of all the nobler and diviner mysteries. Execrable image of life in death and death in life, I warn you back from the cities and homes of healthful men! back to the ruins of departed empires! back to the deserts of nature unredeemed!'

There answered me a whisper so musical, so potently musical, that it seemed to enter into my whole being and subdue me despite myself. Thus it said:

'I have sought one like you for the last hundred years. Now I have found you, we part not till I know what I desire. The vision that sees through the past and cleaves through the veil of the future is in you at this hour – never before, never to come again. The vision of no pulling, fantastic girl, of no sick-bed somnambule, but of a strong man with a vigorous brain. Soar, and look forth!'

As he spoke, I felt as if I rose out of myself upon eagle wings. All the weight seemed gone from air, roofless the room, roofless the dome of space. I was not in the body – where, I knew not; but aloft over time, over earth.

Again I heard the melodious whisper:

'You say right. I have mastered great secrets by the power of will. True, by will and by science I can retard the process of years, but death comes not by age alone. Can I frustrate the accidents which bring death upon the young?'

'No; every accident is a providence. Before a providence snaps every human will.'

'Shall I die at last, ages and ages hence, by the slow though inevitable growth of time, or by the cause that I call accident?'

'By a cause you call accident.'

'Is not the end still remote?' asked the whisper, with a slight tremor.

'Regarded as my life regards time, it is still remote.'

'And shall I, before then, mix with the world of men as I did ere I learned these secrets; resume eager interest in their strife and their trouble; battle with ambition, and use the power of the sage to win the power that belongs to kings?'

'You will yet play a part on the earth that will fill earth with commotion and amaze. For wondrous designs have you, a wonder yourself, been permitted to live on through the centuries. All the secrets you have stored will then have their uses; all that now makes you a stranger amid the generations will contribute then to make you their lord. As the trees and the straws are drawn into a whirlpool, as they spin round, are sucked to the deep, and again tossed aloft by the eddies, so shall races and thrones be drawn into your vortex. Awful destroyer! but in destroying, made, against your own will, a constructor.'

'And that date, too, is far off?'

'Far off; when it comes, think your end in this world is at hand!'

'How and what is the end? Look east, west, south, and north.'

'In the north, where you never yet trod, towards the point whence your instincts have warned you, there a spectre will seize you. 'Tis Death! I see a ship; it is haunted; 'tis chased! it sails on. Baffled navies sail after that ship. It enters the region of ice. It passes a sky red with meteors. Two moons stand on high, over ice-reefs. I see the ship locked between white defiles; they are ice-rocks. I see the dead strew the decks,

stark and livid, green mould on their limbs. All are dead but one man –
it is you! But years, though so slowly they come, have then scathed you.
There is the coming of age on your brow, and the will is relaxed in the
cells of the brain. Still that will, though enfeebled, exceeds all that man
knew before you; through the will you live on, gnawed with famine. And
Nature no longer obeys you in that death-spreading region; the sky is a
sky of iron, and the air has iron clamps, and the ice-rocks wedge in the
ship. Hark how it cracks and groans! Ice will imbed it as amber imbeds
a straw. And a man has gone forth, living yet, from the ship and its dead;
and he has clambered up the spikes of an iceberg, and the two moons
gaze down on his form. That man is yourself, and terror is on you –
terror; and terror has swallowed up your will.

'And I see, swarming up the steep ice-rock, grey, grizzly things. The
bears of the North have scented their quarry; they come nearer and
nearer, shambling, and rolling their bulk. In that day every moment
shall seem to you longer than the centuries through which you have
passed. Heed this: after life, moments continued make the bliss or the
hell of eternity.'

'Hush!' said the whisper. 'But the day, you assure me, is far off, very
far! I go back to the almond and rose of Damascus! Sleep!'

The room swam before my eyes. I became insensible. When I recovered, I found G— holding my hand and smiling. He said, 'You, who
have always declared yourself proof against mesmerism, have suc-
cumbed at last to my friend Richards.'

'Where is Mr Richards?'

'Gone, when you passed into a trance, saying quietly to me, "Your
friend will not wake for an hour." '

I asked, as collectedly as I could, where Mr Richards lodged.

'At the Trafalgar Hotel.'

'Give me your arm,' said I to G—. 'Let us call on him; I have something to say.'

When we arrived at the hotel we were told that Mr Richards had
returned twenty minutes before, paid his bill, left directions with his
servant (a Greek) to pack his effects, and proceed to Malta by the
steamer that should leave Southampton the next day. Mr Richards had
merely said of his own movements that he had visits to pay in the
neighbourhood of London, and it was uncertain whether he should be
able to reach Southampton in time for that steamer; if not, he should
follow in the next one.

The waiter asked me my name. On my informing him, he gave me a
note that Mr Richards had left for me in case I called.

The note was as follows:

I wished you to utter what was in your mind. You obeyed. I have therefore established power over you. For three months from this day you can communicate to no living man what has passed between us. You cannot even show this note to the friend by your side. During three months silence complete as to me and mine. Do you doubt my power to lay on you this command? Try to disobey me. At the end of the third month the spell is raised. For the rest, I spare you. I shall visit your grave a year and a day after it has received you.

So ends this strange story, which I ask no one to believe. I write it down exactly three months after I received the above note. I could not write it before, nor could I show to G——, in spite of his urgent request, the note which I read under the gas lamp by his side.

Edgar Allan Poe

The Masque of the Red Death

The 'Red Death' had long devastated the country. No pestilence had ever been so fatal, or so hideous. Blood was its Avatar and its seal – the redness and horror of blood. There were sharp pains, and sudden dizziness, and then profuse bleeding at the pores, with dissolution. The scarlet stains upon the body and especially upon the face of the victim, were the pest ban which shut him out from the aid and from the sympathy of his fellow-men. And the whole seizure, progress, and termination of the disease, were the incidents of half an hour.

But the Prince Prospero was happy and dauntless and sagacious. When his dominions were half-depopulated, he summoned to his presence a thousand hale and light-hearted friends from among the knights and dames of his court, and with these retired to the deep seclusion of one of his castellated abbeys. This was an extensive and magnificent structure, the creation of the prince's own eccentric yet august taste. A strong and lofty wall girdled it in. This wall had gates of iron. The courtiers, having entered, brought furnaces and massy hammars and welded the bolts. They resolved to leave means neither of ingress nor egress to the sudden impulses of despair or of frenzy from within. The abbey was amply provisioned. With such precautions the courtiers might bid defiance to contagion. The external world could take care of itself. In the meantime it was folly to grieve, or to think. The prince had provided all the appliances of pleasure. There were buffoons, there were improvisatori, there were ballet-dancers, there were musicians, there was Beauty, there was wine. All these and security were within. Without was the 'Red Death'.

It was toward the close of the fifth or sixth month of his seclusion, and while the pestilence raged most furiously abroad, that the Prince Prospero entertained his thousand friends at a masked ball of the most unusual magnificence.

It was a voluptuous scene, that masquerade. But first let me tell of the rooms in which it was held. These were seven – an imperial suite. In many palaces, however, such suites form a long and straight vista, while the folding doors slide back nearly to the walls on either hand, so that the view of the whole extent is scarcely impeded. Here the case was very different, as might have been expected from the duke's love of the *bizarre*. The apartments were so irregularly disposed that the vision embraced but little more than one at a time. There was a sharp turn at every twenty or thirty yards, and at each turn a novel effect. To the right and left, in the middle of each wall, a tall and narrow Gothic window looked out upon a closed corridor which pursued the windings of the suite. These windows were of stained glass whose colour varied in accordance with the prevailing hue of the decorations of the chamber into which it opened. That at the eastern extremity was hung, for example, in blue – and vividly blue were its windows. The second chamber was purple in its ornaments and tapestries, and here the panes were purple. The third was green throughout, and so were the casements. The fourth was furnished and lighted with orange – the fifth with white – the sixth with violet. The seventh apartment was closely shrouded in black velvet tapestries that hung all over the ceiling and down the walls, falling in heavy folds upon a carpet of the same material and hue. But in this chamber only, the colour of the windows failed to correspond with the decorations. The panes here were scarlet – a deep blood colour. Now in no one of the seven apartments was there any lamp or candelabrum, amid the profusion of golden ornaments that lay scattered to and fro or depended from the roof. There was no light of any kind emanating from lamp or candle within the suite of chambers. But in the corridors that followed the suite there stood, opposite to each window, a heavy tripod, bearing a brazier of fire, that projected its rays through the tinted glass and so glaringly illumined the room. And thus were produced a multitude of gaudy and fantastic appearances. But in the western or black chamber the effect of the fire-light that streamed upon the dark hangings through the blood-tinted panes was ghastly in the extreme, and produced so wild a look upon the countenances of those who entered, that there were few of the company bold enough to set foot within its precincts at all.

It was in this apartment, also, that there stood against the western wall, a gigantic clock of ebony. Its pendulum swung to and fro with a dull, heavy, monotonous clang; and when the minute-hand made the circuit of the face, and the hour was to be stricken, there came from the brazen lungs of the clock a sound which was clear and loud and deep and exceedingly musical, but of so peculiar a note and emphasis that, at each lapse of an hour, the musicians of the orchestra were constrained to pause, momentarily, in their performance, to harken to the sound; and thus the waltzers perforce ceased their evolutions; and there was a brief disconcert of the whole gay company; and, while the chimes of the clock yet rang, it was observed that the giddiest grew pale, and the more aged and sedate passed their hands over their brows as if in confused reverie or meditation. But when the echoes had fully ceased, a light laughter at once pervaded the assembly; the musicians looked at each other and smiled as if at their own nervousness and folly, and made whispering vows, each to the other, that the next chiming of the clock should produce in them no similar emotion; and then, after the lapse of sixty minutes (which embrace three thousand and six hundred seconds of the Time that flies), there came yet another chiming of the clock, and then were the same disconcert and tremulousness and meditation as before.

But, in spite of these things, it was a gay and magnificent revel. The tastes of the duke were peculiar. He had a fine eye for colours and effects. He disregarded the *decora* of mere fashion. His plans were bold and fiery, and his conceptions glowed with barbaric lustre. There are some who would have thought him mad. His followers felt that he was not. It was necessary to hear and see and touch him to be *sure* that he was not.

He had directed, in great part, the movable embellishments of the seven chambers, upon occasion of this great *fête*; and it was his own guiding taste which had given character to the masqueraders. Be sure they were grotesque. There were much glare and glitter and piquancy and phantasm — much of what has been since seen in *Hernani*. There were arabesque figures with unsuited limbs and appointments. There were delirious fancies such as the madman fashions. There were much of the beautiful, much of the wanton, much of the *bizarre*, something of the terrible, and not a little of that which might have excited disgust. To and fro in the seven chambers there stalked, in fact, a multitude of dreams. And these — the dreams — writhed in and about, taking hue from the rooms, and causing the wild music of the orchestra to seem as the echo of their steps. And, anon, there strikes the ebony clock which stands in the hall of the velvet. And then, for a moment, all is still, and all is silent save the voice of the clock. The dreams are stiff-frozen as they stand. But the echoes of the chime die away — they have endured but an instant — and a light, half-subdued laughter floats after them as they depart. And now again the music swells, and the dreams live, and writhe to and fro more merrily than ever, taking hue from the many-tinted windows through which stream the rays from the tripods. But to the chamber which lies most westwardly of the seven there are now none of the maskers who venture; for the night is waning away; and there flows a ruddier light through the blood-coloured panes; and the blackness of the sable drapery appals; and to him whose foot falls upon the sable carpet, there comes from the near clock of ebony a muffled peal more solemnly emphatic than any which reaches *their* ears who indulged in the more remote gaieties of the other apartments.

But these other apartments were densely crowded, and in them beat feverishly the heart of life. And the revel went whirlingly on, until at length there commenced the sounding of midnight upon the clock. And then the music ceased, as I have told; and the evolutions of the waltzers were quieted; and there was an uneasy cessation of all things as before. But now there were twelve strokes to be sounded by the bell of the clock; and thus it happened, perhaps, that more of thought crept, with more of time, into the meditations of the thoughtful among those who revelled. And thus too, it happened, perhaps, that before the last echoes of the last chime had utterly sunk into silence, there were many individuals in the crowd who had found leisure to become aware of the presence of a masked figure which had arrested the attention of no single individual before. And the rumour of this new presence having spread itself whisperingly around, there arose at length from the whole company a buzz, or murmur, expressive of disapprobation and surprise – then, finally, of terror, of horror, and of disgust.

In an assembly of phantasms such as I have painted, it may well be supposed that no ordinary appearance could have excited such sensation. In truth the masquerade licence of the night was nearly unlimited; but the figure in question had out-Heroded Herod, and gone beyond the bounds of even the prince's indefinite decorum. There are chords in the hearts of the most reckless which cannot be touched without emotion. Even with the utterly lost, to whom life and death are equally jests, there are matters of which no jest can be made. The whole company, indeed, seemed now deeply to feel that in the costume and bearing of the stranger neither wit nor propriety existed. The figure was tall and gaunt, and shrouded from head to foot in the habiliments of the grave. The mask which concealed the visage was made so nearly to resemble the countenance of a stiffened corpse that the closest scrutiny must have had difficulty in detecting the cheat. And yet all this might have been endured, if not approved, by the mad revellers around. But the mummer had gone so far as to assume the type of the Red Death. His vesture was dabbled in *blood* – and his broad brow, with all the features of the face, was besprinkled with the scarlet horror.

When the eyes of Prince Prospero fell upon this spectral image (which, with a slow and solemn movement, as if more fully to sustain its *rôle*, stalked to and fro among the waltzers) he was seen to be convulsed in the first moment with a strong shudder either of terror or distaste; but, in the next, his brow reddened with rage.

'Who dares,' – he demanded hoarsely of the courtiers who stood near him – 'who dares insult us with this blasphemous mockery? Seize him and unmask him – that we may know whom we have to hang, at sunrise, from the battlements!'

It was in the eastern or blue chamber in which stood the Prince Prospero as he uttered these words. They rang throughout the seven rooms loudly and clearly, for the prince was a bold and robust man, and the music had become hushed at the waving of his hand.

It was in the blue room where stood the prince, with a group of pale courtiers by his side. At first, as he spoke, there was a slight rushing movement of this group in the direction of the intruder, who at the moment was also near at hand, and now, with deliberate and stately step, made closer approach to the speaker. But from a certain nameless awe with which the mad assumptions of the mummer had inspired the whole party, there were found none who put forth hand to seize him; so that, unimpeded, he passed within a yard of the prince's person; and, while the vast assembly, as if with one impulse, shrank from the centres of the rooms to the walls, he made his way uninterruptedly, but with the same solemn and measured step which had distinguished him from the first, through the blue chamber to the purple – through the purple to the green – through the green to the orange – through this again to the white – and even thence to the violet, ere a decided movement had been made to arrest him. It was then, however, that the Prince Prospero, maddening with rage and the shame of his own momentary cowardice, rushed hurriedly through the six chambers, while none followed him on account of a deadly terror that had seized upon all. He bore aloft a drawn dagger, and had approached, in rapid impetuosity, to within three or four feet of the retreating figure, when the latter, having attained the extremity of the velvet apartment, turned suddenly and confronted his pursuer. There was a sharp cry – and the dagger dropped gleaming upon the sable carpet, upon which, instantly afterward, fell prostrate in death the Prince Prospero. Then, summoning the wild courage of despair, a throng of the revellers at once threw themselves into the black apartment, and, seizing the mummer, whose tall figure stood erect and motionless within the shadow of the ebony clock, gasped in unutterable horror at finding the grave cerements and corpse-like mask, which they handled with so violent a rudeness, untenanted by any tangible form.

And now was acknowledged the presence of the Red Death. He had come like a thief in the night. And one by one dropped the revellers in the blood-bedewed halls of their revel, and died each in the despairing posture of his fall. And the life of the ebony clock went out with that of the last of the gay. And the flames of the tripods expired. And Darkness and Decay and the Red Death held illimitable dominion over all.

Edgar Allan Poe

The Facts in the Case of M. Valdemar

Of course I shall not pretend to consider it any matter for wonder, that the extraordinary case of M. Valdemar has excited discussion. It would have been a miracle had it not – especially under the circumstances. Through the desire of all parties concerned, to keep the affair from the public, at least for the present, or until we had farther opportunities for investigation – through our endeavours to effect this – a garbled or exaggerated account made its way into society, and became the source of many unpleasant misrepresentations, and, very naturally, of a great deal of disbelief.

It is now rendered necessary that I give the *facts* – as far as I comprehend them myself. They are, succinctly, these:

My attention, for the last three years, had been repeatedly drawn to the subject of Mesmerism; and, about nine months ago, it occurred to me, quite suddenly, that in the series of experiments made hitherto, there had been a very remarkable and most unaccountable omission: – no person had as yet been mesmerised *in articulo mortis*. It remained to be seen, first, whether, in such condition, there existed in the patient any susceptibility to the magnetic influence; secondly, whether, if any existed, it was impaired or increased by the condition; thirdly, to what extent, or for how long a period, the encroachments of Death might be arrested by the process. There were other points to be ascertained, but these most excited my curiosity – the last in especial, from the immensely important character of its consequences.

In looking around me for some subject by whose means I might test these particulars, I was brought to think of my friend, M. Ernest Valdemar, the well-known compiler of the *Bibliotheca Forensica*, and author (under the *nom de plume* of Issachar Marx) of the Polish versions

of *Wallenstein* and *Gargantua*. M. Valdemar, who has resided principally at Harlaem, N.Y., since the year 1839, is (or was) particularly
noticeable for the extreme spareness of his person – his lower limbs much
resembling those of John Randolph; and, also, for the whiteness of his
whiskers, in violent contrast to the blackness of his hair – the latter, in
consequence, being very generally mistaken for a wig. His temperament
was markedly nervous, and rendered him a good subject for mesmeric
experiment. On two or three occasions I had put him to sleep with little
difficulty, but was disappointed in other results which his peculiar constitution had naturally led me to anticipate. His will was at no period
positively, or thoroughly, under my control, and in regard to *clair-
voyance*, I could accomplish with him nothing to be relied upon. I
always attributed my failure at these points to the disordered state of his
health. For some months previous to my becoming acquainted with him,
his physicians had declared him in a confirmed phthisis. It was his custom, indeed, to speak calmly of his approaching dissolution, as of a
matter neither to be avoided nor regretted.

When the ideas to which I have alluded first occurred to me, it was of
course very natural that I should think of M. Valdemar. I knew the
steady philosophy of the man too well to apprehend any scruples from
him; and he had no relatives in America who would be likely to interfere. I spoke to him frankly upon the subject; and, to my surprise, his
interest seemed vividly excited. I say to my surprise; for, although he had
always yielded his person freely to my experiments, he had never before
given me any tokens of sympathy with what I did. His disease was of
that character which would admit of exact calculation in respect to the
epoch of its termination in death; and it was finally arranged between us
that he would send for me about twenty-four hours before the period
announced by his physicians as that of his decease.

It is now rather more than seven months since I received, from M.
Valdemar himself, the subjoined note:

MY DEAR P—,
   You may as well come *now*. D— and F— are agreed that I cannot
hold out beyond to-morrow midnight; and I think they have hit the
time very nearly.

                                                      VALDEMAR.

I received this note within half an hour after it was written, and in
fifteen minutes more I was in the dying man's chamber. I had not seen
him for ten days, and was appalled by the fearful alteration which the
brief interval had wrought in him. His face wore a leaden hue; the eyes
were utterly lustreless; and the emaciation was so extreme that the skin

THE FACTS IN THE CASE OF M. VALDEMAR

had been broken through by the cheek-bones. His expectoration was excessive. The pulse was barely perceptible. He retained, nevertheless, in a very remarkable manner, both his mental power and a certain degree of physical strength. He spoke with distinctness – took some palliative medicines without aid – and, when I entered the room, was occupied in pencilling memoranda in a pocket-book. He was propped up in the bed by pillows. Doctors D— and F— were in attendance.

After pressing Valdemar's hand, I took these gentlemen aside, and obtained from them a minute account of the patient's condition. The left lung had been for eighteen months in a semi-osseous or cartilaginous state, and was, of course, entirely useless for all purposes of vitality. The right, in its upper portion, was also partially, if not thoroughly, ossified, while the lower region was merely a mass of purulent tubercles, running one into another. Several extensive perforations existed; and, at one point, permanent adhesion to the ribs had taken place. These appearances in the right lobe were of comparatively recent date. The ossification had proceeded with very unusual rapidity; no sign of it had been discovered a month before, and the adhesion had only been observed during the three previous days. Independently of the phthisis, the patient was suspected of aneurism of the aorta; but on this point the osseous symptoms rendered an exact diagnosis impossible. It was the opinion of both physicians that M. Valdemar would die about midnight on the morrow (Sunday). It was then seven o'clock on Saturday evening.

On quitting the invalid's bed-side to hold conversation with myself, Doctors D— and F— had bidden him a final farewell. It had not been their intention to return; but, at my request, they agreed to look in upon the patient about ten the next night.

When they had gone, I spoke freely with M. Valdemar on the subject of his approaching dissolution, as well as, more particularly, of the experiment proposed. He still professed himself quite willing and even anxious to have it made, and urged me to commence it at once. A male and a female nurse were in attendance; but I did not feel myself altogether at liberty to engage in a task of this character with no more reliable witnesses than these people, in case of sudden accident, might prove. I therefore postponed operations until about eight the next night, when the arrival of a medical student with whom I had some acquaintance (Mr Theodore L—l), relieved me from farther embarrassment. It had been my design, originally, to wait for the physicians; but I was induced to proceed, first, by the urgent entreaties of M. Valdemar, and secondly, by my conviction that I had not a moment to lose, as he was evidently sinking fast.

Mr L—l was so kind as to accede to my desire that he would take notes of all that occurred; and it is from his memoranda that what I now have to relate is, for the most part, either condensed or copied *verbatim*.

It wanted about five minutes of eight when, taking the patient's hand, I begged him to state, as distinctly as he could, to Mr L—l, whether he (M. Valdemar) was entirely willing that I should make the experiment of mesmerising him in his then condition.

He replied feebly, yet quite audibly, 'Yes, I wish to be mesmerised' – adding immediately afterwards, 'I fear you have deferred it too long.'

While he spoke thus, I commenced the passes which I had already found most effectual in subduing him. He was evidently influenced with the first lateral strokes of my hand across his forehead; but although I exerted all my powers, no farther perceptible effect was induced until some minutes after ten o'clock, when Doctors D— and F— called, according to appointment. I explained to them, in a few words, what I designed, and as they opposed no objection, saying that the patient was already in the death agony, I proceeded without hesitation – exchanging, however, the lateral passes for downward ones, and directing my gaze entirely into the right eye of the sufferer.

By this time his pulse was imperceptible and his breathing was stertorous, and at intervals of half a minute.

This condition was nearly unaltered for a quarter of an hour. At the expiration of this period, however, a natural although a very deep sigh escaped the bosom of the dying man, and the stertorous breathing ceased – that is to say, its stertorousness was no longer apparent; the intervals were undiminished. The patient's extremities were of an icy coldness.

At five minutes before eleven I perceived unequivocal signs of the mesmeric influence. The glassy roll of the eye was changed for that expression of uneasy *inward* examination which is never seen except in cases of sleep-walking, and which it is quite impossible to mistake. With a few rapid lateral passes I made the lids quiver, as in incipient sleep, and with a few more I closed them altogether. I was not satisfied, however, with this, but continued the manipulation vigorously, and with the fullest exertion of the will, until I had completely stiffened the limbs of the slumberer, after placing them in a seemingly easy position. The legs were at full length; the arms were nearly so, and reposed on the bed at a moderate distance from the loins. The head was very slightly elevated.

When I had accomplished this, it was fully midnight, and I requested the gentlemen present to examine M. Valdemar's condition. After a few experiments, they admitted him to be in an unusually perfect state of mesmeric trance. The curiosity of both physicians was greatly excited. Dr D— resolved at once to remain with the patient all night, while Dr F— took leave with a promise to return at daybreak. Mr L—l and the nurses remained.

THE FACTS IN THE CASE OF M. VALDEMAR

We left M. Valdemar entirely undisturbed until about three o'clock in the morning, when I approached him and found him in precisely the same condition as when Dr F— went away – that is to say, he lay in the same position; the pulse was imperceptible; the breathing was gentle (scarcely noticeable, unless through the application of a mirror to the lips); the eyes were closed naturally; and the limbs were as rigid and as cold as marble. Still, the general appearance was certainly not that of death.

As I approached M. Valdemar I made a kind of half effort to influence his right arm into pursuit of my own, as I passed the latter gently to and fro above his person. In such experiments with this patient I had never perfectly succeeded before, and assuredly I had little thought of succeeding now; but to my astonishment, his arm very readily, although feebly, followed every direction I assigned it with mine. I determined to hazard a few words of conversation.

'M. Valdemar,' I said, 'are you asleep?' He made no answer, but I perceived a tremor about the lips, and was thus induced to repeat the question, again and again. At its third repetition, his whole frame was agitated by a very slight shivering; the eyelids unclosed themselves so far as to display a white line of the bell; the lips moved sluggishly, and from between them, in a barely audible whisper, issued the words:

'Yes; – asleep now. Do not wake me! – let me die so!'

I here felt the limbs and found them as rigid as ever. The right arm, as before, obeyed the direction of my hand. I questioned the sleep-waker again:

'Do you still feel pain in the breast, M. Valdemar?'

The answer now was immediate, but even less audible than before:

'No pain – I am dying.'

I did not think it advisable to disturb him farther just then, and nothing more was said or done until the arrival of Dr F—, who came a little before sunrise, and expressed unbounded astonishment at finding the patient still alive. After feeling the pulse and applying a mirror to the lips, he requested me to speak to the sleep-waker again. I did so, saying:

'M. Valdemar, do you still sleep?'

As before, some minutes elapsed ere a reply was made; and during the interval the dying man seemed to be collecting his energies to speak. At my fourth repetition of the question, he said very faintly, almost inaudibly:

'Yes; still asleep – dying.'

It was now the opinion, or rather the wish, of the physicians, that M. Valdemar should be suffered to remain undisturbed in his present apparently tranquil condition, until death should intervene – and this, it was generally agreed, must now take place within a few minutes. I concluded, however, to speak to him once more, and merely repeated my previous question.

While I spoke, there came a marked change over the countenance of the sleep-waker. The eyes rolled themselves slowly open, the pupils disappearing upwardly; the skin generally assumed a cadaverous hue, resembling not so much parchment as white paper; and the circular hectic spots which, hitherto, had been strongly defined in the centre of each cheek, *went out* at once. I use this expression, because the suddenness of their departure put me in mind of nothing so much as the extinguishment of a candle by a puff of the breath. The upper lip, at the same time, writhed itself away from the teeth, which it had previously covered completely; while the lower jaw fell with an audible jerk, leaving the mouth widely extended, and disclosing in full view the swollen and blackened tongue. I presume that no member of the party then present had been unaccustomed to death-bed horrors; but so hideous beyond conception was the appearance of M. Valdemar at this moment, that there was a general shrinking back from the region of the bed.

I now feel that I have reached a point of this narrative at which every reader will be startled into positive disbelief. It is my business, however, simply to proceed.

There was no longer the faintest sign of vitality in M. Valdemar; and concluding him to be dead, we were consigning him to the charge of the nurses, when a strong vibratory motion was observable in the tongue. This continued for perhaps a minute. At the expiration of this period, there issued from the distended and motionless jaws a voice – such as it would be madness in me to attempt describing. There are, indeed, two or three epithets which might be considered as applicable to it in parts; I might say for example, that the sound was harsh, and broken, and hollow; but the hideous whole is indescribable, for the simple reason that no similar sounds have ever jarred upon the ear of humanity. There were two particulars, nevertheless, which I thought then, and still think, might fairly be stated as characteristic of the intonation – as well adapted to convey some idea of its unearthly peculiarity. In the first place, the voice seemed to reach our ears – at least mine – from a vast distance, or from some deep cavern within the earth. In the second place, it impressed me (I fear, indeed, that it will be impossible to make myself comprehended) as gelatinous or glutinous matters impress the sense of touch.

I have spoken both of 'sound' and of 'voice.' I mean to say that the sound was one of distinct – of even wonderfully, thrilling distinct – syllabification. M. Valdemar *spoke* – obviously in reply to the question I had propounded to him a few minutes before. I had asked him, it will be remembered, if he still slept. He now said:

'Yes; – no; – I *have been* sleeping – and now – now – *I am dead.*'

No person present even affected to deny, or attempted to repress, the unutterable, shuddering horror which these few words, thus uttered, were so well calculated to convey. Mr L—l (the student) swooned. The nurses immediately left the chamber, and could not be induced to return. My own impressions I would not pretend to render intelligible to the reader. For nearly an hour, we busied ourselves, silently – without the utterance of a word – in endeavours to revive Mr L—l. When he came to himself, we addressed ourselves again to an investigation of M. Valdemar's condition.

It remained in all respects as I have last described it, with the exception that the mirror no longer afforded evidence of respiration. An attempt to draw blood from the arm failed. I should mention, too, that this limb was no farther subject to my will. I endeavoured in vain to make it follow the direction of my hand. The only real indication, indeed, of the mesmeric influence, was now found in the vibratory movement of the tongue, whenever I addressed M. Valdemar a question. He seemed to be making an effort to reply, but had no longer sufficient volition. To queries put to him by any other person than myself he seemed utterly insensible – althoug I endeavoured to place each member of the company in mesmeric *rapport* with him. I believe that I have now related all that is necessary to an understanding of the sleep-waker's state at this epoch. Other nurses were procured; and at ten o'clock I left the house in company with the two physicians and Mr L—l.

In the afternoon we all called again to see the patient. His condition remained precisely the same. We had now some discussion as to the propriety and feasibility of awakening him; but we had little difficulty in agreeing that no good purpose would be served by so doing. It was evident that, so far, death (or what is usually termed death) had been arrested by the mesmeric process. It seemed clear to us all that to awaken M. Valdemar would be merely to insure his instant, or at least his speedy dissolution.

From this period until the close of last week – *an interval of nearly seven months* – we continued to make daily calls at M. Valdemar's house, accompanied now and then, by medical and other friends. All this time the sleep-waker remained *exactly* as I have last described him. The nurses' attentions were continual.

It was on Friday last that we finally resolved to make the experiment of awakening, or attempting to awaken him; and it is the (perhaps) unfortunate result of this latter experiment which has given rise to so much discussion in private circles – to so much of what I cannot help thinking unwarranted popular feeling.

For the purpose of relieving M. Valdemar from the mesmeric trance, I made use of the customary passes. These, for a time, were unsuccessful. The first indication of revival was afforded by a partial descent of the iris. It was observed, as especially remarkable, that this lowering of the pupil was accompanied by the profuse out-flowing of a yellowish ichor (from beneath the lids) of a pungent and highly offensive odour.

It was now suggested that I should attempt to influence the patient's arm, as heretofore. I made the attempt and failed. Dr. F— then intimated a desire to have me put a question. I did so, as follows:

'M. Valdemar, can you explain to us what are your feelings or wishes now?'

There was an instant return of the hectic circles on the cheeks; the tongue quivered, or rather rolled violently in the mouth (although the jaws and lips remained rigid as before); and at length the same hideous voice which I have already described, broke forth:

'For God's sake! – quick! – quick! – put me to sleep – or, quick! – waken me! – quick! – *I say to you that I am dead!*'

I was thoroughly unnerved, and for an instant remained undecided what to do. At first I made an endeavour to re-compose the patient; but, failing in this through total abeyance of the will, I retraced my steps and as earnestly struggled to awaken him. In this attempt I soon saw that I should be successful – or at least I soon fancied that my success would be complete – and I am sure that all in the room were prepared to see the patient awaken.

For what really occurred, however, it is quite impossible that any human being could have been prepared.

As I rapidly made the mesmeric passes, amid ejaculations of 'dead! dead!' absolutely *bursting* from the tongue and not from the lips of the suffered, his whole frame at once – within the space of a single minute, or even less, shrunk – crumbled – absolutely *rotted* away beneath my hands. Upon the bed, before that whole company, there lay a nearly liquid mass of loathsome – of detestable putridity.

Edgar Allan Poe

Ligeia

And the will therein lieth, which dieth not. Who knoweth the
mysteries of the will, with its vigour? For God is but a great will
pervading all things by nature of its intentness. Man doth not yield
himself to the angels, nor unto death utterly, save only through the
weakness of his feeble will.—JOSEPH GLANVILL.

I cannot, for my soul, remember how, when, or even precisely where, I
first became acquainted with the Lady Ligeia. Long years have since
elapsed, and my memory is feeble through much suffering. Or, perhaps, I
cannot *now* bring these points to mind, because, in truth, the character
of my beloved, her rare learning, her singular yet placid cast of beauty,
and the thrilling and enthralling eloquence of her low musical language,
made their way into my heart by paces so steadily and stealthily pro-
gressive that they have been unnoticed and unknown. Yet I believe that
I met her first and most frequently in some large, old, decaying city near
the Rhine. Of her family – I have surely heard her speak. That it is of a
remotely ancient date cannot be doubted. Ligeia! Ligeia! Buried in
studies of a nature more than all else adapted to deaden impressions of
the outward world, it is by that sweet word alone – by Ligeia – that I
bring before mine eyes in fancy the image of her who is no more. And
now, while I write, a recollection flashes upon me that I have *never
known* the paternal name of her who was my friend and my betrothed,
and who became the partner of my studies, and finally the wife of my
bosom. Was it a playful charge on the part of my Ligeia? or was it a
test of my strength of affection, that I should institute no inquiries upon
this point? or was it rather a caprice of my own – a wildly romantic
offering on the shrine of the most passionate devotion? I but indistinctly

recall the fact itself – what wonder that I have utterly forgotten the circumstances which originated or attended it? And, indeed, if ever that spirit which is entitled *Romance* – if ever she, the wan and the misty-winged *Ashtophet* of idolatrous Egypt, presided, as they tell, over marriages ill-omened, then most surely she presided over mine.

There is one dear topic, however, on which my memory fails me not. It is the *person* of Ligeia. In stature she was tall, somewhat slender, and, in her latter days, even emaciated. I would in vain attempt to portray the majesty, the quiet ease, of her demeanour, or the incomprehensible lightness and elasticity of her footfall. She came and departed as a shadow. I was never made aware of her entrance into my closed study save by the dear music of her sweet voice, as she placed her marble hand upon my shoulder. In beauty of face no maiden ever equalled her. It was the radiance of an opium-dream – an airy and spirit-lifting vision more wildly divine than the phantasies which hovered about the slumbering souls of the daughters of Delos. Yet her features were not of that regular mould which we have been falsely taught to worship in the classical labours of the heathen. 'There is no exquisite beauty,' says Bacon, Lord Verulam, speaking truly of all the forms and *genera* of beauty, 'without some *strangeness* in the proportion.' Yet, although I saw that the features of Ligeia were not of a classic regularity – although I perceived that her loveliness was indeed 'exquisite', and felt that there was much of 'strangeness' pervading it, yet I have tried in vain to detect the irregularity and to trace home my own perception of 'the strange'. I examined the contour of the lofty and pale forehead – it was faultless – how cold indeed that word when applied to a majesty so divine! – the skin rivalling the purest ivory, the commanding extent and repose, the gentle prominence of the regions above the temples; and then the raven-black, the glossy, the luxuriant and naturally-curling tresses, setting forth the full force of the Homeric epithet, 'hyacinthine'! I looked at the delicate outlines of the nose – and nowhere but in the graceful medallions of the Hebrews had I beheld a similar perfection. There were the same luxurious smoothness of surface, the same scarcely perceptible tendency to the aquiline, the same harmoniously curved nostrils speaking the free spirit. I regarded the sweet mouth. Here was indeed the triumph of all things heavenly – the magnificent turn of the short upper lip – the soft, voluptuous slumber of the under – the dimples which sported, and the colour which spoke – the teeth glancing back, with a brilliancy almost startling, every ray of the holy light which fell upon them in her serene and placid, yet most exultingly radiant of all smiles. I scrutinized the formation of the chin – and here, too, I found the gentleness of breadth, the softness and the majesty, the fullness and the spirituality, of the Greek – the contour which the god Apollo revealed but in a dream, to

LIGEIA

Cleomenes, the son of the Athenian. And then I peered into the large eyes of Ligeia.

For eyes we have no models in the remotely antique. It might have been, too, that in these eyes of my beloved lay the secret to which Lord Verulam alludes. They were, I must believe, far larger than the ordinary eyes of our own race. They were even fuller than the fullest of the gazelle eyes of the tribe of the valley of Nourjahad. Yet it was only at intervals – in moments of intense excitement – that this peculiarity became more than slightly noticeable in Ligeia. And at such moments was her beauty – in my heated fancy thus it appeared perhaps – the beauty of beings either above or apart from the earth – the beauty of the fabulous Houri of the Turk. The hue of the orbs was the most brilliant of black, and, far over them, hung jetty lashes of great length. The brows, slightly irregular in outline, had the same tint. The 'strangeness', however, which I found in the eyes, was of a nature distinct from the formation, or the colour, or the brilliancy of the features, and must, after all, be referred to the *expression*. Ah, word of no meaning! behind whose vast latitude of mere sound we entrench our ignorance of so much of the spiritual. The expression of the eye of Ligeia! How for long hours have I pondered upon it! How have I, through the whole of a midsummer night, struggled to fathom it! What was it – that something more profound than the well of Democritus – which lay far within the pupils of my beloved? What *was* it? I was possessed with a passion to discover. Those eyes! those large, those shining, those divine orbs! they became to me twin stars of Leda, and I to them devoutest of astrologers.

There is no point, among the many incomprehensible anomalies of the science of mind, more thrillingly exciting than the fact – never, I believe, noticed in the schools – that, in our endeavours to recall to memory something long forgotten, we often find ourselves *upon the very verge* of remembrance, without being able, in the end, to remember. And thus how frequently, in my intense scrutiny of Ligeia's eyes, have I felt approaching the full knowledge of their expression – felt it approaching – yet not quite be mine – and so at length entirely depart! And (strange, oh, strangest mystery of all!) I found, in the commonest objects of the universe, a circle of analogies to that expression. I mean to say that, subsequently to the period when Ligeia's beauty passed into my spirit, there dwelling as in a shrine, I derived, from many existences in the material world, a sentiment such as I felt always aroused within me by her large and luminous orbs. Yet not the more could I define that sentiment, or analyse, or even steadily view it. I recognized it, let me repeat, sometimes in the survey of a rapidly-growing vine – in the contemplation of a moth, a butterfly, a chrysalis, a stream of running water. I have felt it in the ocean; in the falling of a meteor. I have felt it in the glances of unusually aged people. And there are one or two stars in heaven (one especially, a star of the sixth magnitude, double and changeable, to be found near the large star in Lyra) in a telescopic scrutiny of which I have been made aware of the feeling. I have been filled with it by certain sounds from stringed instruments, and not un-frequently by passages from books. Among innumerable other instances, I well remember something in a volume of Joseph Glanvill, which (per-haps merely from its quaintness – who shall say?) never failed to inspire me with the sentiment: 'And the will therein lieth, which dieth not. Who knoweth the mysteries of the will, with its vigour? For God is but a great will pervading all things by nature of its intentness. Man doth not yield himself to the angels, nor unto death utterly, save only through the weakness of his feeble will.'

Length of years, and subsequent reflection, have enabled me to trace, indeed, some remote connection between this passage in the English moralist and a portion of the character of Ligeia. An *intensity* in thought, action, or speech, was possibly, in her, a result, or at least an index, of that gigantic volition which, during our long intercourse, failed to give other and more immediate evidence of its existence. Of all the women whom I have ever known, she, the outwardly calm, the ever-placid Ligeia, was the most violently a prey to the tumultuous vultures of stern passion. And of such passion I could form no estimate, save by the miraculous expansion of those eyes which at once so delighted and appalled me – by the almost magical melody, modulation, distinctness, and placidity of her very low voice – and by the fierce energy (rendered doubly effective by contrast with her manner of utterance) of the wild words which she habitually uttered.

I have spoken of the learning of Ligeia: it was immense – such as I have never known in woman. In the classical tongues was she deeply proficient, and as far as my own acquaintance extended in regard to the modern dialects of Europe, I have never known her at fault. Indeed upon any theme of the most admired, because simply the most abstruse, of the boasted erudition of the academy, have I *ever* found Ligeia at fault? How singularly – how thrillingly, this one point in the nature of my wife has forced itself, at this late period only, upon my attention! I said her knowledge was such as I have never known in woman – but where breathes the man who has traversed, and successfully, *all* the wide areas of moral, physical, and mathematical science? I saw not then what I now clearly perceive, that the acquisitions of Ligeia were gigantic, were astounding; yet I was sufficiently aware of her infinite supremacy to resign myself, with a childlike confidence, to her guidance through the chaotic world of metaphysical investigation at which I was most busily occupied during the earlier years of our marriage. With how vast a triumph – with how vivid a delight – with how much of all that is ethereal in hope – did I *feel*, as she bent over me in studies but little sought – but less known – that delicious vista by slow degrees expanding before me, down whose long, gorgeous, and all untrodden path, I might at length pass onward to the goal of a wisdom too divinely precious not to be forbidden!

How poignant, then, must have been the grief with which, after some years, I beheld my well-grounded expectations take wings to themselves and fly away! Without Ligeia I was but as a child groping benighted. Her presence, her readings alone, rendered vividly luminous the many mysteries of the transcendentalism in which we were immersed. Wanting the radiant lustre of her eyes, letters, lambent and golden, grew duller than Saturnian lead. And now those eyes shone less and less frequently upon the pages over which I pored. Ligeia grew ill. The wild eyes blazed with a too – too glorious effulgence; the pale fingers became of the transparent waxen hue of the grave, and the blue veins upon the lofty forehead swelled and sank impetuously with the tides of the most gentle emotion. I saw that she must die – and I struggled desperately in spirit with the grim Azrael. And the struggles of the passionate wife were, to my astonishment, even more energetic than my own. There had been much in her stern nature to impress me with the belief that, to her, death would have come without its terrors; but not so. Words are impotent to convey any just idea of the fierceness of resistance with which she wrestled with the Shadow. I groaned in anguish at the pitiable spectacle. I would have soothed – I would have reasoned; but, in the intensity of her wild desire for life – for life – *but* for life – solace and reason were alike the uttermost of folly. Yet not until the last instance, amid the most convulsive writhings of her fierce spirit, was shaken the external placidity of her demeanour. Her voice grew more gentle – grew more low – yet I would not wish to dwell upon the wild meaning of the quietly uttered words. My brain reeled as I hearkened entranced, to a melody more than mortal – to assumptions and aspirations which mortality had never before known.

That she loved me I should not have doubted; and I might have been easily aware that, in a bosom such as hers, love would have reigned no ordinary passion. But in death only, was I fully impressed with the strength of her affection. For long hours, detaining my hand, would she pour out before me the overflowing of a heart whose more than passionate devotion amounted to idolatry. How had I deserved to be so blessed by such confessions? – how had I deserved to be so cursed with the removal of my beloved in the hour of her making them? But upon this subject I cannot bear to dilate. Let me say only, that in Ligeia's more than womanly abandonment to a love, alas! all unmerited, all un-

worthily bestowed, I at length recognized the principle of her longing
with so wildly earnest a desire for the life which was now fleeing so
rapidly away. It is this wild longing – it is this eager vehemence of desire
for life – *but* for life – that I have no power to portray – no utterance
capable of expressing.

At high noon of the night in which she departed, beckoning me,
peremptorily, to her side she made me repeat certain verses composed by
herself not many days before. I obeyed her. They were these:

> Lo! 'tis a gala night
>   Within the lonesome latter years!
> An angel throng, bewinged, bedight
>   In veils, and drowned in tears,
> Sit in a theatre, to see
>   A play of hopes and fears,
> While the orchestra breathes fitfully
>   The music of the spheres.
>
> Mimes, in the form of God on high,
>   Mutter and mumble low,
> And hither and thither fly –
>   Mere puppets they, who come and go
> At bidding of vast formless things
>   That shift the scenery to and fro,
> Flapping from out their condor wings
>   Invisible Woe!
>
> That motley drama! – oh, be sure
>   It shall not be forgot!
> With its Phantom chased for ever more,
>   By a crowd that seize it not,
> Through a circle that ever returneth in
>   To the self-same spot,
> And much of Madness and more of Sin
>   And Horror the soul of the plot.
>
> But see, amid the mimic rout,
>   A crawling shape intrude!
> A blood-red thing that writhes from out
>   The scenic solitude!
> It writhes! – it writhes! – with mortal pangs
>   The mimes become its food,
> And the seraphs sob at vermin fangs
>   In human gore imbued.

LIGEIA

Out – out are the lights – out all!
  And over each quivering form,
The curtain, a funeral pall,
  Comes down with the rush of a storm,
And the angels, all pallid and wan,
  Uprising, unveiling, affirm
That the play is the tragedy, 'Man',
  And its hero the Conqueror Worm.

'O God!' half shrieked Ligeia, leaping to her feet and extending her arms aloft with a spasmodic movement, as I made an end of these lines: 'O God! O Divine Father! – shall these things be undeviatingly so? – shall this Conqueror be not once conquered? Are we not part and parcel in Thee? Who – who knoweth the mysteries of the will with its vigour? Man doth not yield him to the angels, *nor unto death utterly*, save only through the weakness of his feeble will.'

And now, as if exhausted with emotion, she suffered her white arms to fall, and returned solemnly to her bed of death. And as she breathed her last sighs, there came mingled with them a low murmur from her lips. I bent to them my ear and distinguished, again, the concluding words of the passage in Glanvill: *'Man doth not yield himself to the angels, nor unto death utterly, save only through the weakness of his feeble will.'*

She died; and I, crushed into the very dust with sorrow, could no longer endure the lonely desolation of my dwelling in the dim and decaying city by the Rhine. I had no lack of what the world calls wealth. Ligeia had brought me far more, very far more than ordinarily falls to the lot of mortals. After a few months, therefore, of weary and aimless wandering, I purchased, and put in some repair, an abbey, which I shall not name, in one of the wildest and least frequented portions of fair England. The gloomy and dreary grandeur of the building, the almost savage aspect of the domain, the many melancholy and time-honoured memories connected with both, had much in unison with the feelings of utter abandonment which had driven me into that remote and unsocial region of the country. Yet although the external abbey, with its verdant decay hanging about it, suffered but little alteration, I gave way, with a childlike perversity, and perchance with a faint hope of alleviating my sorrows, to a display of more than regal magnificence within. For such follies, even in childhood, I had imbibed a taste, and now they came back to me as if in the dotage of grief. Alas, I feel how much even of incipient madness might have been discovered in the gorgeous and fantastic draperies, in the solemn carvings of Egypt, in the wild cornices and furniture, in the Bedlam patterns of the carpets of tufted gold! I had become a bounden slave in the trammels of opium, and my labours and my orders had taken a colouring from my dreams. But these absurdities I must not pause to detail. Let me speak only of that one chamber, ever accursed, whither, in a moment of mental alienation, I led from the altar as my bride – as the successor of the unforgotten Ligeia – the fair-haired and blue-eyed Lady Rowena Trevanion, of Tremaine.

There is no individual portion of the architecture and decoration of that bridal chamber, which is not now visibly before me. Where were the souls of the haughty family of the bride, when, through thirst of gold, they permitted to pass the threshold of an apartment *so* bedecked, a maiden and a daughter so beloved? I have said that I minutely remember the details of the chamber – yet I am sadly forgetful on topics of deep moment – and here there was no system, no keeping, in the fantastic display, to take hold upon the memory. The room lay in a high turret of the castellated abbey, was pentagonal in shape, and of capacious size. Occupying the whole southern face of the pentagon was the sole window – an immense sheet of unbroken glass from Venice – a single pane, and tinted of a leaden hue, so that the rays of either the sun or moon, passing through it, fell with a ghastly lustre on the objects within. Over the upper portion of this huge window, extended the trellis-work of an aged vine, which clambered up the massy walls of the turret. The ceiling, of gloomy-looking oak, was excessively lofty, vaulted, and elaborately fretted with the wildest and most grotesque specimens of a semi-Gothic, semi-Druidical device. From out the most central recess of this melancholy vaulting, depended, by a single chain of gold with long links, a huge censer of the same metal, Saracenic in pattern, and with many perforations so contrived that there writhed in and out of them, as if endued with a serpent vitality, a continual succession of particoloured fires.

Some few ottomans and golden candelabra, of Eastern figure, were in various stations about; and there was the couch, too – the bridal couch – of an Indian model, and low, and sculptured of solid ebony, with a pall-like canopy above. In each of the angles of the chamber stood on end a gigantic sarcophagus of black granite, from the tombs of the kings over against Luxor, with their aged lids full of immemorial sculpture. But in the draping of the apartment lay, alas! the chief phantasy of all. The lofty walls, gigantic in height – even unproportionably so – were hung from summit to foot, in vast folds, with a heavy and massive-looking tapestry – tapestry of a material which was found alike as a carpet on the floor, as a covering for the ottomans and the ebony bed, as a canopy for the bed, and as the gorgeous volutes of the curtains which partially shaded the window. The material was the richest cloth of gold. It was spotted all over, at irregular intervals, with arabesque figures, about a foot in diameter, and wrought upon the cloth in patterns of the

LIGEIA

most jetty black. But these figures partook of the true character of the
arabesque only when regarded from a single point of view. By a contrivance now common, and indeed traceable to a very remote period of
antiquity, they were made changeable in aspect. To one entering the
room, they bore the appearance of simple monstrosities; but upon a
farther advance, this appearance gradually departed; and step by step, as
the visitor moved his station in the chamber, he saw himself surrounded
by an endless succession of the ghastly forms which belong to the superstition of the Norman, or arise in the guilty slumbers of the monk. The
phantasmagoric effect was vastly heightened by the artificial introduction
of a strong continual current of wind behind the draperies – giving a
hideous and uneasy animation to the whole.

In halls such as these – in a bridal chamber such as this – I passed,
with the Lady of Tremaine, the unhallowed hours of the first month of
our marriage – passed them with but little disquietude. That my wife
dreaded the fierce moodiness of my temper – that she shunned me and
loved me but little – I could not help perceiving; but it gave me rather
pleasure than otherwise. I loathed her with a hatred belonging more to
demon than to man. My memory flew back (oh, with what intensity of
regret!) to Ligeia, the beloved, the august, the beautiful, the entombed. I
revelled in recollections of her purity, of her wisdom, of her lofty, her
ethereal nature, of her passionate, her idolatrous love. Now, then, did my
spirit fully and freely burn with more than all the fires of her own. In the
excitement of my opium dreams (for I was habitually fettered in the
shackles of the drug) I would call aloud upon her name, during the
silence of the night, or among the sheltered recesses of the glens by day,
as if, through the wild eagerness, the solemn passion, the consuming
ardour of my longing for the departed, I could restore her to the pathway she had abandoned – ah, *could* it be for ever? – upon the earth.

About the commencement of the second month of the marriage, the
Lady Rowena was attacked with sudden illness, from which her recovery
was slow. The fever which consumed her rendered her nights uneasy;
and in her perturbed state of half-slumber, she spoke of sounds, and of
motions, in and about the chamber of the turret, which I concluded had
no origin save in the distemper of her fancy, or perhaps in the phantasmagoric influences of the chamber itself. She became at length con-
valescent – finally well. Yet but a brief period elapsed, ere a second more
violent disorder again threw her upon a bed of suffering; and from this
attack her frame, at all times feeble, never altogether recovered. Her
illnesses were, after this epoch, of alarming character, and of more
alarming recurrence, defying alike the knowledge and the great exertions
of her physicians. With the increase of the chronic disease which had
thus, apparently, taken too sure hold upon her constitution to be eradi-

cated by human means, I could not fail to observe a similar increase in the nervous irritation of her temperament, and in her excitability by trivial causes of fear. She spoke again, and now more frequently and pertinaciously, of the sounds – of the slight sounds – and of the unusual motions among the tapestries, to which she had formerly alluded.

One night, near the closing in of September, she pressed this distressing subject with more than usual emphasis upon my attention. She had just awakened from an unquiet slumber, and I had been watching, with feelings half of anxiety, half of vague terror, the workings of her emaciated countenance. I sat by the side of her ebony bed, upon one of the ottomans of India. She partly rose, and spoke, in an earnest low whisper, of sounds which she *then* heard, but which I could not hear – of motions which she *then* saw, but which I could not perceive. The wind was rushing hurriedly behind the tapestries, and I wished to show her (what, let me confess it, I could not *all* believe) that those almost inarticulate breathings, and those very gentle variations of the figures upon the wall, were but the natural effects of that customary rushing of the wind. But a deadly pallor, overspreading her face, had proved to me that my exertions to reassure her would be fruitless. She appeared to be fainting, and no attendants were within call. I remembered where was deposited a decanter of light wine which had been ordered by her physicians, and hastened across the chamber to procure it. But, as I stepped beneath the light of the censer, two circumstances of a startling nature attracted my attention. I had felt that some palpable although invisible object had passed lightly by my person; and I saw that there lay upon the golden carpet, in the very middle of the rich lustre thrown from the censer, a shadow – a faint, indefinite shadow of angelic aspect – such as might be fancied for the shadow of a shade. But I was wild with the excitement of an immoderate dose of opium, and heeded these things but little, nor spoke of them to Rowena. Having found the wine, I recrossed the chamber, and poured out a gobletful, which I held to the lips of the fainting lady. She had now partially recovered, however, and took the vessel herself, while I sank upon an ottoman near me, with my eyes fastened upon her person. It was then that I became distinctly aware of a gentle footfall upon the carpet, and near the couch; and in a second thereafter, as Rowena was in the act of raising the wine to her lips, I saw, or may have dreamed that I saw, fall within the goblet, as if from some invisible spring in the atmosphere of the room, three or four large drops of a brilliant and ruby-coloured fluid. If this I saw – not so Rowena. She swallowed the wine unhesitatingly, and I forbore to speak to her of a circumstance which must, after all, I considered, have been but the suggestion of a vivid imagination, rendered morbidly active by the terror of the lady, by the opium, and by the hour.

LIGEIA

Yet I cannot conceal it from my own perception that, immediately subsequent to the fall of the ruby-drops, a rapid change for the worse took place in the disorder of my wife; so that, on the third subsequent night, the hands of her menials prepared her for the tomb, and on the fourth, I sat alone, with her shrouded body, in that fantastic chamber which had received her as my bride. Wild visions, opium-engendered, flitted, shadow-like, before me. I gazed with unquiet eye upon the sarcophagi in the angles of the room, upon the varying figures of the drapery, and upon the writhing of the particoloured fires in the censer overhead. My eyes then fell, as I called to mind the circumstances of a former night, to the spot beneath the glare of the censer where I had seen the faint traces of the shadow. It was there, however, no longer; and breathing with greater freedom, I turned my glances to the pallid and rigid figure upon the bed. Then rushed upon me a thousand memories of Ligeia – and then back came upon my heart, with the turbulent violence of a flood, the whole of that unutterable woe with which I had regarded *her* thus enshrouded. The night waned; and still, with a bosom full of bitter thoughts of the only one and supremely beloved, I remained gazing upon the body of Rowena.

It might have been midnight, or perhaps earlier, or later, for I had taken no note of time, when a sob, low, gentle, but very distinct, startled me from my reverie. I *felt* that it came from the bed of ebony – the bed of death. I listened in an agony of superstitious terror – but there was no repetition of the sound. I strained my vision to detect any motion in the corpse – but there was not the slightest perceptible. Yet I could not have been deceived. I *had* heard the noise, however faint, and my soul was awakened within me. I resolutely and perseveringly kept my attention riveted upon the body. Many minutes elapsed before any circumstances occurred tending to throw light upon the mystery. At length it became evident that a slight, a very feeble, and barely noticeable tinge of colour had flushed up within the cheeks, and along the sunken small veins of the eyelids. Through a species of unutterable horror and awe, for which the language of mortality has no sufficiently energetic expression, I felt my heart cease to beat, my limbs grow rigid where I sat. Yet a sense of duty finally operated to restore my self-possession. I could no longer doubt that we had been precipitate in our preparations – that Rowena still lived. It was necessary that some immediate exertion be made; yet the turret was altogether apart from the portion of the abbey tenanted by the servants – there were none within call – I had no means of summoning them to my aid without leaving the room for many minutes – and this I could not venture to do. I therefore struggled alone in my endeavours to call back the spirit still hovering. In a short period it was certain, however, that a relapse had taken place; the colour disappeared from both eyelid and cheek, leaving a wanness even more than that of marble; the lips became doubly shrivelled and pinched up in the ghastly expression of death; a repulsive clamminess and coldness overspread rapidly the surface of the body; and all the usual rigorous stiffness immediately supervened. I fell back with a shudder upon the couch from which I had been so startlingly aroused, and again gave myself up to passionate waking visions of Ligeia.

An hour thus elapsed when (could it be possible?) I was a second time aware of some vague sound issuing from the region of the bed. I listened – in extremity of horror. The sound came again – it was a sigh. Rushing to the corpse, I saw – distinctly saw – a tremor upon the lips. In a minute afterwards they relaxed, disclosing a bright line of the pearly teeth. Amazement now struggled in my bosom with the profound awe which had hitherto reigned there alone. I felt that my vision grew dim, that my reason wandered; and it was only by a violent effort that I at length succeeded in nerving myself to the task which duty thus once more had pointed out. There was now a partial glow upon the forehead and upon the cheek and throat; a perceptible warmth pervaded the whole frame; there was even a slight pulsation at the heart. The lady *lived*; and with redoubled ardour I betook myself to the task of restoration. I chafed and bathed the temples and the hands, and used every exertion which experience, and no little medical reading, could suggest. But in vain. Suddenly, the colour fled, the pulsation ceased, the lips resumed the expression of the dead, and, in an instant afterwards, the whole body took upon itself the icy chilliness, the livid hue, the intense rigidity, the sunken outline, and all the loathsome peculiarities of that which has been, for many days, a tenant of the tomb.

And again I sunk into visions of Ligeia – and again (what marvel that I shudder while I write?), *again* there reached my ears a low sob from the region of the ebony bed. But why shall I minutely detail the unspeakable horrors of that night? Why shall I pause to relate how, time after time, until near the period of the grey dawn, this hideous drama of revivification was repeated; how each terrific relapse was only into a sterner and apparently more irredeemable death; how each agony wore the aspect of a struggle with some invisible foe; and how each struggle was succeeded by I know not what of wild change in the personal appearance of the corpse? Let me hurry to a conclusion.

The greater part of the fearful night had worn away, and she who had been dead, once again stirred – and now more vigorously than hitherto, although arousing from a dissolution more appalling in its utter hopelessness than any. I had long ceased to struggle or to move, and remained sitting rigidly upon the ottoman, a helpless prey to a whirl of violent emotions, of which extreme awe was perhaps the least terrible, the least consuming. The corpse, I repeat, stirred, and now more vigorously than before. The hues of life flushed up with unwonted energy into the countenance – the limbs relaxed – and, save that the eyelids were yet pressed heavily together, and that the bandages and draperies of the grave still imparted their charnel character to the figure, I might have dreamed that Rowena had indeed shaken off, utterly, the fetters of Death. But if this idea was not, even then, altogether adopted, I could at least doubt no longer, when arising from the bed, tottering, with feeble steps, with closed eyes, and with the manner of one bewildered in a dream, the thing that was enshrouded advanced boldly and palpably into the middle of the apartment.

I trembled not – I stirred not – for a crowd of unutterable fancies connected with the air, the stature, the demeanour of the figure, rushing hurriedly through my brain, had paralysed – had chilled me into stone. I stirred not – but gazed upon the apparition. There was a mad disorder in my thoughts – a tumult unappeasable. Could it, indeed, be the *living* Rowena who confronted me? Could it indeed be Rowena *at all* – the fair-haired, the blue-eyed Lady Rowena Trevanion of Tremaine? Why, *why* should I doubt it? The bandage lay heavily about the mouth – but then might it not be the mouth of the breathing Lady of Tremaine? And the cheeks – there were the roses as in her noon of life – yes, these might indeed be the fair cheeks of the living Lady of Tremaine. And the chin, with its dimples, as in health, might it not be hers? – but *had she then grown taller since her malady?* What inexpressible madness seized me with that thought? One bound, and I had reached her feet! Shrinking from my touch, she let fall from her head, unloosened, the ghastly cerements which had confined it, and there streamed forth, into the rushing atmosphere of the chamber, huge masses of long and dishevelled hair; *it was blacker than the raven wings of the midnight!* And now slowly opened the *eyes* of the figure which stood before me. 'Here then, at least,' I shrieked aloud, 'can I never – can I never be mistaken – these are the full, and the black, and the wild eyes – of my lost love – of the Lady – of the LADY LIGEIA.'

Joseph Sheridan Le Fanu

Carmilla

PROLOGUE

Upon a paper attached to the Narrative which follows, Doctor Hesselius has written a rather elaborate note, which he accompanies with a reference to his Essay on the strange subject which the MS. illuminates.

This mysterious subject he treats, in that Essay, with his usual learning and acumen, and with remarkable directness and condensation. It will form but one volume of the series of that extraordinary man's collected papers.

As I publish the case, in this volume, simply to interest the 'laity', I shall forestall the intelligent lady, who relates it, in nothing; and, after due consideration, I have determined, therefore, to abstain from presenting any *précis* of the learned Doctor's reasoning, or extract from his statement on a subject which he describes as 'involving, not improbably, some of the profoundest arcana of our dual existence, and its intermediates.'

I was anxious, on discovering this paper, to re-open the correspondence commenced by Doctor Hesselius, so many years before, with a person so clever and careful as his informant seems to have been. Much to my regret, however, I found that she had died in the interval.

She, probably, could have added little to the Narrative which she communicates in the following pages, with, so far as I can pronounce, such a conscientious particularity.

CARMILLA

CHAPTER I

AN EARLY FRIGHT

In Styria, we, though by no means magnificent people, inhabit a castle, or schloss. A small income, in that part of the world, goes a great way. Eight or nine hundred a year does wonders. Scantily enough ours would have answered among wealthy people at home. My father is English, and I bear an English name, although I never saw England. But here, in this lonely and primitive place, where everything is so marvellously cheap, I really don't see how ever so much more money would at all materially add to our comforts, or even luxuries.

My father was in the Austrian service, and retired upon a pension and his patrimony, and purchased this feudal residence, and the small estate on which it stands, a bargain.

Nothing can be more picturesque or solitary. It stands on a slight eminence in a forest. The road, very old and narrow, passes in front of its drawbridge, never raised in my time, and its moat, stocked with perch, and sailed over by many swans, and floating on its surface white fleets of water-lilies.

Over all this the schloss shows its many-windowed front; its towers, and its Gothic chapel.

The forest opens in an irregular and very picturesque glade before its gate, and at the right a steep Gothic bridge carries the road over a stream that winds in deep shadow through the wood.

I have said that this is a very lonely place. Judge whether I say truth. Looking from the hall door towards the road, the forest in which our castle stands extends fifteen miles to the right, and twelve to the left. The nearest inhabited village is about seven of your English miles to the left. The nearest inhabited schloss of any historic associations, is that of old General Spielsdorf, nearly twenty miles away to the right.

I have said 'the nearest *inhabited* village', because there is, only three miles westward, that is to say in the direction of General Spielsdorf's schloss, a ruined village, with its quaint little church, now roofless, in the aisle of which are the mouldering tombs of the proud family of Karnstein, now extinct, who once owned the equally-desolate château which, in the thick of the forest, overlooks the silent ruins of the town.

Respecting the cause of the desertion of this striking and melancholy spot, there is a legend which I shall relate to you another time.

I must tell you now, how very small is the party who constitute the inhabitants of our castle. I don't include servants, or those dependants who occupy rooms in the buildings attached to the schloss. Listen, and wonder! My father, who is the kindest man on earth, but growing old; and I, at the date of my story, only nineteen. Eight years have passed since then. I and my father constituted the family at the schloss. My mother, a Styrian lady, died in my infancy, but I had a good-natured governess, who had been with me from, I might almost say, my infancy. I could not remember the time when her fat, benignant face was not a familiar picture in my memory. This was Madame Perrodon, a native of Berne, whose care and good nature in part supplied to me the loss of my mother, whom I do not even remember, so early I lost her. She made a third at our little dinner party. There was a fourth, Mademoiselle De Lafontaine, a lady such as you term, I believe, a 'finishing governess'. She spoke French and German, Madame Perrodon French and broken English, to which my father and I added English, which, partly to prevent its becoming a lost language among us, and partly from patriotic motives, we spoke every day. The consequence was a Babel, at which strangers used to laugh, and which I shall make no attempt to reproduce in this narrative. And there were two or three young lady friends besides, pretty nearly of my own age, who were occasional visitors, for longer or shorter terms; and these visits I sometimes returned.

These were our regular social resources; but of course there were chance visits from 'neighbours' of only five or six leagues' distance. My life was, notwithstanding, rather a solitary one, I can assure you.

My gouvernantes had just so much control over me as you might conjecture such sage persons would have in the case of a rather spoiled girl, whose only parent allowed her pretty nearly her own way in everything.

The first occurrence in my existence, which produced a terrible impression upon my mind, which, in fact, never has been effaced, was one of the very earliest incidents of my life which I can recollect. Some people will think it so trifling that it should not be recorded here. You will see, however, by-and-by, why I mention it. The nursery, as it was called, though I had it all to myself, was a large room in the upper story of the castle, with a steep oak roof. I can't have been more than six years old, when one night I awoke, and looking round the room from my bed, failed to see the nursery-maid. Neither was my nurse there; and I thought myself alone. I was not frightened, for I was one of those happy children who are studiously kept in ignorance of ghost stories, of fairy tales, and of all such lore as makes us cover up our heads when the door creaks suddenly, or the flicker of an expiring candle makes the shadow of a bed-post dance upon the wall, nearer to our faces. I was vexed and insulted at finding myself, as I conceived, neglected, and I began to whimper, preparatory to a hearty bout of roaring; when to my surprise, I saw a solemn, but very pretty face looking at me from the side of the bed. It was that of a young lady who was kneeling, with her hands under the coverlet. I looked at her with a kind of pleased wonder, and ceased whimpering. She caressed me with her hands, and lay down beside me on the bed, and drew me towards her, smiling; I felt immediately delightfully soothed, and fell asleep again. I was wakened by a sensation as if two needles ran into my breast very deep at the same moment, and I cried loudly. The lady started back, with her eyes fixed on me, and then slipped down upon the floor, and, as I thought, hid herself under the bed.

I was now for the first time frightened, and I yelled with all my might and main. Nurse, nursery-maid, housekeeper, all came running in, and hearing my story, they made light of it, soothing me all they could meanwhile. But, child as I was, I could perceive that their faces were pale with an unwonted look of anxiety, and I saw them look under the bed, and about the room, and peep under tables and pluck open cupboards; and the housekeeper whispered to the nurse: 'Lay your hand along that hollow in the bed; some one *did* lie there, so sure as you did not; the place is still warm.'

I remember the nursery-maid petting me, and all three examining my chest, where I told them I felt the puncture, and pronouncing that there was no sign visible that any such thing had happened to me.

The housekeeper and the two other servants who were in charge of the nursery, remained sitting up all night; and from that time a servant always sat up in the nursery until I was about fourteen.

I was very nervous for a long time after this. A doctor was called in, he was pallid and elderly. How well I remember his long saturnine face, slightly pitted with small-pox, and his chestnut wig. For a good while, every second day, he came and gave me medicine, which of course I hated.

The morning after I saw this apparition I was in a state of terror, and could not bear to be left alone, daylight though it was, for a moment.

I remember my father coming up and standing at the bedside, and talking cheerfully, and asking the nurse a number of questions, and laughing very heartily at one of the answers; and patting me on the shoulder, and kissing me, and telling me not to be frightened, that it was nothing but a dream and could not hurt me.

But I was not comforted, for I knew the visit of the strange woman was *not* a dream; and I was *awfully* frightened.

I was a little consoled by the nursery-maid's assuring me that it was she who had come and looked at me, and lain down beside me in the bed, and that I must have been half-dreaming not to have known her face. But this, though supported by the nurse, did not quite satisfy me.

I remember, in the course of that day, a venerable old man, in a black cassock, coming into the room with the nurse and housekeeper, and talking a little to them, and very kindly to me; his face was very sweet and gentle, and he told me they were going to pray, and joined my hands together, and desired me to say, softly, while they were praying, 'Lord, hear all good prayers for us, for Jesus' sake.' I think these were the very words, for I often repeated them to myself, and my nurse used for years to make me say them in my prayers.

I remember so well the thoughtful sweet face of that white-haired old man, in his black cassock, as he stood in that rude, lofty, brown room, with the clumsy furniture of a fashion three hundred years old, about him, and the scanty light entering its shadowy atmosphere through the small lattice. He kneeled, and the three women with him, and he prayed aloud with an earnest quavering voice for, what appeared to me, a long time. I forget all my life preceding that event, and for some time after it is all obscure also; but the scenes I have just described stand out vivid as the isolated pictures of the phantasmagoria surrounded by darkness.

CHAPTER II

A GUEST

I am now going to tell you something so strange that it will require all your faith in my veracity to believe my story. It is not only true, nevertheless, but truth of which I have been an eye-witness.

It was a sweet summer evening, and my father asked me, as he sometimes did, to take a little ramble with him along that beautiful forest vista which I have mentioned as lying in front of the schloss.

'General Spielsdorf cannot come to us so soon as I had hoped,' said my father, as we pursued our walk.

He was to have paid us a visit of some weeks, and we had expected his arrival next day. He was to have brought with him a young lady, his niece and ward, Mademoiselle Rheinfeldt, whom I had never seen, but whom I had heard described as a very charming girl, and in whose society I had promised myself many happy days. I was more disappointed than a young lady living in a town, or a bustling neighbourhood can possibly imagine. This visit, and the new acquaintance it promised, had furnished my day dream for many weeks.

'And how soon does he come?' I asked.

'Not till autumn. Not for two months, I dare say,' he answered. 'And I am very glad now, dear, that you never knew Mademoiselle Rheinfeldt.'

'And why?' I asked, both mortified and curious.

'Because the poor young lady is dead,' he replied. 'I quite forgot I had not told you, but you were not in the room when I received the General's letter this evening.'

I was very much shocked. General Spielsdorf had mentioned in his first letter, six or seven weeks before, that she was not so well as he would wish her, but there was nothing to suggest the remotest suspicion of danger.

'Here is the General's letter,' he said, handing it to me. 'I am afraid he is in great affliction; the letter appears to me to have been written very nearly in distraction.'

We sat down on a rude bench, under a group of magnificent lime trees. The sun was setting with all its melancholy splendour behind the sylvan horizon, and the stream that flows beside our home, and passes under the steep old bridge I have mentioned, wound through many a group of noble trees, almost at our feet, reflecting in its current the fading crimson of the sky. General Spieldorf's letter was so extraordinary, so vehement, and in some places so self-contradictory, that I read it twice over – the second time aloud to my father – and was still unable to account for it, except by supposing that grief had unsettled his mind.

It said, 'I have lost my darling daughter, for as such I loved her. During the last days of dear Bertha's illness I was not able to write to you. Before then I had no idea of her danger. I have lost her, and now learn *all*, too late. She died in the peace of innocence, and in the glorious hope of a blessed futurity. The fiend who betrayed our infatuated hospitality has done it all. I thought I was receiving into my house innocence, gaiety, a charming companion for my lost Bertha. Heavens! what a fool have I been! I thank God my child died without a suspicion of the cause of her sufferings. She is gone without so much as conjecturing the nature of her illness, and the accursed passion of the agent of all this misery. I devote my remaining days to tracking and extinguishing a monster. I am told I may hope to accomplish my righteous and merciful purpose. At present there is scarcely a gleam of light to guide me. I curse my conceited incredulity, my despicable affectation of superiority, my blindness, my obstinacy – all – too late. I cannot write or talk collectedly now. I am distracted. So soon as I shall have a little recovered, I mean to devote myself for a time to enquiry, which may possibly lead me as far as Vienna. Some time in the autumn, two months hence, or earlier if I live, I will see you – that is, if you permit me; I will then tell you all that I scarce dare put upon paper now. Farewell. Pray for me, dear friend.'

In these terms ended this strange letter. Though I had never seen Bertha Rheinfeldt, my eyes filled with tears at the sudden intelligence; I was startled, as well as profoundly disappointed.

The sun had now set, and it was twilight by the time I had returned the General's letter to my father.

It was a soft clear evening, and we loitered, speculating upon the possible meanings of the violent and incoherent sentences which I had just been reading. We had nearly a mile to walk before reaching the road that passes the schloss in front, and by that time the moon was shining brilliantly. At the drawbridge we met Madame Perrodon and Mademoiselle De Lafontaine, who had come out, without their bonnets, to enjoy the exquisite moonlight.

We heard their voices gabbling in animated dialogue as we approached. We joined them at the drawbridge, and turned about to admire with them the beautiful scene.

The glade through which we had just walked lay before us. At our left the narrow road wound away under clumps of lordly trees, and was lost to sight amid the thickening forest. At the right the same road crosses the steep and picturesque bridge, near which stands a ruined tower, which once guarded that pass; and beyond the bridge an abrupt eminence rises, covered with trees, and showing in the shadow some grey ivy-clustered rocks.

Over the sward and low grounds, a thin film of mist was stealing like smoke, marking the distances with a transparent veil; and here and there we could see the river faintly flashing in the moonlight.

No softer, sweeter scene could be imagined. The news I had just heard made it melancholy; but nothing could disturb its character of profound serenity, and the enchanted glory and vagueness of the prospect.

My father, who enjoyed the picturesque, and I, stood looking in silence over the expanse beneath us. The two good governesses, standing a little way behind us, discoursed upon the scene, and were eloquent upon the moon.

Madame Perrodon was fat, middle-aged, and romantic, and talked and sighed poetically. Mademoiselle De Lafontaine – in right of her father, who was a German, assumed to be psychological, metaphysical, and something of a mystic – now declared that when the moon shone with a light so intense it was well known that it indicated a special spiritual activity. The effect of the full moon in such a state of brilliancy was manifold. It acted on dreams, it acted on lunacy, it acted on nervous people; it had marvellous physical influences connected with life. Mademoiselle related that her cousin, who was mate of a merchant ship, having taken a nap on deck on such a night, lying on his back, with his face full in the light of the moon, had awakened, after a dream of an old woman clawing him by the cheek, with his features horribly drawn to one side; and his countenance had never quite recovered its equilibrium.

'The moon, this night,' she said, 'is full of odylic and magnetic influence – and see, when you look behind you at the front of the schloss, how all its windows flash and twinkle with that silvery splendour, as if unseen hands had lighted up the rooms to receive fairy guests.'

There are indolent states of the spirits in which, indisposed to talk ourselves, the talk of others is pleasant to our listless ears; and I gazed on, pleased with the tinkle of the ladies' conversation.

'I have got into one of my moping moods to-night,' said my father, after a silence, and quoting Shakespeare, whom, by way of keeping up our English, he used to read aloud, he said: –

> ' "In truth I know not why I am so sad:
> It wearies me; you say it wearies you;
> But how I got it – came by it."

'I forget the rest. But I feel as if some great misfortune were hanging over us. I suppose the poor General's afflicted letter has had something to do with it.'

At this moment the unwonted sound of carriage wheels and many hoofs upon the road, arrested our attention.

They seemed to be approaching from the high ground overlooking the bridge, and very soon the equipage emerged from that point. Two horsemen first crossed the bridge, then came a carriage drawn by four horses, and two men rode behind.

It seemed to be the travelling carriage of a person of rank; and we were all immediately absorbed in watching that very unusual spectacle. It became, in a few moments, greatly more interesting, for just as the carriage had passed the summit of the steep bridge, one of the leaders, taking fright, communicated his panic to the rest, and, after a plunge or two, the whole team broke into a wild gallop together, and dashing between the horsemen who rode in front, came thundering along the road towards us with the speed of a hurricane.

The excitement of the scene was made more painful by the clear, long-drawn screams of a female voice from the carriage window.

We all advanced in curiosity and horror; my father in silence, the rest with various ejaculations of terror.

Our suspense did not last long. Just before you reach the castle draw-bridge, on the route they were coming, there stands by the roadside a magnificent lime tree, on the other stands an ancient stone cross, at sight of which the horses, now going at a pace that was perfectly frightful, swerved so as to bring the wheel over the projecting roots of the tree.

I knew what was coming. I covered my eyes, unable to see it out, and turned my head away; at the same moment I heard a cry from my lady-friends, who had gone on a little.

Curiosity opened my eyes, and I saw a scene of utter confusion. Two of the horses were on the ground, the carriage lay upon its side, with two wheels in the air; the men were busy removing the traces, and a lady, with a commanding air and figure had got out, and stood with clasped hands, raising the handkerchief that was in them every now and then to her eyes. Through the carriage door was now lifted a young lady, who appeared to be lifeless. My dear old father was already beside the elder lady, with his hat in his hand, evidently tendering his aid and the resources of his schloss. The lady did not appear to hear him, or to have eyes for anything but the slender girl who was being placed against the slope of the bank.

I approached; the young lady was apparently stunned, but she was certainly not dead. My father, who piqued himself on being something of a physician, had just had his fingers to her wrist and assured the lady, who declared herself her mother, that her pulse, though faint and irregular, was undoubtedly still distinguishable. The lady clasped her hands and looked upward, as if in a momentary transport of gratitude; but immediately she broke out again in that theatrical way which is, I believe, natural to some people.

She was what is called a fine-looking woman for her time of life, and must have been handsome; she was tall, but not thin, and dressed in black velvet, and looked rather pale, but with a proud and commanding countenance, though now agitated strangely.

'Was ever being so born to calamity?' I heard her say, with clasped hands, as I came up. 'Here am I, on a journey of life and death, in prosecuting which to lose an hour is possibly to lose all. My child will not have recovered sufficiently to resume her route for who can say how long. I must leave her; I cannot, dare not, delay. How far on, sir, can you tell, is the nearest village? I must leave her there; and shall not see my darling, or even hear of her till my return, three months hence.'

I plucked my father by the coat, and whispered earnestly in his ear, 'Oh! papa, pray ask her to let her stay with us – it would be so delightful. Do, pray.'

'If Madame will entrust her child to the care of my daughter and of her good gouvernante, Madame Perrodon, and permit her to remain as our guest, under my charge, until her return, it will confer a distinction and an obligation upon us, and we shall treat her with all the care and devotion which so sacred a trust deserves.'

'I cannot do that, sir, it would be to task your kindness and chivalry too cruelly,' said the lady, distractedly.

'It would, on the contrary, be to confer on us a very great kindness at the moment when we most need it. My daughter has just been disappointed by a cruel misfortune, in a visit from which she had long anticipated a great deal of happiness. If you confide this young lady to our care it will be her best consolation. The nearest village on your route is distant, and affords no such inn as you could think of placing your daughter at; you cannot allow her to continue her journey for any considerable distance without danger. If, as you say, you cannot suspend your journey, you must part with her to-night, and nowhere could you do so with more honest assurances of care and tenderness than here.'

There was something in this lady's air and appearance so distinguished, and even imposing, and in her manner so engaging, as to impress one, quite apart from the dignity of her equipage, with a conviction that she was a person of consequence.

By this time the carriage was replaced in its upright position, and the horses, quite tractable, in the traces again.

The lady threw on her daughter a glance which I fancied was not quite so affectionate as one might have anticipated from the beginning of the scene; then she beckoned slightly to my father and withdrew two or three steps with him out of hearing; and talked to him with a fixed and stern countenance, not at all like that with which she had hitherto spoken.

I was filled with wonder that my father did not seem to perceive the change, and also unspeakably curious to learn what it could be that she was speaking, almost in his ear, with so much earnestness and rapidity.

Two or three minutes at most, I think, she remained thus employed, then she turned, and a few steps brought her to where her daughter lay, supported by Madame Perrodon. She kneeled beside her for a moment and whispered, as Madame supposed, a little benediction in her ear; then hastily kissing her, she stepped into her carriage, the door was closed, the footmen in stately liveries jumped up behind, the outriders spurred on, the postilions cracked their whips, the horses plunged and broke suddenly into a furious canter that threatened soon again to become a gallop, and the carriage whirled away, followed at the same rapid pace by the two horsemen in the rear.

CHAPTER III

WE COMPARE NOTES

We followed the *cortège* with our eyes until it was swiftly lost to sight in the misty wood; and the very sound of the hoofs and wheels died away in the silent night air.

Nothing remained to assure us that the adventure had not been an illusion for a moment but the young lady, who just at that moment opened her eyes. I could not see, for her face was turned from me, but she raised her head, evidently looking about her, and I heard a very sweet voice ask complainingly, 'Where is mamma?'

Our good Madame Perrodon answered tenderly, and added some comfortable assurances.

I then heard her ask:

'Where am I? What is this place?' and after that she said, 'I don't see the carriage; and Matska, where is she?'

Madame answered all her questions in so far as she understood them; and gradually the young lady remembered how the misadventure came about, and was glad to hear that no one in, or in attendance on, the carriage was hurt; and on learning that her mamma had left her here, till her return in about three months, she wept.

I was going to add my consolations to those of Madame Perrodon when Mademoiselle De Lafontaine placed her hand upon my arm, saying:

'Don't approach, one at a time is as much as she can at present converse with; a very little excitement would possibly overpower her now.'

As soon as she is comfortably in bed, I thought, I will run up to her room and see her.

My father in the meantime had sent a servant on horseback for the physician, who lived about two leagues away; and a bedroom was being prepared for the young lady's reception.

The stranger now rose, and leaning on Madame's arm, walked slowly over the drawbridge and into the castle gate.

In the hall the servants waited to receive her, and she was conducted forthwith to her room.

The room we usually sat in as our drawing-room is long, having four windows, that looked over the moat and drawbridge, upon the forest scene I have just described.

It is furnished in old carved oak, with large carved cabinets, and the chairs are cushioned with crimson Utrecht velvet. The walls are covered with tapestry, and surrounded with great gold frames, the figures being as large as life, in ancient and very curious costume, and the subjects represented are hunting, hawking, and generally festive. It is not too stately to be extremely comfortable; and here we had our tea, for with his usual patriotic leanings he insisted that the national beverage should make its appearance regularly with our coffee and chocolate.

We sat here this night, and with candles lighted, were talking over the adventure of the evening.

Madame Perrodon and Mademoiselle De Lafontaine were both of our party. The younger stranger had hardly lain down in her bed when she sank into a deep sleep; and those ladies had left her in the care of a servant.

'How do you like our guest?' I asked, as soon as Madame entered. 'Tell me all about her?'

'I like her extremely,' answered Madame, 'she is, I almost think, the prettiest creature I ever saw; about your age, and so gentle and nice.'

'She is absolutely beautiful,' threw in Mademoiselle, who had peeped for a moment into the stranger's room.

'And such a sweet voice!' added Madame Perrodon.

'Did you remark a woman in the carriage, after it was set up again, who did not get out,' inquired Mademoiselle, 'but only looked from the window.'

No, we had not seen her.

Then she described a hideous black woman, with a sort of coloured turban on her head, who was gazing all the time from the carriage window, nodding and grinning derisively towards the ladies, with gleaming eyes and large white eye-balls, and her teeth set as if in fury.

'Did you remark what an ill-looking pack of men the servants were?' asked Madame.

'Yes,' said my father, who had just come in, 'ugly, hang-dog looking fellows, as ever I beheld in my life. I hope they mayn't rob the poor lady in the forest. They are clever rogues, however; they got everything to rights in a minute.'

'I dare say they are worn out with too long travelling,' said Madame. 'Besides looking wicked, their faces were so strangely lean, and dark, and sullen. I am very curious, I own; but I dare say the young lady will tell us all about it to-morrow, if she is sufficiently recovered.'

'I don't think she will,' said my father, with a mysterious smile, and a little nod of his head, as if he knew more about it than he cared to tell us.

This made me all the more inquisitive as to what had passed between him and the lady in the black velvet, in the brief but earnest interview that had immediately preceded her departure.

We were scarcely alone, when I entreated him to tell me. He did not need much pressing.

'There is no particular reason why I should not tell you. She expressed a reluctance to trouble us with the care of her daughter, saying she was in delicate health, and nervous, but not subject to any kind of seizure – she volunteered that – nor to any illusion; being, in fact, perfectly sane.'

'How very odd to say all that!' I interpolated. 'It was so unnecessary.'

'At all events it *was* said,' he laughed, 'and as you wish to know all that passed, which was indeed very little, I tell you. She then said, "I am making a long journey of *vital* importance" – she emphasized the word – "rapid and secret; I shall return for my child in three months; in the meantime, she will be silent as to who we are, whence we come, and whither we are travelling." That is all she said. She spoke very pure French. When she said the word "secret," she paused for a few seconds, looking sternly, her eyes fixed on mine. I fancy she makes a great point of that. You saw how quickly she was gone. I hope I have not done a very foolish thing, in taking charge of the young lady.'

For my part, I was delighted. I was longing to see and talk to her; and only waiting till the doctor should give me leave. You who live in towns, can have no idea how great an event the introduction of a new friend is, in such a solitude as surrounded us.

The doctor did not arrive till nearly one o'clock; but I could no more have gone to my bed and slept, than I could have overtaken, on foot, the carriage in which the princess in black velvet had driven away.

When the physician came down to the drawing-room, it was to report very favourably upon his patient. She was now sitting up, her pulse quite regular, apparently perfectly well. She had sustained no injury, and the little shock to her nerves had passed away quite harmlessly. There could be no harm certainly in my seeing her, if we both wished it; and, with this permission, I sent forthwith, to know whether she would allow me to visit her for a few minutes in her room.

The servant returned immediately to say that she desired nothing more.

You may be sure I was not long in availing myself of this permission.

Our visitor lay in one of the handsomest rooms in the schloss. It was, perhaps a little stately. There was a sombre piece of tapestry opposite the foot of the bed, representing Cleopatra with the asp to her bosom; and other solemn classic scenes were displayed, a little faded, upon the other walls. But there was gold carving, and rich and varied colour enough in the other decorations of the room, to more than redeem the gloom of the old tapestry.

There were candles at the bed side. She was sitting up; her slender pretty figure enveloped in the soft silk dressing-gown, embroidered with flowers, and lined with thick quilted silk, which her mother had thrown over her feet as she lay upon the ground.

What was it that, as I reached the bed side and had just begun my little greeting, struck me dumb in a moment, and made me recoil a step or two from before her? I will tell you.

I saw the very face which had visited me in my childhood at night, which remained so fixed in my memory, and on which I had for so many years so often ruminated with horror, when no one suspected of what I was thinking.

It was pretty, even beautiful; and when I first beheld it, wore the same melancholy expression.

But this almost instantly lighted into a strange fixed smile of recognition.

There was a silence of fully a minute, and then at length *she* spoke;

I could not.

'How wonderful!' she exclaimed. 'Twelve years ago, I saw your face in a dream, and it has haunted me ever since.'

'Wonderful indeed!' I repeated, overcoming with an effort the horror that had for a time suspended my utterances. 'Twelve years ago, in vision or reality, *I* certainly saw you. I could not forget your face. It has remained before my eyes ever since.'

Her smile had softened. Whatever I had fancied strange in it, was gone, and it and her dimpling cheeks were now delightfully pretty and intelligent.

I felt reassured, and continued more in the vein which hospitality indicated, to bid her welcome, and to tell her how much pleasure her accidental arrival had given us all, and especially what a happiness it was to me.

I took her hand as I spoke. I was a little shy, as lonely people are, but the situation made me eloquent, and even bold. She pressed my hand, she laid hers upon it, and her eyes glowed, as, looking hastily into mine, she smiled again, and blushed.

She answered my welcome very prettily. I sat down beside her, still wondering; and she said:

'I must tell you my vision about you; it is so very strange that you and I should have had, each of the other so vivid a dream, that each should have seen, I you and you me, looking as we do now, when of course we both were mere children. I was a child about six years old, and I awoke from a confused and troubled dream, and found myself in a room, unlike my nursery, wainscoted clumsily in some dark wood, and with cupboards and bedsteads, and chairs, and benches placed about it. The beds were, I thought, all empty, and the room itself without any one but myself in it; and I, after looking about me for some time, and admiring especially an iron candlestick, with two branches, which I should certainly know again, crept under one of the beds to reach the window; but as I got from under the bed, I heard someone crying; and looking up, while I was still upon my knees, I saw *you* – most assuredly you – as I see you now; a beautiful young lady, with golden hair and large blue eyes, and lips – your lips – you, as you are here. Your looks won me; I climbed on the bed and put my arms about you, and I think we both fell asleep. I was aroused by a scream; you were sitting up screaming. I was frightened, and slipped down upon the ground, and, it seemed to me, lost consciousness for a moment; and when I came to myself, I was again in my nursery at home. Your face I have never forgotten since. I could not be misled by mere resemblance. You *are* the lady whom I then saw.'

It was now my turn to relate my corresponding vision, which I did, to the undisguised wonder of my new acquaintance.

'I don't know which should be most afraid of the other,' she said, again smiling. 'If you were less pretty I think I should be very much afraid of you, but being as you are, and you and I both so young, I feel only that I have made your acquaintance twelve years ago, and have already a right to your intimacy; at all events, it does seem as if we were destined, from our earliest childhood, to be friends. I wonder whether you feel as strangely drawn towards me as I do to you; I have never had a friend – shall I find one now?' She sighed, and her fine dark eyes gazed passionately on me.

Now the truth is, I felt rather unaccountably towards the beautiful stranger. I did feel, as she said, 'drawn towards her,' but there was also something of repulsion. In this ambiguous feeling, however, the sense of attraction immensely prevailed. She interested and won me; she was so beautiful and so indescribably engaging.

I perceived now something of languor and exhaustion stealing over her, and hastened to bid her good-night.

'The doctor thinks,' I added, 'that you ought to have a maid to sit up with you to-night; one of ours is waiting, and you will find her a very useful and quiet creature.'

'How kind of you, but I could not sleep, I never could with an attendant in the room. I shan't require any assistance – and, shall I confess my weakness, I am haunted with a terror of robbers. Our house was robbed once, and two servants murdered, so I always lock my door. It has become a habit – and you look so kind I know you will forgive me. I see there is a key in the lock.'

She held me close in her pretty arms for a moment and whispered in my ear, 'Good-night, darling, it is very hard to part with you, but good-night; to-morrow, but not early, I shall see you again.'

She sank back on the pillow with a sigh, and her fine eyes followed me with a fond and melancholy gaze, and she murmured again, 'Good-night, dear friend.'

Young people like, and even love, on impulse. I was flattered by the evident, though as yet undeserved, fondness she showed me. I liked the confidence with which she at once received me. She was determined that we should be very dear friends.

Next day came and we met again. I was delighted with my companion; that is to say, in many respects.

Her looks lost nothing in daylight – she was certainly the most beautiful creature I had ever seen, and the unpleasant remembrance of the face presented in my early dream, had lost the effect of the first unexpected recognition.

She confessed that she had experienced a similar shock on seeing me, and precisely the same faint antipathy that had mingled with my admiration of her. We now laughed together over our momentary horrors.

CHAPTER IV

HER HABITS – A SAUNTER

I told you that I was charmed with her in most particulars.

There were some that did not please me so well.

She was above the middle height of women. I shall begin by describing her. She was slender, and wonderfully graceful. Except that her movements were languid – *very* languid – indeed, there was nothing in her appearance to indicate an invalid. Her complexion was rich and brilliant; her features were small and beautifully formed; her eyes large, dark, and lustrous; her hair was quite wonderful, I never saw hair so magnificently thick and long when it was down about her shoulders; I have often placed my hands under it, and laughed with wonder at its weight. It was exquisitely fine and soft, and in colour a rich very dark brown, with something of gold. I loved to let it down, tumbling with its own weight, as, in her room, she lay back in her chair talking in her sweet low voice, I used to fold and braid it, and spread it out and play with it. Heavens! If I had but known all!

I said there were particulars which did not please me. I have told you that her confidence won me the first night I saw her; but I found that she exercised with respect to herself, her mother, her history, everything in fact connected with her life, plans, and people, an ever-wakeful reserve. I dare say I was unreasonable, perhaps I was wrong; I dare say I ought to have respected the solemn injunction laid upon my father by the stately lady in black velvet. But curiosity is a restless and unscrupulous passion, and no one girl can endure, with patience, that her's should be baffled by another. What harm could it do anyone to tell me what I so ardently desired to know? Had she no trust in my good sense or honour? Why would she not believe me when I assured her, so solemnly, that I would not divulge one syllable of what she told me to any mortal breathing.

There was a coldness, it seemed to me, beyond her years, in her smiling melancholy persistent refusal to afford me the least ray of light.

I cannot say we quarrelled upon this point, for she would not quarrel upon any. It was, of course, very unfair of me to press her, very ill-bred, but I really could not help it; and I might just as well have let it alone.

What she did tell me amounted, in my unconscionable estimation – to nothing.

It was all summed up in three very vague disclosures.

First.—Her name was Carmilla.

Second.—Her family was very ancient and noble.

Third.—Her home lay in the direction of the west.

She would not tell me the name of her family, nor their armorial bearings, nor the name of their estate, nor even that of the country they lived in.

You are not to suppose that I worried her incessantly on these subjects. I watched opportunity, and rather insinuated than urged my enquiries. Once or twice, indeed, I did attack her more directly. But no matter what my tactics, utter failure was invariably the result. Reproaches and caresses were all lost upon her. But I must add this, that her evasion was conducted with so pretty a melancholy and deprecation, with so many, and even passionate declarations of her liking for me, and trust in my honour, and with so many promises, that I should at last know all, that I could not find it in my heart long to be offended with her.

She used to place her pretty arms about my neck, draw me to her, and laying her cheek to mine, murmur with her lips near my ear, 'Dearest, your little heart is wounded; think me not cruel because I obey the irresistible law of my strength and weakness; if your dear heart is wounded, my wild heart bleeds with yours. In the rapture of my enormous humiliation I live in your warm life, and you shall die – die, sweetly die – into mine. I cannot help it; as I draw near to you, you, in your turn, will draw near to others, and learn the rapture of that cruelty, which yet is love; so, for a while, seek to know no more of me and mine, but trust me with all your loving spirit.'

And when she had spoken such a rhapsody, she would press me more closely in her trembling embrace, and her lips in soft kisses gently glow upon my cheek.

Her agitations and her language were unintelligible to me.

From these foolish embraces, which were not of very frequent occurrence, I must allow, I used to wish to extricate myself; but my energies seemed to fail me. Her murmured words sounded like a lullaby in my ear, and soothed my resistance into a trance, from which I only seemed to recover myself when she withdrew her arms.

In these mysterious moods I did not like her. I experienced a strange tumultuous excitement that was pleasurable, ever and anon, mingled with a vague sense of fear and disgust. I had no distinct thoughts about her while such scenes lasted, but I was conscious of a love growing into adoration, and also of abhorrence. This I know is paradox, but I can make no other attempt to explain the feeling.

I now write, after an interval of more than ten years, with a trembling hand, with a confused and horrible recollection of certain occurrences and situations, in the ordeal through which I was unconsciously passing; though with a vivid and very sharp remembrance of the main current of my story. But, I suspect, in all lives there are certain emotional scenes, those in which our passions have been most wildly and terribly roused, that are of all others the most vaguely and dimly remembered.

Sometimes after an hour of apathy, my strange and beautiful companion would take my hand and hold it with a fond pressure, renewed again and again; blushing softly, gazing in my face with languid and burning eyes, and breathing so fast that her dress rose and fell with the tumultuous respiration. It was like the ardour of a lover; it embarrassed me; it was hateful and yet overpowering; and with gloating eyes she drew me to her, and her hot lips travelled along my cheek in kisses; and she would whisper, almost in sobs, 'You are mine, you *shall* be mine, and you and I are one for ever.' Then she has thrown herself back in her chair, with her small hands over her eyes, leaving me trembling.

'Are we related,' I used to ask; 'what can you mean by all this? I remind you perhaps of some one whom you love; but you must not, I hate it; I don't know you – I don't know myself when you look so and talk so.'

She used to sigh at my vehemence, then turn away and drop my hand.

Respecting these very extraordinary manifestations I strove in vain to form any satisfactory theory – I could not refer them to affectation or trick. It was unmistakably the momentary breaking out of suppressed instinct and emotion. Was she, notwithstanding her mother's volunteered denial, subject to brief visitations of insanity; or was there here a disguise and a romance? I had read in old story books of such things. What if a boyish lover had found his way into the house, and sought to prosecute his suit in masquerade, with the assistance of a clever old adventuress. But here were many things against this hypothesis, highly interesting as it was to my vanity.

I could boast of no little attentions such as masculine gallantry delights to offer. Between these passionate moments there were long intervals of common-place, of gaiety, of brooding melancholy, during which, except that I detected her eyes so full of melancholy fire, following me, at times I might have been as nothing to her. Except in these brief periods of mysterious excitement her ways were girlish; and there was always a languor about her, quite incompatible with a masculine system in a state of health.

In some respects her habits were odd. Perhaps not so singular in the opinion of a town lady like you, as they appeared to us rustic people. She used to come down very late, generally not till one o'clock, she would then take a cup of chocolate, but eat nothing; we then went out for a walk, which was a mere saunter, and she seemed, almost immediately, exhausted, and either returned to the schloss or sat on one of the benches that were placed, here and there, among the trees. This was a bodily

languor in which her mind did not sympathise. She was always an animated talker, and very intelligent.

She sometimes alluded for a moment to her own home, or mentioned
an adventure or situation, or an early recollection, which indicated a
people of strange manners, and described customs of which we knew
nothing. I gathered from these chance hints that her native country was
much more remote than I had at first fancied.

As we sat thus one afternoon under the trees a funeral passed us by. It
was that of a pretty young girl, whom I had often seen, the daughter of
one of the rangers of the forest. The poor man was walking behind the
coffin of his darling; she was his only child, and he looked quite heart-
broken. Peasants walking two-and-two came behind, they were singing a
funeral hymn.

I rose to mark my respect as they passed, and joined in the hymn they
were very sweetly singing.

My companion shook me a little roughly, and I turned surprised.

She said brusquely, 'Don't you perceive how discordant that is?'

'I think it is very sweet, on the contrary,' I answered, vexed at the
interruption, and very uncomfortable, lest the people who composed the
little procession should observe and resent what was passing.

I resumed, therefore, instantly, and was again interrupted. 'You pierce
my ears,' said Carmilla, almost angrily, and stopping her ears with her
tiny fingers. 'Besides, how can you tell that your religion and mine are
the same; your forms wound me, and I hate funerals. What a fuss! Why,
you must die – *everyone* must die; and all are happier when they do.
Come home.'

'My father has gone on with the clergyman to the churchyard. I
thought you knew she was to be buried to-day.'

'*She?* I don't trouble my head about peasants. I don't know who she
is,' answered Carmilla, with a flash from her fine eyes.

'She is the poor girl who fancied she saw a ghost a fortnight ago, and
has been dying ever since, till yesterday, when she expired.'

'Tell me nothing about ghosts. I shan't sleep to-night if you do.'

'I hope there is no plague or fever coming; all this looks very like it,' I
continued. 'The swineherd's young wife died only a week ago, and she
thought something seized her by the throat as she lay in her bed, and
nearly strangled her. Papa says such horrible fancies do accompany some
forms of fever. She was quite well the day before. She sank afterwards,
and died before a week.'

'Well, *her* funeral is over, I hope, and *her* hymn sung; and our ears
shan't be tortured with that discord and jargon. It has made me nervous.
Sit down here, beside me; sit close; hold my hand; press it hard – hard –
harder.'

We had moved a little back, and had come to another seat.

She sat down. Her face underwent a change that alarmed and even terrified me for a moment. It darkened, and became horribly livid; her teeth and hands were clenched, and she frowned and compressed her lips, while she stared down upon the ground at her feet, and trembled all over with a continued shudder as irrepressible as ague. All her energies seemed strained to suppress a fit, with which she was then breathlessly tugging; and at length a low convulsive cry of suffering broke from her, and gradually the hysteria subsided. 'There! That comes of strangling people with hymns!' she said at last. 'Hold me, hold me still. It is passing away.'

And so gradually it did; and perhaps to dissipate the sombre impression which the spectacle had left upon me, she became unusually animated and chatty; and so we got home.

This was the first time I had seen her exhibit any definable symptoms of that delicacy of health which her mother had spoken of. It was the first time, also, I had seen her exhibit anything like temper.

Both passed away like a summer cloud; and never but once afterwards did I witness on her part a momentary sign of anger. I will tell you how it happened.

She and I were looking out of one of the long drawing-room windows, when there entered the court-yard, over the drawbridge, a figure of a wanderer whom I knew very well. He used to visit the schloss generally twice a year.

It was the figure of a hunchback, with the sharp lean features that generally accompany deformity. He wore a pointed black beard, and he was smiling from ear to ear, showing his white fangs. He was dressed in buff, black, and scarlet, and crossed with more straps and belts than I could count, from which hung all manner of things. Behind, he carried a magic-lantern, and two boxes, which I well knew, in one of which was a salamander, and in the other a mandrake. These monsters used to make my father laugh. They were compounded of parts of monkeys, parrots, squirrels, fish, and hedgehogs, dried and stitched together with great neatness and startling effect. He had a fiddle, a box of conjuring apparatus, a pair of foils and masks attached to his belt, several other mysterious cases dangling about him, and a black staff with copper ferrules in his hand. His companion was a rough spare dog, that followed at his heels, but stopped short, suspiciously at the drawbridge, and in a little while began to howl dismally.

In the meantime, the mountebank, standing in the midst of the court-yard, raised his grotesque hat, and made us a very ceremonious bow, paying his compliments very volubly in execrable French, and German not much better. Then, disengaging his fiddle, he began to scrape a lively air, to which he sang with a merry discord, dancing with ludicrous airs and activity, that made me laugh, in spite of the dog's howling.

Then he advanced to the window with many smiles and salutations, and his hat in his left hand, his fiddle under his arm, and with a fluency that never took breath, he gabbled a long advertisement of all his accomplishments, and the resources of the various arts which he placed at our service, and the curiosities and entertainments which it was in his power, at our bidding to display.

'Will your ladyships be pleased to buy an amulet against the oupire, which is going like the wolf, I hear, through these woods,' he said, dropping his hat on the pavement. 'They are dying of it right and left, and here is a charm that never fails; only pinned to the pillow, and you may laugh in his face.'

These charms consisted of oblong slips of vellum, with cabalistic ciphers and diagrams upon them.

Carmilla instantly purchased one, and so did I.

He was looking up, and we were smiling down upon him, amused; at least, I can answer for myself. His piercing black eye, as he looked up in our faces, seemed to detect something that fixed for a moment his curiosity.

In an instant he unrolled a leather case, full of all manner of odd little steel instruments.

'See here, my lady,' he said, displaying it, and addressing me, 'I profess, among other things less useful, the art of dentistry. Plague take the dog!' he interpolated. 'Silence, beast! He howls so that your ladyships can scarcely hear a word. Your noble friend, the young lady at your right, has the sharpest tooth — long, thin, pointed, like an awl, like a needle; ha, ha! With my sharp and long sight, as I look up, I have seen it distinctly; now if it happens to hurt the young lady, and I think it must, here am I, here are my file, my punch, my nippers; I will make it round and blunt, if her ladyship pleases; no longer the tooth of a fish, but of a beautiful young lady as she is. Hey? Is the young lady displeased? Have I been too bold? Have I offended her?'

The young lady, indeed, looked very angry as she drew back from the window.

'How dares that mountebank insult us so? Where is your father? I shall demand redress from him. My father would have had the wretch tied up to the pump, and flogged with a cart-whip, and burnt to the bones with the castle brand!'

She retired from the window a step or two, and sat down, and hardly lost sight of the offender, when her wrath subsided as suddenly as it had risen, and she gradually recovered her usual tone, and seemed to forget the little hunchback and his follies.

My father was out of spirits that evening. On coming in he told us that there had been another case very similar to the two fatal ones which had lately occurred. The sister of a young peasant on his estate, only a mile away, was very ill, had been, as she described it, attacked very nearly in the same way, and was now slowly but steadily sinking.

'All this,' said my father, 'is strictly referable to natural causes. These poor people infect one another with their superstitions, and so repeat in imagination the images of terror that have infested their neighbours.'

'But that very circumstance frightens one horribly,' said Carmilla.

'How so?' inquired my father.

'I am so afraid of fancying I see such things; I think it would be as bad as reality.'

'We are in God's hands; nothing can happen without His permission, and all will end well for those who love Him. He is our faithful creator; He had made us all, and will take care of us.'

'Creator! *Nature!*' said the young lady in answer to my gentle father. 'And this disease that invades the country is natural. Nature. All things proceed from Nature – don't they? All things in the heaven, in the earth, and under the earth, act and live as Nature ordains? I think so.'

'The doctor said he would come here to-day,' said my father, after a silence. 'I want to know what he thinks about it, and what he thinks we had better do.'

'Doctors never did me any good,' said Carmilla.

'Then you have been ill?' I asked.

'More ill than ever you were,' she answered.

'Long ago?'

'Yes, a long time. I suffered from this very illness; but I forget all but my pain and weakness, and they were not so bad as are suffered in other diseases.'

'You were very young then?'

'I dare say; let us talk no more of it. You would not wound a friend?' She looked languidly in my eyes, and passed her arm round my waist lovingly, and led me out of the room. My father was busy over some papers near the window.

'Why does your papa like to frighten us?' said the pretty girl, with a sigh and a little shudder.

'He doesn't, dear Carmilla, it is the very furthest thing from his mind.'

'Are you afraid, dearest?'

'I should be very much if I fancied there was any real danger of my being attacked as those poor people were.'

'You are afraid to die?'

'Yes, every one is.'

'But to die as lovers may – to die together, so that they may live together. Girls are caterpillars while they live in the world, to be finally butterflies when the summer comes; but in the meantime there are grubs and larvæ, don't you see – each with their peculiar propensities, necessities and structure. So says Monsieur Buffon, in his big book, in the next room.'

Later in the day the doctor came, and was closeted with papa for some time. He was a skilful man, of sixty and upwards, he wore powder, and shaved his pale face as smooth as a pumpkin. He and papa emerged from the room together, and I heard papa laugh, and say as they came out:

'Well, I do wonder at a wise man like you. What do you say to hippogriffs and dragons?'

The doctor was smiling, and made answer, shaking his head—

'Nevertheless, life and death are mysterious states, and we know little of the resources of either.'

And so they walked on, and I heard no more. I did not then know what the doctor had been broaching, but I think I guess it now.

CHAPTER V

A WONDERFUL LIKENESS

This evening there arrived from Gratz the grave, dark-faced son of the picture-cleaner, with a horse and cart laden with two large packing-cases, having many pictures in each. It was a journey of ten leagues, and whenever a messenger arrived at the schloss from our little capital of Gratz, we used to crowd about him in the hall, to hear the news.

This arrival created in our secluded quarters quite a sensation. The cases remained in the hall, and the messenger was taken charge of by the servants till he had eaten his supper. Then with assistants, and armed with hammer, ripping chisel, and turnscrew he met us in the hall, where we had assembled to witness the unpacking of the cases.

Carmilla sat looking listlessly on, while one after the other the old pictures, nearly all portraits, which had undergone the process of renovation, were brought to light. My mother was of an old Hungarian family, and most of these pictures, which were about to be restored to their places, had come to us through her.

My father had a list in his hand, from which he read, as the artist rummaged out the corresponding numbers. I don't know that the pictures were very good, but they were, undoubtedly very old, and some of them very curious also. They had, for the most part, the merit of being now seen by me, I may say, for the first time; for the smoke and dust of time had all but obliterated them.

'There is a picture that I have not seen yet,' said my father. 'In one corner, at the top of it, is the name, as well as I could read, "Marcia Karnstein", and the date "1698"; and I am curious to see how it has turned out.'

I remembered it; it was a small picture, about a foot and a half high, and nearly square, without a frame; but it was so blackened by age that I could not make it out.

The artist now produced it, with evident pride. It was quite beautiful; it was startling; it seemed to live. It was the effigy of Carmilla!

'Carmilla, dear, here is an absolute miracle. Here you are, living, smiling, ready to speak, in this picture. Isn't it beautiful, papa? And see, even the little mole on her throat.'

My father laughed, and said 'Certainly it is a wonderful likeness,' but he looked away, and to my surprise seemed but little struck by it, and went on talking to the picture-cleaner, who was also something of an artist, and discoursed with intelligence about the portraits or other works, which his art had just brought into light and colour, while *I* was more and more lost in wonder the more I looked at the picture.

'Will you let me hang this picture in my room, papa?' I asked.

'Certainly, dear,' said he, smiling, 'I'm very glad you think it so like. It must be prettier even than I thought it, if it is.'

The young lady did not acknowledge this pretty speech, did not seem to hear it. She was leaning back in her seat, her fine eyes under their long lashes gazing on me in contemplation, and she smiled in a kind of rapture.

'And now you can read quite plainly the name that is written in the corner. It is not Marcia; it looks as if it was done in gold. The name is Mircalla, Countess Karnstein, and this is a little coronet over it, and underneath A.D. 1698. I am descended from the Karnsteins; that is, mamma was.'

'Ah!' said the lady, languidly, 'so am I, I think, a very long descent, very ancient. Are there any Karnsteins living now?'

'None who bear the name, I believe. The family were ruined, I believe, in some civil wars, long ago but the ruins of the castle are only about three miles away.'

'How interesting!' she said, languidly. 'But see what beautiful moon-light!' She glanced through the hall door, which stood a little open. 'Suppose you take a little ramble round the court and look down at the road and river.'

'It is so like the night you came to us,' I said.

She sighed, smiling.

She rose, and each with her arm about the other's waist, we walked out upon the pavement.

In silence, slowly we walked down to the drawbridge, where the beautiful landscape opened before us.

'And so you were thinking of the night I came here?' she almost whispered. 'Are you glad I came?'

'Delighted, dear Carmilla,' I answered.

'And you ask for the picture you think like me, to hang in your room,' she murmured with a sigh, as she drew her arm closer about my waist, and let her pretty head sink upon my shoulder.

'How romantic you are, Carmilla,' I said. 'Whenever you tell me your story, it will be made up chiefly of some one great romance.'

She kissed me silently.

'I am sure, Carmilla, you have been in love; that there is, at this moment, an affair of the heart going on.'

'I have been in love with no one, and never shall,' she whispered, 'unless it should be with you.'

How beautiful she looked in the moonlight!

Shy and strange was the look with which she quickly hid her face in my neck and hair, with tumultuous sighs, that seemed almost to sob, and pressed in mine a hand that trembled.

Her soft cheek was glowing against mine. 'Darling, darling,' she murmured, 'I live in you; and you would die for me, I love you so.'

I started from her.

She was gazing on me with eyes from which all fire, all meaning had flown, and a face colourless and apathetic.

'Is there a chill in the air, dear?' she said drowsily. 'I almost shiver; have I been dreaming? Let us come in. Come, come; come in.'

'You look ill, Carmilla; a little faint. You certainly must take some wine,' I said.

'Yes, I will. I'm better now. I shall be quite well in a few minutes. Yes, do give me a little wine,' answered Carmilla, as we approached the door. 'Let us look again for a moment; it is the last time, perhaps, I shall see the moonlight with you.'

'How do you feel now, dear Carmilla? Are you really better?' I asked.

I was beginning to take alarm, lest she should have been stricken with the strange epidemic that they said had invaded the country about us.

'Papa, would be grieved beyond measure,' I added, 'if he thought you were ever so little ill, without immediately letting us know. We have a very skilful doctor near this, the physician who was with papa to-day.'

'I'm sure he is. I know how kind you all are; but, dear child, I am quite well again. There is nothing ever wrong with me, but a little weakness. People say I am languid; I am incapable of exertion; I can scarcely walk as far as a child of three years old; and every now and then the little strength I have falters, and I become as you have just seen me. But after all I am very easily set up again; in a moment I am perfectly myself. See how I have recovered.'

So, indeed, she had; and she and I talked a great deal, and very animated she was; and the remainder of that evening passed without any recurrence of what I called her infatuations. I mean her crazy talk and looks, which embarrassed, and even frightened me.

But there occurred that night an event which gave my thoughts quite a new turn, and seemed to startle even Carmilla's languid nature into momentary energy.

CHAPTER VI

A VERY STRANGE AGONY

When we got into the drawing-room, and had sat down to our coffee and chocolate, although Carmilla did not take any, she seemed quite herself again, and Madame, and Mademoiselle De Lafontaine, joined us, and made a little card party, in the course of which papa came in for what he called his 'dish of tea'.

When the game was over he sat down beside Carmilla on the sofa, and asked her, a little anxiously, whether she had heard from her mother since her arrival.

She answered 'No.'

He then asked her whether she knew where a letter would reach her at present.

'I cannot tell,' she answered, ambiguously, 'but I have been thinking of leaving you; you have been already too hospitable and too kind to me. I have given you an infinity of trouble, and I should wish to take a carriage to-morrow, and post in pursuit of her; I know where I shall ultimately find her, although I dare not yet tell you.'

'But you must not dream of any such thing,' exclaimed my father, to my great relief. 'We can't afford to lose you so, and I won't consent to your leaving us, except under the care of your mother, who was so good as to consent to your remaining with us till she should herself return. I should be quite happy if I knew that you heard from her; but this evening the accounts of the progress of the mysterious disease that has invaded our neighbourhood, grow even more alarming; and my beautiful guest, I do feel the responsibility, unaided by advice from your mother, very much. But I shall do my best; and one thing is certain, that you must not think of leaving us without her distinct direction to that effect. We should suffer too much in parting from you to consent to it easily.'

'Thank you, sir, a thousand times for your hospitality,' she answered, smiling bashfully. 'You have all been too kind to me; I have seldom been so happy in all my life before, as in your beautiful château, under your care, and in the society of your dear daughter.'

So he gallantly, in his old-fashioned way, kissed her hand, smiling, and pleased at her little speech.

I accompanied Carmilla as usual to her room, and sat and chatted with her while she was preparing for bed.

'Do you think,' I said, at length, 'that you will ever confide fully in me?'

She turned round smiling, but made no answer, only continued to smile on me.

'You won't answer that?' I said. 'You can't answer pleasantly; I ought not to have asked you.'

'You were quite right to ask me that, or anything. You do not know how dear you are to me, or you could not think any confidence too great to look for. But I am under vows, no nun half so awfully, and I dare not tell my story yet, even to you. The time is very near when you shall know everything. You will think me cruel, very selfish, but love is always selfish; the more ardent the more selfish. How jealous I am you cannot know. You must come with me, loving me, to death; or else hate me, and still come with me, and *hating* me through death and after. There is no such word as indifference in my apathetic nature.'

'Now, Carmilla, you are going to talk your wild nonsense again,' I said hastily.

'Not I, silly little fool as I am, and full of whims and fancies; for your sake I'll talk like a sage. Were you ever at a ball?'

'No, how you do run on. What is it like? How charming it must be.'

'I almost forget, it is years ago.'

I laughed.

'You are not so old. Your first ball can hardly be forgotten yet.'

'I remember everything about it – with an effort. I see it all, as divers see what is going on above them, through a medium, dense, rippling, but transparent. There occurred that night what has confused the picture, and made its colours faint. I was all but assassinated in my bed, wounded *here*,' she touched her breast, 'and never was the same since.'

'Were you near dying?'

'Yes, very – a cruel love – strange love, that would have taken my life. Love will have its sacrifices. No sacrifice without blood. Let us go to sleep now; I feel so lazy. How can I get up just now and lock my door?'

She was lying with her tiny hands buried in her rich wavy hair, under her cheek, her little head upon the pillow, and her glittering eyes followed me wherever I moved, with a kind of shy smile that I could not decipher.

I bid her good-night, and crept from the room with an uncomfortable sensation.

I often wondered whether our pretty guest ever said her prayers. *I* certainly had never seen her upon her knees. In the morning she never came down until long after our family prayers were over, and at night she never left the drawing-room to attend our brief evening prayers in the hall.

If it had not been that it had casually come out in one of our careless talks that she had been baptised, I should have doubted her being a Christian. Religion was a subject on which I had never heard her speak a word. If I had known the world better, this particular neglect or antipathy would not have so much surprised me.

The precautions of nervous people are infectious, and persons of a like temperament are pretty sure, after a time, to imitate them. I had adopted Carmilla's habit of locking her bed-room door, having taken into my head all her whimsical alarms about midnight invaders, and prowling assassins. I had also adopted her precaution of making a brief search through her room, to satisfy herself that no lurking assassin or robber was 'ensconced'.

These wise measures taken, I got into my bed and fell asleep. A light was burning in my room. This was an old habit, of very early date, and which nothing could have tempted me to dispense with.

Thus fortified I might take my rest in peace. But dreams come through stone walls, light up dark rooms, or darken light ones, and their persons make their exits and their entrances as they please, and laugh at lock-smiths.

I had a dream that night that was the beginning of a very strange agony.

I cannot call it a nightmare, for I was quite conscious of being asleep. But I was equally conscious of being in my room, and lying in bed, precisely as I actually was. I saw, or fancied I saw, the room and its furniture just as I had seen it last, except that it was very dark, and I saw something moving round the foot of the bed, which at first I could not accurately distinguish. But I soon saw that it was a sooty-black animal that resembled a monstrous cat. It appeared to me about four or five feet long, for it measured fully the length of the hearth-rug as it passed over it; and it continued to-ing and fro-ing with the lithe sinister restlessness of a beast in a cage. I could not cry out, although as you may suppose, I was terrified. Its pace was growing faster, and the room rapidly darker and darker, and at length so dark that I could no longer see anything of it but its eyes. I felt it spring lightly on the bed. The two broad eyes approached my face, and suddenly I felt a stinging pain as if two large needles darted, an inch or two apart, deep into my breast. I waked with a scream. The room was lighted by the candle that burnt there all through the night, and I saw a female figure standing at the foot of the bed, a little at the right side. It was in a dark loose dress, and its hair was down and covered its shoulders. A block of stone could not have been more still. There was not the slightest stir of respiration. As I stared at it, the figure appeared to have changed its place, and was now nearer the door; then, close to it, the door opened, and it passed out.

I was now relieved, and able to breathe and move. My first thought was that Carmilla had been playing me a trick, and that I had forgotten to secure my door. I hastened to it, and found it locked as usual on the inside. I was afraid to open it – I was horrified. I sprang into my bed and covered my head up in the bed-clothes, and lay there more dead than alive till morning.

CHAPTER VII

DESCENDING

It would be vain my attempting to tell you the horror which, even now, I recall the occurrence of that night. It was no such transitory terror as a dream leaves behind it. It seemed to deepen by time, and communicated itself to the room and the very furniture that had encompassed the apparition.

I could not bear next day to be alone for a moment. I should have told papa, but for two opposite reasons. At one time I thought he would laugh at my story, and I could not bear its being treated as a jest; and at another, I thought he might fancy that I had been attacked by the mysterious complaint which had invaded our neighbourhood. I had myself no misgivings of the kind, and as he had been rather an invalid for some time, I was afraid of alarming him.

I was comfortable enough with my good-natured companions, Madame Perrodon, and the vivacious Mademoiselle Lafontaine. They both perceived that I was out of spirits and nervous, and at length I told them what lay so heavy at my heart.

Mademoiselle laughed, but I fancied that Madame Perrodon looked anxious.

'By-the-by,' said Mademoiselle, laughing, 'the long lime tree walk, behind Carmilla's bedroom window, is haunted!'

'Nonsense!' exclaimed Madame, who probably thought the theme rather inopportune, 'and who tells that story, my dear?'

'Martin says that he came up twice, when the old yard-gate was being repaired before sunrise, and twice saw the same female figure walking down the lime tree avenue.'

'So he well might, as long as there are cows to milk in the river fields,' said Madame.

'I dare say; but Martin chooses to be frightened, and never did I see a fool *more* frightened.'

'You must not say a word about it to Carmilla, because she can see down that walk from her room window,' I interposed, 'and she is, if possible, a greater coward than I.'

Carmilla came down rather later than usual that day.

'I was so frightened last night,' she said, so soon as we were together, 'and I am sure I should have seen something dreadful if it had not been for that charm I bought from the poor little hunchback whom I called such hard names. I had a dream of something black coming round my bed, and I awoke in a perfect horror, and I really thought, for some seconds, I saw a dark figure near the chimney piece, but I felt under my pillow for my charm, and the moment my fingers touched it, the figure disappeared, and I felt quite certain, only that I had it by me, that something frightful would have made its appearance, and perhaps, throttled me, as it did those poor people we heard of.'

'Well, listen to me,' I began and recounted my adventure, at the recital of which she appeared horrified.

'And had you the charm near you?' she asked, earnestly.

'No, I had dropped it into a china vase in the drawing-room, but I shall certainly take it with me to-night, as you have so much faith in it.'

At this distance of time I cannot tell you, or even understand, how I overcame my horror so effectually as to lie alone in my room that night. I remember distinctly that I pinned the charm to my pillow. I fell asleep almost immediately, and slept even more soundly than usual all night.

Next night I passed as well. My sleep was delightfully deep and dreamless. But I wakened with a sense of lassitude and melancholy which, however, did not exceed a degree that was almost luxurious.

'Well, I told you so,' said Carmilla, when I described my quiet sleep, 'I had such delightful sleep myself last night; I pinned the charm to the breast of my nightdress. It was too far away the night before. I am quite sure it was all fancy, except the dreams. I used to think that evil spirits made dreams, but our doctor told me it is no such thing. Only a fever passing by, or some other malady, as they often do, he said, knocks at the door, and not being able to get in, passes on, with that alarm.'

'And what do you think the charm is?' said I.

'It has been fumigated or immersed in some drug, and is an antidote against the malaria,' she answered.

'Then it acts only on the body?'

'Certainly; you don't suppose that evil spirits are frightened by bits of ribbon, or the perfumes of a druggist's shop? No, these complaints, wandering in the air, begin by trying the nerves, and so infect the brain; but before they can seize upon you, the antidote repels them. That I am sure is what the charm has done for us. It is nothing magical, it is simply natural.'

I should have been happier if I could quite have agreed with Carmilla, but I did my best, and the impression was a little losing its force.

For some nights I slept profoundly; but still every morning I felt the same lassitude, and a languor weighed upon me all day. I felt myself a changed girl. A strange melancholy was stealing over me, a melancholy that I would not have interrupted. Dim thoughts of death began to open, and an idea that I was slowly sinking took gentle, and, somehow, not unwelcome possession of me. If it was sad, the tone of mind which this induced was also sweet. Whatever it might be, my soul acquiesced in it.

I would not admit that I was ill, I would not consent to tell my papa, or to have the doctor sent for.

Carmilla became more devoted to me than ever, and her strange paroxysms of languid adoration more frequent. She used to gloat on me with increasing ardour the more my strength and spirits waned. This always shocked me like a momentary glare of insanity.

Without knowing it, I was now in a pretty advanced stage of the strangest illness under which mortal ever suffered. There was an unaccountable fascination in its earlier symptoms that more than reconciled me to the incapacitating effect of that stage of the malady. This fascination increased for a time, until it reached a certain point, when gradually a sense of the horrible mingled itself with it, deepening, as you shall hear, until it discoloured and perverted the whole state of my life.

The first change I experienced was rather agreeable. It was very near the turning point from which began the descent of Avernus.

Certain vague and strange sensations visited me in my sleep. The prevailing one was of that pleasant, peculiar cold thrill which we feel in bathing, when we move against the current of a river. This was soon accompanied by dreams that seemed interminable, and were so vague that I could never recollect their scenery and persons, or any one connected portion of their action. But they left an awful impression, and a sense of exhaustion, as if I had passed through a long period of great mental exertion and danger. After all these dreams there remained on waking a remembrance of having been in a place very nearly dark, and of having spoken to people whom I could not see; and especially of one clear voice, of a female's, very deep, that spoke as if at a distance, slowly, and producing always the same sensation of indescribable solemnity and fear. Sometimes there came a sensation as if a hand was drawn softly along my cheek and neck. Sometimes it was as if warm lips kissed me, and longer and more lovingly as they reached my throat, but there the caress fixed itself. My heart beat faster, my breathing rose and fell rapidly and full drawn; a sobbing, that rose into a sense of strangulation, supervened, and turned into a dreadful convulsion, in which my senses left me, and I became unconscious.

It was now three weeks since the commencement of this unaccountable state. My sufferings had, during the last week, told upon my appearance. I had grown pale, my eyes were dilated and darkened underneath, and the languor which I had long felt began to display itself in my countenance.

My father asked me often whether I was ill; but, with an obstinacy which now seems to me unaccountable, I persisted in assuring him that I was quite well.

In a sense this was true. I had no pain, I could complain of no bodily derangement. My complaint seemed to be one of the imagination, or the nerves, and, horrible as my sufferings were, I kept them, with a morbid reserve, very nearly to myself.

It could not be that terrible complaint which the peasants call the oupire, for I had now been suffering for three weeks, and they were seldom ill for much more than three days, when death put an end to their miseries.

Carmilla complained of dreams and feverish sensations, but by no means of so alarming a kind as mine. I say that mine were extremely alarming. Had I been capable of comprehending my condition, I would have invoked aid and advice on my knees. The narcotic of an unsuspected influence was acting upon me, and my perceptions were benumbed.

I am going to tell you now of a dream that led immediately to an odd discovery.

One night, instead of the voice I was accustomed to hear in the dark, I heard one, sweet and tender, and at the same time terrible, which said, 'Your mother warns you to beware of the assassin.' At the same time a light unexpectedly sprang up, and I saw Carmilla, standing, near the foot of my bed, in her white nightdress, bathed, from her chin to her feet, in one great stain of blood.

I wakened with a shriek, possessed with the one idea that Carmilla was being murdered. I remember springing from my bed, and my next recollection is that of standing on the lobby, crying for help.

Madame and Mademoiselle came scurrying out of their rooms in alarm; a lamp burned always on the lobby, and seeing me, they soon learned the cause of my terror.

I insisted on our knocking at Carmilla's door. Our knocking was unanswered. It soon became a pounding and an uproar. We shrieked her name but all was vain.

We all grew frightened, for the door was locked. We hurried back, in panic, to my room. There we rang the bell long and furiously. If my father's room had been at that side of the house, we would have called him up at once to our aid. But, alas! he was quite out of hearing, and to reach him involved an excursion for which we none of us had courage.

Servants, however, soon came running up the stairs; I had got on my dressing-gown and slippers meanwhile, and my companions were already similarly furnished. Recognising the voices of the servants on the lobby, we sallied out together; and having renewed, as fruitlessly, our summons at Carmilla's door, I ordered the men to force the lock. They did so, and we stood, holding our lights aloft, in the doorway, and so stared into the room.

We called her by name; but there was still no reply. We looked round the room. Everything was undisturbed. It was exactly in the state in which I left it on bidding her good night. But Carmilla was gone.

CHAPTER VIII

SEARCH

At sight of the room, perfectly undisturbed except for our violent entrance, we began to cool a little, and soon recovered our senses sufficiently to dismiss the men. It had struck Mademoiselle that possibly Carmilla had been wakened by the uproar at her door, and in her first panic had jumped from her bed, and hid herself in a press, or behind a curtain, from which she could not, of course, emerge until the major-domo and his myrmidons had withdrawn. We now recommenced our search, and began to call her by name again.

It was all to no purpose. Our perplexity and agitation increased. We examined the windows, but they were secured. I implored of Carmilla, if she had concealed herself, to play this cruel trick no longer – to come out, and to end our anxieties. It was all useless. I was by this time convinced that she was not in the room, nor in the dressing-room, the door of which was still locked on this side. She could not have passed it. I was utterly puzzled. Had Carmilla discovered one of those secret passages which the old housekeeper said were known to exist in the schloss, although the tradition of their exact situation had been lost. A little time would, no doubt, explain all – utterly perplexed as, for the present, we were.

It was past four o'clock, and I preferred passing the remaining hours of darkness in Madame's room. Daylight brought no solution of the difficulty.

The whole household, with my father at its head, was in a state of agitation next morning. Every part of the château was searched. The grounds were explored. Not a trace of the missing lady could be discovered. The stream was about to be dragged; my father was in distraction; what a tale to have to tell the poor girl's mother on her return. I, too, was almost beside myself, though my grief was quite of a different kind.

CARMILLA

The morning was passed in alarm and excitement. It was now one o'clock, and still no tidings. I ran up to Carmilla's room, and found her standing at her dressing-table. I was astounded. I could not believe my eyes. She beckoned me to her with her pretty finger, in silence. Her face expressed extreme fear.

I ran to her in an ecstasy of joy; I kissed and embraced her again and again. I ran to the bell and rang it vehemently, to bring others to the spot, who might at once relieve my father's anxiety.

'Dear Carmilla, what has become of you all this time? We have been in agonies of anxiety about you,' I exclaimed. 'Where have you been? How did you come back?'

'Last night has been a night of wonders,' she said.

'For mercy's sake, explain all you can.'

'It was past two last night,' she said, 'when I went to sleep as usual in my bed, with my doors locked, that of the dressing-room and that opening upon the gallery. My sleep was uninterrupted, and so far as I know, dreamless; but I awoke just now on the sofa in the dressing-room there, and I found the door between the rooms open, and the other door forced. How could all this have happened without my being awakened? It must have been accompanied with a great deal of noise, and I am particularly easily wakened; and how could I have been carried out of my bed without my sleep having been interrupted, I whom the slightest stir startles?'

By this time, Madame, Mademoiselle, my father, and a number of the servants were in the room. Carmilla was, of course, overwhelmed with enquiries, congratulations, and welcomes. She had but one story to tell, and seemed the least able of all the party to suggest any way of accounting for what had happened.

My father took a turn up and down the room, thinking. I saw Carmilla's eye follow him for a moment with a sly, dark glance.

When my father had sent the servants away, Mademoiselle having gone in search of a little bottle of valerian and sal-volatile, and there being no one now in the room with Carmilla except my father, Madame, and myself, he came to her thoughtfully, took her hand very kindly, led her to the sofa, and sat down beside her.

'Will you forgive me, my dear, if I risk a conjecture, and ask a question?'

'Who can have a better right?' she said. 'Ask what you please, and I will tell you everything. But my story is simply one of bewilderment and darkness. I know absolutely nothing. Put any question you please. But you know, of course, the limitations mamma has placed me under.'

'Perfectly, my dear child. I need not approach the topics on which she desires our silence. Now, the marvel of last night consists in your having been removed from your bed and your room without being wakened, and this removal having occurred apparently while the windows were still secured, and the two doors locked upon the inside. I will tell you my theory, and first ask you a question.'

Carmilla was leaning on her hand dejectedly; Madame and I were listening breathlessly.

'Now, my question is this. Have you ever been suspected of walking in your sleep?'

'Never since I was very young indeed.'

'But you did walk in your sleep when you were young?'

'Yes; I know I did. I have been told so often by my old nurse.'

My father smiled and nodded.

'Well, what has happened is this. You got up in your sleep, unlocked the door, not leaving the key, as usual, in the lock, but taking it out and locking it on the outside; you again took the key out, and carried it away with you to some one of the five-and-twenty rooms on this floor, or perhaps upstairs or downstairs. There are so many rooms and closets, so much heavy furniture, and such accumulations of lumber, that it would require a week to search this old house thoroughly. Do you see, now, what I mean?'

'I do, but not all,' she answered.

'And how, papa, do you account for her finding herself on the sofa in the dressing-room, which we had searched so carefully?'

'She came there after you had searched it, still in her sleep, and at last awoke spontaneously, and was as much surprised to find herself where she was as any one else. I wish all mysteries were as easily and innocently explained as yours, Carmilla,' he said, laughing. 'And so we may congratulate ourselves on the certainty that the most natural explanation of the occurrence is one that involves no drugging, no tampering with locks, no burglars, or poisoners, or witches – nothing that need alarm Carmilla, or any one else, for our safety.'

Carmilla was looking charmingly. Nothing could be more beautiful than her tints. Her beauty was, I think enhanced by that graceful languor that was peculiar to her. I think my father was silently contrasting her looks with mine, for he said:—

'I wish my poor Laura was looking more like herself;' and he sighed.

So our alarms were happily ended, and Carmilla restored to her friends.

CARMILLA

CHAPTER IX

THE DOCTOR

As Carmilla would not hear of an attendant sleeping in her room, my father arranged that a servant should sleep outside her door so that she could not attempt to make another such excursion without being arrested at her own door.

That night passed quietly; and next morning early, the doctor, whom my father had sent for without telling me a word about it, arrived to see me.

Madame accompanied me to the library; and there the grave little doctor, with white hair and spectacles, whom I mentioned before, was waiting to receive me.

I told him my story, and as I proceeded he grew graver and graver.

We were standing, he and I, in the recess of one of the windows, facing one another. When my statement was over, he leaned with his shoulders against the wall, and with his eyes fixed on me earnestly with an interest in which was a dash of horror.

After a minute's reflection, he asked Madame if he could see my father.

He was sent for accordingly, and as he entered, smiling, he said:

'I dare say, doctor, you are going to tell me that I am an old fool for having brought you here; I hope I am.'

But his smile faded into shadow as the doctor, with a very grave face, beckoned him to him.

He and the doctor talked for some time in the same recess where I had just conferred with the physician. It seemed an earnest and argumentative conversation. The room is very large, and I and Madame stood together, burning with curiosity, at the further end. Not a word could we hear, however, for they spoke in a very low tone, and the deep recess of the window quite concealed the doctor from view, and very nearly my father, whose foot, arm, and shoulder only could we see; and the voices were, I suppose, all the less audible for the sort of closet which the thick wall and window formed.

After a time my father's face looked into the room; it was pale, thoughtful, and, I fancied, agitated.

'Laura, dear, come here for a moment. Madame, we shan't trouble you, the doctor says, at present.'

Accordingly I approached, for the first time a little alarmed; for, although I felt very weak, I did not feel ill; and strength, one always fancies, is a thing that may be picked up when we please.

My father held out his hand to me as I drew near; but he was looking at the doctor, and he said:

'It certainly *is* very odd; I don't understand it quite. Laura, come here, dear; now attend to Doctor Spielsberg, and recollect yourself.'

'You mentioned a sensation like that of two needles piercing the skin, somewhere about your neck, on the night when you experienced your first horrible dream. Is there still any soreness?'

'None at all,' I answered.

'Can you indicate with your finger about the point at which you think this occurred?'

'Very little below my throat – *here*,' I answered.

I wore a morning dress, which covered the place I pointed to.

'Now you can satisfy yourself,' said the doctor. 'You won't mind your papa's lowering your dress a very little. It is necessary, to detect a symptom of the complaint under which you have been suffering.'

I acquiesced. It was only an inch or two below the edge of my collar.

'God bless me! – so it is,' exclaimed my father, growing pale.

'You see it now with your own eyes,' said the doctor, with a gloomy triumph.

'What is it?' I exclaimed, beginning to be frightened.

'Nothing, my dear young lady, but a small blue spot, about the size of the tip of your little finger; and now,' he continued, turning to papa, 'the question is what is best to be done?'

'Is there any danger?' I urged, in great trepidation.

'I trust not, my dear,' answered the doctor. 'I don't see why you should not recover. I don't see why you should not begin *immediately* to get better. That is the point at which the sense of strangulation begins?'

'Yes,' I answered.

'And – recollect as well as you can – the same point was a kind of centre of that thrill which you described just now, like the current of a cold stream running against you?'

'It may have been; I think it was.'

'Ay, you see?' he added, turning to my father. 'Shall I say a word to Madame?'

'Certainly,' said my father.

He called Madame to him, and said:

'I find my young friend here far from well. It won't be of any great consequence, I hope; but it will be necessary that some steps be taken, which I will explain by-and-by; but in the meantime, Madame, you will be so good as not to let Miss Laura be alone for one moment. That is the only direction I need give for the present. It is indispensable.'

'We may rely upon your kindness, Madame, I know,' added my father.

Madame satisfied him eagerly.

'And you, dear Laura, I know you will observe the doctor's direction.'

'I shall have to ask your opinion upon another patient, whose symptoms slightly resemble those of my daughter, that have just been detailed to you – very much milder in degree, but I believe quite of the same sort. She is a young lady – our guest; but as you say you will be passing this way again this evening, you can't do better than take your supper here, and you can then see her. She does not come down till the afternoon.'

'I thank you,' said the doctor. 'I shall be with you, then, at about seven this evening.'

And then they repeated their directions to me and to Madame, and with this parting charge my father left us, and walked out with the doctor; and I saw them pacing together up and down between the road and the moat, on the grassy platform in front of the castle, evidently absorbed in earnest conversation.

The doctor did not return. I saw him mount his horse there, take his leave, and ride away eastward through the forest. Nearly at the same time I saw the man arrive from Dranfeld with the letters, and dismount and hand the bag to my father.

In the meantime, Madame and I were both busy, lost in conjecture as to the reasons of the singular and earnest direction which the doctor and my father had concurred in imposing. Madame, as she afterwards told me, was afraid the doctor apprehended a sudden seizure, and that, without prompt assistance, I might either lose my life in a fit, or at least be seriously hurt.

This interpretation did not strike me: and I fancied perhaps luckily for my nerves, that the arrangement was prescribed simply to secure a companion, who would prevent my taking too much exercise, or eating unripe fruit, or doing any of the fifty foolish things to which young people are supposed to be prone.

About half-an-hour after, my father came in – he had a letter in his hand – and said:

'This letter had been delayed; it is from General Spielsdorf. He might have been here yesterday, he may not come till to-morrow, or he may be here to-day.'

He put the open letter into my hand; but he did not look pleased, as he used when a guest, especially one so much loved as the General, was coming. On the contrary, he looked as if he wished him at the bottom of the Red Sea. There was plainly something on his mind which he did not choose to divulge.

'Papa, darling, will you tell me this?' said I, suddenly laying my hand on his arm, and looking, I am sure, imploringly in his face.

'Perhaps,' he answered, smoothing my hair caressingly over my eyes.

'Does the doctor think me very ill?'

'No, dear; he thinks, if right steps are taken, you will be quite well again, at least on the high road to a complete recovery, in a day or two,' he answered, a little drily. 'I wish our good friend, the General, had chosen any other time; that is, I wish you had been perfectly well to receive him.'

'But do tell me, papa,' I insisted, '*what* does he think is the matter with me?'

'Nothing; you must not plague me with questions,' he answered, with more irritation than I ever remember him to have displayed before; and seeing that I looked wounded, I suppose, he kissed me, and added, 'You shall know all about it in a day or two; that is, all that *I* know. In the meantime, you are not to trouble your head about it.'

He turned and left the room, but came back before I had done wondering and puzzling over the oddity of all this; it was merely to say that he was going to Karnstein and had ordered the carriage to be ready at twelve, and that I and Madame should accompany him; he was going to see the priest who lived near those picturesque grounds, upon business, and as Carmilla had never seen them, she could follow, when she came down, with Mademoiselle, who would bring materials for what you call a pic-nic, which might be laid for us in the ruined castle.

At twelve o'clock, accordingly, I was ready, and not long after, my father, Madame and I set out upon our projected drive. Passing the drawbridge we turn to the right, and follow the road over the steep Gothic bridge westward, to reach the deserted village and ruined castle of Karnstein.

No sylvan drive can be fancied prettier. The ground breaks into gentle hills and hollows, all clothed with beautiful wood, totally destitute of the comparative formality which artificial planting and early culture and pruning impart.

The irregularities of the ground often lead the road out of its course, and cause it to wind beautifully round the sides of broken hollows and the steeper sides of the hills, among varieties of ground almost inexhaustible.

Turning one of these points, we suddenly encountered our old friend, the General, riding towards us, attended by a mounted servant. His portmanteaus were following in a hired waggon, such as we term a cart.

The General dismounted as we pulled up, and, after the usual greetings, was easily persuaded to accept the vacant seat in the carriage, and send his horse on with his servant to the schloss.

CHAPTER X

BEREAVED

It was about ten months since we had last seen him; but that time had sufficed to make an alteration of years in his appearance. He had grown thinner; something of gloom and anxiety had taken the place of that cordial serenity which used to characterise his features. His dark blue eyes, always penetrating, now gleamed with a sterner light from under his shaggy grey eyebrows. It was not such a change as grief alone usually induces, and angrier passions seemed to have had their share in bringing it about.

We had not long resumed our drive, when the General began to talk, with his usual soldierly directness, of the bereavement, as he termed it, which he had sustained in the death of his beloved niece and ward; and he then broke out in a tone of intense bitterness and fury, inveighing against the 'hellish arts' to which she had fallen a victim, and expressing with more exasperation than piety, his wonder that Heaven should tolerate so monstrous an indulgence of the lusts and malignity of hell.

My father, who saw at once that something very extraordinary had befallen, asked him, if not too painful to him, to detail the circumstances which he thought justified the strong terms in which he expressed himself.

'I should tell you all with pleasure,' said the General, 'but you would not believe me.'

'Why should I not?' he asked.

'Because,' he answered testily, 'you believe in nothing but what consists with your own prejudices and illusions. I remember when I was like you, but I have learned better.'

'Try me,' said my father; 'I am not such a dogmatist as you suppose. Besides which, I very well know that you generally require proof for what you believe, and am, therefore, very strongly predisposed to respect your conclusions.'

'You are right in supposing that I have not been led lightly into a belief in the marvellous – for what I have experienced *is* marvellous – and I have been forced by extraordinary evidence to credit that which ran counter, diametrically, to all my theories. I have been made the dupe of a preternatural conspiracy.'

Notwithstanding his professions of confidence in the General's penetration, I saw my father, at this point, glance at the General, with, as I thought a marked suspicion of his sanity.

The General did not see it, luckily. He was looking gloomily and curiously into the glades and vistas of the woods that were opening before us.

'You are going to the Ruins of Karnstein?' he said. 'Yes, it is a lucky coincidence; do you know I was going to ask you to bring me there to inspect them. I have a special object in exploring. There is a ruined chapel, isn't there, with a great many tombs of that extinct family?'

'So there are – highly interesting,' said my father. 'I hope you are thinking of claiming the title and estates?'

My father said this gaily, but the General did not recollect the laugh, or even the smile, which courtesy exacts for a friend's joke; on the contrary, he looked grave and even fierce, ruminating on a matter that stirred his anger and horror.

'Something very different,' he said, gruffly. 'I mean to unearth some of those fine people. I hope, by God's blessing, to accomplish a pious sacrilege here, which will relieve our earth of certain monsters, and enable honest people to sleep in their beds without being assailed by murderers. I have strange things to tell you, my dear friend, such as I myself would have scouted as incredible a few months since.'

My father looked at him again, but this time not with a glance of suspicion – with an eye, rather, of keen intelligence and alarm.

'The house of Karnstein,' he said, 'has been long extinct: a hundred years at least. My dear wife was maternally descended from the Karnsteins. But the name and title have long ceased to exist. The castle is a ruin; the very village is deserted; it is fifty years since the smoke of a chimney was seen there; not a roof left.'

'Quite true. I have heard a great deal about that since I last saw you; a great deal that will astonish you. But I had better relate everything in the order in which it occurred,' said the General. 'You saw my dear ward – my child, I may call her. No creature could have been more beautiful and only three months ago none more blooming.'

'Yes, poor thing! when I saw her last she was certainly quite lovely,' said my father. 'I was grieved and shocked more than I can tell you, my dear friend; I knew what a blow it was to you.'

He took the General's hand, and they exchanged a kind pressure. Tears gathered in the old soldier's eyes. He did not seek to conceal them. He said:

'We have been very old friends; I knew you would feel for me, childless as I am. She had become an object of very dear interest to me, and repaid my care by an affection that cheered my home and made my life happy. That is all gone. The years that remain to me on earth may not be very long; but by God's mercy I hope to accomplish a service to mankind before I die, and to subserve the vengeance of Heaven upon the fiends who have murdered my poor child in the spring of her hopes and beauty!'

'You said, just now, that you intended relating everything as it occurred,' said my father. 'Pray do; I assure you that it is not mere curiosity that prompts me.'

By this time we had reached the point at which the Drunstall road, by which the General had come, diverges from the road which we were travelling to Karnstein.

'How far is it to the ruins?' enquired the General, looking anxiously forward.

'About half a league,' answered my father. 'Pray let us hear the story you were so good as to promise.'

CHAPTER XI

THE STORY

'With all my heart,' said the General, with an effort; and after a short pause in which to arrange his subject, he commenced one of the strangest narratives I ever heard.

'My dear child was looking forward with great pleasure to the visit you had been so good as to arrange for her to your charming daughter.' Here he made me a gallant but melancholy bow. 'In the meantime we had an invitation to my old friend the Count Carlsfeld, whose schloss is about six leagues to the other side of Karnstein. It was to attend the series of fêtes which, you remember, were given by him in honour of his illustrious visitor, the Grand Duke Charles.'

'Yes; and very splendid, I believe, they were,' said my father.

'Princely! But then his hospitalities are quite regal. He has Aladdin's lamp. The night from which my sorrow dates was devoted to a magnificent masquerade. The grounds were thrown open, the trees hung with coloured lamps. There was such a display of fireworks as Paris itself had never witnessed. And such music – music, you know, is my weakness – such ravishing music! The finest instrumental band, perhaps, in the world, and the finest singers who could be collected from all the great operas in Europe. As you wandered through these fantastically illuminated grounds, the moon-lighted château throwing a rosy light from its long row of windows, you would suddenly hear these ravishing voices stealing from the silence of some grove, or rising from boats upon the lake. I felt myself, as I looked and listened, carried back into the romance and poetry of my early youth.

'When the fireworks were ended, and the ball beginning, we returned to the noble suite of rooms that was thrown open to the dancers. A masked ball, you know, is a beautiful sight; but so brilliant a spectacle of the kind I never saw before.

'It was a very aristocratic assembly. I was myself almost the only "nobody" present.

'My dear child was looking quite beautiful. She wore no mask. Her excitement and delight added an unspeakable charm to her features, always lovely. I remarked a young lady, dressed magnificently, but wearing a mask, who appeared to me to be observing my ward with extraordinary interest. I had seen her, earlier in the evening, in the great hall, and again, for a few minutes, walking near us, on the terrace under the castle windows, similarly employed. A lady, also masked, richly and gravely dressed, and with a stately air, like a person of rank, accompanied her as a chaperon. Had the young lady not worn a mask, I could, of course, have been much more certain upon the question whether she was really watching my poor darling. I am now well assured that she was.

'We were now in one of the *salons*. My poor dear child had been dancing, and was resting a little in one of the chairs near the door; I was standing near. The two ladies I have mentioned had approached, and the younger took the chair next my ward; while her companion stood beside me, and for a little time addressed herself, in a low tone, to her charge.

'Availing herself of the privilege of her mask she turned to me, and in the tone of an old friend, and calling me by my name, opened a conversation with me, which piqued my curiosity a good deal. She referred to many scenes where she had met me – at Court, and at distinguished houses. She alluded to little incidents which I had long ceased to think of, but which, I found, had only lain in abeyance in my memory, for they instantly started into life at her touch.

'I became more and more curious to ascertain who she was, every moment. She parried my attempts to discover very adroitly and pleasantly. The knowledge she showed of many passages in my life seemed to me all but unaccountable; and she appeared to take a not unnatural pleasure in foiling my curiosity, and in seeing me flounder, in my eager perplexity, from one conjecture to another.

'In the meantime the young lady, whom her mother called by the odd name of Millarca, when she once or twice addressed her, had, with the same ease and grace, got into conversation with my ward.

'She introduced herself by saying that her mother was a very old acquaintance of mine. She spoke of the agreeable audacity which a mask rendered practicable; she talked like a friend; she admired her dress, and insinuated very prettily her admiration of her beauty. She amused her with laughing criticisms upon the people who crowded the ballroom, and laughed at my poor child's fun. She was very witty and lively when she pleased, and after a time they had grown very good friends, and the young stranger lowered her mask, displaying a remarkably beautiful face. I had never seen it before, neither had my dear child. But though it was new to us, the features were so engaging, as well as lovely, that it was impossible not to feel the attraction powerfully. My poor girl did so. I never saw anyone more taken with another at first sight, unless indeed, it was the stranger herself, who seemed quite to have lost her heart to her.

'In the meantime, availing myself of the licence of a masquerade, I put not a few questions to the elder lady.

' "You have puzzled me utterly," I said, laughing. "Is that not enough? won't you, now, consent to stand on equal terms, and do me the kindness to remove your mask?"

' "Can any request be more unreasonable?" she replied. "Ask a lady to yield an advantage! Beside, how do you know you should recognise me? Years make changes."

' "As you see," I said, with a bow, and, I suppose, a rather melancholy little laugh.

' "As philosophers tell us," she said; "and how do you know that a sight of my face would help you?"

' "I should take chance for that," I answered. "It is vain trying to make yourself out an old woman; your figure betrays you."

' "Years, nevertheless, have passed since I saw you, rather since you saw me, for that is what I am considering. Millarca, there, is my daughter; I cannot then be young, even in the opinion of people whom time has taught to be indulgent, and I may not like to be compared with what you remember me. You have no mask to remove. You can offer me nothing in exchange."

' "My petition is to your pity, to remove it."

' "And mine to yours, to let it stay where it is," she replied.

' "Well, then, at least you will tell me whether you are French or German; you speak both languages so perfectly."

' "I don't think I shall tell you that, General; you intend to surprise, and are meditating the particular point of attack."

' "At all events, you won't deny this," I said, "that being honoured by your permission to converse, I ought to know how to address you. Shall I say Madame la Comtesse!"

'She laughed, and she would, no doubt, have met me with another evasion – if, indeed, I can treat any occurrence in an interview every circumstance of which was pre-arranged, as I now believe, with the profoundest cunning, as liable to be modified by accident.

' "As to that," she began; but she was interrupted, almost as she opened her lips, by a gentleman, dressed in black, who looked particularly elegant and distinguished, with this drawback, that his face was the most deadly pale I ever saw, except in death. He was in no masquerade – in the plain evening dress of a gentleman; and he said, without a smile, but with a courtly and unusually low bow:—

' "Will Madame la Comtesse permit me to say a very few words which may interest her?"

'The lady turned quickly to him, and touched her lip in token of silence; she then said to me, "Keep my place for me, General; I shall return when I have said a few words."

'And with this injunction, playfully given, she walked a little aside with the gentleman in black, and talked for some minutes, apparently very earnestly. They then walked away slowly together in the crowd, and I lost them for some minutes.

'I spent the interval in cudgelling my brains for conjecture as to the identity of the lady who seemed to remember me so kindly, and I was thinking of turning about and joining in the conversation between my pretty ward and the Countess's daughter, and trying whether, by the time she returned, I might not have a surprise in store for her, by having her name, title, château, and estates at my fingers' ends. But at this moment she returned, accompanied by the pale man in black, who said:

' "I shall return and inform Madame la Comtesse when her carriage is at the door."

'He withdrew with a bow.'

CHAPTER XII

A PETITION

' "Then we are to lose Madame la Comtesse, but I hope only for a few hours," I said, with a low bow.

' "It may be that only, or it may be a few weeks. It was very unlucky his speaking to me just now as he did. Do you now know me?"

'I assured her I did not.

' "You shall know me," she said, "but not at present. We are older and better friends than, perhaps, you suspect. I cannot yet declare myself. I shall in three weeks pass your beautiful schloss about which I have been making enquiries. I shall then look in upon you for an hour or two, and renew a friendship which I never think of without a thousand pleasant recollections. This moment a piece of news has reached me like a thunderbolt. I must set out now, and travel by a devious route, nearly a hundred miles, with all the dispatch I can possibly make. My perplexities multiply. I am only deterred by the compulsory reserve I practise as to my name from making a very singular request of you. My poor child has not quite recovered her strength. Her horse fell with her, at a hunt which she had ridden out to witness, her nerves have not yet recovered the shock, and our physician says that she must on no account exert herself for some time to come. We came here, in consequence, by very easy stages – hardly six leagues a day. I must now travel day and night, on a mission of life and death – a mission the critical and momentous nature of which I shall be able to explain to you when we meet, as I hope we shall, in a few weeks, without the necessity of any concealment."

'She went on to make her petition, and it was in the tone of a person from whom such a request amounted to conferring, rather than seeking a favour. This was only in manner, and, as it seemed, quite unconsciously. Than the terms in which it was expressed, nothing could be more deprecatory. It was simply that I would consent to take charge of her daughter during her absence.

'This was, all things considered, a strange, not to say, an audacious request. She in some sort disarmed me, by stating and admitting everything that could be urged against it, and throwing herself entirely upon my chivalry. At the same moment, by a fatality that seems to have pre-determined all that happened, my poor child came to my side, and, in an undertone, besought me to invite her new friend, Millarca, to pay us a visit. She had just been sounding her, and thought, if her mamma would allow her, she would like it extremely.

'At another time I should have told her to wait a little, until, at least, we knew who they were. But I had not a moment to think in. The two ladies assailed me together, and I must confess the refined and beautiful face of the young lady, about which there was something extremely engaging, as well as the elegance and fire of high birth, determined me; and quite overpowered, I submitted, and undertook, too easily, the care of the young lady, whom her mother called Millarca.

'The Countess beckoned to her daughter, who listened with grave attention while she told her, in general terms, how suddenly and peremptorily she had been summoned, and also of the arrangement she had made for her under my care, adding that I was one of her earliest and most valued friends.

'I made, of course, such speeches as the case seemed to call for, and found myself, on reflection, in a position which I did not half like.

'The gentleman in black returned, and very ceremoniously conducted the lady from the room.

'The demeanour of this gentleman was such as to impress me with the conviction that the Countess was a lady of very much more importance than her modest title alone might have led me to assume.

'Her last charge to me was that no attempt was to be made to learn more about her than I might have already guessed, until her return. Our distinguished host, whose guest she was, knew her reasons.

' "But here," she said, "neither I nor my daughter could safely remain for more than a day. I removed my mask imprudently for a moment, about an hour ago, and, too late, I fancied you saw me. So I resolved to seek an opportunity of talking a little to you. Had I found that you *had* seen me, I should have thrown myself on your high sense of honour to keep my secret for some weeks. As it is, I am satisfied that you did not see me; but if you now *suspect*, or, on reflection, *should* suspect, who I am, I commit myself, in like manner, entirely to your honour. My daughter will observe the same secrecy, and I well know that you will, from time to time, remind her, lest she should thoughtlessly disclose it."

'She whispered a few words to her daughter, kissed her hurriedly twice, and went away, accompanied by the pale gentleman in black, and disappeared in the crowd.

' "In the next room," said Millarca, "there is a window that looks upon the hall door. I should like to see the last of mamma, and to kiss my hand to her."

'We assented, of course, and accompanied her to the window. We looked out, and saw a handsome old-fashioned carriage, with a troop of couriers and footmen. We saw the slim figure of the pale gentleman in black, as he held a thick velvet cloak, and placed it about her shoulders and threw the hood over her head. She nodded to him, and just touched his hand with hers. He bowed low repeatedly as the door closed, and the carriage began to move.

' "She is gone," said Millarca, with a sigh.

' "She is gone," I repeated to myself, for the first time – in the hurried moments that had elapsed since my consent – reflecting upon the folly of my act.

' "She did not look up," said the young lady, plaintively.

' "The Countess had taken off her mask, perhaps, and did not care to show her face," I said; "and she could not know that you were in the window."

'She sighed and looked in my face. She was so beautiful that I relented. I was sorry I had for a moment repented of my hospitality, and I determined to make her amends for the unavowed churlishness of my reception.

'The young lady, replacing her mask, joined my ward in persuading me to return to the grounds, where the concert was soon to be renewed. We did so, and walked up and down the terrace that lies under the castle windows. Millarca became very intimate with us, and amused us with lively descriptions and stories of most of the great people whom we saw upon the terrace. I liked her more and more every minute. Her gossip, without being ill-natured, was extremely diverting to me, who had been so long out of the great world. I thought what life she would give to our sometimes lonely evenings at home.

'This ball was not over until the morning sun had almost reached the horizon. It pleased the Grand Duke to dance till then, so loyal people could not go away, or think of bed.

'We had just got through a crowded saloon, when my ward asked me what had become of Millarca. I thought she had been by my side, and she fancied she was by mine. The fact was, we had lost her.

'All my efforts to find her were vain. I feared that she had mistaken, in the confusion of a momentary separation from us, other people for her new friends, and had, possibly, pursued and lost them in the extensive grounds which were thrown open to us.

'Now, in its full force, I recognised a new folly in my having undertaken the charge of a young lady without so much as knowing her name; and fettered as I was by promises, of the reasons for imposing which I knew nothing, I could not even point my enquiries by saying that the missing young lady was the daughter of the Countess who had taken her departure a few hours before.

'Morning broke. It was clear daylight before I gave up my search. It was not till near two o'clock next day that we heard anything of my missing charge.

'At about that time a servant knocked at my niece's door, to say that he had been earnestly requested by a young lady, who appeared to be in great distress, to make out where she could find the General Baron Spielsdorf and the young lady, his daughter, in whose charge she had been left by her mother.

'There could be no doubt, notwithstanding the slight inaccuracy, that our young friend had turned up; and so she had. Would to Heaven we had lost her!

'She told my poor child a story to account for her having failed to recover us for so long. Very late, she said, she had got into the house-keeper's bedroom in despair of finding us, and had then fallen into a deep sleep which, long as it was, had hardly sufficed to recruit her strength after the fatigues of the ball.

'That day Millarca came home with us. I was only too happy, after all, to have secured so charming a companion for my dear girl.'

CHAPTER XIII

THE WOOD-MAN

'There soon, however, appeared some drawbacks. In the first place, Millarca complained of extreme languor – the weakness that remained after her late illness – and she never emerged from her room till the afternoon was pretty far advanced. In the next place, it was accidentally discovered, although she always locked her door on the inside, and never disturbed the key from its place, till she admitted the maid to assist at her toilet, that she was undoubtedly sometimes absent from her room in the very early morning, and at various times later in the day, before she wished it to be understood that she was stirring. She was repeatedly seen from the windows of the schloss, in the first faint grey of the morning, walking through the trees, in an easterly direction, and looking like a person in a trance. This convinced me that she walked in her sleep. But this hypothesis did not solve the puzzle. How did she pass out from her room, leaving the door locked on the inside. How did she escape from the house without unbarring door or window?

'In the midst of my perplexities, an anxiety of a far more urgent kind presented itself.

'My dear child began to lose her looks and health, and that in a manner so mysterious, and even horrible, that I became thoroughly frightened.

'She was at first visited by appalling dreams; then, as she fancied, by a spectre, something resembling Millarca, sometimes in the shape of a beast, indistinctly seen, walking round the foot of the bed, from side to side. Lastly came sensations. One, not unpleasant, but very peculiar, she said, resembled the flow of an icy stream against her breast. At a later time, she felt something like a pair of large needles pierce her, a little below the throat, with a very sharp pain. A few nights after, followed a gradual and convulsive sense of strangulation; then came unconsciousness.'

I could hear distinctly every word the kind old General was saying, because by this time we were driving upon the short grass that spreads on either side of the road as you approach the roofless village which had not shown the smoke of a chimney for more than half a century.

You may guess how strangely I felt as I heard my own symptoms so exactly described in those which had been experienced by the poor girl who, but for the catastrophe which followed, would have been at that moment a visitor at my father's château. You may suppose, also, how I felt as I heard him detail habits and mysterious peculiarities which were, in fact, those of our beautiful guest, Carmilla!

A vista opened in the forest; we were on a sudden under the chimneys and gables of the ruined village, and the towers and battlements of the dismantled castle, round which gigantic trees are grouped, overhung us from a slight eminence.

In a frightened dream I got down from the carriage, and in silence, for we had each abundant matter for thinking; we soon mounted the ascent, and were among the spacious chambers, winding stairs, and dark corridors of the castle.

'And this was once the palatial residence of the Karnsteins!' said the old General at length, as from a great window he looked out across the village, and saw the wide, undulating expanse of forest. 'It was a bad family, and here its blood-stained annals were written,' he continued. 'It is hard that they should, after death, continue to plague the human race with their atrocious lusts. That is the chapel of the Karnsteins, down there.'

He pointed down to the grey walls of the Gothic building, partly visible through the foliage, a little way down the steep. 'And I hear the axe of a woodman,' he added, 'busy among the trees that surround it; he possibly may give us the information of which I am in search, and point out the grave of Mircalla, Countess of Karnstein. These rustics preserve the local traditions of great families, whose stories die out among the rich and titled as soon as the families themselves become extinct.'

'We have a portrait, at home, of Mircalla, the Countess Karnstein; should you like to see it?' asked my father.

'Time enough, dear friend,' replied the General. 'I believe that I have seen the original; and one motive which has led me to you earlier than I at first intended, was to explore the chapel which we are now approaching.'

'What! see the Countess Mircalla,' exclaimed my father; 'why, she has been dead more than a century!'

'Not so dead as you fancy, I am told,' answered the General.

'I confess, General, you puzzle me utterly,' replied my father, looking at him, I fancied, for a moment with a return of the suspicion I detected before. But although there was anger and detestation, at times, in the old General's manner, there was nothing flighty.

'There remains to me,' he said, as we passed under the heavy arch of the Gothic church – for its dimensions would have justified its being so styled – 'but one object which can interest me during the few years that remain to me on earth, and that is to wreak on her the vengeance which, I thank God, may still be accomplished by a mortal arm.'

'What vengeance can you mean?' asked my father, in increasing amazement.

'I mean, to decapitate the monster,' he answered, with a fierce flush, and a stamp that echoed mournfully through the hollow ruin, and his clenched hand was at the same moment raised, as if it grasped the handle of an axe, while he shook it ferociously in the air.

'What!' exclaimed my father, more than ever bewildered.

'To strike her head off.'

'Cut her head off!'

'Aye, with a hatchet, with a spade, or with anything that can cleave through her murderous throat. You shall hear,' he answered, trembling with rage. And hurrying forward he said:

'That beam will answer for a seat; your dear child is fatigued; let her be seated, and I will, in a few sentences, close my dreadful story.'

The squared block of wood, which lay on the grass-grown pavement of the chapel, formed a bench on which I was very glad to seat myself, and in the meantime the General called to the woodman, who had been removing some boughs which leaned upon the old walls; and, axe in hand, the hardy old fellow stood before us.

He could not tell us anything of these monuments; but there was an old man, he said, a ranger of this forest, at present sojourning in the house of the priest, about two miles away, who could point out every monument of the old Karnstein family and, for a trifle, he undertook to bring him back with him, if we would lend him one of our horses, in little more than half-an-hour.

'Have you been long employed about this forest?' asked my father of the old man.

'I have been a woodman here,' he answered in his *patois*, 'under the forester, all my days; so has my father before me, and so on, as many generations as I can count up. I could show you the very house in the village here, in which my ancestors lived.'

'How came the village to be deserted?' asked the General.

'It was troubled by *revenants*, sir; several were tracked to their graves, there detected by the usual tests, and extinguished in the usual way, by decapitation, by the stake, and by burning; but not until many of the villagers were killed.

'But after all these proceedings according to law,' he continued – 'so many graves opened, and so many vampires deprived of their horrible animation – the village was not relieved. But a Moravian nobleman, who happened to be travelling this way, heard how matters were, and being skilled – as many people are in his country – in such affairs, he offered to deliver the village from its tormentor. He did so thus: There being a bright moon that night, he ascended, shortly after sunset, the tower of the chapel here, from whence he could distinctly see the churchyard beneath him; you can see it from that window. From this point he watched until he saw the vampire come out of his grave, and place near it the linen clothes in which he had been folded, and glide away towards the village to plague its inhabitants.

'The stranger, having seen all this, came down from the steeple, took the linen wrapping of the vampire, and carried them up to the top of the tower, which he again mounted. When the vampire returned from his prowlings and missed his clothes, he cried furiously to the Moravian, whom he saw at the summit of the tower, and who, in reply beckoned him to ascend and take them. Whereupon the vampire, accepting his invitation, began to climb the steeple, and so soon as he had reached the battlements, the Moravian, with a stroke of his sword, clove his skull in twain, hurling him down to the churchyard, whither, descending by the winding stairs, the stranger followed and cut his head off, and next day delivered it and the body to the villagers, who duly impaled and burnt them.

'This Moravian nobleman had authority from the then head of the family to remove the tomb of Mircalla, Countess Karnstein, which he did effectually, so that in a little while its site was quite forgotten.'

'Can you point out where it stood?' asked the General, eagerly.

The forester shook his head and smiled.

'Not a soul living could tell you that now,' he said; 'besides they say her body was removed; but no one is sure of that either.'

Having thus spoken, as time pressed, he dropped his axe and departed, leaving us to hear the remainder of the General's strange story.

CHAPTER XIV

THE MEETING

'My beloved child,' he resumed, 'was now growing rapidly worse. The physician who attended her had failed to produce the slightest impression upon her disease, for such I then supposed it to be. He saw my alarm, and suggested a consultation. I called in an abler physician, from Gratz. Several days elapsed before he arrived. He was a good and pious, as well as a learned man. Having seen my poor ward together, they withdrew to my library to confer and discuss. I, from the adjoining room, where I awaited their summons, heard these two gentlemen's voices raised in something sharper than a strictly philosophical discussion. I knocked at the door and entered, I found the old physician from Gratz maintaining his theory. His rival was combating it with undisguised ridicule, accompanied with bursts of laughter. This unseemly manifestation subsided and the altercation ended on my entrance.

' "Sir," said my first physician, "my learned brother seems to think that you want a conjuror, and not a doctor."

' "Pardon me," said the old physician from Gratz, looking displeased, "I shall state my own view of the case in my own way another time. I grieve, Monsieur le Général, that by my skill and science I can be of no use. Before I go I shall do myself the honour to suggest something to you."

'He seemed thoughtful, and sat down at a table, and began to write. Profoundly disappointed, I made my bow, and as I turned to go, the other doctor pointed over his shoulder to his companion who was writing, and then, with a shrug, significantly touched his forehead.

'This consultation, then, left me precisely where I was. I walked out into the grounds, all but distracted. The doctor from Gratz, in ten or fifteen minutes, overtook me. He apologised for having followed me, but said that he could not conscientiously take his leave without a few words more. He told me that he could not be mistaken; no natural disease exhibited the same symptoms; and that death was already very near. There remained, however, a day, or possibly two, of life. If the fatal seizure were at once arrested, with great care and skill her strength might possibly return. But all hung now upon the confines of the irrevocable. One more assault might extinguish the last spark of vitality which is, every moment, ready to die.

' "And what is the nature of the seizure you speak of?" I entreated.

' "I have stated all fully in this note, which I place in your hands, upon the distinct condition that you send for the nearest clergyman, and open my letter in his presence, and on no account read it till he is with you; you would despise it else, and it is a matter of life and death. Should the priest fail you, then, indeed, you may read it."

'He asked me, before taking his leave finally, whether I would wish to see a man curiously learned upon the very subject, which, after I had read his letter, would probably interest me above all others, and he urged me earnestly to invite him to visit him there; and so took his leave.

'The ecclesiastic was absent, and I read the letter by myself. At another time, or in another case, it might have excited my ridicule. But into what quackeries will not people rush for a last chance, where all accustomed means have failed, and the life of a beloved object is at stake?

'Nothing, you will say, could be more absurd than the learned man's letter. It was monstrous enough to have consigned him to a madhouse. He said that the patient was suffering from the visits of a vampire! The punctures which she described as having occurred near the throat, were, he insisted, the insertion of those two long, thin, and sharp teeth which, it is well known, are peculiar to vampires; and there could be no doubt, he added, as to the well-defined presence of the small livid mark which all concurred in describing as that induced by the demon's lips, and every symptom described by the sufferer was in exact conformity with those recorded in every case of a similar visitation.

'Being myself wholly sceptical as to the existence of any such portent as the vampire, the supernatural theory of the good doctor furnished, in my opinion, but another instance of learning and intelligence oddly associated with some hallucination. I was so miserable, however, that, rather than try nothing, I acted upon the instructions of the letter.

CARMILLA

'I concealed myself in the dark dressing-room, that opened upon the poor patient's room, in which a candle was burning, and watched there till she was fast asleep. I stood at the door, peeping through the small crevice, my sword laid on the table beside me, as my directions prescribed, until, a little after one, I saw a large black object, very ill-defined, crawl, as it seemed to me, over the foot of the bed, and swiftly spread itself up to the poor girl's throat, where it swelled, in a moment, into a great, palpitating mass.

'For a few moments I had stood petrified. I now sprang forward, with my sword in my hand. The black creature suddenly contracted toward the foot of the bed, glided over it, and, standing on the floor about a yard below the foot of the bed, with a glare of skulking ferocity and horror fixed on me, I saw Millarca. Speculating I know not what, I struck at her instantly with my sword; but I saw her standing near the door, unscathed. Horrified, I pursued, and struck again. She was gone! and my sword flew to shivers against the door.

'I can't describe to you all that passed on that horrible night. The whole house was up and stirring. The spectre Millarca was gone. But her victim was sinking fast, and before the morning dawned, she died.'

The old General was agitated. We did not speak to him. My father walked to some little distance, and began reading the inscriptions on the tombstones; and thus occupied, he strolled into the door of a side chapel to prosecute his researches. The General leaned against the wall, dried his eyes, and sighed heavily. I was relieved on hearing the voices of Carmilla and Madame, who were at that moment approaching. The voices died away.

In this solitude, having just listened to so strange a story, connected, as it was, with the great and titled dead, whose monuments were mouldering among the dust and ivy round us, and every incident of which bore so awfully upon my own mysterious case – in this haunted spot, darkened by the towering foliage that rose on every side, dense and high above its noiseless walls – a horror began to steal over me, and my heart sank as I thought that my friends were, after all, not about to enter and disturb this triste and ominous scene.

The old General's eyes were fixed on the ground, as he leaned with his hand upon the basement of a shattered monument.

Under a narrow, arched doorway, surmounted by one of those demoniacal grotesques in which the cynical and ghastly fancy of old Gothic carving delights, I saw very gladly the beautiful face and figure of Carmilla enter the shadowy chapel.

I was just about to rise and speak, and nodded smiling, in answer to her peculiarly engaging smile; when, with a cry, the old man by my side caught up the woodman's hatchet, and started forward. On seeing him a brutalised change came over her features. It was an instantaneous and horrible transformation, as she made a crouching step backwards. Before I could utter a scream, he struck at her with all his force, but she dived under his blow, and unscathed, caught him in her tiny grasp by the wrist. He struggled for a moment to release his arm, but his hand opened, the axe fell to the ground, and the girl was gone.

He staggered against the wall. His grey hair stood upon his head, and a moisture shone over his face, as if he were at the point of death.

The frightful scene had passed in a moment. The first thing I recollect after, is Madame standing before me, and impatiently repeating again and again, the question, 'Where is Mademoiselle Carmilla?'

I answered at length, 'I don't know – I can't tell – she went there,' and I pointed to the door through which Madame had just entered; 'only a minute or two since.'

'But I have been standing there, in the passage, ever since Mademoiselle Carmilla entered; and she did not return.'

She then began to call 'Carmilla' through every door and passage and from the windows, but no answer came.

'She called herself Carmilla?' asked the General, still agitated.

'Carmilla, yes,' I answered.

'Aye,' he said; 'that is Millarca. That is the same person who long ago was called Mircalla, Countess Karnstein. Depart from this accursed ground, my poor child, as quickly as you can. Drive to the clergyman's house, and stay there till we come. Begone! May you never behold Carmilla more; you will not find her here.'

CHAPTER XV

ORDEAL AND EXECUTION

As he spoke one of the strangest-looking men I ever beheld, entered the chapel at the door through which Carmilla had made her entrance and her exit. He was tall, narrow-chested, stooping, with high shoulders, and dressed in black. His face was brown and dried in with deep furrows; he wore an oddly-shaped hat with a broad leaf. His hair, long and grizzled, hung on his shoulders. He wore a pair of gold spectacles, and walked slowly, with an odd shambling gait, and his face sometimes turned up to the sky, and sometimes bowed down toward the ground, seemed to wear a perpetual smile; his long thin arms were swinging, and his lank hands, in old black gloves ever so much too wide for them, waving and gesticulating in utter abstraction.

'The very man!' exclaimed the General, advancing with manifest delight. 'My dear Baron, how happy I am to see you, I had no hope of meeting you so soon.' He signed to my father, who had by this time returned, and leading the fantastic old gentleman, whom he called the Baron, to meet him. He introduced him formally, and they at once entered into earnest conversation. The stranger took a roll of paper from his pocket, and spread it on the worn surface of a tomb that stood by. He had a pencil case in his fingers, with which he traced imaginary lines from point to point on the paper, which from their often glancing from it, together, at certain points of the building, I concluded to be a plan of the chapel. He accompanied, what I may term his lecture, with occasional readings from a dirty little book, whose yellow leaves were closely written over.

They sauntered together down the side aisle, opposite to the spot where I was standing, conversing as they went; then they began measuring distances by paces, and finally they all stood together, facing a piece of the side-wall, which they began to examine with great minuteness; pulling off the ivy that clung over it, and rapping the plaster with the ends of their sticks, scraping here, and knocking there. At length they ascertained the existence of a broad marble tablet, with letters carved in relief upon it.

With the assistance of the woodman, who soon returned, a monumental inscription, and carved escutcheon, were disclosed. They proved to be those of the long lost monument of Mircalla, Countess Karnstein.

The old General, though not I fear given to the praying mood, raised his hands and eyes to heaven, in mute thanksgiving for some moments.

'To-morrow,' I heard him say; 'the commissioner will be here, and the Inquisition will be held according to law.'

Then turning to the old man with the gold spectacles, whom I have described, he shook him warmly by both hands and said:

'Baron, how can I thank you? How can we all thank you? You will have delivered this region from a plague that has scourged its inhabitants for more than a century. The horrible enemy, thank God, is at last tracked.'

My father led the stranger aside, and the General followed. I knew that he had led them out of hearing, that he might relate my case, and I saw them glance often quickly at me, as the discussion proceeded.

My father came to me, kissed me again and again, and leading me from the chapel, said:

'It is time to return, but before we go home, we must add to our party the good priest, who lives but a little way from this; and persuade him to accompany us to the schloss.'

In this quest we were successful: and I was glad, being unspeakably fatigued when we reached home. But my satisfaction was changed to dismay, on discovering that there were no tidings of Carmilla. Of the scene that had occurred in the ruined chapel, no explanation was offered to me, and it was clear that it was a secret which my father for the present determined to keep from me.

The sinister absence of Carmilla made the remembrance of the scene more horrible to me. The arrangements for that night were singular. Two servants and Madame were to sit up in my room that night; and the ecclesiastic with my father kept watch in the adjoining dressing-room.

The priest had performed certain solemn rites that night, the purport of which I did not understand any more than I comprehended the reason of this extraordinary precaution taken for my safety during sleep.

I saw all clearly a few days later.

The disappearance of Carmilla was followed by the discontinuance of my nightly sufferings.

You have heard, no doubt, of the appalling superstition that prevails in Upper and Lower Styria, in Moravia, Silesia, in Turkish Servia, in Poland, even in Russia; the superstition, so we must call it, of the vampire.

If human testimony, taken with every care and solemnity, judicially, before commissions innumerable, each consisting of many members, all chosen for integrity and intelligence, and constituting reports more voluminous perhaps than exist upon any one other class of cases, is worth anything, it is difficult to deny, or even to doubt the existence of such a phenomenon as the vampire.

For my part I have heard no theory by which to explain what I myself have witnessed and experienced, other than that supplied by the ancient and well-attested belief of the country.

The next day the formal proceedings took place in the Chapel of Karnstein. The grave of the Countess Mircalla was opened; and the General and my father recognized each his perfidious and beautiful guest, in the face now disclosed to view. The features, though a hundred and fifty years had passed since her funeral, were tinted with the warmth of life. Her eyes were open; no cadaverous smell exhaled from the coffin. The two medical men, one officially present, the other on the part of the promoter of the enquiry, attested the marvellous fact, that there was a faint but appreciable respiration, and a corresponding action of the heart. The limbs were perfectly flexible, the flesh elastic; and the leaden coffin floated with blood, in which to a depth of seven inches, the body lay immersed. Here then, were all the admitted signs and proofs of vampirism. The body, therefore, in accordance with the ancient practice, was raised, and a sharp stake driven through the heart of the vampire, who uttered a piercing shriek at the moment, in all respects such as might escape from a living person in the last agony. Then the head was struck off, and a torrent of blood flowed from the severed neck. The body and head were next placed on a pile of wood, and reduced to ashes, which were thrown upon the river and borne away, and that territory has never since been plagued by the visits of a vampire.

My father has a copy of the report of the Imperial Commission, with the signatures of all who were present at these proceedings, attached in verification of the statement. It is from this official paper that I have summarised my account of this last shocking scene.

CHAPTER XVI

CONCLUSION

I write all this you suppose with composure. But far from it; I cannot think of it without agitation. Nothing but your earnest desire so repeatedly expressed, could have induced me to sit down to a task that has unstrung my nerves for months to come, and re-induced a shadow of the unspeakable horror which years after my deliverance continued to make my days and nights dreadful, and solitude insupportably terrific.

Let me add a word or two about that quaint Baron Vordenburg, to whose curious lore we were indebted for the discovery of the Countess Mircalla's grave.

He had taken up his abode in Gratz, where, living upon a mere pittance, which was all that remained to him of the once princely estates of his family, in Upper Styria, he devoted himself to the minute and laborious investigation of the marvellously authenticated tradition of vampirism. He had at his fingers' ends all the great and little works upon the subject. *Magia Posthuma, Phlegon de Mirabilibus, Augustinus de curâ pro Mortuis, Philosophicæ et Christianæ Cogitationes de Vampiris,* by John Christofer Herenberg; and a thousand others, among which I remember only a few of those which he lent to my father. He had a voluminous digest of all the judicial cases, from which he had extracted a system of principles that appear to govern – some always, and others occasionally only – the condition of the vampire. I may mention, in passing, that the deadly pallor attributed to that sort of *revenants*, is a mere melodramatic fiction. They present, in the grave, and when they show themselves in human society, the appearance of healthy life. When disclosed to light in their coffins, they exhibit all the symptoms that are enumerated as those which proved the vampire-life of the long-dead Countess Karnstein.

How they escape from their graves and return to them for certain hours every day, without displacing the clay or leaving any trace of disturbance in the state of the coffin or the cerements, has always been admitted to be utterly inexplicable. The amphibious existence of the vampire is sustained by daily renewed slumber in the grave. Its horrible lust for living blood supplies the vigour of its waking existence. The vampire is prone to be fascinated with an engrossing vehemence, resembling the passion of love, by particular persons. In pursuit of these it will exercise inexhaustible patience and stratagem, for access to a particular object may be obstructed in a hundred ways. It will never desist until it has satiated its passion, and drained the very life of its coveted victim. But it will, in these cases, husband and protract its murderous enjoyment with the refinement of an epicure, and heighten it by the gradual approaches of an artful courtship. In these cases it seems to yearn for something like sympathy and consent. In ordinary ones it goes direct to its object, overpowers with violence, and strangles and exhausts often at a single feast.

The vampire is, apparently, subject, in certain situations, to special conditions. In the particular instance of which I have given you a relation, Mircalla seemed to be limited to a name which, if not her real one, should at least reproduce, without the omission or addition of a single letter, those, as we say, anagrammatically, which compose it. *Carmilla* did this; so did *Millarca*.

My father related to the Baron Vordenburg, who remained with us for two or three weeks after the expulsion of Carmilla, the story about the Moravian nobleman and the vampire at Karnstein churchyard, and then he asked the Baron how he had discovered the exact position of the long-concealed tomb of the Countess Millarca. The Baron's grotesque features puckered up into a mysterious smile; he looked down, still smiling on his worn spectacle-case and fumbled with it. Then looking up, he said:

'I have many journals, and other papers, written by that remarkable man; the most curious among them is one treating of the visit of which you speak, to Karnstein. The tradition, of course, discolours and distorts a little. He might have been termed a Moravian nobleman, for he had changed his abode to that territory, and was, beside, a noble. But he was, in truth, a native of Upper Styria. It is enough to say that in very early youth he had been a passionate and favoured lover of the beautiful Mircalla, Countess Karnstein. Her early death plunged him into inconsolable grief. It is the nature of vampires to increase and multiply, but according to an ascertained and ghostly law.

'Assume, at starting, a territory perfectly free from that pest. How does it begin, and how does it multiply itself? I will tell you. A person, more or less wicked, puts an end to himself. A suicide, under certain circumstances, becomes a vampire. That spectre visits living people in their slumbers; *they* die, and almost invariably, in the grave, develop into vampires. This happened in the case of the beautiful Mircalla, who was haunted by one of those demons. My ancestor, Vordenburg, whose title I still bear, soon discovered this, and in the course of the studies to which he devoted himself, learned a great deal more.

'Among other things, he concluded that suspicion of vampirism would probably fall, sooner or later, upon the dead Countess, who in life had been his idol. He conceived a horror, be she what she might, of her remains being profaned by the outrage of a posthumous execution. He has left a curious paper to prove that the vampire, on its expulsion from its amphibious existence, is projected into a far more horrible life; and he resolved to save his once beloved Mircalla from this.

'He adopted the stratagem of a journey here, a pretended removal of her remains, and a real obliteration of her monument. When age had stolen upon him, and from the vale of years he looked back on the scenes he was leaving, he considered, in a different spirit, what he had done, and a horror took possession of him. He made the tracings and notes which have guided me to the very spot, and drew up a confession of the deception that he had practised. If he had intended any further action in this matter, death prevented him; and the hand of a remote descendant has too late for many, directed the pursuit to the lair of the beast.'

We talked a little more, and among other things he said was this:

'One sign of the vampire is the power of the hand. The slender hand of Mircalla closed like a vice of steel on the General's wrist when he raised the hatchet to strike. But its power is not confined to its grasp; it leaves a numbness in the limb it seizes, which is slowly, if ever, recovered from.'

The following Spring my father took me a tour through Italy. We remained away for more than a year. It was long before the terror of recent events subsided; and to this hour the image of Carmilla returns to memory with ambiguous alternations – sometimes the playful, languid, beautiful girl; sometimes the writhing fiend I saw in the ruined church; and often from a reverie I have started, fancying I heard the light step of Carmilla at the drawing-room door.

Guy De Maupassant

Was it a Dream?

I had loved her madly!

Why does one love? Why does one love? How queer it is to see only one being in the world, to have only one thought in one's mind, only one desire in the heart and only one name on the lips – a name which comes up continually, rising, like the water in a spring, from the depths of the soul to the lips, a name which one repeats over and over again, which one whispers ceaselessly, everywhere, like a prayer.

I am going to tell you our story, for love has only one, which is always the same. I met her and lived on her tenderness, on her caresses, in her arms, in her dresses, on her words, so completely wrapped up, bound and absorbed in everything which came from her that I no longer cared whether it was day or night, or whether I was dead or alive, on this old earth of ours.

And then she died. How? I do not know; I no longer know anything. But one evening she came home wet, for it was raining heavily, and the next day she coughed, and she coughed for about a week and took to her bed. What happened I do not remember now, but doctors came, wrote, and went away. Medicines were brought, and some women made her drink them. Her hands were hot, her forehead was burning, and her eyes were bright and sad. When I spoke to her she answered me, but I do not remember what we said. I have forgotten everything, everything, everything! She died, and I very well remember her slight, feeble sigh. The nurse said: 'Ah!' and I understood; I understood!

I knew nothing more, nothing. I saw a priest who said: 'Your mistress?' And it seemed to me as if he were insulting her. As she was dead, nobody had the right to say that any longer, and I turned him out. Another came who was very kind and tender, and I shed tears when he spoke to me about her.

They consulted me about the funeral, but I do not remember anything that they said, though I recollect the coffin and the sound of the hammer when they nailed her down in it. Oh! God, God!

She was buried! Buried! She! In that hole! Some people came – female friends. I made my escape and ran away. I ran and then walked through the streets, went home and the next day started on a journey.

Yesterday I returned to Paris, and when I saw my room again – our room, our bed, our furniture, everything that remains of the life of a human being after death – I was seized by such a violent attack of fresh grief that I felt like opening the window and throwing myself out into the street. I could not remain any longer among these things, between these walls which had inclosed and sheltered her, which retained a thousand atoms of her, of her skin and of her breath, in their imperceptible crevices. I took up my hat to make my escape, and just as I reached the door I passed the large glass in the hall, which she had put there so that she might look at herself every day from head to foot as she went out, to see if her toilet looked well and was correct and pretty, from her little boots to her bonnet.

I stopped short in front of that looking-glass in which she had so often been reflected – so often, so often, that it must have retained her reflection. I was standing there trembling, with my eyes fixed on the glass – on that flat, profound, empty glass – which had contained her entirely and had possessed her as much as I, as my passionate looks had. I felt as if I loved that glass. I touched it; it was cold. Oh, the recollection! Sorrowful mirror, burning mirror, horrible mirror, to make men suffer such torments! Happy is the man whose heart forgets everything that it has contained, everything that has passed before it, everything that has looked at itself in it or has been reflected in its affection, in its love! How I suffer!

I went out without knowing it, without wishing it, and towards the cemetery. I found her simple grave, a white marble cross, with these few words:

She loved, was loved, and died.

She is there below, decayed! How horrible! I sobbed with my forehead on the ground, and I stopped there for a long time, a long time. Then I saw that it was getting dark, and a strange, mad wish, the wish of a despairing lover, seized me. I wished to pass the night, the last night, in weeping on her grave. But I should be seen and driven out.

128

THE BEST GHOST STORIES

How was I to manage? I was cunning and got up and began to roam about in that city of the dead. I walked and walked. How small this city is in comparison with the other, the city in which we live. And yet how much more numerous the dead are than the living. We need high houses, wide streets and much room for the four generations which see the daylight at the same time, drink water from the spring and wine from the vines, and eat bread from the plains.

And for all the generations of the dead, for all that ladder of humanity that has descended down to us, there is scarcely anything, scarcely anything! The earth takes them back, and oblivion effaces them. Adieu!

At the end of the cemetery, I suddenly perceived that I was in its oldest part, where those who had been dead a long time are mingling with the soil, where the crosses themselves are decayed, where possibly newcomers will be put to-morrow. It is full of untended roses, of strong and dark cypress trees – a sad and beautiful garden, nourished on human flesh.

I was alone, perfectly alone. So I crouched under a green tree and hid myself there completely amid the thick and sombre branches. I waited, clinging to the trunk as a shipwrecked man does to a plank.

When it was quite dark I left my refuge and began to walk softly, slowly, inaudibly, through that ground full of dead people. I wandered about for a long time, but could not find her tomb again. I went on with extended arms, knocking against the tombs with my hands, my feet, my knees, my chest, even with my head, without being able to find her. I groped about like a blind man seeking his way; I felt the stones, the crosses, the iron railings, the metal wreaths and the wreaths of faded flowers! I read the names with my fingers, by passing them over the letters. What a night! What a night! I could not find her again!

There was no moon. What a night! I was frightened, horribly frightened in those narrow paths between two rows of graves. Graves! Graves! Graves! Nothing but graves! On my right, on my left, in front of me, around me, everywhere there were graves! I sat down on one of them, for I could not walk any longer; my knees were so weak. I could hear my heart beat! And I heard something else as well. What? A confused, nameless noise. Was the noise in my head, in the impenetrable night, or beneath the mysterious earth, the earth sown with human corpses? I looked all around me, but I cannot say how long I remained there; I was paralysed with terror, cold, with fright, ready to shout out, ready to die.

Suddenly it seemed to me that the slab of marble on which I was sitting was moving. Certainly it was moving, as if it were being raised.

WAS IT A DREAM?

With a bound I sprang on to the neighbouring tomb, and I saw, yes, I distinctly saw the stone which I had just quitted rise upright. Then the dead person appeared, a naked skeleton, pushing the stone back with its bent back. I saw it quite clearly, although the night was so dark. On the cross I could read:

> Here lies Jacques Olivant, who died at the age of fifty-one. He loved his family, was kind and honourable, and died in the grace of the Lord.

The dead man also read what was inscribed on the tombstone; then he picked up a stone off the path, a little, pointed stone, and began to scrape the letters carefully. He slowly effaced them, and with the hollows of his eyes he looked at the place where they had been engraved. Then, with the tip of the bone that had been his forefinger, he wrote in luminous letters, like those lines which boys trace on walls with the tip of a lucifer match:

> Here reposes Jacques Olivant, who died at the age of fifty-one. He hastened his father's death by his unkindness, as he wished to inherit his fortune; he tortured his wife, tormented his children, deceived his neighbours, robbed everyone he could, and died wretched.

When he had finished writing, the dead man stood motionless, looking at his work. On turning around I saw that all the graves were open, that all the dead bodies had emerged from them and that all had effaced the lines inscribed on the gravestones by their relations, substituting the truth instead. And I saw that all had been the tormentors of their neighbours – malicious, dishonest, hypocrites, liars, rogues, calumniators, envious; that they had stolen, deceived, performed every disgraceful, every abominable action, these good fathers, these faithful wives, these devoted sons, these chaste daughters, these honest tradesmen, these men and women who were called irreproachable. They were all writing at the same time, on the threshold of their eternal abode, the truth, the terrible, and the holy truth, of which everybody was ignorant, or pretended to be ignorant, while they were alive.

I thought that *she* also must have written something on her tombstone; and now, running without any fear among the half-open coffins, among the corpses and skeletons, I went towards her, sure that I should find her immediately. I recognized her at once without seeing her face, which was covered by the winding sheet; and on the marble cross where shortly before I had read:

> She loved, was loved, and died.

I now saw:

> Having gone out in the rain one day in order to deceive her lover, she caught cold and died.

> It appears that they found me at daybreak, lying on the grave, unconscious.

Guy De Maupassant

The Horla

May 8. What a lovely day! I have spent all the morning lying in the grass in front of my house, under the enormous plane tree that shades the whole of it. I like this part of the country and I like to live here because I am attached to it by old associations, by those deep and delicate roots which attach a man to the soil on which his ancestors were born and died, which attach him to the ideas and usages of the place as well as to the food, to local expressions, to the peculiar twang of the peasants, to the smell of the soil, of the villages, and of the atmosphere itself.

I love my house in which I grew up. From my windows I can see the Seine which flows alongside my garden, on the other side of the high road, almost through my grounds, the great and wide Seine, which goes to Rouen and Le Havre, and is covered with boats passing to and fro.

On the left, down yonder, lies Rouen, that large town, with its blue roofs, under its pointed Gothic towers. These are innumerable, slender or broad, dominated by the spire of the cathedral, and full of bells which sound through the blue air on fine mornings, sending their sweet and distant iron clang even as far as my home; that song of the metal, which the breeze wafts in my direction, now stronger and now weaker, according as the wind is stronger or lighter.

What a delicious morning it was!

About eleven o'clock, a long line of boats drawn by a steam tug as big as a fly, and which scarcely puffed while emitting its thick smoke, passed my gate.

After two English schooners, whose red flag fluttered in space, there came a magnificent Brazilian three-master; she was perfectly white, and wonderfully clean and shining. I saluted her, I hardly knew why, except that the sight of the vessel gave me great pleasure.

May 12. I have had a slight feverish attack for the last few days, and I feel ill, or rather I feel low-spirited.

Whence come those mysterious influences which change our happiness into discouragement, and our self-confidence into diffidence? One might almost say that the air, the invisible air, is full of unknowable Powers whose mysterious presence we have to endure. I wake up in the best spirits, with an inclination to sing. Why? I go down to the edge of the water, and suddenly, after walking a short distance, I return home wretched, as if some misfortune were awaiting me there. Why? Is it a cold shiver which, passing over my skin, has upset my nerves and given me low spirits? Is it the form of the clouds, the colour of the sky, or the colour of the surrounding objects, which is so changeable, that has troubled my thoughts as they passed before my eyes? Who can tell? Everything that surrounds us, everything that we see, without looking at it, everything that we touch, without knowing it, everything that we handle, without feeling it, all that we meet, without clearly distinguishing it, has a rapid, surprising and inexplicable effect upon us and upon our senses, and, through them, on our ideas and on our heart itself.

How profound that mystery of the Invisible is! We cannot fathom it with our miserable senses, with our eyes which are unable to perceive what is either too small or too great, too near to us, or too far from us – neither the inhabitants of a star nor of a drop of water; nor with our ears that deceive us, for they transmit to us the vibrations of the air in sonorous notes. They are fairies who work the miracle of changing these vibrations into sound, and by that metamorphosis give birth to music, which makes the silent motion of nature musical . . . with our sense of smell which is less keen than that of a dog . . . with our sense of taste which can scarcely distinguish the age of a wine!

Oh! If we only had other organs which would work other miracles in our favour, what a number of fresh things we might discover around us!

May 16. I am ill, decidedly! I was so well last month! I am feverish, horribly feverish, or rather I am in a state of feverish enervation, which makes my mind suffer as much as my body. I have, continually, that horrible sensation of some impending danger, that apprehension of some coming misfortune, or of approaching death; that presentiment which is, no doubt, an attack of some illness which is still unknown, which germinates in the flesh and in the blood.

May 17. I have just come from consulting my physician, for I could no longer get any sleep. He said my pulse was rapid, my eyes dilated, my nerves highly strung, but there were no alarming symptoms. I must take a course of shower baths and of bromide of potassium.

May 25. No change! My condition is really very peculiar. As the evening comes on, an incomprehensible feeling of disquietude seizes me, just as if night concealed some threatening disaster. I dine hurriedly, and then try to read, but I do not understand the words, and can scarcely distinguish the letters. Then I walk up and down my drawing-room, oppressed by a feeling of confused and irresistible fear, the fear of sleep and fear of my bed.

About ten o'clock I go up to my room. As soon as I enter it I double-lock and bolt the door; I am afraid – of what? Up to the present time I have been afraid of nothing. . . . I open my cupboards, and look under my bed; I listen – to what? How strange it is that a simple feeling of discomfort, impeded or heightened circulation, perhaps the irritation of a nerve filament, a slight congestion, a small disturbance in the imperfect delicate functioning of our living machinery, may turn the most light-hearted of men into a melancholy one, and make a coward of the bravest? Then I go to bed, and wait for sleep as a man might wait for the executioner. I wait for its coming with dread, and my heart beats and my legs tremble, while my whole body shivers beneath the warmth of the bedclothes, until all at once I fall asleep, as though one should plunge into a pool of stagnant water in order to drown. I do not feel it coming on as I did formerly, this perfidious sleep which is close to me and watching me, which is going to seize me by the head, to close my eyes and annihilate me.

I sleep – a long time – two or three hours perhaps – then a dream – no – a nightmare lays hold on me. I feel that I am in bed and asleep . . . I feel it and I know it . . . and I feel also that somebody is coming close to me, is looking at me, touching me, is getting on to my bed, is kneeling on my chest, is taking my neck between his hands and squeezing it . . . squeezing it with all his might in order to strangle me.

I struggle, bound by that terrible sense of powerlessness which para-lyses us in our dreams; I try to cry out – but I cannot; I want to move – I cannot do so; I try, with the most violent efforts and breathing hard, to turn over and throw off this being who is crushing and suffocating me – I cannot!

And then, suddenly, I wake up, trembling and bathed in perspiration; I light a candle and find that I am alone, and after that crisis, which occurs every night, I at length fall asleep and slumber tranquilly till morning.

June 2. My condition has grown worse. What is the matter with me? The bromide does me no good, and the shower baths have no effect. Sometimes, in order to tire myself thoroughly, though I am fatigued enough already, I go for a walk in the forest of Roumare. I used to think at first that the fresh light and soft air, impregnated with the odour of herbs and leaves, would instill new blood into my veins and impart fresh energy to my heart. I turned into a broad hunting road, and then turned towards La Bouille, through a narrow path, between two rows of exceedingly tall trees, which placed a thick green, almost black, roof between the sky and me.

A sudden shiver ran through me, not a cold shiver, but a strange shiver of agony, and I hastened my steps, uneasy at being alone in the forest, afraid, stupidly and without reason, of the profound solitude. Suddenly it seemed to me as if I were being followed, as if somebody were walking at my heels, close, quite close to me, near enough to touch me.

I turned round suddenly, but I was alone. I saw nothing behind me except the straight, broad path, empty and bordered by high trees, horribly empty; before me it also extended until it was lost in the distance, and looked just the same – terrible.

I closed my eyes. Why? And then I began to turn round on one heel very quickly, just like a top. I nearly fell down, and opened my eyes; the trees were dancing round me and the earth heaved; I was obliged to sit down. Then, ah! I no longer remembered how I had come! What a strange idea! What a strange, strange idea! I did not in the least know. I started off to the right, and got back into the avenue which had led me into the middle of the forest.

June 3. I have had a terrible night. I shall go away for a few weeks, for no doubt a journey will set me up again.

July 2. I have come back, quite cured, and have had a most delightful trip into the bargain. I have been to Mont Saint-Michel, which I had not seen before.

What a sight, when one arrives as I did, at Avranches towards the end of the day! The town stands on a hill, and I was taken into the public garden at the extremity of the town. I uttered a cry of astonishment. An extraordinarily large bay lay extended before me, as far as my eyes could reach, between two hills which were lost to sight in the mist; and in the middle of this immense yellow bay, under a clear, golden sky, a peculiar hill rose up, sombre and pointed in the midst of the sand. The sun had just disappeared, and under the still flaming sky appeared the outline of that fantastic rock which bears on its summit a fantastic monument.

At daybreak I went out to it. The tide was low, as it had been the night before, and I saw that wonderful abbey rise up before me as I approached it. After several hours' walking, I reached the enormous mass of rocks which supports the little town, dominated by the great church. Having climbed the steep and narrow street, I entered the most wonderful Gothic building that has ever been built to God on earth, as large as a town, full of low rooms which seem buried beneath vaulted roofs, and lofty galleries supported by delicate columns.

THE HORLA

I entered this gigantic granite gem, which is as light as a bit of lace, covered with towers, with slender belfries with spiral staircases, which raise their strange heads that bristle with chimeras, with devils, with fantastic animals, with monstrous flowers, to the blue sky by day, and to the black sky by night, and are connected by finely carved arches.

When I had reached the summit I said to the monk who accompanied me: 'Father, how happy you must be here!' And he replied: 'It is very windy here, monsieur'; and so we began to talk while watching the rising tide, which ran over the sand and covered it as with a steel cuirass.

And then the monk told me stories, all the old stories belonging to the place, legends, nothing but legends.

One of them struck me forcibly. The country people, those belonging to the Mount, declare that at night one can hear voices talking on the sands, and that one then hears two goats bleating, one with a strong, the other with a weak voice. Incredulous people declare that it is nothing but the cry of the sea birds, which occasionally resembles bleatings, and occasionally, human lamentations; but belated fishermen swear that they have met an old shepherd wandering between tides on the sands around the little town. His head is completely concealed by his cloak and he is followed by a billy goat with a man's face, and a nanny goat with a woman's face, both having long, white hair, and talking incessantly and quarrelling in an unknown tongue. Then suddenly they cease and begin to bleat with all their might.

'Do you believe it?' I asked the monk. 'I scarcely know,' he replied, and I continued: 'If there are other beings besides ourselves on this earth, how comes it that we have not known it long since, or why have *you* not seen them? How is it that *I* have not seen them?' He replied: 'Do we see the hundred-thousandth part of what exists? Look here; there is the wind, which is the strongest force in nature, which knocks down men, and blows down buildings, uproots trees, raises the sea into mountains of water, destroys cliffs and casts great ships on the rocks; the wind which kills, which whistles, which sighs, which roars – have you ever seen it, and can you see it? It exists for all that, however.'

I was silent before this simple reasoning. That man was a philosopher, or perhaps a fool; I could not say which exactly, so I held my tongue. What he had said had often been in my own thoughts.

July 3. I have slept badly; certainly there is some feverish influence here, for my coachman is suffering in the same way as I am. When I went back home yesterday, I noticed his singular paleness, and I asked him: 'What is the matter with you, Jean?' 'The matter is that I never get any rest, and my nights devour my days. Since your departure, monsieur, there has been a spell over me.'

However, the other servants are all well, but I am very much afraid of having another attack myself.

July 4. I am decidedly ill again; for my old nightmares have returned. Last night I felt somebody leaning on me and sucking my life from between my lips. Yes, he was sucking it out of my throat, like a leech. Then he got up, satiated, and I woke up, so exhausted, crushed and weak that I could not move. If this continues for a few days, I shall certainly go away again.

July 5. Have I lost my reason? What happened last night is so strange that my head wanders when I think of it!

I had locked my door, as I do now every evening, and then, being thirsty, I drank half a glass of water, and accidentally noticed that the water bottle was full up to the cut-glass stopper.

Then I went to bed and fell into one of my terrible sleeps, from which I was aroused in about two hours by a still more frightful shock.

Picture to yourself a sleeping man who is being murdered and who wakes up with a knife in his lung, and whose breath rattles, who is covered with blood, and who can no longer breathe and is about to die, and does not understand – there you have it.

Having recovered my senses, I was thirsty again, so I lit a candle and went to the table on which stood my water bottle. I lifted it up and tilted it over my glass, but nothing came out. It was. empty! It was completely empty! At first I could not understand it at all, and then suddenly I was seized by such a terrible feeling that I had to sit down, or rather I fell into a chair! Then I sprang up suddenly to look about me; then I sat down again, overcome by astonishment and fear, in front of the transparent glass bottle! I looked at it with fixed eyes, trying to conjecture, and my hands trembled! Somebody had drunk the water, but who? I? I, without any doubt. It could surely only be I. In that case I was a somnambulist; I lived, without knowing it, that mysterious double life which makes us doubt whether there are not two beings in us, or whether a strange, unknowable and invisible being does not at such moments, when our soul is in a state of torpor, animate our captive body, which obeys this other being, as it obeys us, and more than it obeys ourselves.

Oh! Who will understand my horrible agony? Who will understand the emotion of a man who is sound in mind, wide awake, full of common sense, who looks in horror through the glass of a water bottle for a little water that disappeared while he was asleep? I remained thus until it was daylight, without venturing to go to bed again.

July 6. I am going mad. Again all the contents of my water bottle have been drunk during the night – or rather, I have drunk it!

But is it I? Is it I? Who could it be? Who? Oh, God! Am I going mad? Who will save me?

THE HORLA

July 10. I have just been through some surprising ordeals. Decidedly I am mad! And yet! . . .

On 6th July, before going to bed, I put some wine, milk, water, bread and strawberries on my table. Somebody drank – I drank – all the water and a little of the milk, but neither the wine, bread, nor the strawberries were touched.

On the seventh of July I renewed the same experiment, with the same results, and on 8th July, I left out the water and the milk, and nothing was touched.

Lastly, on 9th July I put only water and milk on my table, taking care to wrap up the bottles in white muslin and to tie down the stoppers. Then I rubbed my lips, my beard and my hands with pencil lead, and went to bed.

Irresistible sleep seized me, which was soon followed by a terrible awakening. I had not moved, and there was no mark of lead on the sheets. I rushed to the table. The muslin round the bottles remained intact; I undid the string, trembling with fear. All the water had been drunk, and so had the milk! Ah! Great God! . . .

I must start for Paris immediately.

July 12. Paris. I must have lost my head during the last few days! I must be the plaything of my enervated imagination, unless I am really a somnambulist, or perhaps I have been under the power of one of those hitherto unexplained influences which are called suggestions. In any case, my mental state bordered on madness, and twenty-four hours of Paris sufficed to restore my equilibrium.

Yesterday, after doing some business and paying some visits which instilled fresh and invigorating air into my soul, I wound up the evening at the *Théâtre-Français*. A play by Alexandre Dumas the younger was being acted, and his active and powerful imagination completed my cure. Certainly solitude is dangerous for active minds. We require around us men who can think and talk. When we are alone for a long time, we people space with phantoms.

I returned along the boulevards to my hotel in excellent spirits. Amid the jostling of the crowd I thought, not without irony, of my terrors and surmises of the previous week, because I had believed – yes, I had believed – that an invisible being lived beneath my roof. How weak our brains are, and how quickly they are terrified and led into error by a small incomprehensible fact.

Instead of saying simply: 'I do not understand because I do not know the cause,' we immediately imagine terrible mysteries and supernatural powers.

July 14. Fête of the Republic. I walked through the streets, amused as a child at the firecrackers and flags. Still it is very foolish to be merry on a fixed date, by Government decree. The populace is an imbecile flock of sheep, now stupidly patient, and now in ferocious revolt. Say to it: 'Amuse yourself,' and it amuses itself. Say to it: 'Go and fight with your neighbour,' and it goes and fights. Say to it: 'Vote for the Emperor,' and it votes for the Emperor, and then say to it: 'Vote for the Republic,' and it votes for the Republic.

Those who direct it are also stupid; only, instead of obeying men, they obey principles which can only be stupid, sterile, and false, for the very reason that they are principles, that is to say, ideas which are considered as certain and unchangeable in this world where one is certain of nothing, since light is an illusion and noise is an illusion.

July 16. I saw some things yesterday that troubled me very much.

I was dining at the house of my cousin, Madame Sablé, whose husband is colonel of the 76th Chasseurs at Limoges. There were two young women there, one of whom had married a medical man, Dr Parent, who devotes much attention to nervous diseases and to the remarkable manifestations taking place at this moment under the influence of hypnotism and suggestion.

He related to us at some length the wonderful results obtained by English scientists and by the doctors of the Nancy school; and the facts which he adduced appeared to me so strange that I declared that I was altogether incredulous.

'We are,' he declared, 'on the point of discovering one of the most important secrets of nature; I mean to say, one of its most important secrets on this earth, for there are certainly others of a different kind of importance up in the stars, yonder. Ever since man has thought, ever since he has been able to express and write down his thoughts, he has felt himself close to a mystery which is impenetrable to his gross and imperfect senses, and he endeavours to supplement through his intellect the inefficiency of his senses. As long as that intellect remained in its elementary stage, these apparitions of invisible spirits assumed forms that were commonplace, though terrifying. Thence sprang the popular belief in the supernatural, the legends of wandering spirits, of fairies, of gnomes, ghosts, I might even say the legend of God; for our conceptions of the workman-creator, from whatever religion they may have come down to us, are certainly the most mediocre, the most stupid and the most incredible inventions that ever sprang from the terrified brain of any human beings. Nothing is truer than what Voltaire says: "God made man in His own image, but man has certainly paid Him back in his own coin."

'However, for rather more than a century men seem to have had a presentiment of something new. Mesmer and some others have put us on an unexpected track, and, especially within the last two or three years, we have arrived at really surprising results.'

THE HORLA

My cousin, who is also very incredulous, smiled, and Dr Parent said to her: 'Would you like me to try and send you to sleep, madame?' 'Yes, certainly.'

She sat down in an easy chair, and he began to look at her fixedly, so as to fascinate her. I suddenly felt myself growing uncomfortable, my heart beating rapidly and a choking sensation in my throat. I saw Madame Sablé's eyes becoming heavy, her mouth twitching and her bosom heaving, and at the end of ten minutes she was asleep.

'Go behind her,' the doctor said to me, and I took a seat behind her. He put a visiting card into her hands, and said to her: 'This is a looking-glass; what do you see in it?' And she replied: 'I see my cousin.' 'What is he doing?' 'He is twisting his moustache.' 'And now?' 'He is taking a photograph out of his pocket.' 'Whose photograph is it?' 'His own.'

That was true, and the photograph had been given me that same evening at the hotel.

'What is his attitude in this portrait?' 'He is standing up with his hat in his hand.'

She saw, therefore, on that card, on that piece of white pasteboard, as if she had seen it in a mirror.

The young women were frightened and exclaimed: 'That is enough! Quite, quite enough!'

But the doctor said to Madame Sablé authoritatively: 'You will rise at eight o'clock to-morrow morning; then you will go and call on your cousin at his hotel and ask him to lend you five thousand francs which your husband demands of you, and which he will ask for when he sets out on his coming journey.'

Then he woke her up.

On returning to my hotel, I thought over this curious séance, and I was assailed by doubts, not as to my cousin's absolute and undoubted good faith, for I had known her as well as if she were my own sister ever since she was a child, but as to a possible trick on the doctor's part. Had he not, perhaps, kept a glass hidden in his hand, which he showed to the young woman in her sleep, at the same time as he did the card? Professional conjurors do things that are just as singular.

So I went home and to bed, and this morning, at about half-past eight, I was awakened by my valet, who said to me: 'Madame Sablé has asked to see you immediately, monsieur.' I dressed hastily and went to her.

She sat down in some agitation, with her eyes on the floor, and without raising her veil she said to me: 'My dear cousin, I am going to ask a great favour of you.' 'What is it, cousin?' 'I do not like to tell you, and yet I must. I am in absolute need of five thousand francs.' 'What, you?' 'Yes, I, or rather my husband, who has asked me to procure them for him.'

I was so thunderstruck that I stammered out my answers. I asked myself whether she had not really been making fun of me with Dr Parent, if it was not merely a very well-acted farce which had been rehearsed beforehand. On looking at her attentively, however, all my doubts disappeared. She was trembling with grief, so painful was this step to her, and I was convinced that her throat was full of sobs.

I knew that she was very rich and I continued: 'What! Has not your husband five thousand francs at his disposal? Come, think. Are you sure that he commissioned you to ask me for them?'

She hesitated for a few seconds, as if she were making a great effort to search her memory, and then she replied: 'Yes . . . yes, I am quite sure of it.' 'He has written to you?'

She hesitated again and reflected, and I guessed the torture of her thoughts. She did not know. She only knew that she was to borrow five thousand francs of me for her husband. So she told a lie. 'Yes, he has written to me.' 'When, pray? You did not mention it to me yesterday.' 'I received his letter this morning.' 'Can you show it me?' 'No . . . no . . . no . . . it contains private matters . . . things too personal to ourselves. . . . I burned it.' 'So your husband runs into debt?'

She hesitated again, and then murmured: 'I do not know.' Thereupon I said bluntly: 'I have not five thousand francs at my disposal at this moment, my dear cousin.'

She uttered a kind of cry as if she were in pain and said: 'Oh! oh! I beseech you, I beseech you to get them for me. . . .'

She got excited and clasped her hands as if she were praying to me! I heard her voice change its tone; she wept and stammered, harassed and dominated by the irresistible order that she had received.

'Oh! oh! I beg you to . . . if you knew what I am suffering . . . I want them to-day.'

I had pity on her: 'You shall have them by and by, I swear to you.' 'Oh! thank you! thank you! How kind you are.'

I continued: 'Do you remember what took place at your house last night?' 'Yes.' 'Do you remember that Dr Parent sent you to sleep?' 'Yes.' 'Oh! Very well, then; he ordered you to come to me this morning to borrow five thousand francs, and at this moment you are obeying that suggestion.'

She considered for a few moments, and then replied: 'But as it is my husband who wants them—'

For a whole hour I tried to convince her, but could not succeed, and when she had gone I went to the doctor. He was just going out, and he listened to me with a smile, and said: 'Do you believe now?' 'Yes, I cannot help it.' 'Let us go to your cousin's.'

She was already half asleep on a reclining chair, overcome with fatigue. The doctor felt her pulse, looked at her for some time with one hand raised towards her eyes, which she closed by degrees under the irresistible power of this magnetic influence, and when she was asleep, he said:

'Your husband does not require the five thousand francs any longer! You must, therefore, forget that you asked your cousin to lend them to you, and, if he speaks to you about it, you will not understand him.'

Then he woke her up, and I took out a pocketbook and said: 'Here is what you asked me for this morning, my dear cousin.' But she was so surprised that I did not venture to persist; nevertheless, I tried to recall the circumstance to her, but she denied it vigorously, thought I was making fun of her, and, in the end, very nearly lost her temper.

There! I have just come back, and I have not been able to eat any lunch, for this experiment has altogether upset me.

July 19. Many people to whom I told the adventure laughed at me. I no longer know what to think. The wise man says: 'It may be!'

July 21. I dined at Bougival, and then I spent the evening at a boatman's ball. Decidedly everything depends on place and surroundings. It would be the height of folly to believe in the supernatural on the Ile de la Grenouilliere . . . but on the top of Mont Saint-Michel? . . . and in India? We are terribly influenced by our surroundings. I shall return home next week.

July 30. I came back to my own house yesterday. Everything is going on well.

August 2. Nothing new; it is splendid weather, and I spent my days in watching the Seine flowing past.

August 4. Quarrels among my servants. They declare that the glasses are broken in the cupboards at night. The footman accuses the cook, who accuses the seamstress, who accuses the other two. Who is the culprit? It is a clever person who can tell.

August 6. This time I am not mad. I have seen . . . I have seen . . . I have seen! . . . I can doubt no longer . . . I have seen it! . . .

I was walking at two o'clock among my rose trees, in the full sunlight . . . in the walk bordered by autumn roses which are beginning to fall. As I stopped to look at a Géant de Bataille, which had three splendid blossoms, I distinctly saw the stalk of one of the roses near me bend, as if an invisible hand had bent it, and then break, as if that hand had picked it! Then the flower raised itself, following the curve which a hand would have described in carrying it towards a mouth, and it remained suspended in the transparent air, all alone and motionless, a terrible red spot, three yards from my eyes. In desperation I rushed at it to take it! I found nothing; it had disappeared. Then I was seized with furious rage against myself, for a reasonable and serious man should not have such hallucinations.

But was it an hallucination? I turned round to look for the stalk, and I found it at once, on the bush, freshly broken, between two other roses which remained on the branch. I returned home then, my mind greatly disturbed; for I am certain now, as certain as I am of the alternation of day and night, that there exists close to me an invisible being that lives on milk and water, that can touch objects, take them and change their places; that is, consequently, endowed with a material nature, although it is imperceptible to our senses, and that lives as I do, under my roof.

August 7. I slept tranquilly. He drank the water out of my decanter, but did not disturb my sleep.

I wonder if I am mad. As I was walking just now in the sun by the riverside, doubts as to my sanity arose in me; not vague doubts such as I have had hitherto, but definite, absolute doubts. I have seen mad people, and I have known some who have been quite intelligent, lucid, even clear-sighted at every concern of life, except on one point. They spoke clearly, readily, profoundly on everything, when suddenly their mind struck upon the shoals of their madness and broke to pieces there, and scattered and foundered in that furious and terrible sea, full of rolling waves, fogs and squalls, which is called *madness*.

I certainly should think that I was mad, absolutely mad, if I were not conscious, did not perfectly know my condition, did not fathom it by analysing it with the most complete lucidity. I should, in fact, be only a rational man who was labouring under an hallucination. Some unknown disturbance must have arisen in my brain, one of those disturbances which physiologists of the present day try to note and to verify; and that disturbance must have caused a deep gap in my mind and in the sequence and logic of my ideas. Similar phenomena occur in dreams which lead us among the most unlikely phantasmagoria, without causing us any surprise, because our verifying apparatus and our organ of control are asleep, while our imaginative faculty is awake and active. Is it not possible that one of the imperceptible notes of the cerebral keyboard has been paralysed in me? Some men lose the recollection of proper names, of verbs, or of numbers, or merely of dates, in consequence of an accident. The localization of all the variations of thought has been established nowadays; why, then, should it be surprising if my faculty of controlling the unreality of certain hallucinations were dormant in me for the time being?

I thought of all this as I walked by the side of the water. The sun shone brightly on the river and made earth delightful, while it filled me with a love for life, for the swallows, whose agility always delights my eye, for the plants by the riverside, the rustle of whose leaves is a pleasure to my ears.

By degrees, however, an inexplicable feeling of discomfort seized me. It seemed as if some unknown force were numbing and stopping me, were preventing me from going farther, and were calling me back. I felt that painful wish to return which oppresses you when you have left a beloved invalid at home, and when you are seized with a presentiment that he is worse.

I, therefore, returned in spite of myself, feeling certain that I should find some bad news awaiting me, a letter or a telegram. There was nothing, however, and I was more surprised and uneasy than if I had had another fantastic vision.

August 8. I spent a terrible evening yesterday. He does not show himself any more, but I feel that he is near me, watching me, looking at me, penetrating me, dominating me, and more redoubtable when he hides himself thus than if he were to manifest his constant and invisible presence by supernatural phenomena. However, I slept.

August 9. Nothing, but I am afraid.

August 10. Nothing; what will happen to-morrow?

August 11. Still nothing; I cannot stop at home with this fear hanging over me and these thoughts in my mind; I shall go away.

August 12. Ten o'clock at night. All day long I have been trying to get away, and have not been able. I wished to accomplish this simple and easy act of freedom – to go out – to get into my carriage in order to go to Rouen – and I have not been able to do it. What is the reason?

August 13. When we are attacked by certain maladies, all the springs of our physical being appear to be broken, all our energies destroyed, all our muscles relaxed; our bones, too, have become as soft as flesh, and our bodies as liquid as water. I am experiencing these sensations in my moral being in a strange and distressing manner. I have no longer any strength, any courage, any self-control, not even any power to set my own will in motion. I have no power left to will anything; but someone does it for me and I obey.

August 14. I am lost! Somebody possesses my soul and dominates it. Somebody orders all my acts, all my movements, all my thoughts. I am no longer anything in myself, nothing except an enslaved and terrified spectator of all the things I do. I wish to go out; I cannot. He does not wish to, and so I remain, trembling and distracted, in the armchair in which he keeps me sitting. I merely wish to get up and to rouse myself; I cannot! I am riveted to my chair, and my chair adheres to the ground in such a manner that no power could move us.

Then, suddenly, I must, I must go to the bottom of my garden to pick some strawberries and eat them, and I go there. I pick the strawberries and eat them! Oh, my God! My God! Is there a God? If there be one,

deliver me! Save me! Succour me! Pardon! Pity! Mercy! Save me!
Oh, what sufferings! What torture! What horror!

August 15. This is certainly the way in which my poor cousin was
possessed and controlled when she came to borrow five thousand francs
of me. She was under the power of a strange will which had entered into
her, like another soul, like another parasitic and dominating soul. Is the
world coming to an end?

But who is he, this invisible being that rules me? This unknowable
being, this rover of a supernatural race?

Invisible beings exist, then! How is it, then, that since the beginning
of the world they have never manifested themselves precisely as they do
to me? I have never read of anything that resembles what goes on in my
house. Oh, if I could only leave it, if I could only go away, escape, and
never return! I should be saved, but I cannot.

August 16. I managed to escape to-day for two hours, like a prisoner
who finds the door of his dungeon accidentally open. I suddenly felt that
I was free and that he was far away, and so I gave orders to harness the
horses as quickly as possible, and I drove to Rouen. Oh, how delightful
to be able to say to a man who obeys you: 'Go to Rouen!'

I made him pull up before the library, and I begged them to lend me
Dr Herrmann Herestauss' treatise on the unknown inhabitants of the
ancient and modern world.

Then, as I was getting into my carriage, I intended to say: 'To the
railway station!' but instead of this I shouted – I did not say, but I
shouted – in such a loud voice that all the passers-by turned round:
'Home!' and I fell back on the cushion of my carriage, overcome by
mental agony. He had found me again and regained possession of me.

August 17. Oh, what a night! What a night! And yet it seems to me
that I ought to rejoice. I read until one o'clock in the morning! Herestauss, doctor of philosophy and theogony, wrote the history of the manifestation of all those invisible beings which hover around man, or of
whom he dreams. He describes their origin, their domain, their power;
but none of them resembles the one which haunts me. One might say
that man, ever since he began to think, has had a foreboding fear of a
new being, stronger than himself, his successor in this world, and that,
feeling his presence, and not being able to foresee the nature of that
master, he has, in his terror, created the whole race of occult beings, of
vague phantoms born of fear.

Having, therefore, read until one o'clock in the morning, I went and
sat down at the open window, in order to cool my forehead and my
thoughts, in the calm night air. It was very pleasant and warm! How I
should have enjoyed such a night formerly!

There was no moon, but the stars darted out their rays in the dark heavens. Who inhabits those worlds? What forms, what living beings, what animals are there yonder? What do the thinkers in those distant worlds know more than we do? What can they do more than we can? What do they see which we do not know? Will not one of them, some day or other, traversing space, appear on our earth to conquer it, just as the Norsemen formerly crossed the sea in order to subjugate nations more feeble than themselves?

We are so weak, so defenceless, so ignorant, so small, we who live on this particle of mud which revolves in a drop of water.

I fell asleep, dreaming thus in the cool night air, and when I had slept for about three-quarters of an hour, I opened my eyes without moving, awakened by I know not what confused and strange sensation. At first I saw nothing, and then suddenly it appeared to me as if a page of a book which had remained open on my table turned over of its own accord. Not a breath of air had come in at my window, and I was surprised, and waited. In about four minutes, I saw, I saw, yes saw with my own eyes, another page lift itself up and fall down on the others, as if a finger had turned it over. My armchair was empty, appeared empty, but I knew that he was there, he, and sitting in my place, and that he was reading. With a furious bound, the bound of an enraged wild beast that springs at its tamer, I crossed my room to seize him, to strangle him, to kill him! But before I could reach it, the chair fell over as if somebody had run away from me – my table rocked, my lamp fell and went out, and my window closed as if some thief had been surprised and had fled out into the night, shutting it behind him.

So he had run away; he had been afraid; he, afraid of me!

But – but – to-morrow – or later – some day or other – I should be able to hold him in my clutches and crush him against the ground! Do not dogs occasionally bite and strangle their masters?

August 18. I have been thinking the whole day long. Oh, yes, I will obey him, follow his impulses, fulfil all his wishes, show myself humble, submissive, a coward. He is the stronger; but the hour will come—

August 19. I know – I know – I know all! I have just read the following in the *Revue du Monde Scientifique*: 'A curious piece of news comes to us from Rio de Janeiro. Madness, an epidemic of madness, which may be compared to that contagious madness which attacked the people of Europe in the Middle Ages, is at this moment raging in the Province of San-Paolo. The terrified inhabitants are leaving their houses, saying that they are pursued, possessed, dominated like human cattle by invisible, though tangible, beings, a species of vampires, which feed on their life while they are asleep, and which, besides, drink water and milk without appearing to touch any other nourishment.

'Professor Don Pedro Henriques, accompanied by several medical savants, has gone to the Province of San-Paolo, in order to study the origin and the manifestations of this surprising madness on the spot, and to propose such measures to the Emperor as may appear to him to be most fitted to restore the mad population to reason.'

Ah! Ah! I remember now that fine Brazilian three-master which passed in front of my windows as she was going up the Seine, on the 8th day of last May! I thought she looked so pretty, so white and bright! That Being was on board of her, coming from there, where its race originated. And it saw me! It saw my house which was also white, and it sprang from the ship on to the land. Oh, merciful heaven!

Now I know, I can divine. The reign of man is over, and he has come. He who was feared by primitive man; whom disquieted priests exorcised; whom sorcerers evoked on dark nights, without having seen him appear, to whom the imagination of the transient masters of the world lent all the monstrous or graceful forms of gnomes, spirits, genii, fairies, and familiar spirits. After the coarse conceptions of primitive fear, more clear-sighted men foresaw it more clearly. Mesmer divined it, and ten years ago physicians accurately discovered the nature of his power, even before he exercised it himself. They played with this new weapon of the Lord, the sway of a mysterious will over the human soul, which had become a slave. They called it magnetism, hypnotism, suggestion – what do I know? I have seen them amusing themselves like rash children with this horrible power! Woe to us! Woe to man! He has come, the – the – what does he call himself – the – I fancy that he is shouting out his name to me and I do not hear him – the – yes – he is shouting it out – I am listening – I cannot – he repeats it – the – Horla – I hear – the Horla – it is he – the Horla – he has come!

Ah! the vulture has eaten the pigeon; the wolf has eaten the lamb; the lion has devoured the sharp-horned buffalo; man has killed the lion with an arrow, with a sword, with gunpowder; but the Horla will make of man what we have mode of the horse and of the ox; his chattel, his slave, and his food, by the mere power of his will. Woe to us!

But, nevertheless, the animal sometimes revolts and kills the man who has subjugated it. I should also like – I shall be able to – but I must know him, touch him, see him! Scientists say that animals' eyes, being different from ours, do not distinguish objects as ours do. And my eye cannot distinguish this newcomer who is oppressing me.

Why? Oh, now I remember the words of the monk at Mont Saint-Michel: 'Can we see the hundred-thousandth part of what exists? See here; there is the wind, which is the strongest force in nature, which knocks men down, and wrecks buildings, uproots trees, raises the sea into mountains of water, destroys cliffs and casts great ships on the breakers; the wind which kills, which whistles, which sighs, which roars – have you ever seen it, and can you see it? It exists for all that, however!'

And I went on thinking: my eyes are so weak, so imperfect, that they do not even distinguish hard bodies, if they are as transparent as glass! If a glass without tinfoil behind it were to bar my way, I should run into it, just as a bird which has flown into a room breaks its head against the window-panes. A thousand things, moreover, deceive man and lead him astray. Why should it then be surprising that he cannot perceive an unknown body through which the light passes?

A new being! Why not? It was assuredly bound to come! Why should we be the last? We do not distinguish it any more than all the others created before us! The reason is, that its nature is more perfect, its body finer and more finished than ours, that ours is so weak, so awkwardly constructed, encumbered with organs that are always tired, always on the strain like machinery that is too complicated, which lives like a plant and like a beast, nourishing itself with difficulty on air, herbs, and flesh, an animal machine which is a prey to maladies, to malformations, to decay; broken-winded, badly regulated, simple and eccentric, ingeniously badly made, at once a coarse and a delicate piece of workmanship, the rough sketch of a being that might become intelligent and grand.

We are only a few, so few in this world, from the oyster up to man. Why should there not be one more, once that period is passed which separates the successive apparitions from all the different species?

Why not one more? Why not, also, other trees with immense, splendid flowers, perfuming whole regions? Why not other elements besides fire, air, earth, and water? There are four, only four, those nursing fathers of various beings! What a pity! Why are there not forty, four hundred, four thousand? How poor everything is, how mean and wretched! grudgingly produced, roughly constructed, clumsily made! Ah, the elephant and the hippopotamus, what grace! And the camel, what elegance!

But the butterfly, you will say, a flying flower! I dream of one that should be as large as a hundred worlds, with wings whose shape, beauty, colour, and motion I cannot even express. But I see it – it flutters from star to star, refreshing them and perfuming them with the light and harmonious breath of its flight! And the people up there look at it as it passes in an ecstasy of delight!

What is the matter with me? It is he, the Horla, who haunts me, and who makes me think of these foolish things! He is within me, he is becoming my soul; I shall kill him!

August 29. I shall kill him. I have seen him! Yesterday I sat down at my table and pretended to write very assiduously. I knew quite well that he would come prowling round me, quite close to me, so close that I might perhaps be able to touch him, to seize him. And then – then I should have the strength of desperation; I should have my hands, my knees, my chest, my forehead, my teeth to strangle him, to crush him, to bite him, to tear him to pieces. And I watched for him with all my over-excited senses.

I had lighted my two lamps and the eight wax candles on my mantelpiece, as if with this light I could discover him.

My bedstead, my old oak post bedstead, stood opposite to me; on my right was the fireplace; on my left, the door which was carefully closed, after I had left it open for some time in order to attract him; behind me was a very high wardrobe with a looking-glass in it, before which I stood to shave and dress every day, and in which I was in the habit of glancing at myself from head to foot every time I passed it.

I pretended to be writing in order to deceive him, for he also was watching me, and suddenly I felt – I was certain that he was reading over my shoulder, that he was there, touching my ear.

I got up, my hands extended, and turned round so quickly that I almost fell. Eh! well? It was as bright as at midday, but I did not see my reflection in the mirror! It was empty, clear, profound, full of light! But my figure was not reflected in it – and I, I was opposite to it! I saw the large, clear glass from top to bottom, and I looked at it with unsteady eyes; and I did not dare to advance; I did not venture to make a move-ment, feeling that he was there, but that he would escape me again, he whose imperceptible body had absorbed my reflection.

How frightened I was! And then, suddenly, I began to see myself in a mist in the depths of the looking-glass, in a mist as it were a sheet of water; and it seemed to me as if this water were flowing clearer every moment. It was like the end of an eclipse. Whatever it was that hid me did not appear to possess any clearly defined outlines, but a sort of opaque transparency which gradually grew clearer.

At last I was able to distinguish myself completely, as I do every day when I look at myself.

I had seen it! And the horror of it remained with me, and makes me shudder even now.

August 30. How could I kill it, as I could not get hold of it? Poison? But it would see me mix it with the water; and then, would our poisons have any effect on its impalpable body? No – no – no doubt about the matter – Then – then?—

August 31. I sent for a blacksmith from Rouen, and ordered iron shutters for my room, such as some private hotels in Paris have on the ground floor, for fear of burglars, and he is going to make me an iron door as well. I have made myself out a coward, but I do not care about that!

THE HORLA

September 10. Rouen, Hotel Continental. It is done – it is done – but is he dead? My mind is thoroughly upset by what I have seen.

Well, then, yesterday, the locksmith having put on the iron shutters and door, I left everything open until midnight, although it was getting cold.

Suddenly I felt that he was there, and joy, mad joy, took possession of me. I got up softly, and walked up and down for some time, so that he might not suspect anything; then I took off my boots and put on my slipper carelessly; then I fastened the iron shutters, and, going back to the door, quickly double-locked it with a padlock, putting the key into my pocket.

Suddenly I noticed that he was moving restlessly round me, that in his turn he was frightened and was ordering me to let him out. I nearly yielded; I did not, however, but, putting my back to the door, I half opened it, just enough to allow me to go out backward, and as I am very tall my head touched the casing. I was sure that he had not been able to escape, and I shut him up quite alone, quite alone. What happiness! I had him fast. Then I ran downstairs; in the drawing-room, which was under my bedroom, I took the two lamps and I poured all the oil on the carpet, the furniture, everywhere; then I set fire to it and made my escape, after having carefully double-locked the door.

I went and hid myself at the bottom of the garden, in a clump of laurel bushes. How long it seemed! How long it seemed! Everything was dark, silent, motionless, not a breath of air and not a star, but heavy banks of clouds which one could not see, but which weighed, oh, so heavily on my soul.

I looked at my house and waited. How long it was! I already began to think that the fire had gone out of its own accord, or that he had extinguished it, when one of the lower windows gave way under the violence of the flames, and a long, soft, caressing sheet of red flame mounted up the white wall, and enveloped it as far as the roof. The light fell on the trees, the branches, and the leaves, and a shiver of fear pervaded them also! The birds awoke, a dog began to howl, and it seemed to me as if the day were breaking! Almost immediately two other windows flew into fragments, and I saw that the whole of the lower part of my house was nothing but a terrible furnace. But a cry, a horrible, shrill, heart-rending cry, a woman's cry, sounded through the night, and two garret windows were opened! I had forgotten the servants! I saw their terror-stricken faces, and their arms waving fantically.

Then, overwhelmed with horror, I set off to run to the village, shouting: 'Help! help! fire! fire!' I met some people who were already coming to the scene, and I returned with them.

By this time the house was nothing but a horrible and magnificent funeral pile, a monstrous funeral pile which lit up the whole country, a funeral pile where men were burning, and where he was burning also, He, He, my prisoner, that new Being, the new master, the Horla!

Suddenly the whole roof fell in between the walls, and a volcano of flames darted up to the sky. Through all the windows which opened on that furnace, I saw the flames darting, and I thought that he was there, in that kiln, dead.

Dead? Perhaps.—His body? Was not his body, which was transparent, indestructible by such means as would kill ours?

If he were not dead?—Perhaps time alone has power over that Invisible and Redoubtable Being. Why this transparent, unrecognizable body, this body belonging to a spirit, if it also has to fear ills, infirmities and premature destruction?

Premature destruction? All human terror spring from that! After man, the Horla. After him who can die every day, at any hour, at any moment, by any accident, comes the one who will die only at his own proper hour, day, and minute, because he has touched the limits of his existence!

No – no – without any doubt – he is not dead – Then – then – I suppose I must kill *myself!* . . .

M. R. James

Count Magnus

By what means the papers out of which I have made a connected story came into my hands is the last point which the reader will learn from these pages. But it is necessary to prefix to my extracts from them a statement of the form in which I possess them.

They consist, then, partly of a series of collections for a book of travels, such a volume as was a common product of the forties and fifties. Horace Marryat's *Journal of a Residence in Jutland and the Danish Isles* is a fair specimen of the class to which I allude. These books usually treated of some unfamiliar district on the Continent. They were illustrated with woodcuts or steel plates. They gave details of hotel accommodation, and of means of communication, such as we now expect to find in any well-regulated guide-book, and they dealt largely in reported conversations with intelligent foreigners, racy innkeepers and garrulous peasants. In a word, they were chatty.

Begun with the idea of furnishing material for such a book, my papers as they progressed assumed the character of a record of one single personal experience, and this record was continued up to the very eve, almost, of its termination.

The writer was a Mr Wraxall. For my knowledge of him I have to depend entirely on the evidence his writings afford, and from these I deduce that he was a man past middle age, possessed of some private means, and very much alone in the world. He had, it seems, no settled abode in England, but was a denizen of hotels and boarding-houses. It is probable that he entertained the idea of settling down at some future time which never came; and I think it also likely that the Pantechnicon fire in the early seventies must have destroyed a great deal that would have thrown light on his antecedents, for he refers once or twice to property of his that was warehoused at that establishment.

It is further apparent that Mr Wraxall had published a book, and that it treated of a holiday he had once taken in Brittany. More than this I cannot say about his work, because a diligent search in bibliographical works has convinced me that it must have appeared either anonymously or under a pseudonym.

As to his character, it is not difficult to form some superficial opinion. He must have been an intelligent and cultivated man. It seems that he was near being a Fellow of his college at Oxford – Brasenose, as I judge from the Calendar. His besetting fault was pretty clearly that of over-inquisitiveness, possibly a good fault in a traveller, certainly a fault for which this traveller paid dearly enough in the end.

On what proved to be his last expedition, he was plotting another book. Scandinavia, a region not widely known to Englishmen forty years ago, had struck him as an interesting field. He must have lighted on some old books of Swedish history or memoirs, and the idea had struck him that there was room for a book descriptive of travel in Sweden, interspersed with episodes from the history of some of the great Swedish families. He procured letters of introduction, therefore, to some persons of quality in Sweden, and set out thither in the early summer of 1863.

Of his travels in the North there is no need to speak, nor of his residence of some weeks in Stockholm. I need only mention that some *savant* resident there put him on the track of an important collection of family papers belonging to the proprietors of an ancient manor-house in Vestergothland, and obtained for him permission to examine them.

The manor-house, or *herrgård*, in question is to be called Råbäck (pronounced something like Roebeck), though that is not its name. It is one of the best buildings of its kind in all the country, and the picture of it in Dahlenberg's *Suecia antiqua et moderna*, engraved in 1694, shows it very much as the tourist may see it to-day. It was built soon after 1600, and is, roughly speaking, very much like an English house of that period in respect of material – red-brick with stone facings – and style. The man who built it was a scion of the great house of De la Gardie, and his descendants possess it still. De la Gardie is the name by which I will designate them when mention of them becomes necessary.

They received Mr Wraxall with great kindness and courtesy, and pressed him to stay in the house as long as his researches lasted. But, preferring to be independent, and mistrusting his powers of conversing in Swedish, he settled himself at the village inn, which turned out quite sufficiently comfortable, at any rate during the summer months. This arrangement would entail a short walk daily to and from the manor-house of something under a mile. The house itself stood in a park, and was protected – we should say grown up – with large old timber. Near it you found the walled garden, and then entered a close wood fringing one of the small lakes with which the whole country is pitted. Then came the wall of the demesne, and you climbed a steep knoll – a knob of rock lightly covered with soil – and on the top of this stood the church, fenced in with tall dark trees. It was a curious building to English eyes. The nave and aisles were low, and filled with pews and galleries. In the western gallery stood the handsome old organ, gaily painted, and with silver pipes. The ceiling was flat, and had been adorned by a seventeenth-century artist with a strange and hideous 'Last Judgment,' full of lurid flames, falling cities, burning ships, crying souls, and brown and smiling demons. Handsome brass coronæ hung from the roof; the pulpit was like a doll's-house, covered with little painted wooden cherubs and saints; a stand with three hour-glasses was hinged to the preacher's desk. Such sights as these may be seen in many a church in Sweden now, but what distinguished this one was an addition to the original building. At the eastern end of the north aisle the builder of the manor-house had erected a mausoleum for himself and his family. It was a largish, eight-sided building, lighted by a series of oval windows, and it had a domed roof, topped by a kind of pumpkin-shaped object rising into a spire, a form in which Swedish architects greatly delighted. The roof was of copper externally, and was painted black, while the walls, in common with those of the church, were staringly white. To this mausoleum there was no access from the church. It had a portal and steps of its own on the northern side.

Past the churchyard the path to the village goes, and not more than three or four minutes bring you to the inn door.

On the first day of his stay at Råbäck Mr Wraxall found the church door open, and made those notes of the interior which I have epitomized. Into the mausoleum, however, he could not make his way. He could by looking through the keyhole just descry that there were fine marble effigies and sarcophagi of copper, and a wealth of armorial ornament, which made him very anxious to spend some time in investigation.

The papers he had come to examine at the manor-house proved to be of just the kind he wanted for his book. There were family correspondence, journals, and account-books of the earliest owners of the estate, very carefully kept and clearly written, full of amusing and picturesque detail. The first De la Gardie appeared in them as a strong and capable man. Shortly after the building of the mansion there had been a period of distress in the district, and the peasants had risen and attacked several châteaux and done some damage. The owner of Råbäck took a leading part in suppressing the trouble, and there was reference to executions of ringleaders and severe punishments inflicted with no sparing hand.

154

The portrait of this Magnus de la Gardie was one of the best in the house, and Mr Wraxall studied it with no little interest after his day's work. He gives no detailed description of it, but I gather that the face impressed him rather by its power than by its beauty or goodness; in fact, he writes that Count Magnus was an almost phenomenally ugly man.

On this day Mr Wraxall took his supper with the family, and walked back in the late but still bright evening.

'I must remember,' he writes, 'to ask the sexton if he can let me into the mausoleum at the church. He evidently has access to it himself, for I saw him to-night standing on the steps, and, as I thought, locking or unlocking the door.'

I find that early on the following day Mr Wraxall had some conversation with his landlord. His setting it down at such length as he does surprised me at first; but I soon realized that the papers I was reading were, at least in their beginning, the materials for the book he was meditating, and that it was to have been one of those quasi-journalistic productions which admit of the introduction of an admixture of conversational matter.

His object, he says, was to find out whether any traditions of Count Magnus de la Gardie lingered on in the scenes of that gentleman's activity, and whether the popular estimate of him were favourable or not. He found that the Count was decidedly not a favourite. If his tenants came late to their work on the days which they owed to him as Lord of the Manor, they were set on the wooden horse, or flogged and branded in the manor-house yard. One or two cases there were of men who had occupied lands which encroached on the lord's domain, and whose houses had been mysteriously burnt on a winter's night, with the whole family inside. But what seemed to dwell on the innkeeper's mind most – for he returned to the subject more than once – was that the Count had been on the Black Pilgrimage, and had brought something or someone back with him.

You will naturally inquire, as Mr Wraxall did, what the Black Pilgrimage may have been. But your curiosity on the point must remain unsatisfied for the time being, just as his did. The landlord was evidently unwilling to give a full answer, or indeed any answer, on the point, and, being called out for a moment, trotted off with obvious alacrity, only putting his head in at the door a few minutes afterwards to say that he was called away to Skara, and should not be back till evening.

So Mr Wraxall had to go unsatisfied to his day's work at the manor-house. The papers on which he was just then engaged soon put his thoughts into another channel, for he had to occupy himself with glancing over the correspondence between Sophia Albertina in Stockholm and her married cousin Ulrica Leonora at Råbäck in the years 1705–1710. The letters were of exceptional interest from the light they threw upon the culture of that period in Sweden, as anyone can testify who has read the full edition of them in the publications of the Swedish Historical Manuscripts Commission.

In the afternoon he had done with these, and after returning the boxes in which they were kept to their places on the shelf, he proceeded, very naturally, to take down some of the volumes nearest to them, in order to determine which of them had best be his principal subject of investigation next day. The shelf he had hit upon was occupied mostly by a collection of account-books in the writing of the first Count Magnus. But one among them was not an account-book, but a book of alchemical and other tracts in another sixteenth-century hand. Not being very familiar with alchemical literature, Mr Wraxall spends much space which he might have spared in setting out the names and beginnings of the various treatises: The book of the Phœnix, book of the Thirty Words, book of the Toad, book of Miriam, Turba philosophorum, and so forth; and then he announces with a good deal of circumstance his delight at finding, on a leaf originally left blank near the middle of the book, some writing of Count Magnus himself headed 'Liber nigræ peregrinationis.' It is true that only a few lines were written, but there was quite enough to show that the landlord had that morning been referring to a belief at least as old as the time of Count Magnus, and probably shared by him. This is the English of what was written:

'If any man desires to obtain a long life, if he would obtain a faithful messenger and see the blood of his enemies, it is necessary that he should first go into the city of Chorazin, and there salute the prince. . . .' Here there was an erasure of one word, not very thoroughly done, so that Mr Wraxall felt pretty sure that he was right in reading it as *aëris* ('of the air'). But there was no more of the text copied, only a line in Latin: 'Quære reliqua hujus materiei inter secretiora' (See the rest of this matter among the more private things).

It could not be denied that this threw a rather lurid light upon the tastes and beliefs of the Count; but to Mr Wraxall, separated from him by nearly three centuries, the thought that he might have added to his general forcefulness alchemy, and to alchemy something like magic, only made him a more picturesque figure; and when, after a rather prolonged contemplation of his picture in the hall, Mr Wraxall set out on his homeward way, his mind was full of the thought of Count Magnus. He had no eyes for his surroundings, no perception of the evening scents of the woods or the evening light on the lake; and when all of a sudden he pulled up short, he was astonished to find himself already at the gate of the churchyard, and within a few minutes of his dinner. His eyes fell on the mausoleum.

'As,' he said, 'Count Magnus, there you are. I should dearly like to see you.'

'Like many solitary men,' he writes, 'I have a habit of talking to myself aloud; and, unlike some of the Greek and Latin particles, I do not expect an answer. Certainly, and perhaps fortunately in this case, there was neither voice nor any that regarded: only the woman who, I suppose, was cleaning up the church, dropped some metallic object on the floor, whose clang startled me. Count Magnus I think, sleeps sound enough.'

That same evening the landlord of the inn, who had heard Mr Wraxall say that he wished to see the clerk or deacon (as he would be called in Sweden) of the parish, introduced him to that official in the inn parlour. A visit to the De la Gardie tomb-house was soon arranged for the next day, and a little general conversation ensued.

Mr Wraxall, remembering that one function of Scandinavian deacons is to teach candidates for Confirmation, thought he would refresh his own memory on a Biblical point.

'Can you tell me,' he said, 'anything about Chorazin?'

The deacon seemed startled, but readily reminded him how that village had once been denounced.

'To be sure,' said Mr Wraxall; 'it is, I suppose, quite a ruin now?'

'So I expect,' replied the deacon. 'I have heard some of our old priests say that Antichrist is to be born there; and there are tales—'

'Ah! what tales are those?' Mr Wraxall put in.

'Tales, I was going to say, which I have forgotten,' said the deacon; and soon after that he said good night.

The landlord was now alone, and at Mr Wraxall's mercy; and that inquirer was not inclined to spare him.

'Herr Nielson,' he said, 'I have found out something about the Black Pilgrimage. You may as well tell me what you know. What did the Count bring back with him?'

Swedes are habitually slow, perhaps, in answering, or perhaps the landlord was an exception. I am not sure; but Mr Wraxall notes that the landlord spent at least one minute in looking at him before he said anything at all. Then he came close up to his guest, and with a good deal of effort he spoke:

'Mr Wraxall, I can tell you this one little tale, and no more – not any more. You must not ask anything when I have done. In my grandfather's time – that is, ninety-two years ago – there were two men who said: "The Count is dead; we do not care for him. We will go to-night and have a free hunt in his wood" – the long wood on the hill that you have

seen behind Råbäck. Well, those that heard them say this, they said:
"No, do not go; we are sure you will meet with persons walking who
should not be walking. They should be resting, not walking." These men
laughed. There were no forest-men to keep the wood, because no one
wished to hunt there. The family were not here at the house. These men
could do what they wished.

'Very well, they go to the wood that night. My grandfather was sitting
here in this room. It was the summer, and a light night. With the window open, he could see out to the wood, and hear.

'So he sat there, and two or three men with him, and they listened. At
first they hear nothing at all; then they hear someone – you know how
far away it is – they hear someone scream, just as if the most inside part
of his soul was twisted out of him. All of them in the room caught hold
of each other, and they sat so for three-quarters of an hour. Then they
hear someone else, only about three hundred ells off. They hear him
laugh out loud: it was not one of those two men that laughed, and, indeed, they have all of them said that it was not any man at all. After
that they hear a great door shut.

'Then, when it was just light with the sun, they all went to the priest.
They said to him:

' "Father, put on your gown and your ruff, and come to bury these men,
Anders Bjornsen and Hans Thorbjorn."

'You understand that they were sure these men were dead. So they
went to the wood – my grandfather never forgot this. He said they were
all like so many dead men themselves. The priest, too, he was in a white
fear. He said when they came to him:

' "I heard one cry in the night, and I heard one laugh afterwards. If
I cannot forget that, I shall not be able to sleep again."

'So they went to the wood, and they found these men on the edge of
the wood. Hans Thorbjorn was standing with his back against a tree, and
all the time he was pushing with his hands – pushing something away
from him which was not there. So he was not dead. And they led him
away, and took him to the house at Nykjoping, and he died before the
winter; but he went on pushing with his hands. Also Anders Bjornsen
was there; but he was dead. And I tell you this about Anders Bjornsen,
that he was once a beautiful man, but now his face was not there, because the flesh of it was sucked away off the bones. You understand that?
My grandfather did not forget that. And they laid him on the bier which
they brought, and they put a cloth over his head, and the priest walked
before; and they began to sing the psalm for the dead as well as they
could. So, as they were singing the end of the first verse, one fell down,
who was carrying the head of the bier, and the others looked back, and
they saw that the cloth had fallen off, and the eyes of Anders Bjornsen

were looking up, because there was nothing to close over them. And this they could not bear. Therefore the priest laid the cloth upon him, and sent for a spade, and they buried him in that place.'

The next day Mr Wraxall records that the deacon called for him soon after his breakfast, and took him to the church and mausoleum. He noticed that the key of the latter was hung on a nail just by the pulpit, and it occurred to him that, as the church door seemed to be left un-locked as a rule, it would not be difficult for him to pay a second and more private visit to the monuments if there proved to be more of inter-est among them than could be digested at first. The building, when he entered it, he found not unimposing. The monuments, mostly large erec-tions of the seventeenth and eighteenth centuries, were dignified if luxuri-ant, and the epitaphs and heraldry were copious. The central space of the domed room was occupied by three copper sarcophagi, covered with finely-engraved ornament. Two of them had, as is commonly the case in Denmark and Sweden, a large metal crucifix on the lid. The third, that of Count Magnus, as it appeared, had, instead of that, a full-length effigy engraved upon it, and round the edge were several bands of similar ornament representing various scenes. One was a battle, with cannon belching out smoke, and walled towns, and troops of pikemen. Another showed an execution. In a third, among trees, was a man running at full speed, with flying hair and outstretched hands. After him followed a strange form; it would be hard to say whether the artist had intended it for a man, and was unable to give the requisite similitude, or whether it was intentionally made as monstrous as it looked. In view of the skill with which the rest of the drawing was done, Mr Wraxall felt inclined to adopt the latter idea. The figure was unduly short, and was for the most part muffled in a hooded garment which swept the ground. The only part of the form which projected from that shelter was not shaped like any hand or arm. Mr Wraxall compares it to the tentacle of a devil-fish, and continues: 'On seeing this, I said to myself, "This, then, which is evidently an allegorical representation of some kind – a fiend pursuing a hunted soul – may be the origin of the story of Count Magnus and his mysterious companion. Let us see how the huntsman is pictured: doubt-less it will be a demon blowing his horn." ' But, as it turned out, there was no such sensational figure, only the semblance of a cloaked man on a hillock, who stood leaning on a stick, and watching the hunt with an interest which the engraver had tried to express in his attitude.

Mr Wraxall noted the finely-worked and massive steel padlocks – three in number – which secured the sarcophagus. One of them, he saw, was detached, and lay on the pavement. And then, unwilling to delay the deacon longer or to waste his own working-time, he made his way on-ward to the manor-house.

'It is curious,' he notes, 'how on retracing a familiar path one's thoughts engross one to the absolute exclusion of surrounding objects. To-night, for the second time, I had entirely failed to notice where I was going (I had planned a private visit to the tomb-house to copy the epitaphs), when I suddenly, as it were, awoke to consciousness, and found myself (as before) turning in at the churchyard gate, and, I believe, singing or chanting some such words as, "Are you awake, Count Magnus? Are you asleep, Count Magnus?" and then something more which I have failed to recollect. It seemed to me that I must have been behaving in this non-sensical way for some time.'

He found the key of the mausoleum where he had expected to find it, and copied the greater part of what he wanted; in fact, he stayed until the light began to fail him.

'I must have been wrong,' he writes, 'in saying that one of the padlocks of my Count's sarcophagus was unfastened; I see to-night that two are loose. I picked both up, and laid them carefully on the window-ledge, after trying unsuccessfully to close them. The remaining one is still firm, and, though I take it to be a spring lock, I cannot guess how it is opened. Had I succeeded in undoing it, I am almost afraid I should have taken the liberty of opening the sarcophagus. It is strange, the interest I feel in the personality of this, I fear, somewhat ferocious and grim old noble.'

The day following was, as it turned out, the last of Mr Wraxall's stay at Råbäck. He received letters connected with certain investments which made it desirable that he should return to England; his work among the papers was practically done, and travelling was slow. He decided, there-fore, to make his farewells, put some finishing touches to his notes, and be off.

These finishing touches and farewells, as it turned out, took more time than he had expected. The hospitable family insisted on his staying to dine with them – they dined at three – and it was verging on half-past six before he was outside the iron gates of Råbäck. He dwelt on every step of his walk by the lake, determined to saturate himself, now that he trod it for the last time, in the sentiment of the place and hour. And when he reached the summit of the churchyard knoll, he lingered for many minutes, gazing at the limitless prospect of woods near and distant, all dark beneath a sky of liquid green. When at last he turned to go, the thought struck him that surely he must bid farewell to Count Magnus as well as the rest of the De la Gardies. The church was but twenty yards away, and he knew where the key of the mausoleum hung. It was not long before he was standing over the great copper coffin, and, as usual, talking to himself aloud. 'You may have been a bit of a rascal in your time, Magnus,' he was saying, 'but for all that I should like to see you, or, rather—'

'Just at that instant,' he says, 'I felt a blow on my foot. Hastily enough
I drew it back, and something fell on the pavement with a clash. It was
the third, the last of the three padlocks which had fastened the sarcophagus. I stooped to pick it up, and – Heaven is my witness that I am
writing only the bare truth – before I had raised myself there was a
sound of metal hinges creaking, and I distinctly saw the lid shifting
upwards. I may have behaved like a coward, but I could not for my life
stay for one moment. I was outside that dreadful building in less time
than I can write – almost as quickly as I could have said – the words; and
what frightens me yet more, I could not turn the key in the lock. As I sit
here in my room noting these facts, I ask myself (it was not twenty
minutes ago) whether that noise of creaking metal continued, and I cannot tell whether it did or not. I only know that there was something
more than I have written that alarmed me, but whether it was sound or
sight I am not able to remember. What is this that I have done?'

Poor Mr Wraxall! He set out on his journey to England on the next
day, as he had planned, and he reached England in safety; and yet, as I
gather from his changed hand and inconsequent jottings, a broken man.
One of several small notebooks that have come to me with his papers
gives, not a key to, but a kind of inkling of, his experiences. Much of his
journey was made by canal-boat, and I find not less than six painful
attempts to enumerate and describe his fellow-passengers. The entries
are of this kind:

'24. Pastor of village in Skåne. Usual black coat and soft black hat.
'25. Commercial traveller from Stockholm going to Trollhättan.
Black cloak, brown hat.
'26. Man in long black cloak, broad-leafed hat, very old-fashioned.'

This entry is lined out, and a note added: 'Perhaps identical with
No. 13. Have not yet seen his face.' On referring to No. 13, I find that
he is a Roman priest in a cassock.

The net result of the reckoning is always the same. Twenty-eight
people appear in the enumeration, one being always a man in a long
black cloak and broad hat, and the other a 'short figure in dark cloak
and hood.' On the other hand, it is always noted that only twenty-six
passengers appear at meals, and that the man in the cloak is perhaps
absent, and the short figure is certainly absent.

On reaching England, it appears that Mr Wraxall landed at Harwich,
and that he resolved at once to put himself out of the reach of some
person or persons whom he never specifies, but whom he had evidently

come to regard as his pursuers. Accordingly he took a vehicle – it was a closed fly – not trusting the railway, and drove across country to the village of Belchamp St Paul. It was about nine o'clock on a moonlight August night when he neared the place. He was sitting forward, and looking out of the window at the fields and thickets – there was little else to be seen – racing past him. Suddenly he came to a cross-road. At the corner two figures were standing motionless; both were in dark cloaks; the taller one wore a hat, the shorter a hood. He had no time to see their faces, nor did they make any motion that he could discern. Yet the horse shied violently and broke into a gallop, and Mr Wraxall sank back into his seat in something like desperation. He had seen them before.

Arrived at Belchamp St Paul, he was fortunate enough to find a decent furnished lodging, and for the next twenty-four hours he lived, comparatively speaking, in peace. His last notes were written on this day. They are too disjointed and ejaculatory to be given here in full, but the substance of them is clear enough. He is expecting a visit from his pursuers – how or when he knows not – and his constant cry is 'What has he done?' and 'Is there no hope?' Doctors, he knows, would call him mad, policemen would laugh at him. The parson is away. What can he do but lock his door and cry to God?

People still remembered last year at Belchamp St Paul how a strange gentleman came one evening in August years back; and how the next morning but one he was found dead, and there was an inquest; and the jury that viewed the body fainted, seven of 'em did, and none of 'em wouldn't speak to what they see, and the verdict was visitation of God; and how the people as kep' the 'ouse moved out that same week, and went away from that part. But they do not, I think, know that any glimmer of light has ever been thrown, or could be thrown, on the mystery. It so happened that last year the little house came into my hands as part of a legacy. It had stood empty since 1863, and there seemed no prospect of letting it; so I had it pulled down, and the papers of which I have given you an abstract were found in a forgotten cupboard under the window in the best bedroom.

M. R. James

An Episode of Cathedral History

There was once a learned gentleman who was deputed to examine and report upon the archives of the Cathedral of Southminster. The examination of these records demanded a very considerable expenditure of time: hence it became advisable for him to engage lodgings in the city: for though the Cathedral body were profuse in their offers of hospitality, Mr Lake felt that he would prefer to be master of his day. This was recognized as reasonable. The Dean eventually wrote advising Mr Lake, if he were not already suited, to communicate with Mr Worby, the principal Verger, who occupied a house convenient to the church and was prepared to take in a quiet lodger for three or four weeks. Such an arrangement was precisely what Mr Lake desired. Terms were easily agreed upon, and early in December, like another Mr Datchery (as he remarked to himself), the investigator found himself in the occupation of a very comfortable room in an ancient and 'cathedraly' house.

One so familiar with the customs of Cathedral churches, and treated with such obvious consideration by the Dean and Chapter of this Cathedral in particular, could not fail to command the respect of the Head Verger. Mr Worby even acquiesced in certain modifications of statements he had been accustomed to offer for years to parties of visitors. Mr Lake, on his part, found the Verger a very cheery companion, and took advantage of any occasion that presented itself for enjoying his conversation when the day's work was over.

One evening, about nine o'clock, Mr Worby knocked at his lodger's door. 'I've occasion,' he said, 'to go across to the Cathedral, Mr Lake, and I think I made you a promise when I did so next I would give you the opportunity to see what it looks like at night time. It's quite fine and dry outside, if you care to come.'

'To be sure I will; very much obliged to you, Mr Worby, for thinking of it, but let me get my coat.'

'Here it is, sir, and I've another lantern here that you'll find advisable for the steps, as there's no moon.'

'Anyone might think we were Jasper and Durdles, over again, mightn't they?' said Lake, as they crossed the close, for he had ascertained that the Verger had read *Edwin Drood*.

'Well, so they might,' said Mr Worby, with a short laugh, 'though I don't know whether we ought to take it as a compliment. Odd ways, I often think, they had at that Cathedral, don't it seem so to you, sir? Full choral matins at seven o'clock in the morning all the year round. Wouldn't suit our boys' voices nowadays, and I think there's one or two of the men would be applying for a rise if the Chapter was to bring it in – particularly the altos.'

They were now at the south-west door. As Mr Worby was unlocking it, Lake said, 'Did you ever find anybody locked in here by accident?'

'Twice I did. One was a drunk sailor; however he got in I don't know. I s'pose he went to sleep in the service, but by the time I got to him he was praying fit to bring the roof in. Lor'! what a noise that man did make! said it was the first time he'd been inside a church for ten years, and blest if ever he'd try it again. The other was an old sheep: them boys it was, up to their games. That was the last time they tried it on, though. There, sir, now you see what we look like; our late Dean used now and again to bring parties in, but he preferred a moonlight night, and there was a piece of verse he'd coat to 'em, relating to a Scotch cathedral, I understand; but I don't know; I almost think the effect's better when it's all dark-like. Seems to add to the size and heighth. Now if you won't mind stopping somewhere in the nave while I go up into the choir where my business lays, you'll see what I mean.'

Accordingly Lake waited, leaning against a pillar, and watched the light wavering along the length of the church, and up the steps into the choir, until it was intercepted by some screen or other furniture, which only allowed the reflection to be seen on the piers and roof. Not many minutes had passed before Worby reappeared at the door of the choir and by waving his lantern signalled to Lake to rejoin him.

'I suppose it *is* Worby, and not a substitute,' thought Lake to himself, as he walked up the nave. There was, in fact, nothing untoward. Worby showed him the papers which he had come to fetch out of the Dean's stall, and asked him what he thought of the spectacle: Lake agreed that it was well worth seeing. 'I suppose,' he said, as they walked towards the altar-steps together, 'that you're too much used to going about here at night to feel nervous – but you must get a start every now and then, don't you, when a book falls down or a door swings to?'

'No, Mr Lake, I can't say I think much about noises, not nowadays: I'm much more afraid of finding an escape of gas or a burst in the stove pipes than anything else. Still there have been times, years ago. Did you notice that plain altar-tomb there – fifteenth century we say it is, I don't know if you agree to that? Well, if you didn't look at it, just come back and give it a glance, if you'd be so good.' It was on the north side of the choir, and rather awkwardly placed: only about three feet from the enclosing stone screen. Quite plain, as the Verger had said, but for some ordinary stone panelling. A metal cross of some size on the northern side (that next to the screen) was the solitary feature of any interest.

Lake agreed that it was not earlier than the Perpendicular period: 'but,' he said, 'unless it's the tomb of some remarkable person, you'll forgive me for saying that I don't think it's particularly noteworthy.'

'Well, I can't say as it is the tomb of anybody noted in 'istory,' said Worby, who had a dry smile on his face, 'for we don't own any record whatsoever of who it was put up to. For all that, if you've half an hour to spare, sir, when we get back to the house, Mr Lake, I could tell you a tale about that tomb. I won't begin on it now; it strikes cold here, and we don't want to be dawdling about all night.'

'Of course I should like to hear it immensely.'

'Very well, sir, you shall. Now if I might put a question to you,' he went on, as they passed down the choir aisle, 'in our little local guide – and not only there, but in the little book on our Cathedral in the series – you'll find it stated that this portion of the building was erected previous to the twelfth century. Now of course I should be glad enough to take that view, but – mind the step, sir – but, I put it to you – does the lay of the stone 'ere in this portion of the wall (which he tapped with his key), does it to your eye carry the flavour of what you might call Saxon masonry? No, I thought not; no more it does to me: now, if you'll believe me, I've said as much to those men – one's the librarian of our Free Libry here, and the other came down from London on purpose – fifty times, if I have once, but I might just as well have talked to that bit of stonework. But there it is, I suppose every one's got their opinions.'

The discussion of this peculiar trait of human nature occupied Mr Worby almost up to the moment when he and Lake re-entered the former's house. The condition of the fire in Lake's sitting-room led to a suggestion from Mr Worby that they should finish the evening in his own parlour. We find them accordingly settled there some short time afterwards.

Mr Worby made his story a long one, and I will not undertake to tell it wholly in his own words, or in his own order. Lake committed the substance of it to paper immediately after hearing it, together with some few passages of the narrative which had fixed themselves *verbatim* in his mind; I shall probably find it expedient to condense Lake's record to some extent.

Mr Worby was born, it appeared, about the year 1828. His father before him had been connected with the Cathedral, and likewise his grandfather. One or both had been choristers, and in later life both had done work as mason and carpenter respectively about the fabric. Worby himself, though possessed, as he frankly acknowledged, of an indifferent voice, had been drafted into the choir at about ten years of age.

It was in 1840 that the wave of the Gothic revival smote the Cathedral of Southminster. 'There was a lot of lovely stuff went then, sir,' said Worby, with a sigh. 'My father couldn't hardly believe it when he got his orders to clear out the choir. There was a new dean just come in – Dean Burscough it was – and my father had been 'prenticed to a good firm of joiners in the city, and knew what good work was when he saw it. Crool it was, he used to say: all that beautiful wainscot oak, as good as the day it was put up, and garlands-like of foliage and fruit, and lovely old gilding work on the coats of arms and the organ pipes. All went to the timber yard – every bit except some little pieces worked up in the Lady Chapel, and 'ere in this overmantel. Well – I may be mistook, but I say our choir never looked as well since. Still there was a lot found out about the history of the church, and no doubt but what it did stand in need of repair. There was very few winters passed but what we'd lose a pinnicle.' Mr Lake expressed his concurrence with Worby's views of restoration, but owns to a fear about this point lest the story proper should never be reached. Possibly this was perceptible in his manner.

Worby hastened to reassure him, 'Not but what I could carry on about that topic for hours at a time, and do do when I see my opportunity. But Dean Burscough he was very set on the Gothic period, and nothing would serve him but everything must be made agreeable to that. And one morning after service he appointed for my father to meet him in the choir, and he came back after he'd taken off his robes in the vestry, and he'd got a roll of paper with him, and the verger that was then brought in a table, and they begun spreading it out on the table with prayer books to keep it down, and my father helped 'em, and he saw it was a picture of the inside of a choir in a Cathedral; and the Dean – he was a quick-spoken gentleman – he says, "Well, Worby, what do you think of that?" "Why," says my father, "I don't think I 'ave the pleasure of knowing that view. Would that be Hereford Cathedral, Mr Dean?" "No, Worby," says the Dean, "that's Southminster Cathedral as we hope to see it before many years." "In-deed, sir," says my father, and that was all he did say – leastways to the Dean – but he used to tell me he felt reelly faint in himself when he looked round our choir as I can remember it, all comfortable and furnished-like, and then see this nasty little dry picter, as he called it, drawn out by some London architect. Well, there I am again. But you'll see what I mean if you look at this old view.'

Worby reached down a framed print from the wall. 'Well, the long and the short of it was that the Dean he handed over to my father a copy of an order of the Chapter that he was to clear out every bit of the choir – make a clean sweep – ready for the new work that was being designed up in town, and he was to put it in hand as soon as ever he could get the breakers together. Now then, sir, if you look at that view, you'll see where the pulpit used to stand: that's what I want you to notice, if you please.' It was, indeed, easily seen; an unusually large structure of timber with a domed sounding-board, standing at the east end of the stalls on the north side of the choir, facing the bishop's throne. Worby proceeded to explain that during the alterations, services were held in the nave, the members of the choir being thereby disappointed of an anticipated holiday, and the organist in particular incurring the suspicion of having wilfully damaged the mechanism of the temporary organ that was hired at considerable expense from London.

The work of demolition began with the choir screen and organ loft, and proceeded gradually eastwards, disclosing, as Worby said, many interesting features of older work. While this was going on, the members of the Chapter were, naturally, in and about the choir a great deal, and it soon became apparent to the elder Worby – who could not help over-hearing some of their talk – that, on the part of the senior Canons especially, there must have been a good deal of disagreement before the policy now being carried out had been adopted. Some were of opinion that they should catch their deaths of cold in the return-stalls, un-protected by a screen from the draughts in the nave: others objected to being exposed to the view of persons in the choir aisles, especially, they said, during the sermons, when they found it helpful to listen in a posture which was liable to misconstruction. The strongest opposition, however, came from the oldest of the body, who up to the last moment objected to the removal of the pulpit. 'You ought not to touch it, Mr Dean,' he said with great emphasis one morning, when the two were standing before it: 'you don't know what mischief you may do.' 'Mis-chief? it's not a work of any particular merit, Canon.' 'Don't call me Canon,' said the old man with great asperity, 'that is, for thirty years I've been known as Dr Ayloff, and I shall be obliged, Mr Dean, if you would kindly humour me in that matter. And as to the pulpit (which I've preached from for thirty years, though I don't insist on that), all I'll say is, I *know* you're doing wrong in moving it.' 'But what sense could there be, my dear Doctor, in leaving it where it is, when we're fitting up the rest of the choir in a totally different *style*? What reason could be given –

apart from the look of the thing?' 'Reason! reason!' said old Dr Ayloff; 'if you young men – if I may say so without any disrespect, Mr Dean – if you'd only listen to reason a little, and not be always asking for it, we should get on better. But there, I've said my say.' The old gentleman hobbled off, and as it proved, never entered the Cathedral again. The season – it was a hot summer – turned sickly on a sudden. Dr Ayloff was one of the first to go, with some affection of the muscles of the thorax, which took him painfully at night. And at many services the number of choirmen and boys was very thin.

Meanwhile the pulpit had been done away with. In fact, the sounding-board (part of which still exists as a table in a summer-house in the palace garden) was taken down within an hour or two of Dr Ayloff's protest. The removal of the base – not effected without considerable trouble – disclosed to view, greatly to the exultation of the restoring party, an altar-tomb – the tomb, of course, to which Worby had attracted Lake's attention that same evening. Much fruitless research was expended in attempts to identify the occupant; from that day to this he has never had a name put to him. The structure had been most carefully boxed in under the pulpit-base, so that such slight ornament as it possessed was not defaced; only on the north side of it there was what looked like an injury; a gap between two of the slabs composing the side. It might be two or three inches across. Palmer, the mason, was directed to fill it up in a week's time, when he came to do some other small jobs near that part of the choir.

The season was undoubtedly a very trying one. Whether the church was built on a site that had once been a marsh, as was suggested, or for whatever reason, the residents in its immediate neighbourhood had, many of them, but little enjoyment of the exquisite sunny days and the calm nights of August and September. To several of the older people – Dr Ayloff, among others, as we have seen – the summer proved downright fatal, but even among the younger, few escaped either a sojourn in bed for a matter of weeks, or at the least, a brooding sense of oppression, accompanied by hateful nightmares. Gradually there formulated itself a suspicion – which grew into a conviction – that the alterations in the Cathedral had something to say in the matter. The widow of a former old verger, a pensioner of the Chapter of Southminster, was visited by dreams, which she retailed to her friends, of a shape that slipped out of the little door of the south transept as the dark fell in, and flitted – taking a fresh direction every night – about the Close, disappearing for a while in house after house, and finally emerging again when the night sky was paling. She could see nothing of it, she said, but that it was a moving form: only she had an impression that when it returned to the church, as it seemed to do in the end of the dream, it turned its head:

and then, she could not tell why, but she thought it had red eyes. Worby remembered hearing the old lady tell this dream at a tea-party in the house of the chapter clerk. Its recurrence might, perhaps, he said, be taken as a symptom of approaching illness; at any rate before the end of September the old lady was in her grave.

The interest excited by the restoration of this great church was not confined to its own county. One day that summer an F.S.A., of some celebrity, visited the place. His business was to write an account of the discoveries that had been made, for the Society of Antiquaries, and his wife, who accompanied him, was to make a series of illustrative drawings for his report. In the morning she employed herself in making a general sketch of the choir; in the afternoon she devoted herself to details. She first drew the newly-exposed altar-tomb, and when that was finished, she called her husband's attention to a beautiful piece of diaper-ornament on the screen just behind it, which had, like the tomb itself, been completely concealed by the pulpit. Of course, he said, an illustration of that must be made; so she seated herself on the tomb and began a careful drawing which occupied her till dusk.

Her husband had by this time finished his work of measuring and description, and they agreed that it was time to be getting back to their hotel. 'You may as well brush my skirt, Frank,' said the lady, 'it must have got covered with dust, I'm sure.' He obeyed dutifully; but, after a moment, he said, 'I don't know whether you value this dress particularly, my dear, but I'm inclined to think it's seen its best days. There's a great bit of it gone.' 'Gone? Where?' said she. 'I don't know where it's gone, but it's off at the bottom edge behind here.' She pulled it hastily into sight, and was horrified to find a jagged tear extending some way into the substance of the stuff; very much, she said, as if a dog had rent it away. The dress was, in any case, hopelessly spoilt, to her great vexation, and though they looked everywhere, the missing piece could not be found. There were many ways, they concluded, in which the injury might have come about, for the choir was full of old bits of woodwork with nails sticking out of them. Finally, they could only suppose that one of these had caused the mischief, and that the workmen, who had been about all day, had carried off the particular piece with the fragment of dress still attached to it.

It was about this time, Worby thought, that his little dog began to wear an anxious expression when the hour for it to be put into the shed in the back yard approached. (For his mother had ordained that it must not sleep in the house.) One evening, he said, when he was just going to pick it up and carry it out, it looked at him 'like a Christian, and waved its 'and, I was going to say – well, you know 'ow they do carry on sometimes, and the end of it was I put it under my coat, and 'uddled it upstairs – and I'm afraid I as good as deceived my poor mother on the subject. After that the dog acted very artful with 'iding itself under the bed for half an hour or more before bed-time came, and we worked it so as my mother never found out what we'd done.' Of course Worby was glad of its company anyhow, but more particularly when the nuisance that is still remembered in Southminster as 'the crying' set in.

'Night after night,' said Worby, 'that dog seemed to know it was coming; he'd creep out, he would, and snuggle into the bed and cuddle right up to me shivering, and when the crying come he'd be like a wild thing, shoving his head under my arm, and I was fully near as bad. Six or seven times we'd hear it, not more, and when he'd dror out his 'ed again I'd know it was over for that night. What was it like, sir? Well, I never heard but one thing that seemed to hit it off. I happened to be playing about in the Close, and there was two of the Canons met and said "Good morning" one to another. "Sleep well last night?" says one – it was Mr Henslow that one, and Mr Lyall was the other. "Can't say I did," says Mr Lyall, "rather too much of Isaiah xxxiv. 14 for me." "xxxiv. 14," says Mr Henslow, "what's that?" "You call yourself a Bible reader!" says Mr Lyall. (Mr Henslow, you must know, he was one of what used to be termed Simeon's lot – pretty much what we should call the Evangelical party.) "You go and look it up." I wanted to know what he was getting at myself, and so off I ran home and got out my own Bible, and there it was: "the satyr shall cry to his fellow." Well, I thought, is that what we've been listening to these past nights? and I tell you it made me look over my shoulder a time or two. Of course I'd asked my father and mother about what it could be before that, but they both said it was most likely cats: but they spoke very short, and I could see they was troubled. My word! that was a noise – 'ungry-like, as if it was calling after someone that wouldn't come. If ever you felt you wanted company, it would be when you was waiting for it to begin again. I believe two or three nights there was men put on to watch in different parts of the Close; but they all used to get together in one corner, the nearest they could to the High Street, and nothing came of it.

'Well, the next thing was this. Me and another of the boys – he's in business in the city now as a grocer, like his father before him – we'd gone up in the choir after morning service was over, and we heard old Palmer the mason bellowing to some of his men. So we went up nearer, because we knew he was a rusty old chap and there might be some fun going. It appears Palmer 'd told this man to stop up the chink in that old tomb. Well, there was this man keeping on saying he'd done it the best he could, and there was Palmer carrying on like all possessed about it. "Call that making a job of it?" he says. "If you had your rights you'd get the sack for this. What do you suppose I pay you your wages for?

What do you suppose I'm going to say to the Dean and Chapter when they come round, as come they may do any time, and see where you've been bungling about covering the 'ole place with mess and plaster and Lord knows what?" "Well, master, I done the best I could," says the man; "I don't know no more than what you do 'ow it come to fall out this way. I tamped it right in the 'ole," he says, "and now it's fell out," he says, "I never see."

'"Fell out?" says old Palmer, "why it's nowhere near the place. Blowed out, you mean"; and he picked up a bit of plaster, and so did I, that was laying up against the screen, three or four feet off, and not dry yet; and old Palmer he looked at it curious-like, and then he turned round on me and he says, "Now then, you boys, have you been up to some of your games here?" "No," I says, "I haven't, Mr Palmer; there's none of us been about here till just this minute"; and while I was talking the other boy, Evans, he got looking in through the chink, and I heard him draw in his breath, and he came away sharp and up to us, and says he, "I believe there's something in there. I saw something shiny." "What! I dare say!" says old Palmer; "well, I ain't got time to stop about there. You, William, you go off and get some more stuff and make a job of it this time; if not, there'll be trouble in my yard," he says.

'So the man he went off, and Palmer too, and us boys stopped behind, and I says to Evans, "Did you really see anything in there?" "Yes," he says, "I did indeed." So then I says, "Let's shove something in and stir it up." And we tried several of the bits of wood that was laying about, but they were all too big. Then Evans he had a sheet of music he'd brought with him, an anthem or a service, I forget which it was now, and he rolled it up small and shoved it in the chink; two or three times he did it, and nothing happened. 'Give it me, boy,' I said, and I had a try. No, nothing happened. Then, I don't know why I thought of it, I'm sure, but I stooped down just opposite the chink and put my two fingers in my mouth and whistled – you know the way – and at that I seemed to think I heard something stirring, and I says to Evans, "Come away," I says; "I don't like this." "Oh, rot," he says, "give me that roll," and he took it and shoved it in. And I don't think ever I see anyone go so pale as he did. "I say, Worby," he says, "it's caught, or else someone's got hold of it." "Pull it out or leave it," I says. "Come and let's get off." So he gave a good pull, and it came away. Leastways most of it did, but the end was gone. Torn off it was, and Evans looked at it for a second and then he gave a sort of a croak and let it drop, and we both made off out of there as quick as ever we could. When we got outside Evans says to me, "Did you see the end of that paper?" "No," I says, "only it was torn." "Yes, it was," he says, "but it was wet too, and black!" Well, partly because of the fright we had, and partly because that music was wanted in a day or two, and we knew there'd be a set-out about it with the organist, we didn't say nothing to anyone else, and I suppose the workmen they swept up the bit that was left along with the rest of the rubbish. But Evans, if you were to ask him this very day about it, he'd stick to it he saw that paper wet and black at the end where it was torn.'

After that the boys gave the choir a wide berth, so that Worby was not sure what was the result of the mason's renewed mending of the tomb. Only he made out from fragments of conversation dropped by the work-men passing through the choir that some difficulty had been met with, and that the governor – Mr Palmer to wit – had tried his own hand at the job. A little later, he happened to see Mr Palmer himself knocking at the door of the Deanery and being admitted by the butler. A day or so after that, he gathered from a remark his father let fall at breakfast that something a little out of the common was to be done in the Cathedral after morning service on the morrow. 'And I'd just as soon it was to-day,' his father added; 'I don't see the use of running risks.' ' "Father," I says, "what are you going to do in the Cathedral to-morrow?" And he turned on me as savage as I ever see him – he was a wonderful good-tempered man as a general thing, my poor father was. "My lad," he says, "I'll trouble you not to go picking up your elders' and betters' talk: it's not manners and it's not straight. What I'm going to do or not going to do in the Cathedral to-morrow is none of your business: and if I catch sight of you hanging about the place to-morrow after your work's done, I'll send you home with a flea in your ear. Now you mind that." Of course I said I was very sorry and that, and equally of course I went off and laid my plans with Evans. We knew there was a stair up in the corner of the transept which you can get up to the triforium, and in them days the door to it was pretty well always open, and even if it wasn't we knew the key usually laid under a bit of matting hard by. So we made up our minds we'd be putting away music and that, next morning while the rest of the boys was clearing off, and then slip up the stairs and watch from the triforium if there was any signs of work going on.

'Well, that same night I dropped off asleep as sound as a boy does, and all of a sudden the dog woke me up, coming into the bed, and thought I, now we're going to get it sharp, for he seemed more frightened than usual. After about five minutes sure enough came this cry. I can't give you no idea what it was like; and so near too – nearer than I'd heard it yet – and a funny thing, Mr Lake, you know what a place this Close is for an echo, and particular if you stand this side of it. Well, this crying never made no sign of an echo at all. But, as I said, it was dreadful near this night; and on the top of the start I got with hearing it, I got an-other fright; for I heard something rustling outside in the passage. Now to be sure I thought I was done; but I noticed the dog seemed to perk up a bit, and next there was someone whispered outside the door, and I very near laughed out loud, for I knew it was my father and mother that had got out of bed with the noise. "Whatever is it?" says my mother. "Hush! I don't know," says my father, excited-like, "don't disturb the boy. I hope he didn't hear nothing."

'So, me knowing they were just outside, it made me bolder, and I slipped out of bed across to my little window – giving on the Close – but the dog he bored right down to the bottom of the bed – and I looked out. First go off I couldn't see anything. Then right down in the shadow under a buttress I made out what I shall always say was two spots of red – a dull red it was – nothing like a lamp or a fire, but just so as you could pick 'em out of the black shadow. I hadn't but just sighted 'em when it seemed we wasn't the only people that had been disturbed, because I see a window in a house on the left-hand side become lighted up, and the light moving. I just turned my head to make sure of it, and then looked back into the shadow for those two red things, and they were gone, and for all I peered about and stared, there was not a sign more of them. Then come my last fright that night – something come against my bare leg – but that was all right : that was my little dog had come out of bed, and prancing about making a great to-do, only holding his tongue, and me seeing he was quite in spirits again, I took him back to bed and we slept the night out!

'Next morning I made out to tell my mother I'd had the dog in my room, and I was surprised, after all she'd said about it before, how quiet she took it. "Did you?" she says. "Well, by good rights you ought to go without your breakfast for doing such a thing behind my back : but I don't know as there's any great harm done, only another time you ask my permission, do you hear?" A bit after that I said something to my father about having heard the cats again. "*Cats?*" he says; and he looked over at my poor mother, and she coughed and he says, "Oh! ah! yes, cats. I believe I heard 'em myself."

'That was a funny morning altogether: nothing seemed to go right. The organist he stopped in bed, and the minor Canon he forgot it was the 19th day and waited for the *Venite*; and after a bit the deputy he set off playing the chant for evensong, which was a minor; and then the Decani boys were laughing so much they couldn't sing, and when it came to the anthem the solo boy he got took with the giggles, and made out his nose was bleeding, and shoved the book at me what hadn't practised the verse and wasn't much of a singer if I had known it. Well, things was rougher, you see, fifty years ago, and I got a nip from the counter-tenor behind me that I remembered.

'So we got through somehow, and neither the men nor the boys weren't by way of waiting to see whether the Canon in residence – Mr Henslow it was – would come to the vestries and fine 'em, but I don't believe he did: for one thing I fancy he'd read the wrong lesson for the first time in his life, and knew it. Anyhow, Evans and me didn't find no difficulty in slipping up the stairs as I told you, and when we got up we laid ourselves down flat on our stomachs where we could just stretch our heads out over the old tomb, and we hadn't but just done so when we heard the verger that was then, first shutting the iron porch-gates and locking the south-west door, and then the transept door, so we knew there was something up, and they meant to keep the public out for a bit.

'Next thing was, the Dean and the Canon come in by their door on the north, and then I see my father, and old Palmer, and a couple of their best men, and Palmer stood a talking for a bit with the Dean in the middle of the choir. He had a coil of rope and the men had crows. All of 'em looked a bit nervous. So there they stood talking, and at last I heard the Dean say, "Well, I've no time to waste, Palmer. If you think this'll satisfy Southminster people, I'll permit it to be done; but I must say this, that never in the whole course of my life have I heard such arrant nonsense from a practical man as I have from you. Don't you agree with me, Henslow?" As far as I could hear Mr Henslow said something like "Oh well! we're told, aren't we, Mr Dean, not to judge others?" And the Dean he gave a kind of sniff, and walked straight up to the tomb, and took his stand behind it with his back to the screen, and the others they come edging up rather gingerly. Henslow, he stopped on the south side and scratched on his chin, he did. Then the Dean spoke up: "Palmer," he says, "which can you do easiest, get the slab off the top, or shift one of the side slabs?"

'Old Palmer and his men they pottered about a bit looking round the edge of the top slab and sounding the sides on the south and east and west and everywhere but the north. Henslow said something about it being better to have a try at the south side, because there was more light and more room to move about in. Then my father, who'd been watching of them, went round to the north side, and knelt down and felt of the slab by the chink, and he got up and dusted his knees and says to the Dean: "Beg pardon, Mr Dean, but I think if Mr Palmer'll try this here slab he'll find it'll come out easy enough. Seems to me one of the men could prise it out with his crow by means of this chink." "Ah! thank you, Worby," says the Dean; "that's a good suggestion. Palmer, let one of your men do that, will you?"

'So the man come round, and put his bar in and bore on it, and just that minute when they were all bending over, and we boys got our heads well over the edge of the triforium, there come a most fearful crash down at the west end of the choir, as if a whole stack of big timber had fallen down a flight of stairs. Well, you can't expect me to tell you everything that happened all in a minute. Of course there was a terrible commotion. I heard the slab fall out, and the crowbar on the floor, and I heard the Dean say, "Good God!"

'When I looked down again I saw the Dean tumbled over on the floor, the men was making off down the choir, Henslow was just going to help the Dean up, Palmer was going to stop the men (as he said afterwards) and my father was sitting on the altar step with his face in his hands. The Dean he was very cross. "I wish to goodness you'd look where you're coming to, Henslow," he says. "Why you should all take to your heels when a stick of wood tumbles down I cannot imagine"; and all Henslow could do, explaining he was right away on the other side of the tomb, would not satisfy him.

'Then Palmer came back and reported there was nothing to account for this noise and nothing seemingly fallen down, and when the Dean finished feeling of himself they gathered round – except my father, he sat where he was – and someone lighted up a bit of candle and they looked into the tomb. "Nothing there," says the Dean, "what did I tell you? Stay! here's something. What's this? a bit of music paper, and a piece of torn stuff – part of a dress it looks like. Both quite modern – no interest whatever. Another time perhaps you'll take the advice of an educated man" – or something like that, and off he went, limping a bit, and out through the north door, only as he went he called back angry to Palmer for leaving the door standing open. Palmer called out "Very sorry, sir," but he shrugged his shoulders, and Henslow says, "I fancy Mr Dean's mistaken. I closed the door behind me, but he's a little upset." Then Palmer says, "Why, where's Worby?" and they saw him sitting on the step and went up to him. He was recovering himself, it seemed, and wiping his forehead, and Palmer helped him up on to his legs, as I was glad to see.

'They were too far off for me to hear what they said, but my father pointed to the north door in the aisle, and Palmer and Henslow both of them looked very surprised and scared. After a bit, my father and Henslow went out of the church, and the others made what haste they could to put the slab back and plaster it in. And about as the clock struck twelve the Cathedral was opened again and us boys made the best of our way home.

'I was in a great taking to know what it was had given my poor father such a turn, and when I got in and found him sitting in his chair taking a glass of spirits, and my mother standing looking anxious at him, I couldn't keep from bursting out and making confession where I'd been. But he didn't seem to take on, not in the way of losing his temper. "You was there, was you? Well, did you see it?" "I see everything, father," I said, "except when the noise came." "Did you see what it was knocked the Dean over?" he says, "that what come out of the monument? You didn't? Well, that's a mercy." "Why, what was it, father?" I said. "Come, you must have seen it," he says. "*Didn't* you see? A thing like a man, all over hair, and two great eyes to it?"

'Well, that was all I could get out of him that time, and later on he seemed as if he was ashamed of being so frightened, and he used to put me off when I asked him about it. But years after, when I was got to be a grown man, we had more talk now and again on the matter, and he always said the same thing. "Black it was," he'd say, "and a mass of hair, and two legs, and the light caught on its eyes."

'Well, that's the tale of that tomb, Mr Lake; it's one we don't tell to our visitors, and I should be obliged to you not to make any use of it till I'm out of the way. I doubt Mr Evans'll feel the same as I do, if you ask him.'

This proved to be the case. But over twenty years have passed by, and the grass is growing over both Worby and Evans; so Mr Lake felt no difficulty about communicating his notes – taken in 1890 – to me. He accompanied them with a sketch of the tomb and a copy of the short inscription on the metal cross which was affixed at the expense of Dr Lyall to the centre of the northern side. It was from the Vulgate of Isaiah xxxiv., and consisted merely of the three words—

IBI CUBAVIT LAMIA.

M. R. James

Casting the Runes

April 15th, 190–.

DEAR SIR,—I am requested by the Council of the —— Association to return to you the draft of a paper on *The Truth of Alchemy*, which you have been good enough to offer to read at our forthcoming meeting, and to inform you that the Council do not see their way to including it in the programme.

I am,
Yours faithfully,
—— Secretary.

April 18th.

DEAR SIR,—I am sorry to say that my engagements do not permit of my affording you an interview on the subject of your proposed paper. Nor do our laws allow of your discussing the matter with a Committee of our Council, as you suggest. Please allow me to assure you that the fullest consideration was given to the draft which you submitted, and that it was not declined without having been referred to the judgment of a most competent authority. No personal question (it can hardly be necessary for me to add) can have had the slightest influence on the decision of the Council.

Believe me (ut supra).

April 20th.

The Secretary of the —— Association begs repectfully to inform Mr Karswell that it is impossible for him to communicate the name of any person or persons to whom the draft of Mr Karswell's paper may have been submitted; and further desires to intimate that he cannot undertake to reply to any further letters on this subject.

CASTING THE RUNES

'And who *is* Mr Karswell?' inquired the Secretary's wife. She had called at his office, and (perhaps unwarrantably) had picked up the last of these three letters, which the typist had just brought in.

'Why, my dear, just at present Mr Karswell is a very angry man. But I don't know much about him otherwise, except that he is a person of wealth, his address is Lufford Abbey, Warwickshire, and he's an alchemist, apparently, and wants to tell us all about it; and that's about all – except that I don't want to meet him for the next week or two. Now, if you're ready to leave this place, I am.'

'What have you been doing to make him angry?' asked Mrs Secretary.

'The usual thing, my dear, the usual thing: he sent in a draft of a paper he wanted to read at the next meeting, and we referred it to Edward Dunning – almost the only man in England who knows about these things – and he said it was perfectly hopeless, so we declined it. So Karswell has been pelting me with letters ever since. The last thing he wanted was the name of the man we referred his nonsense to; you saw my answer to that. But don't you say anything about it, for goodness' sake.'

'I should think not, indeed. Did I ever do such a thing? I do hope, though, he won't get to know that it was poor Mr Dunning.'

'Poor Mr Dunning? I don't know why you call him that; he's a very happy man, is Dunning. Lots of hobbies and a comfortable home, and all his time to himself.'

'I only meant I should be sorry for him if this man got hold of his name, and came and bothered him.'

'Oh, ah! yes. I dare say he would be poor Mr Dunning then.'

The Secretary and his wife were lunching out, and the friends to whose house they were bound were Warwickshire people. So Mrs Secretary had already settled it in her own mind that she would question them judiciously about Mr Karswell. But she was saved the trouble of leading up to the subject, for the hostess said to the host, before many minutes had passed, 'I saw the Abbot of Lufford this morning.' The host whistled. '*Did* you? What in the world brings him up to town?' 'Goodness knows; he was coming out of the British Museum gate as I drove past.' It was not unnatural that Mrs Secretary should inquire whether this was a real Abbot who was being spoken of. 'Oh, no, my dear: only a neighbour of ours in the country who bought Lufford Abbey a few years ago. His real name is Karswell.' 'Is he a friend of yours?' asked Mr Secretary, with a private wink to his wife. The question let loose a torrent of declamation. There was really nothing to be said for Mr Karswell. Nobody knew what he did with himself: his servants were a hor-

rible set of people; he had invented a new religion for himself, and practised no one could tell what appalling rites; he was very easily offended,
and never forgave anybody: he had a dreadful face (so the lady insisted,
her husband somewhat demurring); he never did a kind action, and whatever influence he did exert was mischievous. 'Do the poor man justice,
dear,' the husband interrupted. 'You forget the treat he gave the school
children.' 'Forget it, indeed! But I'm glad you mentioned it, because it
gives an idea of the man. Now, Florence, listen to this. The first winter
he was at Lufford this delightful neighbour of ours wrote to the clergyman of his parish (he's not ours, but we know him very well) and offered
to show the school children some magic-lantern slides. He said he had
some new kinds, which he thought would interest them. Well, the
clergyman was rather surprised, because Mr Karswell had shown himself
inclined to be unpleasant to the children – complaining of their tres-
passing, or something of the sort; but of course he accepted, and the
evening was fixed, and our friend went himself to see that everything
went right. He said he never had been so thankful for anything as that
his own children were all prevented from being there: they were at a
children's party at our house, as a matter of fact. Because this Mr Karswell had evidently set out with the intention of frightening these poor
village children out of their wits, and I do believe, if he had been allowed
to go on, he would actually have done so. He began with some comparatively mild things. Red Riding Hood was one, and even then, Mr Farrer
said, the wolf was so dreadful that several of the smaller children had to
be taken out: and he said Mr Karswell began the story by producing a
noise like a wolf howling in the distance, which was the most gruesome
thing he had ever heard. All the slides he showed, Mr Farrer said, were
most clever; they were absolutely realistic, and where he had got them
or how he worked them he could not imagine. Well, the show went on,
and the stories kept on becoming a little more terrifying each time, and
the children were mesmerized into complete silence. At last he produced
a series which represented a little boy passing through his own park –
Lufford, I mean – in the evening. Every child in the room could recognize
the place from the pictures. And this poor boy was followed, and at last
pursued and overtaken, and either torn in pieces or somehow made away
with, by a horrible hopping creature in white, which you saw first
dodging about among the trees, and gradually it appeared more and
more plainly. Mr Farrer said it gave him one of the worst nightmares he
ever remembered, and what it must have meant to the children doesn't
bear thinking of. Of course this was too much, and he spoke very sharply
indeed to Mr Karswell, and said it couldn't go on. All *he* said was: 'Oh,
you think it's time to bring our little show to an end and send them home
to their beds? *Very* well!' And then, if you please, he switched on

another slide, which showed a great mass of snakes, centipedes, and disgusting creatures with wings, and somehow or other he made it seem as if they were climbing out of the picture and getting in amongst the audience; and this was accompanied by a sort of dry rustling noise which sent the children nearly mad, and of course they stampeded. A good many of them were rather hurt in getting out of the room, and I don't suppose one of them closed an eye that night. There was the most dreadful trouble in the village afterwards. Of course the mothers threw a good part of the blame on poor Mr Farrer, and, if they could have got past the gates, I believe the fathers would have broken every window in the Abbey. Well, now, that's Mr Karswell: that's the Abbot of Lufford, my dear, and you can imagine how we covet *his* society.'

'Yes, I think he has all the possibilities of a distinguished criminal, has Karswell,' said the host. 'I should be sorry for anyone who got into his bad books.'

'Is he the man, or am I mixing him up with someone else?' asked the Secretary (who for some minutes had been wearing the frown of the man who is trying to recollect something). 'Is he the man who brought out a *History of Witchcraft* some time back – ten years or more?'

'That's the man; do you remember the reviews of it?'

'Certainly I do; and what's equally to the point, I knew the author of the most incisive of the lot. So did you: you must remember John Harrington; he was at John's in our time.'

'Oh, very well indeed, though I don't think I saw or heard anything of him between the time I went down and the day I read the account of the inquest on him.'

'Inquest?' said one of the ladies. 'What has happened to him?'

'Why, what happened was that he fell out of a tree and broke his neck. But the puzzle was, what could have induced him to get up there. It was a mysterious business, I must say. Here was this man – not an athletic fellow, was he? and with no eccentric twist about him that was ever noticed – walking home along a country road late in the evening – no tramps about – well known and liked in the place – and he suddenly begins to run like mad, loses his hat and stick, and finally shins up a tree – quite a difficult tree – growing in the hedgerow: a dead branch gives way, and he comes down with it and breaks his neck, and there he's found next morning with the most dreadful face of fear on him that could be imagined. It was pretty evident, of course, that he had been chased by something, and people talked of savage dogs, and beasts escaped out of menageries; but there was nothing to be made of that. That was in '89, and I believe his brother Henry (whom I remember well at Cambridge, but *you* probably don't) has been trying to get on the track of an explanation ever since. He, of course, insists there was malice in it, but I don't know. It's difficult to see how it could have come in.'

After a time the talk reverted to the *History of Witchcraft*. 'Did you ever look into it?' asked the host.

'Yes, I did,' said the Secretary. 'I went so far as to read it.'

'Was it as bad as it was made out to be?'

'Oh, in point of style and form, quite hopeless. It deserved all the pulverizing it got. But, besides that, it was an evil book. The man believed every word of what he was saying, and I'm very much mistaken if he hadn't tried the greater part of his receipts.'

'Well, I only remember Harrington's review of it, and I must say if I'd been the author it would have quenched my literary ambition for good. I should never have held up my head again.'

'It hasn't had that effect in the present case. But come, it's half-past three; I must be off.'

On the way home the Secretary's wife said, 'I do hope that horrible man won't find out that Mr Dunning had anything to do with the rejection of his paper.' 'I don't think there's much chance of that,' said the Secretary. 'Dunning won't mention it himself, for these matters are confidential, and none of us will for the same reason. Karswell won't know his name, for Dunning hasn't published anything on the same subject yet. The only danger is that Karswell might find out, if he was to ask the British Museum people who was in the habit of consulting alchemical manuscripts: I can't very well tell them not to mention Dunning, can I? It would set them talking at once. Let's hope it won't occur to him.'

However, Mr Karswell was an astute man.

This much is in the way of prologue. On an evening rather later in the same week, Mr Edward Dunning was returning from the British Museum, where he had been engaged in Research, to the comfortable house in a suburb where he lived alone, tended by two excellent women who had been long with him. There is nothing to be added by way of description of him to what we have heard already. Let us follow him as he takes his sober course homewards.

A train took him to within a mile or two of his house, and an electric tram a stage farther. The line ended at a point some three hundred yards from his front door. He had had enough of reading when he got into the car, and indeed the light was not such as to allow him to do more than study the advertisements on the panes of glass that faced him as he sat. As was not unnatural, the advertisements in this particular line of cars were objects of his frequent contemplation, and, with the possible exception of the brilliant and convincing dialogue between Mr Lamplough and an eminent K.C. on the subject of Pyretic Saline, none of them afforded much scope to his imagination. I am wrong: there was one at the corner of the car farthest from him which did not seem familiar. It was in blue letters on a yellow ground, and all that he could read of it was a name – John Harrington – and something like a date. It could be of no interest to him to know more; but for all that, as the car emptied, he was just curious enough to move along the seat until he could read it well. He felt to a slight extent repaid for his trouble; the advertisement was *not* of the usual type. It ran thus: 'In memory of John Harrington, F.S.A., of The Laurels, Ashbrooke. Died Sept. 18, 1889. Three months were allowed.'

The car stopped. Mr Dunning, still contemplating the blue letters on the yellow ground, had to be stimulated to rise by a word from the conductor. 'I beg your pardon,' he said, 'I was looking at that advertisement; it's a very odd one, isn't it?' The conductor read it slowly. 'Well, my word,' he said, 'I never see that one before. Well, that is a cure, ain't it? Someone bin up to their jokes 'ere, I should think.' He got out a duster and applied it, not without saliva, to the pane and then to the outside. 'No,' he said, returning, 'that ain't no transfer; seems to me as if it was reg'lar *in* the glass, what I mean in the substance, as you may say. Don't you think so, sir?' Mr Dunning examined it and rubbed it with his glove, and agreed. 'Who looks after these advertisements, and gives leave for them to be put up? I wish you would inquire. I will just take a note of the words.' At this moment there came a call from the driver: 'Look alive, George, time's up.' 'All right, all right; there's something else what's up at this end. You come and look at this 'ere glass. 'What's gorn with the glass?' said the driver, approaching. 'Well, and oo's 'Arrington? What's it all about?' 'I was just asking who was responsible for putting the advertisements up in your cars, and saying it would be as well to make some inquiry about this one.' 'Well, sir, that's all done at the Company's orfice, that work is: it's our Mr Timms, I believe, looks into that. When we put up to-night I'll leave word, and per'aps I'll be able to tell you to-morrer if you 'appen to be coming this way.'

This was all that passed that evening. Mr Dunning did just go to the trouble of looking up Ashbrooke, and found that it was in Warwickshire.

Next day he went to town again. The car (it was the same car) was too full in the morning to allow of his getting a word with the conductor: he could only be sure that the curious advertisement had been made away with. The close of the day brought a further element of mystery into the transaction. He had missed the tram, or else preferred walking home, but at a rather late hour, while he was at work in his study, one of the maids came to say that two men from the tramways was very anxious to speak to him. This was a reminder of the advertisement, which he had, he says, nearly forgotten. He had the men in – they were the conductor and driver of the car – and when the matter of refreshment had been attended to, asked what Mr Timms had had to say about the advertisement. 'Well, sir, that's what we took the liberty to step round about,' said the conductor. 'Mr Timm's 'e give William 'ere the rough side of his tongue about that: 'cordin' to 'im there warn't no advertisement of that description sent in, nor ordered, nor paid for, nor put up, nor nothink, let alone not bein' there, and we was playing the fool takin' up his time. "Well," I says, "if that's the case, all I ask of you, Mr Timms," I says, "is to take and look at it for yourself," I says. "Of course if it ain't there," I says, "you may take and call me what you like." "Right," he says, "I will": and we went straight off. Now, I leave it to you, sir, if that ad., as we term 'em, with 'Arrington on it warn't as plain as ever you see anythink – blue letters on yeller glass, and as I says at the time, and you borne me out, reg'lar *in* the glass, because, if you remember, you recollect of me swabbing it with my duster.' 'To be sure I do, quite clearly – well?' 'You may say well, I don't think. Mr Timms he gets in that car with a light – no, he told William to 'old the light outside. "Now," he says, "where's your precious ad. what we've 'eard so much about?" " 'Ere it is," I says, "Mr Timms," and I laid my 'and on it.' The conductor paused.

'Well,' said Mr Dunning, 'it was gone, I suppose. Broken?'

'Broke! – not it. There warn't, if you'll believe me, no more trace of them letters – blue letters they was – on that piece o' glass, than – well, it's no good *me* talkin'. *I* never see such a thing. I leave it to William here if – but there, as I says, where's the benefit in me going on about it?'

'And what did Mr Timms say?'

'Why 'e did what I give 'im leave to – called us pretty much anythink he liked, and I don't know as I blame him so much neither. But what we thought, William and me did, was as we seen you take down a bit of a note about that – well that letterin'—'

'I certainly did that, and I have it now. Did you wish me to speak to Mr Timms myself, and show it to him? Was that what you came in about?'

'There, didn't I say as much?' said William. 'Deal with a gent if you can get on the track of one, that's my word. Now perhaps, George, you'll allow as I ain't took you very far wrong to-night.'

'Very well, William, very well; no need for you to go on as if you'd 'ad to frog's-march me 'ere. I come quiet, didn't I? All the same for that, we 'adn't ought to take up your time this way, sir; but if it so 'appened you could find time to step round to the Company's orfice in the morning and tell Mr Timms what you seen for yourself, we should lay under a very 'igh obligation to you for the trouble. You see it ain't bein' called –

well, one thing and another, as we mind, but if they got it into their
'ead at the orfice as we seen things as warn't there, why, one thing leads
to another, and where we should be a twelvemunce 'ence – well, you
can understand what I mean.'

Amid further elucidations of the proposition, George, conducted by
William, left the room.

The incredulity of Mr Timms (who had a nodding acquaintance with
Mr Dunning) was greatly modified on the following day by what the
latter could tell and show him; and any bad mark that might have
been attached to the names of William and George was not suffered to
remain on the Company's books; but explanation there was none.

Mr Dunning's interest in the matter was kept alive by an incident of
the following afternoon. He was walking from his club to the train, and
he noticed some way ahead a man with a handful of leaflets such as are
distributed to passers-by by agents of enterprising firms. This agent had
not chosen a very crowded street for his operations: in fact, Mr Dunning
did not see him get rid of a single leaflet before he himself reached the
spot. One was thrust into his hand as he passed: the hand that gave it
touched his, and he experienced a sort of little shock as it did so. It
seemed unnaturally rough and hot. He looked in passing at the giver,
but the impression he got was so unclear that, however much he tried to
reckon it up subsequently, nothing would come. He was walking quickly,
and as he went on glanced at the paper. It was a blue one. The name of
Harrington in large capitals caught his eye. He stopped, startled, and
felt for his glasses. The next instant the leaflet was twitched out of his
hand by a man who hurried past, and was irrecoverably gone. He ran
back a few paces, but where was the passer-by? and where the distri-
butor?

It was in a somewhat pensive frame of mind that Mr Dunning passed
on the following day into the Select Manuscript Room of the British
Museum, and filled up tickets for Harley 3586, and some other volumes.
After a few minutes they were brought to him, and he was settling the
one he wanted first upon the desk, when he thought he heard his own
name whispered behind him. He turned round hastily, and in doing so,
brushed his little portfolio of loose papers on to the floor. He saw no one
he recognized except one of the staff in charge of the room, who nodded
to him, and he proceeded to pick up his papers. He thought he had them
all, and was turning to begin work, when a stout gentleman at the table
behind him, who was just rising to leave, and had collected his own
belongings, touched him on the shoulder, saying, 'May I give you this? I
think it should be yours,' and handed him a missing quire. 'It is mine,
thank you,' said Mr Dunning. In another moment the man had left the
room. Upon finishing his work for the afternoon, Mr Dunning had some

conversation with the assistant in charge, and took occasion to ask who the stout gentleman was. 'Oh, he's a man named Karswell,' said the assistant; 'he was asking me a week ago who were the great authorities on alchemy, and of course I told him you were the only one in the country. I'll see if I can catch him: he'd like to meet you, I'm sure.'

'For heaven's sake don't dream of it!' said Mr Dunning, 'I'm particularly anxious to avoid him.'

'Oh! very well,' said the assistant, 'he doesn't come here often: I dare say you won't meet him.'

More than once on the way home that day Mr Dunning confessed to himself that he did not look forward with his usual cheerfulness to a solitary evening. It seemed to him that something ill-defined and impalpable had stepped in between him and his fellow-men – had taken him in charge, as it were. He wanted to sit close up to his neighbours in the train and in the tram, but as luck would have it both train and car were markedly empty. The conductor George was thoughtful, and appeared to be absorbed in calculations as to the number of passengers. On arriving at his house he found Dr Watson, his medical man, on his doorstep. 'I've had to upset your household arrangements, I'm sorry to say, Dunning. Both your servants *hors de combat*. In fact, I've had to send them to the Nursing Home.'

'Good heavens! what's the matter?'

'It's something like ptomaine poisoning, I should think: you've not suffered yourself, I can see, or you wouldn't be walking about. I think they'll pull through all right.'

'Dear, dear! Have you any idea what brought it on?'

'Well, they tell me they bought some shell-fish from a hawker at their dinner-time. It's odd. I've made inquiries, but I can't find that any hawker has been to other houses in the street. I couldn't send word to you; they won't be back for a bit yet. You come and dine with me to-night, anyhow, and we can make arrangements for going on. Eight o'clock. Don't be too anxious.'

The solitary evening was thus obviated; at the expense of some distress and inconvenience, it is true. Mr Dunning spent the time pleasantly enough with the doctor (a rather recent settler), and returned to his lonely home at about 11.30. The night he passed is not one on which he looks back with any satisfaction. He was in bed and the light was out. He was wondering if the charwoman would come early enough to get him hot water next morning, when he heard the unmistakable sound of his study door opening. No step followed it on the passage floor, but the sound must mean mischief, for he knew that he had shut the door that evening after putting his papers away in his dsek. It was rather shame than courage that induced him to slip out into the passage and lean over the banister in his nightgown, listening. No light was visible; no further sound came: only a gust of warm, or even hot air played for an instant round his shins. He went back and decided to lock himself into his room. There was more unpleasantness, however. Either an economical suburban company had decided that their light would not be required in the small hours, and had stopped working, or else something was wrong with the meter; the effect was in any case that the electric light was off. The obvious course was to find a match, and also to consult his watch: he might as well know how many hours of discomfort awaited him. So he put his hand into the well-known nook under the pillow: only, it did not get so far. What he touched was, according to his account, a mouth, with teeth, and with hair about it, and, he declares, not the mouth of a human being. I do not think it is any use to guess what he said or did; but he was in a spare room with the door locked and his ear to it before he was clearly conscious again. And there he spent the rest of a most miserable night, looking every moment for some fumbling at the door: but nothing came.

The venturing back to his own room in the morning was attended with many listenings and quiverings. The door stood open, fortunately, and the blinds were up (the servants had been out of the house before the hour of drawing them down); there was, to be short, no trace of an inhabitant. The watch, too, was in its usual place; nothing was disturbed, only the wardrobe door had swung open, in accordance with its confirmed habit. A ring at the back door now announced the charwoman, who had been ordered the night before, and nerved Mr Dunning, after letting her in, to continue his search in other parts of the house. It was equally fruitless.

The day thus begun went on dismally enough. He dared not go to the Museum: in spite of what the assistant had said, Karswell might turn up there, and Dunning felt he could not cope with a probably hostile stranger. His own house was odious; he hated sponging on the doctor. He spent some little time in a call at the Nursing Home, where he was slightly cheered by a good report of his housekeeper and maid. Towards lunch-time he betook himself to his club, again experiencing a gleam of satisfaction at seeing the Secretary of the Association. At luncheon Dunning told his friend the more material of his woes, but could not bring himself to speak of those that weighed most heavily on his spirits. 'My poor dear man,' said the Secretary, 'what an upset! Look here: we're alone at home, absolutely. You must put up with us. Yes! no excuse: send your things in this afternoon.' Dunning was unable to stand out: he was, in truth, becoming acutely anxious, as the hours went on, as to what that night might have waiting for him. He was almost happy as he hurried home to pack up.

His friends, when they had time to take stock of him, were rather shocked at his lorn appearance, and did their best to keep him up to the mark. Not altogether without success: but, when the two men were smoking alone later, Dunning became dull again. Suddenly he said, 'Gayton, I believe that alchemist man knows it was I who got his paper rejected.' Gayton whistled. 'What makes you think that?' he said. Dunning told of his conversation with the Museum assistant, and Gayton could only agree that the guess seemed likely to be correct. 'Not that I care much,' Dunning went on, 'only it might be a nuisance if we were to meet. He's a bad-tempered party, I imagine.' Conversation dropped again; Gayton became more and more strongly impressed with the desolateness that came over Dunning's face and bearing, and finally – though with a considerable effort – he asked him point-blank whether something serious was not bothering him. Dunning gave an exclamation of relief. 'I was perishing to get it off my mind,' he said. 'Do you know anything about a man named John Harrington?' Gayton was thoroughly startled, and at the moment could only ask why. Then the complete story of Dunning's experiences came out – what had happened in the tramcar, in his own house, and in the street, the troubling of spirit that had crept over him, and still held him; and he ended with the question he had begun with. Gayton was at a loss how to answer him. To tell the story of Harrington's end would perhaps be right; only, Dunning was in a nervous state, the story was a grim one, and he could not help asking himself whether there were not a connecting link between these two cases, in the person of Karswell. It was a difficult concession for a scientific man, but it could be eased by the phrase 'hypnotic suggestion'. In the end he decided that his answer to-night should be guarded; he would talk the situation over with his wife. So he said that he had known Harrington at Cambridge, and believed he had died suddenly in 1889, adding a few details about the man and his published work. He did talk over the matter with Mrs Gayton, and, as he had anticipated, she leapt at once to the conclusion which had been hovering before him. It was she who reminded him of the surviving brother, Henry Harrington, and she also who suggested that he might be got hold of by means of their hosts of the day before. 'He might be a hopeless crank,' objected Gayton. 'That could be ascertained from the Bennetts, who knew him,' Mrs Gayton retorted; and she undertook to see the Bennetts the very next day.

It is not necessary to tell in further detail the steps by which Henry Harrington and Dunning were brought together.

The next scene that does require to be narrated is a conversation that took place between the two. Dunning had told Harrington of the strange ways in which the dead man's name had been brought before him, and had said something, besides, of his own subsequent experiences. Then he had asked if Harrington was disposed, in return, to recall any of the circumstances connected with his brother's death. Harrington's surprise at what he heard can be imagined: but his reply was readily given.

'John,' he said, 'was in a very odd state, undeniably, from time to time, during some weeks before, though not immediately before, the catastrophe. There were several things; the principal notion he had was that he thought he was being followed. No doubt he was an impression-able man, but he never had had such fancies as this before. I cannot get it out of my mind that there was ill-will at work, and what you tell me about yourself reminds me very much of my brother. Can you think of any possible connecting link?'

'There is just one that has been taking shape vaguely in my mind. I've been told that your brother reviewed a book very severely not long be-fore he died, and just lately I have happened to cross the path of the man who wrote that book in a way he would resent.'

'Don't tell me the man was called Karswell.'

'Why not? that is exactly his name.'

Henry Harrington leant back. 'That is final to my mind. Now I must explain further. From something he said, I feel sure that my brother John was beginning to believe – very much against his will – that Kars-well was at the bottom of his trouble. I want to tell you what seems to me to have a bearing on the situation. My brother was a great musician, and used to run up to concerts in town. He came back, three months before he died, from one of these, and gave me his programme to look at – an analytical programme: he always kept them. "I nearly missed this one," he said. "I suppose I must have dropped it: anyhow, I was looking for it under my seat and in my pockets and so on, and my neigh-bour offered me his: said 'might he give it me, he had no further use for it,' and he went away just afterwards. I don't know who he was – a stout, clean-shaven man. I should have been sorry to miss it; of course I could have bought another, but this cost me nothing." At another time he told me that he had been very uncomfortable both on the way to his hotel and during the night. I piece things together now in thinking it over. Then, not very long after, he was going over these programmes, putting them in order to have them bound up, and in this particular one (which by the way I had hardly glanced at), he found quite near the beginning a strip of paper with some very odd writing on it in red and black – most carefully done – it looked to me more like Runic letters than anything else. "Why," he said, "this must belong to my fat neighbour. It looks as if it might be worth returning to him; it may be a copy of something; evidently someone has taken trouble over it. How can I find his address?" We talked it over for a little and agreed that it wasn't worth advertising about, and that my brother had better look out for the man at the next concert, to which he was going very soon. The paper was lying on the book and we were both by the fire; it was a cold, windy summer evening. I suppose the door blew open, though I didn't notice it: at any rate a gust – a warm gust it was – came quite suddenly between us, took the paper and blew it straight into the fire: it was light, thin paper, and flared and went up the chimney in a single ash. "Well," I said, "you can't give it back now." He said nothing for a minute: then rather crossly, "No, I can't; but why you should keep on saying so I don't know." I remarked that I didn't say it more than once. "Not more than four times, you mean," was all he said. I remember all that very clearly, without any good reason; and now to come to the point. I don't know if you looked at that book of Karswell's which my unfortunate brother reviewed. It's not likely that you should: but I did, both before his death and after it. The first time we made game of it together. It was written in no style at all – split infinitives, and every sort of thing that makes an Oxford gorge rise. Then there was nothing that the man didn't swallow: mixing up classical myths, and stories out of the *Golden Legend* with reports of savage customs of to-day – all very proper, no doubt, if you know how to use them, but he didn't: he seemed to put the *Golden Legend* and the *Golden Bough* on a par, and to believe both: a pitiable exhibition, in short. Well, after the misfortune, I looked over the book again. It was no better than before, but the impression which it left this time on my mind was different. I suspected – as I told you – that Karswell had borne ill-will to my brother, even that he was in some way responsible for what had happened; and now his book seemed to me to be a very sinister performance indeed. One chapter in particular struck me, in which he spoke of "casting the Runes" on people, either for the purpose of gaining their affection or of getting them out of the way – perhaps more especially the latter: he spoke of all this in a way that really seemed to me to imply actual knowledge. I've not time to go into details, but the upshot is that I am pretty sure from information received that the civil man at the concert was Karswell: I suspect – I more than suspect – that the paper was of importance: and I do believe that if my brother had been able to give it back, he might have been alive now. Therefore, it occurs to me to ask you whether you have anything to put beside what I have told you.'

By way of answer, Dunning had the episode in the Manuscript Room at the British Museum to relate. 'Then he did actually hand you some papers; have you examined them? No? because we must, if you'll allow it, look at them at once, and very carefully.'

They went to the still empty house – empty, for the two servants were not yet able to return to work. Dunning's portfolio of papers was gathering dust on the writing-table. In it were the quires of small-sized scribbling paper which he used for his transcripts: and from one of these, as he took it up, there slipped and fluttered out into the room with uncanny quickness, a strip of thin light paper. The window was open, but Harrington slammed it to, just in time to intercept the paper, which he caught. 'I thought so,' he said; 'it might be the identical thing that was given to my brother. You'll have to look out, Dunning; this may mean something quite serious for you.'

A long consultation took place. The paper was narrowly examined. As Harrington had said, the characters on it were more like Runes than anything else, but not decipherable by either man, and both hesitated to copy them, for fear, as they confessed, of perpetuating whatever evil purpose they might conceal. So it has remained impossible (if I may anticipate a little) to ascertain what was conveyed in this curious message or commission. Both Dunning and Harrington are firmly convinced that it had the effect of bringing its possessors into very undesirable company. That it must be returned to the source whence it came they were agreed, and further, that the only safe and certain way was that of personal service; and here contrivance would be necessary, for Dunning was known by sight to Karswell. He must, for one thing, alter his appearance by shaving his beard. But then might not the blow fall first? Harrington thought they could time it. He knew the date of the concert at which the 'black spot' had been put on his brother: it was June 18th. The death had followed on Sept. 18th. Dunning reminded him that three months had been mentioned on the inscription on the car-window. 'Perhaps,' he added, with a cheerless laugh, 'mine may be a bill at three months too. I believe I can fix it by my diary. Yes, April 23rd was the day at the Museum; that brings us to July 23rd. Now, you know, it becomes extremely important to me to know anything you will tell me about the progress of your brother's trouble, if it is possible for you to speak of it.' 'Of course. Well, the sense of being watched whenever he was alone was the most distressing thing to him. After a time I took to sleeping in his room, and he was the better for that: still, he talked a great deal in his sleep. What about? Is it wise to dwell on that, at least before things are straightened out? I think not, but I can tell you this: two things came for him by post during those weeks, both with a London postmark, and addressed in a commercial hand. One was a woodcut of Bewick's, roughly torn out of the page: one which shows a moonlit road and a man walking along it, followed by an awful demon creature. Under it were written the lines out of the "Ancient Mariner" (which I suppose the cut illustrates) about one who, having once looked round—

> "walks on,
> And turns no more his head,
> Because he knows a frightful fiend
> Doth close behind him tread.'

The other was a calendar, such as tradesmen often send. My brother paid no attention to this, but I looked at it after his death, and found that everything after Sept. 18 had been torn out. You may be surprised at his having gone out alone the evening he was killed, but the fact is that during the last ten days or so of his life he had been quite free from the sense of being followed or watched.'

The end of the consultation was this. Harrington, who knew a neighbour of Karswell's, thought he saw a way of keeping a watch on his movements. It would be Dunning's part to be in readiness to try to cross Karswell's path at any moment, to keep the paper safe and in a place of ready access.

They parted. The next weeks were no doubt a severe strain upon Dunning's nerves: the intangible barrier which had seemed to rise about him on the day when he received the paper, gradually developed into a brooding blackness that cut him off from the means of escape to which one might have thought he might resort. No one was at hand who was likely to suggest them to him, and he seemed robbed of all initiative. He waited with inexpressible anxiety as May, June, and early July passed on, for a mandate from Harrington. But all this time Karswell remained immovable at Lufford.

At last, in less than a week before the date he had come to look upon as the end of his earthly activities, came a telegram: 'Leaves Victoria by boat train Thursday night. Do not miss. I come to you to-night. Harrington.'

He arrived accordingly, and they concocted plans. The train left Victoria at nine and its last stop before Dover was Croydon West. Harrington would mark down Karswell at Victoria, and look out for Dunning at Croydon, calling to him if need were by a name agreed upon. Dunning, disguised as far as might be, was to have no label or initials on any hand luggage, and must at all costs have the paper with him.

Dunning's suspense as he waited on the Croydon platform I need not attempt to describe. His sense of danger during the last days had only been sharpened by the fact that the cloud about him had perceptibly been lighter; but relief was an ominous symptom, and, if Karswell eluded him now, hope was gone: and there were so many chances of that. The rumour of the journey might be itself a device. The twenty minutes in which he paced the platform and persecuted every porter with inquiries as to the boat train were as bitter as any he had spent. Still, the train came, and Harrington was at the window. It was important, of course, that there should be no recognition: so Dunning got in at the farther end of the corridor carriage, and only gradually made his way to the compartment where Harrington and Karswell were. He was pleased, on the whole, to see that the train was far from full.

Karswell was on the alert, but gave no sign of recognition. Dunning took the seat not immediately facing him, and attempted, vainly at first, then with increasing command of his faculties, to reckon the possibilities of making the desired transfer. Opposite to Karswell, and next to Dunning, was a heap of Karswell's coats on the seat. It would be of no use to slip the paper into these – he would not be safe, or would not feel so, unless in some way it could be proffered by him and accepted by the other. There was a handbag, open, and with papers in it. Could he manage to conceal this (so that perhaps Karswell might leave the carriage without it), and then find and give it to him? This was the plan that suggested itself. If he could only have counselled with Harrington! but that could not be. The minutes went on. More than once Karswell rose and went out into the corridor. The second time Dunning was on the point of attempting to make the bag fall off the seat, but he caught Harrington's eye, and read in it a warning. Karswell, from the corridor, was watching: probably to see if the two men recognized each other. He returned, but was evidently restless: and, when he rose the third time, hope dawned, for something did slip off his seat and fall with hardly a sound to the floor. Karswell went out once more, and passed out of range of the corridor window. Dunning picked up what had fallen, and saw that the key was in his hands in the form of one of Cook's ticket-cases, with tickets in it. These cases have a pocket in the cover, and within very few seconds the paper of which we have heard was in the pocket of this one. To make the operation more secure, Harrington stood in the doorway of the compartment and fiddled with the blind. It was done, and done at the right time, for the train was now slowing down towards Dover.

In a moment more Karswell re-entered the compartment. As he did so, Dunning, managing, he knew not how, to suppress the tremble in his voice, handed him the ticket-case, saying, 'May I give you this, sir? I believe it is yours.' After a brief glance at the ticket inside, Karswell uttered the hoped-for response, 'Yes, it is; much obliged to you, sir,' and he placed it in his breast pocket.

Even in the few moments that remained – moments of tense anxiety, for they knew not to what a premature finding of the paper might lead – both men noticed that the carriage seemed to darken about them and to grow warmer; that Karswell was fidgety and oppressed; that he drew the heap of loose coats near to him and cast it back as if it repelled him; and that he then sat upright and glanced anxiously at both. They, with sickening anxiety, busied themselves in collecting their belongings; but they both thought that Karswell was on the point of speaking when the train stopped at Dover Town. It was natural that in the short space between town and pier they should both go into the corridor.

At the pier they got out, but so empty was the train that they were forced to linger on the platform until Karswell should have passed ahead of them with his porter on the way to the boat, and only then was it safe for them to exchange a pressure of the hand and a word of concentrated congratulation. The effect upon Dunning was to make him almost faint. Harrington made him lean up against the wall, while he himself went forward a few yards within sight of the gangway to the boat, at which Karswell had now arrived. The man at the head of it examined his ticket, and, laden with coats, he passed down into the boat. Suddenly the official called after him, 'You, sir, beg pardon, did the other gentleman show his ticket?' 'What the devil do you mean by the other gentleman?' Karswell's snarling voice called back from the deck. The man bent over and looked at him. 'The devil? Well, I don't know, I'm sure,' Harrington heard him say to himself, and then aloud, 'My mistake, sir; must have been your rugs! ask your pardon.' And then, to a subordinate near him, ''Ad he got a dog with him, or what? Funny thing: I could 'a' swore 'e wasn't alone. Well, whatever it was, they'll 'ave to see to it aboard. She's off now. Another week and we shall be gettin' the 'oliday customers.' In five minutes more there was nothing but the lessening lights of the boat, the long line of the Dover lamps, the night breeze, and the moon.

Long and long the two sat in their room at the 'Lord Warden'. In spite of the removal of their greatest anxiety, they were oppressed with a doubt, not of the lightest. Had they been justified in sending a man to his death, as they believed they had? Ought they not to warn him, at least? 'No,' said Harrington; 'if he is the murderer I think him, we have done no more than is just. Still, if you think it better – but how and where can you warn him?' 'He was booked to Abbeville only,' said Dunning. 'I saw that. If I wired to the hotels there in Joanne's Guide, "Examine your ticket-case, Dunning," I should feel happier. This is the 21st: he will have a day. But I am afraid he has gone into the dark.' So telegrams were left at the hotel office.

It is not clear whether these reached their destination, or whether, if they did, they were understood. All that is known is that, on the afternoon of the 23rd, an English traveller, examining the front of St Wulfram's Church at Abbeville, then under extensive repair, was struck on

ASTING THE RUNES

the head and instantly killed by a stone falling from the scaffold erected
round the north-western tower, there being, as was clearly proved, no
workman on the scaffold at that moment: and the traveller's papers
identified him as Mr Karswell.

Only one detail shall be added. At Karswell's sale a set of Bewick,
sold with all faults, was acquired by Harrington. The page with the
woodcut of the traveller and the demon was, as he had expected,
mutilated. Also, after a judicious interval, Harrington repeated to Dunning something of what he had heard his brother say in his sleep: but it
was not long before Dunning stopped him.

O. Henry

The Furnished Room

Restless, shifting, fugacious as time itself, is a certain vast bulk of the population of the red brick district of the lower West Side. Homeless, they have a hundred homes. They flit from furnished room to furnished room, transients for ever – transients in abode, transients in heart and mind. They sing 'Home, Sweet Home' in ragtime; they carry their *lares et penates* in a bandbox; their vine is entwined about a picture hat; a rubber plant is their fig tree.

Hence the houses of this district, having had a thousand dwellers, should have a thousand tales to tell, mostly dull ones, no doubt; but it would be strange if there could not be found a ghost or two in the wake of all these vagrant guests.

One evening after dark a young man prowled among these crumbling red mansions, ringing their bells. At the twelfth he rested his lean hand baggage upon the step and wiped the dust from his hatband and forehead. The bell sounded faint and far away in some remote, hollow depths.

To the door of this, the twelfth house whose bell he had rung, came a housekeeper who made him think of an unwholesome, surfeited worm that had eaten its nut to a hollow shell and now sought to fill the vacancy with edible lodgers.

He asked if there was a room to let.

'Come in,' said the housekeeper. Her voice came from her throat; her throat seemed lined with fur. 'I have the third-floor-back, vacant since a week back. Should you wish to look at it?'

The young man followed her up the stairs. A faint light from no particular source mitigated the shadows of the halls. They trod noiselessly upon a stair carpet that its own loom would have forsworn. It seemed to have become vegetable; to have degenerated in that rank, sunless air to lush lichen or spreading moss that grew in patches to the staircase and was viscid under the foot like organic matter. At each turn of the stairs were vacant niches in the wall. Perhaps plants had once been set within them. If so they had died in that foul and tainted air. It may be that statues of the saints had stood there, but it was not difficult to conceive that imps and devils had dragged them forth in the darkness and down to the unholy depths of some furnished pit below.

'This is the room,' said the housekeeper, from her furry throat. 'It's a nice room. It ain't often vacant. I had some most elegant people in it last summer – no trouble at all, and paid in advance to the minute. The water's at the end of the hall. Sprowls and Mooney kept it three months. They done a vaudeville sketch. Miss B'retta Sprowls – you may have heard of her – oh, that was just the stage names – right there over the dresser is where the marriage certificate hung, framed. The gas is here, and you see there is plenty of closet room. It's a room everybody likes. It never stays idle long.'

'Do you have many theatrical people rooming here?' asked the young man.

'They comes and goes. A good proportion of my lodgers is connected with the theatres. Yes, sir, this is the theatrical district. Actor people never stays long anywhere. I get my share. Yes, they comes and they goes.'

He engaged the room, paying for a week in advance. He was tired, he said, and would take possession at once. He counted out the money. The room had been made ready, she said, even to towels and water. As the housekeeper moved away he put, for the thousandth time, the question that he carried at the end of his tongue.

'A young girl – Miss Vashner – Miss Eloise Vashner – do you remember such a one among your lodgers? She would be singing on the stage, most likely. A fair girl, of medium height and slender, with reddish, gold hair and a dark mole near her left eyebrow.'

'No, I don't remember the name. Them stage people has names they change as often as their rooms. They comes and they goes. No, I don't call that one to mind.'

No. Always no. Five months of ceaseless interrogation and the inevitable negative. So much time spent by days in questioning managers, agents, schools and choruses; by night among the audiences of theatres from all-star casts down to music halls so low that he dreaded to find what he most hoped for. He who had loved her best had tried to find her. He was sure that since her disappearance from home this great, water-girt city held her somewhere, but it was like a monstrous quicksand, shifting its particles constantly, with no foundation, its upper granules of to-day buried to-morrow in ooze and slime.

The furnished room received its latest guest with a first glow of pseudo hospitality, a hectic, haggard, perfunctory welcome like the specious smile of a demirep. The sophistical comfort came in reflected gleams from the decayed furniture, the ragged brocade upholstery of a couch and two chairs, a foot-wide cheap pier glass between the two windows, from one or two gilt picture frames and a brass bedstead in a corner.

The guest reclined, inert, upon a chair, while the room, confused in speech as though it were an apartment in Babel, tried to discourse to him of its divers tenantry.

A polychromatic rug like some brilliant-flowered rectangular, tropical islet lay surrounded by a billowy sea of soiled matting. Upon the gay-papered wall were those pictures that pursue the homeless one from house to house – 'The Huguenot Lovers', 'The First Quarrel', 'The Wedding Breakfast', 'Psyche at the Fountain'. The mantel's chastely severe outline was ingloriously veiled behind some pert drapery drawn rakishly askew like the sashes of the Amazonian ballet. Upon it was some desolate flotsam cast aside by the room's marooned when a lucky sail had borne them to a fresh port – a trifling vase or two, pictures of actresses, a medicine bottle, some stray cards out of a deck.

One by one, as the characters of a cryptograph become explicit, the little signs left by the furnished room's procession of guests developed a significance. The threadbare space in the rug in front of the dresser told that lovely women had marched in the throng. The tiny fingerprints on the wall spoke of little prisoners trying to feel their way to sun and air. A splattered stain, raying like the shadow of a bursting bomb, witnessed where a hurled glass or bottle had splintered with its contents against the wall. Across the pier glass had been scrawled with a diamond in staggering letters the name 'Marie'. It seemed that the succession of dwellers in the furnished room had turned in fury – perhaps tempted beyond forebearance by its garish coldness – and wreaked upon it their passions. The furniture was chipped and bruised; the couch, distorted by bursting springs, seemed a horrible monster that had been slain during the stress of some grotesque convulsion. Some more potent upheaval had cloven a great slice from the marble mantel. Each plank in the floor owned its particular cant and shriek as from a separate and individual agony. It seemed incredible that all this malice and injury had been wrought upon the room by those who had called it for a time their home; and yet it may have been the cheated home instinct surviving blindly, the resentful rage at false household gods that had kindled their wrath. A hut that is our own we can sweep and adorn and cherish.

The young tenant in the chair allowed these thoughts to file, soft shod, through his mind, while there drifted into the room furnished sounds and furnished scents. He heard in one room a tittering and incontinent, slack laughter; in others the monologue of a scold, the rattling of dice, a lullaby, and one crying dully; above him a banjo tinkled with spirit. Doors banged somewhere; the elevated trains roared intermittently; a cat yowled miserably upon a back fence. And he breathed the breath of the house – a dank savour rather than a smell – a cold, musty effluvium as from underground vaults mingled with the reeking exhalations of linoleum and mildewed and rotten woodwork.

Then suddenly, as he rested there, the room was filled with the strong, sweet odour of mignonette. It came as upon a single buffet of wind with such sureness and fragrance and emphasis that it almost seemed a living visitant. And the man cried aloud: 'What, dear?' as if he had been called, and sprang up and faced about. The rich odour clung to him and wrapped him around. He reached out his arms for it, all his senses for the time confused and commingled. How could one be peremptorily called by an odour? Surely it must have been a sound. But, was it not the sound that had touched, that had caressed him?

'She has been in this room,' he cried, and he sprang to wrest from it a token, for he knew he would recognize the smallest thing that had belonged to her or that she had touched. This enveloping scent of mignonette, the odour that she had loved and made her own – whence came it?

The room had been but carelessly set in order. Scattered upon the flimsy dresser scarf were half a dozen hairpins – those discreet, indistinguishable friends of womankind, feminine of gender, infinite of mood and uncommunicative of tense. These he ignored, conscious of their triumphant lack of identity. Ransacking the drawers of the dresser he came upon a discarded, tiny, ragged handkerchief. He pressed it to his face. It was racy and insolent with heliotrope; he hurled it to the floor. In another drawer he found odd buttons, a theatre programme, a pawnbroker's card, two lost marshmallows, a book on the divination of dreams. In the last was a woman's black satin hair bow, which halted him, poised between ice and fire. But the black satin hair bow also is femininity's demure, impersonal common ornament and tells no tales.

And then he traversed the room like a hound on the scent, skimming the walls, considering the corners of the bulging matting on his hands and knees, rummaging mantel and tables, the curtains and hangings, the drunken cabinet in the corner, for a visible sign, unable to perceive that she was there beside, around, against, within, above him, clinging to him, wooing him, calling him so poignantly through the finer senses that even his grosser ones became cognizant of the call. Once again he answered loudly: 'Yes, dear!' and turned, wild-eyed, to gaze on vacancy, for he could not yet discern form and colour and love and outstretched arms in the odour of mignonette. Oh, God! whence that odour, and since when have odours had a voice to call? Thus he groped.

He burrowed in crevices and corners, and found corks and cigarettes. These he passed in passive contempt. But once he found in a fold of the matting a half-smoked cigar, and this he ground beneath his heel with a green and trenchant oath. He sifted the room from end to end. He found dreary and ignoble small records of many a peripatetic tenant; but of her whom he sought, and who may have lodged there, and whose spirit seemed to hover there, he found no trace.

And then he thought of the housekeeper.

He ran from the haunted room downstairs and to a door that showed a crack of light. She came out to his knock. He smothered his excitement as best he could.

'Will you tell me, madam,' he besought her, 'who occupied the room I have before I came?'

'Yes, sir. I can tell you again. 'Twas Sprowls and Mooney, as I said. Miss B'retta Sprowls it was in the theatres, but Missis Mooney she was. My house is well known for respectability. The marriage certificate hung, framed, on a nail over—'

'What kind of a lady was Miss Sprowls – in looks, I mean?'

'Why, black-haired, sir, short, and stout, with a comical face. They left a week ago Tuesday.'

'And before they occupied it?'

'Why, there was a single gentleman connected with the draying business. He left owing me a week. Before him was Missis Crowder and her two children, that stayed four months; and back of them was old Mr Doyle, whose sons paid for him. He kept the room six months. That goes back a year, sir, and further I do not remember.'

He thanked her and crept back to his room. The room was dead. The essence that had vivified it was gone. The perfume of mignonette had departed. In its place was the old, stale odour of mouldy house furniture, of atmosphere in storage.

The ebbing of his hope drained his faith. He sat staring at the yellow, singing gaslight. Soon he walked to the bed and began to tear the sheets into strips. With the blade of his knife he drove them tightly into every crevice around windows and door. When all was snug and taut he turned out the light, turned the gas full on again, and laid himself gratefully upon the bed.

It was Mrs McCool's night to go with the can for beer. So she fetched it and sat with Mrs Purdy in one of those subterranean retreats where housekeepers foregather and the worm dieth seldom.

THE FURNISHED ROOM

'I rented out my third-floor-back this evening,' said Mrs Purdy, across a fine circle of foam. 'A young man took it. He went up to bed two hours ago.'

'Now, did ye, Mrs Purdy, ma'am?' said Mrs McCool, with intense admiration. 'You do be a wonder for rentin' rooms of that kind. And did ye tell him, then?' she concluded in a husky whisper laden with mystery.

'Rooms,' said Mrs Purdy, in her furriest tones, 'are furnished for to rent. I did not tell him, Mrs McCool.'

' 'Tis right ye are, ma'am; 'tis by renting rooms we kape alive. Ye have the rale sense for business, ma'am. There be many people will rayjict the rentin' of a room if they be tould a suicide has been after dyin' in the bed of it.'

'As you say, we has our living to be making,' remarked Mrs Purdy.

'Yis, ma'am; 'tis true. 'Tis just one wake ago this day I helped ye lay out the third-floor-back. A pretty slip of a colleen she was to be killin' herself wid the gas – a swate little face she had, Mrs Purdy, ma'am.'

'She'd a-been called handsome, as you say,' said Mrs Purdy, assenting but critical, 'but for that mole she had a-growin' by her left eyebrow. Do fill up your glass again, Mrs McCool.'

W. W. Jacobs

The Monkey's Paw

I

Without, the night was cold and wet, but in the small parlour of Lakesnam Villa the blinds were drawn and the fire burned brightly. Father and son were at chess, the former, who possessed ideas about the game involving radical changes, putting his king into such sharp and unnecessary perils that it even provoked comment from the white-haired old lady knitting placidly by the fire.

'Hark at the wind,' said Mr White, who, having seen a fatal mistake after it was too late, was amiably desirous of preventing his son from seeing it.

'I'm listening,' said the latter, grimly surveying the board as he stretched out his hand. 'Check.'

'I should hardly think that he'd come to-night,' said his father, with his hand poised over the board.

'Mate,' replied the son.

'That's the worst of living so far out,' bawled Mr White, with sudden and unlooked-for violence; 'of all the beastly, slushy, out-of-the-way places to live in, this is the worst. Pathway's a bog, and the road's a torrent. I don't know what people are thinking about. I suppose because only two houses on the road are let, they think it doesn't matter.'

'Never mind, dear,' said his wife soothingly; 'perhaps you'll win the next one.'

Mr White looked up sharply, just in time to intercept a knowing glance between mother and son. The words died away on his lips, and he hid a guilty grin in his thin grey beard.

'There he is,' said Herbert White, as the gate banged-to loudly and heavy footsteps came towards the door.

The old man rose with hospitable haste, and opening the door, was heard condoling with the new arrival. The new arrival also condoled with himself, so that Mrs White said, 'Tut, tut!' and coughed gently as her husband entered the room, followed by a tall burly man, beady of eye and rubicund of visage.

'Sergeant-major Morris,' he said, introducing him.

The sergeant-major shook hands, and taking the proffered seat by the fire, watched contentedly while his host got out whisky and tumblers and stood a small copper kettle on the fire.

At the third glass his eyes got brighter, and he began to talk, the little family circle regarding with eager interest this visitor from distant parts, as he squared his broad shoulders in the chair and spoke of strange scenes and doughty deeds, of wars and plagues and strange peoples.

'Twenty-one years of it,' said Mr White, nodding at his wife and son. 'When he went away he was a slip of a youth in the warehouse. Now look at him.'

'He don't look to have taken much harm,' said Mrs White politely.

'I'd like to go to India myself,' said the old man, 'just to look round a bit, you know.'

'Better where you are,' said the sergeant-major, shaking his head. He put down the empty glass and, sighing softly, shook it again.

'I should like to see those old temples and fakirs and jugglers,' said the old man. 'What was that you started telling me the other day about a monkey's paw or something, Morris?'

'Nothing,' said the soldier hastily. 'Leastways, nothing worth hearing.'

'Monkey's paw?' said Mrs White curiously.

'Well, it's just a bit of what you might call magic, perhaps,' said the sergeant-major off-handedly.

His three listeners leaned forward eagerly. The visitor absent-mindedly put his empty glass to his lips and then set it down again. His host filled it for him.

'To look at,' said the sergeant-major, fumbling in his pocket, 'it's just an ordinary little paw, dried to a mummy.'

He took something out of his pocket and proffered it. Mrs White drew back with a grimace, but her son, taking it, examined it curiously.

'And what is there special about it?' inquired Mr White, as he took it from his son and, having examined it, placed it upon the table.

'It had a spell put on it by an old fakir,' said the sergeant-major, 'a very holy man. He wanted to show that fate ruled people's lives, and that those who interfered with it did so to their sorrow. He put a spell on it so that three separate men could have three wishes from it.'

His manner was so impressive that his hearers were conscious that their light laughter jarred somewhat.

'Well, why don't you have three, sir?' said Herbert White cleverly.

The soldier regarded him in the way that middle age is wont to regard presumptuous youth. 'I have,' he said quietly, and his blotchy face whitened.

'And did you really have the three wishes granted?' asked Mrs White.

'I did,' said the sergeant-major, and his glass tapped against his strong teeth.

'And has anybody else wished?' inquired the old lady.

'The first man had his three wishes, yes,' was the reply. 'I don't know what the first two were, but the third was for death. That's how I got the paw.'

His tones were so grave that a hush fell upon the group.

'If you've had your three wishes, it's no good to you now, then, Morris,' said the old man at last. 'What do you keep it for?'

The soldier shook his head. 'Fancy, I suppose,' he said slowly. 'I did have some idea of selling it, but I don't think I will. It has caused enough mischief already. Besides, people won't buy. They think it's a fairy tale, some of them, and those who do think anything of it want to try it first and pay me afterwards.'

'If you could have another three wishes,' said the old man, eyeing him keenly, 'would you have them?'

'I don't know,' said the other. 'I don't know.'

He took the paw, and dangling it between his front finger and thumb, suddenly threw it upon the fire. White, with a slight cry, stooped down and snatched it off.

'Better let it burn,' said the soldier solemnly.

'If you don't want it, Morris,' said the old man, 'give it to me.'

'I won't,' said his friend doggedly. 'I threw it on the fire. If you keep it, don't blame me for what happens. Pitch it on the fire again, like a sensible man.'

The other shook his head and examined his new possession closely. 'How do you do it?' he inquired.

'Hold it up in your right hand and wish aloud,' said the sergeant-major, 'but I warn you of the consequences.'

'Sounds like the *Arabian Nights*,' said Mrs White, as she rose and began to set the supper. 'Don't you think you might wish for four pairs of hands for me?'

Her husband drew the talisman from his pocket and then all three burst into laughter as the sergeant-major, with a look of alarm on his face, caught him by the arm.

'If you must wish,' he said gruffly, 'wish for something sensible.'

Mr White dropped it back into his pocket, and placing chairs, motioned his friend to the table. In the business of supper the talisman was partly forgotten, and afterwards the three sat listening in an enthralled fashion to a second instalment of the soldier's adventures in India.

'If the tale about the monkey's paw is not more truthful than those he has been telling us,' said Herbert, as the door closed behind their guest, just in time for him to catch the last train, 'we shan't make much out of it.'

'Did you give him anything for it, Father?' inquired Mrs White, regarding her husband closely.

'A trifle,' said he, colouring slightly. 'He didn't want it, but I made him take it. And he pressed me again to throw it away.'

'Likely,' said Herbert, with pretended horror. 'Why, we're going to be rich, and famous, and happy. Wish to be an emperor, father, to begin with; then you can't be henpecked.'

He darted round the table, pursued by the maligned Mrs White armed with an antimacassar.

Mr White took the paw from his pocket and eyed it dubiously. 'I don't know what to wish for, and that's a fact,' he said slowly. 'It seems to me I've got all I want.'

'If you only cleared the house, you'd be quite happy, wouldn't you?' said Herbert, with his hand on his shoulder. 'Well, wish for two hundred pounds, then; that'll just do it.'

His father, smiling shamefacedly at his own credulity, held up the talisman, as his son, with a solemn face somewhat marred by a wink at his mother, sat down at the piano and struck a few impressive chords.

'I wish for two hundred pounds,' said the old man distinctly.

A fine crash from the piano greeted the words, interrupted by a shuddering cry from the old man. His wife and son ran towards him.

'It moved,' he cried, with a glance of disgust at the object as it lay on the floor. 'As I wished it twisted in my hands like a snake.'

'Well, I don't see the money,' said his son, as he picked it up and placed it on the table, 'and I bet I never shall.'

'It must have been your fancy, Father,' said his wife, regarding him anxiously.

He shook his head. 'Never mind, though; there's no harm done, but it gave me a shock all the same.'

They sat down by the fire again while the two men finished their pipes. Outside, the wind was higher than ever, and the old man started nervously at the sound of a door banging upstairs. A silence unusual and depressing settled upon all three, which lasted until the old couple rose to retire for the night.

'I expect you'll find the cash tied up in a big bag in the middle of your bed,' said Herbert, as he bade them good-night, 'and something horrible squatting up on top of the wardrobe watching you as you pocket your ill-gotten gains.'

II

In the brightness of the wintry sun next morning as it streamed over the breakfast table, Herbert laughed at his fears. There was an air of prosaic wholesomeness about the room which it had lacked on the previous night, and the dirty, shrivelled little paw was pitched on the sideboard with a carelessness which betokened no great belief in its virtues.

'I suppose all old soldiers are the same,' said Mrs White. 'The idea of our listening to such nonsense! How could wishes be granted in these days? And if they could, how could two hundred pounds hurt you, Father?'

'Might drop on his head from the sky,' said the frivolous Herbert.

'Morris said the things happened so naturally,' said his father, 'that you might, if you so wished, attribute it to coincidence.'

'Well, don't break into the money before I come back,' said Herbert, as he rose from the table. 'I'm afraid it'll turn you into a mean, avaricious man, and we shall have to disown you.'

His mother laughed, and following him to the door, watched him down the road, and returning to the breakfast table, was very happy at the expense of her husband's credulity. All of which did not prevent her from scurrying to the door at the postman's knock, nor prevent her from referring somewhat shortly to retired segeant-majors of bibulous habits when she found that the post brought a tailor's bill.

'Herbert will have some more of his funny remarks, I expect, when he comes home,' she said, as they sat at dinner.

'I dare say,' said Mr White, pouring himself out some beer; 'but for all that, the thing moved in my hand; that I'll swear to.'

'You thought it did,' said the old lady soothingly.

'I say it did,' replied the other. 'There was no thought about it; I had just — What's the matter?'

His wife made no reply. She was watching the mysterious movements of a man outside, who, peering in an undecided fashion at the house, appeared to be trying to make up his mind to enter. In mental connection with the two hundred pounds, she noticed that the stranger was well-dressed and wore a silk hat of glossy newness. Three times he paused at the gate, and then walked on again. The fourth time he stood with his hand upon it, and then with sudden resolution flung it open and walked up the path. Mrs White at the same moment placed her hands behind her, and hurriedly unfastening the strings of her apron, put that useful article of apparel beneath the cushion of her chair.

She brought the stranger, who seemed ill at ease, into the room. He gazed furtively at Mrs White, and listened in a preoccupied fashion as the old lady apologized for the appearance of the room, and her husband's coat, a garment which he usually reserved for the garden. She then waited as patiently as her sex would permit for him to broach his business, but he was at first strangely silent.

'I – was asked to call,' he said at last, and stooped and picked a piece of cotton from his trousers. 'I come from Maw and Meggins.'

The old lady started. 'Is anything the matter?' she asked breathlessly. 'Has anything happened to Herbert? What is it? What is it?'

Her husband interposed. 'There, there, mother,' he said hastily. 'Sit down, and don't jump to conclusions. You've not brought bad news, I'm sure, sir,' and he eyed the other wistfully.

'I'm sorry—' began the visitor.

'Is he hurt?' demanded the mother.

The visitor bowed in assent. 'Badly hurt,' he said quietly, 'but he is not in any pain.'

'Oh, thank God!' said the old woman, clasping her hands. 'Thank God for that! Thank—'

She broke off suddenly as the sinister meaning of the assurance dawned upon her and she saw the awful confirmation of her fears in the other's averted face. She caught her breath, and turning to her slower-witted husband, laid her trembling old hand upon his. There was a long silence.

'He was caught in the machinery,' said the visitor at length, in a low voice.

'Caught in the machinery,' repeated Mr White, in a dazed fashion, 'yes.'

He sat staring blankly out at the window, and taking his wife's hand between his own, pressed it as he had been wont to do in their old courting days nearly forty years before.

'He was the only one left us,' he said, turning gently to the visitor. 'It is hard.'

The other coughed, and rising, walked slowly to the window. 'The firm wished me to convey their sincere sympathy with you in your great loss,' he said, without looking round. 'I beg that you will understand I am only their servant and merely obeying orders.'

There was no reply; the old woman's face was white, her eyes staring, and her breath inaudible; on the husband's face was a look such as his friend the sergeant might have carried into his first action.

'I was to say that Maw and Meggins disclaim all responsibility,' continued the other. 'They admit no liability at all, but in consideration of your son's services they wish to present you with a certain sum as compensation.'

Mr White dropped his wife's hand, and rising to his feet, gazed with a look of horror at his visitor. His dry lips shaped the words, 'How much?'

'Two hundred pounds,' was the answer.

Unconscious of his wife's shriek, the old man smiled faintly, put out his hands like a sightless man, and dropped, a senseless heap, to the floor.

III

In the huge new cemetery, some two miles distant, the old people buried their dead, and came back to a house steeped in shadow and silence. It was all over so quickly that at first they could hardly realize it, and remained in a state of expectation as though of something else to happen – something else which was to lighten this load, too heavy for old hearts to bear. But the days passed, and expectation gave place to resignation – the hopeless resignation of the old, sometimes miscalled apathy. Sometimes they hardly exchanged a word, for now they had nothing to talk about, and their days were long to weariness.

It was about a week after that that the old man, waking suddenly in the night, stretched out his hand and found himself alone. The room was in darkness, and the sound of subdued weeping came from the window. He raised himself in bed and listened.

'Come back,' he said tenderly. 'You will be cold.'

'It is colder for my son,' said the old woman, and wept afresh.

The sound of her sobs died away on his ears. The bed was warm, and his eyes heavy with sleep. He dozed fitfully, and then slept until a sudden wild cry from his wife awoke him with a start.

'The monkey's paw!' she cried wildly. 'The monkey's paw!'

He started up in alarm. 'Where? Where is it? What's the matter?'

She came stumbling across the room towards him. 'I want it,' she said quietly. 'You've not destroyed it?'

'It's in the parlour, on the bracket,' he replied, marvelling. 'Why?'

She cried and laughed together, and bending over, kissed his cheek.

'I only just thought of it,' she said hysterically. 'Why didn't I think of it before? Why didn't you think of it?'

'Think of what?' he questioned.

'The other two wishes,' she replied rapidly. 'We've only had one.'

'Was not that enough?' he demanded fiercely.

'No,' she cried triumphantly; 'we'll have one more. Go down and get it quickly, and wish our boy alive again.'

THE MONKEY'S PAW

The man sat up in bed and flung the bedclothes from his quaking limbs. 'Good God, you are mad!' he cried, aghast.

'Get it,' she panted; 'get it quickly, and wish – Oh, my boy, my boy!'

Her husband struck a match and lit the candle. 'Get back to bed,' he said unsteadily. 'You don't know what you are saying.'

'We had the first wish granted,' said the old woman feverishly; 'why not the second?'

'A coincidence,' stammered the old man.

'Go and get it and wish,' cried the old woman, and dragged him towards the door.

He went down in the darkness, and felt his way to the parlour, and then to the mantelpiece. The talisman was in its place, and a horrible fear that the unspoken wish might bring his mutilated son before him ere he could escape from the room seized upon him, and he caught his breath as he found that he had lost the direction of the door. His brow cold with sweat, he felt his way round the table, and groped along the wall until he found himself in the small passage with the unwholesome thing in his hand.

Even his wife's face seemed changed as he entered the room. It was white and expectant, and to his fears seemed to have an unusual look upon it. He was afraid of her.

'Wish!' she cried, in a strong voice.

'It is foolish and wicked,' he faltered.

'Wish!' repeated his wife.

He raised his hand. 'I wish my son alive again.'

The talisman fell to the floor, and he regarded it shudderingly. Then he sank trembling into a chair as the old woman, with burning eyes, walked to the window, and raised the blind.

He sat until he was chilled with the cold, glancing occasionally at the figure of the old woman peering through the window. The candle end, which had burnt below the rim of the china candlestick, was throwing pulsating shadows on the ceiling and walls, until, with a flicker larger than the rest, it expired. The old man, with an unspeakable sense of relief at the failure of the talisman, crept back to his bed, and a minute or two afterwards the old woman came silently and apathetically beside him.

Neither spoke, but both lay silently listening to the ticking of the clock. A stair creaked, and a squeaky mouse scurried noisily through the wall. The darkness was oppressive, and after lying for some time screwing up his courage, the husband took the box of matches, and striking one, went downstairs for a candle.

At the foot of the stairs the match went out, and he paused to strike another, and at the same moment a knock, so quiet and stealthy as to be scarcely audible, sounded on the front door.

The matches fell from his hand. He stood motionless, his breath suspended until the knock was repeated. Then he turned and fled swiftly back to his room, and closed the door behind him. A third knock sounded through the house.

'What's that?' cried the old woman, starting up.

'A rat,' said the old man, in shaking tones – 'a rat. It passed me on the stairs.'

His wife sat up in bed, listening. A loud knock resounded through the house.

'It's Herbert!' she screamed. 'It's Herbert!'

She ran to the door, but her husband was before her, and catching her by the arm, held her tightly.

'What are you going to do?' he whispered hoarsely.

'It's my boy; it's Herbert!' she cried, struggling mechanically. 'I forgot it was two miles away. What are you holding me for? Let go. I must open the door.'

'For God's sake don't let it in,' cried the old man, trembling.

'You're afraid of your own son,' she cried struggling. 'Let me go. I'm coming, Herbert; I'm coming.'

There was another knock, and another. The old woman with a sudden wrench broke free and ran from the room. Her husband followed to the landing, and called after her appealingly as she hurried downstairs. He heard the chain rattle back and the bottom bolt drawn slowly and stiffly from the socket. Then the old woman's voice strained and panting.

'The bolt,' she cried loudly. 'Come down. I can't reach it.'

But her husband was on his hands and knees groping wildly on the floor in search of the paw. If he could only find it before the thing outside got in. A perfect fusillade of knocks reverberated through the house, and he heard the scraping of a chair as his wife put it down in the passage against the door. He heard the creaking of the bolt as it came slowly back, and at the same moment, he found the monkey's paw, and frantically breathed his third and last wish.

The knocking ceased suddenly, although the echoes of it were still in the house. He heard the chair drawn back and the door opened. A cold wind rushed up the staircase, and a long loud wail of disappointment and misery from his wife gave him courage to run down to her side, and then to the gate beyond. The street lamp flickering opposite shone on a quiet and deserted road.

Arthur Machen

The Great God Pan

1. *The Experiment*

'I am glad you came, Clarke; very glad indeed. I was not sure you could
spare the time.'

'I was able to make arrangements for a few days; things are not very
lively just now. But have you no misgivings, Raymond? Is it absolutely
safe?'

The two men were slowly pacing the terrace in front of Dr Raymond's
house. The sun still hung above the western mountain line, but it shone
with a dull red glow that cast no shadows, and all the air was quiet; a
sweet breath came from the great wood on the hillside above, and with
it, at intervals, the soft murmuring call of the wild doves. Below, in the
long lovely valley, the river wound in and out between the lonely hills,
and, as the sun hovered and vanished into the west, a faint mist, pure
white, began to rise from the banks. Dr Raymond turned sharply to his
friend.

'Safe? Of course it is. In itself the operation is a perfectly simple one;
any surgeon could do it.'

'And there is no danger at any other stage?'

'None; absolutely no physical danger whatever, I give you my word.
You are always timid, Clarke, always; but you know my history. I have
devoted myself to transcendental medicine for the last twenty years. I
have heard myself called quack and charlatan and impostor, but all the
while I knew I was on the right path. Five years ago I reached the goal,
and since then every day has been a preparation for what we shall do
to-night.'

'I should like to believe it is all true.' Clarke knit his brows, and looked doubtfully at Dr Raymond. 'Are you perfectly sure, Raymond, that your theory is not a phantasmagoria – a splendid vision, certainly, but a mere vision after all?'

Dr Raymond stopped in his walk and turned sharply. He was a middle-aged man, gaunt and thin, of a pale yellow complexion, but as he answered Clarke and faced him, there was a flush on his cheek.

'Look about you, Clarke. You see the mountain, and hill following after hill, as wave on wave, you see the woods and orchards, the fields of ripe corn, and the meadows reaching to the reed beds by the river. You see me standing here beside you, and hear my voice; but I tell you that all these things – yes, from that star that has just shone out in the sky to the solid ground beneath our feet – I say that all these are but dreams and shadows: the shadows that hide the real world from our eyes. There *is* a real world, but it is beyond this glamour and this vision, beyond these "chases in Arras, dreams in a career," beyond them all as beyond a veil. I do not know whether any human being has ever lifted that veil; but I do know, Clarke, that you and I shall see it lifted this very night from before another's eyes. You may think all this strange nonsense; it may be strange, but it is true, and the ancients knew what lifting the veil means. They called it seeing the god Pan.'

Clarke shivered; the white mist gathering over the river was chilly.

'It is wonderful indeed,' he said. 'We are standing on the brink of a strange world, Raymond, if what you say is true. I suppose the knife is absolutely necessary?'

'Yes; a slight lesion in the grey matter, that is all; a trifling rearrangement of certain cells, a microscopical alteration that would escape the attention of ninety-nine brain specialists out of a hundred. I don't want to bother you with "shop", Clarke; I might give you a mass of technical detail which would sound very imposing, and would leave you as enlightened as you are now. But I suppose you have read, casually, in out-of-the-way corners of your paper, that immense strides have been made recently in the physiology of the brain. I saw a paragraph the other day about Digby's theory, and Browne Faber's discoveries. Theories and discoveries! Where they are standing now, I stood fifteen years ago, and I need not tell you that I have not been standing still for the last fifteen years. It will be enough if I say that five years ago I made the discovery to which I alluded when I said that then I reached the goal. After years of labour, after years of toiling and groping in the dark, after days and nights of disappointment and sometimes of despair, in which I used now and then to tremble and grow cold with the thought that perhaps there were others seeking for what I sought, at last, after so long, a pang of sudden joy thrilled my soul, and I knew the long journey was at an end.

By what seemed then and still seems a chance, the suggestion of a moment's idle thought followed up upon familiar lines and paths that I had tracked a hundred times already, the great truth burst upon me, and I saw, mapped out in lines of light, a whole world, a sphere unknown; continents and islands, and great oceans in which no ship has sailed (to my belief) since Man first lifted up his eyes and beheld the sun, and the stars of heaven, and the quiet earth beneath. You will think all this high-flown language, Clarke, but it is hard to be literal. And yet; I do not know whether what I am hinting at cannot be set forth in plain and homely terms. For instance, this world of ours is pretty well girded now with the telegraph wires and cables; thought, with something less than the speed of thought, flashes from sunrise to sunset, from north to south, across the floods and the desert places. Suppose that an electrician of to-day were suddenly to perceive that he and his friends have merely been playing with pebbles and mistaking them for the foundations of the world; suppose that such a man saw uttermost space lie open before the current, and words of men flash forth to the sun and beyond the sun into the systems beyond, and the voices of articulate-speaking men echo in the waste void that bounds our thought. As analogies go, that is a pretty good analogy of what I have done; you can understand now a little of what I felt as I stood here one evening; it was a summer evening, and the valley looked much as it does now; I stood here, and saw before me the unutterable, the unthinkable gulf that yawns profound between two worlds, the world of matter and the world of spirit; I saw the great empty deep stretch dim before me, and in that instant a bridge of light leapt from the earth to the unknown shore, and the abyss was spanned. You may look in Browne Faber's book, if you like, and you will find that to the present day men of science are unable to account for the presence, or to specify the functions of a certain group of nerve-cells in the brain. That group is, as it were, land to let, a mere waste place for fanciful theories. I am not in the position of Browne Faber and the specialists, I am perfectly instructed as to the possible functions of those nerve-centres in the scheme of things. With a touch I can bring them into play, with a touch, I say, I can set free the current, with a touch I can complete the communication between this world of sense and – we shall be able to finish the sentence later on. Yes, the knife is necessary; but think what that knife will effect. It will level utterly the solid wall of sense, and probably, for the first time since man was made, a spirit will gaze on a spirit world. Clarke, Mary will see the god Pan!'

'But you remember what you wrote to me? I thought it would be requisite that she—'

He whispered the rest into the doctor's ear.

'Not at all, not at all. That is nonsense, I assure you. Indeed, it is better as it is; I am quite certain of that.'

'Consider the matter well, Raymond. It's a great responsibility. Something might go wrong; you would be a miserable man for the rest of your days.'

'No, I think not, even if the worst happened. As you know, I rescued Mary from the gutter, and from almost certain starvation, when she was a child; I think her life is mine, to use as I see fit. Come, it is getting late; we had better go in.'

Dr Raymond led the way into the house, through the hall, and down a long dark passage. He took a key from his pocket and opened a heavy door, and motioned Clare into his laboratory. It had once been a billiard-room, and was lighted by a glass dome in the centre of the ceiling, whence there still shone a sad grey light on the figure of the doctor as he lit a lamp with a heavy shade and placed it on a table in the middle of the room.

Clarke looked about him. Scarcely a foot of wall remained bare; there were shelves all around laden with bottles and phials of all shapes and colours, and at one end stood a little Chippendale bookcase. Raymond pointed to this.

'You see that parchment Oswald Crollius? He was one of the first to show me the way, though I don't think he ever found it himself. That is a strange saying of his: "In every grain of wheat there lies hidden the soul of a star." '

There was not much of furniture in the laboratory. The table in the centre, a stone slab with a drain in one corner, the two arm-chairs on which Raymond and Clarke were sitting; that was all, except an odd-looking chair at the furthest end of the room. Clarke looked at it, and raised his eyebrows.

'Yes, that is the chair,' said Raymond. 'We may as well place it in position.' He got up and wheeled the chair to the light, and began raising and lowering it, letting down the seat, setting the back at various angles, and adjusting the foot-rest. It looked comfortable enough, and Clarke passed his hand over the soft green velvet, as the doctor manipulated the levers.

'Now, Clarke, make yourself quite comfortable. I have a couple of hours' work before me; I was obliged to leave certain matters to the last.'

Raymond went to the stone slab, and Clarke watched him drearily as he bent over a row of phials and lit the flame under the crucible. The doctor had a small hand-lamp, shaded as the larger one, on a ledge above his apparatus, and Clarke, who sat in the shadows, looked down the great dreary room, wondering at the bizarre effects of brilliant light and undefined darkness contrasting with one another. Soon he became conscious of an odd odour, at first the merest suggestion of odour, in the

room; and as it grew more decided he felt surprised that he was not reminded of the chemist's shop or the surgery. Clarke found himself idly
endeavouring to analyse the sensation, and, half conscious, he began to
think of a day, fifteen years ago, that he had spent in roaming through
the woods and meadows near his old home. It was a burning day at the
beginning of August, the heat had dimmed the outlines of all things and
all distances with a faint mist, and people who observed the ther-
mometer spoke of an abnormal register, of a temperature that was
almost tropical. Strangely that wonderful hot day of the 'fifties rose up in
Clarke's imagination; the sense of dazzling all-pervading sunlight seemed
to blot out the shadows and the lights of the laboratory, and he felt again
the heated air beating in gusts about his face, saw the shimmer rising
from the turf, and heard the myriad murmur of the summer.

'I hope the smell doesn't annoy you, Clarke; there's nothing unwholesome about it. It may make you a bit sleepy, that's all.'

Clarke heard the words quite distinctly, and knew that Raymond was
speaking to him, but for the life of him he could not rouse himself from
his lethargy. He could only think of the lonely walk he had taken fifteen
years ago; it was his last look at the fields and woods he had known
since he was a child, and now it all stood out in brilliant light, as a
picture, before him. Above all there came to his nostrils the scent of
summer, the smell of flowers mingled, and the odour of the woods, of
cool shaded places, deep in the green depths, drawn forth by the sun's
heat; and the scent of the good earth, lying as it were with arms stretched
forth, and smiling lips, overpowered all. His fancies made him wander,
as he had wandered long ago, from the fields into the wood, tracking a
little path between the shining undergrowth of beech-trees; and the
trickle of water dropping from the limestone rock sounded as a clear
melody in the dream. Thoughts began to go astray and to mingle with
other recollections; the beech alley was transformed to a path beneath
ilex-trees, and here and there a vine climbed from bough to bough, and
sent up waving tendrils and drooped with purple grapes, and the sparse
grey-green leaves of a wild olive-tree stood out against the dark shadows
of the ilex. Clarke, in the deep folds of dream, was conscious that the
path from his father's house had led him into an undiscovered country,
and he was wondering at the strangeness of it all, when suddenly, in
place of the hum and murmur of the summer, an infinite silence seemed
to fall on all things, and the wood was hushed, and for a moment of time
he stood face to face there with a presence, that was neither man nor
beast, neither the living nor the dead, but all things mingled, the form of
all things but devoid of all form. And in that moment, the sacrament of
body and soul was dissolved, and a voice seemed to cry 'Let us go hence,'

and then the darkness of darkness beyond the stars, the darkness of ever-lasting.

When Clarke woke up with a start he saw Raymond pouring a few drops of some oily fluid into a green phial, which he stoppered tightly.

'You have been dozing,' he said: 'the journey must have tired you out. It is done now. I am going to fetch Mary; I shall be back in ten minutes.'

Clarke lay back in his chair and wondered. It seemed as if he had but passed from one dream into another. He half expected to see the walls of the laboratory melt and disappear, and to awake in London, shudder-ing at his own sleeping fancies. But at last the door opened, and the doctor returned, and behind him came a girl of about seventeen, dressed all in white. She was so beautiful that Clarke did not wonder at what the doctor had written to him. She was blushing now over face and neck and arms, but Raymond seemed unmoved.

'Mary,' he said, 'the time has come. You are quite free. Are you willing to trust yourself to me entirely?'

'Yes, dear.'

'You hear that, Clarke? You are my witness. Here is the chair, Mary. It is quite easy. Just sit in it and lean back. Are you ready?'

'Yes, dear, quite ready. Give me a kiss before you begin.'

The doctor stooped and kissed her mouth, kindly enough. 'Now shut your eyes,' he said. The girl closed her eyelids, as if she were tired, and longed for sleep, and Raymond held the green phial to her nostrils. Her face grew white, whiter than her dress; she struggled faintly, and then with the feeling of submission strong within her, crossed her arms upon her breast as a little child about to say her prayers. The bright light of the lamp beat full upon her, and Clarke watched changes fleeting over that face as the changes of the hills when the summer clouds float across the sun. And then she lay all white and still, and the doctor turned up one of her eyelids. She was quite unconscious. Raymond pressed hard on one of the levers and the chair instantly sank back. Clarke saw him cutting away a circle, like a tonsure, from her hair, and the lamp was moved nearer. Raymond took a small glittering instrument from a little case, and Clarke turned away shuddering. When he looked again the doctor was binding up the wound he had made.

'She will awake in five minutes.' Raymond was still perfectly cool. 'There is nothing more to be done; we can only wait.'

The minutes passed slowly; they could hear a slow, heavy ticking. There was an old clock in the passage. Clarke felt sick and faint; his knees shook beneath him, he could hardly stand.

Suddenly, as they watched, they heard a long-drawn sigh, and sud-denly did the colour that had vanished return to the girl's cheeks, and suddenly her eyes opened. Clarke quailed before them. They shone with an awful light, looking far away, and a great wonder fell upon her face, and her hands stretched out as if to touch what was invisible; but in an instant the wonder faded, and gave place to the most awful terror. The muscles of her face were hideously convulsed, she shook from head to foot; the soul seemed struggling and shuddering within the house of flesh. It was a horrible sight, and Clarke rushed forward, as she fell shrieking to the floor.

Three days later Raymond took Clarke to Mary's bedside. She was lying wide-awake, rolling her head from side to side, and grinning vacantly.

'Yes,' said the doctor, still quite cool, 'it is a great pity; she is a hopeless idiot. However, it could not be helped; and, after all, she has seen the Great God Pan.'

2. *Mr Clarke's Memoirs*

Mr Clarke, the gentleman chosen by Dr Raymond to witness the strange experiment of the god Pan, was a person in whose character caution and curiosity were oddly mingled; in his sober moments he thought of the unusual and the eccentric with undisguised aversion, and yet, deep in his heart, there was a wide-eyed inquisitiveness with respect to all the more recondite and esoteric elements in the nature of men. The latter tendency had prevailed when he accepted Raymond's invitation, for though his considered judgment had always repudiated the doctor's theories as the wildest nonsense, yet he secretly hugged a belief in fantasy, and would have rejoiced to see that belief confirmed. The horrors that he witnessed in the dreary laboratory were to a certain extent salutary; he was conscious of being involved in an affair not altogether reputable, and for many years afterwards he clung bravely to the commonplace, and rejected all occasions of occult investigation. Indeed, on some homœopathic principle, he for some time attended the séances of distinguished mediums, hoping that the clumsy tricks of these gentlemen would make him altogether disgusted with mysticism of every kind, but the remedy, though caustic, was not efficacious. Clarke knew that he still pined for the unseen, and little by little, the old passion began to reassert itself, as the face of Mary, shuddering and convulsed with an unknowable terror, faded slowly from his memory. Occupied all day in pursuits both serious and lucrative, the temptation to relax in the evening was too great, especially in the winter months, when the fire cast a warm glow over his snug bachelor apartment, and a bottle of some choice claret stood ready by his elbow. His dinner digested, he would make a brief pretence of reading the evening paper, but the mere catalogue of news soon palled upon him, and Clarke would find himself casting glances of warm desire in the direction of an old Japanese bureau, which stood at a pleasant distance from the hearth. Like a boy before a jam-closet, for a few minutes he would hover indecisive, but lust always prevailed, and Clarke ended by drawing up his chair, lighting a candle, and sitting down before the bureau. Its pigeon-holes and drawers teemed with documents on the most morbid subjects, and in the well reposed a large manuscript volume, in which he had painfully entered the gems of his collection. Clarke had a fine contempt for published literature; the most ghostly story ceased to interest him if it happened to be printed; his sole pleasure was in the reading, compiling, and rearranging what he called his 'Memoirs to Prove the Existence of the Devil,' and engaged in this pursuit the evening seemed to fly and the night appeared too short.

On one particular evening, an ugly December night, black with fog, and raw with frost, Clarke hurried over his dinner, and scarcely deigned to observe his customary ritual of taking up the paper and laying it down again. He paced two or three times up and down the room, and opened the bureau, stood still a moment, and sat down. He leant back, absorbed in one of those dreams to which he was subject, and at length drew out his book, and opened it at the last entry. There were three or four pages densely covered with Clarke's round, set penmanship, and at the beginning he had written in a somewhat larger hand:

Singular Narrative told me by my Friend, Dr Phillips. He assures me that all the facts related therein are strictly and wholly True, but refuses to give either the Surnames of the Persons concerned, or the Place where these Extraordinary Events occurred.

Mr Clarke began to read over the account for the tenth time, glancing now and then at the pencil notes he had made when it was told him by his friend. It was one of his humours to pride himself on a certain literary ability; he thought well of his style, and took pains in arranging the circumstances in dramatic order. He read the following story:—

The persons concerned in this statement are Helen V., who, if she is still alive, must now be a woman of twenty-three, Rachel M., since deceased, who was a year younger than the above, and Trevor W., an imbecile, aged eighteen. These persons were at the period of the story inhabitants of a village on the borders of Wales, a place of some importance in the time of the Roman occupation, but now a scattered hamlet, of not more than five thousand souls. It is situated on rising ground, about six miles from the sea, and is sheltered by a large and picturesque forest.

THE GREAT GOD PAN

Some eleven years ago, Helen V. came to the village under rather peculiar circumstances. It is understood that she, being an orphan, was adopted in her infancy by a distant relative, who brought her up in his own house till she was twelve years old. Thinking, however, that it would be better for the child to have playmates of her own age, he advertised in several local papers for a good home in a comfortable farmhouse for a girl of twelve, and this advertisement was answered by Mr R., a well-to-do farmer in the above-mentioned village. His references proving satisfactory, the gentleman sent his adopted daughter to Mr. R., with a letter, in which he stipulated that the girl should have a room to herself, and stated that her guardians need be at no trouble in the matter of education, as she was already sufficiently educated for the position in life which she would occupy. In fact, Mr R. was given to understand that the girl was to be allowed to find her own occupations, and to spend her time almost as she liked. Mr R. duly met her at the nearest station, a town some seven miles away from his house, and seems to have remarked nothing extraordinary about the child, except that she was reticent as to her former life and her adopted father. She was, however, of a very difficult type from the inhabitants of the village; her skin was a pale, clear olive, and her features were strongly marked, and of a somewhat foreign character. She appears to have settled down easily enough into farmhouse life, and became a favourite with the children, who sometimes went with her on her rambles in the forest, for this was her amusement. Mr R. states that he has known her to go out by herself directly after their early breakfast, and not return till after dusk, and that, feeling uneasy at a young girl being out alone for so many hours, he communicated with her adopted father, who replied in a brief note that Helen must do as she chose. In the winter, when the forest paths are impassable, she spent most of her time in her bedroom, where she slept alone, according to the instructions of her relative. It was on one of these expeditions to the forest that the first of the singular incidents with which this girl is connected occurred, the date being about a year after her arrival at the village. The preceding winter had been remarkably severe, the snow drifting to a great depth, and the frost continuing for an unexampled period, and the summer following was as noteworthy for its extreme heat. On one of the very hottest days in this summer, Helen V. left the farmhouse for one of her long rambles in the forest, taking with her, as usual, some bread and meat for lunch. She was seen by some men in the fields making for the old Roman Road, a green causeway which traverses the highest part of the wood, and they were astonished to observe that the girl had taken off her hat, though the heat of the sun was already almost tropical. As it happened, a labourer, Joseph W. by name, was working in the forest near the Roman Road, and at twelve o'clock his little son, Trevor, brought the man his dinner of bread and cheese. After the meal, the boy, who was about seven years old at the time, left his father at work, and, as he said, went to look for flowers in the wood, and the man, who could hear him shouting with delight over his discoveries, felt no uneasiness. Suddenly, however, he was horrified at hearing the most dreadful screams, evidently the result of great terror, proceeding from the direction in which his son had gone, and he hastily threw down his tools and ran to see what had happened. Tracing his path by the sound, he met the little boy, who was running headlong, and was evidently terribly frightened, and on questioning him the man at last elicited that after picking a posy of flowers he felt tired, and lay down on the grass and fell asleep. He was suddenly awakened, as he stated, by a peculiar noise, a sort of singing he called it, and on peeping through the branches he saw Helen V. playing on the grass with a 'strange naked man,' whom he seemed unable to describe more fully. He said he felt dreadfully frightened, and ran away crying for his father. Joseph W. proceeded in the direction indicated by his son, and found Helen V. sitting on the grass in the middle of a glade or open space left by charcoal burners. He angrily charged her with frightening his little boy, but she entirely denied the accusation and laughed at the child's story of a 'strange man,' to which he himself did not attach much credence. Joseph W. came to the conclusion that the boy had woke up with a sudden fright, as children sometimes do, but Trevor persisted in his story, and continued in such evident distress that at last his father took him home, hoping that his mother would be able to soothe him. For many weeks, however, the boy gave his parents much anxiety; he became nervous and strange in his manner, refusing to leave the cottage by himself, and constantly alarming the household by waking in the night with cries of 'The man in the wood! Father! Father!'

In course of time, however, the impression seemed to have worn off, and about three months later he accompanied his father to the house of a gentleman in the neighbourhood, for whom Joseph W. occasionally did work. The man was shown into the study, and the little boy was left sitting in the hall, and a few minutes later, while the gentleman was giving W. his instructions, they were both horrified by a piercing shriek and the sound of a fall, and rushing out they found the child lying senseless on the floor, his face contorted with terror. The doctor was immediately summoned, and after some examination he pronounced the child to be suffering from a kind of fit, apparently produced by a sudden shock. The boy was taken to one of the bedrooms, and after some time recovered consciousness, but only to pass into a condition described by the medical man as one of violent hysteria. The doctor exhibited a strong sedative, and in the course of two hours pronounced him fit to walk home, but in passing through the hall the paroxysms of fright returned and with additional violence. The father perceived that the child was pointing at some object and heard the old cry, 'The man in the wood,' and looking in the direction indicated saw a stone head of grotesque appearance, which had been built into the wall above one of the doors. It seems that the owner of the house had recently made alterations in his premises, and on digging the foundation for some offices, the men had found a curious head, evidently of the Roman period, which had been placed in the hall in the manner described. The head is pronounced by the most experienced archæologists of the district to be that of a faun or satyr.[1]

From whatever cause arising, this second shock seemed too severe for the boy Trevor, and at the present date he suffers from a weakness of intellect, which gives but little promise of amending. The matter caused a good deal of sensation at the time, and the girl Helen was closely questioned by Mr R., but to no purpose, she steadfastly denying that she had frightened or in any way molested Trevor.

The second event with which this girl's name is connected took place about six years ago, and is of a still more extraordinary character.

At the beginning of the summer of 1882 Helen contracted a friendship of a peculiarly intimate character with Rachel M., the daughter of a prosperous farmer in the neighbourhood. This girl, who was a year younger than Helen, was considered by most people to be the prettier of the two, though Helen's features had to a great extent softened as she became older. The two girls, who were together on every available opportunity, presented a singular contrast, the one with her clear, olive skin and almost Italian appearance, and the other of the proverbial red and white of our rural districts. It must be stated that the payments made to Mr R. for the maintenance of Helen were known in the village for their excessive liberality, and the impression was general that she would one day inherit a large sum of money from her relative. The parents of Rachel were therefore not averse from their daughter's friendship with the girl, and even encouraged the intimacy, though they now bitterly regret having done so. Helen still retained her extraordinary fondness for the forest, and on several occasions Rachel accompanied her, the two friends setting out early in the morning, and remaining in the wood till dusk. Once or twice after these excursions Mrs M. thought her daughter's manner rather peculiar; she seemed languid and dreamy, and as it has been expressed, 'different from herself,' but these peculiarities seem to have been thought too trifling for remark. One evening, however, after Rachel had come home, her mother heard a noise which

1 Dr Phillips tells me that he has seen the head in question, and assures me that he has never received such a vivid presentment of intense evil.

sounded like suppressed weeping in the girl's room, and on going in found her lying, half undressed, upon the bed, evidently in the greatest distress. As soon as she saw her mother, she exclaimed, 'Ah, Mother, Mother, why did you let me go to the forest with Helen?' Mrs M. was astonished at so strange a question, and proceeded to make inquiries. Rachel told her a wild story. She said—

Clarke closed the book with a snap, and turned his chair towards the fire. When his friend sat one evening in that very chair, and told his story, Clarke had interrupted him at a point a little subsequent to this, had cut short his words in a paroxysm of horror. 'My God!' he had exclaimed, 'think, think what you are saying. It is too incredible, too monstrous; such things can never be in this quiet world, where men and women live and die, and struggle, and conquer, or maybe fail, and fall down under sorrow, and grieve and suffer strange fortunes for many a year; but not this, Phillips, not such things as this. There must be some explanation, some way out of the terror. Why, man, if such a case were possible, our earth would be a nightmare.'

But Phillips had told his story to the end, concluding:

'Her flight remains a mystery to this day; she vanished in broad sunlight; they saw her walking in a meadow, and a few moments later she was not there.'

Clarke tried to conceive the thing again, as he sat by the fire, and again his mind shuddered and shrank back, appalled before the sight of such awful, unspeakable elements enthroned as it were, and triumphant in human flesh. Before him stretched the long dim vista of the green causeway in the forest, as his friend had described it; he saw the swaying leaves and the quivering shadows on the grass, he saw the sunlight and the flowers, and far away, far in the long distance, the two figures moved toward him. One was Rachel, but the other?

Clarke had tried his best to disbelieve it all, but at the end of the account, as he had written it in his book, he had placed the inscription:

ET DIABOLUS INCARNATUS EST. ET HOMO FACTUS EST.

3. The City of Resurrections

'Herbert! Good God! Is it possible?'

'Yes, my name's Herbert. I think I know your face too, but I don't remember your name. My memory is very queer.'

'Don't you recollect Villiers of Wadham?'

'So it is, so it is. I beg your pardon, Villiers, I didn't think I was begging of an old college friend. Good-night.'

'My dear fellow, this haste is unnecessary. My rooms are close by, but we won't go there just yet. Suppose was walk up Shaftesbury Avenue a little way? But how in heaven's name have you come to this pass, Herbert?'

'It's a long story, Villiers, and a strange one too, but you can hear it if you like.'

'Come on, then. Take my arm, you don't seem very strong.'

The ill-assorted pair moved slowly up Rupert Street; the one in dirty, evil-looking rags, and the other attired in the regulation uniform of a man about town, trim, glossy, and eminently well-to-do. Villiers had emerged from his restaurant after an excellent dinner of many courses, assisted by an ingratiating little flask of Chianti, and, in that frame of mind which was with him almost chronic, had delayed a moment by the door, peering round in the dimly lighted street in search of those mysterious incidents and persons with which the streets of London teem in every quarter and at every hour. Villiers prided himself as a practised explorer of such obscure mazes and byways of London life, and in this unprofitable pursuit he displayed an assiduity which was worthy of more serious employment. Thus he stood beside the lamp-post surveying the passers-by with undisguised curiosity, and with that gravity only known to the systematic diner, had just enunciated in his mind the formula: 'London has been called the city of encounters; it is more than that, it is the city of resurrections,' when these reflections were suddenly interrupted by a piteous whine at his elbow, and a deplorable appeal for alms. He looked around in some irritation, and with a sudden shock found himself confronted with the embodied proof of his somewhat stilted fancies. There, close beside him, his face altered and disfigured by poverty and disgrace, his body barely covered by greasy ill-fitting rags, stood his old friend Charles Herbert, who had matriculated on the same day as himself, with whom he had been merry and wise for twelve revolving terms. Different occupations and varying interests had interrupted the friendship, and it was six years since Villiers had seen Herbert; and now he looked upon this wreck of a man with grief and dismay, mingled with a certain inquisitiveness as to what dreary chain of circumstance had dragged him down to such a doleful pass. Villiers felt together with compassion all the relish of the amateur in mysteries, and congratulated himself on his leisurely speculations outside the restaurant.

They walked on in silence for some time, and more than one passer-by stared in astonishment at the unaccustomed spectacle of a well-dressed man with an unmistakable beggar hanging on to his arm, and observing this, Villiers led the way to an obscure street in Soho. Here he repeated his question.

'How on earth has it happened, Herbert? I always understood you would succeed to an excellent position in Dorsetshire. Did your father disinherit you? Surely not?'

'No, Villiers; I came into all the property at my poor father's death; he died a year after I left Oxford. He was a very good father to me, and I mourned his death sincerely enough. But you know what young men are; a few months later I came up to town and went a good deal into society. Of course I had excellent introductions, and I managed to enjoy myself very much in a harmless sort of way. I played a little, certainly, but never for heavy stakes, and the few bets I made on races brought me in money – only a few pounds, you know, but enough to pay for cigars and such petty pleasures. It was in my second season that the tide turned. Of course you have heard of my marriage?'

'No, I never heard anything about it.'

'Yes, I married, Villiers. I met a girl, a girl of the most wonderful and most strange beauty, at the house of some people whom I knew. I cannot tell you her age; I never knew it, but, so far as I can guess, I should think she must have been about nineteen when I made her acquaintance. My friends had come to know her at Florence; she told them she was an orphan, the child of an English father and an Italian mother, and she charmed them as she charmed me. The first time I saw her was at an evening party. I was standing by the door talking to a friend, when suddenly above the hum and babble of conversation, I heard a voice which seemed to thrill to my heart. She was singing an Italian song. I was introduced to her that evening, and in three months I married Helen. Villiers, that woman, if I can call her "woman," corrupted my soul. The night of the wedding I found myself sitting in her bedroom in the hotel, listening to her talk. She was sitting up in bed, and I listened to her as she spoke in her beautiful voice, spoke of things which even now I would not dare whisper in blackest night, though I stood in the midst of a wilderness. You, Villiers, you may think you know life, and London, and what goes on day and night in this dreadful city; for all I can say you may have heard the talk of the vilest, but I tell you you can have no conception of what I know, not in your most fantastic, hideous dreams can you have imaged forth the faintest shadow of what I have heard – and seen. Yes, seen. I have seen the incredible, such horrors that even I myself sometimes stop in the middle of the street, and ask whether it is possible for a man to hold such things and live. In a year, Villiers, I was a ruined man, in body and soul – in body and soul.'

'But your property, Herbert? You had land in Dorset.'

'I sold it all; the fields and woods, the dear old house – everything.'

'And the money?'

'She took it all from me.'

'And then left you?'

'Yes; she disappeared one night. I don't know where she went, but I am sure if I saw her again it would kill me. The rest of my story is of no interest; sordid misery, that is all. You may think, Villiers, that I have exaggerated and talked for effect; but I have not told you half. I could tell you certain things which would convince you, but you would never know a happy day again. You would pass the rest of your life, as I pass mine, a haunted man, a man who has seen hell.'

Villiers took the unfortunate man to his rooms, and gave him a meal. Herbert could eat little, and scarcely touched the glass of wine set before him. He sat moody and silent by the fire, and seemed relieved when Villiers sent him away with a small present of money.

'By the way, Herbert,' said Villiers, as they parted at the door, 'what was your wife's name? You said Helen, I think? Helen what?'

'The name she passed under when I met her was Helen Vaughan, but what her real name was I can't say. I don't think she had a name. No, no, not in that sense. Only human beings have names, Villiers; I can't say any more. Good-bye; yes, I will not fail to call if I see any way in which you can help me. Good-night.'

The man went out into the bitter night, and Villiers returned to his fireside. There was something about Herbert which shocked him inexpressibly; not his poor rags nor the marks which poverty had set upon his face, but rather an indefinite terror which hung about him like a mist. He had acknowledged that he himself was not devoid of blame; the woman, he had avowed, had corrupted him body and soul, and Villiers felt that this man, once his friend, had been an actor in scenes evil beyond the power of words. His story needed no confirmation: he himself was the embodied proof of it. Villiers mused curiously over the story he had heard, and wondered whether he had heard both the first and the last of it. 'No,' he thought, 'certainly not the last, probably only the beginning. A case like this is like a nest of Chinese boxes; you open one after another and find a quainter workmanship in every box. Most likely poor Herbert is merely one of the outside boxes; there are stranger ones to follow.'

Villiers could not take his mind away from Herbert and his story, which seemed to grow wilder as the night wore on. The fire began to burn low, and the chilly air of the morning crept into the room; Villiers got up with a glance over his shoulder, and shivering slightly, went to bed.

A few days later he saw at his club a gentleman of his acquaintance, named Austin, who was famous for his intimate knowledge of London life, both in its tenebrous and luminous phases. Villiers, still full of his encounter in Soho and its consequences, thought Austin might possibly be able to shed some light on Herbert's history, and so after some casual talk he suddenly put the question:

'Do you happen to know anything of a man named Herbert – Charles Herbert?'

Austin turned round sharply and stared at Villiers with some astonishment.

'Charles Herbert? Weren't you in town three years ago? No; then you have not heard of the Paul Street case? It caused a good deal of sensation at the time.'

'What was the case?'

'Well, a gentleman, a man of very good position, was found dead, stark dead, in the area of a certain house in Paul Street, off Tottenham Court Road. Of course the police did not make the discovery; if you happen to be sitting up all night and have a light in your window, the constable will ring the bell, but if you happen to be lying dead in somebody's area, you will be left alone. In this instance as in many others the alarm was raised by some kind of vagabond; I don't mean a common tramp, or a public-house loafer, but a gentleman, whose business or pleasure, or both, made him a spectator of the London streets at five o'clock in the morning. This individual was, as he said, 'going home,' it did not appear whence or whither, and had occasion to pass through Paul Street between four and five a.m. Something or other caught his eye at Number 20; he said, absurdly enough, that the house had the most unpleasant physiognomy he had ever observed, but, at any rate, he glanced down the area, and was a good deal astonished to see a man lying on the stones, his limbs all huddled together, and his face turned up. Our gentleman thought his face looked peculiarly ghastly, and so set off at a run in search of the nearest policeman. The constable was at first inclined to treat the matter lightly, suspecting common drunkenness; however, he came, and after looking at the man's face, changed his tone, quickly enough. The early bird, who had picked up this fine worm, was sent off for a doctor, and the policeman rang and knocked at the door till a slatternly servant girl came down looking more than half asleep. The constable pointed out the contents of the area to the maid, who screamed loudly enough to wake up the street, but she knew nothing of the man; had never seen him at the house, and so forth. Meanwhile the original discoverer had come back with a medical man, and the next thing was to get into the area. The gate was open, so the whole quartet stumped down the steps. The doctor hardly needed a moment's examination; he said the poor fellow had been dead for several hours, and it was then the case began to get interesting. The dead man had not been robbed, and in one of his pockets were papers identifying him as – well, as a man of good family and means, a favourite in society, and nobody's enemy, so far as could be known. I don't give his name, Villiers, because it has nothing to do with the story, and because it's no good raking up these affairs about the dead when there are no relations living. The next curious point was that the medical men couldn't agree as to how he met his death. There were some slight bruises on his shoulders, but they were so slight that it looked as if he had been pushed roughly out of the kitchen door, and not thrown over the railings from the street or even dragged down the steps. But there were positively no other marks of violence about him, certainly none that would account for his death; and when they came to the autopsy there wasn't a trace of poison of any kind. Of course the police wanted to know all about the people at Number 20, and here again, so I have heard from private sources, one or two other very curious points came out. It appears that the occupants of the house were a Mr and Mrs Charles Herbert; he was said to be a landed proprietor, though it struck most people that Paul Street was not exactly the place to look for county gentry. As for Mrs Herbert, nobody seemed to know who or what she was, and, between ourselves, I fancy the divers after her history found themselves in rather strange waters. Of course they both denied knowing anything about the deceased, and in default of any evidence against them they were discharged. But some very odd things came out about them. Though it was between five and six in the morning when the dead man was removed, a large crowd had collected, and several of the neighbours ran to see what was going on. They were pretty free with their comments, by all accounts, and from these it appeared that Number 20 was in very bad odour in Paul Street. The detectives tried to trace down these rumours to some solid foundation of fact, but could not get hold of anything. People shook their heads and raised their eyebrows and thought the Herberts rather "queer", "would rather not be seen going into their house," and so on, but there was nothing tangible. The authorities were morally certain that the man met his death in some way or another in the house and was thrown out by the kitchen door, but they couldn't prove it, and the absence of any indications of violence or poisoning left them helpless. An odd case, wasn't it? But curiously enough, there's something more that I haven't told you. I happened to know one of the doctors who was consulted as to the cause of death, and some time after the inquest I met him, and asked him about it. 'Do you really mean to tell me,' I said, 'that you were baffled by the case, that you actually don't know what the man died of?' 'Pardon me,' he replied, 'I know perfectly well what caused death. Blank died of fright, of sheer, awful terror; I never saw features so hideously contorted in the entire course of my practice, and I have seen the faces of a whole host of dead.' The doctor was usually a cool customer enough, and a certain vehemence in his manner struck me, but I couldn't get anything more out of him. I suppose the Treasury didn't see their way to prosecuting the Herberts for frightening a man to death; at any rate, nothing was done, and the case dropped out of men's minds. Do you happen to know anything of Herbert?'

'Well,' replied Villiers, 'he was an old college friend of mine.'

'You don't say so? Have you ever seen his wife?'

'No, I haven't. I have lost sight of Herbert for many years.'

'It's queer, isn't it, parting with a man at the college gate or at Paddington, seeing nothing of him for years, and then finding him pop up his head in such an odd place. But I should like to have seen Mrs Herbert; people said extraordinary things about her.'

'What sort of things?'

'Well, I hardly know how to tell you. Every one who saw her at the police court said she was at once the most beautiful woman and the most repulsive they had ever set eyes on. I have spoken to a man who saw her, and I assure you he positively shuddered as he tried to describe the woman, but he couldn't tell why. She seems to have been a sort of enigma; and I expect if that one dead man could have told tales, he would have told some uncommonly queer ones. And there you are again in another puzzle; what could a respectable country gentleman like Mr Blank (we'll call him that if you don't mind) want in such a very queer house as Number 20? It's altogether a very odd case, isn't it?'

'It is indeed, Austin; an extraordinary case. I didn't think, when I asked you about my old friend, I should strike on such strange metal. Well, I must be off; good-day.'

Villiers went away, thinking of his own conceit of the Chinese boxes; here was quaint workmanship indeed.

4. *The Discovery in Paul Street*

A few months after Villiers's meeting with Herbert, Mr Clarke was sitting, as usual, by his after-dinner hearth, resolutely guarding his fancies from wandering in the direction of the bureau. For more than a week he had succeeded in keeping away from the 'Memoirs', and he cherished hopes of a complete self-reformation; but, in spite of his endeavours, he could not hush the wonder and the strange curiosity that that last case he had written down had excited within him. He had put the case, or rather the outline of it, conjecturally to a scientific friend, who shook his head, and thought Clarke getting queer, and on this particular evening Clarke was making an effort to rationalize the story, when a sudden knock at his door roused him from his meditations.

'Mr Villiers to see you, sir.'

'Dear me, Villiers, it is very kind of you to look me up; I have not seen you for many months; I should think nearly a year. Come in, come in. And how are you, Villiers? Want any advice about investments?'

'No, thanks, I fancy everything I have in that way is pretty safe. No, Clarke, I have really come to consult you about a rather curious matter that has been brought under my notice of late. I am afraid you will think it all rather absurd when I tell my tale. I sometimes think so myself, and that's just why I made up my mind to come to you, as I know you're a practical man.'

Mr Villiers was ignorant of the 'Memoirs to Prove the Existence of the Devil.'

'Well, Villiers, I shall be happy to give you my advice, to the best of my ability. What is the nature of the case?'

'It's an extraordinary thing altogether. You know my ways; I always keep my eyes open in the streets, and in my time I have chanced upon some queer customers, and queer cases too, but this, I think, beats all. I was coming out of a restaurant one nasty winter night about three months ago; I had had a capital dinner and a good bottle of Chianti, and I stood for a moment on the pavement, thinking what a mystery there is about London streets and the companies that pass along them. A bottle of red wine encourages these fancies, Clarke, and I dare say I should have thought a page of small type, but I was cut short by a beggar who had come behind me, and was making the usual appeals. Of course I looked round, and this beggar turned out to be what was left of an old friend of mine, a man named Herbert. I asked him how he had come to such a wretched pass, and he told me. We walked up and down one of those long dark Soho streets, and there I listened to his story. He said he had married a beautiful girl, some years younger than himself, and, as he put it, she had corrupted him body and soul. He wouldn't go into details; he said he dare not, that what he had seen and heard haunted him by night and day, and when I looked in his face I knew he was speaking the truth. There was something about the man that made me shiver. I don't know why, but it was there. I gave him a little money and sent him away, and I assure you that when he was gone I gasped for breath. His presence seemed to chill one's blood.'

'Isn't all this just a little fanciful, Villiers? I suppose the poor fellow had made an imprudent marriage, and, in plain English, gone to the bad.'

'Well, listen to this.' Villiers told Clarke the story he had heard from Austin.

'You see,' he concluded, 'there can be but little doubt that this Mr Blank, whoever he was, died of sheer terror; he saw something so awful, so terrible that it cut short his life. And what he saw, he most certainly saw in that house, which, somehow or other, had got a bad name in the neighbourhood. I had the curiosity to go and look at the place for myself. It's a saddening kind of street; the houses are old enough to be mean and dreary, but not old enough to be quaint. As far as I could see most of them are let in lodgings, furnished and unfurnished, and almost every door has three bells to it. Here and there the ground floors have been made into shops of the commonest kind; it's a dismal street in every way. I found Number 20 was to let, and I went to the agent's and got the key. Of course I should have heard nothing of the Herberts in that quarter, but I asked the man, fair and square, how long they had left the house, and whether there had been other tenants in the meanwhile. He looked at me queerly for a minute, and told me the Herberts had left immediately after the unpleasantness, as he called it, and since then the house had been empty.'

Mr Villiers paused for a moment.

'I have always been rather fond of going over empty houses; there's a sort of fascination about the desolate empty rooms, with the nails sticking in the walls, and the dust thick upon the window-sills. But I didn't enjoy going over Number 20, Paul Street. I had hardly put my foot inside the passage before I noticed a queer, heavy feeling about the air of the house. Of course all empty houses are stuffy, and so forth, but this was something quite different; I can't describe it to you, but it seemed to stop the breath. I went into the front room and the back room, and the kitchens downstairs; they were all dirty and dusty enough, as you would expect, but there was something strange about them all. I couldn't define it to you, I only know I felt queer. It was one of the rooms on the first floor, though, that was the worst. It was a largish room, and once on a time the paper must have been cheerful enough, but when I saw it, paint, paper, and everything were most doleful. But the room was full of horror; I felt my teeth grinding as I put my hand on the door, and when I went in, I thought I should have fallen fainting to the floor. However, I pulled myself together, and stood against the end wall, wondering what on earth there could be about the room to make my limbs tremble, and my heart beat as if I were at the hour of death. In one corner there was a pile of newspapers littered about on the floor, and I began looking at them; they were papers of three or four years ago, some of them half torn, and some crumpled as if they had been used for packing. I turned the whole pile over, and amongst them I found a curious drawing; I will show it you presently. But I couldn't stay in the room; I felt it was overpowering me. I was thankful to come out, safe and sound, into the open air. People stared at me as I walked along the street, and one man said I was drunk. I was staggering about from one side of the pavement to the other, and it was as much as I could do to take the key back to the agent and get home. I was in bed for a week, suffering from what my doctor called nervous shock and exhaustion. One of those days I was reading the evening paper, and happened to notice a paragraph headed:

"Starved to Death". It was the usual style of thing; a model lodging-house in Marylebone, a door locked for several days, and a dead man in his chair when they broke in. "The deceased," said the paragraph, "was known as Charles Herbert, and is believed to have been once a prosperous country gentleman. His name was familiar to the public three years ago in connection with the mysterious death in Paul Street, Tottenham Court Road, the deceased being the tenant of the house Number 20, in the area of which a gentleman of good position was found dead under circumstances not devoid of suspicion." A tragic ending, wasn't it? But after all, if what he told me were true, which I am sure it was, the man's life was all a tragedy, and a tragedy of a stranger sort than they put on the boards.'

'And that is the story, is it?' said Clarke musingly.

'Yes, that is the story.'

'Well, really, Villiers, I scarcely know what to say about it. There are, no doubt, circumstances in the case which seem peculiar, the finding of the dead man in the area of Herbert's house, for instance, and the extraordinary opinion of the physician as to the cause of death; but, after all, it is conceivable that the facts may be explained in a straightforward manner. As to your own sensations, when you went to see the house, I would suggest that they were due to a vivid imagination; you must have been brooding, in a semi-conscious way, over what you had heard. I don't exactly see what more can be said or done in the matter; you evidently think there is a mystery of some kind, but Herbert is dead; where then do you propose to look?'

'I propose to look for the woman; the woman whom he married. *She* is the mystery.'

The two men sat silent by the fireside; Clarke secretly congratulating himself on having successfully kept up the character of advocate of the commonplace, and Villiers wrapt in his gloomy fancies.

'I think I will have a cigarette,' he said at last, and put his hand in his pocket to feel for the cigarette-case.

'Ah!' he said, starting slightly, 'I forgot I had something to show you. You remember my saying that I had found a rather curious sketch amongst the pile of old newspapers at the house in Paul Street? Here it is.'

Villiers drew out a small thin parcel from his pocket. It was covered with brown paper, and secured with string, and the knots were troublesome. In spite of himself Clarke felt inquisitive; he bent forward on his chair as Villiers painfully undid the string, and unfolded the outer covering. Inside was a second wrapping of tissue, and Villiers took it off and handed the small piece of paper to Clarke without a word.

There was dead silence in the room for five minutes or more; the two men sat so still that they could hear the ticking of the tall old-fashioned clock that stood outside in the hall, and in the mind of one of them the slow monotony of sound woke up a far, far memory. He was looking intently at the small pen-and-ink sketch of the woman's head; it had evidently been drawn with great care, and by a true artist, for the woman's soul looked out of the eyes, and the lips were parted with a strange smile. Clarke gazed still at the face; it brought to his memory one summer evening long ago; he saw again the long lovely valley, the river winding between the hills, the meadows and the cornfields, the dull red sun, and the cold white mist rising from the water. He heard a voice speaking to him across the waves of many years, and saying: 'Clarke, Mary will see the God Pan!' and then he was standing in the grim room beside the doctor, listening to the heavy ticking of the clock, waiting and watching, watching the figure lying on the green chair beneath the lamp-light. Mary rose up, and he looked into her eyes, and his heart grew cold within him.

'Who is this woman?' he said at last. His voice was dry and hoarse.

'That is the woman whom Herbert married.'

Clarke looked again at the sketch; it was not Mary after all. There certainly was Mary's face, but there was something else, something he had not seen on Mary's features when the white-clad girl entered the laboratory with the doctor, nor at her terrible awakening, nor when she lay grinning on the bed. Whatever it was, the glance that came from those eyes, the smile on the full lips, or the expression of the whole face, Clarke shuddered before it in his inmost soul, and thought, unconsciously, of Dr Phillips's words, 'the most vivid presentment of evil I have ever seen.' He turned the paper over mechanically in his hand and glanced at the back.

'Good God! Clarke, what is the matter? You are as white as death.'

Villiers had started wildly from his chair, as Clarke fell back with a groan, and let the paper drop from his hands.

'I don't feel very well, Villiers, I am subject to these attacks. Pour me out a little wine; thanks, that will do. I shall feel better in a few minutes.'

Villiers picked up the fallen sketch and turned it over as Clarke had done.

'You saw that?' he said. 'That's how I identified it as being a portrait of Herbert's wife, or I should say his widow. How do you feel now?'

'Better, thanks, it was only a passing faintness. I don't think I quite catch your meaning. What did you say enabled you to identify the picture?'

'This word – "Helen" – written on the back. Didn't I tell you her name was Helen? Yes; Helen Vaughan.'

Clarke groaned; there could be no shadow of doubt.

'Now, don't you agree with me,' said Villiers, 'that in the story I have told you to-night, and in the part this woman plays in it, there are some very strange points?'

'Yes, Villiers,' Clarke muttered, 'it is a strange story indeed; a strange story indeed. You must give me time to think it over; I may be able to help you or I may not. Must you be going now? Well, good-night, Villiers, good-night. Come and see me in the course of a week.'

5. *The Letter of Advice*

'Do you know, Austin,' said Villiers, as the two friends were pacing sedately along Piccadilly one pleasant morning in May, 'do you know I am convinced that what you told me about Paul Street and the Herberts is a mere episode in an extraordinary history? I may as well confess to you that when I asked you about Herbert a few months ago I had just seen him.'

'You had seen him? Where?'

'He begged of me in the street one night. He was in the most pitiable plight, but I recognized the man, and I got him to tell me his history, or at least the outline of it. In brief, it amounted to this – he had been ruined by his wife.'

'In what manner?'

'He would not tell me; he would only say that she had destroyed him, body and soul. The man is dead now.'

'And what has become of his wife?'

'Ah, that's what I should like to know, and I mean to find her sooner or later. I know a man named Clarke, a dry fellow, in fact a man of business, but shrewd enough. You understand my meaning; not shrewd in the mere business sense of the word, but a man who really knows something about men and life. Well, I laid the case before him, and he was evidently impressed. He said it needed consideration, and asked me to come again in the course of a week. A few days later I received this extraordinary letter.'

Austin took the envelope, drew out the letter, and read it curiously. It ran as follows:—

My dear Villiers. – I have thought over the matter on which you consulted me the other night, and my advice to you is this. Throw the portrait into the fire, blot out the story from your mind. Never give it another thought, Villiers, or you will be sorry. You will think, no doubt, that I am in possession of some secret information, and to a certain extent that is the case. But I only know a little; I am like a traveller who has peered over an abyss, and has drawn back in terror. What I know is strange enough and horrible enough, but beyond my knowledge there are depths and horrors more frightful still, more incredible than any tale told of winter nights about the fire. I have resolved, and nothing shall shake that resolve, to explore no whit farther, and if you value your happiness you will make the same determination.

Come and see me by all means; but we will talk on more cheerful topics than this.

Austin folded the letter methodically, and returned it to Villiers.

'It is certainly an extraordinary letter,' he said; 'what does he mean by the portrait?'

'Ah! I forgot to tell you I have been to Paul Street and have made a discovery.'

Villiers told his story as he had told it to Clarke, and Austin listened in silence He seemed puzzled.

'How very curious that you should experience such an unpleasant sensation in that room!' he said at length. 'I hardly gather that it was a mere matter of the imagination; a feeling of repulsion, in short.'

'No, it was more physical than mental. It was as if I were inhaling at every breath some deadly fume, which seemed to penetrate to every nerve and bone and sinew of my body. I felt racked from head to foot, my eyes began to grow dim; it was like the entrance of death.'

'Yes, yes, very strange, certainly. You see, your friend confesses that there is some very black story connected with this woman. Did you notice any particular emotion in him when you were telling your tale?'

'Yes, I did. He became very faint, but he assured me that it was a mere passing attack to which he was subject.'

'Did you believe him?'

'I did at the time, but I don't now. He heard what I had to say with a good deal of indifference, till I showed him the portrait. It was then he was seized with the attack of which I spoke. He looked ghastly, I assure you.'

'Then he must have seen the woman before. But there might be another explanation; it might have been the name, and not the face, which was familiar to him. What do you think?'

'I couldn't say. To the best of my belief it was after turning the portrait in his hands that he nearly dropped from his chair. The name, you know, was written on the back.'

'Quite so. After all, it is impossible to come to any resolution in a case like this. I hate melodrama, and nothing strikes me as more commonplace and tedious than the ordinary ghost story of commerce; but really,

Villiers, it looks as if there were something very queer at the bottom of all this.'

The two men had, without noticing it, turned up Ashley Street, leading northward from Piccadilly. It was a long street, and rather a gloomy one, but here and there a brighter taste had illuminated the dark houses with flowers, and gay curtains, and a cheerful paint on the doors. Villiers glanced up as Austin stopped speaking, and looked at one of these houses; geraniums, red and white, drooped from every sill, and daffodil-coloured curtains were draped back from each window.

'It looks cheerful, doesn't it?' he said.

'Yes, and the inside is still more cheery. One of the pleasantest houses of the season, so I have heard. I haven't been there myself, but I've met several men who have, and they tell me it's uncommonly jovial.'

'Whose house is it?'

'A Mrs Beaumont's.'

'And who is she?'

'I couldn't tell you. I have heard she comes from South America, but, after all, who she is is of little consequence. She is a very wealthy woman, there's no doubt of that, and some of the best people have taken her up. I heard she has some wonderful claret, really marvellous wine, which must have cost a fabulous sum. Lord Argentine was telling me about it; he was there last Sunday evening. He assures me he has never tasted such a wine, and Argentine, as you know, is an expert. By the way, that reminds me, she must be an oddish sort of woman, this Mrs Beaumont. Argentine asked her how old the wine was, and what do you think she said? 'About a thousand years, I believe.' Lord Argentine thought she was chaffing him, you know, but when he laughed she said she was speaking quite seriously, and offered to show him the jar. Of course, he couldn't say anything more after that; but it seems rather antiquated for a beverage, doesn't it? Why, here we are at my rooms. Come in, won't you?'

'Thanks, I think I will. I haven't seen the curiosity-shop for some time.'

It was a room furnished richly, yet oddly, where every chair and bookcase and table, and every rug and jar and ornament seemed to be a thing apart, preserving each its own individuality.

'Anything fresh lately?' said Villiers after a while.

'No; I think not; you saw those queer jugs, didn't you? I thought so. I don't think I have come across anything for the last few weeks.'

Austin glanced round the room from cupboard to cupboard, from shelf to shelf, in search of some new oddity. His eyes fell at last on an old chest, pleasantly and quaintly carved, which stood in a dark corner of the room.

'Ah,' he said, 'I was forgetting, I have got something to show you.'
Austin unlocked the chest, drew out a thick quarto volume, laid it on the
table, and resumed the cigar he had put down.

'Did you know Arthur Meyrick the painter, Villiers?'

'A little; I met him two or three times at the house of a friend of mine.
What has become of him? I haven't heard his name mentioned for some
time.'

'He's dead.'

'You don't say so! Quite young, wasn't he?'

'Yes; only thirty when he died.'

'What did he die of?'

'I don't know. He was an intimate friend of mine, and a thoroughly
good fellow. He used to come here and talk to me for hours, and he was
one of the best talkers I have met. He could even talk about painting,
and that's more than can be said of most painters. About eighteen
months ago he was feeling rather overworked, and partly at my suggestion he went off on a sort of roving expedition, with no very definite end
or aim about it. I believe New York was to be his first port, but I never
heard from him. Three months ago I got this book, with a very civil
letter from an English doctor practising at Buenos Aires, stating that he
had attended the late Mr Meyrick during his illness, and that the
deceased had expressed an earnest wish that the enclosed packet should
be sent to me after his death. That was all.'

'And haven't you written for further particulars?'

'I have been thinking of doing so. You would advise me to write to the
doctor?'

'Certainly. And what about the book?'

'It was sealed up when I got it. I don't think the doctor had seen it.'

'It is something very rare? Meyrick was a collector, perhaps?'

'No, I think not, hardly a collector. Now, what do you think of those
Ainu jugs?'

'They are peculiar, but I like them. But aren't you going to show me
poor Meyrick's legacy?'

'Yes, yes, to be sure. The fact is, it's rather a peculiar sort of thing, and
I haven't shown it to any one. I wouldn't say anything about it if I were
you. There it is.'

Villiers took the book, and opened it at haphazard.

'It isn't a printed volume then?' he said.

'No. It is a collection of drawings in black and white by my poor
friend Meyrick.'

Villiers turned to the first page, it was blank; the second bore a brief
inscription, which he read:

THE GREAT GOD PAN

Silet per diem universus, nec sine horrore secretus est; lucet nocturnis ignibus, chorus Ægipanum undique personatur: audiuntur et cantus tibiarum, et tinnitus cymbalorum per oram maritimam.

On the third page was a design which made Villiers start and look up at Austin; he was gazing abstractedly out of the window. Villiers turned page after page, absorbed, in spite of himself, in the frightful Walpurgis-night of evil, strange monstrous evil, that the dead artist had set forth in hard black and white. The figures of fauns and satyrs and Ægipans danced before his eyes, the darkness of the thicket, the dance on the mountain-top, the scenes by lonely shores, in green vineyards, by rocks and desert places, passed before him: a world before which the human soul seemed to shrink back and shudder. Villiers whirled over the remaining pages; he had seen enough, but the picture on the last leaf caught his eye, as he almost closed the book.

'Austin!'

'Well, what is it?'

'Do you know who that is?'

It was a woman's face, alone on the white page.

'Know who it is? No, of course not.'

'I do.'

'Who is it?'

'It is Mrs Herbert.'

'Are you sure?'

'I am perfectly certain of it. Poor Meyrick! He is one more chapter in her history.'

'But what do you think of the designs?'

'They are frightful. Lock the book up again, Austin. If I were you I would burn it; it must be a terrible companion even though it be in a chest.'

'Yes, they are singular drawings. But I wonder what connection there could be between Meyrick and Mrs Herbert, or what link between her and these designs?'

'Ah, who can say? It is possible that the matter may end here, and we shall never know, but in my own opinion this Helen Vaughan, or Mrs Herbert, is only the beginning. She will come back to London, Austin; depend upon it, she will come back, and we shall hear more about her then. I don't think it will be very pleasant news.'

6. *The Suicides*

Lord Argentine was a great favourite in London society. At twenty he had been a poor man, decked with the surname of an illustrious family, but forced to earn a livelihood as best he could, and the most speculative of money-lenders would not have entrusted him with fifty pounds on the chance of his ever changing his name for a title, and his poverty for a great fortune. His father had been near enough to the fountain of good things to secure one of the family livings, but the son, even if he had taken orders, would scarcely have obtained so much as this, and moreover felt no vocation for the ecclesiastical estate. Thus he fronted the world with no better armour than the bachelor's gown and the wits of a younger son's grandson, with which equipment he contrived in some way to make a very tolerable fight of it. At twenty-five Mr Charles Aubernoun saw himself still a man of struggles and of warfare with the world, but out of the seven who stood between him and the high places of his family three only remained. These three, however, were 'good lives', but yet not proof against the Zulu assegais and typhoid fever, and so one morning Aubernoun woke up and found himself Lord Argentine, a man of thirty who had faced the difficulties of existence, and had conquered. The situation amused him immensely, and he resolved that riches should be as pleasant to him as poverty had always been. Argentine, after some little consideration, came to the conclusion that dining, regarded as a fine art, was perhaps the most amusing pursuit open to fallen humanity, and thus his dinners became famous in London, and an invitation to his table a thing covetously desired. After ten years of lordship and dinners Argentine still declined to be jaded, still persisted in enjoying life, and by a kind of infection had become recognized as the cause of joy in others, in short, as the best of company. His sudden and tragical death therefore caused a wide and deep sensation. People could scarce believe it, even though the newspaper was before their eyes, and the cry of 'Mysterious Death of a Nobleman' came ringing up from the street. But there stood the brief paragraph: 'Lord Argentine was found dead this morning by his valet under distressing circumstances. It is stated that there can be no doubt that his lordship committed suicide, though no motive can be assigned for the act. The deceased nobleman was widely known in society, and much liked for his genial manner and sumptuous hospitality. He is succeeded by,' etc., etc.

By slow degrees the details came to light, but the case still remained a mystery. The chief witness at the inquest was the dead nobleman's valet, who said that the night before his death Lord Argentine had dined with a lady of good position, whose name was suppressed in the newspaper reports. At about eleven o'clock Lord Argentine had returned, and informed his man that he should not require his services till the next morning. A little later the valet had occasion to cross the hall and was somewhat astonished to see his master quietly letting himself out at the front door. He had taken off his evening clothes, and was dressed in a

Norfolk coat and knickerbockers, and wore a low brown hat. The valet had no reason to suppose that Lord Argentine had seen him, and though his master rarely kept late hours, thought little of the occurrence till the next morning, when he knocked at the bedroom door at a quarter to nine as usual. He received no answer, and, after knocking two or three times, entered the room, and saw Lord Argentine's body leaning forward at an angle from the bottom of the bed. He found that his master had tied a cord securely to one of the short bedposts, and, after making a running noose and slipping it round his neck, the unfortunate man must have resolutely fallen forward, to die by slow strangulation. He was dressed in the light suit in which the valet had seen him go out, and the doctor who was summoned pronounced that life had been extinct for more than four hours. All papers, letters, and so forth seemed in perfect order, and nothing was discovered which pointed in the most remote way to any scandal either great or small. Here the evidence ended; nothing more could be discovered. Several persons had been present at the dinner-party at which Lord Argentine had assisted, and to all these he seemed in his usual genial spirits. The valet, indeed, said he thought his master appeared a little excited when he came home, but he confessed that the alteration in his manner was very slight, hardly noticeable, indeed. It seemed hopeless to seek for any clue, and the suggestion that Lord Argentine had been suddenly attacked by acute suicidal mania was generally accepted.

It was otherwise, however, when within three weeks, three more gentlemen, one of them a nobleman, and the two others men of good position and ample means, perished miserably in almost precisely the same manner. Lord Swanleigh was found one morning in his dressing-room, hanging from a peg affixed to the wall, and Mr Collier-Stuart and Mr Herries had chosen to die as Lord Argentine. There was no explanation in either case; a few bald facts; a living man in the evening, and a dead body with a black swollen face in the morning The police had been forced to confess themselves powerless to arrest or to explain the sordid murders of Whitechapel; but before the horrible suicides of Piccadilly and Mayfair they were dumbfoundered, for not even the mere ferocity which did duty as an explanation of the crimes of the East End, could be of service in the West. Each of these men who had resolved to die a tortured shameful death was rich, prosperous, and to all appearances in love with the world, and not the acutest research could ferret out any shadow of a lurking motive in either case. There was a horror in the air, and men looked at one another's faces when they met, each wondering whether the other was to be the victim of the fifth nameless tragedy. Journalists sought in vain in their scrap-books for materials whereof to concoct reminiscent articles; and the morning paper was unfolded in many a house with a feeling of awe; no man knew when or where the blow would next light.

A short while after the last of these terrible events, Austin came to see Mr Villiers. He was curious to know whether Villiers had succeeded in discovering any fresh traces of Mrs Herbert, either through Clarke or by other sources, and he asked the question soon after he had sat down.

'No,' said Villiers, 'I wrote to Clarke, but he remains obdurate, and I have tried other channels, but without any result. I can't find out what became of Helen Vaughan after she left Paul Street, but I think she must have gone abroad. But to tell the truth, Austin, I haven't paid very much attention to the matter for the last few weeks; I knew poor Herries intimately, and his terrible death has been a great shock to me, a great shock.'

'I can well believe it,' answered Austin gravely; 'you know Argentine was a friend of mine. If I remember rightly, we were speaking of him that day you came to my rooms.'

'Yes; it was in connection with that house in Ashley Street, Mrs Beaumont's house. You said something about Argentine's dining there.'

'Quite so. Of course you know it was there Argentine dined the night before – before his death.'

'No, I haven't heard that.'

'Oh yes; the name was kept out of the papers to spare Mrs Beaumont. Argentine was a great favourite of hers, and it is said she was in a terrible state for some time after.'

A curious look came over Villiers's face; he seemed undecided whether to speak or not. Austin began again.

'I never experienced such a feeling of horror as when I read the account of Argentine's death. I didn't understand it at the time, and I don't now. I knew him well, and it completely passes my understanding for what possible cause he – or any of the others for the matter of that – could have resolved in cold blood to die in such an awful manner. You know how men babble away each other's characters in London, you may be sure any buried scandal or hidden skeleton would have been brought to light in such a case as this; but nothing of the sort has taken place. As for the theory of mania, that is very well, of course, for the coroner's jury, but everybody knows that it's all nonsense. Suicidal mania is not smallpox.'

Austin relapsed into gloomy silence. Villiers sat silent also, watching his friend. The expression of indecision still fleeted across his face; he seemed as if weighing his thoughts in the balance, and the considerations he was revolving left him still silent. Austin tried to shake off the remembrance of tragedies as hopeless and perplexed as the labyrinth of Dædalus, and began to talk in an indifferent voice of the more pleasant incidents and adventures of the season.

'That Mrs Beaumont,' he said, 'of whom we were speaking, is a great success; she has taken London almost by storm. I met her the other night at Fulham's; she is really a remarkable woman.'

'You have met Mrs Beaumont?'

'Yes; she had quite a court around her. She would be called very handsome, I suppose, and yet there is something about her face which I didn't like. The features are exquisite, but the expression is strange. And all the time I was looking at her, and afterwards, when I was going home, I had a curious feeling that that very expression was in some way or other familiar to me.'

'You must have seen her in the Row.'

'No, I am sure I never set eyes on the woman before; it is that which makes it puzzling. And to the best of my belief I have never seen anybody like her; what I felt was a kind of dim far-off memory, vague but persistent. The only sensation I can compare it to, is that odd feeling one sometimes has in a dream, when fantastic cities and wondrous lands and phantom personages appear familiar and accustomed.'

Villiers nodded and glanced aimlessly round the room, possibly in search of something on which to turn the conversation. His eyes fell on an old chest somewhat like that in which the artist's strange legacy lay hid beneath a Gothic scutcheon.

'Have you written to the doctor about poor Meyrick?' he asked.

'Yes; I wrote asking for full particulars as to his illness and death. I don't expect to have an answer for another three weeks or a month. I thought I might as well inquire whether Meyrick knew an English-woman named Herbert, and if so, whether the doctor could give me any information about her. But it's very possible that Meyrick fell in with her at New York, or Mexico, or San Francisco; I have no idea as to the extent or direction of his travels.'

'Yes, and it's very possible that the woman may have more than one name.'

'Exactly. I wish I had thought of asking you to lend me the portrait of her which you possess. I might have enclosed it in my letter to Dr Matthews.'

'So you might; that never occurred to me. We might send it now. Hark! what are those boys calling?'

While the two men had been talking together a confused noise of shouting had been gradually growing louder. The noise rose from the eastward and swelled down Piccadilly, drawing nearer and nearer, a very torrent of sound; surging up streets usually quiet, and making every window a frame for a face, curious or excited. The cries and voices came echoing up the silent street where Villiers lived, growing more distinct as they advanced, and, as Villiers spoke, an answer rang up from the pavement:

THE WEST END HORRORS; ANOTHER AWFUL SUICIDE; FULL DETAILS!

Austin rushed down the stairs and bought a paper and read out the paragraph to Villiers as the uproar in the street rose and fell. The window was open and the air seemed full of noise and terror.

Another gentleman has fallen a victim to the terrible epidemic of suicide which for the last month has prevailed in the West End. Mr Sidney Crashaw, of Stoke House, Fulham, and King's Pomeroy, Devon, was found, after a prolonged search, hanging from the branch of a tree in his garden at one o'clock to-day. The deceased gentleman dined last night at the Carlton Club and seemed in his usual health and spirits. He left the Club at about ten o'clock, and was seen walking leisurely up St James's Street a little later. Subsequent to this his movements cannot be traced. On the discovery of the body medical aid was at once summoned, but life had evidently been long extinct. So far as is known, Mr Crashaw had no trouble or anxiety of any kind. This painful suicide, it will be remembered, is the fifth of the kind in the last month. The authorities at Scotland Yard are unable to suggest any explanation of these terrible occurrences.

Austin put down the paper in mute horror.

'I shall leave London to-morrow,' he said, 'it is a city of nightmares. How awful this is, Villiers!'

Mr Villiers was sitting by the window quietly looking out into the street. He had listened to the newspaper report attentively, and the hint of indecision was no longer on his face.

'Wait a moment, Austin,' he replied, 'I have made up my mind to mention a little matter that occurred last night. It is stated, I think, that Crashaw was last seen alive in St James's Street shortly after ten?'

'Yes, I think so. I will look again. Yes, you are quite right.'

'Quite so. Well, I am in a position to contradict that statement at all events. Crashaw was seen after that; considerably later indeed.'

'How do you know?'

'Because I happened to see Crashaw myself at about two o'clock this morning.'

'You saw Crashaw? You, Villiers?'

'Yes, I saw him quite distinctly; indeed, there were but a few feet between us.'

'Where, in Heaven's name, did you see him?'

'Not far from here. I saw him in Ashley Street. He was just leaving a house.'

'Did you notice what house it was?'

'Yes. It was Mrs Beaumont's.'

'Villiers! Think what you are saying; there must be some mistake. How could Crashaw be in Mrs Beaumont's house at two o'clock in the morning? Surely, surely, you must have been dreaming, Villiers, you were always rather fanciful.'

'No; I was wide awake enough. Even if I had been dreaming as you say, what I saw would have roused me effectually.'

'What you saw? What did you see? Was there anything strange about Crashaw? But I can't believe it; it is impossible.'

'Well, if you like I will tell you what I saw, or if you please, what I think I saw, and you can judge for yourself.'

'Very good, Villiers.'

The noise and clamour of the street had died away, though now and then the sound of shouting still came from the distance, and the dull, leaden silence seemed like the quiet after an earthquake or a storm. Villiers turned from the window and began speaking.

'I was at a house near Regent's Park last night, and when I came away the fancy took me to walk home instead of taking a hansom. It was a clear pleasant night enough, and after a few minutes I had the streets pretty much to myself. It's a curious thing, Austin, to be alone in London at night, the gas-lamps stretching away in perspective, and the dead silence, and then perhaps the rush and clatter of a hansom on the stones, and the fire starting up under the horse's hoofs. I walked along pretty briskly, for I was feeling a little tired of being out in the night, and as the clocks were striking two I turned down Ashley Street, which, you know, is on my way. It was quieter than ever there, and the lamps were fewer; altogether, it looked as dark and gloomy as a forest in winter. I had done about half the length of the street when I heard a door closed very softly, and naturally I looked up to see who was abroad like myself at such an hour. As it happens, there is a street lamp close to the house in question, and I saw a man standing on the step. He had just shut the door and his face was towards me, and I recognized Crashaw directly. I never knew him to speak to, but I had often seen him, and I am positive that I was not mistaken in my man. I looked into his face for a moment, and then – I will confess the truth – I set off at a good run, and kept it up till I was within my own door.'

'Why?'

'Why? Because it made my blood run cold to see that man's face. I could never have supposed that such an infernal medley of passions could have glared out of any human eyes; I almost fainted as I looked. I knew I had looked into the eyes of a lost soul, Austin, the man's outward form remained, but all hell was within it. Furious lust, and hate that was like fire, and the loss of all hope and horror that seemed to shriek aloud to the night, though his teeth were shut; and the utter blackness of despair. I am sure he did not see me; he saw nothing that you or I can see, but he saw what I hope we never shall. I do not know when he died; I suppose in an hour, or perhaps two, but when I passed down Ashley Street and heard the closing door, that man no longer belonged to this world; it was a devil's face I looked upon.'

There was an interval of silence in the room when Villiers ceased speaking. The light was failing, and all the tumult of an hour ago was quite hushed. Austin had bent his head at the close of the story, and his hand covered his eyes.

'What can it mean?' he said at length.

'Who knows, Austin, who knows? It's a black business, but I think we had better keep it to ourselves, for the present at any rate. I will see if I cannot learn anything about that house through private channels of information, and if I do light upon anything I will let you know.'

7. *The Encounter in Soho*

Three weeks later Austin received a note from Villiers, asking him to call either that afternoon or the next. He chose the nearer date, and found Villiers sitting as usual by the window, apparently lost in meditation on the drowsy traffic of the street. There was a bamboo table by his side, a fantastic thing, enriched with gilding and queer painted scenes, and on it lay a little pile of papers arranged and docketed as neatly as anything in Mr Clarke's office.

'Well, Villiers, have you made any discoveries in the last three weeks?'

'I think so; I have here one or two memoranda which struck me as singular, and there is a statement to which I shall call your attention.'

'And these documents relate to Mrs Beaumont? It was really Crashaw whom you saw that night standing on the doorstep of the house in Ashley Street?'

'As to that matter my belief remains unchanged, but neither my inquiries nor their results have any special relation to Crashaw. But my investigations have had a strange issue. I have found out who Mrs Beaumont is!'

'Who she is? In what way do you mean?'

'I mean that you and I know her better under another name.'

'What name is that?'

'Herbert.'

'Herbert!' Austin repeated the word, dazed with astonishment.

'Yes, Mrs Herbert of Paul Street, Helen Vaughan of earlier adventures unknown to me. You had reason to recognize the expression of her face; when you go home look at the face in Meyrick's book of horrors, and you will know the sources of your recollection.'

'And you have proof of this?'

'Yes, the best of proof; I have seen Mrs Beaumont, or shall we say Mrs Herbert?'

'Where did you see her?'

'Hardly in a place where you would expect to see a lady who lives in Ashley Street, Piccadilly. I saw her entering a house in one of the meanest and most disreputable streets in Soho. In fact, I had made an appointment, though not with her, and she was precise both to time and place.'

'All this seems very wonderful, but I cannot call it incredible. You must remember, Villiers, that I have seen this woman, in the ordinary adventure of London society, talking and laughing, and sipping her coffee in a commonplace drawing-room with commonplace people. But you know what you are saying.'

'I do; I have not allowed myself to be led by surmises or fancies. It was with no thought of finding Helen Vaughan that I searched for Mrs Beaumont in the dark waters of the life of London, but such has been the issue.'

'You must have been in strange places, Villiers.'

'Yes, I have been in very strange places. It would have been useless, you know, to go to Ashley Street, and ask Mrs Beaumont to give me a short sketch of her previous history. No; assuming, as I had to assume, that her record was not of the cleanest, it would be pretty certain that at some previous time she must have moved in circles not quite so refined as her present ones. If you see mud on the top of a stream, you may be sure that it was once at the bottom. I went to the bottom. I have always been fond of diving into Queer Street for my amusement, and I found my knowledge of that locality and its inhabitants very useful. It is, perhaps, needless to say that my friends had never heard the name of Beaumont, and as I had never seen the lady, and was quite unable to describe her, I had to set to work in an indirect way. The people there know me; I have been able to do some of them a service now and again, so they made no difficulty about giving their information; they were aware I had no communication direct or indirect with Scotland Yard. I had to cast out a good many lines, though, before I got what I wanted, and when I landed the fish I did not for a moment suppose it was my fish. But I listened to what I was told out of a constitutional liking for useless information, and I found myself in possession of a very curious story, though, as I imagined, not the story I was looking for. It was to this effect. Some five or six years ago, a woman named Raymond suddenly made her appearance in the neighbourhood to which I am refer-

THE BEST GHOST STORIES

ring. She was described to me as being quite young, probably not more than seventeen or eighteen, very handsome, and looking as if she came from the country. I should be wrong in saying that she found her level in going to this particular quarter, or associating with these people, for from what I was told, I should think the worst den in London far too good for her. The person from whom I got my information, as you may suppose, no great Puritan, shuddered and grew sick in telling me of the nameless infamies which were laid to her charge. After living there for a year, or perhaps a little more, she disappeared as suddenly as she came, and they saw nothing of her till about the time of the Paul Street case. At first she came to her old haunts only occasionally, then more frequently, and finally took up her abode there as before, and remained for six or eight months. It's of no use my going into details as to the life that woman led; if you want particulars you can look at Meyrick's legacy. Those designs were not drawn from his imagination. She again disappeared, and the people of the place saw nothing of her till a few months ago. My informant told me that she had taken some rooms in a house which he pointed out, and these rooms she was in the habit of visiting two or three times a week and always at ten in the morning. I was led to expect that one of these visits would be paid on a certain day about a week ago, and I accordingly managed to be on the look-out in company with my cicerone at a quarter to ten, and the hour and the lady came with equal punctuality. My friend and I were standing under an archway, a little way back from the street, but she saw us, and gave me a glance that I shall be long in forgetting. That look was quite enough for me; I knew Miss Raymond to be Mrs Herbert; as for Mrs Beaumont she had quite gone out of my head. She went into the house, and I watched it till four o'clock, when she came out, and then I followed her. It was a long chase, and I had to be very careful to keep a long way in the background, and yet not lose sight of the woman. She took me down to the Strand, and then to Westminster, and then up St James's Street, and along Piccadilly. I felt queerish when I saw her turn up Ashley Street; the thought that Mrs Herbert was Mrs Beaumont came into my mind, but it seemed too improbable to be true. I waited at the corner, keeping my eye on her all the time, and I took particular care to note the house at which she stopped. It was the house with the gay curtains, the house of flowers, the house out of which Crashaw came the night he hanged himself in his garden. I was just going away with my discovery, when I saw an empty carriage come round and draw up in front of the house, and I came to the conclusion that Mrs Herbert was going out for a drive, and I was right. I took a hansom and followed the carriage into the Park. There, as it happened, I met a man I know, and we stood talking together a little distance from the carriage-way, to which I had my back. We had not been there for ten minutes when my friend took off his hat, and I glanced round and saw the lady I had been following all day. "Who is that?" I said, and his answer was, "Mrs Beaumont; lives in Ashley Street." Of course there could be no doubt after that. I don't know whether she saw me, but I don't think she did. I went home at once, and, on consideration, I thought that I had a sufficiently good case with which to go to Clarke.'

'Why to Clarke?'

'Because I am sure that Clarke is in possession of facts about this woman, facts of which I know nothing.'

'Well, what then?'

Mr Villiers leaned back in his chair and looked reflectively at Austin for a moment before he answered:

'My idea was that Clarke and I should call on Mrs Beaumont.'

'You would never go into such a house as that? No, no, Villiers, you cannot do it. Besides, consider; what result. . . .'

'I will tell you soon. But I was going to say that my information does not end here; it has been completed in an extraordinary manner.

'Look at this neat little packet of manuscript; it is paginated, you see, and I have indulged in the civil coquetry of a ribbon of red tape. It has almost a legal air, hasn't it? Run your eye over it, Austin. It is an account of the entertainment Mrs Beaumont provided for her choicer guests. The man who wrote this escaped with his life, but I do not think he will live many years. The doctors tell him he must have sustained some severe shock to the nerves.'

Austin took the manuscript, but never read it. Opening the neat pages at haphazard his eye was caught by a word and a phrase that followed it; and, sick at heart, with white lips and a cold sweat pouring like water from his temples, he flung the paper down.

'Take it away, Villiers, never speak of this again. Are you made of stone, man? Why, the dread and horror of death itself, the thoughts of the man who stands in the keen morning air on the black platform, bound, the bell tolling in his ears, and waits for the harsh rattle of the bolt, are as nothing compared to this. I will not read it; I should never sleep again.'

'Very good. I can fancy what you saw. Yes; it is horrible enough; but after all, it is an old story, an old mystery played in our day, and in dim London streets instead of amidst the vineyards and the olive gardens. We know what happened to those who chanced to meet the Great God Pan, and those who are wise know that all symbols are symbols of something, not of nothing. It was, indeed, an exquisite symbol beneath which men long ago veiled their knowledge of the most awful, most secret forces which lie at the heart of all things; forces before which the souls of men must wither and die and blacken, as their bodies blacken under the electric current. Such forces cannot be named, cannot be spoken, cannot be imagined except under a veil and a symbol, a symbol to the most of us appearing a quaint, poetic fancy, to some a foolish tale. But you and I, at all events, have known something of the terror that may dwell in the secret places of life, manifested under human flesh; that which is without form taking to itself a form. Oh, Austin, how can it be? How is it that the very sunlight does not turn to blackness before this thing, the hard earth melt and boil beneath such a burden?'

Villiers was pacing up and down the room, and the beads of sweat stood out on his forehead. Austin sat silent for a while, but Villiers saw him make a sign upon his breast.

'I say again, Villiers, you will surely never enter such a house as that? You would never pass out alive.'

'Yes, Austin, I shall go out alive – I, and Clarke with me.'

'What do you mean? You cannot, you would not dare. . . .'

'Wait a moment. The air was very pleasant and fresh this morning; there was a breeze blowing, even through this dull street, and I thought I would take a walk. Piccadilly stretched before me a clear, bright vista, and the sun flashed on the carriages and on the quivering leaves in the park. It was a joyous morning, and men and women looked at the sky and smiled as they went about their work or their pleasure, and the wind blew as blithely as upon the meadows and the scented gorse. But somehow or other I got out of the bustle and the gaiety, and found myself walking slowly along a quiet, dull street, where there seemed to be no sunshine and no air, and where the few foot-passengers loitered as they walked, and hung indecisively about corners and archways. I walked along, hardly knowing where I was going or what I did there, but feeling impelled, as one sometimes is, to explore still further, with a vague idea of reaching some unknown goal. Thus I forged up the street, noting the small traffic of the milk-shop, and wondering at the incongruous medley of penny pipes, black tobacco, sweets, newspapers, and comic songs which here and there jostled one another in the short compass of a single window. I think it was a cold shudder that suddenly passed through me that first told me that I had found what I wanted. I looked up from the pavement and stopped before a dusty shop, above which the lettering had faded, where the red bricks of two hundred years ago had grimed to black; where the windows had gathered to themselves the fog and the dirt of winters innumerable. I saw what I required; but I think it was five minutes before I had steadied myself and could walk in and ask for it in a cool voice and with a calm face. I think there must even then have been a tremor in my words, for the old man who came out from his back parlour, and fumbled slowly amongst his goods, looked oddly at me as he tied the parcel. I paid what he asked, and stood leaning by the counter, with a strange reluctance to take up my goods and go. I asked about the business, and learnt that trade was bad and the profits cut down sadly; but then the street was not what it was before traffic had been diverted, but that was done forty years ago, "just before my father died," he said. I got away at last, and walked along sharply; it was a dismal street indeed, and I was glad to return to the bustle and the noise. Would you like to see my purchase?'

Austin said nothing, but nodded his head slightly; he still looked white and sick. Villiers pulled out a drawer in the bamboo table, and showed Austin a long coil of cord, hard and new; and at one end was a running noose.

'It is the best hempen cord,' said Villiers, 'just as it used to be made for the old trade, the man told me. Not an inch of jute from end to end.'

Austin set his teeth hard, and stared at Villiers, growing whiter as he looked.

'You would not do it,' he murmured as last. 'You would not have blood on your hands. My God!' he exclaimed, with sudden vehemence, 'you cannot mean this, Villiers, that you will make yourself a hangman?'

'No. I shall offer a choice, and leave Helen Vaughan alone with this cord in a locked room for fifteen minutes. If when we go in it is not done, I shall call the nearest policeman. That is all.'

'I must go now. I cannot stay here any longer; I cannot bear this. Good-night.'

'Good-night, Austin.'

The door shut, but in a moment it was open again, and Austin stood, white and ghastly, in the entrance.

'I was forgetting,' he said, 'that I too have something to tell. I have received a letter from Dr Harding of Buenos Aires. He says that he attended Meyrick for three weeks before his death.'

'And does he say what carried him off in the prime of life? It was not fever?'

'No, it was not fever. According to the doctor, it was an utter collapse of the whole system, probably caused by some severe shock. But he states that the patient would tell him nothing, and that he was consequently at some disadvantage in treating the case.'

'Is there anything more?'

'Yes. Dr Harding ends his letter by saying: "I think this is all the information I can give you about your poor friend. He had not been long in Buenos Aires, and knew scarcely any one, with the exception of a person who did not bear the best of characters, and has since left – a Mrs Vaughan." '

8. *The Fragments*

Amongst the papers of the well-known physician, Dr Robert Matheson,
of Ashley Street, Piccadilly, who died suddenly, of apoplectic seizure, at
the beginning of 1892, a leaf of manuscript paper was found, covered
with pencil jottings. These notes were in Latin, much abbreviated, and
had evidently been made in great haste. The MS. was only deciphered
with great difficulty, and some words have up to the present time evaded
all the efforts of the expert employed. The date, 'XXV Jul. 1888,' is
written on the right-hand corner of the MS. The following is a translation
of Dr Matheson's manuscript.

Whether science would benefit by these brief notes if they could be
published, I do not know, but rather doubt. But certainly I shall never
take the responsibility of publishing or divulging one word of what is
here written, not only on account of my oath freely given to those two
persons who were present, but also because the details are too
abominable. It is probably that, upon mature consideration, and after
weighing the good and evil, I shall one day destroy this paper, or at
least leave it under seal to my friend D., trusting in his discretion, to
use it or to burn it, as he may think fit.

As was befitting, I did all that my knowledge suggested to make
sure that I was suffering under no delusion. At first astounded, I could
hardly think, but in a minute's time I was sure that my pulse was
steady and regular, and that I was in my real and true senses. I then
fixed my eyes quietly on what was before me.

Though horror and revolting nausea rose up within me, and an
odour of corruption choked my breath, I remained firm. I was then
privileged or accursed, I dare not say which, to see that which was on
the bed, lying there black like ink, transformed before my eyes. The
skin, and the flesh, and the muscles, and the bones, and the firm
structure of the human body that I had thought to be unchangeable,
and permanent as adamant, began to melt and dissolve.

I knew that the body may be separated into its elements by external agencies, but I should have refused to believe what I saw. For
here there was some internal force, of which I knew nothing, that
caused dissolution and change.

Here too was all the work by which man had been made repeated
before my eyes. I saw the form waver from sex to sex, dividing itself
from itself, and then again reunited. Then I saw the body descend to
the beasts whence it ascended, and that which was on the heights go
down to the depths, even to the abyss of all being. The principle of
life, which makes organism, always remained, while the outward

249

form changed.

The light within the room had turned to blackness, not the darkness of night, in which objects are seen dimly, for I could see clearly and without difficulty. But it was the negation of light; objects were presented to my eyes, if I may say so, without any medium, in such a manner that if there had been a prism in the room I should have seen no colours represented in it.

I watched, and at last I saw nothing but a substance as jelly. Then the ladder was ascended again . . . [*here the MS. is illegible*] . . . for one instant I saw a Form, shaped in dimness before me, which I will not farther describe. But the symbol of this form may be seen in ancient sculptures, and in paintings which survived beneath the lava, too foul to be spoken of . . . as a horrible and unspeakable shape, neither man nor beast, was changed into human form, there came finally death.

I who saw all this, not without great horror and loathing of soul, here write my name, declaring all that I have set on this paper to be true.

Robert Matheson, Med. Dr.

. . . Such, Raymond, is the story of what I know and what I have seen. The burden of it was too heavy for me to bear alone, and yet I could tell it to none but you. Villiers, who was with me at the last, knows nothing of that awful secret of the wood, of how what we both saw die, lay upon the smooth, sweet turf amidst the summer flowers, half in sun and half in shadow, and holding the girl Rachel's hand, called and summoned those companions, and shaped in solid form, upon the earth we tread on, the horror which we can but hint at, which we can only name under a figure. I would not tell Villiers of this, nor of that resemblance, which struck me as with a blow upon my heart, when I saw the portrait, which filled the cup of terror at the end. What this can mean I dare not guess. I know that what I saw perish was not Mary, and yet in the last agony Mary's eyes looked into mine. Whether there be any one who can show the last link in this chain of awful mystery, I do not know, but if there be any one who can do this, you, Raymond, are the man. And if you know the secret, it rests with you to tell it or not, as you please.

I am writing this letter to you immediately on my getting back to town. I have been in the country for the last few days; perhaps you may be able to guess in what part. While the horror and wonder of London was at its height – for 'Mrs Beaumont,' as I have told you, was well known in society – I wrote to my friend Dr Phillips, giving some brief outline, or rather hint, of what had happened, and asking him to tell me the name of the village where the events he had related to me occurred. He gave me the name, as he said with the less hesitation, because Rachel's father and mother were dead, and the rest of the family had gone to a relative in the state of Washington six months before. The parents, he said, had undoubtedly died of grief and horror caused by the terrible death of their daughter, and by what had gone before that death. On the evening of the day on which I received Phillips's letter I was at Caermaen, and standing beneath the mouldering Roman walls, white with the winters of seventeen hundred years, I looked over the meadow where once had stood the older temple of the 'God of the Deeps,' and saw a house gleaming in the sunlight. It was the house where Helen had lived. I stayed at Caermaen for several days. The people of the place, I found, knew little and had guessed less. Those whom I spoke to on the matter seemed surprised that an antiquarian (as I professed myself to be) should trouble about a village tragedy, of which they gave a very commonplace version, and, as you may imagine, I told nothing of what I knew. Most of my time was spent in the great wood that rises just above the village and climbs the hillside, and goes down to the river in the valley; such another long lovely valley, Raymond, as that on which we looked one summer night, walking to and fro before your house. For many an hour I strayed through the maze of the forest, turning now to right and now to left, pacing slowly down long alleys of undergrowth, shadowy and chill, even under the midday sun, and halting beneath great oaks; lying on the short turf of a clearing where the faint sweet scent of wild roses came to me on the wind and mixed with the heavy perfume of the elder, whose mingled odour is like the odour of the room of the dead, a vapour of incense and corruption. I stood at the edges of the the wood, gazing at all the pomp and procession of the foxgloves towering amidst the bracken and shining red in the broad sunshine, and beyond them into deep thickets of close undergrowth where springs boil up from the rock and nourish the water-weeds, dank and evil. But in all my wanderings I avoided one part of the wood; it was not till yesterday that I climbed to the summit of the hill, and stood upon the ancient Roman road that threads the highest ridge of the wood. Here they had walked, Helen and Rachel, along this quiet causeway, upon the pavement of green turf, shut in on either side by high banks of red earth, and tall hedges of shining beech, and here I followed in their steps, looking out, now and again, through partings in the boughs, and seeing on one side the sweep of the wood stretching far to right and left, and sinking into the broad level, and beyond, the yellow sea, and the land over the sea. On the other side was the valley and the river and hill following hill as wave on wave, and wood and meadow, and cornfield, and white houses gleaming, and a great wall of mountain, and far blue peaks in the north. And so at last I came to the place. The track went up a gentle slope, and widened out into an open space with a wall of thick undergrowth around it, and then, narrowing again, passed on into the distance and the faint blue mist of summer heat. And into this pleasant summer glade Rachel passed a girl, and left it, who shall say what? I did not stay long there.

In a small town near Caermaen there is a museum, containing for the most part Roman remains which have been found in the neighbourhood at various times. On the day after my arrival at Caermaen I walked over to the town in question, and took the opportunity of inspecting this museum. After I had seen most of the sculptured stones, the coffins, rings, coins, and fragments of tessellated pavement which the place contains, I was shown a small square pillar of white stone, which had been recently discovered in the wood of which I have been speaking, and, as I found on inquiry, in that open space where the Roman road broadens out. On one side of the pillar was an inscription, of which I took a note. Some of the letters have been defaced, but I do not think there can be any doubt as to those which I supply. The inscription is as follows:

> DEVOMNODENT*i*
> FLA*v*SSENILISPOSS*vit*
> PROPTERNVP*tias*
> *qua*SVIDITSVBMBR*a*

'To the great god Nodens (the god of the Great Deep or Abyss) Flavius Senilis has erected this pillar on account of the marriage which he saw beneath the shade.'

The custodian of the museum informed me that local antiquaries were much puzzled, not by the inscription, or by any difficulty in translating it, but as to the circumstance or rite to which allusion is made.

. . . And now, my dear Clarke, as to what you tell me about Helen Vaughan, whom you say you saw die under circumstances of the utmost and almost incredible horror. I was interested in your account, but a good deal, nay all, of what you told me I knew already. I can understand the strange likeness you remarked both in the portrait and in the actual face; you have seen Helen's mother. You remember that still summer night so many years ago, when I talked to you of the world beyond the shadows, and of the god Pan. You remember Mary. She was the mother of Helen Vaughan, who was born nine months after that night.

Mary never recovered her reason. She lay, as you saw her, all the while upon her bed, and a few days after the child was born she died. I fancy that just at the last she knew me; I was standing by the bed, and the old look came into her eyes for a second, and then she shuddered and groaned and died. It was an ill work I did that night when you were present; I broke open the door of the house of life, without knowing or caring what might pass forth or enter it. I recollect your telling me at the time, sharply enough, and rightly enough too, in one sense, that I had ruined the reason of a human being by a foolish experiment, based on an absurd theory. You did well to blame me, but my theory was not all absurdity. What I said Mary would see, she saw, but I forgot that no human eyes could look on such a vision with impunity. And I forgot, as I have just said, that when the house of life is thus thrown open, there may enter in that for which we have no name, and human flesh may become the veil of a horror one dare not express. I played with energies which I did not understand, and you have seen the ending of it. Helen Vaughan did well to bind the cord around her neck and die, though the death was horrible. The blackened face, the hideous form upon the bed, changing and melting before your eyes from woman to man, from man to beast, and from beast to worse than beast, all the strange horror that you witnessed, surprises me but little. What you say the doctor whom you sent for saw and shuddered at I noticed long ago; I knew what I had done the moment the child was born, and when it was scarcely five years old I surprised it, not once or twice but several times with a playmate, you may guess of what kind. It was for me a constant, an incarnate horror, and after a few years I felt I could bear it no longer, and I sent Helen Vaughan away. You know now what frightened the boy in the wood. The rest of the strange story, and all else that you tell me, as discovered by your friend, I have contrived to learn from time to time, almost to the last chapter. And now Helen is with her companions. . . .

Edward Lucas White

Lukundoo

'It stands to reason,' said Twombly, 'that a man must accept the evidence of his own eyes, and when eyes and ears agree, there can be no doubt. He has to believe what he has both seen and heard.'

'Not always,' put in Singleton, softly.

Every man turned towards Singleton. Twombly was standing on the hearthrug, his back to the grate, his legs spread out, with his habitual air of dominating the room. Singleton, as usual, was as much as possible effaced in a corner. But when Singleton spoke he said something. We faced him in that flattering spontaneity of expectant silence which invites utterance.

'I was thinking,' he said, after an interval, 'of something I both saw and heard in Africa.'

Now, if there was one thing we had found impossible, it had been to elicit from Singleton anything definite about his African experiences. As with the Alpinist in the story, who could tell only that he went up and came down, the sum of Singleton's revelations had been that he went there and came away. His words now riveted our attention at once. Twombly faded from the hearthrug, but not one of us could ever recall having seen him go. The room readjusted itself, focused on Singleton, and there was some hasty and furtive lighting of fresh cigars. Singleton lit one also, but it went out immediately, and he never relit it.

I

We were in the Great Forest, exploring for pigmies. Van Rieten had a theory that the dwarfs found by Stanley and others were a mere cross-breed between ordinary negroes and the real pigmies. He hoped to discover a race of men three feet tall at most, or shorter. We had found no trace of any such beings.

Natives were few, game scarce; food, except game, there was none; and the deepest, dankest, drippingest forest all about. We were the only novelty in the country, no native we met had even seen a white man before, most had never heard of white men. All of a sudden, late one afternoon, there came into our camp an Englishman, and pretty well used up he was, too. We had heard no rumour of him; he had not only heard of us but had made an amazing five-day march to reach us. His guide and two bearers were nearly as done up as he. Even though he was in tatters and had five days' beard on, you could see he was naturally dapper and neat and the sort of man to shave daily. He was small, but wiry. His face was the sort of British face from which emotion has been so carefully banished that a foreigner is apt to think the wearer of the face incapable of any sort of feeling; the kind of face which, if it has any expression at all, expresses principally the resolution to go through the world decorously, without intruding upon or annoying anyone.

His name was Etcham. He introduced himself modestly, and ate with us so deliberately that we should never have suspected, if our bearers had not had it from his bearers, that he had had but three meals in the five days, and those small. After we had lit up he told us why he had come.

'My chief is ve'y seedy,' he said between puffs. 'He is bound to go out if he keeps this way. I thought perhaps...'

He spoke quietly in a soft, even tone, but I could see little beads of sweat oozing out on his upper lip under his stubby moustache, and there was a tingle of repressed emotion in his tone, a veiled eagerness in his eye, a palpitating inward solicitude in his demeanour that moved me at once. Van Rieten had no sentiment in him; if he was moved he did not show it. But he listened. I was surprised at that. He was just the man to refuse at once. But he listened to Etcham's halting, difficult hints. He even asked questions.

'Who is your chief?'

'Stone,' Etcham lisped.

That electrified both of us.

'Ralph Stone?' we ejaculated together.

Etcham nodded.

For some minutes Van Rieten and I were silent. Van Rieten had never seen him, but I had been a classmate of Stone's, and Van Rieten and I had discussed him over many a camp fire. We had heard of him two years before, south of Luebo in the Balunda country, which had been ringing with his theatrical strife against a Balunda witch-doctor, ending in the sorcerer's complete discomfiture and the abasement of his tribe before Stone. They had even broken the fetish-man's whistle and given

Stone the pieces. It had been like the triumph of Elijah over the prophets of Baal, only more real to the Balunda.

We had thought of Stone as far off, if still in Africa at all, and here he turned up ahead of us and probably forestalling our quest.

II

Etcham's naming of Stone brought back to us all his tantalizing story, his fascinating parents, their tragic death; the brilliance of his college days; the dazzle of his millions; the promise of his young manhood; his wide notoriety, so nearly real fame; his romantic elopement with the meteoric authoress whose sudden cascade of fiction had made her so great a name so young, whose beauty and charm were so much heralded; the frightful scandal of the breach-of-promise suit that followed; his bride's devotion through it all; their sudden quarrel after it was all over; their divorce; the too much advertised announcement of his approaching marriage to the plaintiff in the breach-of-promise suit; his precipitate re-marriage to his divorced bride; their second quarrel and second divorce; his departure from his native land; his advent in the dark continent. The sense of all this rushed over me and I believe Van Rieten felt it too, as he sat silent.

Then he asked:

'Where is Werner?'

'Dead,' said Etcham. 'He died before I joined Stone.'

'You were not with Stone above Luebo?'

'No,' said Etcham, 'I joined him at Stanley Falls.'

'Who is with him?' Van Rieten asked.

'Only his Zanzibar servants and the bearers,' Etcham replied.

'What sort of bearers?' Van Rieten demanded.

'Mang-Battu men,' Etcham responded simply.

Now that impressed both Van Rieten and myself greatly. It bore out Stone's reputation as a notable leader of men. For up to that time no one had been able to use Mang-Battu as bearers outside of their own country, or to hold them for long or difficult expeditions.

'Were you long among the Mang-Battu?' was Van Rieten's next question.

'Some weeks,' said Etcham. 'Stone was interested in them and made up a fair-sized vocabulary of their words and phrases. He had a theory that they are an offshoot of the Balunda and he found much con-firmation in their customs.'

'What do you live on?' Van Rieten inquired.

'Game, mostly,' Etcham lisped.

'How long has Stone been laid up?' Van Rieten next asked.

'More than a month,' Etcham answered.

'And you have been hunting for the camp?' Van Rieten exclaimed.

Etcham's face, burnt and flayed as it was, showed a flush.

'I missed some easy shots,' he admitted ruefully. 'I've not felt ve'y fit myself.'

'What's the matter with your chief?' Van Rieten inquired.

'Something like carbuncles,' Etcham replied.

'He ought to get over a carbuncle or two,' Van Rieten declared.

'They are not carbuncles,' Etcham explained. 'Nor one or two. He has had dozens, sometimes five at once. If they had been carbuncles he would have been dead long ago. But in some ways they are not so bad, though in others they are worse.'

'How do you mean?' Van Rieten queried.

'Well,' Etcham hesitated, 'they do not seem to inflame so deep nor so wide as carbuncles, nor to be so painful, nor to cause so much fever. But then they seem to be part of a disease that affects his mind. He let me help him dress the first, but the others he has hidden most carefully, from me and from the men. He keeps his tent when they puff up, and will not let me change the dressings or be with him at all.'

'Have you plenty of dressings?' Van Rieten asked.

'We have some,' said Etcham doubtfully. 'But he won't use them; he washes out the dressings and uses them over and over.'

'How is he treating the swellings?' Van Rieten inquired.

'He slices them off clear down to flesh level, with his razor.'

'What?' Van Rieten shouted.

Etcham made no answer but looked him steadily in the eyes.

'I beg pardon,' Van Rieten hastened to say. 'You startled me. They can't be carbuncles. He'd have been dead long ago.'

'I thought I had said they are not carbuncles,' Etcham lisped.

'But the man must be crazy!' Van Rieten exclaimed.

'Just so,' said Etcham. 'He is beyond my advice or control.'

'How many has he treated that way?' Van Rieten demanded.

'Two, to my knowledge,' Etcham said.

'Two?' Van Rieten queried.

Etcham flushed again.

'I saw him,' he confessed, 'through a crack in the hut. I felt impelled to keep a watch on him, as if he was not responsible.'

'I should think not,' Van Rieten agreed. 'And you saw him do that twice?'

'I conjecture,' said Etcham, 'that he did the like with all the rest.'

'How many has he had?' Van Rieten asked.

'Dozens,' Etcham lisped.

'Does he eat?' Van Rieten inquired.

'Like a wolf,' said Etcham. 'More than any two bearers.'

'Can he walk?' Van Rietén asked.

'He crawls a bit, groaning,' said Etcham simply.

'Little fever, you say,' Van Rieten ruminated.

'Enough and too much,' Etcham declared.

'Has he been delirious?' Van Rieten asked.

'Only twice,' Etcham replied; 'once when the first swelling broke, and once later. He would not let anyone come near him then. But we could hear him talking, talking steadily, and it scared the natives.'

'Was he talking their patter in delirium?' Van Rieten demanded.

'No,' said Etcham, 'but he was talking some similar lingo. Hamed Burghash said he was talking Balunda. I know too little Balunda. I do not learn languages readily. Stone learned more Mang-Battu in a week than I could have learned in a year. But I seemed to hear words like Mang-Battu words. Anyhow, the Mang-Battu bearers were scared.'

'Scared?' Van Rieten repeated, questioningly.

'So were the Zanzibar men, even Hamed Burghash, and so was I,' said Etcham, 'only for a different reason. He talked in two voices.'

'In two voices,' Van Rieten reflected.

'Yes,' said Etcham, more excitedly than he had yet spoken. 'In two voices, like a conversation. One was his own, one a small thin, bleaty voice like nothing I ever heard. I seemed to make out, among the sounds the deep voice made, something like Mang-Battu words I knew, as *nedru, metababa,* and *nedo,* their terms for "head," "shoulder," "thigh," and perhaps *kudra* and *nekere* ("speak" and "whistle"); and among the noises of the shrill voice *matomipa, angunzi,* and *kamomami* ("kill," "death," and "hate"). Hamed Burghash said he also heard those words. He knew Mang-Battu far better than I.'

'What did the bearers say?' Van Rieten asked.

'They said, "*Lukundoo, Lukundoo!*" ' Etcham replied. 'I did not know that word; Hamed Burghash said it was Mang-Battu for "leopard." '

'It's Mang-Battu for "witchcraft," ' said Van Rieten.

'I don't wonder they thought so,' said Etcham. 'It was enough to make one believe in sorcery to listen to those two voices.'

'One voice answering the other?' Van Rieten asked perfunctorily.

Etcham's face went grey under his tan.

'Sometimes both at once,' he answered huskily.

'Both at once!' Van Rieten ejaculated.

'It sounded that way to the men, too,' said Etcham. 'And that was not all.'

He stopped and looked helplessly at us for a moment.

'Could a man talk and whistle at the same time?' he asked.

'How do you mean?' Van Rieten queried.

'We could hear Stone talking away, his big, deep-chested baritone rumbling along, and through it all we could hear a high, shrill whistle, the oddest, wheezy sound. You know, no matter how shrilly a grown man may whistle, the note has a different quality from the whistle of a boy or a woman or a little girl. They sound more treble, somehow. Well, if you can imagine the smallest girl who could whistle keeping it up tunelessly right along, that whistle was like that, only even more piercing, and it sounded right through Stone's bass tones.'

'And you didn't go to him?' Van Rieten cried.

'He is not given to threats,' Etcham disclaimed. 'But he had threatened, not volubly, nor like a sick man, but quietly and firmly, that if any man of us (he lumped me in with the men) came near him while he was in his trouble, that man should die. And it was not so much his word as his manner. It was like a monarch commanding respected privacy for a deathbed. One simply could not transgress.'

'I see,' said Van Rieten shortly.

'He's ve'y seedy,' Etcham repeated helplessly. 'I thought perhaps . . .'

His absorbing affection for Stone, his real love for him, shone out through his envelope of conventional training. Worship of Stone was plainly his master passion.

Like many competent men, Van Rieten had a streak of hard selfishness in him. It came to the surface then. He said we carried our lives in our hands from day to day just as genuinely as Stone; that he did not forget the ties of blood and calling between any two explorers, but that there was no sense in imperilling one party for a very problematical benefit to a man probably beyond any help; that it was enough of a task to hunt for one party; that if two were united, providing food would be more than doubly difficult; that the risk of starvation was too great. Deflecting our march seven full days' journey (he complimented Etcham on his marching powers) might ruin our expedition entirely.

III

Van Rieten had logic on his side and he had a way with him. Etcham sat there apologetic and deferential, like a fourth-form schoolboy before a headmaster. Van Rieten wound up.

'I am after pigmies, at the risk of my life. After pigmies I go.'

'Perhaps, then, these will interest you,' said Etcham, very quietly.

He took two objects out of the side-pocket of his blouse, and handed them to Van Rieten. They were round, bigger than big plums, and smaller than small peaches, about the right size to enclose in an average hand. They were black, and at first I did not see what they were.

'Pigmies!' Van Rieten exclaimed. 'Pigmies, indeed! Why, they wouldn't be two feet high! Do you mean to claim that these are adult heads?'

'I claim nothing,' Etcham answered evenly. 'You can see for yourself.'

Van Rieten passed one of the heads to me. The sun was just setting and I examined it closely. A dried head it was, perfectly preserved, and the flesh as hard as Argentine jerked beef. A bit of a vertebra stuck out where the muscles of the vanished neck had shrivelled into folds. The puny chin was sharp on a projecting jaw, the minute teeth white and even between the retracted lips, the tiny nose was flat, the little forehead retreating, there were inconsiderable clumps of stunted wool on the Lilliputian cranium. There was nothing babyish, childish or youthful about the head; rather it was mature to senility.

'Where did these come from?' Van Rieten inquired.

'I do not know,' Etcham replied precisely. 'I found them among Stone's effects while rummaging for medicines or drugs or anything that could help me to help him. I do not know where he got them. But I'll swear he did not have them when we entered this district.'

'Are you sure?' Van Rieten queried, his eyes big and fixed on Etcham's.

'Ve'y sure,' lisped Etcham.

'But how could he have come by them without your knowledge?' Van Rieten demurred.

'Sometimes we were apart ten days at a time hunting,' said Etcham. 'Stone is not a talking man. He gave me no account of his doings, and Hamed Burghash keeps a still tongue and a tight hold on the men.'

'You have examined these heads?' Van Rieten asked.

'Minutely,' said Etcham.

Van Rieten took out his notebook. He was a methodical chap. He tore out a leaf, folded it and divided it equally into three pieces. He gave one to me and one to Etcham.

'Just for a test of my impressions,' he said, 'I want each of us to write separately just what he is most reminded of by these heads. Then I want to compare the writings.'

I handed Etcham a pencil and he wrote. Then he handed the pencil back to me and I wrote.

'Read the three,' said Van Rieten, handing me his piece.

Van Rieten had written:

'An old Balunda witch-doctor.'

Etcham had written:

'An old Mang-Battu fetish-man.'

I had written:

'An old Katongo magician.'

'There!' Van Rieten exclaimed. 'Look at that! There is nothing

Wagabi or Batwa or Wambuttu or Wabotu about these heads. Nor anything pigmy either.'

'I thought as much,' said Etcham.

'And you say he did not have them before?'

'To a certainty he did not,' Etcham asserted.

'It is worth following up,' said Van Rieten. 'I'll go with you. And first of all, I'll do my best to save Stone.'

He put out his hand and Etcham clasped it silently. He was grateful all over.

IV

Nothing but Etcham's fever of solicitude could have taken him in five days over the track. It took him eight days to retrace with full knowledge of it and our party to help. We could not have done it in seven, and Etcham urged us on, in a repressed fury of anxiety, no mere fever of duty to his chief, but a real ardour of devotion, a glow of personal adoration for Stone which blazed under his dry conventional exterior and showed in spite of him.

We found Stone well cared for. Etcham had seen to a good high thorn *zareeba* round the camp, the huts were well built and thatched, and Stone's was as good as their resources would permit. Hamed Burghash was not named after two Seyyids for nothing. He had in him the making of a sultan. He had kept the Mang-Battu together, not a man had slipped off, and he had kept them in order. Also he was a deft nurse and a faithful servant.

The two other Zanzibaris had done some creditable hunting. Though all were hungry, the camp was far from starvation.

Stone was on a canvas cot and there was a sort of collapsible camp-stool-table, like a Turkish tabouret, by the cot. It had a water-bottle and some vials on it and Stone's watch, also his razor in its case.

Stone was clean and not emaciated, but he was far gone; not unconscious, but in a daze; past commanding or resisting anyone. He did not seem to see us enter or to know we were there. I should have recognized him anywhere. His boyish dash and grace had vanished utterly, of course. But his head was even more leonine; his hair was still abundant, yellow and wavy; the close, crisped blond beard he had grown during his illness did not alter him. He was big and big-chested yet. His eyes were dull and he mumbled and babbled mere meaningless syllables, not words.

Etcham helped Van Rieten to uncover him and look him over. He was in good muscle for a man so long bedridden. There were no scars on him except about his knees, shoulders and chest. On each knee and above it he had a full score of roundish cicatrices, and a dozen or more on each

shoulder, all in front. Two or three were open wounds and four or five
barely healed. He had no fresh swellings, except two, one on each side,
on his pectoral muscles, the one on the left being higher up and farther
out than the other. They did not look like boils or carbuncles, but as if
something blunt and hard were being pushed up through the fairly
healthy flesh and skin, not much inflamed.

'I should not lance those,' said Van Rieten, and Etcham assented.

They made Stone as comfortable as they could, and just before sunset
we looked in at him again. He was lying on his back, and his chest showed
big and massive yet, but he lay as if in a stupor. We left Etcham with
him and went into the next hut, which Etcham had resigned to us. The
jungle noises were no different there than anywhere else for months
past, and I was soon fast asleep.

V

Some time in the pitch dark I found myself awake and listening. I
could hear two voices, one Stone's, the other sibilant and wheezy. I knew
Stone's voice after all the years that had passed since I heard it last. The
other was like nothing I remembered. It had less volume than the wail
of a new-born baby, yet there was an insistent carrying power to it, like
the shrilling of an insect. As I listened I heard Van Rieten breathing
near me in the dark; then he heard me and realized that I was listening
too. Like Etcham I knew little Balunda, but I could make out a word or
two. The voices alternated, with intervals of silence between.

Then suddenly both sounded at once and fast. Stone's baritone basso,
full as if he were in perfect health, and that incredibly stridulous falsetto,
both jabbering at once like the voices of two people quarrelling and
trying to talk each other down.

'I can't stand this,' said Van Rieten. 'Let's have a look at him.'

He had one of those cylindrical electric night-candles. He fumbled
about for it, touched the button and beckoned me to come with him.
Outside the hut he motioned me to stand still, and instinctively turned
off the light, as if seeing made listening difficult.

Except for a faint glow from the embers of the bearers' fire we were
in complete darkness, little starlight struggled through the trees, the
river made but a faint murmur. We could hear the two voices together
and then suddenly the creaking voice changed into a razor-edged, slicing
whistle, indescribably cutting, continuing right through Stone's grumbling torrent of croaking words.

'Good God!' exclaimed Van Rieten.

Abruptly he turned on the light.

We found Etcham utterly asleep, exhausted by his long anxiety and the exertions of his phenomenal march, and relaxed completely now that the load was in a sense shifted from his shoulders to Van Rieten's. Even the light on his face did not wake him.

The whistle had ceased and the two voices sounded together. Both came from Stone's cot, where the concentrated white ray showed him lying just as we had left him, except that he had tossed his arms above his head and had torn the coverings and bandages from his chest.

The swelling on the right breast had broken. Van Rieten aimed the centre line of the light at it and we saw it plainly. From his flesh, grown out of it, there protruded a head, such a head as the dried specimens Etcham had shown us, as if it were a miniature of the head of a Balunda fetish-man. It was black, shining black as the blackest African skin; it rolled the whites of its wicked, wee eyes and showed its microscopic teeth between lips repulsively negroid in their red fullness, even in so diminutive a face. It had crisp, fuzzy wool on its miniskin skull, it turned malignantly from side to side and chittered incessantly in that inconceivable falsetto. Stone babbled brokenly against its patter.

Van Rieten turned from Stone and waked Etcham, with some difficulty. When he was awake and saw it all, Etcham stared and said not one word.

'You saw him slice off two swellings?' Van Rieten asked.

Etcham nodded, chokingly.

'Did he bleed much?' Van Rieten demanded.

'Ve'y little,' Etcham replied.

'You hold his arms,' said Van Rieten to Etcham.

He took up Stone's razor and handed me the light. Stone showed no sign of seeing the light or of knowing we were there. But the little head mewled and screeched at us.

Van Rieten's hand was steady, and the sweep of the razor even and true. Stone bled amazingly little and Van Rieten dressed the wound as if it had been a bruise or scrape.

Stone had stopped talking the instant the excrescent head was severed. Van Rieten did all that could be done for Stone and then fairly grabbed the light from me. Snatching up a gun he scanned the ground by the cot and brought the butt down once and twice, viciously.

We went back to our hut, but I doubt if I slept.

VI

Next day, near noon, in broad daylight, we heard the two voices from Stone's hut. We found Etcham dropped asleep by his charge. The swelling on the left had broken, and just such another head was there miauling and spluttering. Etcham woke up and the three of us stood there and glared. Stone interjected hoarse vocables into the tinkling gurgle of the portent's utterance.

Van Rieten stepped forward, took up Stone's razor and knelt down by the cot. The atomy of a head squealed a wheezy snarl at him.

Then suddenly Stone spoke English.

'Who are you with my razor?'

Van Rieten started back and stood up.

Stone's eyes were clear now and bright, they roved about the hut.

'The end,' he said; 'I recognize the end. I seem to see Etcham, as if in life. But Singleton! Ah, Singleton! Ghosts of my boyhood come to watch me pass! And you, strange spectre with the black beard and my razor! Aroint ye all!'

'I'm no ghost, Stone,' I managed to say. 'I'm alive. So are Etcham and Van Rieten. We are here to help you.'

'Van Rieten!' he exclaimed. 'My work passes on to a better man. Luck go with you, Van Rieten.'

Van Rieten went nearer to him.

'Just hold still a moment, old man,' he said soothingly. 'It will be only one twinge.'

'I've held still for many such twinges,' Stone answered quite distinctly. 'Let me be. Let me die in my own way. The hydra was nothing to this. You can cut off ten, a hundred, a thousand heads, but the curse you can not cut off, or take off. What's soaked into the bone won't come out of the flesh, any more than what's bred there. Don't hack me any more. Promise!'

His voice had all the old commanding tone of his boyhood and it swayed Van Rieten as it always had swayed everybody.

'I promise,' said Van Rieten.

Almost as he said the word Stone's eyes filmed again.

Then we three sat about Stone and watched that hideous, gibbering prodigy grow up out of Stone's flesh, till two horrid, spindling little black arms disengaged themselves. The infinitesimal nails were perfect to the barely perceptible moon at the quick, the pink spot on the palm was horridly natural. These arms gesticulated and the right plucked towards Stone's blond beard.

'I can't stand this,' Van Rieten exclaimed and took up the razor again.

Instantly Stone's eyes opened, hard and glittering.

'Van Rieten break his word?' he enunciated slowly. 'Never!'

'But we must help you,' Van Rieten gasped.

'I am past all help and all hurting,' said Stone. 'This is my hour. This curse is not put on me; it grew out of me, like this horror here. Even now I go.'

His eyes closed and we stood helpless, the adherent figure spouting shrill sentences.

In a moment Stone spoke again.

'You speak all tongues?' he asked quickly.

And the mergent minikin replied in sudden English:

'Yea, verily, all that you speak,' putting out its microscopic tongue, writhing its lips and wagging its head from side to side. We could see the thready ribs on its exiguous flanks heave as if the thing breathed.

'Has she forgiven me?' Stone asked in a muffled strangle.

'Not while the moss hangs from the cypresses,' the head squeaked. 'Not while the stars shine on Lake Pontchartrain will she forgive.'

And then Stone, all with one motion, wrenched himself over on his side. The next instant he was dead.

When Singleton's voice ceased the room was hushed for a space. We could hear each other breathing. Twombly, the tactless, broke the silence.

'I presume,' he said, 'you cut off the little minikin and brought it home in alcohol.'

Singleton turned on him a stern countenance.

'We buried Stone,' he said, 'unmutilated as he died.'

'But,' said the unconscionable Twombly, 'the whole thing is incredible.'

Singleton stiffened.

'I did not expect you to believe it,' he said; 'I began by saying that although I heard and saw it, when I look back on it I cannot credit it myself.'

E. F. Benson

The Man Who Went Too Far

The little village of St Faith's nestles in a hollow of wooded hill up on the north bank of the river Fawn in the county of Hampshire, huddling close round its grey Norman church as if for spiritual protection against the fays and fairies, the trolls and 'little people', who might be supposed still to linger in the vast empty spaces of the New Forest, and to come after dusk and do their doubtful businesses. Once outside the hamlet you may walk in any direction (so long as you avoid the high road which leads to Brockenhurst) for the length of a summer afternoon without seeing sign of human habitation, or possibly even catching sight of another human being. Shaggy wild ponies may stop their feeding for a moment as you pass, the white scuts of rabbits will vanish into their burrows, a brown viper perhaps will glide from your path into a clump of heather, and unseen birds will chuckle in the bushes, but it may easily happen that for a long day you will see nothing human. But you will not feel in the least lonely; in summer, at any rate, the sunlight will be gay with butterflies, and the air thick with all those woodland sounds which like instruments in an orchestra combine to play the great symphony of the yearly festival of June. Winds whisper in the birches, and sigh among the firs; bees are busy with their redolent labour among the heather, a myriad birds chirp in the green temples of the forest trees, and the voice of the river prattling over stony places, bubbling into pools, chuckling and gulping round corners, gives you the sense that many presences and companions are near at hand.

Yet, oddly enough, though one would have thought that these benign and cheerful influences of wholesome air and spaciousness of forest were very healthful comrades for a man, in so far as nature can really influence this wonderful human genus which has in these centuries learned

to defy her most violent storms in its well-established houses, to bridle
her torrents and make them light its streets, to tunnel her mountains
and plough her seas, the inhabitants of St Faith's will not willingly venture into the forest after dark. For in spite of the silence and loneliness
of the hooded night it seems that a man is not sure in what company he
may suddenly find himself, and though it is difficult to get from these
villagers any very clear story of occult appearances, the feeling is wide-
spread. One story indeed I have heard with some definiteness, the tale of
a monstrous goat that has been seen to skip with hellish glee about the
woods and shady places, and this perhaps is connected with the story
which I have here attempted to piece together. It too is well-known to
them; for all remember the young artist who died here not long ago, a
young man, or so he struck the beholder, of great personal beauty, with
something about him that made men's faces to smile and brighten when
they looked on him. His ghost they will tell you 'walks' constantly by the
stream and through the woods which he loved so, and in especial it
haunts a certain house, the last of the village, where he lived, and its
garden in which he was done to death. For my part I am inclined to
think that the terror of the Forest dates chiefly from that day. So, such
as the story is, I have set it forth in connected form. It is based partly on
the accounts of the villagers, but mainly on that of Darcy, a friend of
mine and a friend of the man with whom these events were chiefly
concerned.

The day had been one of untarnished midsummer splendour, and as
the sun drew near to its setting, the glory of the evening grew every
moment more crystalline, more miraculous. Westward from St Faith's
the beechwood which stretched for some miles toward the heathery
upland beyond already cast its veil of clear shadow over the red roofs of
the village, but the spire of the grey church, overtopping all, still
pointed a flaming orange finger into the sky. The river Fawn, which runs
below, lay in sheets of sky-reflected blue, and wound its dreamy devious
course round the edge of this wood, where a rough two-planked bridge
crossed from the bottom of the garden of the last house in the village,
and communicated by means of a little wicker gate with the wood itself.
Then once out of the shadow of the wood the stream lay in flaming
pools of the molten crimson of the sunset, and lost itself in the haze of
woodland distances.

This house at the end of the village stood outside the shadow, and the
lawn which sloped down to the river was still flecked with sunlight.
Garden-beds of dazzling colour lined its gravel walks, and down the
middle of it ran a brick pergola, half-hidden in clusters of rambler-rose
and purple with starry clematis. At the bottom end of it, between two of

its pillars, was slung a hammock containing a shirt-sleeved figure.

The house itself lay somewhat remote from the rest of the village, and a footpath leading across two fields, now tall and fragrant with hay, was its only communication with the high road. It was low-built, only two stories in height, and like the garden, its walls were a mass of flowering roses. A narrow stone terrace ran along the garden front, over which was stretched an awning, and on the terrace a young silent-footed man-servant was busied with the laying of the table for dinner. He was neat-handed and quick with his job, and having finished it he went back into the house, and reappeared again with a large rough bath-towel on his arm. With this he went to the hammock in the pergola.

'Nearly eight, sir,' he said.

'Has Mr Darcy come yet?' asked a voice from the hammock.

'No, sir.'

'If I'm not back when he comes, tell him that I'm just having a bathe before dinner.'

The servant went back to the house, and after a moment or two Frank Halton struggled to a sitting posture, and slipped out on to the grass. He was of medium height and rather slender in build, but the supple ease and grace of his movements gave the impression of great physical strength: even his descent from the hammock was not an awkward performance. His face and hands were of very dark complexion, either from constant exposure to wind and sun, or, as his black hair and dark eyes tended to show, from some strain of southern blood. His head was small, his face of an exquisite beauty of modelling, while the smoothness of its contour would have led you to believe that he was a beardless lad still in his teens. But something, some look which living and experience alone can give, seemed to contradict that, and finding yourself completely puzzled as to his age, you would next moment probably cease to think about that, and only look at this glorious specimen of young manhood with wondering satisfaction.

He was dressed as became the season and the heat, and wore only a shirt open at the neck, and a pair of flannel trousers. His head, covered very thickly with a somewhat rebellious crop of short curly hair, was bare as he strolled across the lawn to the bathing-place that lay below. Then for a moment there was silence, then the sound of splashed and divided waters, and presently after, a great shout of ecstatic joy, as he swam up-stream with the foamed water standing in a frill round his neck. Then after some five minutes of limb-stretching struggle with the flood, he turned over on his back, and with arms thrown wide, floated down-stream, ripple-cradled and inert. His eyes were shut, and between half-parted lips he talked gently to himself.

'I am one with it,' he said to himself, 'the river and I, I and the river.

The coolness and splash of it is I, and the water-herbs that wave in it are I also. And my strength and my limbs are not mine but the river's. It is all one, all one, dear Fawn.'

A quarter of an hour later he appeared again at the bottom of the lawn, dressed as before, his wet hair already drying into its crisp short curls again. There he paused a moment, looking back at the stream with the smile with which men look on the face of a friend, then turned towards the house. Simultaneously his servant came to the door leading on to the terrace, followed by a man who appeared to be some half-way through the fourth decade of his years. Frank and he saw each other across the bushes and garden-beds, and each quickening his step, they met suddenly face to face round an angle of the garden walk, in the fragrance of syringa.

'My dear Darcy,' cried Frank, 'I am charmed to see you.'

But the other stared at him in amazement.

'Frank!' he exclaimed.

'Yes, that is my name,' he said laughing, 'what is the matter?'

Darcy took his hand.

'What have you done to yourself?' he asked. 'You are a boy again.'

'Ah, I have a lot to tell you,' said Frank. 'Lots that you will hardly believe, but I shall convince you—'

He broke off suddenly, and held up his hand.

'Hush, there is my nightingale,' he said.

The smile of recognition and welcome with which he had greeted his friend faded from his face, and a look of rapt wonder took its place, as of a lover listening to the voice of his beloved. His mouth parted slightly, showing the white line of teeth, and his eyes looked out and out till they seemed to Darcy to be focused on things beyond the vision of man. Then something perhaps startled the bird, for the song ceased.

'Yes, lots to tell you,' he said. 'Really I am delighted to see you. But you look rather white and pulled down; no wonder after that fever. And there is to be no nonsense about this visit. It is June now, you stop here till you are fit to begin work again. Two months at least.'

'Ah, I can't trespass quite to that extent.'

Frank took his arm and walked him down the grass.

'Trespass? Who talks of trespass? I shall tell you quite openly when I am tired of you, but you know when we had the studio together, we used not to bore each other. However, it is ill talking of going away on the moment of your arrival. Just a stroll to the river, and then it will be dinner-time.'

Darcy took out his cigarette case, and offered it to the other.

Frank laughed.

'No, not for me. Dear me, I suppose I used to smoke once. How very odd!'

'Given it up?'

'I don't know. I suppose I must have. Anyhow I don't do it now. I would as soon think of eating meat.'

'Another victim on the smoking altar of vegetarianism?'

'Victim?' asked Frank. 'Do I strike you as such?'

He paused on the margin of the stream and whistled softly. Next moment a moor-hen made its splashing flight across the river, and ran up the bank. Frank took it very gently in his hands and stroked its head, as the creature lay against his shirt.

'And is the house among the reeds still secure?' he half-crooned to it. 'And is the missus quite well, and are the neighbours flourishing? There, dear, home with you,' and he flung it into the air.

'That bird's very tame,' said Darcy, slightly bewildered.

'It is rather,' said Frank, following its flight.

During dinner Frank chiefly occupied himself in bringing himself up-to-date in the movements and achievements of this old friend whom he had not seen for six years. Those six years, it now appeared, had been full of incident and success for Darcy; he had made a name for himself as a portrait painter which bade fair to outlast the vogue of a couple of seasons, and his leisure time had been brief. Then some four months previously he had been through a severe attack of typhoid, the result of which as concerns this story was that he had come down to this sequestered place to recruit.

'Yes, you've got on,' said Frank at the end. 'I always knew you would. A.R.A. with more in prospect. Money? You roll in it, I suppose, and, O Darcy, how much happiness have you had all these years? That is the only imperishable possession. And how much have you learned? Oh, I don't mean in Art. Even I could have done well in that.'

Darcy laughed.

'Done well? My dear fellow, all I have learned in these six years you knew, so to speak, in your cradle. Your old pictures fetch huge prices. Do you never paint now?'

Frank shook his head.

'No, I'm too busy,' he said.

'Doing what? Please tell me. That is what everyone is for ever asking me.'

'Doing? I suppose you would say I do nothing.'

Darcy glanced up at the brilliant young face opposite him.

'It seems to suit you, that way of being busy,' he said. 'Now, it's your turn. Do you read? Do you study? I remember you saying that it would do us all – all us artists, I mean – a great deal of good if we would study any one human face carefully for a year, without recording a line. Have you been doing that?'

Frank shook his head again.

'I mean exactly what I say,' he said, 'I have been *doing* nothing. And I have never been so occupied. Look at me; have I not done something to myself to begin with?'

'You are two years younger than I,' said Darcy, 'at least you used to be. You therefore are thirty-five. But had I never seen you before I should say you were just twenty. But was it worth while to spend six years of greatly-occupied life in order to look twenty? Seems rather like a woman of fashion.'

Frank laughed boisterously.

'First time I've ever been compared to that particular bird of prey,' he said. 'No, that has not been my occupation – in fact I am only very rarely conscious that one effect of my occupation has been that. Of course, it must have been if one comes to think of it. It is not very important. Quite true my body has become young. But that is very little; I have become young.'

Darcy pushed back his chair and sat sideways to the table looking at the other.

'Has that been your occupation then?' he asked.

'Yes, that anyhow is one aspect of it. Think what youth means! It is the capacity for growth, mind, body, spirit, all grow, all get stronger, all have a fuller, firmer life every day. That is something, considering that every day that passes after the ordinary man reaches the full-blown flower of his strength, weakens his hold on life. A man reaches his prime, and remains, we say, in his prime, for ten years, or perhaps twenty. But after his primest prime is reached, he slowly, insensibly weakens. These are the signs of age in you, in your body, in your art probably, in your mind. You are less electric than you were. But I, when I reach my prime – I am nearing it – ah, you shall see.'

The stars had begun to appear in the blue velvet of the sky, and to the east the horizon seen above the black silhouette of the village was grow- ing dove-coloured with the approach of moon-rise. White moths hovered dimly over the garden-beds, and the footsteps of night tip-toed through the bushes. Suddenly Frank rose.

'Ah, it is the supreme moment,' he said softly. 'Now more than at any other time the current of life, the eternal imperishable current runs so close to me that I am almost enveloped in it. Be silent a minute.'

He advanced to the edge of the terrace and looked out standing stretched with arms outspread. Darcy heard him draw a long breath into his lungs, and after many seconds expel it again. Six or eight times he did this, then turned back into the lamplight.

'It will sound to you quite mad, I expect,' he said, 'but if you want to hear the soberest truth I have ever spoken and shall ever speak, I will tell you about myself. But come into the garden if it is not too damp for you. I have never told anyone yet, but I shall like to tell you. It is long, in fact, since I have even tried to classify what I have learned.'

They wandered into the fragrant dimness of the pergola, and sat down. Then Frank began:

'Years ago, do you remember,' he said, 'we used often to talk about the decay of joy in the world. Many impulses, we settled, had contributed to this decay, some of which were good in themselves, others that were quite completely bad. Among the good things, I put what we may call certain Christian virtues, renunciation, resignation, sympathy with suffering, and the desire to relieve sufferers. But out of those things spring very bad ones, useless renunciations, asceticism for its own sake, mortification of the flesh with nothing to follow, no corresponding gain that is, and that awful and terrible disease which devastated England some centuries ago, and from which by heredity of spirit we suffer now, Puritanism. That was a dreadful plague, the brutes held and taught that joy and laughter and merriment were evil: it was a doctrine the most profane and wicked. Why, what is the commonest crime one sees? A sullen face. That is the truth of the matter.

'Now all my life I have believed that we are intended to be happy, that joy is of all gifts the most divine. And when I left London, abandoned my career, such as it was, I did so because I intended to devote my life to the cultivation of joy, and, by continuous and unsparing effort, to be happy. Among people, and in constant intercourse with others, I did not find it possible; there were too many distractions in towns and work-rooms, and also too much suffering. So I took one step backwards or forwards, as you may choose to put it, and went straight to Nature, to trees, birds, animals, to all those things which quite clearly pursue one aim only, which blindly follow the great native instinct to be happy without any care at all for morality, or human law or divine law. I wanted, you understand, to get all joy first-hand and unadulterated, and I think it scarcely exists among men; it is obsolete.'

Darcy turned in his chair.

'Ah, but what makes birds and animals happy?' he asked. 'Food, food and mating.'

Frank laughed gently in the stillness.

'Do not think I became a sensualist,' he said. 'I did not make that mistake. For the sensualist carries his miseries pick-a-back, and round his feet is wound the shroud that shall soon enwrap him. I may be mad, it is true, but I am not so stupid anyhow as to have tried that. No, what is it that makes puppies play with their own tails, that sends cats on their prowling ecstatic errands at night?'

He paused a moment.

'So I went to Nature,' he said. 'I sat down here in this New Forest, sat down fair and square, and looked. That was my first difficulty, to sit here quiet without being bored, to wait without being impatient, to be receptive and very alert, though for a long time nothing particular happened. The change in fact was slow in those early stages.'

'Nothing happened?' asked Darcy rather impatiently, with the sturdy revolt against any new idea which to the English mind is synonymous with nonsense. 'Why, what in the world *should* happen?'

Now Frank as he had known him was the most generous but most quick-tempered of mortal men; in other words his anger would flare to a prodigious beacon, under almost no provocation, only to be quenched again under a gust of no less impulsive kindliness. Thus the moment Darcy had spoken, an apology for his hasty question was half-way up his tongue. But there was no need for it to have travelled even so far, for Frank laughed again with kindly, genuine mirth.

'Oh, how I should have resented that a few years ago,' he said. 'Thank goodness that resentment is one of the things I have got rid of. I certainly wish that you should believe my story – in fact, you are going to – but that you at this moment should imply that you do not, does not concern me.'

'Ah, your solitary sojournings have made you inhuman,' said Darcy, still very English.

'No, human,' said Frank. 'Rather more human, at least rather less of an ape.'

'Well, that was my first quest,' he continued, after a moment, 'the deliberate and unswerving pursuit of joy, and my method, the eager contemplation of Nature. As far as motive went, I daresay it was purely selfish, but as far as effect goes, it seems to me about the best thing one can do for one's fellow-creatures, for happiness is more infectious than small-pox. So, as I said, I sat down and waited; I looked at happy things, zealously avoided the sight of anything unhappy, and by degrees a little trickle of the happiness of this blissful world began to filter into me. The trickle grew more abundant, and now, my dear fellow, if I could for a moment divert from me into you one half of the torrent of joy that pours through me day and night, you would throw the world, art, everything aside, and just live, exist. When a man's body dies, it passes into trees and flowers. Well, that is what I have been trying to do with my soul before death.'

The servant had brought into the pergola a table with syphons and spirits, and had set a lamp upon it. As Frank spoke he leaned forward towards the other, and Darcy for all his matter-of-fact common-sense could have sworn that his companion's face shone, was luminous in itself. His dark brown eyes glowed from within, the unconscious smile of a child irradiated and transformed his face. Darcy felt suddenly excited, exhilarated.

'Go on,' he said. 'Go on. I can feel you are somehow telling me sober truth. I daresay you are mad; but I don't see that matters.'

Frank laughed again.

'Mad?' he said. 'Yes, certainly, if you wish. But I prefer to call it sane. However, nothing matters less than what anybody chooses to call things. God never labels his gifts; He just puts them into our hands; just as he put animals in the garden of Eden, for Adam to name if he felt disposed.'

'So by the continual observance and study of things that were happy,' continued he, 'I got happiness, I got joy. But seeking it, as I did, from Nature, I got much more which I did not seek, but stumbled upon originally by accident. It is difficult to explain, but I will try.

'About three years ago I was sitting one morning in a place I will show you to-morrow. It is down by the river brink, very green, dappled with shade and sun, and the river passes there through some little clumps of reeds. Well, as I sat there, doing nothing, but just looking and listening, I heard the sound quite distinctly of some flute-like instrument playing a strange unending melody. I thought at first it was some musical yokel on the highway and did not pay much attention. But before long the strangeness and indescribable beauty of the tune struck me. It never repeated itself, but it never came to an end, phrase after phrase ran its sweet course, it worked gradually and inevitably up to a climax, and having attained it, it went on; another climax was reached and another and another. Then with a sudden gasp of wonder I localised where it came from. It came from the reeds and from the sky and from the trees. It was everywhere, it was the sound of life. It was, my dear Darcy, as the Greks would have said, it was Pan playing on his pipes, the voice of Nature. It was the life-melody, the world-melody.'

Darcy was far too interested to interrupt, though there was a question he would have liked to ask, and Frank went on:

'Well, for the moment I was terrified, terrified with the impotent horror of nightmare, and I stopped my ears and just ran from the place and got back to the house panting, trembling, literally in a panic. Unknowingly, for at that time I only pursued joy. I had begun, since I drew my joy from Nature, to get in touch with Nature. Nature, force, God, call it what you will, had drawn across my face a little gossamer web of essential life. I saw that when I emerged from my terror, and I went very humbly back to where I had heard the Pan-pipes. But it was nearly six months before I heard them again.'

'Why was that?' asked Darcy.

'Surely because I had revolted, rebelled, and worst of all been frightened. For I believe that just as there is nothing in the world which so injures one's body as fear, so there is nothing that so much shuts up the soul. I was afraid, you see, of the one thing in the world which has real existence. No wonder its manifestation was withdrawn.'

'And after six months?'

'After six months one blessed morning I heard the piping again. I wasn't afraid that time. And since then it has grown louder, it has become more constant. I now hear it often, and I can put myself into such an attitude towards Nature that the pipes will almost certainly sound. And never yet have they played the same tune, it is always something new, something fuller, richer, more complete than before.'

'What do you mean by "such an attitude towards Nature"?' asked Darcy.

'I can't explain that; but by translating it into a bodily attitude it is this.'

Frank sat up for a moment quite straight in his chair, then slowly sunk back with arms outspread and head drooped.

'That;' he said, 'an effortless attitude, but open, resting, receptive. It is just that which you must do with your soul.'

Then he sat up again.

'One word more,' he said, 'and I will bore you no further. Nor unless you ask me questions shall I talk about it again. You will find me, in fact, quite sane in my mode of life. Birds and beasts, you will see behaving somewhat intimately to me, like that moor-hen, but that is all. I will walk with you, ride with you, play golf with you, and talk with you on any subject you like. But I wanted you on the threshold to know what has happened to me. And one thing more will happen.'

He paused again, and a slight look of fear crossed his eyes.

'There will be a final revelation,' he said, 'a complete and blinding stroke which will throw open to me, once and for all, the full knowledge, the full realisation and comprehension that I am one, just as you are, with life. In reality there is no "me", no "you", no "it". Everything is part of the one and only thing which is life. I know that that is so, but the realisation of it is not yet mine. But it will be, and on that day, so I take it, I shall see Pan. It may mean death, the death of my body, that is, but I don't care. It may mean immortal, eternal life lived here and now and for ever. Then having gained that, ah, my dear Darcy, I shall preach such a gospel of joy, showing myself as the living proof of the truth, that Puritanism, the dismal religion of sour faces, shall vanish like a breath of smoke, and be dispersed and disappear in the sunlit air. But first the full knowledge must be mine.'

Darcy watched his face narrowly.

'You are afraid of that moment,' he said.

Frank smiled at him.

'Quite true; you are quick to have seen that. But when it comes I hope I shall not be afraid.'

For some little time there was silence; then Darcy rose.

'You have bewitched me, you extraordinary boy,' he said. 'You have been telling me a fairy-story, and I find myself saying, "Promise me it is true."'

'I promise you that,' said the other.

'And I know I shan't sleep,' added Darcy.

Frank looked at him with a sort of mild wonder as if he scarcely understood.

'Well, what does that matter?' he said.

'I assure you it does. I am wretched unless I sleep.'

'Of course I can make you sleep if I want,' said Frank in a rather bored voice.

'Well do.'

'Very good: go to bed. I'll come upstairs in ten minutes.'

Frank busied himself for a little after the other had gone, moving the table back under the awning of the verandah and quenching the lamp. Then he went with his quick silent tread upstairs and into Darcy's room. The latter was already in bed, but very wide-eyed and wakeful, and Frank with an amused smile of indulgence, as for a fretful child, sat down on the edge of the bed.

'Look at me,' he said, and Darcy looked.

'The birds are sleeping in the brake,' said Frank softly, 'and the winds are asleep. The sea sleeps, and the tides are but the heaving of its breast. The stars swing slow, rocked in the great cradle of the Heavens, and—'

He stopped suddenly, gently blew out Darcy's candle, and left him sleeping.

Morning brought Darcy a flood of hard common-sense, as clear and crisp as the sunshine that filled his room. Slowly as he woke he gathered together the broken threads of the memories of the evening which had ended, so he told himself, in a trick of common hypnotism. That accounted for it all; the whole strange talk he had had was under a spell of suggestion from the extraordinary vivid boy who had once been a man; all his own excitement, his acceptance of the incredible had been merely the effect of a stronger, more potent will imposed on his own. How strong that will was, he guessed from his own instantaneous obedience to Frank's suggestion of sleep. And armed with impenetrable common-sense he came down to breakfast. Frank had already begun, and

was consuming a large plateful of porridge and milk with the most
prosaic and healthy appetite.

'Slept well?' he asked.

'Yes, of course. Where did you learn hypnotism?'

'By the side of the river.'

'You talked an amazing quantity of nonsense last night,' remarked
Darcy, in a voice prickly with reason.

'Rather. I felt quite giddy. Look, I remembered to order a dreadful
daily paper for you. You can read about money markets or politics or
cricket matches.'

Darcy looked at him closely. In the morning light Frank looked even
fresher, younger, more vital than he had done the night before, and the
sight of him somehow dinted Darcy's armour of common-sense.

'You are the most extraordinary fellow I ever saw,' he said. 'I want to
ask you some more questions.'

'Ask away,' said Frank.

For the next day or two Darcy plied his friend with many questions,
objections and criticisms on the theory of life and gradually got out of
him a coherent and complete account of his experience. In brief then,
Frank believed that 'by lying naked', as he put it, to the force which
controls the passage of the stars, the breaking of a wave, the budding of
a tree, the love of a youth and maiden, he had succeeded in a way
hitherto undreamed of in possessing himself of the essential principle of
life. Day by day, so he thought, he was getting nearer to, and in closer
union with the great power itself which caused all life to be, the spirit of
nature, of force, or the spirit of God. For himself, he confessed to what
others would call paganism; it was sufficient for him that there existed a
principle of life. He did not worship it, he did not pray to it, he did not
praise it. Some of it existed in all human beings, just as it existed in
trees and animals, to realise and make living to himself the fact that it
was all one, was his sole aim and object.

Here perhaps Darcy would put in a word of warning.

'Take care,' he said. 'To see Pan meant death, did it not.'

Frank's eyebrows would rise at this.

'What does that matter?' he said. 'True, the Greeks were always right,
and they said so, but there is another possibility. For the nearer I get to
it, the more living, the more vital and young I become.'

'What then do you expect the final revelation will do for you?'

'I have told you,' said he. 'It will make me immortal.'

But it was not so much from speech and argument that Darcy grew to
grasp his friend's conception, as from the ordinary conduct of his life.
They were passing, for instance, one morning down the village street,

when an old woman, very bent and decrepit, but with an extraordinary cheerfulness of face, hobbled out from her cottage. Frank instantly stopped when he saw her.

'You old darling! How goes it all?' he said.

But she did not answer, her dim old eyes were riveted on his face; she seemed to drink in like a thirsty creature the beautiful radiance which shone there. Suddenly she put her two withered old hands on his shoulders.

'You're just the sunshine itself,' she said, and he kissed her and passed on.

But scarcely a hundred yards further a strange contradiction of such tenderness occurred. A child running along the path towards them fell on its face, and set up a dismal cry of fright and pain. A look of horror came into Frank's eyes, and, putting his fingers in his ears, he fled at full speed down the street, and did not pause till he was out of hearing. Darcy, having ascertained that the child was not really hurt, followed him in bewilderment.

'Are you without pity then?' he asked.

Frank shook his head impatiently.

'Can't you see?' he asked. 'Can't you understand that that sort of thing, pain, anger, anything unlovely throws me back, retards the coming of the great hour! Perhaps when it comes I shall be able to piece that side of life on to the other, on to the true religion of joy. At present I can't.'

'But the old woman. Was she not ugly?'

Frank's radiance gradually returned.

'Ah, no. She was like me. She longed for joy, and knew it when she saw it, the old darling.'

Another question suggested itself.

'Then what about Christianity?' asked Darcy.

'I can't accept it. I can't believe in any creed of which the central doctrine is that God who is Joy should have had to suffer. Perhaps it was so; in some inscrutable way I believe it may have been so, but I don't understand how it was possible. So I leave it alone; my affair is joy.'

They had come to the weir above the village, and the thunder of riotous cool water was heavy in the air. Trees dipped into the translucent stream with slender trailing branches, and the meadow where they stood was starred with midsummer blossomings. Larks shot up carolling into the crystal dome of blue, and a thousand voices of June sang round them. Frank, bare-headed as was his wont, with his coat slung over his arm and his shirt sleeves rolled up above the elbow, stood there like some beautiful wild animal with eyes half-shut and mouth half-open, drinking in the scented warmth of the air. Then suddenly he flung himself face downwards on the grass at the edge of the stream, burying his face in the daisies and cowslips, and lay stretched there in wide-armed ecstasy, with his long fingers pressing and stroking the dewy herbs of the field. Never before had Darcy seen him thus fully possessed by his idea; his caressing fingers, his half-buried face pressed close to the grass, even the clothed lines of his figure were instinct with a vitality that somehow was different from that of other men. And some faint glow from it reached Darcy, some thrill, some vibration from that charged recumbent body passed to him, and for a moment he understood as he had not understood before, despite his persistent questions and the candid answers they received, how real, and how realised by Frank, his idea was.

Then suddenly the muscles in Frank's neck became stiff and alert, and he half-raised his head.

'The Pan-pipes, the Pan-pipes,' he whispered. 'Close, oh, so close.'

Very slowly, as if a sudden movement might interrupt the melody, he raised himself and leaned on the elbow of his bent arm. His eyes opened wider, the lower lids drooped as if he focused his eyes on something very far away, and the smile on his face broadened and quivered like sunlight on still water, till the exultance of its happiness was scarcely human. So he remained motionless and rapt for some minutes, then the look of listening died from his face, and he bowed his head satisfied.

'Ah, that was good,' he said. 'How is it possible you did not hear? Oh, you poor fellow! Did you really hear nothing?'

A week of this outdoor and stimulating life did wonders in restoring to Darcy the vigour and health which his weeks of fever had filched from him, and as his normal activity and higher pressure of vitality returned, he seemed to himself to fall even more under the spell which the miracle of Frank's youth cast over him. Twenty times a day he found himself saying to himself suddenly at the end of some ten minutes' silent resistance to the absurdity of Frank's idea: 'But it isn't possible; it can't be possible,' and from the fact of his having to assure himself so frequently of this, he knew that he was struggling and arguing with a conclusion which already had taken root in his mind. For in any case a visible living miracle confronted him, since it was equally impossible that this youth, this boy, trembling on the verge of manhood, was thirty-five. Yet such was the fact.

July was ushered in by a couple of days of blustering and fretful rain, and Darcy, unwilling to risk a chill, kept to the house. But to Frank this weeping change of weather seemed to have no bearing on the behaviour of man, and he spent his days exactly as he did under the suns of June, lying in his hammock, stretched on the dripping grass, or making huge rambling excursions into the forest, the birds hopping from tree to tree after him, to return in the evening, drenched and soaked, but with the same unquenchable flame of joy burning within him.

'Catch cold?' he would ask, 'I've forgotten how to do it, I think. I suppose it makes one's body more sensible always to sleep out-of-doors. People who live indoors always remind me of something peeled and skinless.'

'Do you mean to say you slept out-of-doors last night in that deluge?' asked Darcy. 'And where, may I ask?'

Frank thought a moment.

'I slept in the hammock till nearly dawn,' he said. 'For I remember the light blinked in the east when I awoke. Then I went – where did I go – oh, yes, to the meadow where the Pan-pipes sounded so close a week ago. You were with me, do you remember? But I always have a rug if it is wet.'

And he went whistling upstairs.

Somehow that little touch, his obvious effort to recall where he had slept, brought strangely home to Darcy the wonderful romance of which he was the still half-incredulous beholder. Sleep till close on dawn in a hammock, then the tramp – or probably scamper – underneath the windy and weeping heavens to the remote and lonely meadow by the weir! The picture of other such nights rose before him; Frank sleeping perhaps by the bathing-place under the filtered twilight of the stars, or the white blaze of moon-shine, a stir and awakening at some dead hour, perhaps a space of silent wide-eyed thought, and then awandering through the hushed woods to some other dormitory, alone with his happiness, alone with the joy and the life that suffused and enveloped him, without other thought or desire or aim except the hourly and never-ceasing communion with the joy of nature.

They were in the middle of dinner that night, talking on indifferent subjects, when Darcy suddenly broke off in the middle of a sentence.

'I've got it,' he said. 'At last I've got it.'

'I congratulate you,' said Frank. 'But what?'

'The radical unsoundness of your idea. It is this: "All Nature from highest to lowest is full, crammed full of suffering; every living organism in nature preys on another, yet in your aim to get close to, to be one with nature, you leave suffering altogether out; you run away from it, you refuse to recognise it. And you are waiting, you say, for the final revelation.'

Frank's brow clouded slightly.

'Well,' he asked, rather wearily.

'Cannot you guess then when the final revelation will be? In joy you are supreme, I grant you that; I did not know a man could be so master of it. You have learned perhaps practically all that nature can teach. And if, as you think, the final revelation is coming to you, it will be the revelation of horror, suffering, death, pain in all its hideous forms. Suffering does exist : you hate it and fear it.'

Frank held up his hand.

'Stop; let me think,' he said.

There was silence for a long minute.

'That never struck me,' he said at length. 'It is possible that what you suggest is true. Does the sight of Pan mean that, do you think? Is it that nature, take it altogether, suffers horribly, suffers to a hideous inconceivable extent? Shall I be shown all the suffering?'

He got up and came round to where Darcy sat.

'If it is so, so be it,' he said. 'Because, my dear fellow, I am near, so splendidly near to the final revelation. To-day the pipes have sounded almost without pause. I have even heard the rustle in the bushes, I believe, of Pan's coming. I have seen, yes, I saw to-day, the bushes pushed aside as if by a hand, and piece of a face, not human, peered through. But I was not frightened, at least I did not run away this time.'

He took a turn up to the window and back again.

'Yes, there is suffering all through,' he said, 'and I have left it all out of my search. Perhaps, as you say, the revelation will be that. And in that case, it will be good-bye. I have gone on one line. I shall have gone too far along one road, without having explored the other. But I can't go back now. I wouldn't if I could; not a step would I retrace! In any case, whatever the revelation is, it will be God. I'm sure of that.'

The rainy weather soon passed, and with the return of the sun Darcy again joined Frank in long rambling days. It grew extraordinarily hotter, and with the fresh bursting of life, after the rain, Frank's vitality seemed to blaze higher and higher. Then, as is the habit of the English weather, one evening clouds began to bank themselves up in the west, the sun went down in a glare of coppery thunder-rack, and the whole earth broiling under an unspeakable oppression and sultriness paused and panted for the storm. After sunset the remote fires of lightning began to wink and flicker on the horizon, but when bed-time came the storm seemed to have moved no nearer, though a very low unceasing noise of thunder was audible. Weary and oppressed by the stress of the day, Darcy fell at once into a heavy uncomforting sleep.

He woke suddenly into full consciousness, with the din of some appalling explosion of thunder in his ears, and sat up in bed with racing heart. Then for a moment, as he recovered himself from the panic-land which lies between sleeping and waking, there was silence, except for the steady hissing of rain on the shrubs outside his window. But suddenly that silence was shattered and shredded into fragments by a scream from somewhere close at hand outside in the black garden, a scream of supreme and despairing terror. Again and once again it shrilled up, and then a babble of awful words was interjected. A quivering sobbing voice that he knew, said:

'My God, oh, my God; oh, Christ!'

And then followed a little mocking, bleating laugh. Then was silence again; only the rain hissed on the shrubs.

All this was but the affair of a moment, and without pause either to put on clothes or light a candle, Darcy was already fumbling at his door-handle. Even as he opened it he met a terror-stricken face outside, that of the man-servant who carried a light.

'Did you hear?' he asked.

The man's face was bleached to a dull shining whiteness.

'Yes, sir,' he said. 'It was the master's voice.'

Together they hurried down the stairs, and through the dining-room where an orderly table for breakfast had already been laid, and out on to the terrace. The rain for the moment had been utterly stayed, as if the tap of the heavens had been turned off, and under the lowering black sky, not quite dark, since the moon rode somewhere serene behind the conglomerated thunder-clouds, Darcy stumbled into the garden, followed by the servant with the candle. The monstrous leaping shadow of himself was cast before him on the lawn; lost and wandering odours of rose and lily and damp earth were thick about him, but more pungent was some sharp and acrid smell that suddenly reminded him of a certain châlet in which he had once taken refuge in the Alps. In the blackness of the hazy light from the sky, and the vague tossing of the candle behind him, he saw that the hammock in which Frank so often lay was tenanted. A gleam of white shirt was there, as if a man sitting up in it, but across that there was an obscure dark shadow, and as he approached the acrid odour grew more intense.

He was now only some few yards away, when suddenly the black shadow seemed to jump into the air, then came down with tappings of hard hoofs on the brick path that ran down the pergola, and with frolicsome skippings galloped off into the bushes. When that was gone Darcy could see quite clearly that a shirted figure sat up in the hammock. For one moment, from sheer terror of the unseen, he hung on his step, and the servant joining him they walked together to the hammock.

It was Frank. He was in shirt and trousers only, and he sat up with braced arms. For one half-second he stared at them, his face a mask of horrible contorted terror. His upper lip was drawn back so that the gums of the teeth appeared, and his eyes were focused not on the two who approached him but on something quite close to him; his nostrils were widely expanded, as if he panted for breath, and terror incarnate and repulsion and deathly anguish ruled dreadful lines on his smooth cheeks and forehead. Then even as they looked the body sank backwards, and the ropes of the hammock wheezed and strained.

Darcy lifted him out and carried him indoors. Once he thought there was a faint convulsive stir of the limbs that lay with so dead a weight in his arms, but when they got inside, there was no trace of life. But the look of supreme terror and agony of fear had gone from his face, a boy tired with play but still smiling in his sleep was the burden he laid on the floor. His eyes had closed, and the beautiful mouth lay in smiling curves, even as when a few mornings ago, in the meadow by the weir, it had quivered to the music of the unheard melody of Pan's pipes. Then they looked further.

Frank had come back from his bathe before dinner that night in his usual costume of shirt and trousers only. He had not dressed, and during dinner, so Darcy remembered, he had rolled up the sleeves of his shirt to above the elbow. Later, as they sat and talked after dinner on the close sultriness of the evening, he had unbuttoned the front of his shirt to let what little breath of wind there was play on his skin. The sleeves were rolled up now, the front of the shirt was unbuttoned, and on his arms and on the brown skin of his chest were strange discolorations which grew momently more clear and defined, till they saw that the marks were pointed prints, as if caused by the hoofs of some monstrous goat that had leaped and stamped upon him.

E. F. Benson

Negotium Perambulans . . .

The casual tourist in West Cornwall may just possibly have noticed, as he bowled along over the bare high plateau between Penzance and Land's End, a dilapidated signpost pointing down a steep lane and bearing on its battered finger the faded inscription 'Polearn 2 miles', but probably very few have had the curiosity to traverse those two miles in order to see a place to which their guide-books award so cursory a notice. It is described there, in a couple of unattractive lines, as a small fishing village with a church of no particular interest except for certain carved and painted wooden panels (originally belonging to an earlier edifice) which form an altar-rail. But the church at St Creed (the tourist is reminded) has a similar decoration far superior in point of preservation and interest, and thus even the ecclesiastically disposed are not lured to Polearn. So meagre a bait is scarce worth swallowing, and a glance at the very steep lane which in dry weather presents a carpet of sharp-pointed stones, and after a rain a muddy watercourse, will almost certainly decide him not to expose his motor or his bicycle to risks like these in so sparsely populated a district. Hardly a house has met his eye since he left Penzance, and the possible trundling of a punctured bicycle for half a dozen weary miles seems a high price to pay for the sight of a few painted panels.

Polearn, therefore, even in the high noon of the tourist season, is little liable to invasion, and for the rest of the year I do not suppose that a couple of folk a day traverse those two miles (long ones at that) of steep and stony gradient. I am not forgetting the postman in this exiguous estimate, for the days are few when, leaving his pony and cart at the top of the hill, he goes as far as the village, since but a few hundred yards down the lane there stands a large white box, like a sea-trunk, by the side of the road, with a slit for letters and a locked door. Should he have in his wallet a registered letter or be the bearer of a parcel too large for insertion in the square lips of the sea-trunk, he must needs trudge down the hill and deliver the troublesome missive, leaving it in person on the owner, and receiving some small reward of coin or refreshment for his kindness. But such occasions are rare, and his general routine is to take out of the box such letters as may have been deposited there, and insert in their place such letters as he has brought. These will be called for, perhaps that day or perhaps the next, by an emissary from the Polearn post-office. As for the fishermen of the place, who, in their export trade, constitute the chief link of movement between Polearn and the outside world, they would not dream of taking their catch up the steep lane and so, with six miles farther of travel, to the market at Penzance. The sea route is shorter and easier, and they deliver their wares to the pier-head. Thus, though the sole industry of Polearn is sea-fishing, you will get no fish there unless you have bespoken your requirements to one of the fishermen. Back come the trawlers as empty as a haunted house, while their spoils are in the fish-train that is speeding to London.

Such isolation of a little community, continued, as it has been, for centuries, produces isolation in the individual as well, and nowhere will you find greater independence of character than among the people of Polearn. But they are linked together, so it has always seemed to me, by some mysterious comprehension: it is as if they had all been initiated into some ancient rite, inspired and framed by forces visible and invisible. The winter storms that batter the coast, the vernal spell of the spring, the hot, still summers, the season of rains and autumnal decay, have made a spell which, line by line, has been communicated to them, concerning the powers, evil and good, that rule the world, and manifest themselves in ways benignant or terrible . . .

I came to Polearn first at the age of ten, a small boy, weak and sickly, and threatened with pulmonary trouble. My father's business kept him in London, while for me abundance of fresh air and a mild climate were considered essential conditions if I was to grow to manhood. His sister had married the vicar of Polearn, Richard Bolitho, himself native to the place, and so it came about that I spent three years, as a paying guest, with my relations. Richard Bolitho owned a fine house in the place, which he inhabited in preference to the vicarage, which he let to a young artist, John Evans, on whom the spell of Polearn had fallen, for from year's beginning to year's end he never left it. There was a solid roofed shelter, open on one side to the air, built for me in the garden, and here I lived and slept, passing scarcely one hour out of the twenty-four behind walls and windows. I was out on the bay with the fisher-folk, or wandering along the gorse-clad cliffs that climbed steeply to right and left of

NEGOTIUM PERAMBULANS

the deep combe where the village lay, or pottering about on the pier-head, or birds' nesting in the bushes with the boys of the village. Except on Sunday and for the few daily hours of my lessons, I might do what I pleased so long as I remained in the open air. About the lessons, there was nothing formidable; my uncle conducted me through flowering by-paths among the thickets of arithmetic, and made pleasant excursions into the elements of Latin grammar, and above all, he made me daily give him an account, in clear and grammatical sentences, of what had been occupying my mind or my movements. Should I select to tell him about a walk along the cliffs, my speech must be orderly, not vague, slip-shod notes of what I had observed. In this way, too, he trained my observation, for he would bid me tell him what flowers were in bloom, and what birds hovered fishing over the sea or were building in the bushes. For that I owe him a perennial gratitude, for to observe and to express my thoughts in the clear spoken word became my life's pro-fession.

But far more formidable than my weekday tasks was the prescribed routine for Sunday. Some dark embers compounded of Calvinism and mysticism smouldered in my uncle's soul, and made it a day of terror. His sermon in the morning scorched us with a foretaste of the eternal fires reserved for unrepentant sinners, and he was hardly less terrifying at the children's service in the afternoon. Well do I remember his exposi-tion of the doctrine of guardian angels. A child, he said, might think himself secure in such angelic care, but let him beware of committing any of those numerous offences which would cause his guardian to turn his face from him, for as sure as there were angels to protect us, there were also evil and awful presences which were ready to pounce; and on them he dwelt with peculiar gusto. Well, too, do I remember in the morning sermon his commentary on the carved panels of the altar-rails to which I have already alluded. There was the angel of Annunciation there, and the angel of Resurrection, but not less was there the witch of Endor, and, on the fourth panel, a scene that concerned me most of all. This fourth panel (he came down from his pulpit to trace its time-worn features) represented the lych-gate of the church-yard at Polearn itself, and indeed the resemblance when thus pointed out was remarkable. In the entry stood the figure of a robed priest holding up a Cross, with which he faced a terrible creature like a gigantic slug, that reared itself up in front of him. That, so ran my uncle's interpretation, was some evil agency, such as he had spoken about to us children, of almost infinite malignity and power, which could alone be combated by firm faith and a pure heart. Below ran the legend *'Negotium perambulans in tenebris'* from the ninety-first Psalm. We should find it translated there, 'the pestilence that walketh in darkness,' which but feebly rendered the

Latin. It was more deadly to the soul than any pestilence that can only kill the body: it was the Thing, the Creature, the Business that trafficked in the outer Darkness, a minister of God's wrath on the unrighteous . . .

I could see, as he spoke, the looks which the congregation exchanged with each other, and knew that his words were evoking a surmise, a remembrance. Nods and whispers passed between them, they understood to what he alluded, and with the inquisitiveness of boyhood I could not rest till I had wormed the story out of my friends among the fisher-boys, as, next morning, we sat basking and naked in the sun after our bathe. One knew one bit of it, one another, but it pieced together into a truly alarming legend. In bald outline it was as follows:

A church far more ancient than that in which my uncle terrified us every Sunday had once stood not three hundred yards away, on the shelf of level ground below the quarry from which its stones were hewn. The owner of the land had pulled this down, and erected for himself a house on the same site out of these materials, keeping, in a very ecstasy of wickedness, the altar, and on this he dined and played dice afterwards. But as he grew old some black melancholy seized him, and he would have lights burning there all night, for he had deadly fear of the darkness. On one winter evening there sprang up such a gale as was never before known, which broke in the windows of the room where he had supped, and extinguished the lamps. Yells of terror brought in his servants, who found him lying on the floor with the blood streaming from his throat. As they entered some huge black shadow seemed to move away from him, crawled across the floor and up the wall and out of the broken window.

'There he lay a-dying,' said the last of my informants, 'and him that had been a great burly man was withered to a bag o' skin, for the critter had drained all the blood from him. His last breath was a scream, and he hollered out the same words as passon read off the screen.'

'*Negotium perambulans in tenebris*,' I suggested eagerly.

'Thereabouts. Latin anyhow.'

'And after that?' I asked.

'Nobody would go near the place, and the old house rotted and fell in ruins till three years ago, when along come Mr Dooliss from Penzance, and built the half of it up again. But he don't care much about such critters, nor about Latin, neither. He takes his bottle of whisky a day and gets drunk's a lord in the evening. Eh, I'm gwine home to my dinner.'

Whatever the authenticity of the legend, I had certainly heard the truth about Mr Dooliss from Penzance, who from that day became an object of keen curiosity on my part, the more so because the quarry-house adjoined my uncle's garden. The Thing that walked in the dark failed to stir my imagination, and already I was so used to sleeping alone in my shelter that the night had no terrors for me. But it would be intensely exciting to wake at some timeless hour and hear Mr Dooliss yelling, and conjecture that the Thing had got him.

But by degrees the whole story faded from my mind, overscored by the more vivid interests of the day, and, for the last two years of my out-door life in the vicarage gardens, I seldom thought about Mr Dooliss and the possible fate that might await him for this temerity in living in the place where that Thing of darkness had done business. Occasionally I saw him over the garden fence, a great yellow lump of a man, with slow and staggering gait, but never did I set eyes on him outside his gate, either in the village street or down on the beach. He interfered with none, and no one interfered with him. If he wanted to run the risk of being the prey of the legendary nocturnal monster, or quietly drink himself to death, it was his affair. My uncle, so I gathered, had made several attempts to see him when first he came to live at Polearn, but Mr Dooliss appeared to have no use for parsons, but said he was not at home and never returned the call.

After three years of sun, wind, and rain, I had completely outgrown my early symptoms and had become a tough, strapping youngster of thirteen. I was sent to Eton and Cambridge, and in due course ate my dinners and became a barrister. In twenty years from that time I was earning a yearly income of five figures, and had already laid by in sound securities a sum that brought me dividends which would, for one of my simple tastes and frugal habits, supply me with all the material comforts I needed on this side of the grave. The great prizes of my profession were already within my reach, but I had no ambition beckoning me on, nor did I want a wife and children, being, I must suppose, a natural celibate. In fact there was only one ambition which through these busy years had held the lure of blue and far-off hills to me, and that was to get back to Polearn, and live once more isolated from the world with the sea and the gorse-clad hills for play-fellows, and the secrets that lurked there for exploration. The spell of it had been woven about my heart, and I can truly say that there had hardly passed a day in all those years in which the thought of it and the desire for it had been wholly absent from my mind. Though I had been in frequent communication with my uncle there during his lifetime, and, after his death, with his widow who still lived there, I had never been back to it since I embarked on my profession, for I knew that if I went there, it would be a wrench beyond my power to tear myself away again. But I had made up my mind that when once I had provided for my own independence, I would go back there not to leave it again. And yet I did leave it again, and now nothing in the world would induce me to turn down the lane from the road that leads from Penzance to Land's End, and see the sides of the combe rise steep above the roofs of the village and hear the gulls chiding as they fish in the bay. One of the things invisible, of the dark powers, leaped into light, and I saw it with my eyes.

The house where I had spent those three years of boyhood had been left for life to my aunt, and when I made known to her my intention of coming back to Polearn, she suggested that, till I found a suitable house or found her proposal unsuitable, I should come to live with her.

'The house is too big for a lone old woman,' she wrote, 'and I have often thought of quitting and taking a little cottage sufficient for me and my requirements. But come and share it, my dear, and if you find me troublesome, you or I can go. You may want solitude – most people in Polearn do – and will leave me. Or else I will leave you: one of the main reasons of my stopping here all these years was a feeling that I must not let the old house starve. Houses starve, you know, if they are not lived in. They die a lingering death; the spirit of them grows weaker and weaker, and at last fades out of them. Isn't this nonsense to your London notions? . . .'

Naturally I accepted with warmth this tentative arrangement, and on an evening in June found myself at the head of the lane leading down to Polearn, and once more I descended into the steep valley between the hills. Time had stood still apparently for the combe, the dilapidated signpost (or its successor) pointed a rickety finger down the lane, and a few hundred yards farther on was the white box for the exchange of letters. Point after remembered point met my eye, and what I saw was not shrunk, as is often the case with the revisited scenes of childhood, into a smaller scale. There stood the post-office, and there the church and close beside it the vicarage, and beyond, the tall shrubberies which separated the house for which I was bound from the road, and beyond that again the grey roofs of the quarry-house damp and shining with the moist evening wind from the sea. All was exactly as I remembered it, and, above all, that sense of seclusion and isolation. Somewhere above the tree-tops climbed the lane which joined the main road to Penzance, but all that had become immeasurably distant. The years that had passed since last I turned in at the well-known gate faded like a frosty breath, and vanished in this warm, soft air. There were law-courts somewhere in memory's dull book which, if I cared to turn the pages, would tell me that I had made a name and a great income there. But the dull book was closed now, for I was back in Polearn, and the spell was woven around me.

And if Polearn was unchanged, so too was Aunt Hester, who met me at the door. Dainty and china-white she had always been, and the years had not aged but only refined her. As she sat and talked after dinner she spoke of all that had happened in Polearn in that score of years, and yet somehow the changes of which she spoke seemed but to confirm the immutability of it all. As the recollection of names came back to me, I asked her about the quarry-house and Mr Dooliss, and her face gloomed a little as with a shadow of a cloud on a spring day.

'Yes, Mr Dooliss,' she said, 'poor Mr Dooliss, how well I remember him, though it must be ten years and more since he died. I never wrote to you about it, for it was all very dreadful, my dear, and I did not want to darken your memories of Polearn. Your uncle always thought that something of the sort might happen if he went on in his wicked, drunken ways, and worse than that, and though nobody knew exactly what took place, it was the sort of thing that might have been anticipated.'

'But what more or less happened, Aunt Hester?' I asked.

'Well, of course I can't tell you everything, for no one knew it. But he was a very sinful man, and the scandal about him at Newlyn was shocking. And then he lived, too, in the quarry-house . . . I wonder if by any chance you remember a sermon of your uncle's when he got out of the pulpit and explained that panel in the altar-rail, the one, I mean, with the horrible creature rearing itself up outside the lych-gate?'

'Yes, I remember perfectly,' said I.

'Ah. It made an impression on you, I suppose, and so it did on all who heard him, and that impression got stamped and branded on us all when the catastrophe occurred. Somehow Mr Dooliss got to hear about your uncle's sermon, and in some drunken fit he broke into the church and smashed the panel to atoms. He seems to have thought that there was some magic in it, and that if he destroyed that he would get rid of the terrible fate that was threatening him. For I must tell you that before he committed that dreadful sacrilege he had been a haunted man: he hated and feared darkness, for he thought that the creature on the panel was on his track, but that as long as he kept lights burning it could not touch him. But the panel, to his disordered mind, was the root of his terror, and so, as I said, he broke into the church and attempted – you will see why I said "attempted" – to destroy it. It certainly was found in splinters next morning, when your uncle went into church for matins, and knowing Mr Dooliss's fear of the panel, he went across to the quarry-house afterwards and taxed him with its destruction. The man never denied it; he boasted of what he had done. There he sat, though it was early morning, drinking his whisky.

' "I've settled your Thing for you," he said, "and your sermon too. A fig for such superstitions."

'Your uncle left him without answering his blasphemy, meaning to go straight into Penzance and give information to the police about this outrage to the church, but on his way back from the quarry-house he went into the church again, in order to be able to give details about the damage, and there in the screen was the panel, untouched and uninjured. And yet he had himself seen it smashed, and Mr Dooliss had confessed that the destruction of it was his work. But there it was, and whether the power of God had mended it or some other power, who knows?'

This was Polearn indeed, and it was the spirit of Polearn that made me accept all Aunt Hester was telling me as attested fact. It had happened like that. She went on in her quiet voice.

'Your uncle recognised that some power beyond police was at work, and he did not go to Penzance or give information about the outrage, for the evidence of it had vanished.'

A sudden spate of scepticism swept over me.

'There must have been some mistake,' I said. 'It hadn't been broken . . .'

She smiled.

'Yes, my dear, but you have been in London so long,' she said. 'Let me, anyhow, tell you the rest of my story. That night, for some reason, I could not sleep. It was very hot and airless; I dare say you will think that the sultry conditions accounted for my wakefulness. Once and again, as I went to the window to see if I could admit more air, I could see from it the quarry-house, and I noticed the first time that I left my bed that it was blazing with lights. But the second time I saw that it was all in darkness, and as I wondered at that, I heard a terrible scream, and the moment afterwards the steps of some one coming at full speed down the road outside the gate. He yelled as he ran; "Light, light!" he called out. "Give me light, or it will catch me!" It was very terrible to hear that, and I went to rouse my husband, who was sleeping in the dressing-room across the passage. He wasted no time, but by now the whole village was aroused by the screams, and when he got down to the pier he found that all was over. The tide was low, and on the rocks at its foot was lying the body of Mr Dooliss. He must have cut some artery when he fell on those sharp edges of stone, for he had bled to death, they thought, and though he was a big burly man, his corpse was but skin and bones. Yet there was no pool of blood round him, such as you would have expected. Just skin and bones as if every drop of blood in his body had been sucked out of him!'

She leaned forward.

'You and I, my dear, know what happened,' she said, 'or at least can guess. God has His instruments of vengeance on those who bring wickedness into places that have been holy. Dark and mysterious are His ways.'

Now what I should have thought of such a story if it had been told me in London I can easily imagine. There was such an obvious explanation: the man in question had been a drunkard, what wonder if the demons of delirium pursued him? But here in Polearn it was different.

'And who is in the quarry-house now?' I asked. 'Years ago the fisher-boys told me the story of the man who first built it and of his horrible end. And now again it has happened. Surely no one has ventured to inhabit it once more?'

I saw in her face, even before I asked that question, that somebody had done so.

'Yes, it is lived in again,' she said, 'For there is no end to the blindness ... I don't know if you remember him. He was the tenant of the vicarage many years ago.'

'John Evans,' said I.

'Yes. Such a nice fellow he was too. Your uncle was pleased to get so good a tenant. And now—'

She rose.

'Aunt Hester, you shouldn't leave your sentences unfinished,' I said.

She shook her head.

'My dear, that sentence will finish itself,' she said. 'But what a time of night! I must go to bed, and you too, or they will think we have to keep lights burning here through the dark hours.'

Before getting into bed I drew my curtains wide and opened all the windows to the warm tide of the sea air that flowed softly in. Looking out into the garden I could see in the moonlight the roof of the shelter, in which for three years I had lived, gleaming with dew. That, as much as anything, brought back the old days to which I had now returned, and they seemed of one piece with the present, as if no gap of more than twenty years sundered them. The two flowed into one like globules of mercury uniting into a softly shining globe, of mysterious lights and reflections. Then, raising my eyes a little, I saw against the black hillside the windows of the quarry-house still alight.

Morning, as is so often the case, brought no shattering of my illusion. As I began to regain consciousness, I fancied that I was a boy again waking up in the shelter in the garden, and though, as I grew more widely awake, I smiled at the impression, that on which it was based I found to be indeed true. It was sufficient now as then to be here, to wander again on the cliffs, and hear the popping of the ripened seed-pods on the gorse-bushes; to stray along the shore to the bathing-cove, to float and drift and swim in the warm tide, and bask on the sand, and watch the gulls fishing, to lounge on the pier-head with the fisher-folk, to see in their eyes and hear in their quiet speech the evidence of secret things not so much known to them as part of their instincts and their very being. There were powers and presences about me; the white poplars that stood by the stream that babbled down the valley knew of them, and showed a glimpse of their knowledge sometimes, like the gleam of their white

underleaves; the very cobbles that paved the street were soaked in it . . .
All that I wanted was to lie there and grow soaked in it too; unconsciously, as a boy, I had done that but now the process must be conscious.
I must know what stir of forces, fruitful and mysterious, seethed along
the hill-side at noon, and sparkled at night on the sea. They could be
known, they could even be controlled by those who were masters of the
spell, but never could they be spoken of, for they were dwellers in the
innermost, grafted into the eternal life of the world. There were dark
secrets as well as these clear, kindly powers, and to these no doubt
belonged the *negotium perambulans in tenebris* which, though of deadly
malignity, might be regarded not only as evil, but as the avenger of
sacrilegious and impious deeds . . . All this was part of the spell of Polearn, of which the seeds had long lain dormant in me. But now they were
sprouting, and who knew what strange flower would unfold on their
stems?

It was not long before I came across John Evans. One morning, as I
lay on the beach, there came shambling across the sand a man stout
and middle-aged with the face of Silenus. He paused as he drew near and
regarded me from narrow eyes.

'Why, you're the little chap that used to live in the parson's garden,'
he said. 'Don't you recognise me?'

I saw who it was when he spoke: his voice, I think instructed me, and
recognising it, I could see the features of the strong, alert young man in
this gross caricature.

'Yes, you're John Evans,' I said. 'You used to be very kind to me: you
used to draw pictures for me.'

'So I did, and I'll draw you some more. Been bathing? That's a risky
performance. You never know what lives in the sea, nor what lives on
the land for that matter. Not that I heed them. I stick to work and
whisky. God! I've learned to paint since I saw you, and drink too for
that matter. I live in the quarry-house, you know, and it's a powerful
thirsty place. Come and have a look at my things if you're passing. Staying with your aunt, are you? I could do a wonderful portrait of her.
Interesting face; she knows a lot. People who live at Polearn get to know
a lot, though I don't take much stock in that sort of knowledge myself.'

I do not know when I have been at once so repelled and interested.
Behind the mere grossness of his face there lurked something which,
while it appalled, yet fascinated me. His thick lisping speech had the
same quality. And his paintings, what would they be like? . . .

'I was just going home,' I said. 'I'll gladly come in, if you'll allow
me.'

He took me through the untended overgrown garden into the house
which I had never yet entered. A great grey cat was sunning itself in the

window, and an old woman was laying lunch in a corner of the cool hall into which the door opened. It was built of stone, and the carved mouldings let into the walls, the fragments of gargoyles and sculptured images, bore testimony to the truth of its having been built out of the demolished church. In one corner was an oblong and carved wooden table littered with a painter's apparatus and stacks of canvases leaned against the walls.

He jerked his thumb towards a head of an angel that was built into the mantelpiece and giggled.

'Quite a sanctified air,' he said, 'so we tone it down for the purposes of ordinary life by a different sort of art. Have a drink? No? Well, turn over some of my pictures while I put myself to rights.'

He was justified in his own estimate of his skill: he could paint (and apparently he could paint anything), but never have I seen pictures so inexplicably hellish. There were exquisite studies of trees, and you knew that something lurked in the flickering shadows. There was a drawing of his cat sunning itself in the window, even as I had just now seen it, and yet it was no cat but some beast of awful malignity. There was a boy stretched naked on the sands, not human, but some evil thing which had come out of the sea. Above all, there were pictures of his garden overgrown and jungle-like, and you knew that in the bushes were presences ready to spring out on you . . .

'Well, do you like my style?' he said as he came up, glass in hand. (The tumbler of spirits that he held had not been diluted.) 'I try to paint the essence of what I see, not the mere husk and skin of it, but its nature, where it comes from and what gives it birth. There's much in common between a cat and a fuchsia-bush if you look at them closely enough. Everything came out of the slime of the pit, and it's all going back there. I should like to do a picture of you some day. I'd hold the mirror up to Nature, as that old lunatic said.'

After this first meeting I saw him occasionally throughout the months of that wonderful summer. Often he kept to his house and to his painting for days together, and then perhaps some evening I would find him lounging on the pier, always alone, and every time we met thus the repulsion and interest grew, for every time he seemed to have gone farther along a path of secret knowledge towards some evil shrine where complete initiation awaited him . . . And then suddenly the end came.

I had met him thus one evening on the cliffs while the October sunset still burned in the sky, but over it with amazing rapidity there spread from the west a great blackness of cloud such as I have never seen for denseness. The light was sucked from the sky, the dusk fell in ever thicker layers. He suddenly became conscious of this.

'I must get back as quick as I can,' he said. 'It will be dark in a few minutes, and my servant is out. The lamps will not be lit.'

He stepped out with extraordinary briskness for one who shambled and could scarcely lift his feet, and soon broke out into a stumbling run. In the gathering darkness I could see that his face was moist with the dew of some unspoken terror.

'You must come with me,' he panted, 'for so we shall get the lights burning the sooner. I cannot do without light.'

I had to exert myself to the full to keep up with him, for terror winged him, and even so I fell behind, so that when I came to the garden gate, he was already half-way up the path to the house. I saw him enter, leaving the door wide, and found him fumbling with matches. But his hand so trembled that he could not transfer the light to the wick of the lamp.

'But what's the hurry about?' I asked.

Suddenly his eyes focused themselves on the open door behind me, and he jumped from his seat beside the table which had once been the altar of God, with a gasp and a scream.

'No, no!' he cried. 'Keep it off! . . .'

I turned and saw what he had seen. The Thing had entered and now was swiftly gliding across the floor towards him, like some gigantic caterpillar. A stale phosphorescent light came from it, for though the dusk had grown to darkness outside, I could see it quite distinctly in the awful light of its own presence. From it too there came an odour of corruption and decay, as from slime that has long lain below water. It seemed to have no head, but on the front of it was an orifice of puckered skin which opened and shut and slavered at the edges. It was hairless, and slug-like in shape and in texture. As it advanced its fore-part reared itself from the ground, like a snake about to strike, and it fastened on him. . . .

At that sight, and with the yells of his agony in my ears, the panic which had struck me relaxed into a hopeless courage, and with palsied, impotent hands I tried to lay hold of the Thing. But I could not: though something material was there, it was impossible to grasp it; my hands sunk in it as in thick mud. It was like wrestling with a nightmare.

I think that but a few seconds elapsed before all was over. The screams of the wretched man sank to moans and mutterings as the Thing fell on him: he panted once or twice and was still. For a moment longer there came gurglings and sucking noises, and then it slid out even as it had entered. I lit the lamp which he had fumbled with, and there on the floor he lay, no more than a rind of skin in loose folds over projecting bones.

Saki

Gabriel-Ernest

'There is a wild beast in your woods,' said the artist Cunningham, as he was being driven to the station. It was the only remark he had made during the drive, but as Van Cheele had talked incessantly his companion's silence had not been noticeable.

'A stray fox or two and some resident weasels. Nothing more formidable,' said Van Cheele. The artist said nothing.

'What did you mean about a wild beast?' said Van Cheele later, when they were on the platform.

'Nothing. My imagination. Here is the train,' said Cunningham.

That afternoon Van Cheele went for one of his frequent rambles through his woodland property. He had a stuffed bittern in his study, and knew the names of quite a number of wild flowers, so his aunt had possibly some justification in describing him as a great naturalist. At any rate, he was a great walker. It was his custom to take mental notes of everything he saw during his walks, not so much for the purpose of assisting contemporary science as to provide topics for conversation afterwards. When the bluebells began to show themselves in flower he made a point of informing every one of the fact, the season of the year might have warned his hearers of the likelihood of such an occurrence, but at least they felt that he was being absolutely frank with them.

What Van Cheele saw on this particular afternoon was, however, something far removed from his ordinary range of experience. On a shelf of smooth stone overhanging a deep pool in the hollow of an oak coppice a boy of about sixteen lay asprawl, drying his wet brown limbs luxuriously in the sun. His wet hair, parted by a recent dive, lay close to his head, and his light-brown eyes, so light that there was an almost tigerish gleam in them, were turned towards Van Cheele with a certain lazy watchfulness. It was an unexpected apparition, and Van Cheele found himself engaged in the novel process of thinking before he spoke. Where on earth could this wild-looking boy hail from? The miller's wife had lost a child some two months ago, supposed to have been swept away by the mill-race, but that had been a mere baby, not a half-grown lad.

'What are you doing here?' he demanded.

'Obviously, sunning myself,' replied the boy.

'Where do you live?'

'Here, in these woods.'

'You can't live in the woods,' said Van Cheele.

'They are very nice woods,' said the boy, with a touch of patronage in his voice.

'But where do you sleep at night?'

'I don't sleep at night; that's my busiest time.'

Van Cheele began to have an irritated feeling that he was grappling with a problem that was eluding him.

'What do you feed on?' he asked.

'Flesh,' said the boy, and he pronounced the word with slow relish, as though he were tasting it.

'Flesh! What flesh?'

'Since it interests you, rabbits, wild-fowl, hares, poultry, lambs in their season, children when I can get any; they're usually too well locked in at night, when I do most of my hunting. It's quite two months since I tasted child-flesh.'

Ignoring the chaffing nature of the last remark, Van Cheele tried to draw the boy on the subject of possible poaching operations.

'You're talking rather through your hat when you speak of feeding on hares.' (Considering the nature of the boy's toilet, the simile was hardly an apt one.) 'Our hillside hares aren't easily caught.'

'At night I hunt on four feet,' was the somewhat cryptic response.

'I suppose you mean you hunt with a dog?' hazarded Van Cheele.

The boy rolled slowly over on to his back, and laughed a weird low laugh, that was pleasantly like a chuckle and disagreeably like a snarl.

'I don't fancy any dog would be very anxious for my company, especially at night.'

Van Cheele began to feel that there was something positively uncanny about the strange-eyed, strange-tongued youngster.

'I can't have you staying in these woods,' he declared authoritatively.

'I fancy you'd rather have me here than in your house,' said the boy.

The prospect of this wild, nude animal in Van Cheele's primly ordered house was certainly an alarming one.

'If you don't go I shall have to make you,' said Van Cheele.

The boy turned like a flash, plunged into the pool, and in a moment had flung his wet and glistening body halfway up the bank where Van Cheele was standing. In an otter the movement would not have been remarkable; in a boy Van Cheele found it sufficiently startling. His foot slipped as he made an involuntary backward movement, and he found himself almost prostrate on the slippery weed-grown bank, with those tigerish yellow eyes not very far from his own. Almost instinctively he half-raised his hand to his throat. The boy laughed again, a laugh in which the snarl had nearly driven out the chuckle, and then, with another of his astonishing lightning movements, plunged out of view into a yielding tangle of weed and fern.

'What an extraordinary wild animal!' said Van Cheele as he picked himself up. And then he recalled Cunningham's remark, 'There is a wild beast in your woods.'

Walking slowly homeward, Van Cheele began to turn over in his mind various local occurrences which might be traceable to the existence of this astonishing young savage.

Something had been thinning the game in the woods lately, poultry had been missing from the farms, hares were growing unaccountably scarcer, and complaints had reached him of lambs being carried off bodily from the hills. Was it possible that this wild boy was really hunting the countryside in company with some clever poacher dog? He had spoken of hunting 'four footed' by night, but then, again, he had hinted strangely at no dog caring to come near him, 'especially at night.' It was certainly puzzling. And then, as Van Cheele ran his mind over the various depredations that had been committed during the last month or two, he suddenly came to a dead stop, alike in his walk and his specu-lations. The child missing from the mill two months ago – the accepted theory was that it had tumbled into the mill-race and been swept away; but the mother had always declared she had heard a shriek on the hill side of the house, in the opposite direction from the water. It was un-thinkable, of course, but he wished that the boy had not made that un-canny remark about child-flesh eaten two months ago. Such dreadful things should not be said even in fun.

Van Cheele, contrary to his usual wont, did not feel disposed to be communicative about his discovery in the wood. His position as a parish councillor and justice of the peace seemed somehow compromised by the fact that he was harbouring a personality of such doubtful repute on his property; there was even a possibility that a heavy bill of damages for raided lambs and poultry might be laid at his door. At dinner that night he was quite unusually silent.

'Where's your voice gone to?' said his aunt. 'One would think you had seen a wolf.'

Van Cheele, who was not familiar with the old saying, thought the remark rather foolish; if he *had* seen a wolf on his property his tongue would have been extraordinarily busy with the subject.

At breakfast next morning Van Cheele was conscious that his feeling of uneasiness regarding yesterday's episode had not wholly disappeared, and he resolved to go by train to the neighbouring cathedral town, hunt up Cunningham, and learn from him what he had really seen that had prompted the remark about a wild beast in the woods. With this resolution taken, his usual cheerfulness partially returned, and he hummed a bright little melody as he sauntered to the morning-room for his customary cigarette. As he entered the room the melody made way abruptly for a pious invocation. Gracefully asprawl on the ottoman, in an attitude of almost exaggerated repose, was the boy of the woods. He was drier than when Van Cheele had last seen him, but no other alteration was noticeable in his toilet.

'How dare you come here?' asked Van Cheele furiously.

'You told me I was not to stay in the woods,' said the boy calmly.

'But not to come here. Supposing my aunt should see you!'

And with a view to minimizing the catastrophe Van Cheele hastily obscured as much of his unwelcome guest as possible under the folds of a *Morning Post*. At that moment his aunt entered the room.

'This is a poor boy who has lost his way – and lost his memory. He doesn't know who he is or where he comes from,' explained Van Cheele desperately, glancing apprehensively at the waif's face to see whether he was going to add inconvenient candour to his other savage propensities.

Miss Van Cheele we enormously interested.

'Perhaps his underlinen is marked,' she suggested.

'He seems to have lost most of that, too,' said Van Cheele, making frantic little grabs at the *Morning Post* to keep it in its place.

A naked homeless child appealed to Miss Van Cheele as warmly as a stray kitten or derelict puppy would have done.

'We must do all we can for him,' she decided, and in a very short time a messenger, dispatched to the rectory, where a page-boy was kept, had returned with a suit of pantry clothes, and the necessary accessories of shirt, shoes, collar, etc. Clothed, clean, and groomed, the boy lost none of his uncanniness in Van Cheele's eyes, but his aunt found him sweet.

'We must call him something till we know who he really is,' she said. 'Gabriel-Ernest, I think; those are nice suitable names.'

Van Cheele agreed, but he privately doubted whether they were being grafted on to a nice suitable child. His misgivings were not diminished by the fact that his staid and elderly spaniel had bolted out of the house at the first incoming of the boy, and now obstinately remained shivering and yapping at the farther end of the orchard, while the canary, usually as vocally industrious at Van Cheele himself, had put itself on an allowance of frightened cheeps. More than ever he was resolved to consult Cunningham without loss of time.

As he drove off to the station his aunt was arranging that Gabriel-Ernest should help her to entertain the infant members of her Sunday-school class at tea that afternoon.

Cunningham was not at first disposed to be communicative.

'My mother died of some brain trouble,' he explained, 'so you will understand why I am averse to dwelling on anything of an impossibly fantastic nature that I may see or think that I have seen.'

'But what *did* you see?' persisted Van Cheele.

'What I thought I saw was something so extraordinary that no really sane man could dignify it with the credit of having actually happened. I was standing, the last evening I was with you, half-hidden in the hedgegrowth by the orchard gate, watching the dying glow of the sunset. Suddenly I became aware of a naked boy, a bather from some neighbouring pool, I took him to be, who was standing out on the bare hillside also watching the sunset. His pose was so suggestive of some wild faun of Pagan myth that I instantly wanted to engage him as a model, and in another moment I think I should have hailed him. But just then the sun dipped out of view, and all the orange and pink slid out of the landscape, leaving it cold and grey. And at the same moment an astounding thing happened – the boy vanished too!'

'What! vanished away into nothing?' asked Van Cheele excitedly.

'No; that is the dreadful part of it,' answered the artist; 'on the open hillside where the boy had been standing a second ago, stood a large wolf, blackish in colour, with gleaming fangs and cruel, yellow eyes. You may think—'

But Van Cheele did not stop for anything as futile as thought. Already he was tearing at top speed towards the station. He dismissed the idea of a telegram. 'Gabriel-Ernest is a werewolf' was a hopelessly inadequate effort at conveying the situation, and his aunt would think it was a code message to which he had omitted to give her the key. His one hope was that he might reach home before sundown. The cab which he chartered at the other end of the railway journey bore him with what seemed exasperating slowness along the country roads, which were pink and mauve with the flush of the sinking sun. His aunt was putting away some unfinished jams and cake when he arrived.

'Where is Gabriel-Ernest?' he almost screamed.

'He is taking the little Toop child home,' said his aunt. 'It was getting so late, I thought it wasn't safe to let it go back alone. What a lovely sunset, isn't it?'

But Van Cheele, although not oblivious of the glow in the western sky, did not stay to discuss its beauties. At a speed for which he was scarcely geared he raced along the narrow lane that led to the home of the Toops. On one side ran the swift current of the mill-stream, on the other rose the stretch of bare hillside. A dwindling rim of red sun showed still on the skyline, and the next turning must bring him in view of the ill-assorted couple he was pursuing. Then the colour went suddenly out of things and a grey light settled itself with a quick shiver over the land-scape. Van Cheele heard a shrill wail of fear, and stopped running.

Nothing was ever again seen of the Toop child or Gabriel-Ernest, but the latter's discarded garments were found lying in the road, so it was assumed that the child had fallen into the water, and that the boy had stripped and jumped in, in a vain endeavour to save it. Van Cheele and some workmen who were near by at the time testified to having heard a child scream loudly just near the spot where the clothes were found. Mrs Toop, who had eleven other children, was decently resigned to her bereavement, but Miss Van Cheele sincerely mourned her lost foundling. It was on her initiative that a memorial brass was put up in the parish church to 'Gabriel-Ernest, an unknown boy, who bravely sacrificed his life for another.'

Van Cheele gave way to his aunt in most things, but he flatly refused to subscribe to the Gabriel-Ernest memorial.

Saki

The Music on the Hill

Sylvia Seltoun ate her breakfast in the morning-room at Yessney with
a pleasant sense of ultimate victory, such as a fervent Ironside might have
permitted himself on the morrow of Worcester fight. She was scarcely
pugnacious by temperament, but belonged to that more successful class
of fighters who are pugnacious by circumstance. Fate had willed that her
life should be occupied with a series of small struggles, usually with the
odds slightly against her, and usually she had just managed to come
through winning. And now she felt that she had brought her hardest
and certainly her most important struggle to a successful issue. To have
married Mortimer Seltoun, 'Dead Mortimer' as his more intimate enemies called him, in the teeth of the cold hostility of his family, and in
spite of his unaffected indifference to women, was indeed an achievement that had needed some determination and adroitness to carry
through; yesterday she had brought her victory to its concluding stage
by wrenching her husband away from Town and its group of satellite
watering-places and 'settling him down,' in the vocabulary of her kind, in
this remote wood-girt manor farm which was his country house.

'You will never get Mortimer to go,' his mother had said carpingly,
'but if he once goes he'll stay; Yessney throws almost as much a spell
over him as Town does. One can understand what holds him to Town,
but Yessney—' and the dowager had shrugged her shoulders.

There was a sombre almost savage wildness about Yessney that was
certainly not likely to appeal to town-bred tastes, and Sylvia, notwithstanding her name, was accustomed to nothing much more sylvan than
'leafy Kensington.' She looked on the country as something excellent and
wholesome in its way, which was apt to become troublesome if you encouraged it overmuch. Distrust of town-life had been a new thing with

her, born of her marriage with Mortimer, and she had watched with satisfaction the gradual fading of what she called 'the Jermyn-Street-look' in his eyes as the woods and heather of Yessney had closed in on them yesternight. Her will-power and strategy had prevailed; Mortimer would stay.

Outside the morning-room windows was a triangular slope of turf, which the indulgent might call a lawn, and beyond its low hedge of neglected fuchsia bushes a steeper slope of heather and bracken dropped down into cavernous combes overgrown with oak and yew. In its wild open savagery there seemed a stealthy linking of the joy of life with the terror of unseen things. Sylvia smiled complacently as she gazed with a School-of-Art appreciation at the landscape, and then of a sudden she almost shuddered.

'It is very wild,' she said to Mortimer, who had joined her; 'one could almost think that in such a place the worship of Pan had never quite died out.'

'The worship of Pan never has died out,' said Mortimer. 'Other newer gods have drawn aside his votaries from time to time, but he is the Nature-God to whom all must come back at last. He has been called the Father of all the Gods, but most of his children have been stillborn.'

Sylvia was religious in an honest, vaguely devotional kind of way, and did not like to hear her beliefs spoken of as mere aftergrowths, but it was at least something new and hopeful to hear Dead Mortimer speak with such energy and conviction on any subject.

'You don't really believe in Pan?' she asked incredulously.

'I've been a fool in most things,' said Mortimer quietly, 'but I'm not such a fool as not to believe in Pan when I'm down here. And if you're wise you won't disbelieve in him too boastfully while you're in his country.'

It was not until a week later, when Sylvia had exhausted the attractions of the woodland walks round Yessney, that she ventured on a tour of inspection of the farm buildings. A farmyard suggested in her mind a scene of cheerful bustle, with churns and flails and smiling dairymaids, and teams of horses drinking knee-deep in duck-crowded ponds. As she wandered among the gaunt grey buildings of Yessney manor farm her first impression was one of crushing stillness and desolation, as though she had happened on some lone deserted homestead long given over to owls and cobwebs; then came a sense of furtive watchful hostility, the same shadow of unseen things that seemed to lurk in the wooded combes and coppices. From behind heavy doors and shuttered windows came the restless stamp of hoof or rasp of chain halter, and at times a muffled bellow from some stalled beast. From a distant corner a shaggy dog watched her with intent unfriendly eyes; as she drew near it slipped quietly into its kennel, and slipped out again as noiselessly when she had passed by. A few hens, questing for food under a rick, stole away under a gate at her approach. Sylvia felt that if she had come across any human beings in this wilderness of barn and byre they would have fled wraith-like from her gaze. At last, turning a corner quickly, she came upon a living thing that did not fly from her. Astretch in a pool of mud was an enormous sow, gigantic beyond the town-woman's wildest computation of swine-flesh, and speedily alert to resent and if necessary repel the unwonted intrusion. It was Sylvia's turn to make an unobtrusive retreat. As she threaded her way past rickyards and cowsheds and long blank walls, she started suddenly at a strange sound – the echo of a boy's laughter, golden and equivocal. Jan, the only boy employed on the farm, a tow-headed, wizen-faced yokel, was visibly at work on a potato clear-ing half-way up the nearest hillside, and Mortimer, when questioned, knew of no other probable or possible begetter of the hidden mockery that had ambushed Sylvia's retreat. The memory of that untraceable echo was added to her other impressions of a furtive sinister 'something' that hung around Yessney.

Of Mortimer she saw very little; farm and woods and trout-streams seemed to swallow him up from dawn till dusk. Once, following the direction she had seen him take in the morning, she came to an open space in a nut copse, further shut in by huge yew trees, in the centre of which stood a stone pedestal surmounted by a small bronze figure of a youthful Pan. It was a beautiful piece of workmanship, but her attention was chiefly held by the fact that a newly cut bunch of grapes had been placed as an offering at its feet. Grapes were none too plentiful at the manor house, and Sylvia snatched the bunch angrily from the pedestal. Contemptuous annoyance dominated her thoughts as she strolled slowly homeward, and then gave way to a sharp feeling of something that was very near fright; across a thick tangle of undergrowth a boy's face was scowling at her, brown and beautiful, with unutterably evil eyes. It was a lonely pathway, all pathways round Yessney were lonely for the matter of that, and she sped forward without waiting to give a closer scrutiny to this sudden apparition. It was not till she had reached the house that she discovered that she had dropped the bunch of grapes in her flight.

'I saw a youth in the wood today,' she told Mortimer that evening, 'brown-faced and rather handsome, but a scoundrel to look at. A gipsy lad, I suppose.'

'A reasonable theory,' said Mortimer, 'only there aren't any gipsies in these parts at present.'

'Then who was he?' asked Sylvia, and as Mortimer appeared to have no theory of his own, she passed on to recount her finding of the votive offering.

'I suppose it was your doing,' she observed; 'it's a harmless piece of lunacy, but people would think you dreadfully silly if they knew of it.'

'Did you meddle with it in any way?' asked Mortimer.

'I – I threw the grapes away. It seemed so silly,' said Sylvia, watching Mortimer's impassive face for a sign of annoyance.

'I don't think you were wise to do that,' he said reflectively. 'I've heard it said that the Wood Gods are rather horrible to those who molest them.'

'Horrible perhaps to those that believe in them, but you see I don't,' retorted Sylvia.

'All the same,' said Mortimer in his even, dispassionate tone, 'I should avoid the woods and orchards if I were you, and give a wide berth to the horned beasts on the farm.'

It was all nonsense, of course, but in that lonely wood-girt spot non-sense seemed able to rear a bastard brood of uneasiness.

'Mortimer,' said Sylvia suddenly, 'I think we will go back to Town some time soon.'

Her victory had not been so complete as she had supposed; it had carried her on to ground that she was already anxious to quit.

'I don't think you will ever go back to Town,' said Mortimer. He seemed to be paraphrasing his mother's prediction as to himself.

Sylvia noted with dissatisfaction and some self-contempt that the course of her next afternoon's ramble took her instinctively clear of the network of woods. As to the horned cattle, Mortimer's warning was scarcely needed for she had always regarded them as of doubtful neu-trality at the best; her imagination unsexed the most matronly dairy cows and turned them into bulls liable to 'see red' at any moment. The ram who fed in the narrow paddock below the orchards she had adjudged, after ample and cautious probation, to be of docile temper; today, how-ever, she decided to leave his docility untested, for the usually tranquil beast was roaming with every sign of restlessness from corner to corner of his meadow. A low, fitful piping, as of some reedy flute, was coming from the depth of a neighbouring copse, and there seemed to be some subtle connection between the animal's restless pacing and the wild music from the wood. Sylvia turned her steps in an upward direction and climbed the heather-clad slopes that stretched in rolling shoulders high above Yessney. She had left the piping notes behind her, but across the wooded combes at her feet the wind brought her another kind of music, the straining bay of hounds in full chase. Yessney was just on the outskirts of the Devon-and-Somerset country, and the hunted deer some-times came that way. Sylvia could presently see a dark body, breasting hill after hill, and sinking again and again out of sight as he crossed the combes, while behind him steadily swelled that relentless chorus, and she grew tense with the excited sympathy that one feels for any hunted thing in whose capture one is not directly interested. And at last he broke through the outermost line of oak scrub and fern and stood panting in the open, a fat September stag carrying a well-furnished head. His obvious course was to drop down to the brown pools of Undercombe, and thence make his way towards the red deer's favoured sanctuary, the sea. To Sylvia's surprise, however, he turned his head to the upland slope and came lumbering resolutely onward over the heather. 'It will be dreadful,' she thought, 'the hounds will pull him down under my very eyes.' But the music of the pack seemed to have died away for a moment, and in its place she heard again that wild piping, which rose now on this side, now on that, as though urging the failing stag to a final effort. Sylvia stood well aside from his path, half hidden in a thick growth of whortle bushes, and watched him swing stiffly upward, his flanks dark with sweat, the coarse hair on his neck showing light by contrast. The pipe music suddenly shrilled around her, seeming to come from the bushes at her very feet, and at the same moment the great beast slewed round and bore directly down upon her. In an instant her pity for the hunted animal was changed to wild terror at her own danger; the thick heather roots mocked her scrambling efforts at flight, and she looked frantically downward for a glimpse of oncoming hounds. The huge antler spikes were within a few yards of her, and in a flash of numbing fear she remembered Mortimer's warning, to beware of horned beasts on the farm. And then with a quick throb of joy she saw that she was not alone; a human figure stood a few paces aside, knee-deep in the whortle bushes.

'Drive it off!' she shrieked. But the figure made no answering movement.

The antlers drove straight at her breast, the acrid smell of the hunted animal was in her nostrils, but her eyes were filled with the horror of something she saw other than her oncoming death. And in her ears rang the echo of a boy's laughter, golden and equivocal.

E. M. Forster

The Story of a Panic

I

Eustace's career – if career it can be called – certainly dates from that afternoon in the chestnut woods above Ravello. I confess at once that I am a plain, simple man, with no pretensions to literary style. Sill, I do flatter myself that I can tell a story without exaggerating, and I have therefore decided to give an unbiased account of the extraordinary events of eight years ago.

Ravello is a delightful place with a delightful little hotel in which we met some charming people. There were the two Miss Robinsons, who had been there for six weeks with Eustace, their nephew, then a boy of about fourteen. Mr Sandbach had also been there some time. He had held a curacy in the north of England, which he had been compelled to resign on account of ill-health, and while he was recruiting at Ravella he had taken in hand Eustace's education – which was then sadly deficient – and was endeavouring to fit him for one of our great public schools. Then there was Mr Leyland, a would-be artist, and, finally, there was the nice landlady, Signora Scafetti, and the nice English-speaking waiter, Emmanuele – though at the time of which I am speaking Emmanuele was away, visiting a sick father.

To this little circle, I, my wife, and my two daughters made, I venture to think, a not unwelcome addition. But though I liked most of the company well enough, there were two of them to whom I did not take at all. They were the artist, Leyland, and the Miss Robinsons' nephew, Eustace.

Leyland was simply conceited and odious, and, as those qualities will be amply illustrated in my narrative, I need not enlarge upon them here.

But Eustace was something besides: he was indescribably repellent.

I am fond of boys as a rule, and was quite disposed to be friendly. I and my daughters offered to take him out – 'No, walking was such a fag.' Then I asked him to come and bathe – 'No, he could not swim.'

'Every English boy should be able to swim,' I said, 'I will teach you myself.'

'There, Eustace, dear,' said Miss Robinson; 'here is a chance for you.'

But he said he was afraid of the water! – a boy afraid! – and of course I said no more.

I would not have minded so much if he had been a really studious boy, but he neither played hard nor worked hard. His favourite occupations were lounging on the terrace in an easy chair and loafing along the high road, with his feet shuffling up the dust and his shoulders stooping forward. Naturally enough, his features were pale, his chest contracted, and his muscles undeveloped. His aunts thought him delicate; what he really needed was discipline.

That memorable day we all arranged to go for a picnic up in the chestnut woods – all, that is, except Janet, who stopped behind to finish her water-colour of the Cathedral – not a very successful attempt, I am afraid.

I wander off into these irrelevant details because in my mind I cannot separate them from an account of the day; and it is the same with the conversation during the picnic: all is imprinted on my brain together. After a couple of hours' ascent, we left the donkeys that had carried the Miss Robinsons and my wife, and all proceeded on foot to the head of the valley – Vallone Fontana Caroso is its proper name, I find.

I have visited a good deal of fine scenery before and since, but have found little that has pleased me more. The valley ended in a vast hollow, shaped like a cup, into which radiated ravines from the precipitous hills around. Both the valley and the ravines and the ribs of hill that divided the ravines were covered with leafy chestnut, so that the general appearance was that of a many-fingered green hand, palm upwards, which was clutching convulsively to keep us in its grasp. Far down the valley we could see Ravello and the sea, but that was the only sign of another world.

'Oh, what a perfectly lovely place,' said my daughter Rose. 'What a picture it would make!'

'Yes,' said Mr Sandbach. 'Many a famous European gallery would be proud to have a landscape a tithe as beautiful as this upon its walls.'

'On the contrary,' said Leyland, 'it would make a very poor picture. Indeed, it is not paintable at all.'

'And why is that?' said Rose, with far more deference than he deserved.

'Look, in the first place,' he replied, 'how intolerably straight against the sky is the line of the hill. It would need breaking up and diversifying. And where we are standing the whole thing is out of perspective. Besides, all the colouring is monotonous and crude.'

'I do not know anything about pictures,' I put in, 'and I do not pretend to know: but I know what is beautiful when I see it, and I am thoroughly content with this.'

'Indeed, who could help being contented!' said the elder Miss Robinson; and Mr Sandbach said the same.

'Ah!' said Leyland, 'you all confuse the artistic view of Nature with the photographic.'

Poor Rose had brought her camera with her, so I thought this positively rude. I did not wish any unpleasantness; so I merely turned away and assisted my wife and Miss Mary Robinson to put out the lunch – not a very nice lunch.

'Eustace dear,' said his aunt, 'come and help us here.'

He was in a particularly bad temper that morning. He had, as usual, not wanted to come, and his aunts had nearly allowed him to stop at the hotel to vex Janet. But I, with their permission, spoke to him rather sharply on the subject of exercise; and the result was that he had come, but was even more taciturn and moody than usual.

Obedience was not his strong point. He invariably questioned every command, and only executed it grumbling. I should always insist on prompt and cheerful obedience, if I had a son.

'I'm – coming – Aunt – Mary,' he at last replied, and dawdled to cut a piece of wood to make a whistle, taking care not to arrive till we had finished.

'Well, well, sir!' said I, 'you stroll in at the end and profit by our labours.' He sighed, for he could not endure being chaffed. Miss Mary, very unwisely, insisted on giving him the wing of the chicken, in spite of all my attempts to prevent her. I remember that I had a moment's vexation when I thought that, instead of enjoying the sun, and the air, and the woods, we were all engaged in wrangling over the diet of a spoilt boy.

But, after lunch, he was a little less in evidence. He withdrew to a tree trunk, and began to loosen the bark from his whistle. I was thankful to see him employed, for once in a way. We reclined, and took a *dolce far niente*.

Those sweet chestnuts of the South are puny striplings compared with our robust Northerners. But they clothed the contours of the hills and valleys in a most pleasing way, their veil being only broken by two clearings, in one of which we were sitting.

And because these few trees were cut down, Leyland burst into a petty indictment of the proprietor.

'All the poetry is going from Nature,' he cried, 'her lakes and marshes are drained, her seas banked up, her forests cut down. Everywhere we see the vulgarity of desolation spreading.'

I have had some experience of estates, and answered that cutting was very necessary for the health of the larger trees. Besides, it was unreasonable to expect the proprietor to derive no income from his lands.

'If you take the commercial side of landscape, you may feel pleasure in the owner's activity. But to me the mere thought that a tree is convertible into cash is disgusting.'

'I see no reason,' I observed politely, 'to despise the gifts of Nature because they are of value.'

It did not stop him. 'It is no matter,' he went on, 'we are all hopelessly steeped in vulgarity. I do not except myself. It is through us, and to our shame, that the Nereids have left the waters and the Oreads the mountains, that the woods no longer give shelter to Pan.'

'Pan!' cried Mr Sandbach, his mellow voice filling the valley as if it had been a great green church, 'Pan is dead. That is why the woods do not shelter him.' And he began to tell the striking story of the mariners who were sailing near the coast at the time of the birth of Christ, and three times heard a loud voice saying: 'The great God Pan is dead.'

'Yes. The great God Pan is dead,' said Leyland. And he abandoned himself to that mock misery in which artistic people are so fond of indulging. His cigar went out, and he had to ask me for a match.

'How very interesting,' said Rose. 'I do wish I knew some ancient history.'

'It is not worth your notice,' said Mr Sandbach. 'Eh, Eustace?'

Eustace was finishing his whistle. He looked up, with the irritable frown in which his aunts allowed him to indulge, and made no reply.

The conversation turned to various topics and then died out. It was a cloudless afternoon in May, and the pale green of the young chestnut leaves made a pretty contrast with the dark blue of the sky. We were all sitting at the edge of the small clearing for the sake of the view, and the shade of the chestnut saplings behind us was manifestly insufficient. All sounds died away – at least that is my account: Miss Robinson says that the clamour of the birds was the first sign of uneasiness that she discerned. All sounds died away, except that, far in the distance, I could hear two boughs of a great chestnut grinding together as the tree swayed. The grinds grew shorter and shorter, and finally that sound stopped also. As I looked over the green fingers of the valley, everything was absolutely motionless and still; and that feeling of suspense which one so often experiences when Nature is in repose began to steal over me.

Suddenly we were all electrified by the excruciating noise of Eustace's whistle. I never heard any instrument give forth so ear-splitting and discordant a sound.

'Eustace dear,' said Miss Mary Robinson, 'you might have thought of your poor Aunt Julia's head.'

Leyland, who had apparently been asleep, sat up.

'It is astonishing how blind a boy is to anything that is elevating or beautiful,' he observed. 'I should not have thought he could have found the wherewithal out here to spoil our pleasure like this.'

Then the terrible silence fell upon us again. I was now standing up and watching a cat's-paw of wind that was running down one of the ridges opposite, turning the light green to dark as it travelled. A fanciful feeling of foreboding came over me; so I turned away, to find to my amazement, that all the others were also on their feet, watching it too.

It is not possible to describe coherently what happened next: but I, for one, am not ashamed to confess that, though the fair blue sky was above me, and the green spring woods beneath me, and the kindest of friends around me, yet I became terribly frightened, more frightened than I ever wish to become again, frightened in a way I never have known either before or after. And in the eyes of the others, too, I saw blank, expressionless fear, while their mouths strove in vain to speak and their hands to gesticulate. Yet, all around us were prosperity, beauty, and peace, and all was motionless, save the cat's-paw of wind, now travelling up the ridge on which we stood.

Who moved first has never been settled. It is enough to say that in one second we were tearing away along the hillside. Leyland was in front, then Mr Sandbach, then my wife. But I only saw for a brief moment: for I ran across the little clearing and through the woods and over the undergrowth and the rocks and down the dry torrent beds into the valley below. The sky might have been black as I ran, and the trees, short grass, and the hillside a level road; for I saw nothing and heard nothing and felt nothing, since all the channels of sense and reason were blocked. It was not the spiritual fear that one has known at other times, but brutal, overmastering, physical fear, stopping up the ears, and dropping clouds before the eyes, and filling the mouth with foul tastes. And it was no ordinary humiliation that survived; for I had been afraid, not as a man, but as a beast.

II

I cannot describe our finish any better than our start; for our fear passed away as it had come, without cause. Suddenly I was able to see, and hear, and cough, and clear my mouth. Looking back, I saw that the others were stopping too; and, in a short time, we were all together, though it was long before we could speak, and longer before we dared to.

No one was seriously injured. My poor wife had sprained her ankle, Leyland had torn one of his nails on a tree trunk, and I myself had scraped and damaged my ear. I never noticed it till I had stopped.

We were all silent, searching one another's faces. Suddenly Miss Mary Robinson gave a terrible shriek. 'Oh, merciful heavens! where is Eustace?' And then she would have fallen if Mr Sandbach had not caught her.

'We must go back, we must go back at once,' said my Rose, who was quite the most collected of the party. 'But I hope – I feel he is safe.'

Such was the cowardice of Leyland, that he objected. But, finding himself in a minority, and being afraid of being left alone, he gave in. Rose and I supported my poor wife, Mr Sandbach and Miss Robinson helped Miss Mary, and we returned slowly and silently, taking forty minutes to ascend the path that we had descended in ten.

Our conversation was naturally disjointed, as no one wished to offer an opinion on what had happened. Rose was the most talkative: she startled us all by saying that she had very nearly stopped where she was.

'Do you mean to say that you weren't – that you didn't feel compelled to go?' said Mr Sandbach.

'Oh, of course, I did feel frightened' – she was the first to use the word – 'but I somehow felt that if I could stop on it would be quite different, that I shouldn't be frightened at all, so to speak.' Rose never did express herself clearly: still, it is greatly to her credit that she, the youngest of us, should have held on so long at that terrible time.

'I should have stopped, I do believe,' she continued, 'if I had not seen mamma go.'

Rose's experience comforted us a little about Eustace. But a feeling of terrible foreboding was on us all as we painfully climbed the chestnut-covered slopes and neared the little clearing. When we reached it our tongues broke loose. There, at the farther side, were the remains of our lunch, and close to them, lying motionless on his back, was Eustace.

With some presence of mind I at once cried out: 'Hey, you young monkey! jump up!' But he made no reply, nor did he answer when his poor aunts spoke to him. And, to my unspeakable horror, I saw one of those green lizards dart out from under his shirt-cuff as we approached.

We stood watching him as he lay there so silently, and my ears began to tingle in expectation of the outbursts of lamentations and tears.

Miss Mary fell on her knees beside him and touched his hand, which was convulsively entwined in the long grass.

As she did so, he opened his eyes and smiled.

I have often seen that peculiar smile since, both on the possessor's face and on the photographs of him that are beginning to get into the illustrated papers. But, till then, Eustace had always worn a peevish, discontented frown; and we were all unused to this disquieting smile, which always seemed to be without adequate reason.

His aunts showered kisses on him, which he did not reciprocate, and then there was an awkward pause. Eustace seemed so natural and undisturbed; yet, if he had not had astonishing experiences himself, he ought to have been all the more astonished at our extraordinary behaviour. My wife, with ready tact, endeavoured to behave as if nothing had happened.

'Well, Mr Eustace,' she said, sitting down as she spoke, to ease her foot, 'how have you been amusing yourself since we have been away?'

'Thank you, Mrs Tytler, I have been very happy.'

'And where have you been?'

'Here.'

'And lying down all the time, you idle boy?'

'No, not all the time.'

'What were you doing before?'

'Oh; standing or sitting.'

'Stood and sat doing nothing! Don't you know the poem "Satan finds some mischief still for—"'

'Oh, my dear madam, hush! hush!' Mr Sandbach's voice broke in; and my wife, naturally mortified by the interruption, said no more and moved away. I was surprised to see Rose immediately take her place, and, with more freedom than she generally displayed, ran her fingers through the boy's tousled hair.

'Eustace! Eustace!' she said hurriedly, 'tell me everything – every single thing.'

Slowly he sat up – till then he had lain on his back.

'Oh, Rose—,' he whispered, and, my curiosity being aroused, I moved nearer to hear what he was going to say. As I did so, I caught sight of some goat's footmarks in the moist earth beneath the trees.

'Apparently you have had a visit from some goats,' I observed. 'I had no idea they fed up here.'

Eustace laboriously got on to his feet and came to see; and when he saw the footmarks he lay down and rolled on them, as a dog rolls in dirt.

After that there was a grave silence, broken at length by the solemn speech of Mr Sandbach.

'My dear friends,' he said, 'it is best to confess the truth bravely. I know that what I am going to say now is what you are all now feeling. The Evil One has been very near us in bodily form. Time may yet discover some injury that he has wrought among us. But, at present, for myself at all events, I wish to offer up thanks for a merciful deliverance.'

THE STORY OF A PANIC

With that he knelt down, and, as the others knelt, I knelt too, though I do not believe in the Devil being allowed to assail us in visible form, as I told Mr Sandbach afterwards. Eustace came too, and knelt quietly enough between his aunts after they had beckoned to him. But when it was over he at once got up, and began hunting for something.

'Why! Someone has cut my whistle in two,' he said. (I had seen Leyland with an open knife in his hand – a superstitious act which I could hardly approve.)

'Well, it doesn't matter,' he continued.

'And why doesn't it matter?' said Mr Sandbach, who has ever since tried to entrap Eustace into an account of that mysterious hour.

'Because I don't want it any more.'

'Why?'

At that he smiled; and, as no one seemed to have anything more to say, I set off as fast as I could through the wood, and hauled up a donkey to carry my poor wife home. Nothing occurred in my absence, except that Rose had again asked Eustace to tell her what had happened; and he, this time, had turned away his head, and had not answered her a single word.

As soon as I returned, we all set off. Eustace walked with difficulty, almost with pain, so that, when we reached the other donkeys, his aunts wished him to mount one of them and ride all the way home. I make it a rule never to interfere between relatives, but I put my foot down at this. As it turned out, I was perfectly right, for the healthy exercise, I suppose, began to thaw Eustace's sluggish mood and loosen his stiffened muscles. He stepped out manfully, for the first time in his life, holding his head up and taking deep draughts of air into his chest. I observed with satisfaction to Miss Mary Robinson that Eustace was at last taking some pride in his personal appearance.

Mr Sandbach sighed, and said that Eustace must be carefully watched, for we none of us understood him yet. Miss Mary Robinson being very much – over much, I think – guided by him, sighed too.

'Come, come, Miss Robinson,' I said, 'there's nothing wrong with Eustace. Our experiences are mysterious, not his. He was astonished at our sudden departure, that's why he was so strange when we returned. He's right enough – improved, if anything.'

'And is the worship of athletics, the cult of insensate activity, to be counted as an improvement?' put in Leyland, fixing a large, sorrowful eye on Eustace, who had stopped to scramble on to a rock to pick some cyclamen. 'The passionate desire to rend from Nature the few beauties that have been still left her – that is to be counted as an improvement too?'

It is mere waste of time to reply to such remarks, especially when they come from an unsuccessful artist suffering from a damaged finger. I changed the conversation by asking what we should say at the hotel. After some discussion, it was agreed that we should say nothing, either there or in our letters home. Importunate truth-telling, which brings only bewilderment and discomfort to the hearers, is, in my opinion, a mistake; and, after a long discussion, I managed to make Mr Sandbach acquiesce in my view.

Eustace did not share in our conversation. He was racing about, like a real boy, in the wood to the right. A strange feeling of shame prevented us from openly mentioning our fright to him. Indeed, it seemed almost reasonable to conclude that it had made but little impression on him. So it disconcerted us when he bounded back with an armful of flowering acanthus, calling out:

'Do you suppose Gennaro'll be there when we get back?'

Gennaro was the stop-gap waiter, a clumsy, impertinent fisher-lad, who had been had up from Minori in the absence of the nice English-speaking Emmanuele. It was to him that we owed our scrappy lunch; and I could not conceive why Eustace desired to see him, unless it was to make mock with him of our behaviour.

'Yes, of course he will be there,' said Miss Robinson. 'Why do you ask, dear?'

'Oh, I thought I'd like to see him.[1]

'And why?' snapped Mr Sandbach.

'Because, because I do, I do; because, because I do.' He danced away into the darkening wood to the rhythm of his words.

'This is very extraordinary,' said Mr Sandbach. 'Did he like Gennaro before?'

'Gennaro has been here only two days,' said Rose, 'and I know that they haven't spoken to each other a dozen times.'

Each time Eustace returned from the wood his spirits were higher. Once he came whooping down on us as a wild Indian, and another time he made believe to be a dog. The last time he came back with a poor dazed hare, too frightened to move, sitting on his arm. He was getting too uproarious, I thought; and we were all glad to leave the wood, and start upon the steep staircase path that leads down into Ravello. It was late and turning dark; and we made all the speed we could, Eustace scurrying in front of us like a goat.

Just where the staircase path debouches on the white high road, the next extraordinary incident of this extraordinary day occurred. Three old women were standing by the wayside. They, like ourselves, had come down from the woods, and they were resting their heavy bundles of fuel on the low parapet of the road. Eustace stopped in front of them, and, after a moment's deliberation, stepped forward and – kissed the left-hand one on the cheek!

'My good fellow!' exclaimed Mr Sandbach, 'are you quite crazy?'

Eustace said nothing, but offered the old woman some of his flowers, and then hurried on. I looked back; and the old woman's companions seemed as much astonished as the proceeding as we were. But she herself had put the flowers in her bosom, and was murmuring blessings.

This salutation of the old lady was the first example of Eustace's strange behaviour, and we were both surprised and alarmed. It was useless talking to him, for he either made silly replies, or else bounded away without replying at all.

He made no reference on the way home to Gennaro, and I hoped that that was forgotten. But when we came to the Piazza, in front of the Cathedral, he screamed out: 'Gennaro! Gennaro!' at the top of his voice, and began running up the little alley that led to the hotel. Sure enough, there was Gennaro at the end of it, with his arms and legs sticking out of the nice little English-speaking waiter's dress suit, and a dirty fisherman's cap on his head – for, as the poor landlady truly said, however much she superintended his toilette, he always managed to introduce something incongruous into it before he had done.

Eustace sprang to meet him, and leapt right up into his arms, and put his own arms round his neck. And this in the presence, not only of us, but also of the landlady, the chambermaid, the facchino, and of two American ladies who were coming for a few days' visit to the little hotel.

I always make a point of behaving pleasantly to Italians, however little they may deserve it; but this habit of promiscuous intimacy was perfectly intolerable, and could only lead to familiarity and mortification for all. Taking Miss Robinson aside, I asked her permission to speak seriously to Eustace on the subject of intercourse with social inferiors. She granted it; but I determined to wait till the absurd boy had calmed down a little from the excitement of the day. Meanwhile, Gennaro, instead of attending to the wants of the two new ladies, carried Eustace into the house, as if it was the most natural thing in the world.

'Ho capito,' I heard him say as he passed me. 'Ho capito' is the Italian for 'I have understood'; but, as Eustace had not spoken to him, I could not see the force of the remark. It served to increase our bewilderment, and, by the time we sat down at the dinner-table, our imaginations and our tongues were alike exhausted.

I omit from this account the various comments that were made, as few of them seem worthy of being recorded. But, for three or four hours, seven of us were pouring forth our bewilderment in a stream of appropriate and inappropriate exclamations. Some traced a connexion between our behaviour in the afternoon and the behaviour of Eustace now. Others saw no connexion at all. Mr Sandbach still held to the possibility of infernal influences, and also said that he ought to have a doctor. Leyland only saw the development of 'that unspeakable Philistine, the boy'. Rose maintained, to my surprise, that everything was excusable; while I began to see that the young gentleman wanted a sound thrashing. The poor Miss Robinsons swayed helplessly about between these diverse opinions; inclining now to careful supervision, now to acquiescence, now to corporal chastisement, now to Eno's Fruit Salt.

Dinner passed off fairly well, though Eustace was terribly fidgety, Gennaro as usual dropping the knives and spoons, and hawking and clearing his throat. He only knew a few words of English, and we were all reduced to Italian for making known our wants. Eustace, who had picked up a little somehow, asked for some oranges. To my annoyance, Gennaro, in his answer, made use of the second person singular – a form only used when addressing those who are both intimates and equals. Eustace had brought it on himself; but an impertinence of this kind was an affront to us all, and I was determined to speak, and to speak at once.

When I heard him clearing the table I went in, and, summoning up my Italian, or rather Neapolitan – the Southern dialects are execrable – I said, 'Gennaro! I heard you address Signor Eustace with "Tu".'

'It is true.'

'You are not right. You must use "Lei" or "Voi" – more polite forms. And remember that, though Signor Eustace is sometimes silly and foolish – this afternoon for example – yet you must always behave respectfully to him; for he is a young English gentleman, and you are a poor Italian fisher-boy.'

I know that speech sounds terribly snobbish, but in Italian one can say things that one would never dream of saying in English. Besides, it is no good speaking delicately to persons of that class. Unless you put things plainly, they take a vicious pleasure in misunderstanding you.

An honest English fisherman would have landed me one in the eye in a minute for such a remark, but the wretched down-trodden Italians have no pride. Gennaro only sighed, and said: 'It is true'.

'Quite so,' I said, and turned to go. To my indignation I heard him add: 'But sometimes it is not important.'

'What do you mean?' I shouted.

He came close up to me with horrid gesticulating fingers.

'Signor Tytler, I wish to say this. If Eustazio asks me to call him "Voi", I will call him "Voi". Otherwise, no.'

With that he seized up a tray of dinner things, and fled from the room with them; and I heard two more wine-glasses go on the courtyard floor.

I was now fairly angry, and strode out to interview Eustace. But he had gone to bed, and the landlady, to whom I also wished to speak, was engaged. After more vague wonderings, obscurely expressed owing to the presence of Janet and the two American ladies, we all went to bed, too, after a harassing and most extraordinary day.

III

But the day was nothing to the night.

I suppose I had slept for about four hours, when I woke suddenly thinking I heard a noise in the garden. And, immediately, before my eyes were open, cold terrible fear seized me – not fear of something that was happening, like the fear in the wood, but fear of something that might happen.

Our room was on the first floor, looking out on to the garden – or terrace, it was rather a wedge-shaped block of ground covered with roses and vines, and intersected with little asphalt paths. It was bounded on the small side by the house; round the two long sides ran a wall, only three feet above the terrace level, but with a good twenty feet drop over it into the olive yards, for the ground fell very precipitously away.

Trembling all over, I stole to the window. There, pattering up and down the asphalt paths, was something white. I was too much alarmed to see clearly; and in the uncertain light of the stars the thing took all manner of curious shapes. Now it was a great dog, now an enormous white bat, now a mass of quickly travelling cloud. It would bounce like a ball, or take short flights like a bird, or glide slowly like a wraith. It gave no sound – save the pattering sound of what, after all, must be human feet. And at last the obvious explanation forced itself upon my disordered mind; and I realized that Eustace had got out of bed, and that we were in for something more.

I hastily dressed myself, and went down into the dining-room which opened upon the terrace. The door was already unfastened. My terror had almost entirely passed away, but for quite five minutes I struggled with a curious cowardly feeling, which bade me not interfere with the poor strange boy, but leave him to his ghostly patterings, and merely watch him from the window to see he took no harm.

But better impulses prevailed and, opening the door, I called out:

'Eustace! what on earth are you doing? Come in at once.'

He stopped his antics and said: 'I hate my bedroom. I could not stop in it, it is too small.'

'Come! come! I'm tired of affectation. You've never complained of it before.'

'Besides, I can't see anything – no flowers, no leaves, no sky: only a stone wall.' The outlook of Eustace's room certainly was limited; but, as I told him, he had never complained of it before.

'Eustace, you talk like a child. Come in! Prompt obedience, if you please.'

He did not move.

'Very well: I shall carry you in by force,' I added, and made a few steps towards him. But I was soon convinced of the futility of pursuing a boy through a tangle of asphalt paths, and went in instead to call Mr Sandbach and Leyland to my aid.

When I returned with them he was worse than ever. He would not even answer us when we spoke, but began singing and chattering to himself in a most alarming way.

'It's a case for the doctor now,' said Mr Sandbach, gravely tapping his forehead.

He had stopped his running, and was singing, first low, then loud – singing five-finger exercises, scales, hymn tunes, scraps of Wagner – anything that came into his head. His voice – a very untuneful voice – grew stronger and stronger, and he ended with a tremendous shout which boomed like a gun among the mountains, and awoke everyone who was still sleeping in the hotel. My poor wife and the two girls appeared at their respective windows, and the American ladies were heard violently ringing their bell.

'Eustace,' we all cried, 'stop! stop, dear boy, and come into the house.'

He shook his head, and started off again – talking this time. Never have I listened to such an extraordinary speech. At any other time it would have been ludicrous, for here was a boy, with no sense of beauty and a puerile command of words, attempting to tackle themes which the greatest poets have found almost beyond their power. Eustace Robinson, aged fourteen, was standing in his nightshirt saluting, praising, and blessing the great forces and manifestations of Nature.

He spoke first of night and the stars and planets above his head, of the swarms of fireflies below him, of the invisible sea below the fireflies, of the great rocks covered with anemones and shells that were slumbering in the invisible sea. He spoke of the rivers and waterfalls, of the ripening bunches of grapes, of the smoking cone of Vesuvius and the hidden fire-channels that made the smoke, of the myriads of lizards who were lying curled up in the crannies of the sultry earth, of the showers of white rose-leaves that were tangled in his hair. And then he spoke of the rain and the wind by which all things are changed, of the air through which all things live, and of the woods in which all things can be hidden.

Of course, it was all absurdly high faluting: yet I could have kicked Leyland for audibly observing that it was 'a diabolical caricature of all that was most holy and beautiful in life.'

'And then' – Eustace was going on in the pitiable conversational doggerel which was his only mode of expression – 'and then there are men, but I can't make them out so well.' He knelt down by the parapet, and rested his head on his arms.

'Now's the time,' whispered Leyland. I hate stealth, but we darted forward and endeavoured to catch hold of him from behind. He was away in a twinkling, but turned round at once to look at us. As far as I could see in the starlight, he was crying. Leyland rushed at him again, and we tried to corner him among the asphalt paths, but without the slightest approach to success.

We returned, breathless and discomfited, leaving him to his madness in the farther corner of the terrace. But my Rose had an inspiration.

'Papa,' she called from the window, 'if you get Gennaro, he might be able to catch him for you.'

I had no wish to ask a favour of Gennaro, but, as the landlady had by now appeared on the scene, I begged her to summon him from the charcoal-bin in which he slept, and make him try what he could do.

She soon returned, and was shortly followed by Gennaro, attired in a dress coat, without either waistcoat, shirt, or vest, and a ragged pair of what had been trousers, cut short above the knees for purposes of wading. The landlady, who had quite picked up English ways, rebuked him for the incongruous and even indecent appearance which he presented.

'I have a coat and I have trousers. What more do you desire?'

'Never mind, Signora Scafetti,' I put in. 'As there are no ladies here, it is not of the slightest consequence.' Then, turning to Gennaro, I said: 'The aunts of Signor Eustace wish you to fetch him into the house.'

He did not answer.

'Do you hear me? He is not well. I order you to fetch him into the house.'

'Fetch! fetch!' said Signora Scafetti, and shook him roughly by the arm.

'Eustazio is well where he is.'

'Fetch! fetch!' Signora Scafetti screamed, and let loose a flood of Italian, most of which, I am glad to say, I could not follow. I glanced up nervously at the girl's window, but they hardly know as much as I do, and I am thankful to say that none of us caught one word of Gennaro's answer.

The two yelled and shouted at each other for quite ten minutes, at the end of which Gennaro rushed back to his charcoal-bin and Signora Scafetti burst into tears, as well she might, for she greatly valued her English guests.

'He says,' she sobbed, 'that Signor Eustace is well where is, and that he will not fetch him. I can do no more.'

But I could, for, in my stupid British way, I have got some insight into the Italian character. I followed Mr Gennaro to his place of repose, and found him wriggling down on to a dirty sack.

'I wish you to fetch Signor Eustace to me,' I began.

He hurled at me an unintelligible reply.

'If you fetch him, I will give you this.' And out of my pocket I took a new ten-lira note.

This time he did not answer.

'This note is equal to ten lire in silver,' I continued, for I knew that the poor-class Italian is unable to conceive of a single large sum.

'I know it.'

'That is, two hundred soldi.'

'I do not desire them. Eustazio is my friend.'

I put the note into my pocket.

'Besides, you would not give it me.'

'I am an Englishman. The English always do what they promise.'

'That is true.' It is astonishing how the most dishonest of nations trust us. Indeed, they often trust us more than we trust one another. Gennaro knelt up on his sack. It was too dark to see his face, but I could feel his warm garlicky breath coming out in gasps, and I knew that the eternal avarice of the South had laid hold upon him.

'I could not fetch Eustazio to the house. He might die there.'

'You need not do that,' I replied patiently. 'You need only bring him to me; and I will stand outside in the garden.' And to this, as if it were something quite different, the pitiable youth consented.

'But give me first the ten lire.'

'No' – for I knew the kind of person with whom I had to deal. Once faithless, always faithless.

We returned to the terrace, and Gennaro, without a single word, pattered off towards the pattering that could be heard at the remoter end. Mr Sandbach, Leyland, and myself moved away a little from the house, and stood in the shadow of the white climbing roses, practically invisible.

We heard 'Eustazio' called, followed by absurd cries of pleasure from the poor boy. The pattering ceased, and we heard them talking. Their voices got nearer, and presently I could discern them through the creepers, the grotesque figure of the young man, and the slim little white-robed boy. Gennaro had his arm round Eustace's neck, and Eustace was talking away in his fluent, slip-shod Italian.

'I understand almost everything,' I heard him say. 'The trees, hills, stars, water, I can see all. But isn't it odd! I can't make out men a bit. Do you know what I mean?'

'Ho capito,' said Gennaro gravely, and took his arm off Eustace's shoulder. But I made the new note crackle in my pocket; and he heard it. He stuck his hand out with a jerk; and the unsuspecting Eustace gripped it in his own.

'It is odd!' Eustace went on – they were quite close now – 'It almost seems as if – as if—'

I darted out and caught hold of his arm, and Leyland got hold of the other arm, and Mr Sandbach hung on to his feet. He gave shrill heart-piercing screams; and the white roses, which were falling early that year, descended in showers on him as we dragged him into the house.

As soon as we entered the house he stopped shrieking; but floods of tears silently burst forth and spread over his upturned face.

'Not to my room,' he pleaded. 'It is so small.'

His infinitely dolorous look filled me with strange pity, but what could I do? Besides, his window was the only one that had bars to it.

'Never mind, dear boy,' said kind Mr Sandbach. 'I will bear you company till the morning.'

At this his convulsive struggles began again. 'Oh, please, not that. Anything but that. I will promise to lie still and not to cry more than I can help, if I am left alone.'

So we laid him on the bed, and drew the sheets over him, and left him sobbing bitterly, and saying: 'I nearly saw everything, and now I can see nothing at all.'

We informed the Miss Robinsons of all that had happened, and returned to the dining-room, where we found Signora Scafetti and Gennaro whispering together. Mr Sandbach got pen and paper, and began writing to the English doctor at Naples. I at once drew out the note, and flung it down on the table to Gennaro.

'Here is your pay,' I said sternly, for I was thinking of the Thirty Pieces of Silver.

'Thank you very much, sir,' said Gennaro, and grabbed it.

He was going off, when Leyland, whose interest and indifference were always equally misplaced, asked him what Eustace had meant by saying 'he could not make out men a bit'.

'I cannot say. Signor Eustazio' (I was glad to observe a little deference at last) 'has a subtle brain. He understands many things.'

'But I heard you say you understood,' Leyland persisted.

'I understand, but I cannot explain. I am a poor Italian fisher-lad. Yet, listen: I will try.' I saw to my alarm that his manner was changing, and tried to stop him. But he sat down on the edge of the table and started off, with some absolutely incoherent remarks.

'It is sad,' he observed at last. 'What has happened is very sad. But what can I do? I am poor. It is not I.'

I turned away in contempt. Leyland went on asking questions. He wanted to know who it was that Eustace had in his mind when he spoke.

'That is easy to say,' Gennaro gravely answered. 'It is you, it is I. It is all in this house, and many outside it. If he wishes for mirth, we discomfort him. If he asks to be alone, we disturb him. He longed for a friend, and found none for fifteen years. Then he found me, and the first night I – I who have been in the woods and understood things too – betray him to you and send him in to die. But what could I do?'

'Gently, gently,' said I.

'Oh, assuredly he will die. He will lie in the small room all night, and in the morning he will be dead. That I know for certain.'

'There, that will do,' said Mr Sandbach. 'I shall be sitting with him.'

'Filomena Giusti sat all night with Caterina, but Caterina was dead in the morning. They would not let her out, though I begged, and prayed, and cursed, and beat the door, and climbed the wall. They were ignorant fools, and thought I wished to carry her away. And in the morning she was dead.'

'What is all this?' I asked Signora Scafetti.

'All kinds of stories will get about,' she replied, 'and he, least of anyone, has reason to repeat them.'

'And I am alive now,' he went on, 'because I had neither parents nor relatives nor friends, so that, when the first night came, I could run through the woods, and climb the rocks, and plunge into the water, until I had accomplished my desire!'

We heard a cry from Eustace's room – a faint but steady sound, like the sound of wind in a distant wood heard by one standing in tranquillity.

'That,' said Gennaro, 'was the last noise of Caterina. I was hanging on to her window then, and it blew out past me.'

And, lifting up his hand, in which my ten-lira note was safely packed, he solemnly cursed Mr Sandbach, and Leyland, and myself, and Fate, because Eustace was dying in the upstairs room. Such is the working of the Southern mind; and I verily believe that he would not have moved even then, had not Leyland, that unspeakable idiot, upset the lamp with his elbow. It was a patent self-extinguishing lamp, bought by Signora Scafetti, at my special request, to replace the dangerous thing that she was using. The result was, that it went out; and the mere physical change from light to darkness had more power over the ignorant animal nature of Gennaro than the most obvious dictates of logic and reason.

I felt, rather than saw, that he had left the room, and shouted out to Mr Sandbach: 'Have you got the key to Eustace's room in your pocket?' But Mr Sandbach and Leyland were both on the floor, having mistaken each other for Gennaro, and some more precious time was wasted in finding a match. Mr Sandbach had only just time to say that he had left the key in the door, in case the Miss Robinsons wished to pay Eustace a visit, when we heard a noise on the stairs, and there was Gennaro, carrying Eustace down.

We rushed out and blocked up the passage, and they lost heart and retreated to the upper landing.

'Now they are caught,' cried Signora Scafetti. 'There is no other way out.'

We were cautiously ascending the staircase, when there was a terrific scream from my wife's room, followed by a heavy thud on the asphalt path. They had leapt out of her window.

I reached the terrace just in time to see Eustace jumping over the parapet of the garden wall. This time I knew for certain he would be killed. But he alighted in an olive tree, looking like a great white moth, and from the tree he slid on to the earth. And as soon as his bare feet touched the clods of earth he uttered a strange loud cry, such as I should not have thought the human voice could have produced, and disappeared among the trees below.

'He has understood and he is saved,' cried Gennaro, who was still sitting on the asphalt path. 'Now, instead of dying he will live!'

'And you, instead of keeping the ten lire, will give them up,' I retorted, for at this theatrical remark I could contain myself no longer.

'The ten lire are mine,' he hissed back in a scarcely audible voice. He clasped his hand over his breast to protect his ill-gotten gains, and, as he did so, he swayed forward and fell upon his face on the path. He had not broken any limbs, and a leap like that would never have killed an Englishman, for the drop was not great. But those miserable Italians have no stamina. Something had gone wrong inside him, and he was dead.

The morning was still far off, but the morning breeze had begun, and more rose leaves fell on us as we carried him in. Signora Scafetti burst into screams at the sight of the dead body, and, far down the valley towards the sea, there still resounded the shouts and the laughter of the escaping boy.

Karen Blixen

The Sailor-Boy's Tale

The barque *Charlotte* was on her way from Marseille to Athens, in grey weather, on a high sea, after three day's heavy gale. A small sailor-boy, named Simon, stood on the wet, swinging deck, held on to a shroud, and looked up towards the drifting clouds, and to the upper top-gallant yard of the main-mast.

A bird, that had sought refuge upon the mast, had got her feet entangled in some loose tackle-yarn of the halliard, and, high up there, struggled to get free. The boy on the deck could see her wings flapping and her head turning from side to side.

Through his own experience of life he had come to the conviction that in this world everyone must look after himself, and expect no help from others. But the mute, deadly fight kept him fascinated for more than an hour. He wondered what kind of bird it would be. These last days a number of birds had come to settle in the barque's rigging: swallows, quails, and a pair of peregrine falcons; he believed that this bird was a peregrine falcon. He remembered how, many years ago, in his own country and near his home, he had once seen a peregrine falcon quite close, sitting on a stone and flying straight up from it. Perhaps this was the same bird. He thought: 'That bird is like me. Then she was there, and now she is here.'

At that a fellow-feeling rose in him, a sense of common tragedy; he stood looking at the bird with his heart in his mouth. There were none of the sailors about to make fun of him; he began to think out how he might go up by the shrouds to help the falcon out. He brushed his hair back and pulled up his sleeves, gave the deck round him a great glance, and climbed up. He had to stop a couple of times in the swaying rigging.

THE SAILOR BOY'S TALE

It was indeed, he found when he got to the top of the mast, a pere-grine falcon. As his head was on a level with hers, she gave up her strug-gle, and looked at him with a pair of angry, desperate, yellow eyes. He had to take hold of her with one hand while he got his knife out, and cut off the tackle-yarn. He was scared as he looked down, but at the same time he felt that he had been ordered up by nobody, but that this was his own venture, and this gave him a proud, steadying sensation, as if the sea and the sky, the ship, the bird and himself were all one. Just as he had had freed the falcon, she hacked him in the thumb, so that the blood ran, and he nearly let her go. He grew angry with her, and gave her a clout on the head, then he put her inside his jacket and climbed down again.

When he reached the deck the mate and the cook were standing there, looking up; they roared to him to ask what he had had to do in the mast. He was so tired that the tears were in his eyes. He took the falcon out and showed her to them, and she kept still within his hands. They laughed and walked off. Simon set the falcon down, stood back and watched her. After a while he reflected that she might not be able to get up from the slippery deck, so he caught her once more, walked away with her and placed her upon a bolt of canvas. A little after she began to trim her feathers, made two or three sharp jerks forward, and then suddenly flew off. The boy could follow her flight above the troughs of the grey sea. He thought: 'There flies my falcon.'

When the *Charlotte* came home, Simon signed aboard another ship, and two years later he was a light hand on the schooner *Hebe* lying at Bodø, high up the coast of Norway, to buy herrings.

To the great herring-markets of Bodø ships came together from all corners of the world; here were Swedish, Finnish and Russian boats, a forest of masts, and on shore a turbulent, irregular display of life, with many languages spoken, and mighty fights. On the shore booths had been set up, and the Lapps, small yellow people, noiseless in their movements, with watchful eyes, whom Simon had never seen before, came down to sell bead-embroidered leather-goods. It was April, the sky and the sea were so clear that it was difficult to hold one's eyes up against them – salt, infinitely wide, and filled with bird-shrieks – as if someone were incessantly whetting invisible knives, on all sides, high up in Heaven.

Simon was amazed at the lightness of these April evenings. He knew no geography, and did not assign it to the latitude, but he took it as a sign of an unwonted good-will in the Universe, a favour. Simon had been small for his age all his life, but this last winter he had grown, and had become strong of limb. That good luck, he felt, must spring from the very same source as the sweetness of the weather, from a new benevo-

326

THE BEST GHOST STORIES

lence in the world. He had been in need of such encouragement, for he
was timid by nature; now he asked for no more. The rest he felt to be
his own affair. He went about slowly, and proudly.

One evening he was ashore with land-leave, and walked up to the
booth of a small Russian trader, a Jew who sold gold watches. All the
sailors knew that his watches were made from bad metal, and would not
go, still they bought them, and paraded them about. Simon looked at
these watches for a long time, but did not buy. The old Jews had divers
goods in his shop, and amongst others a case of oranges. Simon had
tasted oranges on his journeys; he bought one and took it with him. He
meant to go up on a hill, from where he could see the sea, and suck it
there.

As he walked on, and had got to the outskirts of the place, he saw a
little girl in a blue frock, standing at the other side of a fence and looking
at him. She was thirteen or fourteen years old, as slim as an eel, but with
a round, clear, freckled face, and a pair of long plaits. The two looked
at one another.

'Who are you looking out for?' Simon asked, to say something. The
girl's face broke into an ecstatic, presumptuous smile. 'For the man I am
going to marry, of course,' she said. Something in her countenance made
the boy confident and happy; he grinned a little at her. 'That will perhaps be me,' he said. 'Ha, ha,' said the girl, 'he is a few years older than
you, I can tell you.' 'Why,' said Simon, 'you are not grown up yourself.'
The little girl shook her head solemnly. 'Nay,' she said, 'but when I
grow up I will be exceedingly beautiful, and wear brown shoes with
heels, and a hat.' 'Will you have an orange?' asked Simon, who could
give her none of the things she had named. She looked at the orange and
at him. 'They are very good to eat,' said he. 'Why do you not eat it yourself then?' she asked. 'I have eaten so many already,' said he, 'when I
was in Athens. Here I had to pay a mark for it.' 'What is your name?'
asked she. 'My name is Simon,' said he. 'What is yours?' 'Nora,' said the
girl. 'What do you want for your orange now, Simon?'

When he heard his name in her mouth Simon grew bold. 'Will you
give me a kiss for the orange?' he asked. Nora looked at him gravely for
a moment. 'Yes,' she said, 'I should not mind giving you a kiss.' He grew
as warm as if he had been running quickly. When she stretched out her
hand for the orange he took hold of it. At that moment somebody in the
house called out for her. 'That is my father,' said she, and tried to give
him back the orange, but he would not take it. 'Then come again to-
morrow,' she said quickly, 'then I will give you a kiss.' At that she
slipped off. He stood and looked after her, and a little later went back
to his ship.

Simon was not in the habit of making plans for the future, and now he did not know whether he would be going back to her or not.

The following evening he had to stay aboard, as the other sailors were going ashore, and he did not mind that either. He meant to sit on the deck with the ship's dog, Balthasar, and to practise upon a concertina that he had purchased some time ago. The pale evening was all round him, the sky was faintly roseate, the sea was quite calm, like milk-and-water, only in the wake of the boats going inshore it broke into streaks of vivid indigo. Simon sat and played; after a while his own music began to speak to him so strongly that he stopped, got up and looked upwards. Then he saw that the full moon was sitting high on the sky.

The sky was so light that she hardly seemed needed there; it was as if she had turned up by a caprice of her own. She was round, demure and presumptuous. At that he knew that he must go ashore, whatever it was to cost him. But he did not know how to get away, since the others had taken the yawl with them. He stood on the deck for a long time, a small lonely figure of a sailor-boy on a boat, when he caught sight of a yawl coming in from a ship farther out, and hailed her. He found that it was the Russian crew from a boat named *Anna*, going ashore. When he could make himself understood to them, they took him with them; they first asked him for money for his fare, then, laughingly, gave it back to him. He thought: 'These people will be believing that I am going in to town, wenching.' And then he felt, with some pride, that they were right, although at the same time they were infinitely wrong, and knew nothing about anything.

When they came ashore they invited him to come in and drink in their company, and he would not refuse, because they had helped him. One of the Russians was a giant, as big as a bear; he told Simon that his name was Ivan. He got drunk at once, and then fell upon the boy with a bear-like affection, pawed him, smiled and laughed into his face, made him a present of a gold watch chain, and kissed him on both cheeks. At that Simon reflected that he also ought to give Nora a present when they met again, and as soon as he could get away from the Russians he walked up to a booth that he knew of, and bought a small blue silk handkerchief, the same colour as her eyes.

It was Saturday evening, and there were many people amongst the houses; they came in long rows, some of them singing, all keen to have some fun that night. Simon, in the midst of this rich, bawling life under the clear moon, felt his head light with the flight from the ship and the strong drinks. He crammed the handkerchief in his pocket; it was silk, which he had never touched before, a present for his girl.

He could not remember the path up to Nora's house, lost his way, and came back to where he had started. Then he grew deadly afraid that he should be too late, and began to run. In a small passage between two wooden huts he ran straight into a big man, and found that it was Ivan once more. The Russian folded his arms round him and held him. 'Good! Good!' he cried in high glee, 'I have found you, my little chicken. I have looked for you everywhere, and poor Ivan has wept because he lost his friend.' 'Let me go, Ivan,' cried Simon. 'Oho,' said Ivan, 'I shall go with you and get you what you want. My heart and my money are all yours, all yours; I have been seventeen years old myself, a little lamb of God, and I want to be so again to-night.' 'Let me go,' cried Simon, 'I am in a hurry.' Ivan held him so that it hurt, and patted him with his other hand. 'I feel it, I feel it,' he said. 'Now trust to me, my little friend. Nothing shall part you and me. I hear the others coming; we will have such a night together as you will remember when you are an old grandpapa.'

Suddenly he crushed the boy to him, like a bear that carries off a sheep. The odious sensation of male bodily warmth and the bulk of a man close to him made the lean boy mad. He thought of Nora waiting, like a slender ship in the dim air, and of himself, here, in the hot embrace of a hairy animal. He struck Ivan with all his might. 'I shall kill you, Ivan,' he cried out, 'if you do not let me go.' 'Oh, you will be thankful to me later on,' said Ivan, and began to sing. Simon fumbled in his pocket for his knife, and got it opened. He could not lift his hand, but he drove the knife, furiously, in under the big man's arm. Almost immediately he felt the blood spouting out, and running down in his sleeve. Ivan stopped short in the song, let go his hold of the boy and gave two long deep grunts. The next second he tumbled down on his knees. 'Poor Ivan, poor Ivan,' he groaned. He fell straight on his face. At that moment Simon heard the other sailors coming along, singing, in the by-street.

He stood still for a minute, wiped his knife, and watched the blood spread into a dark pool underneath the big body. Then he ran. As he stopped for a second to choose his way, he heard the sailors behind him scream out over their dead comrade. He thought: 'I must get down to the sea, where I can wash my hand.' But at the same time he ran the other way. After a little while he found himself on the path that he had walked on the day before, and it seemed as familiar to him as if he had walked it many hundred times in his life.

He slackened his pace to look round, and suddenly saw Nora standing on the other side of the fence; she was quite close to him when he caught sight of her in the moonlight. Wavering and out of breath he sank down on his knees. For a moment he could not speak. The little girl looked down at him. 'Good evening, Simon,' she said in her small coy voice. 'I have waited for you a long time,' and after a moment she added: 'I have eaten your orange.'

THE SAILOR BOY'S TALE

'Oh, Nora,' cried the boy. 'I have killed a man.' She stared at him, but did not move. 'Why did you kill a man?' she asked after a moment. 'To get here,' said Simon. 'Because he tried to stop me. But he was my friend.' Slowly he got on to his feet. 'He loved me!' the boy cried out, and at that burst into tears. 'Yes,' said she slowly and thoughtfully. 'Yes, because you must be here in time.' 'Can you hide me?' he asked. 'For they are after me.'

'Nay,' said Nora, 'I cannot hide you. For my father is the parson here at Bodø, and he would be sure to hand you over to them, if he knew that you had killed a man.' 'Then,' said Simon, 'give me something to wipe my hands on.' 'What is the matter with your hands?' she asked, and took a little step forward. He stretched out his hands to her. 'Is that your own blood?' she asked. 'No,' said he, 'it is his.' She took the step back again. 'Do you hate me now?' he asked. 'No, I do not hate you,' said she. 'But do put your hands at your back.'

As he did so she came up close to him, at the other side of the fence, and clasped her arms round his neck. She pressed her young body to his, and kissed him tenderly. He felt her face, cool as the moonlight, upon his own, and when she released him, his head swam, and he did not know if the kiss had lasted a second or an hour. Nora stood up straight, her eyes wide open. 'Now,' she said slowly and proudly, 'I promise you that I will never marry anybody, as long as I live.' The boy kept standing with his hands at his back, as if she had tied them there. 'And now,' she said, 'you must run, for they are coming.' They looked at one another. 'Do not forget Nora,' said she. He turned and ran.

He leaped over a fence, and when he was down amongst the houses he walked. He did not know at all where to go. As he came to a house, from where music and noise streamed out, he slowly went through the door. The room was full of people; they were dancing in here. A lamp hung from the ceiling, and shone down on them; the air was thick and brown with the dust rising from the floor. There were some women in the room, but many of the men danced with each other, and gravely or laughingly stamped the floor. A moment after Simon had come in the crowd withdrew to the walls to clear the floor for two sailors, who were showing a dance from their own country.

Simon thought: 'Now, very soon, the men from the boat will come round to look for their comrade's murderer, and from my hands they will know that I have done it.' These five minutes during which he stood by the wall of the dancing-room, in the midst of the gay, sweating dancers, were of great significance to the boy. He himself felt it, as if during this time he grew up, and became like other people. He did not entreat his destiny, nor complain. Here he was, he had killed a man, and had kissed a girl. He did not demand any more from life, nor did life now demand more from him. He was Simon, a man like the men round him, and going to die, as all men are going to die.

He only became aware of what was going on outside him, when he saw that a woman had come in, and was standing in the midst of the cleared floor, looking round her. She was a short, broad old woman, in the clothes of the Lapps, and she took her stand with such majesty and fierceness as if she owned the whole place. It was obvious that most of the people knew her, and were a little afraid of her, although a few laughed; the din of the dancing-room stopped when she spoke.

'Where is my son?' she asked in a high shrill voice, like a bird's. The next moment her eyes fell on Simon himself, and she steered through the crowd, which opened up before he, stretched out her old skinny, dark hand, and took him by the elbow. 'Come home with me now,' she said. 'You need not dance here to-night. You may be dancing a high enough dance soon.'

Simon drew back, for he thought that she was drunk. But as she looked him straight in the face with her yellow eyes, it seemed to him that he had met her before, and that he might do well in listening to her. The old woman pulled him with her across the floor, and he followed her without a word. 'Do not birch your boy too badly, Sunniva,' one of the men in the room cried to her. 'He has done no harm, he only wanted to look at the dance.'

At the same moment as they came out through the door, there was an alarm in the street, a flock of people came running down it, and one of them, as he turned into the house, knocked against Simon, looked at him and the old woman, and ran on.

While the two walked along the street, the old woman lifted up her skirt, and put the hem of it into the boy's hand. 'Wipe your hand on my skirt,' she said. They had not gone far before they came to a small wooden house, and stopped; the door to it was so low that they must bend to get through it. As the Lapp woman went in before Simon, still holding on to his arm, the boy looked up for a moment. The night had grown misty; there was a wide ring round the moon.

The old woman's room was narrow and dark, with but one small window to it; a lantern stood on the floor and lighted it up dimly. It was all filled with reindeer skins and wolf skins, and with reindeer horn, such as the Lapps use to make their carved buttons and knife-handles, and the air in here was rank and stifling. As soon as they were in, the woman turned to Simon, took hold of his head, and with her crooked fingers parted his hair and combed it down in Lapp fashion. She clapped a Lapp cap on him and stood back to glance at him. 'Sit down on my stool, now,' she said. 'But first take out your knife.' She was so commanding in voice and manner that the boy could not but choose to do

THE SAILOR BOY'S TALE

as she told him; he sat down on the stool, and he could not take his eyes off her face, which was flat and brown, and as if smeared with dirt in its net of fine wrinkles. As he sat there he heard many people come along outside, and stop by the house; then someone knocked at the door, waited a moment and knocked again. The old woman stood and listened, as still as a mouse.

'Nay,' said the boy and got up. 'This is no good, for it is me that they are after. It will be better for you to let me go out to them.' 'Give me your knife,' said she. When he handed it to her, she stuck it straight into her thumb, so that the blood spouted out, and she let it drip all over her skirt. 'Come in, then,' she cried.

The door opened, and two of the Russian sailors came and stood in the opening; there were more people outside. 'Has anybody come in here?' they asked. 'We are after a man who has killed our mate, but he has run away from us. Have you seen or heard anybody this way?' The old Lapp woman turned upon them, and her eyes shone like gold in the lamplight. 'Have I seen or heard anyone?' she cried, 'I have heard you shriek murder all over the town. You frightened me, and my poor silly boy there, so that I cut my thumb as I was ripping the skin-rug that I sew. The boy is too scared to help me, and the rug is all ruined. I shall make you pay me for that. If you are looking for a murderer, come in and search my house for me, and I shall know you when we meet again.' She was so furious that she danced where she stood, and jerked her head like an angry bird of prey.

The Russian came in, looked round the room, and at her and her blood-stained hand and skirt. 'Do not put a curse on us now, Sunniva,' he said timidly. 'We know that you can do many things when you like. Here is a mark to pay you for the blood you have spilled.' She stretched out her hand, and he placed a piece of money in it. She spat on it. 'Then go, and there shall be no bad blood between us,' said Sunniva, and shut the door after them. She stuck her thumb in her mouth, and chuckled a little.

The boy got up from his stool, stood straight up before her and stared into her face. He felt as if he were swaying high up in the air, with but a small hold. 'Why have you helped me?' he asked her. 'Do you not know?' she answered. 'Have you not recognized me yet? But you will remember the peregrine falcon which was caught in the tackle-yarn of your boat, the *Charlotte*, as she sailed in the Mediterranean. That day you climbed up by the shrouds of the top-gallant mast to help her out, in a stiff wind, and with a high sea. That falcon was me. We Lapps often fly in such a manner, to see the world. When I first met you I was on my way to Africa, to see my younger sister and her children. She is a falcon too, when she chooses. By that time she was living at Takaunga, within an old ruined tower, which down there they call a minaret.' She swathed a corner of her skirt round her thumb, and bit at it. 'We do not forget,' she said. 'I hacked your thumb, when you took hold of me; it is only fair that I should cut my thumb for you to-night.'

She came close to him, and gently rubbed her two brown, claw-like fingers against his forehead. 'So you are a boy,' she said, 'who will kill a man rather than be late to meet your sweetheart? We hold together, the females of this earth. I shall mark your forehead now, so that the girls will know of that, when they look at you, and they will like you for it.' She played with the boy's hair, and twisted it round her finger.

'Listen now, my little bird,' said she. 'My great-grandson's brother-in-law is lying with his boat by the landing-place at this moment; he is to take a consignment of skins out to a Danish boat. He will bring you back to your boat, in time, before your mate comes. The *Hebe* is sailing to-morrow morning, is it not so? But when you are aboard, give him back my cap for me.' She took up his knife, wiped it in her skirt and handed it to him. 'Here is your knife,' she said. 'You will stick it into no more men; you will not need to, for from now you will sail the seas like a faithful seaman. We have enough trouble with our sons as it is.'

The bewildered boy began to stammer his thanks to her. 'Wait,' said she, 'I shall make you a cup of coffee, to bring back your wits, while I wash your jacket.' She went and rattled an old copper kettle upon the fireplace. After a while she handed him a hot, strong, black drink in a cup without a handle to it. 'You have drunk with Sunniva now,' she said; 'you have drunk down a little wisdom, so that in the future all your thoughts shall not fall like raindrops into the salt sea.'

When he had finished and set down the cup, she led him to the door and opened it for him. He was surprised to see that it was almost clear morning. The house was so high up that the boy could see the sea from it, and a milky mist about it. He gave her his hand to say good-bye.

She stared into his face. 'We do not forget,' she said. 'And you, you knocked me on the head there, high up in the mast. I shall give you that blow back.' With that she smacked him on the ear as hard as she could, so that his head swam. 'Now we are quits,' she said, gave him a great, mischievous, shining glance, and a little push down the doorstep, and nodded to him.

In this way the sailor-boy got back to his ship, which was to sail the next morning, and lived to tell the story.

H. P. Lovecraft

Pickman's Model

You needn't think I'm crazy, Eliot – plenty of others have queerer prejudices than this. Why don't you laugh at Oliver's grandfather, who won't ride in a motor? If I don't like that damned subway, it's my own business; and we got here more quickly anyhow in the taxi. We'd have had to walk up the hill from Park Street if we'd taken the car.

I know I'm more nervous than I was when you saw me last year, but you don't need to hold a clinic over it. There's plenty of reason, God knows, and I fancy I'm lucky to be sane at all. Why the third degree? You didn't use to be so inquisitive.

Well, if you must hear it, I don't know why you shouldn't. Maybe you ought to, anyhow, for you kept writing me like a grieved parent when you heard I'd begun to cut the Art Club and keep away from Pickman. Now that he's disappeared I go round to the club once in a while, but my nerves aren't what they were.

No, I don't know what's become of Pickman, and I don't like to guess. You might have surmised I had some inside information when I dropped him – and that's why I don't want to think where he's gone. Let the police find what they can – it won't be much, judging from the fact that they don't know yet of the old North End place he hired under the name of Peters. I'm not sure that I could find it again myself – not that I'd ever try, even in broad daylight! Yes, I do know, or am afraid I know, why he maintained it. I'm coming to that. And I think you'll understand before I'm through why I don't tell the police. They would ask me to guide them, but I couldn't go back there even if I knew the way. There was something there – and now I can't use the subway or (and you may as well have your laugh at this, too) go down into cellars any more.

I should think you'd have known I didn't drop Pickman for the same silly reasons that fussy old women like Dr. Reid or Joe Minot or Rosworth did. Morbid art doesn't shock me, and when a man has the genius Pickman had I feel it an honour to know him, no matter what direction his work takes. Boston never had a greater painter than Richard Upton Pickman. I said it at first and I say it still, and I never swerved an inch, either, when he showed that 'Ghoul Feeding'. That, you remember, was when Minot cut him.

You know, it takes profound art and profound insight into Nature to turn out stuff like Pickman's. Any magazine-cover hack can splash paint around wildly and call it a nightmare or a Witches' Sabbath or a portrait of the devil, but only a great painter can make such a thing really scare or ring true. That's because only a real artist knows the actual anatomy of the terrible or the physiology of fear – the exact sort of lines and proportions that connect up with latent instincts or hereditary memories of fright, and the proper colour contrasts and lighting effects to stir the dormant sense of strangeness. I don't have to tell you why a Fuseli really brings a shiver while a cheap ghost-story frontispiece merely makes us laugh. There's something those fellows catch – beyond life – that they're able to make us catch for a second. Doré had it. Sime has it. Angarola of Chicago has it. And Pickman had it as no man ever had it before or – I hope to Heaven – ever will again.

Don't ask me what it is they see. You know, in ordinary art, there's all the difference in the world between the vital, breathing things drawn from Nature or models and the artificial truck that commercial small fry reel off in a bare studio by rule. Well, I should say that the really weird artist has a kind of vision which makes models, or summons up what amounts to actual scenes from the spectral world he lives in. Anyhow, he manages to turn out results that differ from the pretender's mince-pie dreams in just about the same way that the life painter's results differ from the concoctions of a correspondence-school cartoonist. If I had ever seen what Pickman saw – but no! Here, let's have a drink before we get any deeper. Gad, I wouldn't be alive if I'd ever seen what that man – if he was a man – saw!

You recall that Pickman's forte was faces. I don't believe anybody since Goya could put so much of sheer hell into a set of features or a twist of expression. And before Goya you have to go back to the mediaeval chaps who did the gargoyles and chimaeras on Notre Dame and Mont Saint-Michel. They believed all sorts of things – and maybe they saw all sorts of things, too, for the Middle Ages had some curious phases. I remember your asking Pickman yourself once, the year before you went away, wherever in thunder he got such ideas and visions. Wasn't that a nasty laugh he gave you? It was partly because of that laugh that Reid dropped him. Reid, you know, had just taken up comparative pathology, and was full of pompous 'inside stuff' about the biological or evolutionary significance of this or that mental or physical symptom. He said Pickman repelled him more and more every day, and almost frightened him towards the last – that the fellow's features and expression were slowly developing in a way he didn't like; in a way that wasn't human. He had a lot of talk about diet, and said Pickman must be abnormal and eccentric to the last degree. I suppose you told Reid, if you and he had any correspondence over it, that he'd let Pickman's paintings get on his nerves or harrow up his imagination. I know I told him that myself – then.

But keep in mind that I didn't drop Pickman for anything like this. On the contrary, my admiration for him kept growing; for that 'Ghoul Feeding' was a tremendous achievement. As you know, the club wouldn't exhibit it, and the Museum of Fine Arts wouldn't accept it as a gift; and I can add that nobody would buy it, so Pickman had it right in his house till he went. Now his father has it in Salem – you know Pickman comes of old Salem stock, and had a witch ancestor hanged in 1692.

I got into the habit of calling on Pickman quite often, especially after I began making notes for a monograph on weird art. Probably it was his work which put the idea into my head, and anyhow, I found him a mine of data and suggestions when I came to develop it. He showed me all the paintings and drawings he had about; including some pen-and-ink sketches that would, I verily believe, have got him kicked out of the club if many of the members had seen them. Before long I was pretty nearly a devotee, and would listen for hours like a schoolboy to art theories and philosophic speculations wild enough to qualify him for the Danvers asylum. My hero-worship, coupled with the fact that people generally were commencing to have less and less to do with him, made him get very confidential with me; and one evening he hinted that if I were fairly close-mouthed and none too squeamish, he might show me something rather unusual – something a bit stronger than anything he had in the house.

'You know,' he said, 'there are things that won't do for Newbury Street – things that are out of place here, and that can't be conceived here, anyhow. It's my business to catch the overtones of the soul, and you won't find those in a parvenu set of artificial streets on made land. Back Bay isn't Boston – it isn't anything yet, because it's had no time to pick up memories and attract local spirits. If there are any ghosts here, they're the tame ghosts of a salt marsh and a shallow cove; and I want human ghosts – the ghosts of beings highly organized enough to have looked on hell and known the meaning of what they saw.

'The place for an artist to live is the North End. If any aesthete were sincere, he'd put up with the slums for the sake of the massed traditions.

God, man! Don't you realize that places like that weren't merely *made*, but actually *grew*? Generation after generation lived and felt and died there, and in days when people weren't afraid to live and feel and die. Don't you know there was a mill on Copp's Hill in 1632, and that half the present streets were laid out by 1650? I can show you houses that have stood two centuries and a half and more; houses that have witnessed what would make a modern house crumble into powder. What do moderns know of life and the forces behind it? You call the Salem witchcraft a delusion, but I'll wager my four-times-great-grandmother could have told you things. They hanged her on Gallows Hill, with Cotton Mather looking sanctimoniously on. Mather, damn him, was afraid somebody might succeed in kicking free of this accursed cage of monotony – I wish someone had laid a spell on him or sucked his blood in the night!

'I can show you a house he lived in, and I can show you another one he was afraid to enter in spite of all his fine bold talk. He knew things he didn't dare put into that stupid *Magnalia* or that puerile *Wonders of the Invisible World*. Look here, do you know the whole North End once had a set of tunnels that kept certain people in touch with each other's houses, and the burying ground, and the sea? Let them prosecute and persecute above ground – things went on every day that they couldn't reach, and voices laughed at night that they couldn't place!

'Why, man, out of ten surviving houses built before 1700 and not moved since I'll wager that in eight I can show you something queer in the cellar. There's hardly a month that you don't read of workmen finding bricked-up arches and wells leading nowhere in this or that old place as it comes down – you could see one near Henchman Street from the elevated last year. There were witches and what their spells summoned; pirates and what they brought in from the sea; smugglers; privateers – and I tell you, people knew how to live, and how to enlarge the bounds of life, in the old time! This wasn't the only world a bold and wise man could know – faugh! And to think of today in contrast, with such pale-pink brains that even a club of supposed artists gets shudders and convulsions if a picture goes beyond the feelings of a Beacon Street tea-table!

'The only saving grace of the present is that it's too damned stupid to question the past very closely. What do maps and records and guide-books really tell of the North End? Bah! At a guess I'll guarantee to lead you to thirty or forty alleys and networks of alleys north of Prince Street that aren't suspected by ten living beings outside of the foreigners that swarm them. And what do those Dagoes know of their meaning? No, Thurber, these ancient places are dreaming gorgeously and overflowing with wonder and terror and escapes from the commonplace, and yet there's not a living soul to understand or profit by them. Or rather, there's only one living soul – for I haven't been digging around in the past for nothing!

'See here, you're interested in this sort of thing. What if I told you that I've got another studio up there, where I can catch the night-spirit of antique horror and paint things that I couldn't even think of in Newbury Street? Naturally I don't tell those cursed old maids at the club – with Reid, damn him, whispering even as it is that I'm a sort of monster bound down the toboggan of reverse evolution. Yes, Thurber, I decided long ago that one must paint terror as well as beauty from life, so I did some exploring in places where I had reason to know terror lives.

'I've got a place that I don't believe three living Nordic men besides myself have ever seen. It isn't so very far from the elevated as distance goes, but it's centuries away as the soul goes. I took it because of the queer old brick well in the cellar – one of the sort I told you about. The shack's almost tumbling down so that nobody else would live there, and I'd hate to tell you how little I pay for it: The windows are boarded up, but I like that all the better, since I don't want daylight for what I do. I paint in the cellar, where the inspiration is thickest, but I've other rooms furnished on the ground floor. A Sicilian owns it, and I've hired it under the name of Peters.

'Now, if you're game, I'll take you there tonight. I think you'd enjoy the pictures, for, as I said, I've let myself go a bit there. It's no vast tour – I sometimes do it on foot, for I don't want to attract attention with a taxi in such a place. We can take the shuttle at the South Station for Battery Street, and after that the walk isn't much.'

Well, Eliot, there wasn't much for me to do after that harangue but to keep myself from running instead of walking for the first vacant cab we could sight. We changed to the elevated at the South Station, and at about twelve o'clock had climbed down the steps at Battery Street and struck along the old waterfront past Constitution Wharf. I didn't keep track of the cross streets, and can't tell you yet which it was we turned up, but I know it wasn't Greenough Lane.

When we did turn, it was to climb through the deserted length of the oldest and dirtiest alley I ever saw in my life, with crumbling-looking gables, broken small-paned windows, and archaic chimneys that stood out half-disintegrated against the moonlit sky. I don't believe there were three houses in sight that hadn't been standing in Cotton Mather's time – certainly I glimpsed at least two with an overhang, and once I thought I saw a peaked roof-line of the almost forgotten pre-gambrel type, though antiquarians tell us there are none left in Boston.

From that alley, which had a dim light, we turned to the left into an equally silent and still narrower alley with no light at all: and in a minute made what I think was an obtuse-angled bend towards the right in the dark. Not long after this Pickman produced a flashlight and revealed an antediluvian ten-panelled door that looked damnably worm-eaten. Unlocking it, he ushered me into a barren hallway with what was once splendid dark-oak panelling – simple, of course, but thrillingly suggestive of the times of Andros and Phipps and the Witchcraft. Then he took me through a door on the left, lighted an oil lamp, and told me to make myself at home.

Now, Eliot, I'm what the man in the street would call fairly 'hard-boiled,' but I'll confess that what I saw on the walls of that room gave me a bad turn. They were his pictures, you know – the ones he couldn't paint or even show in Newbury Street – and he was right when he said he had 'let himself go.' Here – have another drink – I need one anyhow!

There's no use in my trying to tell you what they were like, because the awful, the blasphemous horror, and the unbelievable loathsomeness and moral foetor came from simple touches quite beyond the power of words to classify. There was none of the exotic technique you see in Sidney Sime, none of the trans-Saturnian landscapes and lunar fungi that Clark Ashton Smith uses to freeze the blood. The backgrounds were mostly old churchyards, deep woods, cliffs by the sea, brick tunnels, ancient panelled rooms, or simple vaults of masonry. Copp's Hill Bury-ing Ground, which could not be many blocks away from this very house, was a favourite scene.

The madness and monstrosity lay in the figures in the foreground – for Pickman's morbid art was pre-eminently one of daemoniac portraiture. These figures were seldom completely human, but often approached humanity in varying degree. Most of the bodies, while roughly bipedal, had a forward slumping, and a vaguely canine cast. The texture of the majority was a kind of unpleasant rubberiness. Ugh! I can see them now! Their occupations – well, don't ask me to be too precise. They were usually feeding – I won't say on what. They were sometimes shown in groups in cemeteries or underground passages, and often appeared to be in battle over their prey – or rather, their treasure-trove. And what damnable expressiveness Pickman sometimes gave the sightless faces of this charnel booty! Occasionally the things were shown leaping through open windows at night, or squatting on the chests of sleepers, worrying at their throats. One canvas showed a ring of them baying about a hanged witch on Gallows Hill, whose dead face held a close kinship to theirs.

But don't get the idea that it was all this hideous business of theme and setting which struck me faint. I'm not a three-year-old kid, and I'd seen much like this before. It was the *faces*, Eliot, those accursed *faces*, that leered and slavered out of the canvas with the very breath of life! By God, man, I verily believe they *were* alive! That nauseous wizard had waked the fires of hell in pigment, and his brush had been a nightmare-spawning wand. Give me that decanter, Eliot!

There was one thing called 'The Lesson' – Heaven pity me, that I ever saw it! Listen – can you fancy a squatting circle of nameless doglike things in a churchyard teaching a small child how to feed like themselves? The price of a changeling, I suppose – you know the old myth about how the weird people leave their spawn in cradles in exchange for the human babes they steal. Pickman was showing what happens to those stolen babes – how they grow up – and then I began to see a hideous relationship in the faces of the human and non-human figures. He was, in all his gradations of morbidity between the frankly nonhuman and the degradedly human, establishing a sardonic linkage and evolution. The dog-things were developed from mortals!

And no sooner had I wondered what he made of their own young as left with mankind in the form of changelings, than my eye caught a picture embodying that very thought. It was that of an ancient Puritan interior – a heavily beamed room with lattice windows, a settle, and clumsy seventeenth-century furniture, with the family sitting about while the father read from the Scriptures. Every face but one showed nobility and reverence, but that one reflected the mockery of the pit. It was that of a young man in years, and no doubt belonged to a supposed son of that pious father, but in essence it was the kin of the unclean things. It was their changeling – and in a spirit of supreme irony Pickman had given the features a very perceptible resemblance to his own.

By this time Pickman had lighted a lamp in an adjoining room and was politely holding open the door for me; asking me if I would care to see his 'modern studies.' I hadn't been able to give him much of my opinions – I was too speechless with fright and loathing – but I think he fully understood and felt highly complimented. And now I want to assure you again, Eliot, that I'm no mollycoddle to scream at anything which shows a bit of departure from the usual. I'm middle-aged and decently sophisticated, and I guess you saw enough of me in France to know I'm not easily knocked out. Remember, too, that I'd just about recovered my wind and gotten used to those frightful pictures which turned colonial New England into a kind of annexe of hell. Well, in spite of all this, that next room forced a real scream out of me, and I had to clutch at the doorway to keep from keeling over. The other chamber had shown a pack of ghouls and witches over-running the world of our forefathers, but this one brought the horror right into our own daily life!

Gad, how that man could paint! There was a study called 'Subway

Accident,' in which a flock of the vile things were clambering up from some unknown catacomb through a crack in the floor of the Boylston Street subway and attacking a crowd of people on the platform. Another showed a dance on Copp's Hill among the tombs with the background of today. Then there were any number of cellar views, with monsters creeping in through holes and rifts in the masonry and grinning as they squatted behind barrels or furnaces and waited for their first victim to descend the stairs.

One disgusting canvas seemed to depict a vast cross-section of Beacon Hill, with ant-like armies of the mephitic monsters squeezing themselves through burrows that honeycombed the ground. Dances in the modern cemeteries were freely pictured, and another conception somehow shocked me more than all the rest – a sense in an unknown vault, where scores of the beasts crowded about one who held a well-known Boston guidebook and was evidently reading aloud. All were pointing to a certain passage, and every face seemed so distorted with epileptic and reverberant laughter that I almost thought I heard the fiendish echoes. The title of the picture was, 'Holmes, Lowell and Longfellow Lie Buried in Mount Auburn.'

As I gradually steadied myself and got readjusted to this second room of deviltry and morbidity, I began to analyse some of the points in my sickening loathing. In the first place, I said to myself, these things repelled because of the utter inhumanity and callous cruelty they showed in Pickman. The fellow must be a relentless enemy of all mankind to take such glee in the torture of brain and flesh and the degradation of the mortal tenement. In the second place, they terrified because of their very greatness. Their art was the art that convinced – when we saw the pictures we saw the daemons themselves and were afraid of them. And the queer part was, that Pickman got none of his power from the use of selectiveness or bizarrerie. Nothing was blurred, distorted, or conventionalized; outlines were sharp and lifelike, and details were almost painfully defined. And the faces!

It was not any mere artist's interpretation that we saw; it was pandemonium itself, crystal clear in stark objectivity. That was it, by Heaven! The man was not a fantaisiste or romanticist at all – he did not even try to give us the churning, prismatic ephemera of dreams, but coldly and sardonically reflected some stable, mechanistic, and well-established horror-world which he saw fully, brilliantly, squarely, and unfalteringly. God knows what that world can have been, or where he ever glimpsed the blasphemous shapes that loped and trotted and crawled through it; but whatever the baffling source of his images, one thing was plain. Pickman was in every sense – in conception and in execution – a thorough, painstaking, and almost scientific *realist*.

PICKMAN'S MODEL

My host was now leading the way down the cellar to his actual studio, and I braced myself for some hellish efforts among the unfinished canvases. As we reached the bottom of the damp stairs he turned his flashlight to a corner of the large open space at hand, revealing the circular brick curb of what was evidently a great well in the earthen floor. We walked nearer, and I saw that it must be five feet across, with walls a good foot thick and some six inches above the ground level – solid work of the seventeenth century, or I was much mistaken. That, Pickman said, was the kind of thing he had been talking about – an aperture of the network of tunnels that used to undermine the hill. I noticed idly that it did not seem to be bricked up, and that a heavy disc of wood formed the apparent cover. Thinking of the things this well must have been connected with if Pickman's wild hints had not been mere rhetoric, I shivered slightly; then turned to follow him up a step and through a narrow door into a room of fair size, provided with a wooden floor and furnished as a studio. An acetylene gas outfit gave the light necessary for work.

The unfinished pictures on easels or propped against the walls were as ghastly as the finished ones upstairs, and showed the painstaking methods of the artist. Scenes were blocked out with extreme care, and pencilled guide lines told of the minute exactitude which Pickman used in getting the right perspective and proportions. The man was great – I say it even now, knowing as much as I do. A large camera on a table excited my notice, and Pickman told me that he used it in taking scenes for backgrounds, so that he might paint them from photographs in the studio instead of carting his oufit around the town for this or that view. He thought a photograph quite as good as an actual scene or model for sustained work, and declared he employed them regularly.

There was something very disturbing about the nauseous sketches and half-finished monstrosities that leered round from every side of the room, and when Pickman suddenly unveiled a huge canvas on the side away from the light I could not for my life keep back a loud scream – the second I had emitted that night. It echoed and echoed through the dim vaultings of that ancient and nitrous cellar, and I had to choke back a flood of reaction that threatened to burst out as hysterical laughter. Merciful Creator! Eliot, but I don't know how much was real and how much was feverish fancy. It doesn't seem to me that earth can hold a dream like that!

It was a colossal and nameless blasphemy with glaring red eyes, and it held in bony claws a thing that had been a man, gnawing at the head as a child nibbles at a stick of candy. Its position was a kind of crouch, and as one looked one felt that at any moment it might drop its present prey and seek a juicier morsel. But damn it all, it wasn't even the fiendish subject that made it such an immortal fountain-head of all panic – not that, nor the dog face with its pointed ears, bloodshot eyes, flat nose, and drooling lips. It wasn't the scaly claws nor the mould-caked body nor the half-hooved feet – none of these, though any one of them might well have driven an excitable man to madness.

It was the technique, Eliot – the cursed, the impious, the unnatural technique! As I am a living being, I never elsewhere saw the actual breath of life so fused into a canvas. The monster was there – it glared and gnawed and gnawed and glared – and I knew that only a suspension of Nature's laws could ever let a man paint a thing like that without a model – without some glimpse of the nether world which no mortal unsold to the Fiend has ever had.

Pinned with a thumb-tack to a vacant part of the canvas was a piece of paper now badly curled up – probably, I thought, a photograph from which Pickman meant to paint a background as hideous as the nightmare it was to enhance. I reached out to uncurl and look at it, when suddenly I saw Pickman start as if shot. He had been listening with peculiar intensity ever since my shocked scream had waked unaccustomed echoes in the dark cellar, and now he seemed struck with a fright which, though not comparable to my own, had in it more of the physical than of the spiritual. He drew a revolver and motioned me to silence, then stepped out into the main cellar and closed the door behind him.

I think I was paralysed for an instant. Imitating Pickman's listening, I fancied I heard a faint scurrying sound somewhere, and a series of squeals or beats in a direction I couldn't determine. I thought of huge rats and shuddered. Then there came a subdued sort of clatter which somehow set me all in gooseflesh – a furtive, groping kind of clatter, though I can't attempt to convey what I mean in words. It was like heavy wood falling on stone or brick – wood on brick – what did that make me think of?

It came again, and louder. There was a vibration as if the wood had fallen farther than it had fallen before. After that followed a sharp grating noise, a shouted gibberish from Pickman, and the deafening discharge of all six chambers of a revolver, fired spectacularly as a lion-tamer might fire in the air for effect. A muffled squeal or squawk, and a thud. Then more wood and brick grating, a pause, and the opening of the door – at which I'll confess I started violently. Pickman reappeared with his smoking weapon, cursing the bloated rats that infested the ancient well.

'The deuce knows what they eat, Thurber,' he grinned, 'for those archaic tunnels touched graveyard and witch-den and sea-coast. But whatever it is, they must have run short, for they were devilish anxious to get out. Your yelling stirred them up, I fancy. Better be cautious in these old places – our rodent friends are the one drawback, though I sometimes think they're a positive asset by way of atmosphere and colour.'

Well, Eliot, that was the end of the night's adventure. Pickman had promised to show me the place, and Heaven knows he had done it. He led me out of that tangle of alleys in another direction, it seems, for when we sighted a lamp-post we were in a half-familiar street with monotonous rows of mingled tenement blocks and old houses. Charter Street, it turned out to be, but I was too flustered to notice just where we hit it. We were too late for the elevated, and walked back downtown through Hanover Street. I remember that walk. We switched from Tremont up Beacon, and Pickman left me at the corner of Joy, where I turned off. I never spoke to him again.

Why did I drop him? Don't be impatient. Wait till I ring for coffee. We've had enough of the other stuff, but I for one need something. No – it wasn't the paintings I saw in that place; though I'll swear they were enough to get him ostracised in nine-tenths of the homes and clubs of Boston, and I guess you won't wonder now why I have to steer clear of subways and cellars. It was – something I found in my coat the next morning. You know, the curled-up paper tacked to the frightful canvas in the cellar; the thing I thought was a photograph of some scene he meant to use as a background for that monster. That last scare had come while I was reaching to uncurl it, and it seems I had vacantly crumpled it into my pocket. But here's the coffee – take it black, Eliot, if you're wise.

Yes, that paper was the reason I dropped Pickman; Richard Upton Pickman, the greatest artist I have ever known – and the foulest being that ever leaped the bounds of life into the pits of myth and madness. Eliot – old Reid was right. He wasn't strictly human. Either he was born in strange shadow, or he'd found a way to unlock the forbidden gate. It's all the same now, for he's gone – back into the fabulous darkness he loved to haunt. Here, let's have the chandelier going.

Don't ask me to explain or even conjecture about what I burned. Don't ask me, either, what lay behind that mole-like scrambling Pickman was so keen to pass off as rats. There are secrets, you know, which might have come down from old Salem times, and Cotton Mather tells even stranger things. You know how damned lifelike Pickman's paintings were – how we all wondered where he got those faces.

Well – that paper wasn't a photograph of any background, after all. What it showed was simply the monstrous being he was painting on that awful canvas. It was the model he was using – and its background was merely the wall of the cellar studio in minute detail. But by God, Eliot, *it was a photograph from life.*

H. P. Lovecraft

The Dunwich Horror

Gorgons and Hydras, and Chimaeras – dire stories of Celaeno and
the Harpies – may reproduce themselves in the brain of superstition
– *but they were there before.* They are transcripts, types – the arch-
types are in us, and eternal. How else should the recital of that which
we know in a waking sense to be false come to affect us all? Is it that
we naturally conceive terror from such objects, considered in their
capacity of being able to inflict upon us bodily injury? O, least of all!
These terrors are of older standing. They date beyond body – or without the body, they would have been the same. . . . That the kind of fear
here treated is purely spiritual – that it is strong in proportion as it is
objectless on earth, that it predominates in the period of our sinless
infancy – are difficulties the solution of which might afford some probable insight into our ante-mundane condition, and a peep at least into
the shadowland of pre-existence.

> – CHARLES LAMB: Witches and Other Night-Fears

I

When a traveller in north central Massachusetts takes the wrong fork at
the junction of Aylesbury pike just beyond Dean's Corners he comes upon
a lonely and curious country. The ground gets higher, and the brier-
bordered stone walls press closer and closer against the ruts of the dusty,
curving road. The trees of the frequent forest belts seem too large, and
the wild weeds, brambles and grasses attain a luxurance not often found
in settled regions. At the same time the planted fields appear singularly
few and barren; while the sparsely scattered houses wear a surprisingly
uniform aspect of age, squalor, and dilapidation. Without knowing why,

one hesitates to ask directions from the gnarled solitary figures spied now and then on crumbling doorsteps or on the sloping, rock-strewn meadows. Those figures are so silent and furtive that one feels somehow confronted by forbidden things, with which it would be better to have nothing to do. When a rise in the road brings the mountains in view above the deep woods, the feeling of strange uneasiness is increased. The summits are too rounded and symmetrical to give a sense of comfort and naturalness, and sometimes the sky silhouettes with especial clearness the queer circles of tall stone pillars with which most of them are crowned.

Gorges and ravines of problematical depth intersect the way, and the crude wooden bridges always seem of dubious safety. When the road dips again there are stretches of marshland that one instinctively dislikes, and indeed almost fears at evening when unseen whippoorwills chatter and the fireflies come out in abnormal profusion to dance to the raucous, creepily insistent rhythms of stridently piping bull-frogs. The thin, shining line of the Miskatonic's upper reaches has an oddly serpent-like suggestion as it winds close to the feet of the domed hills among which it rises.

As the hills draw nearer, one heeds their wooded sides more than their stone-crowned tops. Those sides loom up so darkly and precipitously that one wishes they would keep their distance, but there is no road by which to escape them. Across a covered bridge one sees a small village huddled between the stream and the vertical slope of Round Mountain, and wonders at the cluster of rotting gambrel roofs bespeaking an earlier architectural period than that of the neighbouring region. It is not reassuring to see, on a closer glance, that most of the houses are deserted and falling to ruin, and that the broken-steepled church now harbours the one slovenly mercantile establishment of the hamlet. One dreads to trust the tenebrous tunnel of the bridge, yet there is no way to avoid it. Once across, it is hard to prevent the impression of a faint, malign odour about the village street, as of the massed mould and decay of centuries. It is always a relief to get clear of the place, and to follow the narrow road around the base of the hills and across the level country beyond till it rejoins the Aylesbury pike. Afterwards one sometimes learns that one has been through Dunwich.

Outsiders visit Dunwich as seldom as possible, and since a certain season of horror all the signboards pointing towards it have been taken down. The scenery, judged by an ordinary aesthetic canon, is more than commonly beautiful; yet there is no influx of artists or summer tourists. Two centuries ago, when talk of witch-blood, Satan-worship, and strange forest presences was not laughed at, it was the custom to give reasons for avoiding the locality. In our sensible age – since the Dunwich horror of 1928 was hushed up by those who had the town's and the world's welfare at heart – people shun it without knowing exactly why. Perhaps one reason – though it cannot apply to uninformed strangers – is that the natives are now repellently decadent, having gone far along that path of retrogression so common in many New England backwaters. They have come to form a race by themselves, with the well-defined mental and physical stigmata of degeneracy and in-breeding. The average of their intelligence is woefully low, whilst their annals reek of overt viciousness and of half-hidden murders, incests, and deeds of almost unnameable violence and perversity. The old gentry, representing the two or three armigerous families which came from Salem in 1692, have kept somewhat above the general level of ɛecay; though many branches are sunk into the sordid populace so deeply that only their names remain as a key to the origin they disgrace. Some of the Whateleys and Bishops still send their eldest sons to Harvard and Miskatonic, though those sons seldom return to the mouldering gambrel roofs under which they and their ancestors were born.

No one, even those who have the facts concerning the recent horror, can say just what is the matter with Dunwich; though old legends speak of unhallowed rites and conclaves of the Indians, amidst which they called forbidden shapes of shadow out of the great rounded hills, and made wild orgiastic prayers that were answered by loud crackings and rumblings from the ground below. In 1747 the Reverend Abijah Hoadley, newly come to the Congregational Church at Dunwich Village, preached a memorable sermon on the close presence of Satan and his imps; in which he said:

It must be allow'd, that these Blasphemies of an infernall Train of Daemons are Matters of too common Knowledge to be deny'd; the cursed Voices of *Azazel* and *Buzrael*, of *Beelzebub* and *Belial*, being heard now from under Ground by above a Score of credible Witnesses now living. I myself did not more than a Fortnight ago catch a very plain Discourse of evill Powers in the Hill behind my House; wherein there were a Rattling and Rolling, Groaning, Screeching, and Hissing, such as no Things of this Earth cou'd raise up, and which must needs have come from those Caves that only black Magick can discover, and only the Divell unlock.

Mr Hoadley disappeared soon after delivering this sermon, but the text, printed in Springfield, is still extant. Noises in the hills continued to be reported from year to year, and still form a puzzle to geologists and physiographers.

Other traditions tell of foul odours near the hill-crowning circles of stone pillars, and of rushing airy presences to be heard faintly at certain hours from stated points at the bottom of the great ravines; while still others try to explain the Devil's Hop Yard – a bleak, blasted hillside where no tree, shrub, or grass-blade will grow. Then, too, the natives are mortally afraid of the numerous whippoorwills which grow vocal on warm nights. It is vowed that the birds are psychopomps lying in wait for the souls of the dying, and that they time their eerie cries in unison with the sufferer's struggling breath. If they can catch the fleeing soul when it leaves the body, they instantly flutter away chittering in daemoniac laughter; but if they fail, they subside gradually into a disappointed silence.

These tales, of course, are obsolete and ridiculous; because they come down from very old times. Dunwich is indeed ridiculously old – older by far than any of the communities within thirty miles of it. South of the village one may still spy the cellar walls and chimney of the ancient Bishop house, which was built before 1700; whilst the ruins of the mill at the falls, built in 1806, form the most modern piece of architecture to be seen. Industry did not flourish here, and the nineteenth-century factory movement proved short-lived. Oldest of all are the great rings of rough-hewn stone columns on the hilltops, but these are more generally attributed to the Indians than to the settlers. Deposits of skulls and bones, found within these circles and around the sizeable table-like rock on Sentinel Hill, sustain the popular belief that such spots were once the burial-places of the Pocumtucks; even though many ethnologists, disregarding the absurd improbability of such a theory, persist in believing the remains Caucasian.

II

It was in the township of Dunwich, in a large and partly inhabited farmhouse set against a hillside four miles from the village and a mile and a half from any other dwelling, that Wilbur Whateley was born at 5 a.m. on Sunday, the second of February, 1913. This date was recalled because it was Candlemas, which people in Dunwich curiously observe under another name; and because the noises in the hills had sounded, and all the dogs of the countryside had barked persistently, throughout the night before. Less worthy of notice was the fact that the mother was one of the decadent Whateleys, a somewhat deformed, unattractive albino woman of 35, living with an aged and half-insane father about whom the most frightful tales of wizardry had been whispered in his youth. Lavinia Whateley had no known husband, but according to the custom of the region made no attempt to disavow the child; concerning the other side of whose ancestry the country folk might – and did – speculate as widely as they chose. On the contrary, she seemed strangely proud of the dark, goatish-looking infant who formed such a contrast to her own sickly and pink-eyed albinism, and was heard to mutter many curious prophecies about its unusual powers and tremendous future.

Lavinia was one who would be apt to mutter such things, for she was a lone creature given to wandering amidst thunderstorms in the hills and trying to read the great odorous books which her father had inherited through two centuries of Whateleys, and which were fast falling to pieces with age and wormholes. She had never been to school, but was filled with disjointed scraps of ancient lore that Old Whateley had taught her. The remote farmhouse had always been feared because of Old Whateley's reputation for black magic, and the unexplained death by violence of Mrs Whateley when Lavinia was twelve years old had not helped to make the place popular. Isolated among strange influences, Lavinia was fond of wild and grandiose day-dreams and singular occupations; nor was her leisure much taken up by household cares in a home from which all standards of order and cleanliness had long since disappeared.

There was a hideous screaming which echoed above even the hill noises and the dogs' barking on the night Wilbur was born, but no known doctor or midwife presided at his coming. Neighbours knew nothing of him till a week afterward, when Old Wateley drove his sleigh through the snow into Dunwich Village and discoursed incoherently to the group of loungers at Osborne's general store. There seemed to be a change in the old man – an added element of furtiveness in the clouded brain which subtly transformed him from an object to a subject of fear – though he was not one to be perturbed by any common family event. Amidst it all he showed some trace of the pride later noticed in his daughter, and what he said of the child's paternity was remembered by many of his hearers years afterward.

'I dun't keer what folks think – ef Lavinny's boy looked like his pa, he wouldn't look like nothin' ye expeck. Ye needn't think the only folks is the folks hereabouts. Lavinny's read some, an' has seed some things the most o' ye only tell abaout. I calc'late her man is as good a husban' as ye kin find this side of Aylesbury; an' ef ye knowed as much abaout the hills as I dew, ye wouldn't ast no better church weddin' nor her'n. Let me tell ye suthin – *some day yew folks'll hear a child o' Lavinny's a-callin' its father's name on the top o' Sentinel Hill!*'

The only person who saw Wilbur during the first month of his life were old Zechariah Whateley, of the undecayed Whateleys, and Earl Sawyer's common-law wife, Mamie Bishop. Mamie's visit was frankly one of curiosity, and her subsequent tales did justice to her observations; but Zechariah came to lead a pair of Alderney cows which Old Whateley had bought of his son Curtis. This marked the beginning of a course of cattle-buying on the part of small Wilbur's family which ended only in

1928, when the Dunwich horror came and went; yet at no time did the ramshackle Wateley barn seem overcrowded with livestock. There came a period when people were curious enough to steal up and count the herd that grazed precariously on the steep hillside above the old farmhouse, and they could never find more than ten or twelve anaemic, bloodless-looking specimens. Evidently some blight or distemper, perhaps sprung from the unwholesome pasturage or the diseased fungi and timbers of the filthy barn, caused a heavy mortality amongst the Whateley animals. Odd wounds or sores, having something of the aspect of incisions, seemed to afflict the visible cattle; and once or twice during the earlier months certain callers fancied they could discern similar sores about the throats of the grey, unshaven old man and his slatternly, crinkly-haired albino daughter.

In the spring after Wilbur's birth Lavinia resumed her customary rambles in the hills, bearing in her misproportioned arms the swarthy child. Public interest in the Whateley's subsided after most of the country folk had seen the baby, and no one bothered to comment on the swift development which that newcomer seemed every day to exhibit. Wilbur's growth was indeed phenomenal, for within three months of his birth he had attained a size and muscular power not usually found in infants under a full year of age. His motions and even his vocal sounds showed a restraint and deliberateness highly peculiar in an infant, and no one was really unprepared when, at seven months, he began to walk unassisted, with falterings which another month was sufficient to remove.

It was somewhat after this time – on Hallowe'en – that a great blaze was seen at midnight on the top of Sentinel Hill where the old tablelike stone stands amidst its tumulus of ancient bones. Considerable talk was started when Silas Bishop – of the undecayed Bishops – mentioned having seen the boy running sturdily up that hill ahead of his mother about an hour before the blaze was remarked. Silas was rounding up a stray heifer, but he nearly forgot his mission when he fleetingly spied the two figures in the dim light of his lantern. They darted almost noiselessly through the underbrush, and the astonished watcher seemed to think they were entirely unclothed. Afterwards he could not be sure about the boy, who may have had some kind of a fringed belt and a pair of dark trunks or trousers on. Wilbur was never subsequently seen alive and conscious without complete and tightly buttoned attire, the disarrangement or threatened disarrangement of which always seemed to fill him with anger and alarm. His contrast with his squalid mother and grandfather in this respect was thought very notable until the horror of 1928 suggested the most valid of reasons.

The next January gossips were mildly interested in the fact that 'Lavinny's black brat' had commenced to talk, and at the age of only eleven months. His speech was somewhat remarkable both because of its difference from the ordinary accents of the region, and because it displayed a freedom from infantile lisping of which many children of three or four might well be proud. The boy was not talkative, yet when he spoke he seemed to reflect some elusive element wholly unpossessed by Dunwich and its denizens. The strangeness did not reside in what he said, or even in the simple idioms he used; but seemed vaguely linked with his intonation or with the internal organs that produced the spoken sounds. His facial aspect, too, was remarkable for its maturity; for though he shared his mother's and grandfather's chinlessness, his firm and precociously shaped nose united with the expression of his large, dark, almost Latin eyes to give him an air of quasi-adulthood and well-nigh preternatural intelligence. He was, however, exceedingly ugly despite his appearance of brilliancy; there being something almost goatish or animalistic about his thick lips, large-pored, yellowish skin, coarse crinkly hair, and oddly elongated ears. He was soon disliked even more decidedly than his mother and grandsire, and all conjectures about him were spiced with references to the bygone magic of Old Whateley, and how the hills once shook when he shrieked the dreadful name of *Yog-Sothoth* in the midst of a circle of stones with a great book open in his arms before him. Dogs abhorred the boy, and he was always obliged to take various defensive measures against their barking menace.

III

Meanwhile Old Whateley continued to buy cattle without measurably increasing the size of his herd. He also cut timber and began to repair the unused parts of his house – a spacious, peak-roofed affair whose rear end was buried entirely in the rocky hillside, and whose three least-ruined ground-floor rooms had always been sufficient for himself and his daughter. There must have been prodigious reserves of strength in the old man to enable him to accomplish so much hard labour; and though he still babbled dementedly at times, his carpentry seemed to show the effects of sound calculation. It had already begun as soon as Wilbur was born, when one of the many tool sheds had been put suddenly in order, clapboarded, and fitted with a stout fresh lock. Now, in restoring the abandoned upper storey of the house, he was a no less thorough craftsman. His mania showed itself only in his tight boarding-up of all the windows in the reclaimed section – though many declared that it was a crazy thing to bother with the reclamation at all. Less inexplicable was his fitting up of another downstairs room for his new grandson – a room which several callers saw, though no one was ever admitted to the closely-boarded upper storey. This chamber he lined with tall, firm shelving, along which he began gradually to arrange, in apparently careful order, all the rotting ancient books and parts of books which during his own day had been heaped promiscuously in odd corners of the various rooms.

'I made some use of 'em,' he would say as he tried to mend a torn black-letter page with paste prepared on the rusty kitchen stove, 'but the boy's fitten to make better use of 'em. He'd orter hev 'em as well so as he kin, for they're goin' to be all of his larnin'.'

When Wilbur was a year and seven months old – in September of 1914 – his size and accomplishments were almost alarming. He had grown as large as a child of four, and was a fluent and incredibly intelligent talker. He ran freely about the fields and hills, and accompanied his mother on all her wanderings. At home he would pore dilligently over the queer pictures and charts in his grandfather's books, while Old Whateley would instruct and catechise him through long, hushed afternoons. By this time the restoration of the house was finished, and those who watched it wondered why one of the upper windows had been made into a solid plank door. It was a window in the rear of the east gable end, close against the hill; and no one could imagine why a cleated wooden runway was built up to it from the ground. About the period of this work's completion people noticed that the old tool-house, tightly locked and windowlessly clapboarded since Wilbur's birth, had been abandoned again. The door swung listlessly open, and when Earl Sawyer once stepped within after a cattle-selling call on Old Whateley he was quite discomposed by the singular odour he encountered – such a stench, he averred, as he had never before smelt in all his life except near the Indian circles on the hills, and which could not come from anything sane or of this earth. But then, the homes and sheds of Dunwich folk have never been remarkable for olfactory immaculateness.

The following months were void of visible events, save that everyone swore to a slow but steady increase in the mysterious hill noises. On May Eve of 1915 there were tremors which even the Aylesbury people felt, whilst the following Hallowe'en produced an underground rumbling queerly synchronized with bursts of flame – 'them witch Whateleys' doin's' – from the summit of Sentinel Hill. Wilbur was growing up uncannily, so that he looked like a boy of ten as he entered his fourth year. He read avidly by himself now; but talked much less than formerly. A settled taciturnity was absorbing him, and for the first time people began to speak specifically of the dawning look of evil in his goatish face. He would sometimes mutter an unfamiliar jargon, and chant in bizarre rhythms which chilled the listener with a sense of unexplainable terror. The aversion displayed towards him by dogs had now become a matter of wide remark, and he was obliged to carry a pistol in order to traverse the countryside in safety. His occasional use of the weapon did not enhance his popularity amongst the owners of canine guardians.

The few callers at the house would often find Lavinia alone on the ground floor, while odd cries and footsteps resounded in the boarded-up second storey. She would never tell what her father and the boy were doing up there, though once she turned pale and displayed an abnormal degree of fear was a jocose fish-pedlar tried the locked door leading to the stairway. That pedlar told the store loungers at Dunwich Village that he thought he heard a horse stamping on that floor above. The loungers reflected, thinking of the door and runway, and of the cattle that so swiftly disappeared. Then they shuddered as they recalled tales of Old Whateley's youth, and of the strange things that are called out of the earth when a bullock is sacrificed at the proper time to certain heathen gods. It had for some time been noticed that dogs had begun to hate and fear the whole Whateley place as violently as they hated and feared young Wilbur personally.

In 1917 the war came, and Squire Sawyer Whateley, as chairman of the local draft board, had hard work finding a quota of young Dunwich men fit even to be sent to development camp. The government, alarmed at such signs of wholesale regional decadence, sent several officers and medical experts to investigate; conducting a survey which New England newspaper readers may still recall. It was the publicity attending this investigation which set reporters on the track of the Whateleys, and caused the *Boston Globe* and *Arkham Advertiser* to print flamboyant Sunday stories of young Wilbur's precociousness, Old Whateley's black magic, and the shelves of strange books, the sealed second storey of the ancient farmhouse, and the weirdness of the whole region and its hill noises. Wilbur was four and a half then, and looked like a lad of fifteen. His lips and cheeks were fuzzy with a coarse dark down, and his voice had begun to break.

Earl Sawyer went out to the Whateley place with both sets of reporters and camera men, and called their attention to the queer stench which now seemed to trickle down from the sealed upper spaces. It was, he said, exactly like a smell he had found in the toolshed abandoned when the house was finally repaired; and like the faint odours which he sometimes thought he caught near the stone circle on the mountains. Dunwich folk read the stories when they appeared, and grinned over the obvious mistakes. They wondered, too, why the writers made so much of the fact that Old Whateley always paid for his cattle in gold pieces of extremely ancient date. The Whateleys had received their visitors with ill-concealed distaste, though they did not dare court further publicity by a violent resistance or refusal to talk.

THE DUNWICH HORROR

IV

For a decade the annals of the Whateleys sink indistinguishably into the general life of a morbid community used to their queer ways and hardened to their May Eve and All-Hallows orgies. Twice a year they would light fires on the top of Sentinel Hill, at which times the mountain rumblings would recur with greater and greater violence; while at all seasons there were strange and portentous doings at the lonely farmhouse. In the course of time callers professed to hear sounds in the sealed upper storey even when all the family were downstairs, and they wondered how swiftly or how lingeringly a cow or bullock was usually sacrificed. There was talk of a complaint to the Society for the Prevention of Cruelty to Animals but nothing ever came of it, since Dunwich folk are never anxious to call the outside world's attention to themselves.

About 1923, when Wilbur was a boy of ten whose mind, voice, stature, and bearded face gave all the impressions of maturity, a second great siege of carpentry went on at the old house. It was all inside the sealed upper part, and from bits of discarded lumber people concluded that the youth and his grandfather had knocked out all the partitions and even removed the attic floor, leaving only one vast open void between the ground storey and the peaked roof. They had torn down the great central chimney, too, and fitted the rusty range with a flimsy outside tin stovepipe.

In the spring after this event Old Whateley noticed the growing number of whippoorwills that would come out of Cold Spring Glen to chirp under his window at night. He seemed to regard the circumstance as one of great significance, and told the loungers at Osborn's that he thought his time had almost come.

'They whistle jest in tune with my breathin' naow,' he said, 'an' I guess they're gittin' ready to ketch my soul. They know it's a-goin' aout, an' dun't calc'late to miss it. Yew'll know, boys, arter I'm gone, whether they git me er not. Ef they dew, they'll keep up a-singin' an' laffin' till break o' day. Ef they dun't they'll kinder quiet daown like. I expeck them an' the souls they hunts fer hev some pretty tough tussles sometimes.'

On Lammas Night, 1924, Dr Houghton of Aylesbury was hastily summoned by Wilbur Whateley, who had lashed his one remaining horse through the darkness and telephoned from Osborn's in the village. He found Old Whateley in a very grave state, with a cardiac action and stertorous breathing that told of an end not far off. The shapeless albino daughter and oddly bearded grandson stood by the bedside, whilst from the vacant abyss overhead there came a disquieting suggestion of rhythmical surging or lapping, as of the waves on some level beach. The doctor, though, was chiefly disturbed by the chattering night birds outside;

a seemingly limitless legion of whippoorwills that cried their endless message in repetitions timed diabolically to the wheezing gasps of the dying man. It was uncanny and unnatural – too much, thought Dr Houghton, like the whole of the region he had entered so reluctantly in response to the urgent call.

Towards one o'clock Old Whateley gained consciousness, and interrupted his wheezing to choke out a few words to his grandson.

'More space, Willy, more space soon. Yew grows – an' *that* grows faster. It'll be ready to sarve ye soon, boy. Open up the gates to Yog-Sothoth with the long chant that ye'll find on page 751 *of the complete edition*, an *then* put a match to the prison. Fire from airth can't burn it nohaow.'

He was obviously quite mad. After a pause, during which the flock of whippoorwills outside adjusted their cries to the altered tempo while some indications of the strange hill noises came from afar off, he added another sentence or two.

'Feed it reg'lar, Willy, an' mind the quantity; but dun't let it grow too fast fer the place, fer ef it busts quarters or gits aout afore ye opens to Yog-Sothoth, it's all over an' no use. Only them from beyont kin make it multiply an' work. . . . Only them, the old uns as wants to come back. . . .'

But speech gave place to gasps again, and Lavinia screamed at the way the whippoorwills followed the change. It was the same for more than an hour, when the final throaty rattle came. Dr Houghton drew shrunken lids over the glazing grey eyes as the tumult of birds faded imperceptibly to silence. Lavinia sobbed, but Wilbur only chuckled whilst the hill noises rumbled faintly.

'They didn't git him,' he muttered in his heavy bass voice.

Wilbur was by this time a scholar of really tremendous erudition in his one-sided way, and was quietly known by correspondence to many librarians in distant places where rare and forbidden books of old days are kept. He was more and more hated and dreaded around Dunwich because of certain youthful disappearances which suspicion laid vaguely at his door; but was always able to silence inquiry through fear or through use of that fund of old-time gold which still, as in his grandfather's time, went forth regularly and increasingly for cattle-buying. He was now tremendously mature of aspect, and his height, having reached the normal adult limit, seemed inclined to wax beyond that figure. In 1925, when a scholarly correspondent from Miskatonic University called upon him one day and departed pale and puzzled, he was fully six and three-quarters feet tall.

Through all the years Wilbur had treated his half-deformed albino mother with a growing contempt, finally forbidding her to go to the hills with him on May Eve and Hallowmass; and in 1926 the poor creature complained to Mamie Bishop of being afraid of him.

'They's more abaout him as I knows than I kin tell ye, Mamie,' she said, 'an' naowadays they's more nor what I know myself. I vaow afur Gawd, I dun't know what he wants nor what he's a-tryin' to dew.'

That Hallowe'en the hill noises sounded louder than ever, and fire burned on Sentinel Hill as usual; but people paid more attention to the rhythmical screaming of vast flocks of unnaturally belated whippoorwills which seemed to be assembled near the unlighted Whateley farmhouse. After midnight their shrill notes burst into a kind of pandemoniac cachinnation which filled all the countryside, and not until dawn did they finally quiet down. Then they vanished, hurrying southward where they were fully a month overdue. What this meant, no one could quite be certain till later. None of the countryfolk seemed to have died – but poor Lavinia Whateley, the twisted albino, was never seen again.

In the summer of 1927 Wilbur repaired two sheds in the farmyard and began moving his books and effects out to them. Soon afterwards Earl Sawyer told the loungers at Osborn's that more carpentry was going on in the Whateley farmhouse. Wilbur was closing all the doors and windows on the ground floor, and seemed to be taking out partitions as he and his grandfather had done upstairs four years before. He was living in one of the sheds, and Sawyer thought he seemed unusually worried and tremulous. People generally suspected him of knowing something about his mother disappearance, and very few ever approached his neighbourhood now. His height had increased to more than seven feet, and showed no signs of ceasing its development.

V

The following winter brought an event no less strange than Wilbur's first trip outside the Dunwich region. Correspondence with the Widener Library at Harvard, the Bibliothèque Nationale in Paris, the British Museum, the University of Buenos Ayres, and the Library of Miskatonic University at Arkham had failed to get him the loan of a book he desperately wanted; so at length he set out in person, shabby, dirty, bearded, and uncouth of dialect, to consult the copy at Miskatonic, which was the nearest to him geographically. Almost eight feet tall, and carrying a cheap new valise from Osborne's general store, this dark and goatish gargoyle appeared one day in Arkham in quest of the dreaded volume kept under lock and key at the college library – the hideous *Necronomicon* of the mad Arab Abdul Alhazred in Olaus Wormius' Latin version, as printed in Spain in the seventeenth century. He had never seen a city before, but had no thought save to find his way to the university grounds; where indeed, he passed heedlessly by the great white-fanged watchdog that barked with unnatural fury and enmity, and tugged frantically at its stout chain.

Wilbur had with him the priceless but imperfect copy of Dr Dee's English version which his grandfather had bequeathed him, and upon receiving access to the Latin copy he at once began to collate the two texts with the aim of discovering a certain passage which would have come on the 751st page of his own defective volume. This much he could not civilly refrain from telling the librarian – the same erudite Henry Armitage (A.M. Miskatonic, Ph.D. Princeton, Litt.D. Johns Hopkins) who had once called at the farm, and who now politely plied him with questions. He was looking, he had to admit, for a kind of formula or incantation containing the frightful name *Yog-Sothoth*, and it puzzled him to find discrepancies, duplications, and ambiguities which made the matter of determination far from easy. As he copied the formula he finally chose, Dr Armitage looked involuntarily over his shoulder at the open pages; the left-hand one of which, in the Latin version, contained such monstrous threats to the peace and sanity of the world.

Nor is it to be thought [ran the text as Armitage mentally translated it] that man is either the oldest or the last of earth's masters, or that the common bulk of life and substance walks alone. The Old Ones were, the Old Ones are, and the Old Ones shall be. Not in the spaces we know, but *between* them, they walk serene and primal, undimensioned and to us unseen. *Yog-Sothoth* knows the gate. *Yog-Sothoth* is the gate. *Yog-Sothoth* is the key and guardian of the gate. Past, present, future, all are one in *Yog-Sothoth*. He knows where the Old Ones broke through of old, and where They shall break through again. He knows where They had trod earth's fields, and where They still tread them, and why no one can behold Them as They tread. By Their smell can men sometimes know Them near, but of Their semblance can no man know, *saving only in the features of those They have begotten on mankind*; and of those are there many sorts, differing in likeness from man's truest eidolon to that shape without sight or substance which is *Them*. They walk unseen and foul in lonely places where the Words have been spoken and the Rites howled through at their Seasons. The wind gibbers with Their voices, and the earth mutters with Their consciousness. They bend the forest and crush the city, yet may not forest or city behold the hand that smites. Kadath in the cold waste hath known Them, and what man knows Kadath? The ice desert of the South and the sunken isles of Ocean hold stones whereon Their seal is engraven, but who hath seen the deep frozen city or the sealed tower long garlanded with seaweed and barnacles?

Great Cthulhu is Their cousin, yet can he spy Them only dimly. *Iä! Shub-Niggurath!* As a foulness shall ye know Them. Their hand is at your throats, yet ye see Them not; and Their habitation is even one with your guarded threshold. *Yog-Sothoth* is the key to the gate, whereby the spheres meet. Man rules now where They ruled once; They shall soon rule where man rules now. After summer is winter, after winter summer. They wait patient and potent, for here shall They reign again.

Dr Armitage, associating what he was reading with what he had heard of Dunwich and its brooding presences, and of Wilbur Whateley and his dim, hideous aura that stretched from a dubious birth to a cloud of probable matricide, felt a wave of fright as tangible as a draught of the tomb's cold clamminess. The bent, goatish giant before him seemed like the spawn of another planet or dimension; like something only partly of mankind, and linked to black gulfs of essence and entity that stretch like titan phantasms beyond all spheres of force and matter, space and time. Presently Wilbur raised his head and began speaking in that strange, resonant fashion which hinted at sound-producing organs unlike the run of mankind's.

'Mr Armitage,' he said, 'I calc'late I've got to take that book home. They's things in it I've got to try under sarten conditions that I can't git here, an' it 'ud be a mortal sin to let a red-tape rule hold me up. Let me take it along, Sir, an' I'll swar they wun't nobody know the difference. I dun't need to tell ye I'll take good keer of it. It wan't me that put this Dee copy in the shape it is. . . .'

He stopped as he saw firm denial on the librarian's face, and his own goatish features grew crafty. Armitage, half-ready to tell him he might make a copy of what parts he needed, thought suddenly of the possible consequences and checked himself. There was too much responsibility in giving such a being the key to such blasphemous outer spheres. Whateley saw how things stood, and tried to answer lightly.

'Wal, all right, ef ye feel that way abaout it. Maybe Harvard wun't be so fussy as yew be.' And without saying more he rose and strode out of the building, stooping at each doorway.

Armitage heard the savage yelping of the great watchdog, and studied Whateley's gorilla-like lope as he crossed the bit of campus visible from the window. He thought of the wild tales he had heard, and recalled the old Sunday stories in the *Advertiser*; these things, and the lore he had picked up from Dunwich rustics and villagers during his one visit there. Unseen things not of earth – or at least not of tri-dimensional earth – rushed foetid and horrible through New England's glens, and brooded obscenely on the mountain tops. Of this he had long felt certain. Now he seemed to sense the close presence of some terrible part of the intruding horror, and to glimpse a hellish advance in the black dominion of the ancient and once passive nightmare. He locked away the *Necronomicon* with a shudder of disgust, but the room still reeked with an unholy and unidentifiable stench. 'As a foulness shall ye know them,' he quoted. Yes – the odour was the same as that which had sickened him at the Whateley farmhouse less than three years before. He thought of Wilbur, goatish and ominous, once again, and laughed mockingly at the village rumours of his parentage.

'Inbreeding?' Armitage muttered half-aloud to himself. 'Great God, what simpletons! Show them Arthur Machen's Great God Pan and they'll think it a common Dunwich scandal! But what thing – what cursed shapeless influence on or off this three-dimensional earth – was Wilbur Whateley's father? Born on Candlemas – nine months after May Eve of 1912, when the talk about the queer earth noises reached clear to Arkham – what walked on the mountains that May night? What Roodmas horror fastened itself on the world in half-human flesh and blood?'

During the ensuing weeks Dr Armitage set about to collect all possible data on Wilbur Whateley and the formless presences around Dunwich. He got in communication with Dr Houghton of Aylesbury, who had attended Old Whateley in his last illness, and found much to ponder over in the grandfather's last words as quoted by the physician. A visit to Dunwich Village failed to bring out much that was new; but a close survey of the *Necronomicon*, in those parts which Wilbur had sought so avidly, seemed to supply new and terrible clues to the nature, methods, and desires of the strange evil so vaguely threatening this planet. Talks with several students of archaic lore in Boston, and letters to many others elsewhere, gave him a growing amazement which passed slowly through varied degrees of alarm to a state of really acute spiritual fear. As the summer drew on he felt dimly that something ought to be done about the lurking terrors of the upper Miskatonic valley, and about the monstrous being known to the human world as Wilbur Whateley.

VI

The Dunwich horror itself came between Lammas and the equinox in 1928, and Dr Armitage was among those who witnessed its monstrous prologue. He had heard, meanwhile, of Whateley's grotesque trip to Cambridge, and of his frantic efforts to borrow or copy from the *Necronomicon* at the Widener Library. Those efforts had been in vain, since Armitage had issued warnings of the keenest intensity to all librarians having charge of the dreaded volume. Wilbur had been shockingly nervous at Cambridge; anxious for the book, yet almost equally anxious to get home again, as if he feared the results of being away long.

Early in August the half-expected outcome developed, and in the small hours of the third Dr Armitage was awakened suddenly by the wild, fierce cries of the savage watchdog on the college campus. Deep and terrible, the snarling, half-mad growls and barks continued; always in mounting volume, but with hideously significant pauses. Then there rang out a scream from a wholly different throat – such a scream as roused half the sleepers of Arkham and haunted their dreams ever afterwards – such a scream as could come from no being born of earth, or wholly of earth.

Armitage, hastening into some clothing and rushing across the street and lawn to the college buildings, saw that others were ahead of him; and heard the echoes of a burglar-alarm still shrilling from the library. An open window showed black and gaping in the moonlight. What had come had indeed completed its entrance; for the barking and the screaming, now fast fading into a mixed low growling and moaning, proceeded unmistakably from within. Some instinct warned Armitage that what was taking place was not a thing for unfortified eyes to see, so he brushed back the crowd with authority as he unlocked the vestibule door. Among the others he saw Professor Warren Rice and Dr Francis Morgan, men to whom he had told some of his conjectures and misgivings; and these two he motioned to accompany him inside. The inward sounds, except for a watchful, droning whine from the dog, had by this time quite subsided; but Armitage now perceived with a sudden start that a loud chorus of whippoorwills among the shrubbery had commenced a damnably rhythmical piping, as if in unison with the last breaths of a dying man.

The building was full of a frightful stench which Dr Armitage knew too well, and the three men rushed across the hall to the small genealogical reading-room whence the low whining came. For a second nobody dared to turn on the light, then Armitage summoned up his courage and snapped the switch. One of the three – it is not certain which – shrieked aloud at what sprawled before them among disordered tables and overturned chairs. Professor Rice declares that he wholly lost consciousness for an instant, though he did not stumble or fall.

The thing that lay half-bent on its side in a foetid pool of greenish-yellow ichor and tarry stickiness was almost nine feet tall, and the dog had torn off all the clothing and some of the skin. It was not quite dead, but twitched silently and spasmodically while its chest heaved in monstrous unison with the mad piping of the expectant whippoorwills outside. Bits of shoe-leather and fragments of apparel were scattered about the room, and just inside the window an empty canvas sack lay where it had evidently been thrown. Near the central desk a revolver had fallen, a dented but undischarged cartridge later explaining why it had not been fired. The thing itself, however, crowded out all other images at the time. It would be trite and not wholly accurate to say that no human pen could describe it, but one may properly say that it could not be vividly visualized by anyone whose ideas of aspect and contour are too closely bound up with the common life-forms of this planet and of the three known dimensions. It was partly human, beyond a doubt, with very manlike hands and head, and the goatish, chinless face had the stamp of the Whateley's upon it. But the torso and lower parts of the body were teratologically fabulous, so that only generous clothing could ever have enabled it to walk on earth unchallenged or uneradicated.

Above the waist it was semi-anthropomorphic; though its chest, where the dog's rending paws still rested watchfully, had the leathery, reticulated hide of a crocodile or alligator. The back was piebald with yellow and black, and dimly suggested the squamous covering of certain snakes. Below the waist, though, it was the worst; for here all human resemblance left off and sheer phantasy began. The skin was thickly covered with coarse black fur, and from the abdomen a score of long greenish-grey tentacles with red sucking mouths protruded limply. Their arrangement was odd, and seemed to follow the symmetries of some cosmic geometry unknown to earth or the solar system. On each of the hips, deep set in a kind of pinkish, ciliated orbit, was what seemed to be a rudimentary eye; whilst in lieu of a tail there depended a kind of trunk or feeler with purple annular markings, and with many evidences of being an undeveloped mouth or throat. The limbs, save for their black fur, roughly resembled the hind legs of prehistoric earth's giant saurians, and terminated in ridgy-veined pads that were neither hooves nor claws. When the thing breathed, its tail and tentacles rhythmically changed colour, as if from some circulatory cause normal to the non-human greenish tinge, whilst in the tail it was manifest as a yellowish appearance which alternated with a sickly greyish-white in the spaces between the purple rings. Of genuine blood there was none; only the foetid greenish-yellow ichor which trickled along the painted floor beyond the radius of the stickiness, and left a curious discoloration behind it.

As the presence of the three men seemed to rouse the dying thing, it began to mumble without turning or raising its head. Dr Armitage made no written record of its mouthings, but asserts confidently that nothing in English was uttered. At first the syllables defied all correlation with any speech of earth, but towards the last there came some disjointed fragments evidently taken from the *Necronomicon*, that monstrous blasphemy in quest of which the thing had perished. These fragments, as Armitage recalls them, ran something like '*N'gai, n'gha'ghaa, buggshoggog, y'hah: Yog-Sothoth, Yog-Sothoth. . . .*' They trailed off into nothingness as the whippoorwills shrieked in rhythmical crescendos of unholy anticipation.

Then came a halt in the gasping, and the dog raised its head in a long, lugubrious howl. A change came over the yellow, goatish face of the prostrate thing, and the great black eyes fell in appallingly. Outside the window the shrilling of the whippoorwills had suddenly ceased, and above the murmurs of the gathering crowd there came the sound of a panic-struck whirring and fluttering. Against the moon vast clouds of feathery watchers rose and raced from sight, frantic at that which they had sought for prey.

All at once the dog started up abruptly, gave a frightened bark, and leaped nervously out of the window by which it had entered. A cry rose from the crowd, and Dr Armitage shouted to the men outside that no one must be admitted till the police or medical examiner came. He was thankful that the windows were just too high to permit of peering in, and drew the dark curtains carefully down over each one. By this time two policemen had arrived; and Dr Morgan, meeting them in the vestibule, was urging them for their own sakes to postpone entrance to the stench-filled reading-room till the examiner came and the prostrate thing could be covered up.

Meanwhile frightful changes were taking place on the floor. One need not describe the *kind* and *rate* of shrinkage and disintegration that occurred before the eyes of Dr Armitage and Professor Rice; but it is permissible to say that, aside from the external appearance of face and hands, the really human element in Wilbur Whateley must have been very small. When the medical examiner came, there was only a sticky whitish mass on the painted boards, and the monstrous odour had nearly disappeared. Apparently Whateley had had no skull or bony skeleton; at least, in any true or stable sense. He had taken somewhat after his unknown father.

VII

Yet all this was only the prologue of the actual Dunwich horror. Formalities were gone through by bewildered officials, abnormal details were duly kept from press and public, and men were sent to Dunwich and Aylesbury to look up property and notify any who might be heirs of the late Wilbur Whateley. They found the countryside in great agitation, both because of the growing rumblings beneath the domed hills, and because of the unwonted stench and the surging, lapping sounds which came increasingly from the great empty shell formed by Whateley's boarded-up farmhouse. Earl Sawyer, who tended the horse and cattle during Wilbur's absence, had developed a woefully acute case of nerves.

The officials devised excuses not to enter the noisome boarded place; and were glad to confine their survey of the deceased's living quarters, the newly mended sheds, to a single visit. They filed a ponderous report at the courthouse in Aylesbury, and litigations concerning heirship are said to be still in progress amongst the innumerable Whateleys, decayed and undecayed, of the upper Miskatonic valley.

An almost interminable manuscript in strange characters, written in a huge ledger and adjudged a sort of diary because of the spacing and the variations in ink and penmanship, presented a baffling puzzle to those who found it on the old bureau which served as its owner's desk. After a week of debate it was sent to Miskatonic University, together with the deceased's collection of strange books, for study and possible translation; but even the best linguists soon saw that it was not likely to be unriddled with ease. No trace of the ancient gold with which Wilbur and Old Whateley had always paid their debts has yet been discovered.

It was in the dark of September ninth that the horror broke loose. The hill noises had been very pronounced during the evening, and dogs barked frantically all night. Early risers on the tenth noticed a peculiar stench in the air. About seven o'clock Luther Brown, the hired boy at George Corey's, between Cold Spring Glen and the village, rushed frenziedly back from his morning trip to Ten-Acre Meadow with the cows. He was almost convulsed with fright as he stumbled into the kitchen; and in the yard outside the no less frightened herd were pawing and lowing pitifully, having followed the boy back in the panic they shared with him. Between gasps Luther tried to stammer out his tale to Mrs Corey.

'Up thar in the rud beyont the glen, Mis' Corey – they's suthin' ben thar! It smells like thunder, an' all the bushes an' little trees is pushed back from the rud like they'd a haouse ben moved along of it. An' that ain't the wust, nuther. They's *prints* in the rud, Mis' Corey – great raound prints as big as barrel-heads, all sunk dawon deep like a elephant had ben along, *only they's a sight more nor four feet could make*! I looked at one or two afore I run, an' I see every one was covered with lines spreadin' aout from one place, like as if big palm-leaf fans – twict or three times as big as any they is – hed of ben paounded dawon into the rud. An' the smell was awful, like what it is around Wizard Whateley's ol' haouse. . . .'

Here he faltered, and seemed to shiver afresh with the fright that had sent him flying home. Mrs Corey, unable to extract more information, began telephoning the neighbours; thus starting on its rounds the overture of panic that heralded the major terrors. When she got Sally Sawyer, housekeeper at Seth Bishop's, the nearest place to Whateley's, it became her turn to listen instead of transmit; for Sally's boy Chauncey, who slept poorly, had been up on the hill towards Whateley's, and had dashed back in terror after one look at the place, and at the pasturage where Mr Bishop's cows had been left out all night.

'Yes, Mis' Corey,' came Sally's tremulous voice over the party wire, 'Cha'ncey he just come back a-postin', and couldn't haff talk fer bein' scairt! He says Ol' Whateley's house is all bowed up, with timbers scattered raound like they'd ben dynamite inside; only the bottom floor ain't through, but is all covered with a kind o' tar-like stuff that smells awful an' drips daown offen the aidges onto the graoun' whar the side timbers is blowed away. An' they's awful kinder marks in the yard, tew – great raound marks bigger raound than a hogshead, an' all sticky with stuff like is on the blowed-up haouse. Cha'ncey he says they leads off into the medders, whar a great swath wider'n a barn is matted daown, an' all the stun walls tumbled every whichway wherever it goes.

'An' he says, says he, Mis' Corey, as haow he sot to look fer Seth's caows, frightened ez he was an' faound 'em in the upper pasture nigh the Devil's Hop Yard in an awful shape. Haff on 'em's clean gone, an' nigh haff o' them that's left is sucked most dry o' blood, with sores on 'em like they's ben on Whateleys cattle ever senct Lavinny's black brat was born. Seth hes gone aout naow to look at 'em, though I'll vaow he wun't keer ter git very nigh Wizard Whateley's! Cha'ncey didn't look keerful ter see whar the big matted-daown swath led arter it lef the pasturage, but he says he thinks it p'inted towards the glen rud to the village.

'I tell ye, Mis' Corey, they's suthin' abroad as hadn't orter be abroad, an' I for one think that black Wilbur Whateley, as come to the bad end he desarved, is at the bottom of the breedin' of it. He wa'n't all human hisself, I allus says to everybody; an' I think he an' Ol' Whateley must a raised suthin' in that there nailed-up haouse as ain't even so human as he was. They's allus ben unseen things araound Dunwich – livin' things – as ain't human an' ain't good fer human folks.

'The graoun' was a-talkin' las' night, an' towards mornin' Cha'ncey he heered the whippoorwills so laoud in Col' Spring Glen he couldn't sleep nun. Then he thought he heered another faint-like saound over towards Wizard Whateley's – a kinder rippin' or tearin' o' wood, like some big box er crate was bin' opened fur off. What with this an' that, he didn't git to sleep at all till sunup, an' no sooner was he up this mornin', but he's got to go over to Whateley's an' see what's the matter. He see enough I tell ye, Mis' Corey! This dun't mean no good, an' I think as all the men-folks ought to git up a party an' do suthin'. I know suthin' awful's abaout, an' feel my time is nigh, though only Gawd knows jest what it is.

'Did your Luther take accaount o' whar them big tracks led tew? No?

Wal, Mis' Corey, ef they was on the glen rud this side o' the glen, an'
ain't got to your haouse yet, I calc'late they must go into the glen itself.
They would do that. I allus says Col' Spring Glen ain't no healthy nor
decent place. The whippoorwills an' fireflies there never did act like
they was creaters o' Gawd, an' they's them as says ye kin hear strange
things a-rushin' an' a-talkin' in the air dawon thar ef ye stand in the
right place, atween the rock falls an' Bear's Den.'

By that noon fully three-quarters of the men and boys of Dunwich
were trooping over the roads and meadows between the newmade
Whateley ruins and Cold Spring Glen, examining in horror the vast,
monstrous prints, the maimed Bishop cattle, the strange, noisome wreck
of the farmhouse, and the bruised, matted vegetation of the fields and
roadside. Whatever had burst loose upon the world had assuredly gone
down into the great sinister ravine; for all the trees on the banks were
bent and broken, and a great avenue had been gouged in the precipice-
hanging underbrush. It was as though a house, launched by an avalanche,
had slid down through the tangled growths of the almost vertical slope.
From below no sound came, but only a distant, undefinable foetor; and
it is not to be wondered at that the men preferred to stay on the edge
and argue, rather than descend and beard the unknown Cyclopean
horror in its lair. Three dogs that were with the party had barked
furiously at first, but seemed cowed and reluctant when near the glen.
Someone telephoned the news to the *Aylesbury Transcript*; but the
editor, accustomed to wild tales from Dunwich, did no more than concoct a humorous paragraph about it; an item soon afterwards reproduced by the Associated Press.

That night everyone went home, and every house and barn was
barricaded as stoutly as possible. Needless to say, no cattle were allowed
to remain in open pasturage. About two in the morning a frightful
stench and the savage barking of the dogs awakened the household at
Elmer Frye's, on the eastern edge of Cold Spring Glen, and all agreed
that they could hear a sort of muffled swishing or lapping sound from
somewhere outside. Mrs Frye proposed telephoning the neighbours,
and Elmer was about to agree when the noise of splintering wood burst
in upon their deliberations. It came, apparently, from the barn; and was
quickly followed by a hideous screaming and stamping amongst the
cattle. The dogs slavered and crouched close to the feet of the fear-
numbed family. Frye lit a lantern through force of habit, but knew it
would be death to go out into that black farmyard. The children and
the women-folk whimpered, kept from screaming by some obscure,
vestigial instinct of defence which told them their lives depended on
silence. At last the noise of the cattle subsided to a pitiful moaning, and
a great snapping, crashing, and crackling ensued. The Fryes, huddled

together in the sitting-room, did not dare to move until the last echoes died away far down in Cold Spring Glen. Then, amidst the dismal moans from the stable and the daemoniac piping of the late whippoor-wills in the glen, Selina Frye tottered to the telephone and spread what news she could of the second phase of the horror.

The next day all the countryside was in a panic; and cowed, uncom-municative groups came and went where the fiendish thing had oc-curred. Two titan swaths of destruction stretched from the glen to the Frye farmyard, monstrous prints covered the bare patches of ground, and one side of the old red barn had completely caved in. Of the cattle, only a quarter could be found and identified. Some of these were in curious fragments, and all that survived had to be shot. Earl Sawyer suggested that help be asked from Aylesbury or Arkham, but others maintained it would be of no use. Old Zebulon Whateley, of a branch that hovered about halfway between soundness and decadence, made darkly wild suggestions about rites that ought to be practised on the hill-tops. He came of a line where tradition ran strong, and his memo-ries of chantings in the great stone circles were not altogether connected with Wilbur and his grandfather.

Darkness fell upon a stricken countryside too passive to organize for real defence. In a few cases closely related families would band together and watch in the gloom under one roof; but in general there was only a repetition of the barricading of the night before, and a futile, ineffective gesture of loading muskets and setting pitchforks handily about. Noth-ing, however, occurred except some hill noises; and when the day came there were many who hoped that the new horror had gone as swiftly as it had come. There were even bold souls who proposed an offensive expedition down in the glen, though they did not venture to set an actual example to the still reluctant majority.

When night came again the barricading was repeated, though there was less huddling together of families. In the morning both the Frye and the Seth Bishop households reported excitement among the dogs and vague sounds and stenches from afar, while early explorers noted with horror a fresh set of the monstrous tracks in the road skirting Sentinel Hill. As before, the sides of the road showed a bruising indi-cative of the blasphemously stupendous bulk of the horror; whilst the conformation of the tracks seemed to argue a passage in two directions, as if the moving mountain had come from Cold Spring Glen and re-turned to it along the same path. At the base of the hill a thirty-foot swath of crushed shrubbery saplings led steeply upwards, and the seekers gasped when they saw that even the most perpendicular places did not deflect the inexorable trail. Whatever the horror was, it could scale a sheer stony cliff of almost complete verticality; and as the investigators climbed round to the hill's summit by safer routes they saw that the trail ended – or rather, reversed – there.

It was here that the Whateleys used to build their hellish fires and chant their hellish rituals by the table-like stone on May Eve and Hallowmass. Now that very stone formed the centre of a vast space thrashed around by the mountainous horror, whilst upon its slightly concave surface was a thick and foetid deposit of the same tarry stickiness observed on the floor of the ruined Whateley farmhouse when the horror escaped. Men looked at one another and muttered. Then they looked down the hill. Apparently the horror had descended by a route much the same as that of its ascent. To speculate was futile. Reason, logic, and normal ideas of motivation stood confounded. Only old Zebulon, who was not with the group, could have done justice to the situation or suggested a plausible explanation.

Thursday night began much like the others, but it ended less happily. The whippoorwills in the glen had screamed with such unusual persistence that many could not sleep, and about 3 A.M. all the party telephones rang tremulously. Those who took down their receivers heard a fright-mad voice shriek out, 'Help, oh, my Gawd! . . .' and some thought a crashing sound followed the breaking off of the exclamation. There was nothing more. No one dared do anything, and no one knew till morning whence the call came. Then those who had heard it called everyone on the line, and found that only the Fryes did not reply. The truth appeared an hour later, when a hastily assembled group of armed men trudged out to the Frye place at the head of the glen. It was horrible, yet hardly a surprise. There were more swaths and monstrous prints, but there was no longer any house. It had caved in like an eggshell, and amongst the ruins nothing living or dead could be discovered. Only a stench and a tarry stickiness. The Elmer Fryes had been erased from Dunwich.

VIII

In the meantime a quieter yet even more spiritually poignant phase of the horror had been blackly unwinding itself behind the closed door of a shelf-lined room in Arkham. The curious manuscript record or diary of Wilbur Whateley, delivered to Miskatonic University for translation, had caused much worry and bafflement among the experts in language both ancient and modern; its very alphabet, notwithstanding a general resemblance to the heavily-shaded Arabic used in Mesopotamia, being absolutely unknown to any available authority. The final conclusion of the linguists was that the text represented an artificial alphabet, giving the effect of a cipher; though none of the usual methods of cryptographic solution seemed to furnish any clue, even when applied on the basis of every tongue the writer might conceivably have used. The ancient books taken from Whateley's quarters, while absorbingly interesting and in several cases promising to open up new and terrible lines of research among philosophers and men of science, were of no assistance whatever in this matter. One of them, a heavy tome with an iron clasp, was in another unknown alphabet – this one of a very different cast, and resembling Sanskrit more than anything else. The old ledger was at length given wholly into the charge of Dr Armitage, both because of his peculiar interest in the Whateley matter, and because of his wide linguistic learning and skill in the mystical formulae of antiquity and the middle ages.

Armitage had an idea that the alphabet might be something esoterically used by certain forbidden cults which have come down from old times, and which have inherited many forms and traditions from the wizards of the Saracenic world. That question, however, he did not deem vital; since it would be unnecessary to know the origin of the symbols if, as he suspected, they were used as a cipher in a modern language. It was his belief that, considering the great amount of text involved, the writer would scarcely have wished the trouble of using another speech than his own, save perhaps in certain special formulae and incantations. Accordingly he attacked the manuscript with the preliminary assumption that the bulk of it was in English.

Dr Armitage knew, from the repeated failures of his colleagues, that the riddle was a deep and complex one; and that no simple mode of solution could merit even a trial. All through late August he fortified himself with the mass lore of cryptography; drawing upon the fullest resources of his own library, and wading night after night amidst the arcana of Trithemius' *Poligraphia*, Giambattista Porta's *De Furtivis Literarum Notis*, De Vigenere's *Traite des Chiffres*, Falconer's *Cryptomenysis Patefacta*, Davys' and Thicknesse's eighteenth-century treatises, and such fairly modern authorities as Blair, von Marten and Klüber's script itself, and in time became convinced that he had to deal with one of those subtlest and most ingenious of cryptograms, in which many separate lists of corresponding letters are arranged like the multiplication table, and the message built up with arbitrary key-words known only to the initiated. The older authorities seemed rather more helpful than the newer ones, and Armitage concluded that the code of the manuscript was one of great antiquity, no doubt handed down through a long line of mystical experimenters. Several times he seemed near daylight, only to be set back by some unforeseen obstacle. Then, as September approached, the clouds began to clear. Certain letters, as used in certain parts of the manuscript, emerged definitely and unmistakably; and it became obvious that the text was indeed in English.

On the evening of September second the last major barrier gave way, and Dr Armitage read for the first time a continuous passage of Wilbur Whateley's annals. It was in truth a diary, as all had thought; and it was couched in a style clearly showing the mixed occult erudition and general illiteracy of the strange being who wrote it. Almost the first long passage that Armitage deciphered, an entry dated November 26, 1916, proved highly startling and disquieting. It was written, he remembered, by a child of three and a half who looked like a lad of twelve or thirteen.

Today learned the Aklo for the Sabaoth (it ran), which did not like, it being answerable from the hill and not from the air. That upstairs more ahead of me than I had thought it would be, and is not like to have much earth brain. Shot Elam Hutchins's collie Jack when he went to bite me, and Elam says he would kill me if he dast. I guess he won't. Grandfather kept me saying the Dho formula last night, and I think I saw the inner city at the 2 magnetic poles. I shall go to those poles when the earth is cleared off, if I can't break through with the Dho-Hna formula when I commit it. They from the air told me at Sabbat that it will be years before I can clear off the earth, and I guess grandfather will be dead then, so I shall have to learn all the angles of the planes and all the formulas between the Yr and the Nhhngr. They from outside will help, but they cannot take body without human blood. That upstairs looks it will have the right cast. I can see it a little when I make the Voorish sign or blow the powder of Ibn Ghazi at it, and it is near like them at May Eve on the Hill. The other face may wear off some. I wonder how I shall look when the earth is cleared and there are no earth beings on it. He that came with the Aklo Sabaoth said I may be transfigured there being much of outside to work on.

Morning found Dr Armitage in a cold sweat of terror and a frenzy of wakeful concentration. He had not left the manuscript all night, but sat at his table under the electric light turning page after page with shaking hands as fast as he could decipher the cryptic text. He had nervously telephoned his wife he would not be home, and when she brought him a breakfast from the house he could scarcely dispose of a mouthful. All that day he read on, now and then halted maddeningly as a reapplication of the complex key became necessary. Lunch and dinner were brought him, but he ate only the smallest fraction of either. Toward the middle of the next night he drowsed off in his chair, but soon woke out of a tangle of nightmares almost as hideous as the truths and menaces to man's existence that he had uncovered.

THE DUNWICH HORROR

On the morning of September fourth Professor Rice and Dr Morgan insisted on seeing him for a while, and departed trembling and ashen-grey. That evening he went to bed, but slept only fitfully. Wednesday – the next day – he was back at the manuscript, and began to take copious notes both from the current sections and from those he had already deciphered. In the small hours of that night he slept a little in a easy chair in his office, but was at the manuscript again before dawn. Some time before noon his physician, Dr Hartwell, called to see him and insisted that he cease work. He refused; intimating that it was of the most vital importance for him to complete the reading of the diary and promising an explanation in due course of time. That evening, just as twilight fell, he finished his terrible perusal and sank back exhausted. His wife, bringing his dinner, found him in a half-comatose state; but he was conscious enough to warn her off with a sharp cry when he saw her eyes wander toward the notes he had taken. Weakly rising, he gathered up the scribbled papers and sealed them all in a great en-velope, which he immediately placed in his inside coat pocket. He had sufficient strength to get home, but was so clearly in need of medical aid that Dr Hartwell was summoned at once. As the doctor put him to bed he could only mutter over and over again, *'But what, in God's name, can we do?'*

Dr Armitage slept, but was partly delirious the next day. He made no explanations to Hartwell, but in his calmer moments spoke of the im-perative need of a long conference with Rice and Morgan. His wilder wanderings were very startling indeed, including frantic appeals that something in a boarded-up farmhouse be destroyed, and fantastic references to some plan for the extirpation of the entire human race and all animal and vegetable life from the earth by some terrible elder race of beings from another dimension. He would shout that the world was in danger, since the Elder Things wished to strip it and drag it away from the solar system and cosmos of matter into some other plane or phase of entity from which it had once fallen, vigintillions of aeons ago. At other times he would call for the dreaded *Necronomicon* and the *Daemonolatreia* of Remigius, in which he seemed hopeful of finding some formula to check the peril he conjured up.

'Stop them, stop them!' he would shout. 'Those Whateleys meant to let them in, and the worst of all is left! Tell Rice and Morgan we must do something – it's a blind business, but I know how to make the pow-der. . . . It hasn't been fed since the second of August, when Wilbur came here to his death, and at that rate. . . .'

But Armitage had a sound physique despite his seventy-three years, and slept off his disorder that night without developing any real fever. He woke late Friday, clear of head, though sober with a gnawing fear and tremendous sense of responsibility. Saturday afternoon he felt able to go over to the library and summon Rice and Morgan for a conference, and the rest of that day and evening the three men tortured their brains in the wildest speculation and the most desperate debate. Strange and terrible books were drawn voluminously from the stack shelves and from secure places of storage; and diagrams and formulae were copied with feverish haste and in bewildering abundance. Of scepticism there was none. All three had seen the body of Wilbur Whateley as it lay on the floor in a room of that very building, and after that not one of them could feel even slightly inclined to treat the diary as a madman's raving.

Opinions were divided as to notifying the Massachusetts State Police, and the negative finally won. There were things involved which simply could not be believed by those who had not seen a sample, as indeed was made clear during certain subsequent investigations. Late at night the conference disbanded without having developed a definite plan, but all day Sunday Armitage was busy comparing formulae and mixing chemicals obtained from the college laboratory. The more he reflected on the hellish diary, the more he was inclined to doubt the efficacy of any material agent in stamping out the entity which Wilbur Whateley had left behind him – the earth threatening entity which, unknown to him, was to burst forth in a few hours and become the memorable Dunwich horror.

Monday was a repetition of Sunday with Dr Armitage, for the task in hand required an infinity of research and experiment. Further consultations of the monstrous diary brought about various changes of plan, and he knew that even in the end a large amount of uncertainty must remain. By Tuesday he had a definite line of action mapped out, and believed he would try a trip to Dunwich within a week. Then, on Wednesday, the great shock came. Tucked obscurely away in a corner of the *Arkham Advertiser* was a facetious little item from the Associated Press, telling what a record-breaking monster the bootleg whisky of Dunwich had raised up. Armitage, half stunned, could only telephone for Rice and Morgan. Far into the night they discussed, and the next day was a whirlwind of preparation on the part of them all. Armitage knew he would be meddling with terrible powers, yet saw that there was no other way to annul the deeper and more malign meddling which others had done before him.

IX

Friday morning Armitage, Rice, and Morgan set out by motor for Dunwich, arriving at the village about one in the afternoon. The day was pleasant, but even in the brightest sunlight a kind of quiet dread and portent seemed to hover about the strangely domed hills and the deep, shadowy ravines of the stricken region. Now and then on some mountain top a gaunt circle of stones could be glimpsed against the sky. From the air of hushed fright at Osborn's store they knew something hideous had happened, and soon learned of the annihilation of the Elmer Frye house and family. Throughout that afternoon they rode around Dunwich, questioning the natives concerning all that had occurred, and seeing for themselves with rising pangs of horror the drear Frye ruins with their lingering traces of the tarry stickiness, the blasphemous tracks in the Frye yard, the wounded Seth Bishop cattle, and the enormous swaths of disturbed vegetation in various places. The trail up and down Sentinel Hill seemed to Armitage of almost cataclysmic significance, and he looked long at the sinister altar-like stone on the summit.

At length the visitors, apprised of a party of State Police which had come from Aylesbury that morning in response to the first telephone reports of the Frye tragedy, decided to seek out the officers and compare notes as far as practicable. This, however, they found more easily planned than performed; since no sign of the party could be found in any direction. There had been five of them in a car, but now the car stood empty near the ruins in the Frye yard. The natives, all of whom had talked with the policemen, seemed at first as perplexed as Armitage and his companions. Then old Sam Hutchins thought of something and turned pale, nudging Fred Farr and pointing to the dank, deep hollow that yawned close by.

'Gawd,' he gasped, 'I told 'em not ter go daown into the glen, an' I never thought nobody'd dew it with them tracks an' that smell an' the whippoorwills a-screechin' daown thar in the dark o' noonday. . . .'

A cold shudder ran through natives and visitors alike, and every ear seemed strained in a kind of instinctive, unconscious listening. Armitage, now that he had actually come upon the horror and its monstrous work, trembled with the responsibility he felt to be his. Night would soon fall, and it was then that the mountainous blasphemy lumbered upon its eldritch course. *Negotium perambulans in tenebris.* . . . The old librarian rehearsed the formulae he had memorized, and clutched the paper containing the alternative one he had not memorized. He saw that his electric flashlight was in working order. Rice, beside him, took from a valise a metal sprayer of the sort used in combating insects; whilst Morgan uncased the big-game rifle on which he relied despite his colleague's warnings that no material weapon would be of help.

Armitage, having read the hideous diary, knew painfully well what kind of a manifestation to expect; but he did not add to the fright of

the Dunwich people by giving any hints or clues. He hoped that it might
be conquered without any revelation to the world of the monstrous thing
it had escaped. As the shadows gathered, the natives commenced to
disperse homeward, anxious to bar themselves indoors despite the
present evidence that all human locks and bolts were useless before a
force that could bend trees and crush houses when it chose. They shook
their heads at the visitors' plan to stand guard at the Frye ruins near
the glen; and, as they left, had little expectancy of ever seeing the
watchers again.

There were rumblings under the hills that night, and the whippoorwills piped threateningly. Once in a while a wind, sweeping up out of
Cold Spring Glen, would bring a touch of ineffable foetor to the heavy
night air; such a foetor as all three of the watchers had smelled once
before, when they stood above a dying thing that had passed for fifteen
years and a half as a human being. But the looked-for terror did not
appear. Whatever was down there in the glen was biding its time, and
Armitage told his colleagues it would be suicidal to try to attack it in the
dark.

Morning came wanly, and the night-sounds ceased. It was a grey,
bleak day, with now and then a drizzle of rain; and heavier and heavier
clouds seemed to be piling themselves up beyond the hills to the north-
west. The men from Arkham were undecided what to do. Seeking
shelter from the increasing rainfall beneath one of the few undestroyed
Frye outbuildings, they debated the wisdom of waiting, or of taking the
aggressive and going down into the glen in quest of their nameless,
monstrous quarry. The downpour waxed in heaviness, and distant peals
of thunder sounded from far horizons. Sheet lightning shimmered, and
then a forky bolt flashed near at hand, as if descending into the accursed
glen itself. The sky grew very dark, and the watchers hoped that the
storm would prove a short, sharp one followed by clear weather.

It was still gruesomely dark when, not much over an hour later, a
confused babel of voices sounded down the road. Another moment
brought to view a frightened group of more than a dozen men, running,
shouting, and even whimpering hysterically. Someone in the lead began
sobbing out words, and the Arkham men started violently when those
words developed a coherent form.

'Oh, my Gawd, my Gawd,' the voice choked out. 'It's a-goin' agin,
an' this time by day! It's aout – it's aout an' a-movin' this very minute,
an' only the Lord knows when it'll be on us all!'

The speaker panted into silence, but another took up his message.

'Nigh on a haour ago Zeb Whateley here heered the 'phone a-ringin',
an' it was Mis' Corey, George's wife, that lives daown by the junction.
She says the hired boy Luther was aout drivin' in the caows from the

storm arter the big bolt, when he see all the trees a-bendin' at the maouth o' the glen – opposite side ter this – an' smelt the same awful smell like he smelt when he faound the big tracks las' Monday mornin'. An' she says he says they was a swishin' lappin' saound, more nor what the bendin' trees an' bushes could make, an' all on a suddent the trees along the rud begun ter git pushed one side, an' they was a awful stompin' an' splashin' in the mud. But mind ye, Luther he didn't see nothin' at all, only just the bendin' trees an' underbrush.

'Then fur ahead where Bishop's Brook goes under the rud he heerd a awful creakin' an' strainin' on the bridge, an' says he could tell the saound o' wood a-startin' to crack an' split. An' all the whiles he never see a thing, only them trees an' bushes a-bendin'. An' when the swishin' saound got very fur off – on the rud towards Wizard Whateley's an' Sentinel Hill – Luther he had the guts ter step up whar he'd heerd it fust an' look at the graound. It was all mud an' water, an' the sky was dark, an' the rain was wipin' aout all tracks abaout as fast as could be; but beginnin' at the glen maouth, whar the trees hed moved, they was still some o' them awful prints big as bar'ls like he seen Monday.'

At this point the first excited speaker interrupted.

'But *that* ain't the trouble naow – that was only the start. Zeb here was callin' folks up an' everybody was a-listenin' in when a call from Seth Bishop's cut in. His haousekeeper Sally was carryin' on fit to kill – she'd jest seed the trees a-bendin' beside the rud, an' says they was a kind o' mushy saound, like a elephant puffin' an' treadin', a-headin' fer the haouse. Then she up an' spoke suddent of a fearful smell, an' says her boy Cha'ncey was a-screamin' as haow it was jest like what he smelt up to the Whateley rewins Monday mornin'. An' the dogs was all barkin' an' whinin' awful.

'An 'then she let aout a turrible yell, an' says the shed daown the rud had jest caved in like the storm hed blowed it over, only he wind w'an't strong enough to dew that. Everybody was a-listenin', an' we could hear lots o' folks on the wire a-gaspin'. All to onct Sally she yelled again, an' says the front yard picket fence hed just crumbled up, though they wa'n't no sign o' what done it. Then everybody on the line could hear Cha'ncey an' old Seth Bishop a-yellin' tew, an' Sally was shriekin' aout that suthin' heavy hed struck the haouse – not lightnin' nor nothin', but suthin' heavy again the front, that kep' a-launchin' itself agin an' agin, though ye couldn't see nothin' aout the front winders. An' then . . . an' then. . . .'

Lines of fright deepened on every face; and Armitage, shaken as he was, had barely poise enough to prompt the speaker.

'An' then . . . Sally she yelled aout, "O help, the haouse is a-cavin' in" . . . , an' on the wire we could hear a turrible crashin' an' a hull flock o' screamin' . . . jes like when Elmer Frye's place was took, only wuss. . . .'

The man paused, and another of the crowd spoke.

'That's all – not a saound nor squeak over the 'phone arter that. Jest still-like. We that heerd it got aout Fords an' wagons an' rounded up as many able-bodied men-folks as we could git, at Corey's place, an' come up here ter see what yew thought best ter dew. Not but what I think it's the Lord's jedgment fer our iniquities, that no mortal kin ever set aside.'

Armitage saw that the time for positive action had come, and spoke decisively to the faltering group of frightened rustics.

'We must follow it, boys.' He made his voice as reassuring as possible. 'I believe there's a chance of putting it out of business. You men know that those Whateleys were wizards – well, this thing is a thing of wizardry, and must be put down by the same means. I've seen Wilbur Whateley's diary and read some of the strange old books he used to read; and I think I know the right kind of spell to recite to make the thing fade away. Of course, one can't be sure, but we can always take a chance. It's invisible – I knew it would be – but there's powder in this long-distance sprayer that might make it show up for a second. Later on we'll try it. It's a frightful thing to have alive, but it isn't as bad as what Wilbur would have let in if he'd lived longer. You'll never know what the world escaped. Now we've only this one thing to fight, and it can't multiply. It can, though, do a lot of harm; so we mustn't hesitate to rid the community of it.

'We must follow it – and the way to begin is to go to the place that has just been wrecked. Let somebody lead the way – I don't know your roads very well, but I've an idea there might be a shorter cut across lots. How about it?'

The men shuffled about a moment, and then Earl Sawyer spoke softly, pointing with a grimy finger through the steadily lessening rain.

'I guess ye kin git to Seth Bishop's quickest by cuttin' acrost the lower medder here, wadin' the brook at the low place, an' climbin' through Carrier's mowin' an' the timber-lot beyont. That comes aout on the upper rud mighty nigh Seth's – a leetle t'other side.'

Armitage, with Rice and Morgan, started to walk in the direction indicated; and most of the natives followed slowly. The sky was growing lighter, and there were signs that the storm had worn itself away. When Armitage inadvertently took a wrong direction, Joe Osborn warned him and walked ahead to show the right one. Courage and confidence were mounting, though the twilight of the almost perpendicular wooded hill which lay towards the end of their short cut, and among whose fantastic ancient trees they had to scramble as if up a ladder, put these qualities to a severe test.

At length they emerged on a muddy road to find the sun coming out.

They were a little beyond the Seth Bishop place, but bent trees and hideously unmistakable tracks showed what had passed by. Only a few moments were consumed in surveying the ruins just round the bend. It was the Frye incident all over again, and nothing dead or living was found in either of the collapsed shells which had been the Bishop house and barn. No one cared to remain there amidst the stench and tarry stickiness, but all turned instinctively to the line of horrible prints leading on towards the wrecked Whateley farmhouse and the altar-crowned slopes of Sentinel Hill.

As the men passed the site of Wilbur Whateley's abode they shuddered visibly, and seemed again to mix hesitancy with their zeal. It was no joke tracking down something as big as a house that one could not see, but that had all the vicious malevolence of a daemon. Opposite the base of Sentinel Hill the tracks left the road, and there was a fresh bending and matting visible along the broad swath marking the monster's former route to and from the summit.

Armitage produced a pocket telescope of considerable power and scanned the steep green side of the hill. Then he handed the instrument to Morgan, whose sight was keener. After a moment of gazing Morgan cried out sharply, passing the glass to Earl Sawyer and indicating a certain spot on the slope with his finger. Sawyer, as clumsy as most non-users of optical devices are, fumbled a while; but eventually focused the lenses with Armitage's aid. When he did so his cry was less restrained than Morgan's had been.

'Gawd almighty, the grass an' bushes is a'movin'! It's a-goin' up – slow-like – creepin' – up ter the top this minute, heaven only knows what fur!'

Then the germ of panic seemed to spread among the seekers. It was one thing to chase the nameless entity, but quite another to find it. Spells might be all right – but suppose they weren't? Voices began questioning Armitage about what he knew of the thing, and no reply seemed quite to satisfy. Everyone seemed to feel himself in close proximity to phases of Nature and of being utterly forbidden and wholly outside the sane experience of mankind.

X

In the end the three men from Arkham – old, white-bearded Dr Armitage, stocky, iron-grey Professor Rice, and lean, youngish Dr Morgan, ascended the mountain alone. After much patient instruction regarding its focusing and use, they left the telescope with the frightened group that remained in the road; and as they climbed they were watched closely by those among whom the glass was passed round. It was hard going, and Armitage had to be helped more than once. High above the toiling group the great swath trembled as its hellish maker repassed with snail-like deliberateness. Then it was obvious that the pursuers were gaining.

Curtis Whateley – of the undecayed branch – was holding the telescope when the Arkham party detoured radically from the swath. He told the crowd that the men were evidently trying to get to a subordinate peak which overlooked the swath at a point considerably ahead of where the shrubbery was now bending. This, indeed, proved to be true; and the party were seen to gain the minor elevation only a short time after the invisible blasphemy had passed it.

Then Wesley Corey, who had taken the glass, cried out that Armitage was adjusting the sprayer which Rice held, and that something must be about to happen. The crowd stirred uneasily, recalling that his sprayer was expected to give the unseen horror a moment of visibility. Two or three men shut their eyes, but Curtis Whateley snatched back the telescope and strained his vision to the utmost. He saw that Rice, from the party's point of advantage above and behind the entity, had an excellent chance of spreading the potent powder with marvellous effect.

Those without the telescope saw only an instant's flash of grey cloud – a cloud about the size of a moderately large building – near the top of the mountain. Curtis, who held the instrument, dropped it with a piercing shriek into the ankle-deep mud of the road. He reeled, and would have crumbled to the ground had not two or three others seized and steadied him. All he could do was moan half-inaudibly.

'Oh, oh, great Gawd . . . that . . . that. . . .'

There was a pandemonium of questioning, and only Henry Wheeler thought to rescue the fallen telescope and wipe it clean of mud. Curtis was past all coherence, and even isolated replies were almost too much for him.

'Bigger'n a barn . . . all made o' squirmin' ropes . . . hull thing sort o' shaped like a hen's egg bigger'n anything with dozens o' legs like hogsheads that haff shut up when they step . . . nothin' solid abaout it – all like jelly, an' made o' sep'rit wrigglin' ropes pushed clost together . . . great bulgin' eyes all over it . . . ten or twenty maouths or trunks a-stickin' aout all along the sides, big as stove-pipes an all a-tossin' an openin' an' shuttin' . . . all grey, with kinder blue or purple rings . . . *an Gawd in Heaven – that haff face on top . . .*'

This final memory, whatever it was, proved too much for poor Curtis; and he collapsed completely before he could say more. Fred Farr and Will Hutchins carried him to the roadside and laid him on the damp grass. Henry Wheeler, trembling, turned the rescued telescope on the

THE DUNWICH HORROR

mountain to see what he might. Through the lenses were discernible three tiny figures, apparently running towards the summit as fast as the steep incline allowed. Only these – nothing more. Then everyone noticed a strangely unseasonable noise in the deep valley behind, and even in the underbrush of Sentinel Hill itself. It was the piping of unnumbered whippoorwills, and in their shrill chorus there seemed to lurk a note of tense and evil expectancy.

Earl Sawyer now took the telescope and reported the three figures as standing on the topmost ridge, virtually level with the altar-stone but at a considerable distance from it. One figure, he said, seemed to be raising its hands above its head at rhythmic intervals; and as Sawyer mentioned the circumstance the crowd seemed to hear a faint, half-musical sound from the distance, as if a loud chant were accompanying the gestures. The weird silhouette on that remote peak must have been a spectacle of infinite grotesqueness and impressiveness, but no observer was in a mood for aesthetic appreciation. 'I guess he's sayin' the spell,' whispered Wheeler as he snatched back the telescope. The whippoor-wills were piping wildly, and in a singularly curious irregular rhythm quite unlike that of the visible ritual.

Suddenly the sunshine seemed to lessen without the intervention of any discernible cloud. It was a very peculiar phenomenon, and was plainly marked by all. A rumbling sound seemed brewing beneath the hills, mixed strangely with a concordant rumbling which clearly came from the sky. Lightning flashed aloft, and the wondering crowd looked in vain for the portents of storm. The chanting of the men from Arkham now became unmistakable, and Wheeler saw through the glass that they were all raising their arms in the rhythmic incantation. From some farmhouse far away came the frantic barking of dogs.

The change in the quality of the daylight increased, and the crowd gazed about the horizon in wonder. A purplish darkness, born of nothing more than a spectral deepening of the sky's blue, pressed down upon the rumbling hills. Then the lightning flashed again, somewhat brighter than before, and the crowd fancied that it had showed a certain misti-ness around the altar-stone on the distant height. No one, however, had been using the telescope at that instant. The whippoorwills continued their irregular pulsation, and the men of Dunwich braced themselves tensely against some imponderable menace with which the atmosphere seemed surcharged.

Without warning came those deep, cracked, raucous vocal sounds which will never leave the memory of the stricken group who heard them. Not from any human throat were they born, for the organs of man can yield no such acoustic perversions. Rather would one have said they came from the pit itself, had not their source been so unmistakably the altar-stone on the peak. It is almost erroneous to call them *sounds* at all, since so much of their ghastly, infra-bass timbre spoke to dim seats of consciousness and terror far subtler than the ear; yet one must do so, since their form was indisputably though vaguely that of half-articulate *words*. They were loud – loud as the rumblings and the thunder above which they echoed – yet did they come from no visible being. And because imagination might suggest a conjectural source in the world of non-visible beings, the huddled crowd at the mountain's base huddled still closer, and winced as if in expectation of a blow.

'Ygnaiih . . . ygnaiih . . . thflthkh'ngha . . . Yog-Sothoth . . .' rang the hideous croaking out of space. 'Y'bthnk . . . h'ehye – n'grkdl'lh. . . .'

The speaking impulse seemed to falter here, as if some frightful psychic struggle were going on. Henry Wheeler strained his eye at the telescope, but saw only the three grotesquely silhouetted human figures on the peak, all moving their arms furiously in strange gestures as their incantation drew near its culmination. From what black wells of Acherontic fear or feeling, from what unplumbed gulfs of extra-cosmic consciousness or obscure, long-latent heredity, were those half-articulate thunder-croakings drawn? Presently they began to gather renewed force and coherence as they grew in stark, utter, ultimate frenzy

'Eh-y-ya-ya-yahaah – e'yayayaaaa . . . ngh'aaaaa . . . ngh'aaa . . . h'yuh . . . h'yuh . . . HELP! HELP! . . . ff – ff – ff – FATHER! FATHER! YOG-SOTHOTH! . . .'

But that was all. The pallid group in the road, still reeling at the *indisputably English* syllables that had poured thickly and thunderously down from the frantic vacancy beside that shocking altar-stone, were never to hear such syllables again. Instead, they jumped violently at the terrific report which seemed to rend the hills; the deafening, cataclysmic peal whose source, be it inner earth or sky, no hearer was ever able to place. A single lightning bolt shot from the purple zenith to the altar-stone, and a great tidal wave of viewless force and indescribable stench swept down from the hill to all the countryside. Trees, grass, and underbrush were whipped into a fury; and the frightened crowd at the mountain's base, weakened by the lethal foetor that seemed about to asphyxiate them, were almost hurled off their feet. Dogs howled from the distance, green grass and foliage wilted to a curious, sickly yellow-grey, and over field and forest were scattered the bodies of dead whip-poorwills.

The stench left quickly, but the vegetation never came right again. To this day there is something queer and unholy about the growths on and around that fearsome hill. Curtis Whateley was only just regaining consciousness when the Arkham men came slowly down the mountain in the beams of a sunlight once more brilliant and untainted. They were grave and quiet, and seemed shaken by memories and reflections even more terrible than those which had reduced the group of natives to a state of cowed quivering. In reply to a jumble of questions they only shook their heads and reaffirmed one vital fact.

'The thing has gone for ever,' Armitage said. 'It has been split up into what it was originally made of, and can never exist again. It was an impossibility in a normal world. Only the least fraction was really matter in any sense we know. It was like its father – and most of it has gone back to him in some vague realm or dimension outside our material universe; some vague abyss out of which only the most accursed rites of human blasphemy could ever have called him for a moment on the hills.'

There was a brief silence, and in that pause the scattered senses of poor Curtis Whateley began to knit back into a sort of continuity; so that he put his hands to his head with a moan. Memory seemed to pick itself up where it had left off, and the horror of the sight that had prostrated him burst in upon him again.

'*Oh, oh, my Gawd, that haff face – that haff face on top of it . . . that face with the red eyes an' crinkly albino hair, an' no chin, like the Whateleys. . . . It was a octopus, centipede, spider kind o' thing, but they was a haff-shaped man's face on top of it, an' it looked like Wizard Whateley's, only it was yards an' yards acrost. . . .*'

He paused exhausted, as the whole group of natives stared in a bewilderment not quite crystallized into fresh terror. Only old Zebulon Whateley, who wanderingly remembered ancient things but who had been silent heretofore, spoke aloud.

'Fifteen year' gone,' he rambled, 'I heered Ol' Whateley say as haow some day we'd hear a child o' Lavinny's a-callin its father's name on the top o' Sentinel Hill. . . .'

But Joe Osborn interrupted him to question the Arkham men anew.

'*What was it, anyhaow,* an' haowever did young Wizard Whateley call it aout o' the air it come from?'

Armitage chose his words very carefully.

'It was – well, it was mostly a kind of force that doesn't belong in our part of space; a kind of force that acts and grows and shapes itself by other laws than those of our sort of Nature. We have no business calling in such things from outside, and only very wicked people and very wicked cults ever try to. There was some of it in Wilbur Whateley himself – enough to make a devil and a precocious monster of him, and to make his passing out a pretty terrible sight. I'm going to burn his accursed diary, and if you men are wise you'll dynamite that altar-stone up there, and pull down all the rings of standing stones on the other hills. Things like that brought down the beings those Whateleys were so fond of – the beings they were going to let in tangibly to wipe out the human race and drag the earth off to some nameless place for some nameless purpose.

'But as to this thing we've just sent back – the Whateleys raised it for a terrible part in the doings that were to come. It grew fast and big from the same reason that Wilbur grew fast and big – but it beat him because it had a greater share of the *outsideness* in it. You needn't ask how Wilbur called it out of the air. He didn't call it out. *It was his twin brother, but it looked more like the father than he did.*'

H. P. Lovecraft

The Rats in the Walls

On July 16, 1923, I moved into Exham Priory after the last workman had finished his labours. The restoration had been a stupendous task, for little had remained of the deserted pile but a shell-like ruin; yet because it had been the seat of my ancestors, I let no expense deter me. The place had not been inhabited since the reign of James the First, when a tragedy of intensely hideous, though largely unexplained, nature had struck down the master, five of his children, and several servants; and driven forth under a cloud of suspicion and terror the third son, my lineal progenitor and the only survivor of the abhorred line.

With this sole heir denounced as a murderer, the estate had reverted to the Crown, nor had the accused man made any attempt to exculpate himself or regain his property. Shaken by some horror greater than that of conscience or the law, and expressing only a frantic wish to exclude the ancient edifice from his sight and memory, Walter de la Poer, eleventh Baron Exham, fled to Virginia and there founded the family which by the next century had become known as Delapore.

Exham Priory had remained untenanted, though later allotted to the estates of the Norrys family and much studied because of its peculiarly composite architecture; an architecture involving Gothic towers resting on a Saxon or Romanesque substructure, whose foundation in turn was of a still earlier order or blend of orders – Roman, and even Druidic or native Cymric, if legend speaks truly. This foundation was a very singular thing, being merged on one side with the solid limestone of the precipice from whose brink the priory overlooked a desolate valley three miles west of the village of Anchester.

Architects and antiquarians loved to examine this strange relic of forgotten centuries, but the country folk hated it. They had hated it hundreds of years before, when my ancestors lived there, and they hated it now, with the moss and mould of abandonment on it. I had not been a day in Anchester before I knew I came of an accursed house. And this week workmen have blown up Exham Priory, and are busy obliterating the traces of its foundations. The bare statistics of my ancestry I had always known, together with the fact that my first American forebear had come to the colonies under a strange cloud. Of details, however, I had been kept wholly ignorant through the policy of reticence always maintained by the Delapores. Unlike our planter neighbours, we seldom boasted of crusading ancestors or other medieval and Renaissance heroes; nor was any kind of tradition handed down except what may have been recorded in the sealed envelope left before the Civil War by every squire to his eldest son for posthumous opening. The glories we cherished were those achieved since the migration; the glories of a proud and honourable, if somewhat reserved and unsocial Virginia line.

During the war our fortunes were extinguished and our whole existence changed by the burning of Carfax, our home on the banks of the James. My grandfather, advanced in years, had perished in that incendiary outrage, and with him the envelope that bound us all to the past. I can recall that fire to-day as I saw it then at the age of seven, with the Federal soldiers shouting, the women screaming, and the negroes howling and praying. My father was in the army, defending Richmond, and after many formalities my mother and I were passed through the lines to join him.

When the war ended we all moved north, whence my mother had come; and I grew to manhood, middle age, and ultimate wealth as a stolid Yankee. Neither my father nor I ever knew what our hereditary envelope had contained, and as I merged into the greyness of Massachusetts business life I lost all interest in the mysteries which evidently lurked far back in my family tree. Had I suspected their nature, how gladly I would have left Exham Priory to its moss, bats and cobwebs!

My father died in 1904, but without any message to leave to me, or to my only child, Alfred, a motherless boy of ten. It was this boy who reversed the order of family information, for although I could give him only jesting conjectures about the past, he wrote me of some very interesting ancestral legends when the late war took him to England in 1917 as an aviation officer. Apparently the Delapores had a colourful and perhaps sinister history, for a friend of my son's, Capt. Edward Norrys of the Royal Flying Corps, dwelt near the family seat at Anchester and related some peasant superstitions which few novelists could equal for wildness and incredibility. Norrys himself, of course, did not take them seriously; but they amused my son and made good material for his letters to me. It was this legendry which definitely turned my attention to my transatlantic heritage, and made me resolve to purchase and restore the family seat which Norrys showed to Alfred in its picturesque desertion, and offered to get for him at a surprisingly reasonable figure, since his own uncle was the present owner.

I bought Exham Priory in 1918, but was almost immediately distracted from my plans of restoration by the return of my son as a maimed invalid. During the two years that he lived I thought of nothing but his care, having even placed my business under the direction of partners.

In 1921, as I found myself bereaved and aimless, a retired manufacturer no longer young, I resolved to divert my remaining years with my new possession. Visiting Anchester in December, I was entertained by Capt. Norrys, a plump, amiable young man who had thought much of my son, and secured his assistance in gathering plans and anecdotes to guide in the coming restoration. Exham Priory itself I saw without emotion, a jumble of tottering medieval ruins covered with lichens and honeycombed with rooks' nests, perched perilously upon a precipice, and denuded of floors or other interior features save the stone walls of the separate towers.

As I gradually recovered the image of the edifice as it had been when my ancestors left it over three centuries before, I began to hire workmen for the reconstruction. In every case I was forced to go outside the immediate locality, for the Anchester villagers had an almost unbelievable fear and hatred of the place. This sentiment was so great that it was sometimes communicated to the outside labourers, causing numerous desertions; whilst its scope appeared to include both the priory and its ancient family.

My son had told me that he was somewhat avoided during his visits because he was a de la Poer, and I now found myself subtly ostracised for a like reason until I convinced the peasants how little I knew of my heritage. Even then they sullenly disliked me, so that I had to collect most of the village traditions through the mediation of Norrys. What the people could not forgive, perhaps, was that I had come to restore a symbol so abhorrent to them; for, rationally or not, they viewed Exham Priory as nothing less than a haunt of fiends and werewolves.

Piecing together the tales which Norry collected for me, and supplementing them with the accounts of several savants who had studied the ruins, I deduced that Exham Priory stood on the site of a prehistoric temple; a Druidical or ante-Druidical thing which must have been contemporary with Stonehenge. That indescribable rites had been celebrated there, few doubted, and there were unpleasant tales of the transference of these rites into the Cybele-worship which the Romans had introduced.

Inscriptions still visible in the sub-cellar bore such unmistakable letters as 'DIV . . . OPS . . . MAGNA. MAT. . .' sign of the Magna Mater whose dark worship was once vainly forbidden to Roman citizens. Anchester had been the camp of the third Augustan legion, as many remains attest, and it was said that the temple of the Cybele was splendid and thronged with worshippers who performed nameless ceremonies at the bidding of a Phrygian priest. Tales added that the fall of the old religion did not end the orgies at the temple, but that the priests lived on in the new faith without real change. Likewise was it said that the rites did not vanish with the Roman power, and that certain among the Saxons added to what remained of the temple, and gave it the essential outline it subsequently preserved, making it the centre of a cult feared through half the heptarchy. About 1000 A.D. the place is mentioned in a chronicle as being a substantial stone priory housing a strange and powerful monastic order and surrounded by extensive gardens which needed no walls to exclude a frightened populace. It was never destroyed by the Danes, though after the Norman Conquest it must have declined tremendously; since there was no impediment when Henry the Third granted the site to my ancestor, Gilbert de la Poer, First Baron Exham, in 1261.

Of my family before this date there is no evil report, but something strange must have happened then. In one chronicle there is a reference to a de la Poer as 'cursed of God' in 1307, whilst village legendry had nothing but evil and frantic fear to tell of the castle that went up on the foundations of the old temple and priory. The fireside tales were of the most grisly description; all the ghastlier because of their frightened reticence and cloudy evasiveness. They represented my ancestors as a race of hereditary daemons beside whom Gilles de Retz and the Marquis de Sade would seem the veriest tyros, and hinted whisperingly at their responsibility for the occasional disappearances of villagers through several generations.

The worst characters, apparently, were the barons and their direct heirs; at least, most was whispered about these. If of healthier inclinations, it was said, an heir would early and mysteriously die to make way for another more typical scion. There seemed to be an inner cult in the family, presided over by the head of the house, and sometimes closed except to a few members. Temperament rather than ancestry was evidently the basis of this cult, for it was entered by several who married into the family. Lady Margaret Trevor from Cornwall, wife of Godfrey, the second son of the fifth baron, became a favourite bane of children all over the countryside, and the daemon heroine of a particularly horrible old ballad not yet extinct near the Welsh border. Preserved in balladry, too, though not illustrating the same point, is the hideous tale of Lady Mary de la Poer, who shortly after her marriage to the Earl of

Shrewsfield was killed by him and his mother, both of the slayers being absolved and blessed by the priest to whom they confessed what they dared not repeat to the world.

These myths and ballads, typical as they were of crude superstition, repelled me greatly. Their persistence, and their application to so long a line of my ancestors, were especially annoying; whilst the imputations of monstrous habits proved unpleasantly reminiscent of the one known scandal of my immediate forebears – the case of my cousin, young Randolph Delapore of Carfax, who went among the negroes and became a voodoo priest after he returned from the Mexican War.

I was much less disturbed by the vaguer tales of wails and howlings in the barren, windswept valley beneath the limestone cliff; of the graveyard stenches after the spring rains; of the floundering, squealing white thing on which Sir John Clave's horse had trod one night in a lonely field; and of the servant who had gone mad at what he saw in the priory in the full light of day. These things were hackneyed spectral lore, and I was at that time a pronounced sceptic. The accounts of vanished peasants were less to be dismissed, though not especially significant in view of medieval custom. Prying curiosity meant death, and more than one severed head had been publicly shown on the bastions – now effaced – around Exham Priory.

A few of the tales were exceedingly picturesque, and made me wish I had learnt more of comparative mythology in my youth. There was, for instance, the belief that a legion of bat-winged devils kept witches' sabbath each night at the priory – a legion whose sustenance might explain the disproportionate abundance of coarse vegetables harvested in the vast gardens. And, most vivid of all, there was the dramatic epic of the rats – the scampering army of obscene vermin which had burst forth from the castle three months after the tragedy that doomed it to desertion – the lean, filthy, ravenous army which had swept all before it and devoured fowl, cats, dogs, hogs, sheep, and even two hapless human beings before its fury was spent. Around that unforgettable rodent army a whole separate cycle of myths revolves, for it scattered among the village homes and brought curses and horrors in its train.

Such was the lore that assailed me as I pushed to completion, with an elderly obstinacy, the work of restoring my ancestral home. It must not be imagined for a moment that these tales formed my principal psychological environment. On the other hand, I was constantly praised and encouraged by Capt. Norrys and the antiquarians who surrounded and aided me. When the task was done, over two years after its commencement, I viewed the great rooms, wainscotted walls, vaulted ceilings, mullioned windows, and broad staircases with a pride which fully compensated for the prodigious expense of the restoration.

Every attribute of the Middle Ages was cunningly reproduced, and the new parts blended perfectly with the original walls and foundation. The seat of my fathers was complete, and I looked forward to redeeming at last the local fame of the line which ended in me. I would reside here permanently, and prove that a de la Poer (for I had adopted again the original spelling of the name) need not be a fiend. My comfort was perhaps augmented by the fact that, although Exham Priory was medievally fitted, its interior was in truth wholly new and free from old vermin and old ghosts alike.

As I have said, I moved in on 16th July 1923. My household consisted of seven servants and nine cats, of which latter species I am particularly fond. My eldest cat, 'Nigger-Man,' was seven years old and had come with me from my home in Boston, Massachusetts; the others I had accumulated whilst living with Capt. Norrys' family during the restoration of the priory.

For five days our routine proceeded with the utmost placidity, my time being spent mostly in the codification of old family data. I had now obtained some very circumstantial accounts of the final tragedy and flight of Walter de la Poer, which I conceived to be the probable contents of the hereditary paper lost in the fire at Carfax. It appeared that my ancestor was accused with much reason of having killed all the other members of his household, except four servant confederates, in their sleep, about two weeks after a shocking discovery which changed his whole demeanour, but which, except by implication, he disclosed to no one save perhaps the servants who assisted him and afterwards fled beyond reach.

This deliberate slaughter, which included a father, three brothers, and two sisters, was largely condoned by the villagers, and so slackly treated by the law that its perpetrator escaped honoured, unharmed, and undisguised to Virginia; the general whispered sentiment being that he had purged the land of an immemorial curse. What discovery had prompted an act so terrible, I could scarcely even conjecture. Walter de la Poer must have known for years the sinister tales about his family, so that this material could have given him no fresh impulse. Had he, then, witnessed some appalling ancient rite, or stumbled upon some frightful and revealing symbol in the priory or its vicinity? He was reputed to have been a shy, gentle youth in England. In Virginia he seemed not so much hard or bitter as harassed and apprehensive. He was spoken of in the diary of another gentleman adventurer, Francis Harley of Bellview, as a man of unexampled justice, honour, and delicacy.

On 22nd July occurred the first incident which, though lightly dismissed at the time, takes on a preternatural significance in relation to later events. It was so simple as to be almost negligible, and could not possibly have been noticed under the circumstances; for it must be recalled that since I was in a building practically fresh and new except for the walls, and surrounded by a well-balanced staff of servitors, apprehension would have been absurd despite the locality.

What I afterwards remembered is merely this – that my old black cat, whose moods I know so well, was undoubtedly alert and anxious to an extent wholly out of keeping with his natural character. He roved from room to room, restless and disturbed, and sniffed constantly about the walls which formed part of the Gothic structure. I realize how trite this sounds – like the inevitable dog in the ghost story, which always growls before his master sees the sheeted figure – yet I cannot consistently suppress it.

The following day a servant complained of restlessness among all the cats in the house. He came to me in my study, a lofty west room on the second story, with groined arches, black oak panelling, and a triple Gothic window overlooking the limestone cliff and desolate valley; and even as he spoke I saw the jetty form of Nigger-Man creeping along the west wall and scratching at the new panels which overlaid the ancient stone.

I told the man that there must be some singular odour or emanation from the old stonework, imperceptible to human senses, but affecting the delicate organs of cats even through the new woodwork. This I truly believed, and when the fellow suggested the presence of mice or rats, I mentioned that there had been no rats there for three hundred years, and that even the field mice of the surrounding country could hardly be found in these high walls, where they had never been known to stray. That afternoon I called on Capt. Norrys, and he assured me that it would be quite incredible for field mice to infest the priory in such a sudden and unprecedented fashion.

That night, dispensing as usual with a valet, I retired in the west tower chamber which I had chosen as my own, reached from the study by a stone staircase and short gallery – the former partly ancient, the latter entirely restored. This room was circular, very high, and without wainscotting, being hung with arras which I had myself chosen in London.

Seeing that Nigger-Man was with me, I shut the heavy Gothic door and retired by the light of the electric bulbs which so cleverly counterfeited candles, finally switching off the light and sinking on the carved and canopied four-poster, with the venerable cat in his accustomed place across my feet. I did not draw the curtains, but gazed out at the narrow north window which I faced. There was a suspicion of aurora in the sky, and the delicate traceries of the window were pleasantly silhouetted.

At some time I must have fallen quietly asleep, for I recall a distinct sense of leaving strange dreams, when the cat started violently from his placid position. I saw him in the faint auroral glow, head strained forward, forefeet on my ankles, and hind feet stretched behind. He was looking intensely at a point on the wall somewhat west of the window, a point which to my eye had nothing to mark it, but towards which all my attention was now directed.

And as I watched, I knew that Nigger-Man was not vainly excited. Whether the arras actually moved I cannot say. I think it did, very slightly. But what I can swear to is that behind it I heard a low, distinct scurrying as of rats or mice. In a moment the cat had jumped bodily on the screening tapestry, bringing the affected section to the floor with his weight, and exposing a damp, ancient wall of stone; patched here and there by the restorers, and devoid of any trace of rodent prowlers.

Nigger-Man raced up and down the floor by this part of the wall, clawing the fallen arras and seemingly trying at times to insert a paw between the wall and the oaken floor. He found nothing, and after a time returned wearily to his place across my feet. I had not moved, but I did not sleep again that night.

In the morning I questioned all the servants, and found that none of them had noticed anything unusual, save that the cook remembered the actions of a cat which had rested on her window-sill. This cat had howled at some unknown hour of the night, awaking the cook in time for her to see him dart purposefully out of the open door down the stairs. I drowsed away the noontime, and in the afternoon called again on Capt. Norrys, who became exceedingly interested in what I told him. The odd incidents – so slight yet so curious – appealed to his sense of the picturesque, and elicited from him a number of reminiscences of local ghostly lore. We were genuinely perplexed at the presence of rats, and Norrys lent me some traps and Paris green, which I had the servants place in strategic localities when I returned.

I retired early, being very sleepy, but was harassed by dreams of the most horrible sort. I seemed to be looking down from an immense height upon a twilit grotto, knee-deep with filth, where a white-bearded daemon swineherd drove about with his staff a flock of fungous, flabby beasts whose appearance filled me with unutterable loathing. Then, as the swineherd paused and nodded over his task, a mighty swarm of rats rained down on the stinking abyss and fell to devouring beasts and man alike.

From this terrific vision I was abruptly awaked by the motions of Nigger-Man, who had been sleeping as usual across my feet. This time I did not have to question the source of his snarls and hisses, and of the fear which made him sink his claws into my ankle, unconscious of their effect; for on every side of the chamber the walls were alive with nauseous sound – the verminous slithering of ravenous, gigantic rats. There was now no aurora to show the state of the arras – the fallen section of which had been replaced – but I was not too frightened to switch on the light.

As the bulbs leapt into radiance I saw a hideous shaking all over the tapestry, causing the somewhat peculiar designs to execute a singular dance of death. This motion disappeared almost at once, and the sound with it. Springing out of bed, I poked at the arras with the long handle of a warming-pan that rested near, and lifted one section to see what lay beneath. There was nothing but the patched stone wall, and even the cat had lost his tense realization of abnormal presences. When I examined the circular trap that had been placed in the room, I found all of the openings sprung, though no trace remained of what had been caught and had escaped.

Further sleep was out of the question, so, lighting a candle, I opened the door and went out in the gallery towards the stairs to my study, Nigger-Man following at my heels. Before we had reached the stone steps, however, the cat darted ahead of me and vanished down the ancient flight. As I descended the stairs myself, I became suddenly aware of sounds in the great room below; sounds of a nature which could not be mistaken.

The oak-panelled walls were alive with rats, scampering and milling, whilst Nigger-Man was racing about with the fury of a baffled hunter. Reaching the bottom, I switched on the light, which did not this time cause the noise to subside. The rats continued their riot, stampeding with such force and distinctness that I could finally assign to their motions a definite direction. These creatures, in numbers apparently inexhaustible, were engaged in one stupendous migration from inconceivable heights to some depth conceivably or inconceivably below.

I now heard steps in the corridor, and in another moment two servants pushed open the massive door. They were searching the house for some unknown source of disturbance which had thrown all the cats into a snarling panic and caused them to plunge precipitately down several flights of stairs and squat, yowling, before the closed door to the sub-cellar. I asked them if they had heard the rats, but they replied in the negative. And when I turned to call their attention to the sounds in the panels, I realized that the noise had ceased.

With the two men, I went down to the door of the sub-cellar, but found the cats already dispersed. Later I resolved to explore the crypt below, but for the present I merely made a round of the traps. All were sprung, yet all were tenantless. Satisfying myself that no one had heard the rats save the felines and me, I sat in my study till morning, thinking profoundly and recalling every scrap of legend I had unearthed concerning the building I inhabited.

I slept some in the forenoon, leaning back in the one comfortable library chair which my medieval plan of furnishing could not banish. Later I telephoned to Captain Norrys, who came over and helped me explore the sub-cellar.

Absolutely nothing untoward was found, although we could not repress a thrill at the knowledge that this vault was built by Roman hands. Every low arch and massive pillar was Roman – not the debased Romanesque of the bungling Saxons, but the severe and harmonious classicism of the age of the Caesars; indeed, the walls abounded with inscriptions familiar to the antiquarians who had repeatedly explored the place – things like 'P. GETAE. PROP . . . TEMP . . . DONA . . .' and 'L. PRAEC . . . VS PONTIFI . . . ATYS. . . .'

The reference to Atys made me shiver, for I had read Catullus and knew something of the hideous rites of the Eastern god, whose worship was so mixed with that of Cybele. Norrys and I, by the light of lanterns, tried to interpret the odd and nearly effaced designs on certain irregularly rectangular blocks of stone generally held to be altars, but could make nothing of them. We remembered that one pattern, a sort of rayed sun, was held by students to imply a non-Roman origin, suggesting that these altars had merely been adopted by the Roman priests from some older and perhaps aboriginal temple on the same site. On one of these blocks were some brown stains which made me wonder. The largest, in the centre of the room, had certain features on the upper surface which indicated its connection with fire – probably burnt-offerings.

Such were the sights in that crypt before whose door the cats howled, and where Norrys and I now determined to pass the night. Couches were brought down by the servants, who were told not to mind any nocturnal actions of the cats, and Nigger-Man was admitted as much for help as for companionship. We decided to keep the great oak door – a modern replica with slits for ventilation – tightly closed; and, with this attended to, we retired with lanterns still burning to await whatever might occur.

The vault was very deep in the foundations of the priory, and undoubtedly far down on the face of the beetling limestone cliff overlooking the waste valley. That it had been the goal of the scuffling and unexplainable rats I could not doubt, though why, I could not tell. As we lay there expectantly, I found my vigil occasionally mixed with half-formed dreams from which the uneasy motions of the cat across my feet would rouse me.

These dreams were not wholesome, but horribly like the one I had had the night before. I saw again the twilit grotto, and the swineherd with his unmentionable fungous beasts wallowing in filth, and as I looked at these things they seemed nearer and more distinct – so distinct that I could observe their features. Then I did observe the flabby features of one of them – and awaked with such a scream that Nigger-Man started up, whilst Captain Norrys, who had not slept, laughed considerably. Norrys might have laughed more – or perhaps less – had he known what it was that made me scream. But I did not remember myself till later. Ultimate horror often paralyses memory in a merciful way.

Norrys waked me when the phenomena began. Out of the same frightful dream I was called by his gentle shaking and his urging to listen to the cats. Indeed, there was much to listen to, for beyond the closed door at the head of the stone steps was a veritable nightmare of feline yelling and clawing, whilst Nigger-Man, unmindful of his kindred outside, was running excitedly around the bare stone walls, in which I heard the same babel of scurrying rats that had troubled me the night before.

An acute terror now rose within me, for here were anomalies which nothing normal could well explain. These rats, if not the creatures of a madness which I shared with the cats alone, must be burrowing and sliding in Roman walls I had thought to be of solid limestone blocks . . . unless perhaps the action of water through more than seventeen centuries had eaten winding tunnels which rodent bodies had worn clear and ample. . . . But even so, the spectral horror was no less; for if these were living vermin why did not Norrys hear their disgusting commotion? Why did he urge me to watch Nigger-Man and listen to the cats outside, and why did he guess wildly and vaguely at what could have aroused them?

By the time I had managed to tell him, as rationally as I could, what I thought I was hearing, my ears gave me the last fading impression of the scurrying; which had retreated *still downward*, far underneath this deepest of sub-cellars till it seemed as if the whole cliff below were riddled with questing rats. Norrys was not as sceptical as I had anticipated, but instead seemed profoundly moved. He motioned me to notice that the cats at the door had ceased their clamour, as if giving up the rats for lost; whilst Nigger-Man had a burst of renewed restlessness, and was clawing frantically around the bottom of the large stone altar in the centre of the room, which was nearer Norrys' couch than mine.

My fear of the unknown was at this point very great. Something astounding had occurred, and I saw that Captain Norrys, a younger, stouter, and presumably more naturally materialistic man, was affected fully as much as myself – perhaps because of his lifelong and intimate familiarity with local legend. We could for the moment do nothing but watch the old black cat as he pawed with decreasing fervour at the base of the altar, occasionally looking up and mewing to me in that persuasive manner which he used when he wished me to perform some favour for him.

Norrys now took a lantern close to the altar and examined the place where Nigger-Man was pawing; silently kneeling and scraping away the lichens of centuries which joined the massive pre-Roman block to the tessellated floor. He did not find anything, and was about to abandon his efforts when I noticed a trivial circumstance which made me shudder, even though it implied nothing more than I had already imagined.

I told him of it, and we both looked at its almost imperceptible manifestation with the fixedness of fascinated discovery and acknowledgment. It was only this – that the flame of the lantern set down near the altar was slightly but certainly flickering from a draught of air which it had not before received, and which came indubitably from the crevice between floor and altar where Norrys was scraping away the lichens.

We spent the rest of the night in the brilliantly lighted study, nervously discussing what we should do next. The discovery that some vault deeper than the deepest known masonry of the Romans underlay this accursed pile, some vault unsuspected by the curious antiquarians of three centuries, would have been sufficient to excite us without any background of the sinister. As it was, the fascination became two-fold; and we paused in doubt whether to abandon our search and quit the priory forever in superstitious caution, or to gratify our sense of adventure and brave whatever horrors might await us in the unknown depths.

By morning we had compromised, and decided to go to London to gather a group of archæologists and scientific men fit to cope with the mystery. It should be mentioned that before leaving the sub-cellar we had vainly tried to move the central altar which we now recognized as the gate to a new pit of nameless fear. What secret would open the gate, wiser men than we would have to find.

During many days in London Captain Norrys and I presented our facts, conjectures, and legendary anecdotes to five eminent authorities, all men who could be trusted to respect any family disclosures which future explorations might develop. We found most of them little disposed to scoff, but, instead, intensely interested and sincerely sympathetic. It is hardly necessary to name them all, but I may say that they included Sir William Brinton, whose excavations in the Troad excited most of the world in their day. As we all took the train for Anchester I felt myself poised on the brink of frightful revelations, a sensation symbolized by the air of mourning among the many Americans at the unexpected death of the President on the other side of the world.

On the evening of 7th August we reached Exham Priory, where the servants assured me that nothing unusual had occurred. The cats, even old Nigger-Man, had been perfectly placid; and not a trap in the house had been sprung. We were to begin exploring on the following day, awaiting which I assigned well-appointed rooms to all my guests.

I myself retired in my own tower chamber, with Nigger-Man across my feet. Sleep came quickly, but hideous dreams assailed me. There was a vision of a Roman feast like that of Trimalchio, with a horror in a covered platter. Then came that damnable, recurrent thing about the swineherd and his filthy drove in the twilit grotto. Yet when I awoke it was full daylight, with normal sounds in the house below. The rats, living or spectral, had not troubled me; and Nigger-Man was still quietly asleep. On going down, I found that the same tranquillity had prevailed elsewhere; a condition which one of the assembled savants – a fellow named Thornton, devoted to the psychic – rather absurdly laid to the fact that I had now been shown the thing which certain forces had wished to show me.

All was now ready, and at 11 a.m. our entire group of seven men, bearing powerful electric searchlights and implements of excavation, went down to the sub-cellar and bolted the door behind us. Nigger-Man was with us, for the investigators found no occasion to despise his excitability, and were indeed anxious that he be present in case of obscure rodent manifestations. We noted the Roman inscriptions and unknown altar designs only briefly, for three of the savants had already seen them, and all knew their characteristics. Prime attention was paid to the momentous central altar, and within an hour Sir William Brinton had caused it to tilt backward, balanced by some unknown species of counter-weight.

There now lay revealed such a horror as would have overwhelmed us had we not been prepared. Through a nearly square opening in the tiled floor, sprawling on a flight of stone steps so prodigiously worn that it was little more than an inclined plane at the centre, was a ghastly array of human or semi-human bones. Those which retained their collocation as skeletons showed attitudes of panic fear, and over all were the marks of rodent gnawing. The skulls denoted nothing short of utter idiocy, cretinism, or primitive semi-apedom.

Above the hellishly littered steps arched a descending passage seemingly chiselled from the solid rock, and conducting a current of air. This current was not a sudden and noxious rush as from a closed vault, but a cool breeze with something of freshness in it. We did not pause long, but shiveringly began to clear a passage down the steps. It was then that Sir William, examining the hewn walls, made the odd observation that the passage, according to the direction of the strokes, must have been chiselled *from beneath*.

I must be very deliberate now, and choose my words.

After ploughing down a few steps amidst the gnawed bones we saw that there was light ahead; not any mystic phosphorescence, but a filtered daylight which could not come except from unknown fissures in the cliff that overlooked the waste valley. That such fissures had escaped notice from the outside was hardly remarkable, for not only is the valley wholly uninhabited, but the cliff is so high and beetling that only an aeronaut could study its face in detail. A few steps more, and our breaths were literally snatched from us by what we saw; so literally that Thornton, the psychic investigator, actually fainted in the arms of the dazed man who stood behind him. Norrys, his plump face utterly white and flabby, simply cried out inarticulately; whilst I think that what I did was to gasp or hiss, and cover my eyes.

The man behind me – the only one of the party older than I – croaked the hackneyed 'My God!' in the most cracked voice I ever heard. Of seven cultivated men, only Sir William Brinton retained his composure, a thing the more to his credit because he led the party and must have seen the sight first.

It was a twilit grotto of enormous height, stretching away farther than any eye could see; a subterraneous world of limitless mystery and horrible suggestion. There were buildings and other architectural remains – in one terrified glance I saw a weird pattern of tumuli, a savage circle of monoliths, a low-domed Roman ruin, a sprawling Saxon pile, and an early English edifice of wood – but all these were dwarfed by the ghoulish spectacle presented by the general surface of the ground. For yards about the steps extended an insane tangle of human bones, or bones at least as human as those on the steps. Like a foamy sea they stretched, some fallen apart, but others wholly or partly articulated as skeletons; these latter invariably in postures of daemoniac frenzy, either fighting off some menace or clutching other forms with cannibal intent.

When Dr Trask, the anthropologist, stooped to classify the skulls, he found a degraded mixture which utterly baffled him. They were mostly lower than the Piltdown man in the scale of evolution, but in every case definitely human. Many were of higher grade, and a very few were the skulls of supremely and sensitively developed types. All the bones were gnawed, mostly by rats, but somewhat by others of the half-human drove. Mixed with them were many tiny bones of rats – fallen members of the lethal army which closed the ancient epic.

I wonder that any man among us lived and kept his sanity through that hideous day of discovery. Not Hoffman or Huysmans could conceive a scene more wildly incredible, more frenetically repellent, or more Gothically grotesque than the twilit grotto through which we seven staggered; each stumbling on revelation after revelation, and trying to keep for the nonce from thinking of the events which must have taken place there three hundred, or a thousand, or two thousand, or ten thousand years ago. It was the antechamber of hell, and poor Thornton fainted again when Trask told him that some of the skeleton things must have descended as quadrupeds through the last twenty or more generations.

Horror piled on horror as we began to interpret the architectural remains. The quadruped things – with their occasional recruits from the biped class – had been kept in stone pens, out of which they must have broken in their last delirium of hunger or rat-fear. There had been great herds of them, evidently fattened on the coarse vegetables whose remains could be found as a sort of poisonous ensilage at the bottom of huge stone bins older than Rome. I knew now why my ancestors had had such excessive gardens – would to heaven I could forget! The purpose of the herds I did not have to ask.

Sir William, standing with his searchlight in the Roman ruin, translated aloud the most shocking ritual I have ever known; and told of the diet of the antidiluvian cult which the priests of Cybele found and mingled with their own. Norrys, used as he was to the trenches, could not walk straight when he came out of the English building. It was a butcher shop and kitchen – he had expected that – but it was too much to see familiar English implements in such a place, and to read familiar English *graffiti* there, some as recent as 1610. I could not go in that building – that building whose daemon activities were stopped only by the dagger of my ancestor Walter de la Poer.

What I did venture to enter was the low Saxon building whose oaken door had fallen, and there I found a terrible row of ten stone cells with rusty bars. Three had tenants, all skeletons of high grade, and on the bony forefinger of one I found a seal ring with my own coat-of-arms. Sir William found a vault with far older cells below the Roman chapel, but these cells were empty. Below them was a low crypt with cases of formally arranged bones, some of them bearing terrible parallel inscriptions carved in Latin, Greek, and the tongue of Phrygia.

Meanwhile, Dr Trask had opened one of the prehistoric tumuli, and brought to light skulls which were slightly more human than a gorilla's, and which bore indescribable ideographic carvings. Through all this horror my cat stalked unperturbed. Once I saw him monstrously perched atop a mountain of bones, and wondered at the secrets that might lie behind his yellow eyes.

Having grasped to some slight degree the frightful revelations of this twilit area – an area so hideously foreshadowed by my recurrent dream – we turned to that apparently boundless depth of midnight cavern where no ray of light from the cliff could penetrate. We shall never know what sightless Stygian worlds yawn beyond the little distance we went, for it was decided that such secrets are not good for mankind.

But there was plenty to engross us close at hand, for we had not gone far before the searchlights showed that accursed infinity of pits in which the rats had feasted, and whose sudden lack of replenishment had driven the ravenous rodent army first to turn on the living herds of starving things, and then to burst forth from the priory in that historic orgy of devastation which the peasants will never forget.

God! those carrion black pits of sawed, picked bones and opened skulls! Those nightmare chasms choked with the pithecanthropoid, Celtic, Roman, and English bones of countless unhallowed centuries! Some of them were full, and none can say how deep they had once been. Others were still bottomless to our searchlights, and peopled by unnamable fancies. What, I thought, of the hapless rats that stumbled into such traps amidst the blackness of their quests in this grisly Tartarus?

Once my foot slipped near a horribly yawning brink, and I had a moment of ecstatic fear. I must have been musing a long time, for I could not see any of the party but the plump Capt. Norrys. Then there came a sound from that inky, boundless, farther distance that I thought I knew; and I saw my old black cat dart past me like a winged Egyptian god, straight into the illimitable gulf of the unknown. But I was not far behind, for there was no doubt after another second. It was the eldritch scurrying of those fiend-born rats, always questing for new horrors, and determined to lead me on even unto those grinning caverns of earth's centre where Nyarlathotep, the mad faceless god, howls blindly in the darkness to the piping of two amorphous idiot flute-players.

My searchlight expired, but still I ran. I heard voices, and yowls, and echoes, but above all there gently rose that impious, insidious scurrying; gently rising, rising, as a stiff bloated corpse gently rises above an oily river that flows under endless onyx bridges to a black, putrid sea.

Something bumped into me – something soft and plump. It must have been the rats; the viscous, gelatinous, ravenous army that feast on the dead and the living. . . . Why shouldn't rats eat a de la Poer as a de la Poer eats forbidden things? . . . The war ate my boy, damn them all . . . and the Yanks ate Carfax with flames and burnt Grandsire Delapore and the secret. . . . No, no, I tell you, I am *not* that daemon swineherd in the twilit grotto! It was *not* Edward Norrys' fat face on that flabby fungous thing! Who says I am a de la Poer? He lived, but my boy died! . . . Shall a Norrys hold the lands of a de la Poer? . . . It's voodoo, I tell you . . . that spotted snake. . . . Curse you, Thornton, I'll teach you to faint at what my family do! . . . 'Sblood, thou stinkard, I'll learn ye how to gust . . . wolde ye swynke me thilke wys? . . . *Magna Mater! Magna Mater!* . . . *Atys* . . . *Dia ad aghaidh 's ad aodaun . . . agus bas dunach ort! Dhonas 's dholas ort, agus leat-sa!* . . . *Ungl . . . ungl . . .*

THE RATS IN THE WALLS

rrlh . . . chchch . . .

That is what they say I said when they found me in the blackness after three hours – found me crouching in the blackness over the plump, half-eaten body of Capt. Norrys, with my own cat leaping and tearing at my throat. Now they have blown up Exham Priory, taken my Nigger-Man away from me, and shut me into this barred room at Hanwell with fearful whispers about my heredity and experiences. Thornton is in the next room, but they prevent me from talking to him. They are trying, too, to suppress most of the facts concerning the priory. When I speak of poor Norrys they accuse me of a hideous thing, but they must know that I did not do it. They must know it was the rats; the slithering scurrying rats whose scampering will never let me sleep; the daemon rats that race behind the padding in this room and beckon me down to greater horrors than I have ever known; the rats they can never hear; the rats, the rats in the walls.

ACKNOWLEDGEMENTS

The Publishers wish to thank the following for permission to reprint previously published material. Every effort has been made to locate all persons having any rights in the stories appearing in this book but appropriate acknowledgement has been omitted in some cases through lack of information. Such omissions will be corrected in future printings of the book upon written notification to the Publishers.

A.P. Watt, the Estate of E.F. Benson and Panther Books Ltd for 'Negotium Perambulans' from *The Horror Horn and Other Stories* by E.F. Benson.

Sidgwick & Jackson Ltd and Alfred A. Knopf, Inc for 'The Story of a Panic' from *The Collected Tales of E.M. Forster*. Published 1947 by Alfred A. Knopf, Inc..

The Rungstedlund Foundation of Denmark and Chicago University Press for 'The Sailor-Boy's Tale' from *Winter's Tales* by Karen Blixen.

A.M. Heath & Co. Ltd and the Scott Meredith Literary Agency, Inc., 845 Third Avenue, New York, New York 10022 for 'Pickman's Model', 'The Dunwich Horror' and 'The Rats in the Walls' by H.P. Lovecraft.

GINO'S

ITALIAN COASTAL ESCAPE

GINO D'ACAMPO

First published in Great Britain in 2017 by Hodder
& Stoughton
An Hachette UK company

1

Copyright © ITV Ventures Ltd 2017

Recipes copyright © Gino D'Acampo 2017
Photography copyright © Dan Jones 2017

Additional photography copyright © Abbi-Rose Crook
4, 72, 98, 134, 169, 199; Gino D'Acampo 224;
Matt Russell 198; Shutterstock.com 26–27, 78–79,
110–11, 162–63

Television series *Gino's Italian Coastal Escape*
copyright © ITV Studios Limited 2017.
Licensed by ITV Ventures Ltd. All rights reserved.

Map © Louise Lockhart 2017
(The Printed Peanut)

A CIP catalogue record for this title is available from
the British Library

Hardback ISBN 978 1 473 661516
eBook ISBN 978 1 473 66152 3

Editorial Director: Nicky Ross
Project Editor: Polly Boyd
Assistant Editor: Lauren Whelan
Design and art direction: Georgia Vaux
Photography: Dan Jones
Food Stylist: Gee Charman
Props Stylist: Tonia Shuttleworth
Shoot Producer: Ruth Ferrier
Proofreader: Miren Lopategui
Indexer: Caroline Jones

Typeset in Univers
Colour origination by Born
Printed and bound in Germany by Mohn media

Hodder & Stoughton policy is to use papers that
are natural, renewable and recyclable products
and made from wood grown in sustainable forests.
The logging and manufacturing processes are expected
to conform to the environmental regulations of the
country of origin.

Hodder & Stoughton Ltd
Carmelite House
50 Victoria Embankment
London
EC4Y 0DZ

www.hodder.co.uk

GINO'S

ITALIAN COASTAL ESCAPE

A TASTE OF ITALY FROM THE AEOLIAN
ISLANDS TO ELBA

GINO D'ACAMPO

CONTENTS

MAP: ITALY'S COASTLINE 6

INTRODUCTION 7

ANTIPASTI & SOUPS 11

CALABRIAN SPECIALITIES 26

ITALIAN FOR TWO 43

FISH & SEAFOOD 65

CAMPANIAN SPECIALITIES 78

MEAT & POULTRY 91

LAZIO SPECIALITIES 110

PASTA, GNOCCHI & RISOTTO 125

PIZZA & BREADS 151

TUSCAN SPECIALITIES 162

VEGETABLES 175

DESSERTS 195

INDEX 220

INTRODUCTION

On this latest journey to my wonderful homeland to film *Gino's Italian Coastal Escape* I travelled up Italy's west coast visiting the Aeolian Islands, Calabria, Campania, Capri, Lazio, Tuscany (*Toscana*) and Elba. It was an amazing trip in so many ways, and I was reminded once again of the beauty of the Italian coastline, the incredible quality of the ingredients, and how passionate the locals are about their food, especially their regional specialities.

THE AEOLIAN ISLANDS

I was particularly excited about visiting the Aeolian islands, as I'd heard so much about them yet had never been there before. Situated in the Tyrrhenian Sea, 25km northeast of Sicily (the jumping-off point for the ferry), the archipelago consists of seven tiny volcanic islands – Salina and Panarea (both of which we visited), Lipari, Vulcano, Stromboli, Filicudi and Alicudi. All are protected by UNESCO as a World Heritage Site.

Salina is remarkably green and lush because of its natural freshwater springs. As its name (which means 'salt mill' in Italian) implies, salt is a major part of this island's economy, but it is also famous for its delicious capers and exquisite sweet Malvasia wine. Panarea – the smallest and chicest of the islands – has a rocky, dramatic landscape and is inhabited on just one side. Cars aren't allowed, so residents drive around in three-wheel trucks, golf buggies and scooters. Since just about everything has to be shipped in, the ferry arrivals are a riotous affair as lorry loads of goods are stacked precariously onto these tiny, basic vehicles. The surrounding waters are full of fish, crustaceans and squid. I was lucky enough to go fishing off the island and was thrilled to catch one of the local specialities – *totano*, the red squid.

CALABRIA

We then travelled to the mainland, to the region of Calabria. If Sicily is considered the football of Italy, Calabria is the toe of the boot that's kicking it – and because there is only a thin sliver of water separating the two regions, their history is very similar. Calabria has one of the oldest records of human habitation in Italy, dating back to around 700,000 BCE. For some reason relatively few tourists visit Calabria (although numbers are increasing every year), but I really don't understand why – it's a natural paradise, with 485 miles of coastline and spectacular mountains, and it's still remarkably unspoilt.

Food traditions are very important in Calabria. Vegetables and fruit are widely cultivated, with highlights including Tropea onions, aubergines, figs, liquorice and bergamot, which is not grown anywhere else in Italy (see pages 26–27). One thing locals really know about is the art of preserving food – through salting, smoking, oiling and curing – to counteract spoilage that would otherwise occur rapidly in the humid climate. I love the fact that many local festivals (*sagre*) are held each year to honour the regional ingredients. I think Calabria is a very special place that still sees beauty in the simple things in life.

[7]

CAMPANIA & CAPRI

Moving up the boot I then travelled to Campania, which is where I grew up and my family still lives (and that includes 62 crazy cousins!). This wonderful region encompasses hills, mountains, fertile lowland plains and breathtakingly beautiful coastal areas, which give rise to a wonderfully varied cuisine that draws inspiration from both land and sea (see pages 78–79).

Campania is known as one of the poorer regions of Italy, and that may well be the case when it comes to the economy, but to me it's one of the richest in so many ways. The pace of life is slow, the food is outstanding and the people are warm and full of character. I know I'm biased because it's my home, but it really has so much to offer. You can sunbathe on a Sorrento beach, stroll down the cobbled streets of the picturesque cliffside village of Positano, wonder at the beauty and tragic destruction of Pompeii and Herculaneum almost two thousand years ago, feel the brooding presence of Mount Vesuvius – the only active volcano on mainland Europe – and experience the hustle and bustle of the vibrant city of Naples. Everything you could ever want from a holiday is to be found right there. I try not to be too gushing about this region, but I just love everything about it! And of course there is also the gorgeous neighbouring island of Capri, which is pure opulence with its designer shops and elite restaurants. The must-see site on Capri is the Blue Grotto, a dark cavern where the sea glows electric blue. It is truly magical.

If you ever visit Campania – which you really should if you can – you simply must try the buffalo mozzarella; what many of you know as mozzarella is just not the real thing. And the Neapolitan pizzas – wow … and the freshly caught seafood … and the ice cream … ahhhhhhhhh … OK, I'm getting carried away. Maybe I'd better move on to the next region …

LAZIO

My travels then took me to Lazio, in central Italy, home of the capital city of Rome. Of course, everyone loves to visit Rome – its history and architecture are phenomenal and there is so much to do there, but if you visit the city do try to build in more time so you can venture outside to experience the great pleasures that await you in the rest of this fascinating region. Of Lazio's 5.8 million inhabitants 4 million live in Rome, so you can see that once you leave the city you can certainly find plenty of peace and quiet in the surrounding areas. There are spectacular nature reserves, stunning lakes and wonderful old stone-built villages. The ancient coastal city of Gaeta, just over 100km south of Rome, is also a must. There you'll find the distinctive Gaeta olives and *tiella*, a delicious snack food, as well as many other local specialities (see pages 110–11).

The food in Lazio can be sophisticated or simple and down to earth. Generally, it is richer and more robustly flavoured than the cuisine of neighbouring regions. Braised meat and slow-cooked stews are popular, and appetising dishes are made out of traditional 'poor man's' ingredients such as offal. Some of the best-known pasta sauces originate in this region (including *carbonara* and *arrabbiata*), and the pasta itself tends to be thick and chunky. Other staples include *polenta* and *gnocchi*. Pulses and seafood are popular in the region, and fresh vegetables feature prominently in Lazio cuisine, as the fertile volcanic soil around Rome is ideal for their cultivation.

TUSCANY & ELBA

My final stop was Tuscany. This region, especially Florence, is regarded as the birthplace of the Renaissance, and art and fashion are still as important as ever. However, it also has a more rustic side, which I experienced when I spent an amazing day herding cattle with the famous Tuscan cowboys (*butteri*). The Tuscan style of cooking is generally fairly rustic too, and I love it. Locals seek out only the freshest seasonal produce, so incredible meals are created from whatever is at its best in the market that day. Although the cuisine can be regarded as basic, because it generally doesn't include lots of sauces or spices, the amazing quality of the raw ingredients (see pages 162–63) means that dishes are always full of flavour. White truffles are a special treat that appear in October and November in San Miniato, and the beef from the Chiana Valley is outstanding, so perfect for the popular local speciality *bistecca alla fiorentina* (Florentine steak). As well as tasting delicious, Tuscan food is hearty and filling, probably because bread (often unsalted) is served in or with most dishes. Tuscan wine is also excellent.

I must reserve a special mention for Elba – a stunning, quaint island 10km off the coast of Tuscany. It holds particularly fond memories for me, as it was where I spent my first-ever family holiday. As you may know, this is where Napoleon was exiled for nine months. Quite honestly, I don't know why he didn't just stay and enjoy the rest of his life here – it's hard to think of a better place to retire or be banished to! You're constantly reminded of Napoleon's presence on Elba, but funnily enough when I think of the island what comes to mind first is tasting a pizza made with chickpea flour. At first I was sceptical, but after tasting the pizza I was well and truly converted!

In this brief introduction I have tried to describe some of the wonderful places I was lucky enough to visit and have only touched on the exciting regional ingredients and specialities I discovered there, but you'll find plenty more information on these elsewhere in the book. I know that some of you may never visit Italy, but hopefully with these simple and delicious recipes, which were inspired by my recent trip, I can bring a little bit of Italy to you.

Buon appetito!

Gino xxx

Whenever I travel around Italy I can't resist trying out a wide range of new and different antipasti — for me, they're frequently the highlight of the meal. For this book I've chosen recipes that have a real 'wow' factor. They look and taste amazing, yet the ingredients are mostly easy to find and the dishes simple to prepare — I firmly believe 'special' doesn't have to mean complicated. If you're on the Italian coast you'll always find *antipasti di pesce* (seafood antipasti), so I've included a good selection of seafood recipes here, including tuna carpaccio (raw tuna), two fish salads, fritto misto (mixed fried seafood), a seafood gratin and a traditional fish soup. The other dishes feature meat, vegetables, cheese and even fruit. Generally, hot antipasti are served only before a light meal in Italy.

ANTIPASTI & SOUPS

SALT COD & POTATO SALAD WITH RED ONION & CAPERS

TUNA CARPACCIO WITH ROCKET, CAPERS & BALSAMIC

SEARED SALMON SALAD

BEEF CARPACCIO WITH HORSERADISH & PARMESAN CREAM SAUCE

BAKED PEACHES WITH PARMA HAM & BOCCONCINI MOZZARELLA

PEAR, DOLCELATTE & MASCARPONE TART WITH HONEY & THYME

RICE CROQUETTES WITH ARRABBIATA SAUCE

PRAWN & SCALLOP GRATIN

MIXED FRIED SEAFOOD WITH SPICY LEMON MAYONNAISE

CHICKEN LIVER SKEWERS WITH LEMON BUTTER SAUCE

CANNELLINI BEAN, RED LENTIL & CHILLI SOUP

ROASTED LEEK, CELERY & SPINACH SOUP

AMALFI-STYLE FISH SOUP

SALT COD & POTATO SALAD WITH RED ONION & CAPERS

INSALATONA DI BACCALÀ CON PATATE, CIPOLLE ROSSE E CAPPERI

Baccalà is cod that has been preserved in salt and then air-dried. In the days before refrigeration and good transport links it was preserved out of necessity, so those living inland could enjoy fish all year round. Today there is still a great demand for salt cod, even in coastal areas where fresh fish is abundant – in Calabria, which is surrounded by the sea, it is one of the most popular forms of seafood. It is less widely available in Britain, but you can usually find it in large supermarkets, Italian delis or online. Before cooking, always soak the fish in cold water for 48 hours to rehydrate it and remove excess salt.

450g salt cod, cut into 6 equal-sized pieces
500g Charlotte potatoes, scrubbed
1 large red onion, peeled and finely sliced
30g capers, drained
3 tablespoons chopped fresh flat-leaf parsley

For the dressing
60ml freshly squeezed lemon juice
2 garlic cloves, peeled and crushed
100ml extra virgin olive oil
Pinch of salt

Serves 6

1] To prepare the salt cod, rinse thoroughly under cold running water. Place in a large bowl and pour over cold water then cover with cling film and refrigerate. Leave to soak for 48 hours, changing the water often. Drain and rinse.

2] Place the fish in a medium saucepan with 2 litres of cold unsalted water. Bring to the boil then reduce the heat and simmer for 10 minutes. To test if the cod is done, pull back a small piece of flesh with a fork – it should flake easily. Drain and set aside to cool.

3] Put the potatoes in a medium saucepan and cover with cold unsalted water. Bring to the boil. Reduce the heat and simmer for 20 minutes or until the potatoes feel tender when pierced with a knife. Drain and set aside to cool.

4] To make the dressing, put the lemon juice and garlic in a small bowl and gradually whisk in the olive oil. Add the salt.

5] Place the onion, capers and parsley in a large bowl. Using a fork or your fingers, flake the cooled fish into the bowl, discarding any skin and bones.

6] Slice the cooled potatoes into rounds about 1cm thick and add to the bowl with the fish. Pour over the dressing and gently stir to combine. Transfer to a serving platter.

TUNA CARPACCIO WITH ROCKET, CAPERS & BALSAMIC

CARPACCIO DI TONNO CON RUCOLA, CAPPERI E BALSAMICO

This dish looks amazing and requires no cooking whatsoever, so it's perfect for when you're entertaining. To make life even easier, you can assemble it up to an hour ahead while you enjoy an *aperitivo* with your guests. The sweetness of the balsamic glaze and the saltiness of the capers is a combination made in heaven. It's vital to use very fresh, good-quality tuna for this dish. Serve with toasted ciabatta and a bottle of chilled sparkling wine such as Franciacorta.

Serves 4

300g tuna loin fillet
4 tablespoons extra virgin olive oil
60g rocket leaves
3 tablespoons nonpareille capers, drained

4 tablespoons balsamic glaze
Sea salt flakes
Freshly ground black pepper

1] Wrap the tuna tightly in cling film to create a cylindrical shape. Place in the freezer for about 3 hours until firm but not frozen hard. Put 4 flat serving plates in the fridge.

2] Remove the tuna from the freezer and discard the cling film. Place the fish on a board. Using a very sharp, long-bladed knife, cut across into very thin slices, about the same thickness as smoked salmon.

3] Arrange the tuna slices on the chilled plates. Drizzle over the oil and sprinkle over a few sea salt flakes and a little pepper.

4] Arrange the rocket along the top of the tuna and scatter over the capers. Drizzle over the balsamic glaze.

SEARED SALMON SALAD

INSALATA CON SALMONE SCOTTATO

Salmon is not native to southern Italy, but it often features on the menus of trendy establishments. The chefs like to get creative, combining the rich, oily fish with classic Italian flavours like olives, orange, lemon, fennel, tomatoes and extra virgin olive oil. In this recipe you can use rocket instead of spinach if you prefer, and feel free to add olives or capers for added depth of flavour. Serve with warm, crusty bread.

Serves 6

500g skinned salmon fillet
1 tablespoon extra virgin olive oil
350g frozen podded broad beans
350g baby spinach leaves
1 large fennel bulb, cored
Salt and freshly ground black pepper

For the dressing
Grated zest and juice of ½ unwaxed orange
1 teaspoon Dijon mustard
3 tablespoons extra virgin olive oil

1] Brush the salmon with the oil and season both sides with salt. Place a large frying pan over a medium to high heat. When hot, add the salmon and fry for 6 minutes, then turn and fry for a further 3 minutes. Set aside to cool.

2] Put the broad beans in a small pan and cover with water. Bring to the boil, cover and simmer for 3 minutes. Drain and rinse under cold running water then slip the beans out of their skins. Put in a medium bowl and add the spinach.

3] Slice the fennel very finely lengthways, either on a mandolin or using a sharp knife. Put in the bowl with the beans and spinach.

4] To make the dressing, combine the orange zest and juice and mustard in a small bowl. Gradually add the oil, whisking vigorously as you go, then season with salt and pepper.

5] Pour half the dressing over the vegetables and gently toss together. Transfer to a large serving platter.

6] Using a fork or your fingers, flake the cooled fish into large chunks and scatter them over the salad. Drizzle over the remaining dressing and season with salt and pepper.

...sapore intenso
PRODOTTI DI QUALITA'
PERCOCA
...sapore intenso

BEEF CARPACCIO WITH HORSERADISH
& PARMESAN CREAM SAUCE

CARPACCIO DI MANZO CON CREMINA AL PARMIGIANO E RAFANO

Beef carpaccio is one of those dishes that you tend to order in a restaurant, thinking you could never make it at home. It looks so impressive, yet it's actually incredibly simple. The slicing is the hardest part, but if you freeze the beef for 30 minutes first it will be a lot easier. The horseradish and Parmesan cream sauce in this recipe perfectly complement the raw beef. Serve with toasted ciabatta.

300g beef fillet (ideally the centre cut)
35g frisée lettuce
20g Parmesan cheese shavings

For the sauce
100ml double cream
1 teaspoon hot horseradish sauce
1 teaspoon white wine vinegar
1½ tablespoons freshly grated
  Parmesan cheese
Freshly ground black pepper

Serves 4

1] To make the sauce, put the cream, horseradish sauce, vinegar and Parmesan in a small bowl. Season with pepper and stir to combine. Cover with cling film and chill until ready to serve.

2] Using a sharp knife, slice the beef very thinly. Place a slice between two layers of cling film. Using a meat mallet or heavy-based pan, pound the meat as thinly as possible without tearing it. Repeat for all the slices. Arrange the beef on a large serving platter.

3] Pile the frisée lettuce on top of the beef, drizzle over the Parmesan and horseradish cream and scatter over the Parmesan shavings. Season with pepper.

BAKED PEACHES WITH PARMA HAM & BOCCONCINI MOZZARELLA

PESCHE AL FORNO CON PROSCIUTTO CRUDO E BOCCONCINI DI MOZZARELLA

Some of the best peaches are grown in Campania, in southern Italy. In season between June and September, the most widely available are the yellow peach (*pesca gialla*) and the white peach (*pesca bianca*), although many other more unusual varieties are grown on a smaller scale. Roasted peaches were enjoyed in the Roman times, and although they're usually eaten as a dessert today they also work wonderfully in savoury dishes, as in this recipe – the flavour and texture combinations of the sweet, soft fruit with the salty, crisp ham and tangy, smooth mozzarella are sensational. If you prefer, use roasted figs instead of peaches.

Serves 4

4 ripe peaches, halved and stone removed
3 tablespoons extra virgin olive oil
3 tablespoons balsamic glaze
8 large slices of Parma ham
4 slices of ciabatta bread, about 1cm thick

1 garlic clove, peeled
300g bocconcini mozzarella cheese (mini mozzarella, mozzarella pearls), drained
60g rocket leaves
Salt and freshly ground black pepper

1] Preheat the oven to 180°C/gas mark 4. Put the peaches, cut-side up, on a baking sheet. Drizzle over 1 tablespoon each of the oil and balsamic glaze. Season with salt and pepper. Roast for about 20 minutes or until soft (the cooking time depends on ripeness). Remove from the oven and set aside.

2] Arrange the ham on a non-stick baking sheet, about 30 x 38cm. Lay a piece of foil on top then place a smaller baking sheet, about 25 x 35cm, on top of the foil. Bake for 5 minutes or until the ham is very crisp. Remove the top baking sheet and foil. Leave to cool.

3] Toast the ciabatta on both sides until golden and rub all over with the garlic. Drizzle the remaining 2 tablespoons of oil over the toasted side.

4] Divide the bocconcini, rocket, peaches and ham among 4 serving plates. Drizzle over the remaining 2 tablespoons of balsamic glaze and season with salt and pepper. Serve with the toasted ciabatta.

PEAR, DOLCELATTE & MASCARPONE TART
WITH HONEY & THYME

TORTA DI PERE, DOLCELATTE E MASCARPONE CON MIELE E TIMO

I know that buying shop-bought pastry is cheating, but making puff pastry from scratch is a bit of a faff. And besides, with the shop-bought variety this dish can be prepared in about 15 minutes – and if that's what it takes to get you into the kitchen, I've won! The combination of honey and cheese is very popular in Italy, the sweetness of honey contrasting particularly well with cheeses that are mild and creamy (ricotta), salty (pecorino) or sharp (aged blue cheeses). Serve with a crisp, mixed-leaf salad dressed with extra virgin olive oil and balsamic vinegar.

Serves 6

2 conference pears
Plain flour for dusting
320g shop-bought puff pastry
150g Dolcelatte cheese (room temperature)
150g mascarpone cheese (room temperature)
1 medium egg, lightly beaten

15g pine nuts
1 tablespoon fresh thyme leaves
2 tablespoons runny honey
Freshly ground black pepper

1] Preheat the oven to 180°C/gas mark 4. Peel the pears, slice in half through the stem and remove the core. Cut lengthways into slices about 5mm thick. Set aside.

2] Line a baking sheet, about 30 x 38cm, with baking parchment. Lightly dust the work surface with flour. Roll out the pastry into a rectangle slightly smaller than the baking sheet and carefully transfer the pastry to the prepared sheet.

3] Combine the Dolcelatte and mascarpone in a small bowl. Spread the mixture onto the pastry, leaving a border of about 1cm around the edge.

4] Arrange the pears in slightly overlapping rows on top of the cheese mixture and brush the border with the egg. Bake for 15 minutes.

5] Remove from the oven and scatter over the pine nuts and thyme. Return to the oven for a further 5 minutes or until golden. Drizzle over the honey and season with black pepper. Serve warm.

CALABRIAN SPECIALITIES

The southernmost region of mainland Italy, Calabria is the 'toe' to Italy's 'boot'. A narrow strip of land, it is surrounded by sea on three sides and contains some of the highest mountains in the country. Although Calabria is one of the poorest regions in Italy, it has a strong culinary tradition and many wonderful ingredients, some of which are found nowhere else. As in neighbouring Sicily, the food in Calabria is strongly influenced by Arabic cuisine and is often extremely spicy.

PEPERONCINO CALABRESE

The hot red Calabrian chilli *peperoncino calabrese* (see below), grown by almost every household in Calabria, is used to add flavour and heat to any number of dishes, from vegetable sauces and pork *ragù* for pasta to the local delicacy *nduja* (see opposite). No Calabrian meal is complete without these chilli peppers, used fresh, dried, whole or crushed.

AUBERGINES

Vegetables are very widely cultivated in Calabria, particularly aubergines, which were introduced to the Mediterranean by the Arabs when they ruled in the 9th and 10th centuries. They are incredibly popular in the region and are used in a great number of dishes in many ways, including fried, stewed, stuffed, baked or in pâté. One speciality is *ciambotta*, a stewed aubergine recipe that can be eaten hot or cold – it's a delicious must-try.

CAPERS

The Aeolian island of Salina, west of Calabria, is well known for its delicious capers, which thrive in the volcanic soil. They're used in many dishes in the region, in salads and in cooking, and they're sometimes served simply on their own with fresh home-made bread.

TROPEA ONIONS

Calabria is famous for its sweet red onions (*cipolle di Tropea*), which are in season in spring and summer. They're grown around Tropea, in the Vibo Valentia province of Calabria, on the cliffs that lead down to the sea. The bulbs, which vary in shape from round or oval to elongated, are a wonderful deep purple colour. These onions are a chef's favourite, and are either served raw in salads or are used in cooking.

BERGAMOT

Almost a quarter of Italy's citrus fruit is grown in Calabria, including bergamot (see below), which is not cultivated anywhere else in the country. About the size of an orange but greenish yellow in colour, and more bitter-tasting, the pulp is used in marmalade, and the essential oil extracted from the peel is used to flavour Earl Grey tea and in the perfume industry. It is cultivated mainly along a small stretch of land in southern Calabria, where the temperature and soil are ideal. I've included a dessert flavoured with bergamot in this book (see page 196).

FIGS

Calabria is the principal fig-growing region in Italy. Abundant in September, this wonderful fruit is eaten raw or roasted and many are dried. Calabrian green 'Dottato' figs are considered the best in Italy, having smaller seeds and thicker skins than other figs, making them particularly juicy. A great Calabrian delicacy is figs stuffed with candied orange peel and nuts and dipped in chocolate (see pages 202–3).

FISH & FISH PRODUCTS

The seas around Calabria are rich in fish, particularly swordfish, tuna, sardines and anchovies. A local speciality is *mustica* (also known as *rosamarina*), often referred to as 'caviar for the poor'. It is made from newly hatched anchovies (*bianchetti*), which are salted, dried and then preserved in chilli-flavoured oil.

NDUJA

One of the most exciting ingredients in Calabrian cuisine is *nduja* (pronounced 'en-doo-zha', see below) – a spicy, spreadable sausage, or paste, made from pork and flavoured with hot red Calabrian chillies, which give it its rich red colour. It is usually spread on bread or toast, on its own or with cheese. It goes very well with seafood (see page 74) and transforms dishes by giving added fire – add a spoonful to pep up a sauce, stew or pizza. *Nduja* is made mainly in the town of Spilinga, in Vibo Valentia province, which is where it originated.

PORK & PORK PRODUCTS

Pork is by far the most popular meat in Calabria. Traditional breeds raised in the region are particularly large in size and well suited to the mountainous terrain and climate. Many pork products are produced there, including *prosciutto*, *pancetta*, *capocollo di Calabria* and salami, such as *soppressata*.

PITTA CALABRESE

Not to be confused with Middle-eastern pitta, *pitta calabrese* is a key part of the Calabrian diet. A round flatbread, often with a hole in the centre, it is stuffed and seasoned with various ingredients, including peppers, tomatoes, herbs, anchovies and *nduja*.

LIQUORICE

The climate and soil in Calabria are ideal for growing liquorice, particularly on the Ionian coast. Liquorice root (see below) is thought to aid digestion and is used in many dishes (see page 210). The Calabrians are so passionate about this plant that they have even built a museum dedicated to it, in Rossano.

SWEETS & CAKES

As in neighbouring Sicily, cakes and sweets are great delicacies in Calabria and are often infused with Middle-Eastern flavours. They are frequently linked to local traditions and festivals, such as Christmas, Easter and carnival time. *Mostaccioli*, made of honey, almonds and sweet wine, and *torrone di Bagnara*, a kind of nougat, are among the best known.

RICE CROQUETTES WITH ARRABBIATA SAUCE

ARANCINE ALL'ARRABBIATA

This is a Sicilian recipe I've given a Neapolitan twist by using buffalo mozzarella. You can prepare the croquettes a day ahead; just take them out of the fridge 30 minutes before you need them and roll them in the breadcrumbs once more before frying. The sauce can also be prepared ahead and reheated.

Makes 6

Saffron risotto (see page 147, except omit the peas)
200g '00' grade pasta flour
100g frozen peas, defrosted
2 x 125g balls of buffalo mozzarella cheese, drained and cut into small pieces
150g dried fine breadcrumbs
About 1 litre sunflower oil for deep-frying
Freshly ground black pepper

For the sauce
4 tablespoons extra virgin olive oil
2 garlic cloves, peeled and finely chopped
2 fresh, medium-hot red chillies, deseeded and finely sliced
2 x 400g tins of chopped tomatoes
3 tablespoons chopped fresh flat-leaf parsley
Salt

1] First make the sauce. Heat the oil in a large frying pan over a medium heat. Add the garlic and chillies and fry for about 1 minute, stirring continuously. Tip in the tomatoes and parsley and simmer gently for about 15 minutes, stirring occasionally. Season with salt and set aside.

2] Now make Saffron risotto (see page 147, except omit the peas). Cover and leave to cool for 15 minutes.

3] Meanwhile prepare the batter. Put the flour in a large bowl and add 300ml cold water gradually, whisking until smooth and very runny. Set aside.

4] Tip the cooled risotto onto a clean surface. Work the risotto in your hands for about 5 minutes, squeezing it to make it more compact (it helps if your hands are slightly damp). Shape into 6 balls. Place each ball in the palm of your hand and flatten it a little. Place some peas and mozzarella in the hollow part and gently close the rice around the filling. Dip each ball in the batter then roll lightly in the breadcrumbs to coat.

5] Heat a deep-fat fryer to 190°C, or heat the sunflower oil in a deep pan or wok until very hot. To test the temperature, add a small piece of bread; it will sizzle when the oil is hot enough for frying. Fry the rice balls in 2 batches for about 8 minutes or until golden brown. Remove with a slotted spoon and drain on kitchen paper. Gently heat the sauce and serve with the croquettes.

PRAWN & SCALLOP GRATIN

GAMBERONI E CAPESANTE GRATINATI

The Pozzuoli fish market in Campania is a real institution, both for the professional chef and domestic cook, so when I was in the area I couldn't resist stopping to buy some prawns and scallops to make this heavenly concoction. You can either make this in one large dish to share, as here, or in 4 individual gratin dishes, about 10 x 10cm. Serve with crusty bread to mop up the delicious garlicky sauce.

Serves 4

60g white bread (about 2 slices), crusts
  removed
16 raw king prawns (about 160g), peeled and
  deveined
12 fresh red cherry tomatoes, quartered
8 extra-large scallops (about 200g), with corals
  attached if possible

130g salted butter (room temperature)
2 tablespoons chopped fresh flat-leaf parsley
1 garlic clove, peeled and crushed
½ teaspoon chilli powder
Grated zest of ½ unwaxed lemon
Salt

1] Preheat the oven to 150°C/gas mark 2. First make the dried breadcrumbs: cut the bread into 1cm cubes and spread on a baking sheet in a single layer. Bake for about 20 minutes until crisp and dry. Remove from the oven and leave to cool a little. Put the dried bread in a plastic food bag, seal the bag and crush with a rolling pin. Set aside.

2] Increase the oven temperature to 200°C/gas mark 6. Butterfly the prawns: place a prawn on its back and make a cut down the centre, but do not cut right through. Ease open with your thumb. Place the prawns in a baking dish, about 28 x 20cm.

3] Scatter the tomatoes over the prawns. Cut the scallops in half lengthways and arrange on top of the tomatoes.

4] Place the butter in a small bowl with the parsley, garlic, chilli powder and lemon zest and combine using the back of a fork, then season with salt. Stir in the dried breadcrumbs. Spread the buttery crumbs evenly over the scallops.

5] Bake for 10 minutes or until the breadcrumbs are golden. Serve immediately.

MIXED FRIED SEAFOOD WITH SPICY LEMON MAYONNAISE

FRITTO MISTO CON MAIONESE PICCANTE AL LIMONE

You will find fritto misto in every restaurant along Italy's Mediterranean coast. The classic ingredients are large prawns, anchovies, squid, sardines and sometimes whitebait, but the beauty of the dish is that you can use whatever is on offer at your fishmonger's. The coating is simple – just polenta, flour and seasoning – no egg, no milk, no water. You then just coat the fish, deep-fry and *ecco qua* – Italy's answer to fish and chips!

Serves 4

2 whole medium squid, about 200g in total
8 fresh whole anchovies, descaled and gutted
4 fresh whole sardines, descaled and gutted
4 large raw king prawns (head and shell on)
150g fine polenta
150g plain flour
1 litre sunflower oil for deep-frying

1 unwaxed lemon, cut into wedges
Salt and freshly ground black pepper

For the spicy lemon mayonnaise
250g good-quality mayonnaise
1½ teaspoons chilli powder
Juice of ½ lemon

1] To prepare the squid, pull the tentacles from the body. Feel inside the body and remove and discard the 'quill' (a transparent sliver of cartilage). Wash the inside of the body and peel off the outer skin. Cut off the squid tentacles just below the eyes (discard the head and guts). Discard the small, hard beak at the base of the tentacles. Rinse the tentacles and squid body in cold water.

2] Cut open the body pouch of each squid along one side and score the inner side with the tip of a small sharp knife into a fine diamond pattern. Cut each pouch into quarters (lengthways then across) and the tentacles in half. Rinse the anchovies, sardines and prawns.

3] Put the polenta and flour in a large shallow dish or roasting tin, season generously with salt and pepper and mix thoroughly. Carefully coat the squid, anchovies, sardines and prawns in the seasoned mix.

4] Heat a deep-fat fryer to 180°C or heat the oil in a deep pan or a wok until very hot. To test the temperature, drop a pinch of the flour mixture into the oil; it will sizzle when the oil is hot enough for frying.

5] Deep-fry the seafood in batches until golden and crisp, cooking the anchovies, sardines and prawns for about 1 minute and the squid for about 30 seconds. Remove with a slotted spoon and drain on kitchen paper. Meanwhile, combine all the ingredients for the spicy lemon mayonnaise in a small bowl. Serve the fried seafood immediately with the mayonnaise and lemon wedges.

CHICKEN LIVER SKEWERS WITH LEMON BUTTER SAUCE

SPIEDINI DI FEGATO DI POLLO CON SALSETTA AL BURRO E LIMONE

Every celebratory meal in Tuscany starts with chicken liver pâté, but personally I prefer the more robust simplicity of grilled, skewered chicken livers – silky smooth on the inside, with just a hint of crispness on the outside. I usually pop these skewers on the barbecue when I'm in Italy, but in the absence of a sunny day in Britain a kitchen grill will do the job. Make sure that you don't overcook the livers: they should be pink in the middle; if you cook them until they're browned all the way through, they will be dry and crumbly. Serve with a simple salad.

Serves 4

750g chicken livers, trimmed
2 tablespoons extra virgin olive oil
75g salted butter

Juice of 2 lemons
2 tablespoons chopped fresh flat-leaf parsley
Salt and freshly ground black pepper

1] Soak 4 wooden skewers, about 25cm long, in cold water for 30 minutes. Preheat the grill to its highest setting.

2] Thread the skewers with the chicken livers and place them on a large baking tray. Brush all over with the oil and season with salt and pepper. Grill the skewers for about 6 minutes, turning halfway through.

3] Meanwhile, heat the butter and lemon juice in a small saucepan over a low heat. As soon as the butter starts to melt, stir in the parsley.

4] Transfer the skewers to a serving plate and drizzle over the lemon butter.

CANNELLINI BEAN, RED LENTIL & CHILLI SOUP

ZUPPA PICCANTE DI CANNELLINI E LENTICCHIE ROSSE

This was cooked and served to me by my niece, Sara, when I visited her at her college near Viareggio, in Tuscany. If I'm honest, I wasn't expecting much, but I was really impressed by this spicy soup made from inexpensive ingredients. The Tuscans love their bean soups and generally use a lot of cannellini beans in their dishes – white, rich and creamy, they are incredibly versatile and healthy, being high in fibre, protein and antioxidants, and low in fat.

6 tablespoons extra virgin olive oil
1 large red onion, peeled and roughly chopped
2 large carrots, peeled and roughly chopped
2 celery sticks, roughly chopped
2 tablespoons tomato purée
1 teaspoon chilli powder

2 x 400g tins of cannellini beans, rinsed and drained
75g red split lentils, rinsed and drained
1 litre hot vegetable stock
Pinch of dried chilli flakes to garnish
A few parsley leaves to garnish

Serves 4

1] Heat 3 tablespoons of the oil in a medium saucepan over a medium heat. Add the onion, carrots and celery and fry for 15 minutes until softened but not browned, stirring occasionally. Stir in the tomato purée and chilli powder.

2] Add the beans (reserve 4 tablespoons for garnish), lentils and stock. Bring to the boil then reduce the heat, half-cover the pan and simmer for 20 minutes, stirring occasionally.

3] Remove the saucepan from the heat and purée using an electric blender or food processor until smooth. Check for seasoning.

4] To serve, ladle the soup into warm bowls and garnish with the reserved beans, the chilli flakes and parsley. Drizzle over the remaining 3 tablespoons of oil.

ROASTED LEEK, CELERY & SPINACH SOUP

ZUPPA DI PORRI AL FORNO, SEDANO E SPINACI

The depth of flavour in this soup is incredible, not to mention its rich, vibrant colour. Roasting and charring the leeks rather than simply frying them gives a lovely sweet, smoky flavour, while the mascarpone provides a hint of creaminess. I've used vegetable stock in this recipe, so it's suitable for vegetarians, but chicken stock would be fine too. Serve with warm crusty bread.

Serves 6

5 leeks, cut into rounds 3cm thick
6 tablespoons extra virgin olive oil
1 tablespoon fresh thyme leaves
1 large onion, peeled and roughly chopped
5 celery sticks, roughly chopped
150ml dry white wine

1.3 litres hot vegetable stock
250g fresh spinach
100g mascarpone cheese
15g toasted pine nuts
Salt and freshly ground black pepper

1] Preheat the oven to 200°C/gas mark 6. Place the leeks in a shallow roasting tin, about 25 x 35cm. Drizzle over 3 tablespoons of the oil, scatter over the thyme and season with salt and pepper. Use your hands to mix everything together thoroughly. Roast for 25 minutes, stirring halfway through. Remove from the oven and set aside.

2] Heat the remaining 3 tablespoons of oil in a medium saucepan over a medium heat. Add the onion and fry for 5 minutes, stirring occasionally. Add the celery and fry for about 3 minutes.

3] Increase the heat to high. Pour in the wine, bring to the boil and let it bubble for 1–2 minutes. Add the roasted leeks and the stock and bring to the boil. Reduce the heat to low and simmer gently for 20 minutes, stirring occasionally.

4] Stir in the spinach. When it has wilted (this will take a few seconds), remove the pan from the heat. Blend and season with salt and pepper.

5] To serve, ladle the soup into warm bowls. Add a spoonful of mascarpone in the centre and scatter over the pine nuts.

AMALFI-STYLE FISH SOUP

ZUPPA DI PESCE ALL'AMALFITANA

You can find wonderful fish soups and stews along the Amalfi coast. They all tend to be hearty, substantial and big on flavour, but there are many variations on the theme, depending on the cook's preference and what's available in the market on the day. Here I've used a mixture of haddock, red mullet and prawns, but plenty of other types of fish, as well as mussels, squid and clams, are also popular. Serve with plenty of fresh crusty bread to dunk in the liquid.

3 tablespoons extra virgin olive oil
1 large red onion, peeled and finely chopped
1 teaspoon dried chilli flakes
200ml dry white wine
400ml hot fish stock
1 x 400g tin of cherry tomatoes
300g skinless haddock fillet, cut into
  2cm chunks
300g skinless red mullet fillet, cut into
  2cm chunks

20 large raw prawns, peeled and deveined
1 x 400g tin of cannellini beans, rinsed
  and drained
10 fresh yellow cherry tomatoes, halved
4 tablespoons chopped fresh flat-leaf parsley
Grated zest of 1 unwaxed lemon
Salt

Serves 4

1] Heat the oil in a medium saucepan over a medium heat. Add the onion and chilli flakes and fry for 5 minutes, stirring occasionally.

2] Increase the heat to high. Pour in the wine, bring to the boil and let it bubble for 2 minutes. Stir in the stock and tinned cherry tomatoes, season with salt and bring to the boil. Reduce the heat to medium. Simmer for 20 minutes, stirring occasionally.

3] Reduce the heat and add the fish, prawns and beans. Simmer gently for 10 minutes, stirring occasionally.

4] Stir in the fresh cherry tomatoes and parsley and heat gently. Transfer to warm bowls and sprinkle over some lemon zest. Serve immediately.

I can't tell you how many times I've been asked for suggestions for romantic Italian meals for two. So for those who have asked, and for those who would like to know, this chapter is for you. I've included sumptuous dishes for special occasions, such as lobster and oysters, as well as less extravagant, 'cosier' meals, including a frittatina (Italian-style omelette) and the ultimate baked potato stuffed with Taleggio cheese. Of course, these dishes aren't only suitable for lovers — they're also ideal for that perfect evening in with a friend.

ITALIAN FOR TWO

AUBERGINE, MOZZARELLA & ROASTED RED PEPPER STACK

ITALIAN-STYLE SMOKED HADDOCK & PAPRIKA OMELETTE

DEEP-FRIED SPICY OYSTERS WITH BALSAMIC DIPPING SAUCE

SALMON ESCALOPES WITH CREAMY VERMOUTH SAUCE

SORRENTO-STYLE LOBSTER WITH LIMONCELLO & ROCKET

CHICKEN ESCALOPES WITH WILD MUSHROOMS & THYME

TWICE-BAKED JACKET POTATOES WITH LEEKS & TALEGGIO

SLICED RIB-EYE STEAK WITH BLACK PEPPER BUTTER

AUBERGINE, MOZZARELLA & ROASTED RED PEPPER STACK

TORRETTA DI MELANZANE, MOZZARELLA E PEPERONI ROSSI ARROSTITI

When I was filming *Gino's Italian Coastal Escape* I visited Paestum, near Salerno – home to three amazingly well-preserved ancient Greek temples dating back to 600 BCE. I also visited a local farm, where I lost my heart to Ana Maria – a lovely water buffalo whose milk is used to make the most exquisite buffalo mozzarella, a speciality of Campania (see page 78). There I prepared this super-simple but impressive dish, ideal for a first course or a light lunch. Serve with toasted ciabatta.

2 tablespoons chopped fresh flat-leaf parsley
1 tablespoon shredded fresh mint
125ml extra virgin olive oil
¾ teaspoon smoked paprika
Small handful of walnut halves
1 large aubergine

1 x 125g ball of buffalo mozzarella cheese, drained
50g Parmesan cheese shavings
75g roasted peppers in a jar, drained
Balsamic glaze for drizzling
Salt

Serves 2

1] Put the parsley and mint in a small bowl and pour over 100ml of the oil. Add the paprika and walnuts, crushing them roughly with your hands, and season with salt. Stir well and set aside to infuse.

2] Slice the aubergine into rounds, about 1cm thick. Season both sides with salt.

3] Heat the remaining olive oil in a large frying pan over a high heat. Add the aubergine and fry until golden brown and soft. Remove with a slotted spoon and drain on kitchen paper. Meanwhile, cut the mozzarella into rounds about 5mm thick.

4] Place an aubergine slice in the middle of each serving plate and top with some Parmesan shavings, then some roasted pepper and a slice of mozzarella. Drizzle with some of the infused oil. Repeat the process once more and finish with a drizzle of oil and some balsamic glaze. Serve immediately.

ITALIAN-STYLE SMOKED HADDOCK & PAPRIKA OMELETTE

FRITTATINA CON EGLEFINO AFFUMICATO E PAPRICA

Italian-style omelettes, known as frittata or frittatina, are thicker and chunkier than French-style omelettes and are always completely set. All kinds of ingredients are added to the eggs – cheese, vegetables and herbs are the most common – but here I've used smoked haddock and paprika, a great combination. Smoked salmon and black pepper are good too. When making Italian-style omelettes, beat the eggs very lightly (you don't want air bubbles) and cook the omelette slowly. Serve hot with a simply dressed tomato salad.

Serves 2

300ml full-fat milk
3 bay leaves
250g smoked, undyed, skinned haddock fillets
6 medium eggs
1 teaspoon paprika

30g salted butter
2 tablespoons double cream
2 tablespoons chopped fresh chives
Salt

1] Put the milk and 300ml water in a large, shallow pan. Add the bay leaves and bring to the boil. Reduce the heat, add the haddock and simmer gently for about 4 minutes.

2] Transfer the fish to a large plate and leave to cool. Using a fork or your fingers, flake the fish into large chunks. Set aside.

3] Preheat the grill to its highest setting. Break the eggs into a large bowl, add the paprika and season with salt. Whisk and set aside.

4] Melt the butter in a 23cm heavy-based frying pan over a medium heat. Swirl it around to coat the base and sides of the pan. Pour in the eggs and tilt the pan to distribute the eggs evenly over the bottom.

5] When the omelette is set underneath but still very moist on top, sprinkle over the flaked fish and the chives, then drizzle over the cream. Place under the hot grill for about 2 minutes until set firm.

DEEP-FRIED SPICY OYSTERS WITH BALSAMIC DIPPING SAUCE

OSTRICHE FRITTE PICCANTI CON SALSETTA ALL'ACETO BALSAMICO

The ancient Romans loved oysters – they gorged on them at banquets and considered them a great aphrodisiac. British oysters were particularly highly prized and were transported live, packed in barrels of snow, over the Alps to dinner tables in Rome. To satisfy their craving, by the 1st century BCE the Romans had established the world's first oyster farms. Oysters are often eaten raw, but I also like them deep-fried with a piquant dipping sauce, as here.

10 rock oysters
30g plain flour
30g cornflour
1 teaspoon chilli powder
2 tablespoons sesame seeds
150ml chilled bottled soda water

About 1 litre sunflower oil for deep-frying
Salt

For the dipping sauce
3 tablespoons balsamic vinegar
Juice of 1 lemon

Serves 2

1] First remove the oysters from their shells. Place the oyster flat on a tea towel, with the wider end facing you. Wrap your hand in a bundle of tea towels for protection and hold the oyster at the wider end. At the pointed end, insert the tip of a sharp knife (ideally an oyster knife) between the two shells (hold the blade away from you) and prise the shells apart. Remove the oyster and lay on kitchen paper to dry. Repeat for all the oysters, reserving the deeper shells for serving, if desired.

2] To make the dipping sauce, put the vinegar, lemon juice and 3 tablespoons of cold water in a small bowl and whisk to combine. Pour the mixture into a dipping saucer or oyster shell and set aside.

3] To make the batter, put the flour and cornflour in a large bowl with a pinch of salt. Sprinkle over the chilli powder and sesame seeds and mix together. Gradually add the soda water, stirring as you go. The batter should be very thin.

4] Heat the oil in a deep pan or a wok until very hot. To test the temperature, add a small piece of bread; it will sizzle when the oil is hot enough for frying.

5] Dip the oysters in the batter to coat lightly and fry for no more than 1 minute. Drain on kitchen paper. If you like, put the oysters back in their shells. Serve immediately with the dipping sauce alongside.

SALMON ESCALOPES WITH CREAMY VERMOUTH SAUCE

SCALOPPINE DI SALMONE CON SALSA CREMOSA AL VERMOUTH

Light and delicate, these salmon escalopes with a creamy, sweet vermouth sauce are a great option for an elegant supper for two. The fish fillets need to be sliced very thin; to make things simpler, ask your fishmonger to prepare the escalopes for you. Serve with new potatoes and a crispy salad.

Serves 2

400g skinned salmon fillet (middle fillet)
2 tablespoons olive oil

For the sauce
300ml fish stock
100ml double cream

30ml sweet vermouth (e.g. Martini Bianco)
40g salted butter
1 tablespoon freshly squeezed lemon juice
2 tablespoons chopped fresh flat-leaf parsley
White pepper

1] First make the sauce. Heat the stock, half the cream and the vermouth in a medium saucepan over a medium heat. Bring to the boil and let it bubble, stirring occasionally, until the liquid has reduced to about 100ml.

2] Add the remaining cream, butter and lemon juice. Simmer until the sauce has thickened slightly. Stir in the parsley. Set aside.

3] Preheat the grill to its highest setting. Place the salmon, skinned-side down, on a board. Using a long, thin, sharp-bladed knife, cut the fish slightly on the diagonal into 6 slices (escalopes), each about 5mm thick.

4] Line a baking sheet with foil. Lay the escalopes on the sheet and brush both sides with oil. Grill for 30 seconds until just firm and cooked through.

5] Gently warm through the sauce over a low heat. Divide the sauce between 2 serving plates and arrange 3 escalopes per person on top of the sauce. Sprinkle over a little white pepper and serve immediately.

SORRENTO-STYLE LOBSTER WITH LIMONCELLO & ROCKET

ARAGOSTA ALLA SORRENTINA

This is a luxurious dish for a special occasion when you want to impress. Limoncello is a lovely lemon-flavoured liqueur produced in Campania, particularly in the area around Sorrento and Naples (see page 79). It is popular as an *aperitivo* or *digestivo*, but I've used it in this recipe to enhance the dressing, its light, fresh flavour perfectly complementing the richness of the lobster. I have described how to cook live lobsters here, but you can buy cooked lobster from most fishmongers.

Serves 2

2 live lobsters, each about 800g
2 shallots, peeled and very finely sliced
80ml red wine vinegar
5 fresh yellow cherry tomatoes, quartered
5 fresh red cherry tomatoes, quartered
2 tablespoons chopped fresh flat-leaf parsley
Handful of rocket leaves

For the dressing
Juice of ½ lemon
1 tablespoon limoncello liqueur
6 tablespoons extra virgin olive oil
Salt and white pepper

1] Make some air holes in a large plastic bag, place the lobsters in the bag and seal. Transfer immediately to the freezer for 45 minutes.

2] Place the shallots in a small bowl and pour over the vinegar. Leave to marinate for 20 minutes, then drain and set aside.

3] Meanwhile, bring a large pan of water to the boil, add the lobsters and cook for about 8 minutes. Lift out with tongs and set aside to cool.

4] Remove the meat from the lobsters. First twist off the large claws. Using a nutcracker, small hammer or rolling pin, crack the shells of the claws. Pick out the meat and put it in a bowl.

5] Place one lobster body shell on a board, belly-side down. Using a heavy, sharp knife, split the lobster in half lengthways, cutting from the head to the tail. Pull the halves apart. Discard the intestinal tract from the tail and the stomach sac. Remove the meat from the shell and cut into 2cm chunks. Put in the bowl with the claw meat. Retain the shells and remove and discard the legs. Repeat with the second lobster.

6] To make the dressing, put the lemon juice and limoncello in a medium bowl and gradually whisk in the oil. Season with salt and pepper.

7] Transfer the lobster meat to the bowl with the dressing and stir until well coated. Add the tomatoes, drained shallots and parsley and stir to combine. Divide the rocket among the lobster shells and spoon in the lobster mixture.

CHICKEN ESCALOPES WITH WILD MUSHROOMS & THYME

SCALOPPINE DI POLLO CON FUNGHI DI BOSCO E TIMO

Wild mushrooms are extremely popular in Italy, particularly in Calabria – the largest producer of wild mushrooms in Italy – where they grow in the mountainous forests of Sila. The peak season for mushrooms is April to early November, but the season can sometimes extend into late December in the south. Wild mushrooms make a great pairing with chicken and thyme in this classic dish. Serve with a simple tomato salad.

2 skinless, boneless chicken breasts
30g plain flour
1 garlic clove, peeled
6 tablespoons olive oil
1 teaspoon fresh thyme leaves

150g fresh wild mushrooms
4 tablespoons dry white wine
100ml hot chicken stock
1 tablespoon salted butter
Salt and freshly ground black pepper

Serves 2

1] Place the chicken breasts between 2 sheets of cling film. Using a meat mallet or heavy-based saucepan, pound the chicken to make 5mm-thick escalopes. Season both sides with salt and pepper. Coat lightly in the flour and shake off the excess. Set aside. Flatten the garlic with the back of a knife.

2] Heat 3 tablespoons of the oil in a large frying pan over a high heat. Add the garlic and thyme and fry for 30 seconds, stirring continuously. Tip in the mushrooms and fry for 3 minutes. Transfer the mushrooms and garlic to a warm plate and set aside. Wipe the inside of the pan with kitchen paper, ready to be used again.

3] Place the pan over a medium heat and pour in the remaining 3 tablespoons of oil. Add the escalopes and fry for 2 minutes each side. Pour in the wine and cook for 1 minute. When it has evaporated, return the mushrooms and garlic to the pan, add the stock and simmer for 3 minutes. Add the butter and stir for about 30 seconds.

4] To serve, place the escalopes on warmed plates, spoon over the mushrooms (discard the garlic) and pour over the juices from the pan. Serve immediately.

TWICE-BAKED JACKET POTATOES WITH LEEKS & TALEGGIO

PATATE AL FORNO CON PORRI E TALEGGIO

There are few comfort foods that are easier to prepare than baked potatoes, but sometimes they can become a bit repetitive. However, with just a tiny bit more effort you can transform them into something really special for a cosy supper for two. Taleggio is a great melting cheese with a tangy flavour that goes beautifully with the leeks in this recipe. The mascarpone gives a lovely creamy consistency.

Serves 2

2 large baking potatoes
25g salted butter
1 leek, halved lengthways and finely sliced
100g mascarpone cheese

120g Taleggio cheese, rind removed and
 broken into small pieces
Freshly ground black pepper

1] Preheat the oven to 200°C/gas mark 6. Prick the potatoes with a fork several times. Bake for 1½ hours, turning halfway, or until the centre feels soft when you insert a knife into it.

2] Meanwhile, melt the butter in a small pan over a medium heat. Add the leek and fry for 10 minutes or until tender, stirring occasionally. Remove from the heat.

3] Cut the potatoes in half and scoop out the middle, leaving a thin shell. Put the potato flesh and mascarpone into the pan with the leeks. Mash until smooth then stir in the Taleggio.

4] Pile the cheesy potato mixture back into the potato skins and bake for a further 20 minutes. Finish with a few grindings of black pepper. Serve immediately.

SLICED RIB-EYE STEAK WITH BLACK PEPPER BUTTER

TAGLIATA DI MANZO CON BURRO AL PEPE NERO

Tagliata has become increasingly popular in recent years. It is basically a steak that has been cut diagonally into slices and served with the cooking juices and, sometimes, flavoured butter. It is usually placed on a bed of leaves, such as rocket. Here I've given instructions for a medium-rare steak, but if you like it rare, cook it for just 1 minute each side. It's important not to overcook the meat or it will be tasteless and tough. Always remove steaks from the fridge 30 minutes before cooking to bring them to room temperature.

60g salted butter (room temperature)
2 teaspoons coarsely ground black pepper
50g rocket leaves
80g semi-dried tomatoes in oil, drained
2 tablespoons extra virgin olive oil, plus extra
  for brushing

2 rib-eye steaks, about 150g each (room
  temperature)
Sea salt flakes

Serves 2

1] Put the butter in a small bowl with the black pepper and beat together well using a fork or small wooden spoon. Transfer to a sheet of cling film and form into a cylinder by rolling the cling film. Twist the ends to seal and refrigerate for 2 hours. Discard the cling film and slice the butter into 1cm-thick rounds. Return to the fridge.

2] Put the rocket leaves and tomatoes in a bowl, add the oil and toss together. Arrange on a large flat serving platter.

3] Preheat a ridged cast-iron chargrill pan over a high heat for 5–10 minutes or until very hot. Meanwhile, dry the steaks with kitchen paper and brush both sides with oil.

4] Place the steaks in the pan and cook for 2 minutes. Press down with a fish slice but do not move the steaks around while they are cooking. Turn over and place the pepper butter slices on top of the steaks. Sprinkle over a pinch of sea salt flakes. Grill for a further 2 minutes. Remove from the pan and leave to rest for about 2 minutes.

5] To serve, cut the steak diagonally into slices about 1cm thick and arrange on the rocket and tomatoes. Drizzle over any cooking juices from the pan.

Most of Italy's 20 regions have a coastline, so Italians eat a huge amount of fish and shellfish and have a vast selection of wonderful seafood dishes. Even in areas without a coastline, there is plenty of freshwater fish in rivers and lakes, and salt cod (cod that has been preserved in salt and air-dried) is popular throughout the country. Some of the cold dishes in this chapter can be served as a first course, and conversely some of the seafood dishes in the Antipasti & Soups chapter (see pages 11—41) make a good main course — just adjust the portion sizes and add an accompaniment or two.

FISH & SEAFOOD

TUNA TARTARE

SQUID, SPICY SALAMI & BEAN SALAD

SEAFOOD PLATTER WITH TOMATOES & RED CHILLIES

PARMESAN-CRUSTED COD WITH A CREAMY CAPER & PARSLEY SAUCE

CALABRIAN-STYLE KING PRAWNS IN A SPICY TOMATO SAUCE

CAPRI-STYLE PAN-FRIED SEA BREAM

GRILLED TUNA WITH GARLIC GREEN BEANS, TOMATOES & OLIVES

SEA BASS BAKED IN A ROSEMARY-FLAVOURED SALT CRUST

SEA BASS WITH ROASTED VEGETABLES & ANCHOVIES

CREAMY FISH PIE WITH ROASTED RED PEPPERS & VERMOUTH

TUNA TARTARE

TONNO ALLA TARTARA

You'll find variations of this classic dish in restaurants all along the southern Italian coast, especially in Sicily and Calabria. I've tried many different recipes, but this one is my favourite – it's simple, colourful and packed with fresh flavours. When I'm in Italy I drizzle anchovy extract or dripping (*colatura di alici*, see page 79) over the top. This has an amazingly sweet and intense flavour and can be used to enliven plain spaghetti, potatoes, salads and steamed vegetables. You can buy anchovy extract or dripping online and in delicatessens in Britain, but if you can't find it you can drizzle over a little of the olive oil from the anchovy tin.

Serves 4

400g very fresh skinned tuna loin, chopped into 1cm cubes

6 anchovy fillets in oil, drained and roughly chopped

2 tablespoons capers, drained and roughly chopped

3 tablespoons pitted black olives (preferably Leccino), drained and roughly chopped

3 fresh plum tomatoes (preferably San Marzano), deseeded and chopped into 5mm cubes

1 fresh, medium-hot red chilli, deseeded and finely sliced

1 small spring onion, finely chopped

2 tablespoons chopped fresh flat-leaf parsley

2 tablespoons extra virgin olive oil, plus extra for brushing

Grated zest and juice of 1 unwaxed lemon

8 slices of ciabatta

1 garlic clove, peeled

8 leaves of chicory or Little Gem lettuce

2 tablespoons anchovy extract (optional)

1] Put the tuna, anchovies, capers, olives, tomatoes, chilli, spring onion and parsley in a medium bowl. Stir to combine.

2] Pour over the oil and add the lemon zest and juice. Toss everything together gently. Leave for 5 minutes to allow the flavours to combine.

3] Meanwhile, brush both sides of the ciabatta with a little olive oil and toast under the grill until lightly golden. Leave to cool then gently rub the garlic clove over both sides.

4] Place a chicory or lettuce leaf on each plate and pile the tuna mixture into the leaves. Drizzle over the anchovy extract, if using. Serve with the ciabatta.

SQUID, SPICY SALAMI & BEAN SALAD

INSALATA DI CALAMARI CON SALAME PICCANTE E FAGIOLI

I created this dish on the picture postcard Aeolian island of Panarea, where squid is abundant in the surrounding waters. The salad is full of punchy flavours and robust textures and makes a great summer main course.

Serves 4–6

100g tinned chickpeas, rinsed and drained
100g tinned borlotti beans, rinsed and drained
15 fresh red cherry tomatoes, quartered
50g semi-dried cherry tomatoes in oil, drained
125g pitted green olives
1 fresh, medium-hot red chilli, deseeded and
  finely sliced
1 garlic clove, crushed
3 tablespoons chopped fresh flat-leaf parsley

2 tablespoons freshly squeezed lemon juice
8 tablespoons extra virgin olive oil
400g whole medium squid
80g spicy salami, cut into rounds 5mm thick
  and halved
50g rocket leaves
Large handful (about 40g) of fresh basil leaves
Salt

1] Put the chickpeas and beans in a large bowl with the fresh and semi-dried tomatoes, olives, chilli, garlic and parsley. Add the lemon juice and 5 tablespoons of the oil, season with salt and toss well to coat. Set aside.

2] To prepare the squid, pull the tentacles from the body. Feel inside the body and remove and discard the 'quill' (a transparent sliver of cartilage). Wash the inside of the body and peel off the outer skin. Cut off the squid tentacles just below the eyes (discard the head and guts). Discard the small, hard beak at the base of the tentacles. Rinse the tentacles and squid body in cold water.

3] Cut open the body pouch of each squid along one side and score the inner side with the tip of a small sharp knife into a fine diamond pattern. Then cut each pouch lengthways in half and then across into 7cm lengths. Keep the tentacles whole.

4] Heat the remaining 3 tablespoons of oil in a large frying pan over a high heat. Add the squid, scored-side up, and the tentacles. Fry for about 1 minute, turning halfway, or until golden and caramelized. Add the salami, season with salt and cook for 1 minute.

5] Add the rocket to the bean mixture, toss until lightly coated in the dressing, and place on a large serving plate. Scatter over the squid and salami, sprinkle over the basil and serve immediately.

SEAFOOD PLATTER WITH TOMATOES & RED CHILLIES

PIATTO DI MARE

All restaurants along the coast in Calabria will offer their own version of this wonderful, spicy mixed seafood platter. It's a great sharing dish for when you're entertaining: it looks stunning and makes a festive and celebratory centrepiece. Either hand the platter around or put it on the table so that everyone can help themselves. Serve with a chilled bottle of Italian white wine and plenty of crusty bread to mop up the delicious sauce.

Serves 6

1kg live clams
1kg live mussels
2 whole medium squid, about 200g in total
4 garlic cloves, peeled and sliced
4 fresh, medium-hot red chillies, deseeded
  and finely sliced
8 tablespoons extra virgin olive oil

6 large whole raw king prawns
150ml dry white wine
300g fresh red cherry tomatoes, halved
4 tablespoons chopped fresh flat-leaf parsley
Salt

1] Soak the clams in cold salted water for 1 hour, drain well and scrub the shells under cold running water. Discard any open clams or clams with broken shells. Set aside.

2] Scrub the mussels under cold running water. Rinse away the grit and remove barnacles with a small, sharp knife. Remove the 'beards' by pulling the dark, stringy pieces away from the mussels. Discard any open mussels or mussels with broken shells. Set aside.

3] To prepare the squid, pull the tentacles from the body. Feel inside the body and remove and discard the 'quill' (a transparent sliver of cartilage). Wash the inside of the body and peel off the outer skin. Cut off the squid tentacles just below the eyes (discard the head and guts). Discard the small, hard beak at the base of the tentacles. Rinse the tentacles and squid body in cold water, place on a board and cut into 2cm pieces. Set aside.

4] Put the garlic and chillies in a large saucepan. Add the oil and place the pan over a medium heat. As soon as the garlic starts to sizzle, add the mussels and clams. Cover and cook for 1 minute or until the mussels and clams just start to open. Tip in the prawns and squid, cover again and cook for 2 minutes.

5] Increase the heat, pour in the wine and cook for 3 minutes, uncovered. Stir in the tomatoes and parsley and season with salt. Cook for a further 3 minutes, stirring occasionally. Discard any mussels and clams that have not opened. Transfer to a large serving platter. Serve immediately.

PARMESAN-CRUSTED COD WITH
A CREAMY CAPER & PARSLEY SAUCE

MERLUZZO IN CROSTA DI PARMIGIANO E SALSA AL PREZZEMOLO E CAPPERI

Cod is not native to the Mediterranean (hake is the equivalent), but I know how popular it is in Britain so have adapted this Italian recipe accordingly. The lemon and Parmesan crust adds flavour and contrast in texture and keeps the fish beautifully moist, while the piquant sauce adds pizzazz. It's important to buy sustainable cod: look out for the Marine Stewardship Council (MSC) ecolabel.

Serves 4

80g salted butter (room temperature), cubed
80g fresh white breadcrumbs
80g pine nuts
Grated zest of 1 unwaxed lemon
60g freshly grated Parmesan cheese
Olive oil for greasing
1 whole skinless cod fillet, about 800g
Salt and freshly ground black pepper

For the sauce
500ml fish stock
200ml mascarpone cheese
4 tablespoons capers, drained
3 tablespoons chopped fresh flat-leaf parsley

1] To make the crust, place the butter, breadcrumbs, pine nuts, lemon zest and two-thirds of the Parmesan in a food processor. Season with salt and pepper. Blitz until the mixture binds together. Set aside.

2] Lightly oil a baking sheet. Lay the cod on top, skinned-side down. Season with salt and pepper. Spread the crust mixture in an even layer over the top of the fish. Chill for 30 minutes. Meanwhile, preheat the oven to 200°C/gas mark 6.

3] Sprinkle the remaining Parmesan over the fish and bake for 25 minutes.

4] Meanwhile, make the sauce. Heat the stock in a medium saucepan over a medium heat. Bring to the boil and let it bubble for about 10 minutes or until reduced by two-thirds. Remove the pan from the heat and whisk in the mascarpone. Return the pan to a low heat and simmer for 10 minutes, stirring occasionally. Add the capers and parsley and taste for seasoning.

5] Transfer the cod to a large serving platter and serve with the sauce in a jug.

CALABRIAN-STYLE KING PRAWNS IN A SPICY TOMATO SAUCE

GAMBERONI CON NDUJA CALABRESE

Nduja is a spicy salami paste made with hot Calabrian chillies (see pages 26–27). It is so versatile and will seriously transform your cooking – it's hot, sweet and smoky at the same time, and is perfect in sauces or just on its own, spread on thickly sliced bread. Here I paired it with juicy prawns to create the ultimate classy comfort food. You can find nduja online or in Italian delicatessens, but otherwise use 2 teaspoons of dried chilli flakes instead in this recipe – it won't have the same smoky, meaty flavour but will add heat. Serve with toasted ciabatta.

Serves 4

6 tablespoons extra virgin olive oil, plus extra for drizzling
6 anchovy fillets in oil, drained
1 medium red onion, peeled and finely sliced
150g pitted black olives (preferably Leccino), drained

50g fresh nduja
2 tablespoons capers, drained
3 x 400g tins of chopped tomatoes
100g frozen peas, defrosted
20 large raw king prawns (head and shell on)
4 tablespoons chopped fresh flat-leaf parsley

1] Heat the oil in a large frying pan or wok over a medium heat. Add the anchovies and fry for 3 minutes or until they break down, stirring occasionally. Tip in the onion and fry for about 5 minutes or until slightly softened. Stir in the olives, nduja and capers and fry for about 1 minute.

2] Add the tomatoes and peas and simmer for 6–8 minutes, stirring occasionally.

3] Stir in the prawns and parsley. Cook for about 6 minutes, turning the prawns halfway through cooking.

4] To serve, divide the sauce between 4 bowls or plates and place 5 prawns on top. Drizzle over a little oil. Serve immediately.

CAPRI-STYLE PAN-FRIED SEA BREAM

ORATA ALLA CAPRESE

Simple yet so full of flavour, this is a classic dish from Capri, a beautiful island off
the Sorrentine peninsula. Gilthead sea bream is a firm white fish that is extremely
popular along Italy's Mediterranean coast. The British equivalent, black bream,
has a very short season and is usually available only in late spring, so in Britain
you're more likely to find imported gilthead bream. Sea bass, which is similar, and
salmon are also good for this recipe.

6 tablespoons extra virgin olive oil
200g fresh red cherry tomatoes, quartered
200g fresh yellow cherry tomatoes, quartered
150g pitted black olives (preferably Leccino),
 drained and halved

About 20 fresh basil leaves, shredded
Juice and grated zest of 1 unwaxed lemon
4 sea bream fillets (about 170g each), skin on
4 tablespoons olive oil
Salt and freshly ground black pepper

Serves 4

1] Heat the extra virgin olive oil in a medium frying pan over a medium heat. Add
the tomatoes and olives and fry for 1 minute, stirring occasionally. Stir in the basil
and fry for 30 seconds. Add the lemon juice, season with salt and pepper and stir
to combine. Set aside.

2] Place the fish fillets on a board and pat dry with kitchen paper. Using a sharp
knife, score the fish skin by making 3 diagonal cuts to the point where you can
see the flesh. Season with salt and pepper.

3] Heat the olive oil in a large frying pan over a high heat. When the oil is really
hot, place the fillets skin-side down in the pan and fry for 3 minutes or until the
skin is golden and crisp. (The flesh should be opaque two-thirds of the way up
the fillet.) Turn the fillets and fry for 1 further minute.

4] To serve, spoon the tomato and olive mixture onto serving plates and gently
place 1 fish fillet on top, with the skin-side uppermost. If you like, sprinkle over
a little salt and pepper, add a pinch of lemon zest and serve immediately.

CAMPANIAN SPECIALITIES

Situated on the west coast of southern Italy just above Calabria, Campania has some of the most spectacular scenery in Italy – a dramatic coastline, stunning towns and villages perched high up on the cliffs, and terraces filled with lemon and orange trees sloping down to the sea. Naples, the Amalfi coast, Sorrento, Positano, Ravello, Minori, the island of Capri and the brooding Mount Vesuvius are just some of the highlights of this amazing region. For me, Campania is Italy's larder – you'll find all the ingredients that you associate with Italian cuisine – a great array of pasta, pizzas, buffalo mozzarella and large, ruby-red, gem-like tomatoes – as well as many other local specialities.

AMALFI LEMONS

Huge, succulent, intensely flavoured and gloriously aromatic and sweet, the Amalfi lemon (*sfusato d'Amalfi*, see below) is one of the great prizes of Campania. It grows in abundance on the cliffs above the coast, particularly around Sorrento and Amalfi, and is used in many dishes, both savoury and sweet. Locals sometimes grate its zest over pasta, others eat the flesh on its own. It is also the main ingredient of the drink *limoncello* (see opposite) and is used to make other thirst-quenching drinks, such as *spremuta di limone* (freshly squeezed lemon juice) and *granita* (a semi-frozen dessert or drink). Amalfi lemons are best in summer, as the hot weather makes their flavour even more intense.

SAN MARZANO TOMATOES

The San Marzano plum tomato (see below) – which many chefs consider the best tomato in the world for sauces – thrives in the rich volcanic soil around Mount Vesuvius. It is fleshier than most other tomatoes, with smaller seeds and a robust flavour. These tomatoes are exported all over the world, both fresh and tinned. Officially, they have been named the only tomato that can be used in the 'True Neapolitan pizza' (see opposite).

BUFFALO MOZZARELLA

Water buffalos were introduced to Italy from Asia or the Middle East in the Middle Ages and they were used as draught animals; by the 12th century, their milk was being used to make cheese (although buffalo mozzarella didn't emerge until the 18th century). Produced entirely from buffalo milk, and sometimes referred to as 'white gold' or 'the pearl of the table', *mozzarella di bufala* is a fresh, milky white, stringy-textured cheese that is best eaten the day after it's made. It is a key ingredient in Caprese salad (see page 176) and is also used on pizzas (see page 152). Most imported mozzarella is made from cow's milk and has a firmer, springier consistency and less flavour than buffalo mozzarella.

CACIOCAVALLO CHEESE

Made throughout southern Italy, *caciocavallo* (see opposite) is a hard white aged cheese made from cow's or sheep's milk, with a distinctive gourd-like shape. The name *caciocavallo*, which means 'cheese on horseback', comes from the fact that a pair of cheeses are joined together by a rope and are hung over a wooden beam or board to age. *Caciocavallo* is often served on its own at the end of a meal or is used in cooking.

FISH & SHELLFISH

Seafood is a staple food in Campania, where more people live along the coast than inland. Squid, tuna and anchovies (see below) are very popular, as are clams and mussels. As you would expect, some of the most well-known Campanian dishes have seafood as a main ingredient, including Amalfi-style fish soup (see page 41) and *spaghetti vongole* (see page 132).

PASTA

In the 19th century the Neapolitans were known as 'maccheroni eaters' because of their love of pasta, and today pasta remains extremely popular in the region. Industrial production of dried pasta first started near Naples using durum wheat, and the best-grade pasta is still produced in the town of Gragnano, near Naples. The most popular pasta types are spaghetti, linguine, scialatielli (similar to fettuccine but thicker and shorter), fusilli lunghi (see page 137), ziti (like rigatoni, but a little

thinner and ideal for baking) and paccheri (large tubes that are sometimes stuffed). While in northern Italy the preference is for fresh egg pasta, in the south the pasta is usually dried.

PIZZA

Campania – more specifically Naples – is the home of pizza, and the locals are very proud of their heritage. The Associazione Verace Pizza Napoletana (AVPN) was set up in 1984 to monitor the quality of pizzas and certify chefs in making them the traditional way, using hand-formed dough and designated ingredients for the topping, and baking them in a wood-fired oven for 60–90 seconds. Officially, there are only two types of Neapolitan pizzas that qualify for the trademark 'Vera Pizza Napoletana' – *pizza marinara* (San Marzano tomatoes, extra virgin olive oil, oregano and garlic) and *pizza Margherita* (San Marzano tomatoes, extra virgin olive oil, mozzarella or *fior di latte* cheese, sometimes hard grated cheese, and fresh basil).

COLATURA DI ALICI

A key ingredient in Campanian cooking is *colatura di alici*, or anchovy extract or dripping, which is produced in the small fishing village of Cetara, on the Amalfi coast. Similar to the popular Roman sauce *garum*, it is made by fermenting anchovies in brine, then straining off the juice to use as a flavouring. Anchovy extract is used to add punch to pasta dishes, vegetables, salads and sauces.

LIMONCELLO

Enjoyed as an *aperitivo* before a meal or a *digestivo* at the end, *limoncello* is a sweet lemon liqueur from Campania made from lemon zest from Amalfi lemons, alcohol, water and sugar. It is produced mainly in the area around Naples and Sorrento, on the Amalfi coast and on the islands of Capri, Procida and Ischia. *Limoncello* can be used in cooking, in both savoury dishes (see page 56) and sweet (see page 201).

GRILLED TUNA WITH GARLIC GREEN BEANS, TOMATOES & OLIVES

TONNO GRIGLIATO CON FAGIOLINI VERDI ALL'AGLIO, POMODORI E OLIVE

Chargrilled tuna steak on a bed of green beans, tomatoes and olives makes a tasty, colourful dish for a special summer lunch or a quick supper. It's important not to overcook the tuna: it should be pink in the middle or it will be tough and dry. If you prefer, use green pitted olives or capers in brine instead of black olives. Always buy sustainable tuna from a reputable supplier.

400g fine green beans, trimmed and halved across

4 x 200g tuna steaks (preferably from the loin)

4 tablespoons extra virgin olive oil, plus extra for brushing and drizzling

2 garlic cloves, peeled and sliced

3 large fresh plum tomatoes, deseeded and cut into small cubes

100g pitted black olives (preferably Leccino), drained and halved

4 large fresh mint leaves, shredded

Salt and freshly ground black pepper

Serves 4

1] Bring a small saucepan of salted water to the boil and cook the beans for 3–4 minutes or until al dente. Drain and rinse under cold running water (so they retain their colour and crunch), then drain again thoroughly. Set aside.

2] Preheat a ridged cast-iron chargrill pan over a high heat for 5–10 minutes. Pat the tuna dry with kitchen paper and brush each side with a little oil. Season with salt and pepper. Lay the tuna in the hot pan and cook for 2 minutes each side.

3] Meanwhile, heat the oil over a high heat. Add the drained beans, garlic, tomatoes, olives and mint and fry for 2 minutes, stirring occasionally. Season with salt and pepper.

4] Arrange the vegetables on 4 warm serving plates and place a tuna steak on top (cut in half if the steaks are large). Drizzle over a little oil over and around the tuna and vegetables and grind over some black pepper. Serve immediately.

SEA BASS BAKED IN A ROSEMARY-FLAVOURED SALT CRUST

SPIGOLA IN CROSTA DI SALE AL ROSMARINO

This dish really has the 'wow' factor, so is perfect for entertaining. Imagine your guests' reaction as you bring the tin to the table and crack open the salty crust to reveal the perfectly cooked fish beneath. Baking fish in salt is a very old technique that ensures the fish remains moist. Although you might think the fish would taste incredibly salty, it doesn't, as the salt comes off in large chunks and so is removed before eating. Serve with spinach.

Serves 4

1kg whole sea bass, gutted
3kg rock salt
4 tablespoons chopped fresh rosemary
2 unwaxed lemons, roughly sliced
100g bag crispy mixed salad leaves

For the dressing
100ml extra virgin olive oil
Juice of 1 large lemon
2 tablespoons chopped fresh flat-leaf parsley
Salt and freshly ground black pepper

1] Preheat the oven to 220°C/gas mark 7. Rinse the fish under cold running water and pat dry with kitchen paper.

2] Arrange a layer of salt, 1cm thick, over the bottom of a large roasting tin. Tip the remaining salt into a large bowl and add the rosemary. Mix in enough cold water to moisten the salt slightly, but do not over-wet it; you need to create a stiff slush that can be patted into shape.

3] Place the fish on top of the salt in the tin. Stuff the stomach cavity with the lemons. Cover the top and sides of the fish with the rosemary salt, packing it around the fish to encase it completely. Bake for 25 minutes.

4] Meanwhile, make the dressing. Combine the oil and lemon juice in a small bowl. Slowly pour in 50ml cold water, whisking as you go. Stir in the parsley and season with salt and pepper. Put the salad leaves in a large bowl, pour over a quarter of the dressing and toss to coat. Set aside.

5] To serve, crack open the salt crust with a tablespoon and lift away any large pieces of salt. Use a pastry brush to push away any remaining pieces. Remove the skin with a fork and discard. Run the tip of the fork down the centre of the fish, just to one side of the spine. Gently transfer the fillet to a warm serving plate, then do the same for the second fillet. Turn over the fish and repeat.

6] Drizzle the remaining dressing over the fillets. Serve immediately with the salad on the side.

SEA BASS WITH ROASTED VEGETABLES & ANCHOVIES

SPIGOLA AL FORNO CON VERDURE E ACCIUGHE

Everywhere along the Mediterranean coast in southern Italy you'll find very similar recipes to this using a whole sea bream, salmon, trout and even monkfish. The dish is packed with flavour, and as the vegetables are roasted with the fish, it's a substantial meal in itself and no other accompaniment is needed. If you like a bit of kick, sprinkle over a few pinches of dried chilli flakes.

Serves 4

1 whole sea bass (about 1.6kg), scaled, gutted, gilled, fins and tail trimmed and head removed
100ml extra virgin olive oil, plus extra for brushing
Large pinch of saffron threads
1kg Maris Piper potatoes, peeled and cut into slices 1cm thick

4 large fresh plum tomatoes, quartered lengthways
60g anchovy fillets in oil, drained
150ml hot chicken stock
5 red peppers, deseeded and cut into 8 chunks
6 garlic cloves, halved (skin on)
8 small sprigs of fresh oregano
Salt and freshly ground black pepper

1] Pat the fish dry with kitchen paper and place on a board. Using a sharp knife, score the fish on one side, making 5 diagonal cuts just through to the bones. Score again in the opposite direction to give a criss-cross pattern. Brush all over with oil and season both sides with salt and pepper. Set aside.

2] Preheat the oven to 200°C/gas mark 6. Put the saffron in a small bowl or cup, pour over 3 tablespoons of hot water and set aside to infuse.

3] Bring a large saucepan of salted water to the boil. Add the potatoes, bring back to the boil and simmer for 5 minutes. Drain thoroughly. Arrange the potatoes in a large roasting tin (big enough to hold the sea bass lengthways or diagonally), leaving space around the sides for the red peppers. The potatoes will form a bed for the fish.

4] Scatter the tomatoes and anchovies over the potatoes. Pour over the saffron water (with strands) and the stock. Arrange the peppers around the potatoes and sprinkle over the garlic and oregano. Drizzle the oil over the peppers. Season with salt and pepper. Bake for 15–20 minutes.

5] Remove the tin from the oven and place the fish on top of the potatoes. Bake for about 20 minutes (you know the fish is cooked when the flesh near the bone at the thickest part turns white). Serve immediately.

CREAMY FISH PIE WITH ROASTED RED PEPPERS & VERMOUTH

TORTA DI PESCE CREMOSA CON PEPERONI ARROSTO E VERMOUTH

This is a luxury fish pie with an Italian twist. You can prepare it up to a day ahead, refrigerate it and when you're ready to eat simply pop it in the oven to bake. If making the pie ahead, bring it to room temperature before baking.

Serves 6

Olive oil for greasing
200g skinless salmon fillet, cut into bite-sized
  chunks
200g skinless cod fillet, cut into bite-sized
  chunks
200g queen scallops
200g raw king prawns, peeled and deveined
280g roasted red peppers in a jar, drained and
  sliced

For the topping
750g Desirée potatoes, peeled and cut into
  large chunks
80g salted butter (room temperature), cut into
  small cubes

2 large egg yolks
80g freshly grated Grana Padano cheese
Salt and freshly ground black pepper

For the sauce
3 tablespoons olive oil
50g salted butter
1 large red onion, peeled and finely chopped
1 tablespoon fresh thyme leaves
100ml sweet vermouth (e.g. Martini bianco)
4 tablespoons plain flour
250ml hot fish stock
200ml full-fat milk
5 tablespoons double cream
3 tablespoons chopped fresh flat-leaf parsley

1] To make the topping, cook the potatoes in simmering salted water for 15–20 minutes or until tender. Drain then pass through a potato ricer or mash until smooth. Add the butter and leave to cool slightly. Stir in the egg yolks and season with salt and pepper. Set aside. Preheat the oven to 190°C/gas mark 5.

2] To make the sauce, heat the oil and butter in a medium saucepan over a medium heat. Add the onion and thyme and fry for 5–10 minutes, stirring occasionally. Pour in the vermouth and simmer for about 3 minutes. Stir in the flour and cook for 1–2 minutes.

3] Gradually add the stock, stirring constantly, until smooth. Simmer for 5 minutes or until reduced by one-third. Stir in the milk, reduce the heat and simmer for 3 minutes or until the sauce thickens. Stir in the cream and parsley and season with salt and pepper. Set aside.

4] Grease a 2-litre pie dish with oil and place on a baking sheet. Put the fish, scallops, prawns and peppers in the dish. Season with salt and pepper. Pour the sauce over the seafood mixture and stir to combine. Leave to cool.

5] Spread the topping evenly over the surface. Sprinkle over the Grana Padano. Bake for 30 minutes until golden. Leave to stand for 5 minutes before serving.

Although seafood is very prevalent along the coast in Italy, meat is still extremely popular wherever you go. Pork is probably the most widely available meat, both fresh and cured, as well as chicken — a particular favourite in Tuscany. Beef and veal are most popular in the north, where much of the land is pasture, and lamb is eaten mainly in the mountainous central and southern regions. Many other types of meat that are not at all popular in Britain are enjoyed in Italy, including kid and rabbit, and I have provided recipes for both in this chapter. They taste incredible, and I believe it's important to keep on experiencing new things in life — and that includes new foods. So please do try them — you will be really glad that you did!

MEAT & POULTRY

HERB & MUSTARD-CRUSTED RACK OF LAMB

STUFFED PORK ROLLS IN A TOMATO SAUCE

MAMMA ALBA'S MEATBALLS

POT-ROASTED BEEF IN RED WINE

RED WINE & CHERRY GRAVY

BEEF FILLET WITH PARMA HAM & PESTO IN PUFF PASTRY

ROAST BEEF WITH ROASTED VEGETABLES & FRESH HERBS

TUSCAN-STYLE BARBECUED PORK WITH SPICY BEANS

ROASTED KID WITH GARLIC NEW POTATOES

SWEET & SOUR RABBIT WITH BORETTANE ONIONS

CRISPY CHICKEN WITH A SPICY SAUCE & GREEN BEANS

SPICY CHICKEN WITH NEW POTATOES, TOMATOES & RED PEPPERS

ITALIAN-STYLE ROAST CHICKEN WITH NEW POTATOES & RED ONION

CHARGRILLED CHICKEN WITH GARLIC & ROSEMARY POTATOES

HERB & MUSTARD-CRUSTED RACK OF LAMB

COSTOLETTE D'AGNELLO IN CROSTA DI SENAPE ED ERBE

Lamb is eaten mainly in central and southern Italy, although roasted young spring lamb is traditional throughout the country at Easter. Later in the year, a rack of lamb makes a wonderful dish for a special occasion. Cooking the lamb on the bone and coating it in a herb crust keeps the meat really moist and succulent. Serve with roasted baby new potatoes and green beans.

Serves 4

2 racks of lamb (about 350g each), trimmed
 of excess fat
25g fresh white breadcrumbs
2 tablespoons chopped fresh flat-leaf parsley
1 tablespoon chopped fresh rosemary

1 tablespoon chopped fresh mint
15g freshly grated Parmesan cheese
2 tablespoons olive oil
2 tablespoons English mustard
Salt and freshly ground black pepper

1] Preheat the oven to 200°C/gas mark 6. Season the lamb with salt and pepper.

2] Place the breadcrumbs, parsley, rosemary and mint in a food processor and blitz. Tip into a small bowl and stir in the Parmesan. Set aside.

3] Heat the oil in a large non-stick frying pan over a high heat. When very hot, sear the lamb for about 2 minutes each side or until browned.

4] Transfer the lamb to a baking sheet, flesh-side up. Spread over the mustard. Press the herb crumbs into the mustard.

5] Roast for 15–20 minutes. Remove from the oven, cover with foil and leave to rest in a warm place for 5 minutes before serving. To serve, slice into cutlets.

STUFFED PORK ROLLS IN A TOMATO SAUCE

INVOLTINI DI MAIALE IN SALSA DI POMODORO

There are many variations on the theme of stuffed pork rolls in southern Italy – they may be filled with cheese, prosciutto, sultanas, pine nuts and a variety of other ingredients. In this recipe, thin slices of pork are stuffed with minced pork back fat, parsley and garlic, then browned and simmered in a tomato sauce. Your butcher may be able to supply pork back fat if they make their own sausages, but if you can't find it use unsmoked bacon instead.

Serves 6

125g pork back fat, minced
3 tablespoons chopped fresh flat-leaf parsley
4 garlic cloves, peeled (2 crushed, 2 left whole)
6 pork shoulder steaks, trimmed

3 tablespoons olive oil
2 x 400g tins of chopped tomatoes
6 fresh basil leaves, shredded
Salt and freshly ground black pepper

1] Place the pork back fat, parsley and crushed garlic in a small bowl. Season with salt and pepper. Mix until smooth. Set aside.

2] Place each pork steak between 2 sheets of cling film. Using a meat mallet or heavy-based pan, pound the steak to about 5mm thick. Season with salt.

3] Spread the pork back fat mixture evenly over one side of the pork slices. Roll up and tie with kitchen string to secure.

4] Heat the oil in a flameproof casserole over a medium heat. Add the pork rolls in batches and fry for 8 minutes, turning a couple of times until lightly browned on all sides. Using a slotted spoon, transfer the rolls to a plate.

5] Put the 2 whole garlic cloves in the casserole and fry for 1 minute. Add the tomatoes and basil and season with salt. Bring to the boil then return the pork rolls to the casserole together with any meat juices. Gently submerge the rolls in the sauce. Reduce the heat and simmer for 1 hour, uncovered.

6] To serve, divide the sauce among 6 serving plates (discard the garlic), remove the string from the rolls and arrange the rolls on the sauce. If you like, grind over a little black pepper.

MAMMA ALBA'S MEATBALLS

POLPETTE DI MAMMA ALBA

The secret of my mother's meatballs is very simple – always use two types of mincemeat for texture and flavour (in this case pork and beef) and keep the tomato sauce simple, so you can appreciate the flavour of the meatballs. She also used to bake the meatballs before simmering them in the tomato sauce rather than frying them, as is often the case. Always use fresh breadcrumbs rather than dried or toasted, or the meatballs will be tough and chewy. Serve with plenty of warm crusty bread to mop up the sauce.

Olive oil for greasing
400g minced pork
400g minced beef
150g fresh white breadcrumbs
2 garlic cloves, peeled and crushed
5 tablespoons chopped fresh flat-leaf parsley
100g freshly grated Grana Padano cheese
2 medium eggs, lightly beaten
Salt and freshly ground black pepper

For the sauce
2 x 400g tins of chopped tomatoes
690ml jar of passata (sieved tomatoes)
4 tablespoons extra virgin olive oil
½ teaspoon dried chilli flakes
10 fresh basil leaves, plus extra to garnish

Serves 4

1] Preheat the oven to 220°C/gas mark 7. Grease a large baking sheet with oil and set aside. Place the pork, beef, breadcrumbs, garlic, parsley, Grana Padano and eggs in a large bowl. Season with salt and pepper. Mix with your hands until everything is thoroughly combined.

2] Using dampened hands, take small amounts of the meat mixture and roll into 12 equal-sized balls. Place the balls on the baking sheet. Bake for 12 minutes.

3] Meanwhile, make the sauce. Put the tomatoes, passata and oil in a large saucepan over a medium heat. Stir in the chilli flakes, basil and some salt. Bring to the boil. Reduce the heat, partially cover the pan and simmer for 10 minutes, stirring occasionally.

4] Carefully place the meatballs in the tomato sauce and partially cover the pan again. Simmer for 30 minutes, turning the meatballs occasionally. If the sauce gets too thick, add a little hot water. To serve, scatter over a few basil leaves.

POT-ROASTED BEEF IN RED WINE

STUFATO DI MANZO AL VINO ROSSO

Beef is generally more common in northern Italy than in the central and southern parts of the country, but it is the most popular meat in the Lazio region, particularly in Rome. When bought in a single piece it is often braised for a long time in red wine, with onions, carrots, celery and fresh herbs, as in this recipe. The long, slow cooking time allows the meat to cook to a melting softness. Serve with creamy mashed potato.

Serves 4

1kg beef topside, trimmed
4 tablespoons olive oil
2 large red onions, peeled and finely sliced
2 large carrots, peeled and sliced into 5mm
  rounds
2 celery sticks, cut into 5mm slices
300ml hot beef stock

300ml full-bodied red wine
2 tablespoons tomato purée
2 bay leaves
2 sprigs of fresh rosemary
3 sprigs of fresh thyme
Salt and freshly ground black pepper

1] Preheat the oven to 160°C/gas mark 3. Season the beef well all over with salt and pepper.

2] Heat 2 tablespoons of the oil in a large flameproof casserole over a medium heat. Add the onions, carrots and celery and fry for 10 minutes, stirring occasionally. Using a slotted spoon, transfer the vegetables to a large plate and set aside.

3] Heat the remaining 2 tablespoons of oil in the casserole. When the oil is very hot, sear the beef all over for about 3 minutes or until browned. Remove the beef and set aside.

4] Pour in the stock, scraping up all the sticky bits from the bottom of the pan. Add the wine and bring to the boil. Reduce the heat and simmer for 1 minute. Stir in the tomato purée and herbs. Season with salt and pepper.

5] Return the vegetables and meat to the casserole, bring to simmering point and cover. Cook in the oven for 1 hour and 20 minutes, turning the meat and stirring the vegetables after about 50 minutes. Discard the herbs.

6] To serve, slice the beef and arrange it on a large serving platter. Spoon over the vegetables and the sauce.

RED WINE & CHERRY GRAVY

SALSINA AL VINO ROSSO ED AMARENE

This delicious gravy goes beautifully with a variety of beef dishes, including my Beef fillet with Parma ham and pesto in puff pastry (see page 102) and Roast beef with roasted vegetables and fresh herbs (see page 106). I make it using amarena cherries, which grow in the upper plains of Sorrento. They are quite bitter so are usually preserved in syrup. If you can't find amarena cherries, use red cherries in syrup or 2 tablespoons of cherry jam instead.

3 tablespoons olive oil
1 large red onion, peeled and finely sliced
1 teaspoon salt
3 sprigs of fresh rosemary
1 tablespoon runny honey

500ml full-bodied red wine
400ml hot chicken stock
2 tablespoons balsamic vinegar
1½ teaspoons cornflour
200g pitted cherries in syrup

Serves 4

1] Heat the oil in a medium saucepan over a medium heat. Add the onion and salt and fry for 8 minutes, stirring occasionally. Add the rosemary and honey and fry for 1 minute. Pour in the wine and bring to the boil. Reduce the heat to low and simmer gently for 15 minutes, stirring occasionally.

2] Add the stock and vinegar and simmer for 20 minutes, stirring occasionally. Meanwhile, put the cornflour in a small cup or bowl and stir in 3 tablespoons of water. Set aside.

3] Place a sieve over a medium bowl and pour in the gravy. Using the back of a wooden spoon, press the gravy through. Return the sieved gravy to the saucepan and place over a low heat.

4] Stir in the cornflour mixture, whisking constantly for 1 minute to remove any lumps. When it has thickened slightly, add the cherries and stir for 1 minute.

BEEF FILLET WITH PARMA HAM & PESTO IN PUFF PASTRY

FILETTO DI MANZO IN CAMICIA

This is a classic dish that I learnt at catering college in Naples. It is very similar to beef Wellington – fillet steak wrapped in puff pastry and baked – but uses Italian ingredients such as Parma ham and red pesto instead of pâté and mushrooms. For best results, the beef should be medium rare in the middle. Serve with my delicious Red wine and cherry gravy (see page 101).

Serves 4

800g piece of middle-cut beef fillet, trimmed
5 tablespoons olive oil
10 slices of Parma ham
4 tablespoons shop-bought red, sun-dried
  tomato pesto

500g puff pastry
4 egg yolks
Salt and freshly ground black pepper

1] Wrap a tight layer of cling film around the beef to form a cylinder, then wrap it around twice more for reinforcement. Chill overnight.

2] Heat the oil in a large frying pan over a high heat. Remove the cling film from the beef and season with salt and pepper. When the oil is very hot, sear the meat for 1 minute on all sides – it should be brown all over but still rare in the middle. Remove from the pan and leave to cool.

3] Arrange the Parma ham on a large sheet of cling film, overlapping the slices slightly. Spread a layer of red pesto over the ham. Place the beef in the centre of the ham. Using the cling film, wrap the ham around the beef to create a neat, tight log. Twist the ends of the cling film to seal. Chill for 45 minutes.

4] Roll out the pastry on a lightly floured surface to a rectangle large enough to envelop the beef with a little overlap and allowing about 20cm (8in) extra at either end. Remove the cling film and place the beef in the middle of the pastry. Wrap the pastry tightly around the beef to enclose. Press the edges firmly to seal. Wrap tightly with cling film and chill for 1 hour. Meanwhile, preheat the oven to 200°C/gas mark 6.

5] Remove the cling film. Using the back of a knife, lightly score a line down the centre, then diagonal lines either side to create a herringbone pattern. Beat the egg yolks and add 2 tablespoons of water and a pinch of salt. Brush the outside of the pastry case with the egg and season generously with salt and pepper.

6] Bake for 30 minutes for medium rare, or 10 minutes longer for medium. If the pastry browns too quickly, cover with foil. Remove from the oven and leave to rest for 10 minutes. Cut into thick slices to serve – use a serrated knife to slice through the pastry and ham, then finish with a sharp carving knife for the meat.

ROAST BEEF WITH ROASTED VEGETABLES & FRESH HERBS

ARROSTO DI MANZO CON VERDURE ED ERBE FRESCHE

Historically, Italy is associated more with pork than beef, as pigs are less expensive to raise and easier to butcher than cows. However, the post-war boom brought new wealth to Italy and for the first time in the country's history the average Italian began sitting down to beef for dinner. This dish is one of many cooked by the beautiful people from Catanzaro Lido in the Calabria region.
Serve with crispy roast potatoes and Red wine and cherry gravy (see page 101).

Serves 4

2 leeks, roughly chopped
2 medium carrots, peeled and roughly chopped
2 celery sticks, roughly chopped
1 large fennel bulb, cored and quartered
10 garlic cloves (skin on), halved
8 sprigs of fresh thyme

2 sprigs of fresh rosemary
6 sprigs of fresh sage
4 tablespoons extra virgin olive oil
1.5kg beef topside
Salt and freshly ground black pepper

1] Preheat the oven to 240°C/gas mark 9. Put all the vegetables (including the garlic) and herbs in a large roasting tin, about 25 x 30cm. Drizzle over 2 tablespoons of the oil and season with salt and pepper. Using your hands, mix thoroughly so the vegetables are coated in the oil. Spread out the vegetables over the bottom of the tin.

2] Season the beef with salt and pepper and place it on the vegetables. Drizzle over the remaining 2 tablespoons of oil.

3] Reduce the oven temperature to 200°C/gas mark 6 and roast for 1 hour (for medium rare), basting halfway through. Increase the cooking time by 10 minutes if you prefer your beef well done and reduce by 10 minutes if you like it rare.

4] Transfer the beef to a carving board, cover loosely with foil and leave to rest for 10–15 minutes. Meanwhile, transfer the vegetables to a serving dish and keep warm. To serve, cut the meat into slices and serve with the vegetables.

TUSCAN-STYLE BARBECUED PORK WITH SPICY BEANS

MAIALE GRIGLIATO ALLA TOSCANA CON FAGIOLI PICCANTI

After an afternoon of herding cattle with the Tuscan *butteri* (cowboys), I knew the best way to end the day was to have a hearty barbecue on the beach. You just can't beat a pile of sticky ribs, plump sausages, pork chops and steaks and marinated grilled vegetables, washed down with a few beers or a stiff whisky. If you prefer, the meat can be cooked in the oven at 180°C/gas mark 4 (15–30 minutes depending on the meat) and the beans on the hob (about 15 minutes).

Serves 6

4 pork ribs
4 pork loin steaks
6 pork sausages
4 pork chops
2 fennel bulbs, cored and cut into 3 thick
    pieces
6 cobs sweetcorn
2 large red peppers, deseeded and quartered
4 Romano (long, thin) peppers (left whole)

For the marinade
4 tablespoons olive oil
4 tablespoons balsamic vinegar
50ml red wine
2 tablespoons runny honey

3 tablespoons whisky
3 teaspoons chilli powder
2 teaspoons paprika
2 teaspoons fine sea salt

For the beans
2 tablespoons olive oil
2 medium red onions, finely sliced
3 x 400g tins of borlotti beans, rinsed and
    drained
3 teaspoons chilli powder
3 teaspoons paprika
100ml red wine
Small handful of fresh oregano, shredded

1] Put the meat on a large platter or tray. Add the ingredients for the marinade and mix together with your hands until well coated. Ideally, marinate for 4–5 hours (or minimum 30 minutes).

2] Light the barbecue. When the barbecue is ready (the coals will be covered in a fine greyish white ash), make the beans. Heat the oil in a heavy-based saucepan at the edge of the grill (where the temperature is lower). When hot add the onions and fry for about 5 minutes or until soft, stirring frequently. Add the beans, chilli powder and paprika and stir to combine. Pour in the wine and a dash of water and add the oregano. Cook for 20–25 minutes, stirring occasionally.

3] Take the meat out of the marinade (reserve the marinade). Place the ribs on the barbecue and grill for 8–10 minutes, then add the loin steaks and sausages and cook for 7–8 minutes, then the chops and cook for 5–6 minutes. Turn occasionally but do not move the meat around too much. Meanwhile, lightly coat the vegetables in the leftover marinade. Place the fennel and corn on the barbecue and cook for 8–10 minutes then the peppers and cook for 5 minutes.

LAZIO SPECIALITIES

Located in central Italy, between Tuscany in the north and Campania in the south, Lazio lies at the heart of the country. Its capital is Rome, so the region has a longstanding gastronomic tradition of fine food that dates back over two thousand years, as well as simpler, more rustic fare. Beef and veal are the meat of choice, with *saltimbocca* and braised oxtail being two well-known dishes from the region, but pork, chicken, kid, lamb, rabbit and offal are also popular. The fertile volcanic soil is ideal for cultivating vegetables and fruit, including grapes for wine-making.

OLIVES

Southern Lazio is famous for its wonderful black Gaeta olives. Similar to the Greek Kalamata olives, they have a meaty texture and are considered the best olives for cooking (see page 115), but they are also eaten on their own, in salads or chopped and made into a tapenade.

ONANO LENTILS

Known as the 'lentil of the popes', Onano lentils have been cultivated in the sandy volcanic soils around Onano, in the province of Viterbo, north of Rome, for centuries. They are light brown, with grey, pink or green marbling, and have an intense flavour and creamy consistency. In many regions of Italy, lentils are eaten on New Year's Eve or New Year's Day, as they are believed to bring wealth for the forthcoming year, their round shape being reminiscent of small coins.

ARTICHOKES

The best artichokes in Italy are found in the rich soil of Lazio, in the area around Rome. There are many different varieties, including very small ones that are eaten raw or preserved in oil and served as part of a mixed antipasti. The most famous Lazio dishes using artichokes are *carciofi alla giudea*, from Rome's Jewish quarter, in which artichokes are deep-fried whole in olive oil, and *carciofi alla romana*, in which larger artichokes are stuffed with herbs, breadcrumbs and garlic and baked. The famous festival *Sagra del carciofo romanesco*, which takes place each year in April, celebrates this much-loved vegetable.

BACCALÀ

Traditionally eaten on Fridays, which were decreed 'meatless' days by the Roman Catholic Church, *baccalà* (salt cod) is a staple food in Lazio. It is basically cod that has been preserved by salting then drying. Each region of Italy has its own specialities, but in Lazio it is *baccalà alla romana*, which is salt cod coated in a light batter and deep-fried. It is also often cooked in a tomato sauce with onions and white wine (*baccalà in guazzetto*) or eaten cold in a salad with potatoes (see page 13).

FISH & SHELLFISH

Along the Lazio coast seafood is popular, particularly red mullet, octopus and crustaceans. A great delicacy of the region is the delicately flavoured *mazzancolla*, or *gambero imperiale* (see below), which is a kind of giant king prawn harvested in summer and traditionally served fried or grilled. There is also a lot of freshwater fish from rivers and lakes, including eels.

GUANCIALE

Many meats are cured in Lazio, including *guanciale*. Resembling *pancetta*, *guanciale* is pork cheek that has been salted, rolled in pepper and dried. The curing process lasts about three months. It is often used in cooking, and is the main ingredient in Lazio's pasta speciality *spaghetti all'amatriciana*. Good-quality *guanciale* can also be eaten raw.

CHEESE

Lazio has a strong cheese-making tradition, with the sheep's milk cheese *pecorino romano*, buffalo mozzarella (*mozzarella di bufala*) and *ricotta romana* (see below) being the most popular cheeses in the region. *Ricotta romana* is made from sheep's milk and is eaten either fresh, within days of being made, or it is salted and preserved. It is also used in cooking, for example in tarts, pastries and fritters. *Provatura* (a buffalo milk cheese similar to *mozzarella*) is also popular in Lazio.

PASTA

Some of the most well-known pasta sauces originate in Lazio, including *carbonara* (eggs and *pancetta* or *guanciale*), *amatriciana* (*guanciale*, tomatoes, onions and chilli), *puttanesca* (anchovies, chillies and tomatoes) and *arrabbiata* (a very spicy tomato sauce with chilli). The pasta itself is usually long, such as spaghetti, or tube-shaped, to absorb the hearty sauces.

GNOCCHI

Potato gnocchi are very popular in Lazio, where they're usually made from yellow waxy potatoes and egg (in some regions of Italy they're made from starchy potatoes and no egg). Frequently, they're dressed with the local's favourite – *amatriciana* sauce. Another speciality of Lazio is *gnocchi alla romana*, also known as *gnocchi di semolino*, as they're made from semolina instead of potatoes. This type of gnocchi tend to be served with a creamy sauce, such as béchamel, or simply cream and Parmesan.

TIELLA

A speciality of Gaeta, in southern Lazio, *tiella* (see below) is an enclosed pie made from pizza dough and filled with vegetables and sometimes seafood. Popular as a street food, it is named for the round baking dish in which it is cooked (*tiella* in southern Italy, *teglia* in standard Italian); traditionally this was earthenware but today it is usually metal. When I was filming in Gaeta recently I made *tiella* from escarole (a slightly bitter-tasting, leafy green vegetable in the chicory family) and chillies. It's simple food, but oh-so moreish!

ROASTED KID WITH GARLIC NEW POTATOES

CAPRETTO AL FORNO E PATATE NOVELLE ALL'AGLIO

Kid (young goat) is eaten mainly in central and southern Italy, particularly in mountainous regions. It has a delicate flavour and is similar to lamb, but kid is slightly sweeter, leaner and firmer. It hasn't yet taken off in Britain, which is a pity, as it's delicious and relatively healthy too, having fewer calories than beef, pork, lamb and even chicken. It isn't available in supermarkets, but you may find it at a good local butcher's or farmer's market, and there are specialist suppliers online. Kid meat benefits from long, slow cooking and can become tough if cooked at high temperatures or with insufficient liquid. Don't treat it like lamb and serve it rare; it should be cooked thoroughly, or it will be tough.

Serves 6

3kg kid (bone-in), trimmed and cut into
   18 pieces
5 garlic cloves, peeled and crushed
2 tablespoons chopped fresh rosemary
100ml extra virgin olive oil
4 tablespoons runny honey
100ml hot lamb stock
300ml dry white wine
Salt and freshly ground black pepper

For the potatoes
1kg baby new potatoes (preferably Charlotte),
   scrubbed and quartered lengthways into fat
   chips
6 garlic cloves, peeled and crushed
2 tablespoons chopped fresh rosemary
140ml extra virgin olive oil

1] Preheat the oven to 200°C/gas mark 6. Season the meat with salt and pepper and place in a large roasting tin, about 45 x 35cm, in a single layer.

2] Add the garlic and rosemary. Drizzle over the olive oil and honey and, using your hands, mix together thoroughly to coat the meat. Cover the tin with foil.

3] Roast for 1 hour. Remove the tin from the oven and discard the foil. Turn the meat. Pour in the stock and wine. Return to the oven for a further 45 minutes, turning the meat halfway.

4] Meanwhile, divide the potatoes and garlic between 2 smaller roasting tins, about 25 x 30cm each. Sprinkle over the rosemary and drizzle with the olive oil. Using your hands, toss the potatoes and garlic thoroughly until well coated in the oil. Season with salt and pepper. Roast for 1 hour, turning several times.

5] Remove the meat and potatoes from the oven. Tip the potatoes into the roasting tin with the meat and toss gently in the juices. Serve immediately.

SWEET & SOUR RABBIT WITH BORETTANE ONIONS

CONIGLIO IN AGRODOLCE CON CIPOLLE BORETTANE

Many families in Italy make use of the abundant ingredients on their doorstep – fish caught from the sea, and rabbit, vegetables and herbs from their own back gardens. This recipe came from a wonderful farming family who live near Torre del Greco in Campania – the town where I was born. If you don't fancy eating rabbit, use chicken thighs and legs instead, and if you can't get hold of Borettane onions, small pickled onions in balsamic vinegar make a good substitute.

50g plain flour
1 large rabbit (about 1.8kg), including the liver, heart and kidneys, cut into 8 pieces
6 tablespoons olive oil
1 large red onion, peeled and thinly sliced
75g shallots, peeled and sliced
1 celery stick, cut into 1cm cubes
1 large carrot, peeled and cut into 1cm dice
25g sun-dried tomatoes, drained and finely chopped
1 teaspoon fennel seeds
350ml red wine vinegar

50g brown sugar
2 tablespoons tomato purée
1 litre hot chicken stock
100g Borettane onions in balsamic vinegar, drained
75g pitted black olives (preferably Leccino), drained
40g sultanas
1 tablespoon fresh thyme leaves
25g toasted pine nuts
Salt and freshly ground black pepper

Serves 4

1] Preheat the oven to 180°C/gas mark 4. Put the flour on a large plate and season with salt and pepper. Dust the rabbit pieces with the seasoned flour.

2] Heat 4 tablespoons of the oil in a large flameproof casserole over a medium to high heat. When very hot, add half the rabbit and fry for about 5 minutes each side or until golden brown all over. Transfer to a large plate using a slotted spoon and set aside. Repeat for the remaining rabbit.

3] Add the red onion, shallots, celery, carrot, sun-dried tomatoes and fennel seeds. Fry for about 5 minutes, stirring occasionally. Stir in the vinegar, sugar and tomato purée. Cook for 5 minutes, stirring occasionally. Return the rabbit and any juices to the casserole. Add the stock and bring to the boil. Transfer to the oven, uncovered, for 20 minutes.

4] Remove from the oven and add the Borettane onions, olives, sultanas and thyme. Season with salt and pepper. Return to the oven for a further 25 minutes or until the rabbit is cooked through.

5] Heat the remaining 2 tablespoons of oil in a small frying pan. Add the offal and fry for 2 minutes, turning halfway. Season with salt and pepper. To serve, put the rabbit and offal on a serving platter and pour over the juices. Garnish with pine nuts.

CRISPY CHICKEN WITH A SPICY SAUCE & GREEN BEANS

COTOLETTA DI POLLO CON SALSA PICCANTE E FAGIOLINI VERDI

My aunty Clara is the eldest of my mother's nine sisters and has always been like a second mother to me. When I was a little boy I used to spend every Thursday and Friday afternoon with her and she would often cook this wonderful dish for me. I just love the contrast of textures and flavours – the crispy, Parmesan-coated chicken with the spicy tomato and olive sauce.

Serves 4

3 tablespoons plain flour
3 medium eggs
80g freshly grated Parmesan cheese
60g dried breadcrumbs
4 skinless, boneless chicken breasts
4 tablespoons olive oil
40g Parmesan cheese shavings

For the sauce
3 tablespoons olive oil
2 garlic cloves, peeled and sliced

1 teaspoon dried chilli flakes
2 x 400g tins of chopped tomatoes
150g pitted black olives (preferably Gaeta or Leccino), drained
Salt

For the beans
400g fine green beans
50ml extra virgin olive oil
2 tablespoons white wine vinegar

1] First prepare the sauce. Heat the oil in a medium saucepan over a medium heat. Add the garlic. As soon as it starts to sizzle, add the chilli flakes and fry for 1 minute, stirring continually. Tip in the tomatoes and olives and bring to the boil. Reduce the heat and simmer for 20 minutes, uncovered, stirring occasionally. Season with salt. Set aside.

2] Put the flour on a large plate or tray. Beat the eggs in a large bowl and season with salt. Combine the grated Parmesan and breadcrumbs in a shallow dish. Place the chicken breasts between 2 sheets of cling film. Using a rolling pin, meat mallet or heavy-based pan, pound the chicken to about 1cm thick. Dip each chicken breast in the flour, then the eggs, then finally the breadcrumb mixture. Ensure each breast is evenly coated and press the breadcrumbs firmly into the egg so they stick.

3] Heat the oil in a large frying pan over a medium heat. Add the chicken and fry for 4–5 minutes each side. Drain on kitchen paper. Keep warm.

4] Meanwhile, plunge the beans into boiling water for 2–3 minutes or until al dente. Using a slotted spoon, transfer to a large bowl. While still warm, drizzle over the oil and vinegar, season well and toss to coat.

5] Gently warm through the sauce over a low heat. Divide the sauce among 4 serving plates, then place the chicken breast on the sauce. Scatter over the Parmesan shavings. Serve the beans on the side.

SPICY CHICKEN WITH NEW POTATOES, TOMATOES & RED PEPPERS

POLLO PICCANTE CON PATATE NOVELLE, POMODORI E PEPERONI ROSSI

This is an incredibly simple recipe, perfect for a midweek supper – you just put everything in the roasting tin and pop it in the oven. Being a one-pot dish, minimal washing-up is required and there's no need to cook any additional vegetables, although you may like to serve it with a mixed salad. Make sure you use a large enough roasting tin – ideally the ingredients should be in a single layer so the chicken will turn golden brown, the peppers and onion will start to char around the edges and the potatoes will become lovely and crisp all over.

650g baby new potatoes (preferably Charlotte), scrubbed and halved lengthways
6 fresh plum tomatoes, quartered
1 large red onion, peeled, halved and cut into 1cm slices
2 red peppers, deseeded and cut into 2cm chunks

1 tablespoon dried oregano
1kg chicken legs (skin on)
1kg bone-in chicken thighs (skin on)
75ml olive oil
1 teaspoon chilli powder
Salt

Serves 6

1] Preheat the oven to 220°C/gas mark 7. Put the potatoes, tomatoes, onion and red peppers in a large roasting tin, about 45 x 35cm. Sprinkle over the oregano and season with salt.

2] Season the chicken with salt, put it in the tin and drizzle over the oil. Using your hands, mix thoroughly until the vegetables and chicken are well coated in oil. Arrange the chicken on top of the vegetables, skin-side up. Sprinkle over the chilli powder.

3] Roast for 45 minutes. Remove from the oven and turn over the chicken. Return to the oven for 35 minutes.

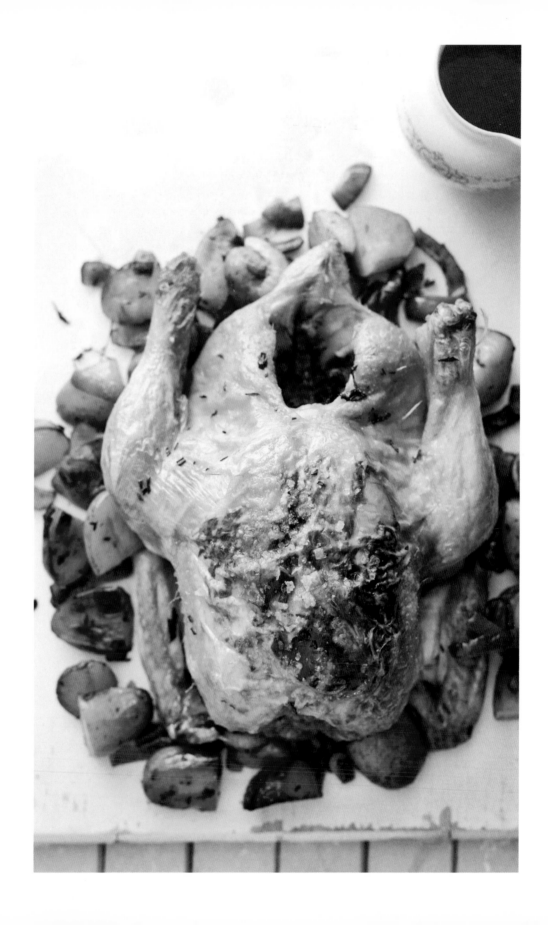

ITALIAN-STYLE ROAST CHICKEN WITH
NEW POTATOES & RED ONION

POLLO ARROSTO CON PATATE NOVELLE E CIPOLLE ROSSE

Italians love the combination of chicken, lemon and fresh herbs. In this recipe I've put a mixture of olive oil, Italian herbs and lemon zest under the skin of the chicken, as it imparts such a lovely delicate flavour and also helps to keep the meat moist. New potatoes and red onion go beautifully with the chicken. You can either use whole baby new potatoes or cut them into chunks, as I've done here. I've used thyme in the potatoes, but feel free to play about with the herbs.

3 tablespoons extra virgin olive oil
Grated zest and juice of 1 unwaxed lemon
1 tablespoon chopped fresh oregano
1 tablespoon chopped fresh rosemary
1 tablespoon shredded fresh basil
1 whole free-range chicken, about 2kg
2 bay leaves
Salt and freshly ground black pepper

For the potatoes
1kg new potatoes, scrubbed and cut into
  large chunks
1 large red onion, peeled, quartered and cut
  into slices 1cm thick
1 tablespoon fresh thyme leaves
2 tablespoons extra virgin olive oil

Serves 6

1] Preheat the oven to 200°C/gas mark 6. Combine the oil, lemon zest and juice, oregano, rosemary and basil in a small bowl.

2] Place the chicken, breast-side up, in a large roasting tin, about 25 x 30cm. Pull back the skin over the breasts (being careful not to tear the skin) and spread the herb mixture over the flesh under the skin. Tuck in the bay leaves and bring the skin back over the flesh. Season the outside of the chicken with salt and pepper.

3] Pour 150ml of water into the tin. Roast the chicken for about 2 hours, basting occasionally. If the water evaporates, add a splash more.

4] Meanwhile, about 40 minutes before the chicken is done, put the potatoes and onion in another roasting tin, about 25 x 30cm. Sprinkle over the thyme and drizzle over the oil. Using your hands, mix thoroughly, ensuring that the potatoes are coated with the oil. Season with salt. Roast for 45 minutes, turning halfway.

5] When the chicken is done (check by inserting a small, sharp knife into the thickest part of the thigh; if the juices run clear, the bird is cooked), remove it from the oven. Transfer it to a board, cover loosely with foil and leave to rest for 10–15 minutes before carving. Pour the cooking juices into a warm jug. Serve the chicken with the potatoes and the juices poured over.

CHARGRILLED CHICKEN WITH GARLIC & ROSEMARY POTATOES

POLLO ALLA GRIGLIA CON PATATE ALL'AGLIO E ROSMARINO

I made this delicious chargrilled chicken dish when we were filming on the wonderful island of Elba, off the coast of Tuscany. There I had the privilege of meeting octogenarian Roberto, who's been studying and working with bees for over 40 years. He taught me how to 'whisper' to the bees and I managed to harvest some fresh honey straight from the hive. I then rubbed it over the meat for added flavour before chargrilling. This is a great way to cook chicken, and the garlic and rosemary potatoes make a wonderful accompaniment.

Serves 4

1.3kg whole free-range chicken
3 tablespoons runny honey
1 tablespoon fresh chopped rosemary
2 garlic cloves, peeled and crushed
3 tablespoons tomato purée
50ml extra virgin olive oil
Juice of ½ lemon
1 tablespoon chopped fresh parsley to garnish
Salt and freshly ground black pepper

For the potatoes
500g new potatoes, scrubbed and halved
75ml extra virgin olive oil
4 garlic cloves, peeled and finely sliced
3 sprigs of rosemary, leaves removed

1] To spatchcock the chicken, remove any trussing string and place the bird breast-side down on a board. Using a sharp knife or poultry shears, cut along both sides of the backbone and discard. Turn the chicken over and, using the heel of your hand, press firmly along the breastbone to break it and flatten the bird.

2] Drizzle the honey over the chicken then scatter over the rosemary and garlic. Spread over the tomato purée and drizzle with oil. Season with salt and pepper. Rub the mixture all over the chicken to coat.

3] Preheat a large ridged cast-iron chargrill pan over a high heat for 5–10 minutes. Once hot, reduce the heat to medium and place the chicken breast-side up on the griddle. Squeeze over the lemon juice. Cook for 15 minutes each side or until golden and cooked through. Leave to rest and keep warm.

4] Meanwhile, bring a pan of salted water to the boil. Parboil the potatoes for 4–5 minutes or until tender and drain thoroughly.

5] Heat the oil in a large frying pan over a medium heat. Add the garlic and as soon as it starts to sizzle add the rosemary and potatoes. Season with salt and pepper. Fry the potatoes for 4–5 minutes or until golden brown, turning often.

6] Cut the chicken into pieces and place on a serving platter with the potatoes. Scatter over the parsley.

I could happily eat pasta every day — and many people in Italy do just that. There are so many different kinds of varying shapes and sizes, and such a vast array of pasta sauces, the possibilities are endless. For centuries, pasta was eaten only in central and southern Italy — in some northern regions it didn't become popular until the 20th century — but today it is the staple food all over Italy. One of the great pasta specialities on the coast is spaghetti vongole, made with clams. I cooked it when we were filming in the Bay of Naples and have included the recipe here. Other popular Italian staples are gnocchi (small dumplings) and risotto, which both originate in northern Italy but are now found throughout the country. Many serve them as a first course or an accompaniment, but I love them as a meal in their own right.

PASTA, GNOCCHI & RISOTTO

LINGUINE WITH PESTO, GREEN BEANS & CAPERS

FETTUCCINE WITH NEAPOLITAN RAGÙ

FETTUCCINE WITH NEAPOLITAN SAUSAGES, MUSHROOMS & PEAS

SPAGHETTI WITH SALAMI & COURGETTE IN A RICH, CREAMY SAUCE

SPAGHETTI WITH CLAMS & MUSSELS

FUSILLI WITH VEGETABLES, PANCETTA, PESTO & MOZZARELLA

PRAWN & RICOTTA RAVIOLI WITH OLIVE OIL & FRESH SAGE

POTATO GNOCCHI WITH COURGETTES & TOMATOES

RICOTTA GNOCCHI WITH RED PEPPERS, COURGETTES, BUTTER & SAGE

SAFFRON RISOTTO WITH PEAS

CHICKEN RISOTTO WITH RED PESTO & ROSEMARY

LINGUINE WITH PESTO, GREEN BEANS & CAPERS

LINGUINE CON PESTO, FAGIOLINI VERDI E CAPPERI

This is a great vegetarian pasta dish that makes a nice change from regular pesto. I created it when filming on the beautiful green, fertile Aeolian island of Salina, which is famous for its capers. For added piquancy, squeeze excess water from the capers into your pasta water.

Serves 4

170ml extra virgin olive oil, plus extra for drizzling
1 large garlic clove, peeled and halved
50g pine nuts
60g large fresh basil leaves

70g freshly grated pecorino cheese
50g capers, drained and chopped
500g dried linguine
150g fine green beans, trimmed and halved
Salt and freshly ground black pepper

1] First make the pesto sauce. Put the oil, garlic and pine nuts in a food processor. Blitz for about 1 minute or until the garlic and pine nuts have broken into really small pieces. Add the basil and blitz until smooth. Transfer the mixture to a large bowl. Stir in the pecorino and capers. Season with salt and pepper and set aside.

2] Cook the linguine in a large pan of boiling, salted water until al dente. About 2 minutes before the end of the cooking time, drop in the beans. Reserve 4 tablespoons of the cooking water. Drain the pasta and beans thoroughly.

3] Tip the pasta and beans into the pesto and add the reserved cooking water. Stir gently for about 30 seconds, drizzle over a little extra oil then serve.

FETTUCCINE WITH NEAPOLITAN RAGÙ

FETTUCCINE AL RAGÙ NAPOLETANO

This Neapolitan ragù recipe has been in my family for over 40 years and my mother has never changed a single ingredient. It works to perfection, and the great thing is that you can prepare the sauce a day ahead and it will taste even better the day after. The meat should be crumbly and as soft as butter. Feel free to use rump steak if you prefer, as fillet steak can be expensive.

Serves 6

4 tablespoons olive oil
1 large red onion, peeled and finely chopped
1 large carrot, peeled and finely chopped
1 celery stick, finely chopped
500g fillet steak, cut into 2cm cubes
300ml full-bodied red wine
100ml hot beef stock

4 tablespoons tomato purée
1 x 680g bottle of passata (sieved tomatoes)
10 fresh basil leaves, shredded
500g dried fettuccine
80g freshly grated Parmesan cheese
Salt and freshly ground black pepper

1] Heat the oil in a medium saucepan over a medium heat. Add the onion, carrot and celery and fry for 8–10 minutes, stirring occasionally.

2] Add the steak and fry for 2 minutes. Pour in the wine and let it simmer for about 2 minutes. Season with salt and pepper. Cover and simmer for 30 minutes, stirring occasionally.

3] Stir in the stock, tomato purée and passata. Bring to the boil. Reduce the heat, re-cover and simmer for 1½ hours, stirring every 20 minutes. Stir in the basil and check for seasoning.

4] Cook the fettuccine in a large pan of boiling, salted water until al dente. Drain the pasta thoroughly and tip it back into the same pan.

5] Pour over the sauce and stir for 30 seconds to allow the flavours to combine. Sprinkle the Parmesan over the top before serving.

FETTUCCINE WITH NEAPOLITAN
SAUSAGES, MUSHROOMS & PEAS

FETTUCCINE CON SALSICCE NAPOLETANE, FUNGHI E PISELLI

If you want a hearty, meaty pasta dish on the table within half an hour, this one is for you. The main differences between British sausages and Italian *salsicce* is that Italian sausages are all meat, and in a natural casing. They are also slightly coarser (the meat is cut by hand) and more highly seasoned. Each region has its own type of sausage – generally, the further south you go the spicier the flavour. If you can't find Neapolitan sausages use any other Italian sausages, or buy good-quality British ones with a high meat content and season really well.

Serves 4

6 tablespoons olive oil
1 leek, halved lengthways and finely sliced
100g chestnut mushrooms, sliced
2 tablespoons chopped fresh rosemary
400g Neapolitan sausages or good-quality pork
  sausages, skin removed

100g frozen peas, defrosted
100ml dry white wine
150ml double cream
500g fresh egg fettuccine
80g freshly grated Parmesan cheese
Salt and freshly ground black pepper

1] Heat the oil in a large frying pan over a medium heat. Add the leek, mushrooms and rosemary and fry for 3 minutes, stirring occasionally.

2] Add the sausage meat and fry for 8–10 minutes, breaking it up with a wooden spoon as you go.

3] Stir in the peas and wine. Let the wine bubble for 2 minutes. Pour in the cream, stir well and simmer for 1 minute. Season with salt and pepper. Set aside.

4] Cook the pasta in a large pan of boiling, salted water until al dente. Drain thoroughly and tip it back into the pan.

5] Pour over the sauce and add half the Parmesan. Stir together for 30 seconds to allow the flavours to combine. Transfer to a warm serving bowl and sprinkle over the remaining Parmesan.

SPAGHETTI WITH SALAMI & COURGETTE IN A RICH, CREAMY SAUCE

SPAGHETTI CON SALAME PICCANTE

I love the contrast of the spicy salami with the creaminess of the eggs and cheese in this recipe, and the courgette adds flavour, colour and a soft texture. You can use any pecorino (sheep's milk cheese) for this recipe, but I particularly like pecorino sardo (from Sardinia), as it has a wonderful salty, piquant flavour. If you prefer, use peas instead of courgettes. As with spaghetti carbonara, the heat from the pasta will cook the egg.

5 tablespoons olive oil

1 large courgette, trimmed and cut into 1cm cubes

200g sliced spicy salami, cut into strips

30g salted butter

4 medium eggs

½ teaspoon freshly ground black pepper

4 tablespoons chopped fresh flat-leaf parsley

4 tablespoons full-fat milk

80g freshly grated pecorino cheese

500g dried spaghetti

Salt

Serves 4

1] Heat the oil in a medium frying pan over a medium heat. Add the courgette and salami and fry for 6 minutes, stirring occasionally. Stir in the butter. Remove from the heat.

2] Crack the eggs into a bowl. Add the pepper, parsley, milk and half the pecorino. Season with salt and set aside.

3] Cook the pasta in a large pan of boiling, salted water until al dente. Drain the pasta thoroughly and tip it back into the same pan. Working quickly off the heat, add the egg and the salami and courgette mixture. Stir for 30 seconds to combine.

4] Transfer to a warm serving bowl and sprinkle over the remaining pecorino.

SPAGHETTI WITH CLAMS & MUSSELS

SPAGHETTI VONGOLE

As a young man I often used to go to the pretty port town of Castellammare, near Naples, to eat platefuls of their famous mussels. When I found myself there again recently, filming *Gino's Italian Coastal Escape*, I couldn't resist making the classic dish of the region – the chilli-spiked spaghetti vongole. Traditionally, spaghetti vongole contains just clams, but as I was in Castellammare, of course I had to include some mussels.

Serves 2

250g live clams
150g live mussels
1 garlic clove, peeled and finely sliced
1 fresh, medium-hot red chilli, finely sliced
3 tablespoons olive oil

150ml dry white wine
3 tablespoons chopped fresh flat-leaf parsley
300g dried spaghetti
12 yellow cherry tomatoes, quartered
Salt

1] Prepare the clams and mussels (see page 70, steps 1 and 2). Bring a large pan of salted water to the boil.

2] Meanwhile, put the garlic and chilli in a large saucepan or wok. Add the oil and place the pan over a medium heat. As soon as the garlic starts to sizzle, add the clams and mussels.

3] Pour in the wine and stir in the parsley. Bring to the boil, cover and cook for about 5–7 minutes or until the mussels have opened. Discard any mussels that remain closed.

4] Meanwhile, cook the spaghetti in the boiling water until al dente. Drain the pasta and tip it into the pan with the clams and mussels. Add the tomatoes and cook for 1 minute, stirring. Tip onto a large serving plate and serve immediately.

FUSILLI WITH VEGETABLES, PANCETTA, PESTO & MOZZARELLA

FUSILLI CON VERDURE, PANCETTA, MOZZARELLA E PESTO

When I was filming in southern Campania, in the medieval town of Felitto, I met the wonderful Rosy – the 'First Lady' of fusilli lunghi (long pasta spirals). She still makes fusilli the traditional way, hand-rolling individual lengths of dough around a square wire to make a long, gently twisty thread of pasta with a small hole in it. As a thank you to her for showing me her techniques, I made this pasta sauce from the locally produced fresh vegetables and mozzarella that the region is so famous for. If you can't find fusilli lunghi in the shops, use any long pasta such as spaghetti, linguine or bucatini.

100ml olive oil
1 large aubergine, cut into 1cm cubes
1 large courgette, cut into 1cm cubes
2 medium red onions, peeled and finely sliced
150g diced pancetta
2 x 400g tins of cherry tomatoes

2 tablespoons fresh or shop-bought basil pesto
500g dried fusilli lunghi
2 x 125g balls of mozzarella cheese, drained
  and cut into small cubes
Salt and freshly ground black pepper

Serves 6

1] Heat the oil in a large frying pan over a medium heat. Add the aubergine and courgette and some salt and fry for 7–8 minutes. Add the onions and pancetta and fry for 8 minutes.

2] Stir in the tomatoes and pesto. Simmer for 15 minutes, stirring occasionally. Season with salt and pepper and set aside.

3] Cook the fusilli lunghi in a large pan of boiling, salted water until al dente. Drain the pasta thoroughly and tip it back into the same saucepan you cooked it in. Pour over the sauce. Stir to combine.

4] Return the pan to a low heat. Add the mozzarella and stir until it starts to melt and go stringy. Serve immediately.

PRAWN & RICOTTA RAVIOLI WITH OLIVE OIL & FRESH SAGE

RAVIOLI DI GAMBERONI E RICOTTA CON OLIO DI OLIVA E SALVIA

Ravioli are popular all over Italy, stuffed with a variety of different ingredients depending on the region and the season. Wherever you are on the coast, you'll usually find them filled with seafood, as in this recipe.

Serves 4

400g '00' grade pasta flour, plus extra for dusting
½ teaspoon fine salt
2 teaspoons very finely ground black pepper
2 egg yolks
3 medium eggs, lightly beaten
230ml extra virgin olive oil
8 large (or 16 medium) fresh sage leaves
½ teaspoon grated lemon zest, to serve

For the filling
750g ricotta cheese
Grated zest of 2 unwaxed lemons
250g cooked king prawns, peeled and finely chopped
3 tablespoons chopped fresh chives
2 medium eggs, lightly beaten
Salt

1] First make the dough: place the flour, salt and pepper in a large bowl. Make a well in the centre and add the egg yolks, beaten eggs and 2 tablespoons of the oil. Using the handle of a wooden spoon, gradually mix the flour into the liquid. Once the texture is crumbly, turn out the mixture onto a well-floured surface.

2] Knead for about 8–10 minutes until you have a soft, smooth dough. The technique is the same as for bread: hold the dough in one hand and fold, push down and stretch the dough away from you with the other hand. Rotate and repeat. Shape the dough into a ball, wrap in cling film and chill for 30 minutes. Meanwhile, put the ricotta, lemon zest, prawns and chives in a large bowl and mix with a fork. Cover with cling film and refrigerate for at least 15 minutes.

3] Remove the cling film from the dough, dust the dough lightly with flour and cut into 2 even-sized pieces. Roll out each piece to about 2mm thick, either using a pasta machine or a rolling pin (dust the rolling pin and work surface with flour first). Dust frequently with flour or the dough can become sticky.

4] Lay 1 piece of dough on a well-dusted work surface. Place a tablespoonful of the filling on the dough and repeat at 5cm intervals over half the sheet only. Lightly brush the spaces around the filling with the 2 beaten eggs. Fold over the dough to cover the filling. Press gently around each spoonful of filling to expel the air. Using a 5.5cm round ravioli stamp cutter, cut out the ravioli. Cover with a tea towel and repeat with the other piece of dough.

5] Cook the ravioli in a large pan of boiling, salted water for 3 minutes. Meanwhile, heat the remaining oil in a large frying pan over a medium heat. Add the sage. As soon as it starts to sizzle, transfer the ravioli using a slotted spoon to the pan with the sage. Gently toss to coat. To serve, sprinkle over a little lemon zest.

POTATO GNOCCHI WITH COURGETTES & TOMATOES

GNOCCHI DI PATATE CON ZUCCHINE E POMODORI

Gnocchi are most commonly made with potatoes but there are many regional variations, so depending on where you are in Italy you'll also find them containing pumpkin, polenta, rice, semolina or ricotta (see page 144); there are even sweet gnocchi in some areas. This is a lovely light recipe for summer, when tomatoes and courgettes are in season.

Serves 4

600g floury potatoes, such as Desirée or Maris Piper, peeled and cut into 5cm chunks
200g plain flour or '00' grade pasta flour, plus extra for dusting
1½ teaspoons salt, plus extra for seasoning
½ teaspoon freshly ground black pepper, plus extra for seasoning
2 medium eggs, lightly beaten

50g salted butter
5 tablespoons extra virgin olive oil
2 medium courgettes, cut into 1cm cubes
3 large fresh plum tomatoes, deseeded and cut into 1cm cubes
60g freshly grated Parmesan cheese
8 large basil leaves, shredded

1] Put the potatoes in a large pan and cover with cold, salted water. Bring to the boil then simmer for 15–20 minutes or until tender. Drain well and leave for 2–3 minutes. Pass the potatoes through a potato ricer set over a large bowl or mash until really smooth. While the potatoes are still warm, add the flour and salt and pepper. Make a well and add the eggs. Using the handle of a wooden spoon, mix thoroughly then turn out onto a floured surface. Knead lightly until you have soft, slightly sticky dough. (Do not overwork or the dough will be tough.)

2] Divide the dough into 4. Roll each piece with your hands into a long sausage shape, about 1.5cm thick. Use a sharp knife to cut across into 2cm lengths. Lay the gnocchi on a lightly floured clean tea towel or tray until ready to cook.

3] Bring a large pan of salted water to the boil. Meanwhile, heat the butter and oil in a large frying pan over a high heat. Add the courgettes and fry for 5 minutes, stirring occasionally. Season with some salt and pepper. Remove the pan from the heat and set aside.

4] Drop the gnocchi into the boiling water and cook for about 2–3 minutes. They will be ready when they float to the surface. Drain thoroughly.

5] Return the frying pan to the heat and tip in the gnocchi. Stir in the tomatoes, half the Parmesan and the basil and fry for 1 minute, stirring continuously. Sprinkle over the remaining Parmesan and serve immediately.

RICOTTA GNOCCHI WITH RED PEPPERS, COURGETTES, BUTTER & SAGE

NDUNDERI CON PEPERONI ROSSI, ZUCCHINE, BURRO E SALVIA

When I was filming recently in Minori – one of the gems of the Amalfi coast – I met expert pasta-maker Claudia, who taught me how to prepare the regional speciality, ndunderi. It's a ricotta and flour-based gnocchi and is named for the sound the pasta makes when it hits your plate. I've dressed the gnocchi in butter, sage and Parmesan – a classic Italian combination – and added red peppers and courgettes for extra flavour, colour and texture. It is important to drain the ricotta the day before or the gnocchi will be soggy and not hold together properly.

Serves 4

400g ricotta cheese
4 egg yolks
60g freshly grated Parmesan cheese
2 teaspoons salt
1 teaspoon ground black pepper
½ teaspoon freshly grated nutmeg
160g '00' grade pasta flour

For the sauce
150ml extra virgin olive oil
2 medium courgettes, cut into 5mm cubes
2 large red peppers, cut into 5mm cubes
8 large fresh sage leaves, shredded
100g salted butter
60g freshly grated Parmesan cheese
Salt and freshly ground black pepper

1] Put the ricotta in a piece of muslin or a clean tea towel and place in a colander. Leave to drain overnight.

2] In a medium bowl, combine the ricotta, egg yolks, Parmesan, salt, pepper and nutmeg. Add the flour. Using the handle of a wooden spoon, gradually mix together thoroughly.

3] Use your hands to bring the dough together into a ball and place on a lightly floured work surface. Divide the dough into 4. Roll each piece beneath the palms of your hands into a long sausage shape, each about 2.5cm thick. Use a sharp knife to cut across into 2.5cm lengths. Dust with a little flour. Press each piece against the tines of a fork to create small grooves on one side. Place the gnocchi on a lightly floured tray or tea towel until ready to cook.

4] To make the sauce, heat the oil in a large frying pan over a high heat. Add the courgettes, red peppers and some salt and fry for about 7 minutes, stirring occasionally. Add the sage and butter, stirring until the butter has melted and everything is well combined. Remove the pan from the heat and set aside.

5] Bring a large pan of salted water to the boil. Drop the gnocchi into the boiling water and cook for about 5 minutes. Once they have floated to the surface, continue to cook for 2 further minutes. Remove the gnocchi with a slotted spoon and stir them into the sauce. Return the frying pan to the heat for 1 minute. Add some black pepper and sprinkle over the Parmesan.

SAFFRON RISOTTO WITH PEAS

RISOTTO ZAFFERANO E PISELLI

This simple risotto is perfect for lunchtime entertaining or a light supper. The saffron gives the dish its wonderful rich golden colour and distinctive flavour, and the peas provide sweetness and contrast in texture and colour. The best saffron in southern Italy comes from Sicily, where they use it in both savoury and sweet dishes. I know it's a bit expensive, but you only need to use a tiny amount and it's worth every penny.

½ teaspoon saffron threads
1.3 litres hot vegetable stock
6 tablespoons olive oil
1 large onion, peeled and finely chopped
400g Arborio or Carnaroli rice

150ml dry rosé or white wine
80g salted butter
200g frozen petit pois, defrosted
80g freshly grated Grana Padano cheese
Salt and white pepper

Serves 4

1] Put the saffron in a small bowl with 4 tablespoons of the stock and set aside to infuse. Meanwhile, heat the olive oil in a large, heavy-based saucepan over a medium heat. Add the onion and fry for 5 minutes or until softened but not browned, stirring occasionally.

2] Add the rice and fry for 3 minutes, stirring constantly, or until the grains are coated and shiny.

3] Pour in the wine and let it bubble for 1 minute or until it has evaporated.

4] Stir in the saffron mixture. Add 2 ladlesful of stock and bring to a simmer. Stir continuously until the liquid has been absorbed. Continue adding the rest of the stock in the same way, until the rice is cooked but still has a slight bite. This will take 16–18 minutes and you may not need to add all the stock.

5] Remove the pan from the heat. Add the butter, peas and Grana Padano and stir for about 30 seconds until creamy. Season with salt and pepper.

CHICKEN RISOTTO WITH RED PESTO & ROSEMARY

RISOTTO CON POLLO, PESTO ROSSO E ROSMARINO

Risotto is the ultimate comfort food, and it's so versatile and quick to make. For this recipe I've used chicken breast, but you can also use cooked chicken left over from a roast – just stir it in as you add the last ladleful of stock. Red pesto is a southern Italian variation of the northern Italian basil pesto – the colour comes from sun-dried tomatoes or red peppers and the sauce adds depth of flavour and piquancy to this dish.

Serves 4

8 tablespoons olive oil
1 large red onion, peeled and finely chopped
250g skinless boneless chicken breast, cut into
  2cm cubes
1 tablespoon chopped fresh rosemary
400g Arborio or Carnaroli rice
150ml dry white wine
1.3 litres hot vegetable stock

50g salted butter
2 tablespoons shop-bought red, sun-dried
  tomato pesto
50g freshly grated Parmesan cheese
50g Parmesan cheese shavings
Extra virgin olive oil for drizzling
Salt and freshly ground black pepper

1] Heat 4 tablespoons of the oil in a large, heavy-based saucepan over a medium heat. Add the onion and fry for 5 minutes until softened but not browned. Add the chicken and rosemary and fry for a further 5 minutes, stirring occasionally. Using a slotted spoon, transfer the chicken and onion to a plate. Cover with foil and set aside.

2] Heat the remaining 4 tablespoons of oil in the same pan. When hot, add the rice and fry for 3 minutes, stirring continuously, until the rice is well coated in the oil. Pour in the wine and let it simmer for 1 minute or until it has evaporated.

3] Pour in 2 ladlesful of stock and bring to a simmer. Stir continuously until the liquid has been absorbed. Continue adding the rest of the stock in the same way, until the rice is cooked but still has a slight bite. This will take 16–18 minutes and you may not need to add all the stock.

4] Take the pan off the heat. Return the chicken and onion to the pan, then stir in the butter, red pesto and grated Parmesan. Stir gently for 30 seconds. Season with salt and pepper. Scatter Parmesan shavings over the top and drizzle over some extra virgin olive oil.

I love making pizza and bread — it's so satisfying, the results are incredible and it's a lot easier than you might think. You can be as creative as you like — once you've got the dough right, more or less anything goes. Here I've included pizzas with seafood toppings, which you'll find along the coast, and have adapted traditional Neapolitan recipes that use simple local ingredients such as buffalo mozzarella and plum tomatoes. My favourite recipe in this chapter has to be my father's calzone — if you like spicy flavours, this one is for you. Among the breads are the familiar and popular ciabatta and focaccia, but I've also included a stuffed focaccia and some sweet rolls, which are a little more unusual and absolutely delicious.

PIZZA & BREADS

NEAPOLITAN PIZZA WITH BUFFALO MOZZARELLA, TOMATOES & BASIL

TOMATO, GARLIC & OREGANO PIZZA

PIZZA TRAY WITH SMOKED SALMON, MASCARPONE & MOZZARELLA

SEAFOOD PIZZA

PIZZA TRAY WITH ANCHOVIES, COURGETTES, GARLIC & CHILLI

PAPA CIRO'S SPICY CALZONE

SWEET SOFT BUTTER ROLLS WITH VANILLA

FOCACCIA WITH TOMATOES, OLIVES, CAPERS & RED PESTO

FOCACCIA STUFFED WITH GORGONZOLA, OLIVES, GARLIC & ROSEMARY

OLIVE & FENNEL SEED CIABATTA

NEAPOLITAN PIZZA WITH BUFFALO MOZZARELLA, TOMATOES & BASIL

PIZZA MARGHERITA

Pizza originated in Naples and it's where the best, most authentic pizza can still be found today – and I'm not just saying that because I'm a Neapolitan! Apparently this topping was created in the 19th century to honour the visit of Queen Margherita to Naples, as it represented the colours of the Italian flag – red, white and green. Try to use buffalo (rather than cow's milk) mozzarella if you can.

Makes 2

200g strong white flour, plus extra for dusting
1 x 7g sachet of fast-action (easy-blend) dried yeast
½ teaspoon salt
2 tablespoons extra virgin olive oil, plus extra for greasing and brushing

For the topping
1 x 400g tin of chopped tomatoes
2 tablespoons extra virgin olive oil
2 x 125g balls of buffalo mozzarella cheese, drained and cut into small cubes
10 fresh basil leaves
Salt and freshly ground black pepper

1] Put the flour in a large bowl. Add the yeast to one side of the bowl and the salt to the other. Make a well in the centre and add the oil then gradually pour in 140ml warm water. Using the handle of a wooden spoon, mix together thoroughly to create a wet dough. Turn out the dough onto a well-floured surface and knead it for about 5 minutes or until smooth and elastic.

2] Shape the dough into a round and place in a large oiled bowl. Brush the top with a little oil and cover with cling film. Leave to rest at room temperature for 20–25 minutes. Preheat the oven to 220°C/gas mark 7.

3] Meanwhile, make the topping. Put the tomatoes, oil, salt and pepper in a small bowl. Using your hands, squeeze the tomatoes to make a fine pulp. Set aside.

4] Turn out the dough onto a lightly floured surface and knead just 3 or 4 times to knock out the air. Halve the dough and place each half in the centre of an oiled baking sheet. Use your fingertips to push each half out from the centre, stretching the dough to create 2 rounds about 25cm in diameter and 1–2cm thick. You can also use a rolling pin if you prefer. Make a small rim by pulling up the edges slightly.

5] Spread the tomato mixture evenly over the pizza bases, avoiding the rim, and top with the mozzarella. Bake for 12–14 minutes or until golden brown.

6] Remove from the oven, scatter over the basil and return to the oven for 1 further minute.

TOMATO, GARLIC & OREGANO PIZZA

PIZZA AL POMODORO, AGLIO E ORIGANO

Simple, tasty and light – this is how a good pizza should be. Always use the best-quality ingredients you can afford, as it will really make a difference to the flavour. In Naples we would use San Marzano tomatoes – a type of plum tomato that grows in the volcanic soil around Mount Vesuvius and has a rich, sweet flavour and dense texture. You can buy tinned San Marzano tomatoes in Britain, but if you can't find them another really good-quality brand of plum tomato will be fine. You can add a few anchovies on top if you like, but generally it's best to keep things simple.

Makes 2

200g strong white flour, plus extra for dusting
1 x 7g sachet of fast-action (easy-blend) dried yeast
½ teaspoon salt
2 tablespoons extra virgin olive oil, plus extra for greasing and brushing

For the topping
1 x 400g tin of chopped tomatoes
2 tablespoons extra virgin olive oil
4 garlic cloves, peeled and finely chopped
1 teaspoon dried oregano
Salt and freshly ground black pepper

1] Put the flour in a large bowl. Add the yeast to one side of the bowl and the salt to the other. Make a well in the centre and add the oil then gradually pour in 140ml warm water. Using the handle of a wooden spoon, mix together thoroughly to create a wet dough. Turn out the dough onto a well-floured surface and knead it for about 5 minutes or until smooth and elastic.

2] Shape the dough into a round and place in a large oiled bowl. Brush the top with a little oil and cover with cling film. Leave to rest at room temperature for 20–25 minutes. Preheat the oven to 220°C/gas mark 7.

3] Meanwhile, make the topping. Put the tomatoes in a small bowl with the oil, salt and pepper. Using your hands, squeeze the tomatoes to make a fine pulp. Set aside.

4] Turn out the dough onto a lightly floured surface and knead just 3 or 4 times to knock out the air. Halve the dough and place each half in the centre of an oiled baking sheet. Use your fingertips to push each half out from the centre, stretching the dough to create 2 rounds about 25cm in diameter and 1–2cm thick. You can also use a rolling pin if you prefer. Make a small rim by pulling up the edges slightly.

5] Spread the tomato mixture evenly over the pizza bases, avoiding the rim. Scatter over the garlic. Bake for 14 minutes or until golden brown. Remove from the oven, sprinkle over the oregano and bake for 1 further minute.

PIZZA TRAY WITH SMOKED SALMON, MASCARPONE & MOZZARELLA

TEGLIA DI PIZZA CON MASCARPONE E SALMONE AFFUMICATO

The first time I tried this pizza topping was on the island of Elba, off the coast of Tuscany. It isn't traditional, but the combination of smoked salmon, soft creamy cheeses and chives works really well and I was seriously impressed. If you've never made homemade pizza before, a pizza tray is probably a good introduction, as you don't have to worry about creating the perfect round pizza shape.

200g strong white flour, plus extra for dusting
1 x 7g sachet of fast-action (easy-blend) dried yeast
½ teaspoon salt
2 tablespoons extra virgin olive oil, plus extra for greasing and brushing

For the topping
250g mascarpone cheese (room temperature)
4 tablespoons full-fat milk
2 tablespoons chopped fresh chives
1 x 125g ball of mozzarella cheese, drained and cut into small cubes
120g smoked salmon trimmings, roughly sliced
Salt and freshly ground black pepper

Serves 2

1] Put the flour in a large bowl. Add the yeast to one side of the bowl and the salt to the other. Make a well in the centre and add the oil then gradually pour in 140ml warm water. Using the handle of a wooden spoon, mix together thoroughly to create a wet dough. Turn out the dough onto a well-floured surface and knead for about 5 minutes or until smooth and elastic.

2] Shape the dough into a round and place in a large oiled bowl. Brush the top with a little oil and cover with cling film. Leave to rest at room temperature for 20–25 minutes.

3] To make the topping, put the mascarpone in a medium bowl and pour over the milk. Add the chives, season with salt and pepper and mix with a fork until smooth. Set aside.

4] Turn out the dough onto a lightly floured surface and knead just 3 or 4 times to knock out the air. Transfer to an oiled traybake tin, about 25 x 23cm and at least 2cm high. Using your fingertips, gently flatten the dough to extend to the sides (it should be about 1cm thick). Brush over a little oil, cover with a tea towel and leave to rise again in a warm place for a further 20 minutes. Preheat the oven to 220°C/gas mark 7.

5] Spread the mascarpone mixture evenly over the pizza tray base, leaving a 1cm border clear. Scatter over the mozzarella and bake for 12 minutes. Remove from the oven, scatter over the smoked salmon and bake for a further 3 minutes.

SEAFOOD PIZZA

PIZZA CON VONGOLE E COZZE

In summer there is an abundance of mussels and clams along the southern Italian coast and they're used frequently as pizza toppings. If you have the good fortune to visit the Amalfi coast you'll find this in most pizzerias.

Makes 2

200g strong white flour, plus extra for dusting
1 x 7g sachet of fast-action (easy-blend)
 dried yeast
½ teaspoon salt
2 tablespoons extra virgin olive oil, plus extra
 for greasing and brushing

For the topping
500g live clams
500g live mussels
4 tablespoons extra virgin olive oil
50ml dry white wine
1 x 400g tin of chopped tomatoes
4 garlic cloves, peeled and finely chopped
2 tablespoons fresh chopped flat-leaf parsley
Salt and freshly ground black pepper

1] To make the topping, first prepare the clams and mussels (see page 70, steps 1 and 2). Heat 2 tablespoons of the oil in a large saucepan over a high heat. Add the clams, mussels and wine. Cover the pan and cook for 5 minutes, shaking the pan every minute or so. Remove from the heat and leave to rest for 20 minutes. Meanwhile, put the tomatoes, remaining 2 tablespoons of oil and salt and pepper in a small bowl. Using your hands, squeeze the tomatoes to make a fine pulp. Remove the clams and mussels from their shells (discard the shells). Set aside.

2] Put the flour in a large bowl. Add the yeast to one side of the bowl and the salt to the other. Make a well in the centre and add the oil then gradually pour in 140ml warm water. Using the handle of a wooden spoon, mix to create a wet dough. Turn out the dough onto a well-floured surface and knead for 5 minutes or until smooth and elastic. Shape the dough into a round and place in a large oiled bowl. Brush the top with a little oil and cover with cling film. Leave to rest at room temperature for 20–25 minutes. Preheat the oven to 220°C/gas mark 7.

3] Turn out the dough onto a lightly floured surface and knead just 3 or 4 times to knock out the air. Halve the dough and place each half in the centre of an oiled baking sheet. Use your fingertips to push each half out from the centre, stretching the dough to create 2 rounds about 25cm in diameter and 1–2cm thick. You can also use a rolling pin if you prefer. Make a small rim by pulling up the edges slightly.

4] Spread the tomato mixture evenly over the pizza bases, avoiding the rim. Scatter over the garlic and bake for 12 minutes. Remove from the oven, scatter over the clams and mussels and return to the oven for 3 minutes. Sprinkle over the parsley.

PIZZA TRAY WITH ANCHOVIES, COURGETTES, GARLIC & CHILLI

TEGLIA DI PIZZA PICCANTE CON ACCIUGHE, ZUCCHINE, E AGLIO

Anchovies are found in large numbers in the Mediterranean, particularly in southern Italy, where they are a staple food and are eaten fresh or preserved in olive oil or salt. They're high in antioxidants, and some research suggests they may be linked to longevity. If you prefer, replace the anchovies with black olives.

Serves 2

200g strong white flour, plus extra for dusting
1 x 7g sachet fast-action (easy-blend)
   dried yeast
½ teaspoon salt
2 tablespoons extra virgin olive oil, plus extra
   for greasing and brushing

For the topping
6 tablespoons oil
2 large courgettes, cut into 1cm cubes
1 x 400g tin of chopped tomatoes
½ teaspoon dried chilli flakes
4 garlic cloves, peeled and finely chopped
16 anchovy fillets in oil, drained
1 teaspoon dried oregano
Salt

1] Put the flour in a large bowl. Add the yeast to one side of the bowl and the salt to the other. Make a well in the centre and add the oil then gradually pour in 140ml warm water. Using the handle of a wooden spoon, mix together thoroughly to create a wet dough. Turn out the dough onto a well-floured surface and knead for about 5 minutes or until smooth and elastic. Shape the dough into a round and place in a large oiled bowl. Brush the top with a little oil and cover with cling film. Leave to rest at room temperature for 20–25 minutes.

2] Meanwhile, make the topping. Heat 4 tablespoons of the oil in a medium pan over a medium heat. Add the courgettes, season with salt and fry for 12 minutes, stirring occasionally. Leave to cool. Put the tomatoes in a small bowl with the remaining 2 tablespoons of the oil, the salt and the chilli flakes. Using your hands (you may want to use gloves to protect your hands and eyes from the chilli), squeeze the tomatoes to create a fine pulp. Set aside.

3] Turn out the dough onto a lightly floured surface and knead just 3 or 4 times to knock out the air. Transfer to an oiled traybake tin, about 25 x 23cm and at least 2cm high. Using your fingertips, gently flatten the dough to extend to the sides (it should be about 1cm thick). Brush over a little oil, cover with a tea towel and leave to rise again in a warm place for a further 20 minutes. Preheat the oven to 220°C/gas mark 7.

4] Remove the tea towel and spread the tomato mixture evenly over the pizza base, leaving a 1cm border clear. Scatter over the garlic and cooled courgettes and lay the anchovies on top. Bake for 12–14 minutes or until golden brown. Remove from the oven, sprinkle over the oregano and bake for 1 further minute.

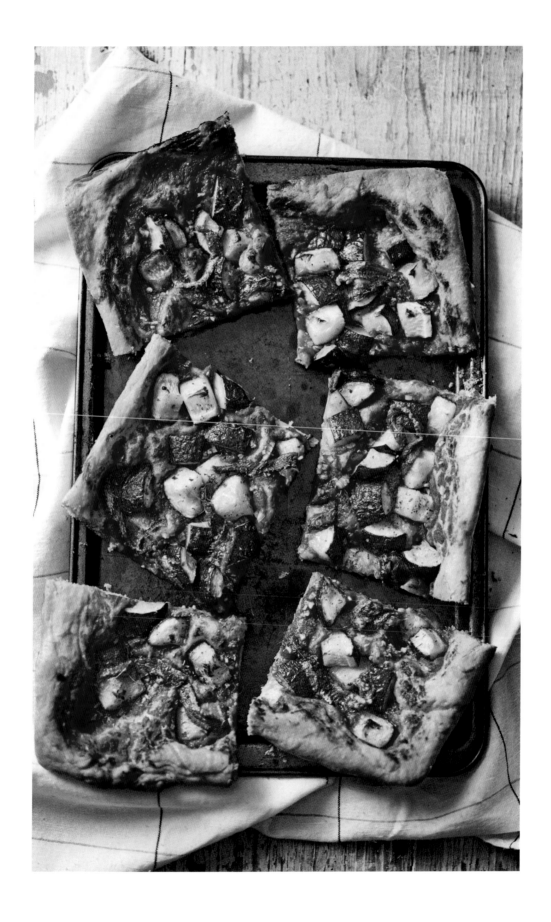

TUSCAN SPECIALITIES

One of the most visited regions in Italy, Tuscany has stunning landscapes that include an extensive coastline, rolling hills and the beautiful neighbouring island of Elba. Generally, Tuscan cuisine is extremely varied, simple and rustic, with its roots in peasant traditions. The raw ingredients are excellent and the flavours strong and punchy, with fresh herbs used widely, but it is the liberal use of olive oil that really defines the food of this region. Soups and meat of all kinds are extremely popular, and bread (often unsalted) is an important staple. Pasta is less popular than in many other regions.

CANNELLINI BEANS

Sometimes referred to as the *mangiafagioli* ('bean eaters'), the Tuscans love their pulses. They are particularly fond of the rich, creamy white cannellini beans (see below). These are often paired with pork and tuna or used in salads, soups and stews, and are sometimes served on their own with sage and garlic. Cannellini beans are a key ingredient of *ribollita* – a classic Tuscan bean soup that contains toasted bread rubbed with garlic.

WILD MUSHROOMS

In Tuscany and on the neighbouring island of Elba, wild mushrooms – particularly the intensely flavoured *porcini* (see below) – grow in abundance in the woods. In autumn, locals rise at dawn to forage for these highly prized delicacies – a tradition that has become a competitive pasttime. Wild mushrooms are served in many ways, sometimes with polenta or risotto, or simply fried in olive oil. A particularly Tuscan method is to sauté them with chicken livers in olive oil flavoured with sage. *Porcini* are often dried, which preserves them and makes their flavour very concentrated in the process.

CHESTNUTS

Although chestnuts (see below) are mainly associated with northern Italy, they also play an important part in the cuisine of Tuscany and the island of Elba. Chestnut trees grow in mountainous regions and the nuts are harvested in the autumn. Tuscany has its own speciality made with chestnuts – *castagnaccio*, which is a cake made with chestnut flour, olive oil, sultanas, pine nuts or walnuts and fennel seeds or rosemary. Its popularity has spread and it is now found throughout Italy.

HONEY

The honey on Elba is arguably the best in Italy – because of the island's great biodiversity, the bees gather nectar from a wide selection of flowers, producing different types of honey, each with its own distinctive flavour and scent. Arbutus honey is perhaps most characteristic of the area, but there is also acacia, wildflower, eucalyptus, rosemary, thistle and chestnut honeys, to name but a few. Honey is used as a sweetener in cooking, but it is also served with cheese at the end of a meal.

OLIVES & OLIVE OIL

Tuscany is well known for its olives (see below), and one of the most distinctive elements of Tuscan cooking is the generous use of olive oil. Although olive oil is produced in 19 out of the 20 regions of Italy, mainly in the south, Tuscan olive oils are considered by many to be some of the best, especially the fruity-flavoured oil from the province of Lucca. Extra virgin olive oil is extracted from the first pressing of the olives and is best for salads and uncooked dishes.

FISH & SHELLFISH

All along the Tuscan coast you'll find wonderful seafood dishes. Grey mullet, cuttlefish and octopus are all popular, as are mussels and clams. The king of Tuscan seafood dishes is *cacciucco* – a chunky seafood soup or stew that originates in Livorno and includes chilli and at least five different types of fish. It is served on slices of toasted bread rubbed with garlic. Elvers (*cieche*), caught at the mouth of the Arno near Pisa, are also a great favourite in Tuscany.

BOTTARGA

Made mainly in Sardinia but also in Orbetello in Tuscany, *bottarga* (see below) is the compressed, salted and dried roe of the grey mullet. It is a magical ingredient and can transform dishes with its intensely savoury, salty flavour. You can grate or shave *bottarga* onto pasta and pizzas, or slice it finely and use it as a topping for toasted ciabatta. It can also be served on its own as an antipasto, sliced and marinated in olive oil and lemon juice. Some *bottarga*, produced mainly in Sicily, is made from the roe of tuna rather than grey mullet.

CHEESE

There is a strong tradition of raising sheep in Tuscany, so many of the cheeses are made from sheep's milk, including *pecorino toscano*, *pecorino di Pienze*, *marzolino del Chianti* and *caciotte*, which is made from a mixture of sheep and cow's milk. The *pecorino* in Tuscany is considered by many to be the best in Italy, and it is often served at the end of a meal. There are also great goat's cheeses from Maremma and Mugello.

WINE

Tuscany is the most established wine-growing region in Italy. Although it doesn't produce the most in terms of quantity, two of Italy's most famous wines are made there: Chianti (in the hills between Florence and Siena) and Brunello di Montalcino (south of Siena). Other quality wines produced in Tuscany include Moscatello di Montalcino, Vernaccia di San Gimignano, Aleatico di Portoferraio and the sweet dessert wine, vin santo.

PAPA CIRO'S SPICY CALZONE

IL CALZONE BRUCIA-CULO DI PAPÀ CIRO

When my late father came to stay with me in London, we were in the kitchen experimenting with different pizzas and toppings and he created this folded pizza filled with peppers, olives, ricotta and chilli. He loved spicy food and was delighted with the results. Be ready for something very special and really hot!

Makes 2

200g strong white flour, plus extra for dusting
1 x 7g sachet of fast-action (easy-blend) dried yeast
½ teaspoon salt
2 tablespoons extra virgin olive oil, plus extra for greasing and brushing
3 tablespoons chilli oil

For the filling
4 tablespoons extra virgin olive oil
1 large red onion, peeled and thinly sliced

1 red pepper, deseeded and sliced into 5mm strips
1 yellow pepper, deseeded and sliced into 5mm strips
1 green pepper, deseeded and sliced into 5mm strips
2 teaspoons dried chilli flakes
100g pitted black olives (preferably Leccino), drained and halved
250g ricotta cheese (room temperature)
Salt

1] To make the filling, heat the oil in a large frying pan over a medium heat. Add the onion, peppers, chilli flakes and some salt and fry for 10 minutes, stirring occasionally. Add the olives and fry for 5 minutes. Set aside. Place the ricotta in a bowl and mash with a fork until smooth, creamy and easy to spread. Set aside.

2] Place the flour in a large bowl. Add the yeast to one side and the salt to the other. Make a well in the centre and add the oil then gradually pour in 140ml warm water. Using the handle of a wooden spoon, mix to create a wet dough. Turn out the dough onto a well-floured surface and knead for about 5 minutes or until smooth and elastic. Shape the dough into a round and place in a large oiled bowl. Brush the top with a little oil and cover with cling film. Leave to rest at room temperature for 20–25 minutes. Preheat the oven to 220°C/gas mark 7.

3] Turn out the dough onto a lightly floured surface and knead just 3 or 4 times to knock out the air. Halve the dough and place each half in the centre of an oiled baking sheet. Use your fingertips to push each half out from the centre, stretching the dough to create 2 rounds about 22cm in diameter.

4] Spread the ricotta evenly over half the surface of each pizza base, leaving a border of 1cm all around, then spoon over the pepper mixture. Fold over the empty side to enclose the filling. Pinch the edges to seal and crimp them by making tucks at regular intervals. Brush the surface with chilli oil and bake for 15 minutes or until golden brown.

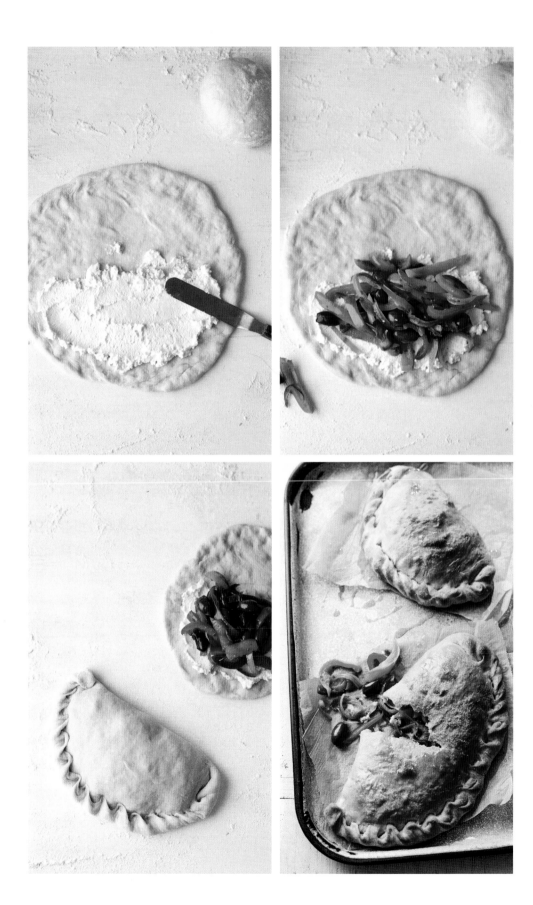

SWEET SOFT BUTTER ROLLS WITH VANILLA

BOCCONCINI DI PANE DOLCE AL BURRO E VANIGLIA

These delicious little rolls are the creation of the Neapolitan baker Vincenzo Mennella. I know his son, Liborio, very well and I've been chasing him for this recipe for the last 21 years. Finally he agreed to give it to me, after I made him an offer he couldn't refuse! The rolls are very versatile – they're great served with savoury antipasti such as Italian cured hams and salami, or with sweet preserves such as strawberry jam.

Makes 16
small rolls

450g strong white flour, plus extra for dusting
10g fast-action (easy blend) dried yeast
1 teaspoon salt
60g caster sugar
150g salted butter, melted

120ml warm full-fat milk
3 medium eggs
1 tablespoon vanilla extract
Icing sugar for dusting

1] Combine the flour, yeast, salt and sugar in a large bowl. Make a well in the centre and pour in 50g of the melted butter and the milk. Mix together using the handle of a wooden spoon. Cover with cling film and leave to rest at room temperature for 30 minutes.

2] Break the eggs into a small bowl. Beat lightly with a fork then stir in the vanilla. Add the eggs gradually to the mixture in the larger bowl, pouring in a steady stream and stirring all the time until thoroughly combined.

3] Turn out the dough onto a well-floured surface and knead for 5–10 minutes or until soft and elastic. Brush the inside of a large bowl with melted butter. Shape the dough into a round and place in the bowl. Brush the top with melted butter and cover with cling film. Leave in a warm, draught-free place for 1½ hours or until doubled in size. Brush a 20cm loose-bottomed round or square cake tin with melted butter.

4] Tip the dough out onto a lightly floured surface and knead 3 or 4 times to knock out the air. Cut the dough into 16 equal-sized pieces and shape into balls. Roll the balls in melted butter and place in the cake tin, spacing them slightly apart. Cover with a tea towel and leave to rise in a warm place for about 1 hour or until doubled in size. Preheat the oven to 190°C/gas mark 5.

5] Brush the rolls with the remaining melted butter. Bake for 25 minutes or until golden brown and firm.

6] Leave to cool slightly or completely on a wire rack, then dust with icing sugar and serve.

FOCACCIA WITH TOMATOES, OLIVES, CAPERS & RED PESTO

FOCACCIA CON POMODORINI, OLIVE, CAPPERI E PESTO ROSSO

As I was filming the new series of *Gino's Italian Coastal Escape* along Italy's beautiful Mediterranean coast I came across this focaccia recipe, which I'd like to share with you all. I also met an elderly lady called Teresa, who told me her top three tips for making the perfect focaccia: always use the best extra virgin olive oil you can afford; work the dough in a warm environment, otherwise it won't rise properly; and the oven temperature must remain constant – if the oven is allowed to cool down, the focaccia will lose its soft texture.

500g strong white flour, plus extra for dusting
1 x 7g sachet of fast-action (easy-blend) dried yeast
2 teaspoons salt
4 tablespoons extra virgin olive oil, plus extra for greasing and brushing

For the topping
2 tablespoons extra virgin olive oil
10 fresh yellow cherry tomatoes
10 fresh red cherry tomatoes
100g pitted black olives, drained
3 tablespoons capers, drained
Large pinch of sea salt flakes
3 tablespoons shop-bought red, sun-dried tomato pesto

Serves 8

1] Place the flour in a large bowl. Add the yeast to one side of the bowl and the salt to the other. Make a well in the centre and add 3 tablespoons of the oil then gradually pour in 300ml warm water. Mix using the handle of a wooden spoon.

2] Tip out the dough onto a lightly floured surface and knead for about 10 minutes or until smooth and elastic, adding a little more flour if it's really sticky. Shape the dough into a round and place in a large oiled bowl. Brush the top with a little oil. Cover with cling film and leave in a warm place for 1 hour or until doubled in size. Grease a large baking sheet with a little oil and set aside.

3] Turn out the dough onto a lightly floured surface. Knead just 3 or 4 times to knock out some of the air. Transfer to the oiled baking sheet. Using your fingertips, push the dough to a rectangle about 30 x 24cm and 2–3 cm thick. Brush with the remaining tablespoon of oil, cover with a tea towel and leave to rise for a further 40 minutes or until doubled in size. Preheat the oven to 200°C/ gas mark 6.

4] Remove the tea towel and press your fingertips into the dough to create indentations. Drizzle over most of the oil for the topping. Press the tomatoes into the indentations, scatter over the olives and capers and sprinkle with the sea salt. Brush with the remaining oil. Bake for 20 minutes or until golden brown. Dot the top with the red pesto and transfer to a wire rack to cool slightly. Serve warm.

FOCACCIA STUFFED WITH GORGONZOLA, OLIVES, GARLIC & ROSEMARY

FOCACCIA RIPIENA DI GORGONZOLA, OLIVE, AGLIO E ROSMARINO

This is the number one bestselling bread in my restaurants. It looks fantastic, fills the kitchen with wonderful smells when it's baking, and the combined flavours of the melting Gorgonzola cheese and Leccino olives pack a huge punch. It's perfect for when you have guests. Serve with a glass or two of prosecco.

Serves 6

350g strong white flour, plus extra for dusting
5g fast-action (easy-blend) dried yeast
1 teaspoon salt
½ teaspoon caster sugar
6 tablespoons extra virgin olive oil, plus extra
  for greasing and brushing
1 tablespoon chopped fresh rosemary

For the filling
250g Gorgonzola cheese, cut into small cubes
150g black olives (preferably Leccino), drained
  and halved
2 garlic cloves, peeled and finely sliced
3 tablespoons chopped fresh flat-leaf parsley
1 teaspoon freshly ground black pepper

1] Place the flour in a large bowl. Add the yeast to one side of the bowl and the salt and sugar to the other. Make a well in the centre and add 3 tablespoons of the oil then gradually pour in 200ml warm water. Mix together using the handle of a wooden spoon to create a soft, sticky dough.

2] Knead the dough on a lightly floured surface for about 10 minutes until smooth and elastic. Shape into a round and transfer to a large, oiled bowl. Brush the top with a little oil, cover with cling film and leave in a warm place for 1 hour or until doubled in size. Grease a large baking sheet with a little oil and set aside.

3] Turn out the dough onto a lightly floured surface and knead just 3 or 4 times to knock out the air. Roll out the dough to a rectangle about 30 x 24cm. Cover with a tea towel and leave to rest for 10 minutes.

4] Scatter the Gorgonzola, olives, garlic and parsley over the dough, leaving a 1cm border clear all around. Sprinkle over the black pepper.

5] Starting from the shorter side, roll up the dough like a Swiss roll. Tuck the side edges under to seal. Transfer the roll, seam-side down, to the oiled baking sheet. Cover with a tea towel and leave to rest for 30 minutes in a warm place. Preheat the oven to 200°C/gas mark 6.

6] Brush the surface of the focaccia with the remaining 3 tablespoons of oil and prick holes all over the bread using a fork. Sprinkle over the rosemary. Bake for 35 minutes or until golden brown. Transfer to a wire rack to cool slightly. Slice and serve warm.

OLIVE & FENNEL SEED CIABATTA

CIABATTA CON OLIVE E FINOCCHIETTO

This long, flattish bread takes its name from the Italian word for slipper, which it's thought to resemble. Note that the 'starter' (known in Italy as the *biga*) needs to be made a day ahead and left to rest overnight.

Makes 4
small
loaves

10g fresh yeast
450g strong white flour, plus extra for dusting
1 teaspoon salt
50ml extra virgin olive oil, plus extra for
  greasing
180g pitted black olives (preferably Leccino),
  drained and quartered
1 tablespoon fennel seeds, crushed

For the starter
5g fresh yeast
350g strong white flour
Olive oil, for greasing

1] To prepare the starter, place the yeast and 180ml warm water in a large bowl. When the yeast has dissolved, add the flour and stir to combine for 5 minutes to form a rough dough. Grease the inside of another large bowl with a little oil and put in the dough. Cover with cling film and leave overnight (ideally for about 20 hours) in a warm, draught-free place.

2] The next day, place the 10g yeast and 340ml warm water in a large bowl. When the yeast has dissolved, add the flour and the starter. Add the salt and pour over the olive oil. Mix thoroughly. Add the olives and fennel seeds and mix until well combined. Transfer the dough to a lightly floured surface and knead for about 10 minutes or until smooth. Place the dough in a large, oiled bowl, cover with cling film and leave to rise in a warm place for 1½–2 hours or until doubled in size.

3] Turn out the dough onto a floured surface and sprinkle over a little flour. Gently press the dough to flatten to a 2cm-thick rectangle, then cut into 4 equal-sized strips. Take one strip of dough, fold one short side of it into the middle, then bring the other side over to meet it. Press down to seal. Fold in half lengthways and press to seal the edges to create a long shape. Repeat with the remaining dough.

4] Cover a tray with a tea towel and sprinkle it with flour. Place the 4 loaves on the tea towel, cover with another tea towel and leave to rest in a warm place for 40 minutes. Preheat the oven to 220°C/gas mark 7. Dust a large baking sheet with flour and lay the loaves on the sheet, spaced apart and with the folded sides down. Gently stretch the dough to create the characteristic 'slipper' shape.

5] Spray the inside of the oven with water or splash a little water using your fingertips. Bake the loaves for 20–22 minutes or until golden brown. Transfer to a wire rack to cool slightly. Serve warm.

In Italy we really celebrate our vegetables and they're often the main attraction of a meal rather than just an accompaniment to meat or fish, especially in the south. Our markets are packed full of wonderful produce and you'll only find vegetables in season, as they're so much fresher and more flavourful. In this chapter I've chosen a wide range of different recipes, many of which are quite unusual and you may not have tried before. They include various salads, vegetables to serve as part of a mixed antipasti selection, finger food, accompaniments and more substantial main course dishes. *Buon appetito!*

VEGETABLES

CAPRESE SALAD

ROASTED ASPARAGUS SALAD WITH RED ONIONS

COURGETTES PRESERVED IN OIL WITH CHILLIES, GARLIC & FRESH MINT

SOUTHERN ITALIAN PICKLED VEGETABLE SALAD

POTATO & ARTICHOKE GRATIN

AUBERGINE BALLS WITH PARMESAN, GARLIC & PARSLEY

SPICY SAUTÉED MUSHROOMS WITH GARLIC & TOMATOES

COURGETTES STUFFED WITH RICOTTA & PECORINO

BAKED COURGETTES WITH MOZZARELLA & PARMESAN

CAPRESE SALAD

INSALATA ALLA CAPRESE

The last time I saw my late father was a few years ago in a restaurant on the Amalfi coast, where we both enjoyed a wonderful Caprese salad. So when I found myself on a boat sailing along the same stretch of coast recently, I made my own version of this traditional salad in his memory. Papà – I dedicate this recipe to you!

Serves 4

4 large fresh plum tomatoes (preferably San Marzano)
3 x 125g balls of buffalo mozzarella cheese, drained
2 large handfuls (about 80g) of fresh basil

4 tablespoons extra virgin olive oil, plus extra for drizzling
Coarse sea salt
Freshly ground black pepper

1] Roughly chop the tomatoes into large chunks and put on a serving plate.

2] Tear the mozzarella and basil into large pieces and add to the plate with the tomatoes.

3] Drizzle with the olive oil.

4] Grind over some salt and black pepper. Gently toss together.

5] Drizzle with a little more oil, toss again and serve.

ROASTED ASPARAGUS SALAD WITH RED ONIONS

INSALATONA DI ASPARAGI E CIPOLLE ROSSE

Asparagus has been popular in Italy since the Roman times. Usually it's boiled or steamed, or a combination of the two in a special pan, but it's also delicious roasted with garlic in a little olive oil and lemon juice. In central Italy wild asparagus grows in abundance in the countryside in spring, often in sandy soil close to the roadside. It's green, much thinner and less woody than cultivated asparagus, and full of flavour. Here I've used fine asparagus spears – the type you buy in the supermarket – and it pairs beautifully with the roasted red onions in this salad. I make it at least once a week during our family holidays in Sardinia.

Serves 4

600g fine asparagus spears, woody ends
  removed
1 garlic clove, peeled and crushed
1 tablespoon freshly squeezed lemon juice
4 tablespoons extra virgin olive oil
2 large red onions, peeled and cut into slices
  1cm thick
140g rocket leaves
50g Parmesan cheese shavings
Salt and freshly ground black pepper

For the dressing
2 tablespoons freshly squeezed lemon juice
1 tablespoon wholegrain mustard
1 teaspoon runny honey
5 tablespoons extra virgin olive oil

1] Preheat the oven to 200°C/gas mark 6. Place the asparagus and garlic in a roasting tin, about 25 x 35cm. Spoon over the lemon juice and 2 tablespoons of the oil. Toss together. Roast for 20 minutes. Remove the tin from the oven and leave to cool slightly. Transfer the asparagus to a plate.

2] Put the onions in the same tin as you cooked the asparagus. Drizzle over the remaining 2 tablespoons of oil and toss to coat. Roast for 25 minutes, turning halfway. Leave to cool slightly.

3] To make the dressing, put the lemon juice, mustard and honey in a large bowl, gradually add the oil and whisk thoroughly until well combined. Add the asparagus and onions and toss to coat. Season with salt and pepper.

4] Scatter the rocket on a plate and arrange the asparagus and onions on top. Serve with the Parmesan shavings on the side or scattered over the salad.

COURGETTES PRESERVED IN OIL WITH CHILLIES, GARLIC & FRESH MINT

ZUCCHINE MARINATE ALLA SCAPECE

Whenever my mother visits she always brings me several jars of preserved courgettes, as she knows how much I've loved them since my childhood. They're wonderful served as part of the antipasti table, for example with Parma ham and creamy burrata cheese (made from mozzarella and cream). You do need to make them at least a couple of weeks before serving. The courgettes will last for up to 1 month in the fridge provided they're always submerged in oil. Remove from the fridge about 1 hour before serving.

Makes
500ml

12 large courgettes
75g sea salt flakes
700ml white wine vinegar
12 fresh mint leaves, roughly chopped

5 garlic cloves, peeled and halved
4 fresh, medium-hot red chillies, halved
125ml extra virgin olive oil, plus extra for
 topping up

1] Cut the courgettes in half lengthways. Using a small teaspoon, scoop out the pulp and seeds and discard. Cut each courgette half into thirds across then slice each piece into strips lengthways, about 5mm thick. Place in a large bowl and sprinkle over the salt. Using your hands, toss together. Cover with a tea towel and leave for 10 hours at room temperature (the salt will draw out the moisture).

2] Drain the courgettes and squeeze out as much water as you can with your hands. Place in a medium saucepan with the vinegar and 250ml water and bring to the boil over a high heat. Reduce the heat to medium, stir and cook for a further 5 minutes.

3] Drain thoroughly in a colander then fill the pan with water and place it on top of the courgettes (the weight of the filled pan will squeeze out more of the liquid). Leave for 20 minutes.

4] Lay the courgettes on tea towels in a single layer and so they are not touching. Cover with another tea towel and leave to dry at room temperature for 24 hours.

5] Place the courgettes in a large bowl with the mint, garlic, chillies and oil. Season with a little salt and gently toss together. Cover with a tea towel and leave to marinate at room temperature for 12 hours.

6] Sterilise a 500ml lidded glass jar (or several smaller jars) by placing in boiling water for about 10–15 minutes. Transfer the courgette mixture to the jar and pack down the contents as tightly as possible to release any air bubbles. Add extra oil to cover, if needed. Seal tightly. Refrigerate for 2 weeks before sampling.

SOUTHERN ITALIAN PICKLED VEGETABLE SALAD

VERDURE IN SALAMOIA

This pickled vegetable salad complements rich meat dishes perfectly, and it's also a great accompaniment to serve with fish. There are many variations of pickled vegetable salad recipes in southern Italy – some contain peppers or carrots, and cloves are often used in the pickling brine. This is my favourite combination of vegetables and flavourings. Plus it's a quick no-nonsense recipe, which means you can eat it pretty much straightaway.

Serves 6

1 large cauliflower (about 1kg), cut into small
  florets
400g purple sprouting broccoli, cut into florets
  and stems sliced into bite-sized pieces
200g Borettane onions in oil or brine, drained
50g sultanas
80g caper berries, drained
50ml extra virgin olive oil

For the pickling brine
1 litre white wine vinegar
50g runny honey
2 bay leaves
4 juniper berries
45g salt
4 black peppercorns

1] Put all the ingredients for the pickling brine in a medium saucepan. Add 1 litre of water. Place over a high heat and bring to the boil.

2] Reduce the heat to medium and add the cauliflower. Simmer for 6 minutes. Using a slotted spoon, lift out the cauliflower and drain in a colander. Add the broccoli to the pan and simmer for 6 minutes. Meanwhile, transfer the cauliflower to a tea towel.

3] Drain the broccoli (discard the brine) and transfer to the tea towel. Leave the vegetables for 30 minutes or until completely dry.

4] Tip the vegetables into a large bowl. Add the Borettane onions, sultanas, caper berries and oil. Gently toss together until all the vegetables are coated in the oil. Transfer to a large serving platter.

POTATO & ARTICHOKE GRATIN

TEGLIA DI PATATE E CARCIOFI GRATINATI

Artichokes are incredibly popular in Italy. They're celebrated throughout April at many food festivals, including the famous *Sagra del carciofo romanesco*, in the central region of Lazio. For this dish I cooked whole raw artichokes, but you can use a jar of chargrilled artichoke hearts in oil if you prefer, provided you drain them well. This is a great accompaniment to roasted meat and poultry.

2 lemons (1 squeezed, 1 quartered)
8 globe artichokes, about 250g each
4 tablespoons olive oil, plus extra for greasing
100g fresh white breadcrumbs
50g freshly grated Grana Padano cheese

2 garlic cloves, peeled and crushed
4 tablespoons chopped fresh flat-leaf parsley
800g Charlotte potatoes, peeled and cut into
  5mm slices
Salt and freshly ground black pepper

Serves 6

1] Preheat the oven to 200°C/gas mark 6. Fill a large bowl with cold water and add the lemon juice.

2] Peel off the dark outer leaves of one of the artichokes until you reach the tender light green leaves. Using a sharp knife, cut off the top third of the artichoke and remove the stem. Trim the base to remove all traces of green. Use a teaspoon to scoop out the hairy choke from the centre of the artichoke and discard. Rub all over with one of the lemon quarters to prevent browning. Cut the heart into quarters and immediately immerse the wedges in the lemon water to prevent discoloration while you prepare the other artichokes in the same way.

3] Heat 2 tablespoons of the oil in a large saucepan over a medium heat. Drain the artichokes and add them to the pan with 130ml of cold water and some salt. Cook for 10 minutes, stirring occasionally, until tender.

4] Meanwhile, combine the breadcrumbs, Grana Padano, garlic and parsley in a medium bowl.

5] Grease a baking dish, about 20 x 28cm, with some oil. Spread half the potatoes over the bottom of the dish. Season with salt and pepper. Scatter over a quarter of the breadcrumb mixture, then half the artichokes. Repeat this stage. To finish, scatter over a quarter of the breadcrumb mixture and lay the remaining potatoes on top. Season with salt and pepper. Scatter over the remaining breadcrumb mixture and drizzle over the remaining 2 tablespoons of oil.

6] Cover with foil and bake for 30 minutes. Remove the foil and bake for a further 45 minutes or until golden brown. Serve hot.

AUBERGINE BALLS WITH PARMESAN, GARLIC & PARSLEY

POLPETTINE DI MELANZANE CON PARMIGIANO, AGLIO E PREZZEMOLO

Most recipes for aubergines come from southern Italy – particularly Calabria and Sicily – where the vegetable has been popular for a lot longer than in the north. This great recipe came from my aunty Rafilina, one of my mother's nine sisters. We used to visit her at weekends, and as we played and chatted by the lake at the bottom of her garden she would continuously supply us with home-made finger food. These aubergine balls were always my favourite – I love the contrast between their crisp coating and their warm, creamy interior.

2 aubergines (about 250g each), cut into 2cm cubes
150g fresh white breadcrumbs
50g freshly grated Parmesan cheese
3 tablespoons chopped fresh flat-leaf parsley

1 garlic clove, peeled and crushed
1 large egg, lightly beaten
50g fine dried breadcrumbs
500ml olive oil
Salt and freshly ground black pepper

Serves 4

1] Bring a large pan of salted water to the boil over a high heat. Drop in the aubergines and bring back to the boil, then reduce the heat to medium. Place a pan lid on top so the aubergine cubes are submerged. Simmer for 10 minutes then drain thoroughly in a colander or sieve. Leave to cool slightly.

2] Using the back of a wooden spoon, press the aubergine against the side of the colander or sieve to remove as much excess liquid as possible. Chop the aubergine finely, then put in a medium bowl with the fresh breadcrumbs, Parmesan, parsley and garlic. Mash with a fork to combine, mix in the egg and season with salt and pepper.

3] Tip the dried breadcrumbs onto a plate. Using your hands, roll the aubergine mixture into small balls about the size of a walnut. Carefully roll each ball in the breadcrumbs and transfer to another plate. You should end up with about 20 balls in total.

4] Heat the oil in a large non-stick frying pan over a high heat. When the oil is very hot, carefully add the balls in a single layer and fry for about 6 minutes, turning them over as they brown. You may need to fry in batches. Transfer to kitchen paper to drain for about 2 minutes then serve.

SPICY SAUTÉED MUSHROOMS WITH GARLIC & TOMATOES

FUNGHI DI BOSCO PICCANTI CON AGLIO E POMODORINI

Wild mushrooms are found throughout Italy in autumn, with the island of Elba and the wooded hills of Sila, in Calabria, being among the best places in the country to forage for them. There are well over 200 varieties, but porcini and chanterelles are certainly the most common. For this recipe you can use whatever mixed mushrooms are available. I suggest you make double quantities and toss the leftovers in pasta the following day – delicious!

900g fresh mixed wild mushrooms (porcini, chanterelle, oyster, chestnut)
4 tablespoons extra virgin olive oil
3 large garlic cloves, peeled and halved
1 tablespoon chopped fresh rosemary

1 teaspoon dried chilli flakes
1 x 400g tin of cherry tomatoes
2 tablespoons chopped fresh flat-leaf parsley
Salt

Serves 4

1] Remove any dirt from the mushrooms with a pastry brush. Cut the mushrooms into slices 5mm thick. Set aside.

2] Heat the oil in a large frying pan over a high heat. Add the garlic and rosemary and fry for 1 minute. Tip in the mushrooms, add the chilli flakes and season with salt. Fry for 10 minutes, stirring occasionally.

3] Add the tomatoes and fry for about 8 minutes. Stir in the parsley and serve hot.

COURGETTES STUFFED WITH RICOTTA & PECORINO

ZUCCHINE AL FORNO RIPIENE DI RICOTTA E PECORINO

As I was filming in Campania I found the most beautiful restaurant in Castel Volturno – a coastal town north of Naples, which has long beaches surrounded by fragrant pine forests. The restaurant is called Da Michele, and if you're ever in the area I suggest a visit. The food is simple and true to the region – hand-made pasta, stuffed home-grown vegetables and simple salads. This courgette dish is one of their most popular offerings and has been on the menu consistently for the past nine years. Serve with a tomato and onion salad dressed with extra virgin olive oil and balsamic vinegar.

Serves 6

6 medium courgettes
5 tablespoons extra virgin olive oil, plus extra
  for greasing
2 garlic cloves, peeled and crushed
40g fresh white breadcrumbs

3 tablespoons chopped fresh flat-leaf parsley
250g ricotta cheese, drained
50g freshly grated pecorino cheese
1 large egg, lightly beaten
Salt and freshly ground black pepper

1] Preheat the oven to 190°C/gas mark 5. Cut the courgettes in half lengthways. Using a teaspoon, carefully scoop out most of the insides. Finely chop the courgette flesh. Lay the courgette shells, cut-side up and in a single layer, on a large oiled baking sheet. Season with salt.

2] To make the stuffing, heat 3 tablespoons of the oil in a medium saucepan over a medium heat. Add the garlic and fry for 30 seconds. Add the courgette flesh and fry for 5 minutes, stirring occasionally. Tip in the breadcrumbs and fry for 3 minutes, stirring continuously.

3] Remove the pan from the heat and add the parsley, ricotta, 40g of the pecorino and the egg. Season with salt and pepper and stir to combine.

4] Fill the courgette shells with the stuffing mixture. Sprinkle over the remaining pecorino and drizzle over the remaining 2 tablespoons of oil.

5] Bake for 30 minutes or until the top is golden.

BAKED COURGETTES WITH MOZZARELLA & PARMESAN

ZUCCHINE AL FORNO CON MOZZARELLA E PARMIGIANO

This dish is extremely popular on the west coast of Italy, where it is often served as an accompaniment to chargrilled fish. The tomato sauce can be made ahead and the whole dish assembled several hours ahead of cooking. Just add on an extra 5 minutes to the cooking time if it's being cooked from cold. Serve with warm, crusty bread.

Serves 6 as a side dish, 4 as a main course

3 tablespoons extra virgin olive oil
2 large garlic cloves, peeled and halved
2 x 400g tins of chopped tomatoes
12 fresh basil leaves, roughly torn
9 large courgettes, cut lengthways into slices 5mm thick

250ml olive oil, plus extra for greasing
80g freshly grated Parmesan cheese
2 x 125g balls of mozzarella cheese, drained and cut into small cubes
Salt and freshly ground black pepper

1] Heat the extra virgin olive oil in a medium saucepan over a medium heat. Add the garlic and fry for 1 minute. Add the tomatoes, 6 basil leaves and salt. Simmer for about 15 minutes, stirring occasionally, until quite thick. Set aside and discard the garlic.

2] Put the courgettes in a colander placed over the sink and sprinkle salt between the layers (this will draw out the moisture). Leave for 15–30 minutes, then rinse in cold water to remove the salt. Drain on kitchen paper and pat dry.

3] Heat the olive oil in a large non-stick frying pan over a medium heat. Add a single layer of courgettes and fry for about 2 minutes each side or until lightly coloured. Drain on kitchen paper, laying kitchen paper between the layers to absorb excess oil. Fry and drain the remaining courgettes in batches in the same way. Set aside.

4] Preheat the oven to 200°C/gas mark 6. Grease a baking dish, about 24 x 28cm, with a little oil. Spread one third of the tomato sauce in the dish. Place half of the courgettes on top, then scatter over half each of the basil, mozzarella and the Parmesan. Season with salt and pepper. Add another one third of the tomato sauce, then arrange the remaining courgettes and remaining basil on top. Season again with salt and pepper. Spread over the remaining tomato sauce and finish with the remaining mozzarella and Parmesan.

5] Bake for 45 minutes until bubbling and golden brown.

We Italians are very proud of our desserts and there is such an amazing variety. Generally, the desserts in southern Italy are less creamy and rich than those in the north and often contain almonds, pistachios and candied fruits — all brought to the region by the Arabs, who ruled Sicily in the 9th and 10th centuries. The south is also famous for its wonderful granitas, sorbets and ice cream. I have included a range of popular desserts in this chapter, such as tiramisù, but I have also added some recipes that are less well known outside Italy, for instance baked aubergines with sweetened ricotta served with a chocolate sauce. I know it sounds really strange, but trust me on this one — it is heavenly.

DESSERTS

FRUIT & PROSECCO JELLIES WITH VANILLA CREAM

ZABAIONE WITH LIMONCELLO & STRAWBERRIES

CHOCOLATE-DIPPED STUFFED FIGS

CHOCOLATE ICE CREAM SANDWICH

BLACKBERRY SORBET

LIQUORICE SEMIFREDDO

HAZELNUT & VANILLA CAKE

CHOCOLATE, PISTACHIO & ALMOND CAKE

BAKED AUBERGINE & SWEETENED RICOTTA WITH CHOCOLATE SAUCE

TIRAMISÙ WITH AMARETTO

FRUIT & PROSECCO JELLIES WITH VANILLA CREAM

GELATINA DI FRUTTA E PROSECCO CON PANNA ALLA VANIGLIA

This is a lovely summery dessert that looks elegant and can easily be made ahead, so it's perfect for entertaining. It contains some rather special ingredients – prosecco and bergamot syrup; this delicious syrup is made from the citrus fruit bergamot, which is cultivated only in Calabria (see page 26). You might not recognise the name or even the fruit itself, but you will certainly recognise the flavour, as it's used to flavour Earl Grey tea. Bergamot syrup is difficult to find in Britain, but you can use a few drops of orange extract as a substitute, and candied orange peel instead of bergamot peel to decorate.

Serves 4

1 Granny Smith apple
Juice of 1 lemon
500ml lemonade
8 sheets of leaf gelatine
75ml bergamot syrup
220g ripe strawberries, hulled and sliced
140ml prosecco
12 small mint leaves and 40g candied
  bergamot peel to decorate

For the vanilla cream
150ml double cream
100g mascarpone cheese
Seeds of 1 vanilla pod

1] Peel, core and cut the apple into bite-sized pieces. Squeeze over the lemon juice. Set aside.

2] To make the jelly mixture, heat half the lemonade in a medium saucepan over a medium heat. When the lemonade is almost boiling, remove from the heat.

3] Meanwhile, soak the gelatine in a bowl of cold water for 4–5 minutes (no longer). Squeeze well to remove any excess moisture then stir the leaves into the hot lemonade until completely dissolved. Stir in the bergamot syrup and the remaining lemonade. Set aside to cool slightly.

4] Divide the strawberries and apple between 4 serving glasses (ideally martini glasses). Pour over the jelly mixture to cover the fruit. Top up with prosecco and stir. Cover with cling film and chill for at least 3 hours or overnight until set.

5] To make the vanilla cream, whip the cream until thick enough to just hold its shape and form soft peaks. Using a metal spoon, fold in the mascarpone and vanilla seeds until smooth. Cover and refrigerate until ready to serve.

6] Remove the jellies from the fridge 20 minutes before serving and spoon a dollop of vanilla cream over each. Decorate with mint leaves and candied bergamot peel.

ZABAIONE WITH LIMONCELLO & STRAWBERRIES

ZABAIONE AL LIMONCELLO CON FRAGOLE

Zabaione is an old Venetian dessert traditionally made with Marsala wine (or sometimes vin santo), but here I've given it a southern Italian twist by using limoncello (see page 79) – a lemon-flavoured liqueur that is produced mainly in Campania. It's made from Amalfi lemons, which are famous for their wonderful sweet flavour and fragrance and exceptionally large size (see page 78). Raspberries are equally delicious with this dessert.

200g ripe strawberries, hulled and sliced
140ml limoncello (lemon-flavoured liqueur)
80g caster sugar
6 egg yolks

Grated zest of 1 unwaxed lemon, plus extra
  for decoration
120ml double cream

Serves 6

1] Put the strawberries in a medium bowl with 4 tablespoons of the limoncello and 2 tablespoons of the sugar. Stir and set aside at room temperature for 1 hour, stirring every 10 minutes.

2] Meanwhile, place the egg yolks in a heatproof bowl (preferably stainless steel) with the lemon zest and remaining sugar. Whisk using a balloon whisk until pale and creamy.

3] Set the bowl over a pan of very gently simmering water. The base of the bowl should not touch the water. Add the remaining limoncello and whisk constantly until the mixture foams and thickens. This should take about 5 minutes; remember, the mixture will thicken further as it cools.

4] Fill a slightly larger bowl with iced water and set the bowl with the zabaione mixture inside it. Leave to cool completely, stirring occasionally (it should take about 25 minutes).

5] Put the cream in a medium bowl and whip until thick enough to form peaks. Gently fold a quarter of the cream into the cooled zabaione, then the remainder.

6] To serve, divide the strawberries and their juices among 6 dessert glasses and top with a large dollop of zabaione. Sprinkle over some grated lemon zest. Serve immediately.

CHOCOLATE-DIPPED STUFFED FIGS

FICHI RIPIENI E RICOPERTI DI CIOCCOLATO

Calabria is Italy's main fig-growing region, and in September the trees in the region are bursting with this wonderful fruit. There is such an abundance of figs that many are preserved, and you'll often see farmers laying out fruit to dry in the sun, sometimes on traditional reed racks (*cannizzole*) as they have done for centuries. In this recipe – a Calabrian favourite – dried figs are stuffed with almonds and candied orange peel and dipped in chocolate. It's an amazing combination. Here I've shown how to make your own candied orange peel (which can be stored in an airtight container for about six weeks), but as a shortcut you can buy it in the shops.

Serves 12

2 large oranges
550g granulated sugar
24 dried figs

48 almonds (with the skin on)
400g dark chocolate

1] First make the candied peel. Cut the oranges into 8 wedges. Remove the flesh, leaving only the skin and pith (keep the flesh for eating later). Slice each piece of peel into 3 or 4 strips, place in a small saucepan and cover with cold water.

2] Bring to the boil, then reduce the heat and simmer for 5 minutes. Drain and return the peel to the pan with 600ml cold water. Bring to the boil, then reduce the heat again and simmer for a further 30 minutes. Transfer the peel to a plate.

3] Reduce the heat to low. Add 500g of the sugar and heat gently until dissolved. Return the peel to the pan. Increase the heat slightly and simmer for 30 minutes. Remove from the heat and leave the peel to cool in the syrup.

4] Preheat the oven to 50°C or the lowest possible gas setting. Using a slotted spoon, lift out the peel and place on a wire rack set over a baking sheet (discard the syrup). Transfer to the oven for 30 minutes to dry out. Place the remaining sugar on a plate and toss the warm peel in the sugar to coat. Spread the strips on a baking sheet for 1 hour to dry at room temperature.

5] Preheat the oven to 120°C/gas mark ¼. To stuff the figs, first remove and discard the tough stems. Cut a slit about 2cm wide and 2cm deep opposite the stem end of each fig to create a pocket. Fill each with an almond and a piece of orange peel then press gently to seal. Place the figs on a baking sheet and bake for 40 minutes, turning halfway. Remove from the oven and leave to cool. Meanwhile, line a tray or baking sheet with baking parchment.

6] Break the chocolate into a large heatproof bowl and set the bowl over a saucepan of gently simmering water. The base of the bowl should not touch the

water. Heat gently until just melted (do not stir), then remove the pan from the heat and stir. Alternatively, melt the chocolate in a microwave on medium in short bursts, stirring in between.

7] Working quickly to keep the chocolate from hardening, drop a fig into the chocolate to submerge it completely, then remove and top with an almond. Transfer the fig to the lined tray or baking sheet. Repeat with the remaining figs. If the chocolate starts to harden, just melt it again over the warm water. Leave the figs to cool and the chocolate to harden. If you like, dip or partially dip any remaining candied orange peel in the chocolate and serve on the side.

CHOCOLATE ICE CREAM SANDWICH

CUCCIOLONE

Chocolate ice cream sandwiched between two cookies – what more do you need from life?! Kids love cucciolone, and in my experience they really enjoy getting involved in making them too. You can use any cookies you like for cucciolone. Here I used choc chip cookies, which worked very well. I've also tried the same recipe with peanut and caramel cookies and it was delicious.

Makes 12

10 egg yolks
150g caster sugar
2 teaspoons vanilla extract

250g chocolate spread (e.g. Nutella)
500ml double cream
24 shop-bought cookies, about 8cm diameter

1] Put the egg yolks, sugar and vanilla in a medium heatproof bowl and set the bowl over a saucepan of simmering water. Ensure the base of the bowl is not touching the water. Stir with a balloon whisk for about 5 minutes or until the sugar has dissolved and the mixture is pale, thick and creamy. Remove from the heat and gently fold in the chocolate spread in 3 stages. Leave to cool completely.

2] Pour the cream into a medium bowl and whisk until thick enough to just hold its shape and form soft peaks. Gently fold the cream into the cooled mixture in 3 stages.

3] Spoon the mixture into a 1-litre rigid freezerproof container. Cover with a lid or cling film and place in the freezer overnight to set.

4] Remove the ice cream from the freezer 5 minutes before you are ready to serve. Arrange 12 cookies on a work surface, with the flat side facing upwards.

5] Place a scoop of ice cream on each cookie then top each with a cookie placed flat-side down to make a sandwich. Gently press the top cookie to spread out the filling. Using a palette knife, smooth the side of the filled cookies.

BLACKBERRY SORBET

SORBETTO ALLE MORE

Blackberry sorbet is always my flavour of choice and brings back memories of foraging with friends when I was a little boy. We'd pick and eat our way through the bushes, and our purple-stained mouths and fingers were always a huge source of amusement – until my mum scrubbed me clean later that evening, practically scraping off the top layer of my skin in the process! This sorbet is perfect served with a chilled bottle of prosecco.

250g caster sugar
600g fresh blackberries
Juice of 2 lemons

Serves 6

1] Put the sugar in a small saucepan with 750ml water. Heat over a low heat for several minutes until the sugar has dissolved, stirring occasionally. Increase the heat to medium and bring to the boil. Boil for 1–2 minutes then remove from the heat and leave to cool.

2] Blitz the blackberries in a food processor or blender until smooth. Place a sieve over a medium bowl and push the blackberries through using the back of a wooden spoon to remove most of the seeds. Discard the seeds.

3] Tip the blackberry purée into the cooled sugar syrup and stir in the lemon juice.

4] Pour the mixture into a 2-litre shallow, rigid freezerproof container, cover and freeze for at least 4 hours or, ideally, overnight.

5] Remove the sorbet from the freezer and blitz the mixture using a food processor or blender (blitzing will break down the ice crystals). When the sorbet is smooth, put it back in the freezer for at least 4 hours or overnight.

6] About 10 minutes before serving, remove the sorbet from the freezer to soften slightly. Serve in scoops in glass dishes or glasses.

LIQUORICE SEMIFREDDO

SEMIFREDDO ALLA LIQUIRIZIA

Liquorice has been grown along the Mediterranean coastline for centuries, particularly in Calabria, where the soil and climate are ideal (see page 27). For this dessert I've used powdered liquorice root, but I've also made it with shop-bought liquorice twists and it works well too. Use 100g liquorice twists in place of the liquorice root powder and cut the twists into tiny pieces before adding them to the milk. They won't dissolve, so you'll need to blend with a hand-held blender before adding the liquorice-flavoured milk to the egg yolk and sugar mixture.

Serves 8

250ml full-fat milk
15g liquorice root powder
4 large eggs, separated

150g caster sugar
Pinch of salt
300ml double cream

1] Dampen the bottom and sides of a 1kg loaf tin using a pastry brush dipped in water then line the tin with cling film, allowing enough to overhang the sides. Set aside. Put the milk and liquorice in a medium saucepan and heat over a low to medium heat, stirring occasionally, until the powder has dissolved and the milk is hot but not yet simmering. Remove from the heat and set aside.

2] Place the egg yolks and 100g of the sugar in a medium bowl and whisk using a balloon whisk for about 5 minutes until thick and pale. Gradually add the liquorice milk to the egg yolks in a steady stream, whisking all the time. Pour the mixture back into the pan (rinse it out first so the mixture doesn't burn) and heat gently over a low to medium heat, stirring constantly for 5 minutes or until the mixture thickens and coats the back of the spoon. Pour the mixture into a heatproof bowl. Place the bowl in a larger bowl filled with iced water. Leave to cool, stirring occasionally.

3] Put the egg whites in a separate bowl, add the salt and whisk with an electric hand whisk on full speed until they form soft peaks. Add the remaining 50g sugar and whisk until firm peaks form. Set aside.

4] Pour the cream into a medium bowl and whip until thick enough to just hold its shape and form soft peaks. Set aside.

5] Remove the liquorice mixture from the water bath. Gently fold one third of the egg whites into the liquorice mixture until well blended. Fold in the remaining egg whites in two stages then the cream. Tip the mixture into the prepared loaf tin. Fold the overhanging cling film over the top and freeze for 8 hours or until set.

6] Remove the tin from the freezer 10 minutes before serving. To serve, turn out the semifreddo onto a serving plate, carefully remove the cling film and slice.

HAZELNUT & VANILLA CAKE

TORTA DI NOCCIOLE E VANIGLIA

This hazelnut and vanilla cake is perfect served with morning coffee, or you could make it more of a special-occasion dessert by cutting it in half and making a sandwich cake with a sweetened ricotta and mascarpone filling. You can also make this cake with pistachios or walnuts if you prefer and use orange zest instead of lemon zest. No flour is used, so it's completely gluten-free.

Butter for greasing
200g hazelnuts
6 medium eggs, separated
140g caster sugar

Grated zest of 1 unwaxed lemon
1 teaspoon vanilla extract
Icing sugar for dusting

Serves 8

1] Preheat the oven to 160°C/gas mark 3. Grease a deep, loose-bottomed round cake tin, 20cm diameter, with butter and line with baking parchment.

2] Grind the hazelnuts in a food processor until fine (it doesn't matter if there are a few slightly larger pieces). Set aside.

3] Put the egg whites in a medium bowl and whisk using an electric hand whisk on full speed until they form soft peaks. Gradually add half the sugar, whisking between each spoonful until stiffer peaks form. Set aside.

4] In a separate medium bowl, whisk the egg yolks and remaining sugar using a balloon whisk for about 5 minutes or until thick and pale. Stir in the lemon zest and vanilla.

5] Using a metal spoon or spatula, fold the egg yolks into the egg whites. Now gently fold the hazelnuts into the mixture in 4 stages.

6] Spoon the mixture into the prepared cake tin and spread it out evenly. Bake for 35 minutes or until well risen and the top springs back when lightly pressed.

7] Stand the tin on a cooling rack and leave the cake to cool. Just before serving, run a knife around the cake and turn it out onto a serving plate. Lightly dust with icing sugar.

CHOCOLATE, PISTACHIO & ALMOND CAKE

TORTA CAPRESE

Capri is the number one island to visit in Italy, and this is one of its fabulous specialities – torta caprese. It's a gloriously rich chocolate cake with nuts, and beautifully sums up the simplicity and elegance of this glittering island. Serve with a little glass of vin santo.

Serves 8

80g shelled pistachio nuts
100g salted butter, plus extra for greasing
250g plain dark chocolate, about 70%
  cocoa solids

4 large eggs, separated
160g icing sugar, plus extra for dusting
150g ground almonds
8 tablespoons mascarpone cheese

1] Put the pistachios in a medium bowl and pour over boiling water. Leave to soak for 3 minutes then drain and peel off the skin. Roughly chop the nuts. Set aside.

2] Preheat the oven to 180°C/gas mark 4. Grease a deep, loose-bottomed cake tin, 23cm diameter, with butter.

3] Break the chocolate into a large heatproof bowl and add the butter. Place the bowl over a saucepan of gently simmering water. The base of the bowl should not touch the water or the chocolate will become bitter. Heat gently until just melted (do not stir), then remove the pan from the heat and stir.

4] Put the egg yolks and icing sugar in a large bowl and whisk using a balloon whisk for about 5 minutes until fluffy and pale.

5] Put the egg whites in a medium bowl and whisk using an electric hand whisk on full speed until firm peaks form.

6] Pour the melted chocolate into the bowl with the egg yolks and sugar and mix thoroughly. Stir in the pistachios and almonds. Gently fold one third of the egg whites into the mixture using a metal spoon. Fold in the remaining egg whites in 2 stages.

7] Pour the mixture into the prepared cake tin and spread it out evenly. Bake for 30 minutes or until well risen and the top springs back when lightly pressed.

8] Stand the tin on a cooling rack and leave to rest for 10 minutes, then turn it out onto the rack and leave to cool. Just before serving lightly dust with icing sugar, then slice and serve with a tablespoon of mascarpone per person.

BAKED AUBERGINE & SWEETENED RICOTTA WITH CHOCOLATE SAUCE

MELANZANE AL CIOCCOLATO

This is traditionally served on 15 August to celebrate the Italian national holiday *Ferragosto*. Historically, this festival celebrated the end of the harvest and provided a period of rest for labourers, but more recently it has become the time Italians take a holiday and visit their families. Southern Italians love combining savoury and sweet flavours with amazing results, and this is a prime example. It may sound strange but it works incredibly well as a dessert – do try it and see.

Serves 6–8

100g plain flour
280g caster sugar, plus extra for dusting
½ teaspoon ground cinnamon
Grated zest of 2 unwaxed lemons
500ml olive oil
5 medium aubergines (about 1.4kg), peeled and cut lengthways into slices 1cm thick
Butter for greasing
Icing sugar for decoration

For the sweetened ricotta
50g blanched almonds
250g ricotta cheese, drained
50g caster sugar
5 amaretti biscuits, crushed
10g candied orange peel, finely chopped (shop-bought or see page 202)
2 large eggs, lightly beaten

For the chocolate sauce
300ml double cream
300g dark chocolate, broken into small pieces

1] Put the flour on a plate and the 280g caster sugar on another. Stir the cinnamon and lemon zest into the sugar.

2] Heat 4 tablespoons of the oil in a large non-stick frying pan over a medium heat until very hot. Lightly coat the aubergines with flour and place in the pan in a single layer. Fry for 3 minutes, then turn over and fry for 2 minutes. Drain on kitchen paper. Repeat for the remaining aubergine, working in batches and adding a little more oil each time. While the aubergine is still warm, dip each slice in the cinnamon sugar to coat on both sides. Set aside.

3] To make the sweetened ricotta, heat a small non-stick frying pan until hot. Add the almonds and dry-fry over a medium to low heat for a few minutes, stirring and shaking the pan constantly so they don't burn. Roughly chop and put into a medium bowl. Add the remaining ingredients and stir to combine. Set aside.

4] To make the chocolate sauce, heat the cream in a medium saucepan over a low heat. When hot, remove from the heat and add the chocolate. Leave for 2 minutes (without stirring) or until the chocolate has melted, then stir until smooth. Set aside.

5] Preheat the oven to 190°C/gas mark 5. Grease a baking dish, 22 x 22cm and at least 6cm high, with butter and dust with caster sugar. Line the bottom and sides of the dish with aubergine slices, allowing some overhang.

6] Spread one third of the sweetened ricotta over the aubergines, then a quarter of the chocolate sauce and top with a layer of aubergines. Repeat twice more, finishing with a layer of aubergines. Fold over the aubergine overhang to enclose the filling. Loosen the remaining chocolate sauce with a little milk, cover and refrigerate.

7] Bake the dish for 25 minutes or until golden brown and bubbling. Remove from the oven and leave to cool completely. Cover and refrigerate for at least 4 hours, or overnight.

8] Remove from the fridge 1 hour before serving. Cut into slices and place on serving plates. Gently warm the chocolate sauce in a pan over a low heat. Drizzle over the chocolate sauce and sprinkle over some icing sugar, then serve.

TIRAMISÙ WITH AMARETTO

TIRAMISÙ CON AMARETTO

Tiramisù (which translates as 'pick me up') is a modern version of a dessert first created in Tuscany, where it was known in the 19th century as 'zuppa inglese' (English soup), because of the popularity of the dessert among the English living in the region. The original dessert had a custard base, but this was later replaced with mascarpone. There are often variations in the liqueur used. Some cooks like to use a coffee liqueur (Tia Maria), while others prefer Irish cream (Baileys), strega (an Italian herbal liqueur containing saffron) or Marsala wine. Personally, I think that nothing beats the almond-flavoured liqueur amaretto.

Serves 8

350ml cold strong black coffee, preferably
  espresso
150ml amaretto (almond liqueur)
200ml double cream
5 medium eggs, separated

6 tablespoons caster sugar
500g mascarpone cheese
36 Savoiardi sponge fingers (ladyfingers)
Cocoa powder for dusting

1] Put the coffee in a medium bowl and stir in 4 tablespoons of the amaretto. Set aside.

2] Pour the cream into a medium bowl and whip until thick enough to just hold its shape and form soft peaks. Set aside.

3] Place the egg yolks and sugar in a large bowl and whisk using a balloon whisk for about 5 minutes until thick and pale. Add the mascarpone and beat thoroughly. Gently fold in the whipped cream and remaining amaretto.

4] Put the egg whites in a separate bowl and whisk with an electric hand whisk on full speed until they form stiff peaks. Using a metal spoon, gently fold one third of the egg whites into the mascarpone mixture until well blended. Fold in the remaining egg whites in 2 stages. Set aside.

5] Dip one of the biscuits in the coffee for 2 seconds (no longer) and place it in the bottom of a 20 x 30 x 7cm ceramic dish, with the sugar-side facing upwards. Repeat until the bottom of the dish is covered with half the biscuits.

6] Spread half the mascarpone mixture over the biscuits, then cover with another layer of the remaining biscuits dipped in coffee as previously. Spread the remaining mascarpone mixture on top and smooth the surface using a palette knife. Cover with cling film and refrigerate for 3 hours. Just before serving, remove the cling film and dust with cocoa powder.

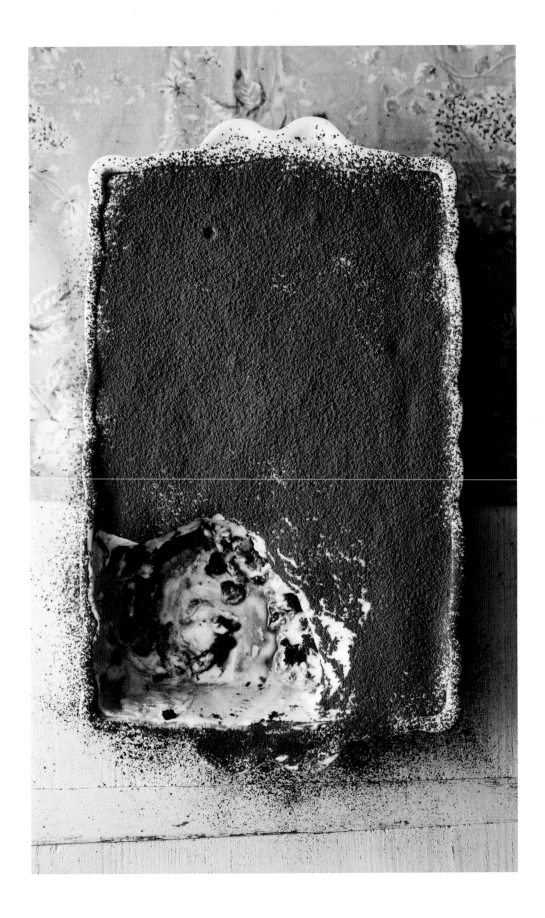

INDEX

A

Aeolian Islands 7
almonds 202–3, 214, 216–17
Amalfi-style Fish Soup 40–41
amaretto 218
anchovies
    Calabrian-style King Prawns in a
        Spicy Tomato Sauce 74–75
    colatura di alici 79
    Mixed Fried Seafood with Spicy
        Lemon Mayonnaise 32–33
    Pizza Tray with Anchovies,
        Courgettes, Garlic & Chilli 160–61
    Sea Bass with Roasted
        Vegetables and Anchovies 86–87
    Tuna Tartare 66–67
Antipasti 10–33
apples 196
Artichoke Gratin, Potato & 183
artichokes 110
Asparagus Salad, Roasted, with
    Red Onions 178–79
aubergines 26
    Aubergine Balls with Parmesan,
        Garlic & Parsley 186–87
    Aubergine, Mozzarella & Roasted
        Red Pepper Stack 44–45
    Baked Aubergine & Sweetened
        Ricotta with Chocolate Sauce
        216–17
    Fusilli with Vegetables, Pancetta,
        Pesto & Mozzarella 136–37

B

baccalà 13, 110
Baked Aubergine & Sweetened
    Ricotta with Chocolate Sauce
    216–17
Baked Courgettes with Mozzarella
    & Parmesan 192–93
Baked Peaches with Parma Ham &
    Bocconcini Mozzarella 22–23
beans
    Cannellini Bean, Red Lentil &
        Chilli Soup 37
    cannellini beans 162
    Crispy Chicken with a Spicy
        Sauce & Green Beans 114–15
    Grilled Tuna with Garlic Green
        Beans, Tomatoes & Olives
        80–81
    Linguine with Pesto, Green Beans
        & Capers 126–27
    Squid, Spicy Salami & Bean Salad
        68–69

Tuscan-style Barbecued Pork with
    Spicy Beans 108–9
beef
    Beef Carpaccio with Horseradish
        & Parmesan Cream Sauce 20–21
    Beef Fillet with Parma Ham &
        Pesto in Puff Pastry 102–3
    Fettuccine with Neapolitan Ragù
        128–29
    Mamma Alba's Meatballs 96–97
    Pot-roasted Beef in Red Wine 100
    Roast Beef with Roasted
        Vegetables & Fresh Herbs 106–7
    Sliced Rib-eye Steak with Black
        Pepper Butter 63
bergamot 26
Blackberry Sorbet 208–9
bottarga 163
bread 150
    Focaccia stuffed with Gorgonzola,
        Olives, Garlic & Rosemary 170–71
    Foccaccia with Tomatoes, Olives,
        Capers & Red Pesto 167
    Olive & Fennel Seed Ciabatta
        172–73
    Sweet Soft Butter Rolls with
        Vanilla 166
broccoli 182

C

caciocavallo cheese 78–79
cakes 211, 214–15
Calabria 7, 26–27
Calabrian-style King Prawns in a
    Spicy Tomato Sauce 74–75
Calzone, Papa Ciro's Spicy 164–65
Campania 8, 78–79
capers 26
    Focaccia with Tomatoes, Olives,
        Capers & Red Pesto 167
    Linguine with Pesto, Green Beans
        & Capers 126–27
    Parmesan-crusted Cod with a
        Creamy Caper & Parsley Sauce 71
    Salt Cod & Potato Salad with Red
        Onion & Capers 12–13
    Tuna Carpaccio with Rocket,
        Capers & Balsamic 14–15
Caprese Salad 176–77
Capri 8
Capri-style Pan-fried Sea Bream
    76–77
cauliflower 182
celery 37, 38, 100, 106, 113, 128
Chargrilled Chicken with Garlic &
    Rosemary Potatoes 122–23
cheese see caciocavallo,
    Gorgonzola, etc.

Cherry Gravy, Red Wine & 101
chestnuts 162
chicken
    Chargrilled Chicken with Garlic
        & Rosemary Potatoes 122–23
    Chicken Escalopes with Wild
        Mushrooms & Thyme 58–59
    Chicken Risotto with Red Pesto
        & Rosemary 148–49
    Crispy Chicken with a Spicy
        Sauce & Green Beans 114–15
    Italian-style Roast Chicken with
        New Potatoes & Red Onion
        120–21
    Spicy Chicken with New
        Potatoes, Tomatoes & Red
        Peppers 118–19
Chicken Liver Skewers with Lemon
    Butter Sauce 36
chickpeas 68
chillies 26, 28, 66–67, 68, 70,
    132, 180
Chocolate
    Chocolate-dipped Stuffed Figs
        202–3
    Chocolate, Pistachio & Almond
        Cake 214–15
    Ice Cream Sandwich 206–7
    Ciabatta, Olive & Fennel Seed
        172–73
clams
    Seafood Pizza 158–59
    Seafood Platter with Tomatoes
        & Red Chillies 70
    Spaghetti with Clams & Mussels
        132–33
cod
    baccalà 13, 110
    Creamy Fish Pie with Roasted Red
        Peppers & Vermouth 88–89
    Parmesan-crusted Cod with a
        Creamy Caper & Parsley Sauce 71
    Salt Cod & Potato Salad with Red
        Onion & Capers 12–13
colatura di alici 79
courgettes
    Baked Courgettes with
        Mozzarella & Parmesan 192–93
    Courgettes Preserved in Oil with
        Chillies, Garlic & Fresh Mint
        180–81
    Courgettes Stuffed with Ricotta
        & Pecorino 190–91
    Fusilli with Vegetables, Pancetta,
        Pesto & Mozzarella 136–37
    Pizza Tray with Anchovies,
        Courgettes, Garlic & Chilli
        160–61

Potato Gnocchi with Courgettes & Tomatoes 140–41

Ricotta Gnocchi with Red Peppers, Courgettes, Butter & Sage 144–45

Spaghetti with Salami & Courgette in a Rich, Creamy Sauce 131

Creamy Fish Pie with Roasted Red Peppers & Vermouth 88–89

Crispy Chicken with a Spicy Sauce & Green Beans 114–15

D, E

Deep-fried Spicy Oysters with Balsamic Dipping Sauce 50–51

Desserts 194–219

Calabrian Specialities 27

Dolcelatte cheese 24

Elba 9

F

fennel bulbs 16, 106, 108

Fettuccine
with Neapolitan Ragù 128–29
with Neapolitan Sausages, Mushrooms & Peas 130

figs 27

Figs, Chocolate-dipped Stuffed 202–3

Fish & seafood 64
Calabrian Specialities 27
Calabrian-style King Prawns in a Spicy Tomato Sauce 74–75
Campanian Specialities 79
Capri-style Pan-fried Sea Bream 76–77
Creamy Fish Pie with Roasted Red Peppers & Vermouth 88–89
Deep-fried Spicy Oysters with Balsamic Dipping Sauce 50–51
Grilled Tuna with Garlic Green Beans, Tomatoes & Olives 80–81
Italian-style Smoked Haddock & Paprika Omelette 46–47
Lazio Specialities 110–11
Parmesan-crusted Cod with a Creamy Caper & Parsley Sauce 71
Salmon Escalopes with Creamy Vermouth Sauce 52–53
Sea Bass in a Rosemary-flavoured Salt Crust 82–83
Sea Bass with Roasted Vegetables and Anchovies 86–87
Seafood Platter with Tomatoes & Red Chillies 70

Sorrento-style Lobster with Limoncello & Rocket 56–57
Squid, Spicy Salami & Bean Salad 68–69
Tuna Tartare 66–67
Tuscan Specialities 163
see also Antipasti & Soups

Focaccia
stuffed with Gorgonzola, Olives, Garlic & Rosemary 170–71
with Tomatoes, Olives, Capers & Red Pesto 167

Fruit & Prosecco Jellies with Vanilla Cream 196–97

Fusilli with Vegetables, Pancetta, Pesto & Mozzarella 136–37

G

Gnocchi 124
Lazio Specialities 111
Potato, with Courgettes & Tomatoes 140–41
Ricotta, with Red Peppers, Courgettes, Butter & Sage 144–45

Gorgonzola cheese 170

Grana Padano cheese 88, 97, 147, 183

Grilled Tuna with Garlic Green Beans, Tomatoes & Olives 80–81

guanciale 111

H

haddock
Amalfi-style Fish Soup 40–41
Italian-style Smoked Haddock & Paprika Omelette 46–47

Hazelnut & Vanilla Cake 211

Herb & Mustard-crusted Rack of Lamb 92–93

honey 163

I

ice cream 206–7

Italian-style Roast Chicken with New Potatoes & Red Onion 120–21

Italian-style Smoked Haddock & Paprika Omelette 46–47

K, L

Kid with Garlic New Potatoes, Roasted 112

Lamb, Herb & Mustard-crusted, Rack of 92–93

Lazio 8–9, 110–11

leeks 38, 62, 106, 130

lemons, Amalfi 78

lentils 37, 110

limoncello 56, 79, 201

Linguine with Pesto, Green Beans & Capers 126–27

liquorice 27

Liquorice Semifreddo 210

Lobster, Sorrento-style, with Limoncello & Rocket 56–57

M

Mamma Alba's Meatballs 96–97

map of Italy's coastline 6

mascarpone cheese
Fruit & Prosecco Jellies with Vanilla Cream 196–97
Parmesan-crusted Cod with a Creamy Caper & Parsley Sauce 71
Pear, Dolcelatte & Mascarpone Tart with Honey & Thyme 24–25
Pizza Tray with Smoked Salmon, Mascarpone & Mozzarella 155
Tiramisù with Amaretto 218–19
Twice-baked Jacket Potatoes with Leeks & Taleggio 62

Mayonnaise, Spicy Lemon 32–33

Meat & Poultry 90–123
see also beef, chicken, etc.

Meatballs, Mamma Alba's 96–97

Mixed Fried Seafood with Spicy Lemon Mayonnaise 32–33

mozzarella
Aubergine, Mozzarella & Roasted Red Pepper Stack 44–45
Baked Courgettes with Mozzarella & Parmesan 192–93
Baked Peaches with Parma Ham & Bocconcini Mozzarella 22–23
Campanian Specialities 78
Caprese Salad 176–77
Fusilli with Vegetables, Pancetta, Pesto & Mozzarella 136–37
Lazio Specialities 111
Neapolitan Pizza with Buffalo Mozzarella, Tomatoes & Basil 152–53
Pizza Tray with Smoked Salmon, Mascarpone & Mozzarella 155
Rice Croquettes with Arrabbiata Sauce 28–29

mushrooms
Chicken Escalopes with Wild Mushrooms & Thyme 58–59
Fettuccine with Neapolitan Sausages, Mushrooms & Peas 130
Spicy Sautéed Mushrooms with Garlic & Tomatoes 188–89
Tuscan Specialities 162

mussels
  Seafood Pizza 158–59
  Seafood Platter with Tomatoes
    & Red Chillies 70
  Spaghetti with Clams & Mussels
    132–33

N, O

nduja 27, 74
Neapolitan Pizza with Buffalo
  Mozzarella, Tomatoes & Basil
  152–53
Olive & Fennel Seed Ciabatta
  172–73
olive oil 163
olives
  Calabrian-style King Prawns in a
    Spicy Tomato Sauce 74–75
  Capri-style Pan-fried Sea Bream
    76–77
  Crispy Chicken with a Spicy
    Sauce & Green Beans 114–15
  Foccaccia with Tomatoes, Olives,
    Capers & Red Pesto 167
  Focaccia stuffed with Gorgonzola,
    Olives, Garlic & Rosemary
    170–71
  Gaeta 110, 115
  Grilled Tuna with Garlic Green
    Beans, Tomatoes & Olives 80–81
  Olive & Fennel Seed Ciabatta
    172–73
  Papa Ciro's Spicy Calzone 164–65
  Squid, Spicy Salami & Bean Salad
    68–69
  Sweet & Sour Rabbit with
    Borettane Onions 113
  Tuna Tartare 66–67
onions
  Borettane onions 113, 182
  Red onions 12–13, 120–121,
    178–79
  Tropea onions 26
oranges 26, 202
Oysters, Deep-fried Spicy, with
  Balsamic Dipping Sauce 50–51

P

pancetta 137
Papa Ciro's Spicy Calzone 164–65
Parma ham
  Baked Peaches with Parma Ham
    & Bocconcini Mozzarella 22–23
  Beef Fillet with Parma Ham
    & Pesto in Puff Pastry 102–3
Parmesan cheese
  Aubergine Balls with Parmesan,
    Garlic & Parsley 186–87

Aubergine, Mozzarella & Roasted
  Red Pepper Stack 44–45
Baked Courgettes with
  Mozzarella & Parmesan 192–93
Beef Carpaccio with Horseradish
  & Parmesan Cream Sauce 20–21
Crispy Chicken with a Spicy
  Sauce & Green Beans 114–15
Parmesan-crusted Cod with a
  Creamy Caper & Parsley
  Sauce 71
  see also Pasta, Gnocchi & Risotto
Parmesan-crusted Cod with a
  Creamy Caper & Parsley Sauce 71
passata 97, 128
Pasta 124
  Campanian Specialities 79
  Fettuccine with Neapolitan Ragù
    128–29
  Fettuccine with Neapolitan
    Sausages, Mushrooms & Peas
    130
  Fusilli with Vegetables, Pancetta,
    Pesto & Mozzarella 136–37
  Lazio Specialities 111
  Linguine with Pesto, Green Beans
    & Capers 126–27
  Prawn & Ricotta Ravioli with
    Olive Oil & Fresh Sage 138–39
  Spaghetti with Clams & Mussels
    132–33
  Spaghetti with Salami &
    Courgette in a Rich, Creamy
    Sauce 131
Peaches, Baked, with Parma Ham
  & Bocconcini Mozzarella 22–23
Pear, Dolcelatte & Mascarpone Tart
  with Honey & Thyme 24–25
peas 28, 74, 130, 147
pecorino cheese 111, 126, 131,
  163, 190
peperoncino calabrese 26
peppers
  Aubergine, Mozzarella & Roasted
    Red Pepper Stack 44–45
  Creamy Fish Pie with Roasted Red
    Peppers & Vermouth 88–89
  Papa Ciro's Spicy Calzone 164–65
  Ricotta Gnocchi with Red
    Peppers, Courgettes, Butter &
    Sage 144–45
  Sea Bass with Roasted
    Vegetables and Anchovies 86–87
  Spicy Chicken with New
    Potatoes, Tomatoes & Red
    Peppers 118–19
  Tuscan-style Barbecued Pork with
    Spicy Beans 108–9

pesto
  Beef Fillet with Parma Ham &
    Pesto in Puff Pastry 102–3
  Chicken Risotto with Red Pesto &
    Rosemary 148–49
  Focaccia with Tomatoes, Olives,
    Capers & Red Pesto 167
  Fusilli with Vegetables, Pancetta,
    Pesto & Mozzarella 136–37
  Linguine with Pesto, Green Beans
    & Capers 126–27
pine nuts 24, 38, 71, 113, 126
pistachio nuts 214
pitta calabrese 27
Pizza 150
  Campanian Specialities 79
  Neapolitan Pizza with Buffalo
    Mozzarella, Tomatoes & Basil
    152–53
  Papa Ciro's Spicy Calzone 164–65
  Pizza Tray with Anchovies,
    Courgettes, Garlic & Chilli 160–61
  Pizza Tray with Smoked Salmon,
    Mascarpone & Mozzarella 155
  Seafood Pizza 158–59
  Tomato, Garlic & Oregano Pizza
    154
pork
  Calabrian Specialities 27
  Fettuccine with Neapolitan
    Sausages, Mushrooms & Peas
    130
  guanciale 111
  Mamma Alba's Meatballs 96–97
  Stuffed Pork Rolls in a Tomato
    Sauce 94–95
  Tuscan-style Barbecued Pork with
    Spicy Beans 108–9
Pot-roasted Beef in Red Wine 100
potatoes
  Creamy Fish Pie with Roasted Red
    Peppers & Vermouth 88–89
  Garlic Potatoes 112, 122–23
  Italian-style Roast Chicken with
    New Potatoes & Red Onion
    120–21
  Potato & Artichoke Gratin 183
  Potato Gnocchi with Courgettes
    & Tomatoes 140–41
  Salt Cod & Potato Salad with Red
    Onion & Capers 12–13
  Sea Bass with Roasted Vegetables
    and Anchovies 86–87
  Spicy Chicken with New
    Potatoes, Tomatoes & Red
    Peppers 118–19
  Twice-baked Jacket Potatoes
    with Leeks & Taleggio 62

prawns
  Amalfi-style Fish Soup 40–41
  Calabrian-style King Prawns in a
    Spicy Tomato Sauce 74–75
  Creamy Fish Pie with Roasted Red
    Peppers & Vermouth 88–89
  Lazio Specialities 110–11
  Mixed Fried Seafood with Spicy
    Lemon Mayonnaise 32–33
  Prawn & Ricotta Ravioli with
    Olive Oil & Fresh Sage 138–39
  Prawn & Scallop Gratin 30–31
  Seafood Platter with Tomatoes
    & Red Chillies 70
Prosecco Jellies, Fruit &, with
  Vanilla Cream 196–97
provatura cheese 111
puff pastry 24, 102–3

R

Rabbit, Sweet & Sour, with
  Borettane Onions 113
Ravioli, Prawn & Ricotta, with Olive
  Oil & Fresh Sage 138–39
red mullet 41
Red Wine & Cherry Gravy 101
Rice Croquettes with Arrabbiata
  Sauce 28–29
ricotta cheese 111
  Baked Aubergine & Sweetened
    Ricotta with Chocolate Sauce
    216–17
  Courgettes Stuffed with Ricotta
    & Pecorino 190–91
  Papa Ciro's Spicy Calzone 164–65
  Prawn & Ricotta Ravioli with
    Olive Oil & Fresh Sage 138–39
  Ricotta Gnocchi with Red Peppers,
    Courgettes, Butter & Sage 144–45
Risotto 124
  Chicken, with Red Pesto &
    Rosemary 148–49
  Saffron, with Peas 146–47
Roast Beef with Roasted
  Vegetables & Fresh Herbs 106–7
Roasted Asparagus Salad with Red
  Onions 178–79
Roasted Kid with Garlic New
  Potatoes 112
Roasted Leek, Celery & Spinach
  Soup 38–39

S

Saffron Risotto with Peas 146–47
Salads
  Caprese Salad 176–77
  Roasted Asparagus Salad with
    Red Onions 178–79

Salt Cod & Potato Salad with Red
  Onion & Capers 12–13
Seared Salmon Salad 16–17
Southern Italian Pickled
  Vegetable Salad 182
Squid, Spicy Salami & Bean Salad
  68–69
salami
  Spaghetti with Salami & Courgette
    in a Rich, Creamy Sauce 131
  Squid, Spicy Salami & Bean Salad
    68–69
salmon
  Creamy Fish Pie with Roasted Red
    Peppers & Vermouth 88–89
  Pizza Tray with Smoked Salmon,
    Mascarpone & Mozzarella 155
  Salmon Escalopes with Creamy
    Vermouth Sauce 52–53
  Seared Salmon Salad 16–17
Salt Cod & Potato Salad with Red
  Onion & Capers 12–13
sardines 32
scallops
  Creamy Fish Pie with Roasted Red
    Peppers & Vermouth 88–89
  Prawn & Scallop Gratin 30–31
Sea Bass
  with Roasted Vegetables and
    Anchovies 86–87
  in a Rosemary-flavoured Salt Crust
    82–83
Sea Bream, Capri-style Pan-fried
  76–77
Seafood
  Seafood Pizza 158–59
  Seafood Platter with Tomatoes
    & Red Chillies 70
  see also Fish & seafood
Seared Salmon Salad 16–17
Semifreddo, Liquorice 210
Sliced Rib-eye Steak with Black
  Pepper Butter 63
Sorbet, Blackberry 208–9
Sorrento-style Lobster with
  Limoncello & Rocket 56–57
Soups 36–41
Southern Italian Pickled Vegetable
  Salad 182
Spaghetti
  with Clams & Mussels 132–33
  with Salami & Courgette in a
    Rich, Creamy Sauce 131
Spicy Chicken with New Potatoes,
  Tomatoes & Red Peppers 118–19
Spicy Lemon Mayonnaise 32–33
Spicy Sautéed Mushrooms with
  Garlic & Tomatoes 188–89

spinach 16, 38
squid
  Mixed Fried Seafood with Spicy
    Lemon Mayonnaise 32–33
  Seafood Platter with Tomatoes
    & Red Chillies 70
  Squid, Spicy Salami & Bean Salad
    68–69
strawberries 196, 201
Stuffed Pork Rolls in a Tomato
  Sauce 94–95
sultanas 113, 182
Sweet & Sour Rabbit with
  Borettane Onions 113
Sweet Soft Butter Rolls with
  Vanilla 166
sweetcorn cobs 108

T

Taleggio cheese 62
tiella 111
Tiramisù with Amaretto 218–19
Tomato, Garlic & Oregano Pizza 154
tomatoes, cherry 31, 41, 56, 68, 70,
  77, 132, 167
tomatoes, fresh plum 66, 81, 86,
  119, 140, 176
tomatoes, San Marzano 78, 154
tomatoes, semi-dried 63, 68
tomatoes, sun-dried 113
tomatoes, tinned 28, 41, 74,
  94, 97, 115, 137, 152, 154, 158,
  160, 189, 192
tuna
  Grilled Tuna with Garlic Green
    Beans, Tomatoes & Olives 80–81
  Tuna Carpaccio with Rocket,
    Capers & Balsamic 14–15
  Tuna Tartare 66–67
Tuscany 9, 162–63
Tuscan-style Barbecued Pork with
  Spicy Beans 108–9
Twice-baked Jacket Potatoes with
  Leeks & Taleggio 62

V, W

Vegetables 174–193
  see also aubergines, peppers, etc.
vermouth 52, 88
walnuts 45
Wine, Red
  & Cherry Gravy 101
  Pot-roasted Beef in 100
wines, Tuscan 163

Z

Zabaione with Limoncello &
  Strawberries 200–201

AUTHOR'S ACKNOWLEDGEMENTS

I am dedicating this book to Comandante Pino Spano for all the wonderful summers we spend on the island of Sardinia in Baia Caddinas. Grazie for your friendship and for looking after my family.

Thank you to everyone involved in the making of my *Gino's Italian Coastal Escape* series and book – you know who you are! Grazie xxx